Penguin Books

Charlie Chan Is Dead

Jessica Hagedorn, poet, multimedia artist, screenwriter, and novelist, was born and raised in the Philippines and moved to the United States in her teens. *Dogeaters*, her first novel (available from Penguin), was nominated for the 1990 National Book Award. *Danger and Beauty*, a collection of selected poetry and short fiction from earlier works and previously unpublished material, was published by Penguin in 1993. She is currently working on another novel.

Charlie Chan Is Dead

An Anthology
of Contemporary
Asian American Fiction

Edited and with an Introduction by
Jessica Hagedorn

With a Preface by
Elaine Kim

Penguin Books

PENGUIN BOOKS
Published by the Penguin Group
Penguin Books USA Inc., 375 Hudson Street,
New York, New York 10014, U.S.A.
Penguin Books Ltd, 27 Wrights Lane, London W8 5TZ, England
Penguin Books Australia Ltd, Ringwood, Victoria, Australia
Penguin Books Canada Ltd, 10 Alcorn Avenue,
Toronto, Ontario, Canada M4V 3B2
Penguin Books (N.Z.) Ltd, 182–190 Wairau Road,
Auckland 10, New Zealand

Penguin Books Ltd, Registered Offices:
Harmondsworth, Middlesex, England

First published in Penguin Books 1993

10 9 8 7 6 5 4 3 2 1

PUBLISHER'S NOTE
These selections are works of fiction. Names, characters, places, and incidents are the product of the authors' imagination or are used fictitiously, and any resemblance to actual persons, living or dead, events, or locales is entirely coincidental.

LIBRARY OF CONGRESS CATALOGING-IN-PUBLICATION DATA
Charlie Chan is dead: an anthology of contemporary Asian American
    fiction/edited and with an introduction by Jessica Hagedorn; with
    a preface by Elaine Kim.
        p. cm.
    ISBN 0 14 02.3111 0
    1. American fiction—Asian American authors.   2. American
fiction—20th century.   3. Asian Americans—Fiction.   I. Hagedorn,
Jessica Tarahata.
PS647.A75C48   1993
813954080895—dc20   93-10703

Printed in the United States of America
Set in Electra
Designed by Cheryl L. Cipriani

For my daughters,
Paloma and Esther Gabrielle

Preface

In the United States, racism's "traveling eye" has created and cordoned off race-based communities, affixing meaning to them according to the degree of threat they are thought to pose to the dominant culture at particular points in time. Asian-origin communities were called "Oriental," east of and peripheral to an unnamed center. Historically, Asian Americans, as we renamed ourselves, have had

ELAINE KIM is a Professor of Asian American Studies, Faculty Assistant for the Status of Women, and former Assistant Dean, College of Letters and Science, at the University of California, Berkeley. A widely respected political activist, feminist, and renowned Asian American scholar, she is the current President of the Association for Asian American Studies. Her publications include the breakthrough *Asian American Literature: An Introduction to the Writings and Their Social Context*, as well as numerous articles and essays. She co-edited *Making Waves: Writings by and about Asian American Women* and *Writing Self, Writing Nation: A Collection of Essays on DICTEE by Theresa Hak Kyung Cha*. Her video documentary credits include "Sa-i-ku: From Korean Women's Perspectives" (co-producer) and "Slaying the Dragon: Asian Women in U.S. Television and Film" (associate producer). She is collaborating on a book with visual artist Betty Kano entitled *Visions and Fierce Dreams: Lives and Work of Asian American Visual Artists*. She is President of the Board of Directors of the Korean Community Center in Oakland, and the founder and member of Asian Women United of California.

no place in the discourse on race and culture in the United States except as "model minorities" on the one hand or as unassimilable aliens on the other, as statements about the ultimate goodness of the dominant culture and the ultimate badness of those who refuse to go along with the program. Faced with sets of mutually exclusive binaries between "East" and "West," between Asia and America, and between suspect alien and patriot, those seeking a third space as "both/and" instead of "either/or" are usually considered racist, un-American, even anti-American. Within the context of these silencing systems of domination, Asian Americans are supposed to deny their cultural heritages, accept positions as sojourning "exotic aliens," or "go back" to Asia.[1]

A generation ago, I attempted to define Asian American literature as work in English by writers of Chinese, Filipino, Japanese, and Korean descent about U.S. American experiences.[2] I admitted at the time that this definition was arbitrary, prompted by my own inability to read Asian languages and my own lack of access to South and Southeast Asian communities. But for these shortcomings, I wrote, I would have included in my introductory study works written in Asian languages and works by writers from Vietnamese American, Indian American, and other communities.

Nonetheless, it is true that I wanted to delineate and draw boundaries around whatever I thought of as Asian American identity and literature. Clearly, Asian American experiences and creative visions had been excluded from or distorted in the established texts: although I had majored in English and American literature in the 1960s at Ivy League universities and at Berkeley, I was never assigned the work of a single writer of color, not even Ralph Ellison or Richard Wright, whose books I had to read on my own, together with the work of many other "Third World" and American writers of color. A century and a

---

1. In "Home Is Where the *Han* Is: A Korean American Perspective on the Los Angeles Upheavals" (in *Reading Rodney King/Reading Urban Uprising*, ed. Robert Gooding-Williams, New York: Routledge, 1993), I quote from the scores of hate letters I have received in response to an essay I wrote for *Newsweek* magazine in May 1992 from Americans living in all parts of the country. These letters provide concrete examples of U.S. American nativist thinking about Asian Americans in the 1990s.
2. *Asian American Literature: An Introduction to the Writings and Their Social Context* (Philadelphia: Temple University Press, 1982).

half of persistent and deeply rooted racist inscriptions in both official and mass literary culture in the United States perpetuated grotesque representations of Asian Americans as alien Others, whether as sinister villains, dragon ladies, brute hordes, helpless heathens, comical servants, loyal sidekicks, Suzy Wongs, or wily asexual detectives. Like many other Asian Americans, I felt an urgent need to insist that these were not "our realities." Our strategy was to assert a self-determined Asian American identity in direct opposition to these dehumanizing characterizations, even if it was limited by being contained within the exclusive binary system that occasioned it.

For the most part, I read Asian American literature as a literature of protest and exile, a literature about place and displacement, a literature concerned with psychic and physical "home"—searching for and claiming a "home" or longing for a final "homecoming." I looked for unifying thematic threads and tidy resolutions that might ease the pain of displacement and heal the exile, heedless of what might be missing from this homogenizing approach and oblivious to the parallels between what I was doing and dominant culture attempts to reduce Asian American experiences to developmental narratives about the movement from "primitive," "Eastern," and foreign immigrant to "civilized," Western, and "Americanized" loyal citizen.

The cultural nationalist defenses we constructed were anti-assimilationist. But while they opposed official nationalisms, the Asian American identity they allowed for was fixed, closed, and narrowly defined, dividing "Asian American" from "Asian" as sharply as possible, privileging race over gender and class, accepting compulsory heterosexuality as "natural," and constructing a hierarchy of authenticity to separate the "real" from the "fake." According to this definition, there were not many ways of being Asian American. The ideal was male, heterosexual, Chinese or Japanese American, and English-speaking. The center of Chinese America was San Francisco or New York Chinatown, and the heart of Japanese America was in Hawaii or along Highway 99, which cut through the agricultural fields the *issei* and *nisei* had lost during World War II. Asian American history was about railroads, "bachelor societies," and internment. The sacred Asian American texts—such as Carlos Bulosan's *America Is in the*

Heart, John Okada's *No-No Boy*, and Louis Chu's *Eat a Bowl of Tea* —were by "dead yellow men" instead of "dead white men." Asian American literary studies usually did not question the concept of canonization but simply posited an alternative canon. It seemed that every film, every article, and even many novels had to be a unidimensional documentary filled with literal and solemnly delivered history lessons. Given the magnitude of general ignorance about Asian Americans, it was difficult to do anything but play a dead straight part. Dealing with subtleties, hybridities, paradoxes, and layers seemed almost out of the question when so much effort had to be expended simply justifying Asian Americans as discursive subjects in the first place.

Cultural nationalist agendas have the potential to contest and disrupt the logic of domination, its exploitation and exclusions. Certainly it was possible for me as a Korean American female to accept the fixed masculinist Asian American identity posited in Asian American cultural nationalism, even when it rendered invisible or at least muted women's oppression, anger, and ways of loving and interpreted Korean Americans as imperfect imitations of Chinese Americans; because I could see in everyday life that not all material and psychic violence to women of color comes from men, and because, as my friends used to say, "No Chinese [American] ever called me 'gook.' " No matter what, some cultural nationalist approaches have the power to render visible what David Lloyd has called "the history of the possible."[3]

While I was preoccupied with defining Asian American identity and culture in the 1970s and with uncovering buried stories from "early" Asian America, changes in U.S. immigration quotas in 1965 were already resulting in massive and highly visible transformations in Asian American communities. Indeed, it might be said that until recent years, Asian American communities and cultures were shaped by legal exclusion and containment, while contemporary experiences are being shaped by the internationalization of the world's political economies and cultures. Yesterday's young Asian immigrant might have worked beside his parents on a pineapple plantation in Hawaii or in a fruit

---

3. "Race Under Representation," *Oxford Literary Review* 13, nos. 1–2 (1991): 62–94, p. 88.

orchard on the Pacific Coast, segregated from the mainstream of American life. Today's Asian immigrant teenager might have only Asian friends, but she probably deals daily with a not necessarily anguishing confusion of divergent influences, a collision of elements she needs to negotiate in her search to define herself. In this regard, she is not unlike other Americans: as Trinh T. Minh-ha has pointed out, "There is a Third World in every First World and vice versa."[4] Her collisions, however, are probably tied to the particularities of her cultural background at a particular point in time. Thus, she might rent Korean language video melodramas from a shopping center in Southern California today, after having watched "MacGyver" and "Entertainment Tonight" on television in Seoul as a child.

During the past two decades, some Asian and Pacific American populations have increased by 500 to 1,000 percent. New Asian American communities have taken root all over the country, as Vietnamese refugees settle in Westminster, California, and Korean immigrants gather in Flushing, New York. Newcomers are diverse in terms of origin and ethnicity, language, social class, political situations, educational backgrounds, and patterns of settlement. They have moved to cities and towns where few Asian Americans had lived before and are doing things to earn their livelihoods that they could not have imagined when they were in their homelands: Cambodians are making doughnuts, Koreans are making burritos, South Asians are operating motels, Filipinos are driving airport shuttle buses. The lines between Asian and Asian American, so crucial to identity formations in the past, are increasingly blurred: transportation to and communication with Asia is no longer daunting, resulting in new crossovers and intersections and different kinds of material and cultural distances today.

Asian American identities are fluid and migratory: the Minnesota social worker who clings to the idea of Hmongs as limited-English-speaking refugees from a pre-literate society may be surprised to encounter a Hmong teenager who composes rap music, plays hockey, and dates Chicano boys or girls. Cultures, whether Asian origin cul-

---

4. Trinh T. Minh-ha, *Woman, Native, Other* (Bloomington: Indiana University Press, 1989), p. 98.

tures or the "majority culture," which is no more monolithic and unitary than "Asian" or "Asian American culture," have never been fixed, continuous, or discrete. The notion of an absolute American past, a single source for American people, a founding identity or wholeness in America, is rooted in the racist fiction of primordial white American universality, as is the fear that "American culture" is now being broken down by rowdy brown and yellow immigrants and other people of color who refuse to melt into the final identity of "just Americans."

I often hear people lament that things are getting worse all the time, that Americans are more divided, that there is less tolerance and more racial violence than ever before. But according to my own experience of the Wonder Bread days before the Civil Rights Movement, there was much more racial violence and much less racial tolerance then than now. Maybe some people remember the "good old days" of the Ozzie and Harriet 1950s as peaceful and harmonious; I don't. The races were more divided in the past, when segregation was the rule and racial hierarchies were accepted as natural and permanent. In Maryland, where I grew up, interracial marriages were illegal, and job announcements routinely stipulated "whites only" as well as "men only." It is true that hate crimes against Asian Americans are more and more frequently in the news. But if anyone thinks that racial violence is a 1990s phenomenon, maybe that's because racial violence in the "good old days" was not documented except in the lived experiences of Americans of color. In my view, the "good old days" were not so good for women and people of color.

The America that is ever "becoming" has always been a polyglot nation of immigrants, but this has never been *all*; it is also the site of Native America, of African slavery and resistances to it, of the war between the United States and Mexico and the yet to be fully honored Treaty of Guadalupe Hidalgo. Knowing that there never has been a unified Mayflower-and-Plymouth Rock beginning to "return to" makes me feel hopeful about the future.

No matter what we wish for, things do not necessarily come to a harmonious resolution. Perhaps after all there is no "home," except for a place of contestation that negates as well as affirms. And identity, like "home," is ever in process, less a refuge than the site of contending, multiple meanings. Inevitably, the Asian American identity offered by cultural nationalism could not but produce conflicts that portended its own undoing: what was excluded and rendered invisible—the unruly, the transgressive, and the disruptive—began to seep out from under the grids and appear from between the cracks. Eventually the seams burst and were exposed. In the case of Asian America, this unruliness has come from women who never stop being both Asian and female, as well as from others rendered marginal by the essentializing aspects of Asian American cultural nationalism.

This book shows us what is now possible as well as what is in store, for without a doubt, there is much more where these stories came from. Charlie Chan is indeed dead, never to be revived. Gone for good his yellowface asexual bulk, his fortune-cookie English, his stereotypical Orientalist version of "the [Confucian] Chinese family," challenged by an array of characters, some hip and articulate, some brooding and sexy, some insolent and others innocent, but all as unexpected as a Korean American who writes in French, a Chinese-Panamanian-German who longs too late to know her father, a mean Japanese American grandmother, a Chinese American flame-diver, or a teenaged Filipino American male prostitute. Instead of "model minorities," we find human beings with rich and complex pasts and brave, often flamboyant dreams of the future. There are dysfunctional families that bear no resemblance to the Charlie Chan version of "Chinese family values," tragic stories of suicide, incest, and child abuse, as well as bittersweet songs about aging, love, and death. The locales span the world, and the writers are old, young, established, and new, reflecting the amazing diversity of Asian American national origins and a wide variety of subject positions. To read them, we will need to go beyond cultural nationalist approaches to employ mixed strategies and critical practices.

For me, this collection celebrates many ways of being Asian American today, when the question need no longer be "either/or." This anthology gives us *both* Asian American literature *and* world literature: Asian American literary work may be about Asian American experiences, but this is never *all* it is about. The writers here are magicians who transform "facts" into meanings, reaching across pain and silences to shape legacies and create new cultures as they open spaces for the historically banished. "One day/I going to write/about you," writes Lois-Ann Yamanaka in "Empty Heart," and she has kept her promise.

Elaine Kim
Oakland, California
1993

Acknowledgments

Thanks to my agent Harold Schmidt, and to my editor, Dawn Seferian, and her assistants, Will Gillham and Michael Hardart, at Viking Penguin.

And thank you to those folks who gave me suggestions, sent me their students' work, and shared invaluable lists of writers: Leonor Briscoe, Carol Bruchac, Luis Francia, Helena Franklin, Marie Hara, Edward Iwata, Zia Jaffrey, Elaine Kim, Maxine Hong Kingston, Alan Chong Lau, Amy Ling, Wing Tek Lum, David Mura, Oscar Peñaranda, and Sam Solberg.

And for their supportive criticism and feedback: *maraming salamat* to Thulani Davis, Russell Leong, Shawn Wong, and John Woo.

And finally—thank you to my anthology assistants, Cheong Kim and Angel Velasco Shaw.

Contents

Introduction

"Role of Dead Man Require Very Little Acting"

from *Charlie Chan's Secret* (1936; 20th Century-Fox),
starring Warner Oland as Charlie Chan

C harlie Chan is our most famous fake "Asian" pop icon—known for his obsequious manner, fractured English, and dainty walk. Absurdly cryptic, pseudo-Confucian sayings rolled off his tongue:

"Observe."
"When weaving nets, all threads counted."
"Woman's intuition like feather on arrow. May help flight to truth."
"Necessity mother of invention, but sometimes stepmother of deception."
"Boy scout knife, like ladies' hairpin. Have many uses."
"Best place for skeleton is in family closet."
"Chinese people interested in all things psychic."
"If strength were all, tiger would not fear scorpion."
"Observe."

The character of Charlie Chan was created by a white man named Earl Derr Biggers in 1925. Ingrained in American popular culture, Charlie Chan is as much a part of the demeaning legacy of stereotypes that includes Fu Manchu, Stepin' Fetchit, Sambo, Aunt Jemima,

Amos N'Andy, Speedy Gonzalez, Tonto, and Little Brown Brother. I grew up in the Philippines watching Hollywood movies featuring yellowface, blackface, and redface actors giving me their versions of myself. It was so easy to succumb to the seductive, insidious power of these skewed, wide-screen images. Better than books, movies were immediate and reached more people—both literate and illiterate. Movies were instantly gratifying. Bigger than life. I was a child. The movies were God. And therefore, true.

The slit-eyed, bucktooth Jap thrusting his bayonet, thirsty for blood. The inscrutable, wily Chinese detective with his taped eyelids and wispy moustache. The childlike, indolent Filipino houseboy. Always giggling. Bowing and scraping. Eager to please, but untrustworthy. The sexless, hairless Asian male. The servile, oversexed Asian female. The Geisha. The sultry, sarong-clad, South Seas maiden. The serpentine, cunning Dragon Lady. Mysterious and evil, eager to please. Effeminate. Untrustworthy. Yellow Peril. Fortune Cookie Psychic. Savage. Dogeater. Invisible. Mute. Faceless peasants breeding too many children. Gooks. Passive Japanese Americans obediently marching off to "relocation camps" during the Second World War.

The images have now evolved into subtler stereotypes. There's the greedy, clever *Japanese Businessman*, ready to buy up New York City and all the Van Goghs in the world. There's the *Ultimate Nerd*, the model minority Asian American student, excelling in math and computer science, obsessed with work, work, work. There's *Miss Saigon*, the contemporary version of Madame Butterfly—tragic victim/whore of wartorn Vietnam, eternally longing for the white boy soldier who has abandoned her and her son. There's *The Lover*, the pathetic Chinese millionaire boy-toy completely dominated by his impoverished, adolescent, blondie waif dominatrix in both Marguerite Duras' popular novel and the recent film version. Often portrayed as loyal servants and children, we are humorless, non-assertive, impotent—yet we are eroticized as exotic playthings in both Western film and literature. In our perceived American character—we are completely non-threatening. We don't complain. We endure humiliation. We are almost inhuman in our patience. *We never get angry.*

I grew up in the Philippines reading the literature of the Western World—Hawthorne, Poe, Cervantes, to name a few. Of course there was also the Old and New Testament of the Bible which we were expected to study and deconstruct in loving detail; we were a majority Catholic country, after all, legendary for our faith and zeal. My reading books in English came from the United States—*Fun with Dick and Jane.* I thought all Americans were blond and freckled, ate apples, and all fairhaired children had dogs like Spot. Everyone lived in modern homes, with mowed lawns and picket fences. It was a David Lynch movie cliche without the perverse undertones. Even though we also studied Tagalog, one of our native languages (now known as Pilipino), and read some of the native literature (I remember Jose Rizal in particular, and an epic, romantic poem by Francisco Balagtas), it was pretty clear to most of us growing up in the fifties and early sixties that what was really important, what was inevitably preferred, was the aping of our mythologized Hollywood universe. The colonization of our imagination was relentless and hard to shake off. Everywhere we turned, the images held up did not match our own. In order to be acknowledged, we had to strive to be as American as possible.

And then I came to the United States of America. We settled in San Francisco, California—a city we probably felt most comfortable in because of its closeness to water (we could leave anytime and go back "home"), and because there was a growing and already visible Asian community (we had easy access to our culture, whether we wanted it or not). The irony was lost on us, back then. We were also confronted by the new and unfamiliar: Chicanos, African Americans (still called "Negroes"), and an incredible variety of white people of various ethnic origins.

I was ignorant of the difficult history and contributions of Asian Americans in this country. I had no idea Filipinos were exploited as cheap farm labor in California places like Watsonville, Salinas, and Stockton; they were firebombed and run out of town by angry mobs threatened by loss of jobs throughout the Western states; they were forbidden to marry white women, harassed openly, and even lynched for being involved with them. Filipino women were outnumbered by Filipino men one to a hundred in the 1920s and '30s, according to Fred Cordova's remarkable book, *Filipinos: Forgotten Asian Americans*. I was unaware of the signs in California public establishments that were a common sight in the 1930s: "Positively No Filipinos Allowed." This had never been taught to us back in Manila, and was certainly not part of my high school social studies in San Francisco in the sixties. Americans were the good guys. For Filipinos, especially, America was generally perceived as our savior, our benefactor, our protector; as Carlos Bulosan wrote so sincerely and poignantly, and as I imagine he believed to the bitter end: *"America Is in the Heart."*

In my American high school classes, I was again reading Hawthorne, Poe, Melville, Dostoevski, Dickens, the occasional Emily Dickinson or Brontë sisters. Sui Sin Far, Richard Wright, John Okada, Lawson Inada, Gwendolyn Brooks, James Baldwin, Toshio Mori, and Carlos Bulosan did not exist in our curriculum. I graduated from high school in 1967, unable to pinpoint the source of my unease. I had been in America exactly four years. There were sit-ins going on, downtown on Van Ness Avenue. A strike at San Francisco State University a few blocks away from my high school. John F. Kennedy and Malcolm X had been assassinated. The Black Panther Party was born. How did I fit in? Chicanos, African Americans, and even militant Asian Americans were forming alliances. Could Asian Americans, in fact, be "militant"? Were we really a part of the Third World? *The Third World.* Not exactly a term my family would take pride in. Back where I came from, "Third World" lacked glamour. It was synonymous with phones that didn't work, roads that were badly in need of repair, corrupt politicians, and naked children with rickety bones and bellies bloated from hunger. Who was I?

Shake syntax, smash the myths, and if you lose, slide on, unearth some new linguistic paths. Do you surprise?
Do you shock? Do you have a choice?

—Trinh T. Minh-ha,
Woman, Native, Other

My mother bought me my first portable typewriter. There was no question. After all, my maternal grandfather had been a writer and a teacher. Everyone in my family enjoyed books. I had always been encouraged to write, although I'm not sure I was taken all that seriously. Poems were my way out of isolation. I read anything I could get my hands on, and by sheer accident, stumbled upon a new wave of irreverent and blasphemous American writers. This was not the white-washed America I'd been taught to revere. These were poems and poets who were talking back to me. These were words that got American people upset. LeRoi Jones' angry incantations. Victor Hernandez Cruz's precocious, sly, and rhythmic ditties. The thrilling indulgence of Allen Ginsberg's "Howl." The fierce drag queens and teenage hustlers of John Rechy's dark "City of Night." The swaggering power of Nikki Giovanni's "EgoTripping." *I am, I am, I am.*

With no real idea of myself as postcolonial Filipino, Asian American, or as a female person of mixed descent, but armed with this new and disturbing inspiration, I began to seriously write and read. I found other provocative books which unsettled me and made me ask questions. In spite of my political ignorance, I was blissfully driven to put word to paper, perhaps to express what I did not know. Words were my favorite instruments of illusion and communication. In slowly discovering the works of other Asian and Asian American writers in the early Seventies, I delighted in my rude awakenings. Some of my first readings included: Jose Garcia Villa's elegant poems and stories; Frank Chin's powerful "Goong Hai Fot Choy" excerpted in Ishmael Reed's seminal multicultural anthology, *19 Necromancers from Now*; Bienvenido Santos' bittersweet portraits of Filipino *manong*s in his short-story collection, *Scent of Apples*; N. V. M. Gonzalez's wistful novel, *The Bamboo Dancers*; John Okada's searing indictment of racist hysteria against Japanese Americans in *No-No Boy*; Toshio Mori's haunting novel of an Issei woman, *Woman from Hiroshima*. Unfortunately, these books were difficult to find back then, and still are now. Many are out-of-print.

And thank god for the other Asian American writers who became my streetwise teachers, co-conspirators, and artistic family in the blossoming Bay Area of the 1970s: the late Serafin Syquia, the late Bayani

Mariano, Al Robles, Janice Mirikitani, Kitty Tsui, Geraldine Kudaka, Oscar Peñaranda, Lou Syquia, Nellie Wong, Russell Leong, Genny Lim, Presco Tabios, Norman Jayo, George Leong . . . all those who volunteered to work with the *manongs* and other senior citizens living at the legendary I-Hotel, all those who passed through the open doors of the Kearny Street Writers Workshop, sharing food, drink, gossip, poems, stories, and first attempts at scripts. We collaborated on many literary projects with other Bay Area writers and artists of color like Ishmael Reed, Roberto Vargas, Thulani Davis, Avotcja Jiltonero, the late Buriel Clay, Alejandro Murguia, Jim Dong, Janet Campbell Hale, Ntozake Shange, and Rupert Garcia, to name a few. Some of us were part of an artistic and media collective known as Third World Communications. We no longer wanted to sit around waiting for the publishing industry to notice us; we raised money, edited, designed, and published our own books, knowing all along that there was a growing readership out there.

The first *Aiiieeeee!* anthology, published in hardback in 1974 and in paperback in 1975, was an absolute breakthrough for Asian Americans. The brash, refreshingly outspoken editors of this landmark collection were Frank Chin, Jeffery Paul Chan, Lawson Fusao Inada, and Shawn Wong. Receiving my copy as a gift from Frank Chin (who declined to be included in this anthology) proved a joyous revelation. I was not alone, pure and simple. There were other writers—poets, essayists, novelists, playwrights—like me, and yet not like me at all. We may share the same yearnings for *adobo* and *pinakbet*, but some of us had worked in Alaskan canneries or as migrant workers in California, and wrote from that brutal experience; others wrote sophisticated existential fiction reeking with black humor; still others wrote of the conflicts and tensions within Asian American families, and the surreal displacement felt by many immigrants. Others owed their anarchic allegiances purely to rock 'n' roll. Some were my contemporaries, immigrants like me. Others had been in America two or three generations. There were many who had experienced firsthand the indignities and harsh realities of incarceration in the so-called "relocation camps" like Manzanar, Tule Lake, or Poston, Arizona. Our histories are often painfully entangled, and yes—we quarrel amongst ourselves. But we are definitely "not new here."

Besides presenting the individual literary work of the editors, the first *Aiiieeeee!* gave us a sampling of the poems, plays, and stories of: Carlos Bulosan. Louis Chu. Hisaye Yamamoto DeSoto. Wakako Yamauchi. Diana Chang. Toshio Mori. Oscar Peñaranda. Sam Tagatac. John Okada. Momoko Iko. Russell Leong, a.k.a. Wallace Lin. My writer's education owes a big debt to this first *Aiiieeeee!* The sound was, and is "more than a whine, shout or scream. This is fifty years of our whole voice."

The energy and interest sparked by *Aiiieeeee!* in the Seventies was essential to Asian American writers because it gave us visibility and credibility as creators of our own specific literature. We could not be ignored; suddenly, we were no longer silent. Like other writers of color in America, we were beginning to challenge the long-cherished concepts of a xenophobic literary canon dominated by white heterosexual males. Obviously, there was room for more than one voice and one vision in this ever-expanding arena.

There were fourteen writers included in the first *Aiiieeeee!* anthology. Since then, there has been more cause for celebration. A number of notable novels, memoirs, essays and collections of Asian American poetry, plays, critical theory, social history and fiction have been published by big and small presses to critical and commercial acclaim in the brief, seventeen-year period spanning 1976 to 1993. (See my suggested reading list.)

And then of course, came *The Big AIIIEEEEE!*, this time billed solely as "An Anthology of Chinese American and Japanese American Literature" and again edited by Chan, Chin, Inada, and Wong and published in 1991. This second volume boasts 619 pages and features twenty-eight writers of fiction, poetry, and essays. *Three Filipino Women*—three novellas by one of the Philippines' most distinguished writers, F. Sionil Jose—were published in one volume in America in 1992. That same year, Trevor Carolan's *The Colors of Heaven*, a collection of Pacific Rim writers from China, Japan, Taiwan, the Philippines, Malaysia, Singapore, Korea, Australia, Indonesia, and New

Zealand, was published. Nineteen ninety-three has already brought us Garrett Hongo's anthology of Asian American poetry, *The Open Boat*; Lawson Fusao Inada's *Legends from Camp*; Luis Francia's anthology of Philippine literature in English, *Brown River, White Ocean*; and Fae Myenne Ng's long-awaited first novel, *Bone*.

Hmmm. We've come a long way, Charlie baby.

In the thirty years I have lived in America, I never really thought I would see the literary landscape change, splitting off into so many challenging and liberating directions. As the first anthology of Asian American fiction by a commercial publisher in this country, *Charlie Chan Is Dead* proudly presents forty-eight writers. Almost half are being published in a major collection for the first time.

The writers selected for this anthology are exhilarating in their differences; there is an array of cultural backgrounds, age range, and literary styles gathered here. No "theme" was imposed on the writers when they were invited to submit. I let it be known that I was definitely more interested in "riskier" work, and that I was eager to subvert the very definition of what was considered "fiction." Unless I had a specific work of theirs in mind, the choice of what to send me was left up to the writer. Even the notion of what is "Asian American" is expanded to include the writer Joy Kogawa, a resident of Canada. The resulting range is enormous, and one almost has to read through these marvelous stories as if one were watching a movie, shifting back and forth in time: Jose Garcia Villa's minimalist "Untitled Story" (first published in 1933) bumps heads with Carlos Bulosan's harrowing "I Would Remember." Meena Alexander's "Manhattan Music" offers an insightful look at the multiculti, trendy New York downtown art scene of the troubled '90s. Wakako Yamauchi evokes a young girl's sexual awakening in the barren desert landscape of "That Was All." Han Ong's tough male hustler prowls the seedy landscape of modern Los Angeles in "The Stranded in the World." R. Zamora Linmark creates playful, tragicomic vignettes of growing up gay and Filipino in Hawaii in "They Like You Because You Eat Dog, So What Are You Gonna Do About It?"

Bienvenido Santos' classic "Immigration Blues" moves us with its unsparing yet tender characterizations of old-time Filipino bachelors seeking love in America. Marilyn Chin's angry, sly voice in "Moon" shocks us and makes us laugh—indeed the quintessential Chinese American girl's "Revenge Tale"—and Marianne Villanueva's voice is elegiac in "Lenox Hill, December 1991." Insolence and heat emanate from the bad boys of Lawrence Chua's "No Sayang Lost." There is a variety of rhythms and language in the genteel madness of Hisaye Yamamoto DeSoto's "Eucalyptus," the jumpy, streetwise rap of Walter Lew's nervy "Black Korea," and the sophisticated repartee of Shawn Wong's sexy, almost too-hip-for-their-own-good lovers in "Eye Contact." The jagged fragments of poetic language slice through Theresa Hak Kyung Cha's complex "Melpomene Tragedy." N. V. M. Gonzalez gives us earthy wisdom in "The Bread of Salt." In the face of loss, stoicism and longing are exhibited by the protagonist of Russell Leong's "Geography One." The haunting junkie ecstasy of Kiana Davenport's "Dragon Seed" is both abhorrent and beautiful. I was intrigued by the sinister psychosexual obsessions explored in both Kerri Sakamoto's "Walk-In Closet" and John Yau's "Photographs for an Album (Third Version)." I was delighted by the sassiness and spunk of Cherylene Lee's "Safe." The rich, funky rhythm-and-blues poetry of pidgin English is captured by both Lois-Ann Yamanaka's "Empty Heart" and Darrell Lum's hilarious "Fourscore and Seven Years Ago." Postmodern conceits are fluidly adapted in the deadpan, contemporary portrait of Chairman Mao in Alex Kuo's "The Connoisseur of Chaos." John Song's "Faith" examines the impact of incest on a family in lyrical yet restrained language that keeps the story from becoming sensational and obvious. Toshio Mori's unforgettable "The Chauvinist" reminds us once again that he was one of our master storytellers.

And there's more. Wonderful stories rich in craft and complex vision by writers such as: Maxine Hong Kingston, Amy Tan, Bharati Mukherjee, Diana Chang, Gish Jen, Fae Myenne Ng, David Wong Louie, David Mura, Cynthia Kadohata, Joy Kogawa, Jeffery Paul Chan, Ninotchka Rosca, Ruthanne Lum McCunn, Fiona Cheong, Kimiko Hahn, Ruxana Meer, Sigrid Nunez, Peter Bacho, Yoji Yamaguchi, Laureen Mar, Jocelyn Lieu, and Sylvia Watanabe.

Some of these writers were originally poets, some still are. Others only write fiction. Some were born in the Philippines, some in Seattle.

A few in Hawaii. Others in Toronto or London. Some live in San Francisco. Oakland. Stockton. Los Angeles. New York City. Santa Fe. Family in Panama. Singapore. Tokyo. Manila. Pusan. Chicago. Hayward. Boston. Brooklyn. Beijing. Mindoro. Washington, D.C. Seoul. Greeley, Colorado. India. Penang. Moscow, Idaho.

Asian American literature? Too confining a term, maybe. World literature? Absolutely.

This is an anthology I created for selfish reasons; a book I wanted to read that had never been available to me. In many of these stories, cultures clash. We are confronted by characters in all their contradictions and complexities. They make love, worry about the future, hurt each other, endure hardships. They grease their hair, conk and lacquer it; dance slick like James Brown, shimmy across the floor, get loud and have fun. They get high. Sell their bodies. They audition for jobs as anchormen and women. They are lost in nostalgia, homesick for their country of origin. Exiled. Displaced. Assimilated. Rebellious. They lie and cheat; they betray themselves and others. They are tough and noble. They survive. They remind us that in our civilized anguish, we are still beautiful and amazing.

In this collection, some of us retell familial and cultural mythology, yet we also write out of more personal and perhaps more terrifying truths. For many of us, what is personal is also political, and vice versa. We are asserting and continually exploring who we are as Asians, Asian Americans, and artists and citizens of what Salman Rushdie calls "a shrinking universe." The choice is more than whether to hyphenate or not. The choice is more than gender, race, or class. First generation, second, third, fourth. Who is authentic or fake. Dead or undead. Mainstream or marginal. Uncle Tom or Charlie Chan. And the language(s) we speak are not necessarily the language(s) in which we dream.

Jessica Hagedorn
New York City
1993

Charlie Chan Is Dead

Manhattan Music

Meena Alexander

1.

A summer ago I thought I would lose my mind.
Riding the subway. Up and down. Down and up, from my
studio to see him. Holding it all together. With a bit of string, torn
rope, a rubber band. My canvas, rolled up, the tools for cutting
wood—litho tools, the sand I had picked up from the edge of the pier.
All the while he was in my head. How hot I was stacked next to a
saxophone player with green antennae, shimmering sequins on his
suit. Hot wet, summertime. Boobooboo, shuushuushuu, he kept going,
growing in me. I clutched my litho tools. I took in the green sequins,
the antennae bobbing on a black man's head.

The doors clanged shut.

"Black bitch," he yelled, the other guy. "Bitch, bitch," he muttered

MEENA ALEXANDER was born in India and raised there and in North Africa. Now she lives and works in Manhattan. Her writing includes poetry: *House of a Thousand Doors*, *The Storm*, and *Night-Scene, the Garden*; a novel, *Nampally Road*; and a recently published memoir, *Fault Lines*. The present selection is an excerpt from a novel-in-progress. She is professor of English and creative writing at Hunter College and the Graduate Center, City University of New York.

under his breath. "Bloody black bitch." I stared down at my hands. I held my head proud. I looked the other way. I saw a small stick figure waving its red hands—jammed tight against a track. A new poster. La via del tren . . . Who am I? Who the hell am I? Stuck in Manhattan's black hole. Who?

Madeleine of Manhattan, you are in search of love.

I said this to myself, in a stage whisper. The young Latino male in the red coat stared at me puckering his lips, twitching the upper part of his face as if he'd been let out of Bellevue.

Toothpaste made my mind wander, the infinite variety. I selected one with multicoloured letters, C red, little r dark blue, e burning turquoise. I let the rest of the letters go. Took it to the checkout counter. Paid, counting out dimes, nickels, flat copper pennies. Getting the sum just right. Three cents off. Something twisted in my head. The morning paper. I touched it as I set foot in the street. Broadway. I knew it by heart. No pictures, nothing. Who needed that? Front page. Bottom right hand corner. New York Times: "5 Dead, Many Hurt in Derailment as Subway Nears Union Square." The train jumped the rail from 4 to 6. Metal carriage split. Five dead, over a hundred injured with the impact of collision.

Some guy from Crown Heights saying: "There was no warning. I thought it was the end of the world." People lying in a daze bleeding. It could have been me. Or Rashid. Trapped there in pig metal.

I could have been trapped on my way to visit him in his white room, set my cheek on the new pillows he picked up at the futon shop. I started complaining about my neck. "I love your brown neck." He kissed me in Arabic, making a word as he kissed. A little roughly. I loved that. "Halati," he crooned. I started complaining about my neck. "It hurts. Rub it for me Rashid. Please. Pretty please."

That neck might have been torn off. Just where he loved to kiss it. Rashid of the rounded lips and the delicate hands with blue veins running. My lover.

"I am New York, you are New York," he sang at me through his coffee cup. That was long ago. His mood changed, abruptly, as it often did:

"They killed me once," he said, looking at me dead straight. This was after we made love with the new pillow under my ass. I was raised as the princesses were raised in pharaonic days, pillows of down under brown asses. As Cleopatra was raised. Or was she fucked from the back?

"They killed me once," he repeated. "Then wore my face many times."

"Whose?" I asked, wiping the tears off my cheek.

"Samih al-Qasim," he replied, "poet of the Occupation. I met him once."

"Beirut," I asked.

"No, Gaza. Eyeless," he smiled at me. His black eyes spread into his face.

He stood by the window in Brooklyn utterly naked. I had the morning paper I had brought him. My tools too. A bit of rope I wanted to use for my installation. There was a tall tree behind him, a green tree waving its new leaves in the spring air, a tree visible through clean glass. And a flagpole. Greene Park. A red, white and blue flag.

"It's just a bloody circus. That's all it is."

My own voice rose in my head and I did not know what to do with it. Or with what was not voice, just sheer unmitigated body. Unredeemable.

"Bloody circus, bloody circus," I kept muttering.

"What's that?" he asked, a quizzical look on his face.

I quieted down immediately. Pretended to look at a tree or a stone, or was that water trembling behind us in Central Park?

"Shall we sit?"

"No, no." Suddenly he was uncomfortable with people around, even the shadow of the tourist from some Slavic country with a camera dangling helplessly from a shoulder. "Let's walk on a bit." How nervous he was getting. They had not yet started bombing Baghdad as we spoke. Raising rubble. Bombing the bridges, the watertanks, the baby milk factory. I could not bear it.

Through rough grass and odd nettles scraping the ankle we strolled to an elaborate arrangement of seats by an oak shaded path. On one side was a disused monument, something round and ugly and bald and grey, with graffiti on it, torn up like the stuff that New York is full of, I stopped and said:

"This bench do? Or can't you bear these faded American monuments, ugly, disused?"

"Why are you so damn symbolic," he snapped, "can't you stop it?" I started laughing as he stared at me. My kinky hair and brown skin started glowing, glowing. I shall invade his dreams for centuries to come.

In each of his births I shall be there.

I stood arms akimbo, legs apart, as if there were a sickle at my waist and a child on my back, its thighs against the GAP T-shirt dull orange with indigo stripes.

It's over now. The shit pile of history. I shall never visit Beirut with him, walk down the Hamra. Nor dream of Alexandria where he went to boarding school, where the wild philosophers roamed. I shall never go to Brooklyn with him, lay my naked body on a down pillow. Nor rendezvous by Columbus' cold statue, stroll with him in Central Park.

No more.

Through Rashid I met Varun.

"Call Sandhya," Varun said.

"Who?"

"Sandhya, my cousin."

"From India?" I asked.

"Yes, from India," he sounded amused. "Have I never mentioned her?"

"No, never."

"Call her, Madeleine. She's so stuck in her flat, husband child and all. An American man, she married in India. Rosenbloom. She's very lonely. Take her to the supermarket."

"The supermarket? You're nuts. Has Rashid been at you?"

He was bewildered. "Rashid is my friend," he said sternly. "We meet very often." Then he changed his tone.

"Take her to Bloomingdale's then. She wants to go shopping with you. Sandhya likes you—you see I spoke to her about you. She wants to learn about America. After all how much can Ronald do? Her husband. He's heavy into stocks these days or is it real estate? She knows there's no Janpath here." And Varun started laughing in that charming trill of his over the phone.

"Where are you calling from?" I asked suddenly.

"Briana's of course."

I heard her rustle something in the background. Or perhaps it was him.

"Look I have to rush to a gallery now," he went on. "They might take some of my shots."

His voice ran on as if he had guessed my thoughts:

"Janpath is the bazaar in Delhi, next to Cottage Industries, where you can pick up anything, a Tibetan tanka, a piece of blue pottery, cheap china, shoes, chappals, a condom, an imitation Gucci watch. You should go there sometime. Ciao. Call her, call her though."

2.

"Consider the roses," I said rather loudly.

"Roses?" She gave me a little smile, not wanting to offend.

I was in her small kitchen, back against pots and pans she'd neatly hooked on a white metal grid picked up at Zabar's the week before. I looked at her long and hard.

"Since you took me out, I've started shopping on my own," she said.

The kitchen was adequate, enough space for two adults to push pots and pans, make do. Enough for one dimpled three year old to shove peanut butter down her throat. Behind my back was Ronald's old toaster, a blender fit to fall apart, cups and saucers, plates and bowls with the blue fish mark one picks up in Chinatown for a dollar fifty a piece. Her housekeeping didn't amount to much, I could tell that.

A pile of dried thyme, mixed with sage, knotted up and hanging from a pin. That caught the light. That and Dora's mess of hair. I wanted to ask her about the herbs. She had her back to me, ladling chili out with a spoon, tossing it into oil, mixing it with turmeric and garam masala. Her back to me. She turned politely, feeling I needed more attention.

"I mean roses," I argued. "You and I. Females of colour. That old man Emerson. Cut off the past. Frisk it, skin it he said. Consider the roses. What are we standing on chile but Turtle Island?"

Something burst in the curved metal pot and she thrust her spoon to stir it, keeping her face away, averting her eyes. Do Indian women avert their eyes when cooking? I wondered. Then to be kind, I touched the rim of her sari. It had some embroidery on it. A sail, and upturned roof, I could not tell. She smiled again, wary I felt.

"Madeleine, please. Have some beer, juice, there's some bourbon too."

Later I sat at the edge of the window seat. Varun was there, Rashid too. Why the hell they asked him and me, all in one pour, when one subway car fixed with strong metals cannot hold us both? And where is that bloody Zeinab I thought, here or in Cairo, she with the bright red nails you dream of in between bombs bursting in air. I taught him that about America. But he knew it already, in his own words, his own rhythms. Beirut was his teacher. I sat staring at Rashid, who kept very still. He had a green shirt on with stripes, open at the neck. His neck was pale, as if cut out of beechwood. I knew every crease in his neck.

"Do you still teach your course on Desire in the Third World?" I asked, sitting very still, at the edge of the window seat. He was poised in that way of his, arms folded about his midriff, but a little nervous.

"Yes, Madeleine."

He said my name. Madeleine. Then Sandhya rushed in, Dora in one arm, the plate full of rice and lentils and fish with coconut poured over it, almost tipping from the other.

"He teaches a most fascinating course on post-colonial texts. Do you know that Madeleine? Do you know?"

"Yes," Ronald murmured, as if he sensed trouble.

"Even Connecticut is in trouble," Ronald said sternly, looking at me. "Unemployment to the hilt, stocks falling, brokers stripped to the skin in swimming pools."

"Eat cake," I laughed, "eat cake."

That was early January, a week before the bombs started falling on

Baghdad. Our bombs. And even the Iraqi rooster was deceived thinking it dawn. Christ the men on the floor in that hotel room in Baghdad, that was what our pool reporting was, saw the light bursting and then the cocks started crowing in the unnatural dawn.

Next time I was in the apartment, I noticed they had changed the cover on the captain's bed that doubled as a couch, something red with tie dye squares. When I admired it, Sandhya said she had picked it up in Ahmedabad, where she had friends. This was before Ronald.

"You know I married him right away," she laughed, with an air of grace, as if she had tricked fate or something. "I so wanted to come to America."

I felt she was evading something, what I didn't know, but still confiding in me as best she could.

"Well you gave birth to a child in the New World." I pointed at Dora's picture, set in a wooden frame. "That's more than me. I was born in Port of Spain, raised here though." I patted my own arm, the skin tingled. It was as if she hadn't heard. Her thoughts ran on:

"I have a cousin, a cardiologist in Kuwait. Masses of money. He had to flee when the Iraqis invaded. With his wife. The children were in college in India. They took the desert road as far as they could. Abandoned the car, got into a truck with some Pakistani workers and ended up in the desert outside Amman. There was barbed wire around in the transit camp."

Her eyes grew bleak as she said this. "There were bombs all around. Shrapnel. Amma told me this on the phone," she said. "I got such a clear line last week."

"American shrapnel, you know that don't you," I said softly, then added, "Iraqi too, I guess."

I bent my back against the wall, crossed my legs, adding, "I have a new friend, Rinaldo."

"O" she said, "O" her black eyes open very wide.

She poured me tea, passed me a plate with little samosas, bought she confided in the frozen food section of the supermarket. She ran off to the kitchen, picked up the container to show me.

"Imagine that," she said, "frozen samosas." She shivered, as if with thoughts of the desert nights when even samosas might freeze.

"I got a very clear line last week," she repeated as if it were such an oddity, "a clear line to Tiruvella. Amma told me that our next door neighbor in Kozencheri, my father's village, has a daughter who lived in Kuwait. She was eight months pregnant when they fled. She gave birth in the sand, in a transit camp outside Amman. There was very little water to wash her or the baby. He lived, a male child." She looked tearful as she said this, clutching Dora who sat quietly on her lap.

"Well, we're here, safe in Manhattan," I said to her, though I did not know where those words were coming from. "And you have Ronald."

"He's in Connecticut all day, you know that don't you?" she said in a small voice. Then staring at her child, her voice even softer:

"Sometimes I remember things. I try not to. Varun called by the way. He asked after you."

3.

At Franklin Furnace, setting eyes on me for the very first time, Rinaldo stared long and hard. It was an AIDS show I had a piece in. I had hung a bit of rope over the neck of a figure sculpted out of condoms, diaphragms, the congealed gel of an Orthotube—the stink smell I can't stand. The figure was blank faced, breastless, neither male nor female. Deliberately.

Spray painted the whole thing in orange, dazzling orange that shimmers in the dark. Set a wooden case around it cut with a peephole, so figure and the rope shone out.

Arrayed myself in Grandma Loulou's old cloak, the one she wore when KKK men spat at her, threatened her with death. Had my hair done in dreadlocks with brilliant orange beads to match the rope.

Just stood there with a sign next to the dark box with the hole in it. A handmade sign I carried it: "Choose your blood. This is America."

The cloak was tattered in parts.

I stood carefully against the wall. Next to me, an old gramophone played Nancy Sinatra's "You Only Live Twice." The music made me want to weep. A Thai woman did that piece and on the spindle she pasted cut outs of bikini clad prostitutes, bottoms twirling. The moral of this piece Sikrit explained to me later, is we are bought and sold for dollars. She started to explain this to Rinaldo when he came in. I noticed the muscular strength of him first.

The other side of me was a white woman's work. A shot of a vulva, delicately open, labia lipped out, clitoris showing, all the fragile softness of it, hair cloaking what would other wise be too black. Under the blown-up photo a sign in black and white: "Read my Lips Before they're sealed." Rosie, the white woman, stood by, placard in hand, well raised: "Our Bodies should be Playgrounds—Not Battlefields: Down with Madness in Wichita and Elsewhere in Our Land." And in smaller letters: "On May 23, 1991, the Supreme Court Upheld the Federal Government's right to deny funds to clinics that provide information about abortion."

"What this have to do with AIDS?" Sikrit asked, nudging at me.

"It's OK gal," I signalled. I could tell she was much struck by the piece.

On her front Rosie from Milwaukee wore a plastic blow up of the image, so magnified labia rippled as she moved in her skin tight leotards. She held up her hands for Rinaldo to see. I was watching quite closely. Black with fingerprint ink.

Other pieces too.

The Virgin of Guadalupe Simon Escobar my next door neighbour did. Him and his lover did it together. Bought the statue from the Botanica in the Bronx that Simon's aunt frequents, plastered it with images of gay couples, Latino and Chicano, Asian American, African American. Made a skirt for the virgin with condom packets. Around the black virgin's neck a rosary, each wax bead sculpted out as a tiny skull. Her eyes were bloodshot, the mad virgin of Guadalupe. She too had dollars round her neck. A hell of a lot of dollars there. The two men, Simon and Juan knelt in front of her. All of us in the show had to put our bodies on the line.

There were a few Jehovah's Witnesses protesting outside, though I think they had the wrong building. In the afternoon a few trickled back saying: "The end is approaching. It is the Lord's will." I took a break, still wearing the cloak. I felt ill. When I returned I saw Rinaldo first. His shoulders rippling under his coat. He looked at Rosie and her labia for a bit. Then walked over to me.

"Aha," he said.

"Yes?" I was quizzical.

"America?" he said in his Italian accent. I didn't know about the Fiat cars or anything then.

Stood straight. Set my shoulders back as Miss Howe my fifth-grader teacher in Nyack had told me. "You and I are coloured women," she pronounced, "we must set our shoulders back." I threw my left arm over the wooden box: "Take a lookie," I invited him. But he just stood there, raised his eyebrows.

"Yes, yes," I muttered, "I too am part of this show. This is America."

"No, no."

I understood. It was the bit about choosing your blood that threw him.

Earlier I had thought about having a spot of the real stuff on the label and writing MISCEGENATION in big letters under it, super-imposed on David Dukes' face, but I feared that would clutter it up.

I understood that he was foreign, that he needed an explanation. "I am born in Port of Spain, most part African American, descended from slaves. I am the pride of the Middle Passage. I am also part Asian American, from Japanese, Chinese, and Filipino blood: railroads in the West, the pineapple and sugarcane fields." I straightened up. "I also have a smattering of white—low European—in me. Hence the slight pallor, I suspect."

He smiled broadly at this.

After this speech I needed a break. When I went out he was there, conversing with one of the Jehovah's witnesses. He had just flown in from Naples, I heard him say.

"Come, come?" he said smiling, arms wide open in all that cold.

Fire, fire, the Jehovah's witnesses were yelling.

How could I resist? I require, dear Rinaldo, love that's made of fire. Remember when we listened to Lady Day together, lying on my floor?

4.

"Who am I? What sort of creature am I?" I asked this of Worthing-ton Arai as I stood arms akimbo, feet apart on the bare floor of the room he wants to sublet from me. My white room in Westbeth, by the Hudson's brink, seven floors up.

"What are we? What are we to do?"

At which he stared at me, a little cockeyed, in the way he's always been, black hair flaring over his head, dead straight, not a kink in it, Asian American male, thirty-seven years old, in good health, hoping not to cease till . . . Looks odd with his Brooks Brothers pin stripes.

"OK? OK NO?" he asked the other day tripping by from Wall Street. "I think I'll try the Health Club." Which one this time? Which one old Manhattanite?

Worthington and I have known each other a hell of a long time, all the way from the high school gym, the tuna fish sandwich in the shopping mall, the French fries I wrapped up for him oh so tenderly, before, before he fell in love's hellfire with Tom I had thought he was all mine, figuring America's side lanes on the back of his Harley.

Shit-shat he crashed, my Worthington, into the pizza store by the Hudson. His papa reared up to his five foot two in the Nyack back yard, in mid-winter, a week before Christmas when the Italian neighbours had set out their Christ child and crib matted with fake holly, the tiny lights gasping: year's out, year's out. And he said:

"I did not suffer with all my sansei blood, internment and all hell broken loose, the barbed wires of America in the small of my back, nor did my Hawaiian grandmother cut pineapples day and night in the fields, nor I sweat in the cannery, so you can crash that goddam bike with girl on the back."

Guilt trip massive as the black pipes they raised around the roadside for the new factory; powerplant sputtering its waste into grey waters.

Mr. Arai dragged him home, flung him into Tufts—the waste lands of Boston where I visited him once—thence to the golden floors of Wall street.

I stand with my back against a bare wall watching waves at my back as barges thrust in, mounded up with all the garbage Texas and Connecticut can't take. Boards by the piers rotting too where gay men pick and flirt with the gulls, with themselves too. We with ourselves.

"Worthington, take me, take me with you," I said to him one day "for the sake of our high school hours."

Hot hands, legs, thighs in the back of his father's Saab, in a side street in Nyack. He did.

"I might meet an old lover there," he muttered, staring at my wall and the bit of rope I had hooked up for my forthcoming Installation. "Would you care?"

"No, noo," I murmured ever so sweetly. I don't know if he heard or not but he zipped into his old leather jacket, gave me that dear cock eyed stare, for which I would follow him almost anywhere.

"You'll need your heavy coat," he said. "Best bring a plant, blend into the jungle."

I plucked an old orchid Rinaldo brought in from Brazil, Peru—God knows where, where ever Fiat is sold—dear Rinaldo without whom I could not—without whose cock I could not—he returns, orchids in his teeth for me. He sets them in my thighs.

"I am thigh brimful of orchids for you, dear cuchicoo," I murmured for him, setting water to boil in my old blue pan, the one I picked up at Orchard Street.

"I am making you cocoa Rinaldo, just as old mama used to."

And I hated myself for saying that, poking fun at him as he sat naked, squatting in the sunlight on my bare boards, a heavy set fifty-year-old man, the hair on him greying. A man . . .

Worthington needs a break. He needs a break from his East Side luxury. From his Wall Street pap. "The Dow Jones Industrial," I trill racing around him on the pier, doing an imitation of NPR, doing the Dow Jones. "What the hell is it, Worthington? A tube, a pile of male bile. There are some women in the pit too, aren't there. The heat of the free world concentrated therein?"

"I need out, Maddy," he said. Sometimes he calls me Maddy. "Let me sublet your room when you go off with Rinaldo." He was delicate about it too. "What does it take?"

"I won't charge you a penny more than I pay. Just rent, utilities and you'll have a perfect view of the waves and water." Listen though,

Worthington, in the month when Rinaldo takes me off, to what vineyard, what silken boudoir in Europe I don't know, you'll have my room.

"Still here I am, an Asian African treasure albeit with a New World stamp" I arranged myself against the window "being carried off on Rinaldo's arm to Europe, to the Indre et Loire to be precise, where pale wines flourish and Jeanne d'Arc was imprisoned. I am the New International. Really Worthington, consider my dark skin, my Asian African blood, a dash of white Florida bootlegger thrown in, consider my orchids."

But he was looking at me rather oddly now:

"Maddy let's have coffee OK. Larry just left for Themesville, cleaned out all his stuff. Makes me feel a little sick."

He sat down heavily, his back to my window, went on: "What choices do we have? Who are we Maddy? Who?"

"Worthington I think I'm going out of my head," I blurted out. "Just like Sandhya did. Remember what she did to herself?"

It was evening, low skies, grey water outside my window, troubled Hudson water. I was trying to pack my suitcase with sketches for the Installation, silk pants, two sets in black, a pink packet of Lo-Ovral, though Rinaldo feels that at my age it's not a good idea to take them, hairbrush, opal beads, toothbrush. Small red suitcase, slightly bashed in.

"Nonsense," he replied. He can be curt like that sometimes.

"I bet she just wants us to think she's vanished. I bet Sandhya's in that motel, right by the Hall of Fame. Her Indian relatives bought it. The Philadelphia bunch. You told me so. Larry may not be so far from there, cleaned me out Maddy. He cleaned me out."

His voice slipped low, his old sorrow. His elegant Larry.

Just this time of day, a year ago almost he brought Larry up and I made tofu in my wok, with capers, scallions, red peppers. And Rinaldo came too, late as usual and we watched the lights on the water, on the barges filled with refuse, the pale roofs of New Jersey.

"It really is another country isn't it?" said Larry. "I always feel that when I go into Hoboken."

Rinaldo picked up at that and went on about the Unity of Europe, crossing over from the Basque lands and almost getting stabbed by a mad voyou in Paris, right by the Tour Eiffel and all that. And Worthington looked a little embarrassed for me, at all my richesses as it were, and Larry and he reminisced about a little fish restaurant in Hoboken, right by the water's edge.

"Larry cleaned me out, Maddy, my insides I mean." Worthington's voice was sad and slow. I stood by my red suitcase, brimful. I decided not to listen to him anymore.

"So where is Sandhya now?" he asked and then added, as if to save himself from thoughts of Larry, "Not in India any more. No, right here, a stone's throw away. Cooperstown I bet, good old Sandhya."

I turned away from Worthington. I set my back to him. I felt the ceaseless present flowing, flowing.

Rico

Peter Bacho

Rico enlisted just before the start of my senior year in high school. I never thought those days would seem as distant as Burma, or Myanmar, as some now call it, or even Vietnam. I was almost seventeen then and Rico was a little more than a year older. We were both starting to peer beyond the boundaries of the poor neighborhood that tied us down but protected us and made us strong. It was our home and, in my view, he ruled it.

He was tall for a Filipino and rather slim. But he made up for his lack of bulk with a big heart and by being strong, fast, and clever— traits that earned him respect even from the bloods, and they were always the hardest to impress.

White girls were a lot easier. Although there were the occasional rich ones from across Lake Washington, Rico usually dated the daughters of working class families in Seattle's nearby South End. They lived

---

PETER BACHO teaches writing in San Francisco. His first novel, *Cebu*, won the 1992 American Book Award. He is currently working on a collection of short stories entitled *First, There Were the Men*. The short story "Rico" is part of that collection.

closer which, when you're poor, young, and travel mainly by bus, was a major consideration. There were other young women Rico could have had—Filipinos, Asians, blacks, all pretty by any standard—but to them he paid no mind. His social tastes were strictly segregated and, the way I see it, he was lured most by the taboo against interracial dating.

There were the inevitable hassles—disapproving looks from the girl's parents and snide remarks and occasional fistfights with her male friends—but Rico never cared.

I once suggested his social course needed a change of direction, and that maybe it was just too much trouble. "Why?" he laughed. "I'm just following tradition."

We both knew the baggage from our fathers' generation; they were young and single, a randy bunch, more Latin than "Oriental" in outlook. In those days they wandered the West Coast, following the crops. Life was hard, but not without occasional rewards. Growing up, we'd hear it in their stories when the old men would gather for rummy and beer: Ticoy, remember that waitress? Blondie. Big one. San Jose was it? No, mebbe Santa Maria.

Unlike other Asians, they didn't worry much about protecting the purity of race and culture, particularly if it interfered with a good time. The Philippines never developed those myths largely because it was a polyglot colony that for centuries had been an open port for the world's conquerors, priests, merchants, deadbeats, and thieves. The oldtimers, products of this bastard milieu, slept freely with women of different races. Like miniature Mandingos, they freely disregarded America's most serious social ban, and brazenly left evidence of their conduct: progeny as varied as the colors of Joseph's coat.

If this meant risking the wrath of local vigilantes, then that's what it meant.

Rico admired their attitude, their defiance, and adopted it. The vigilantes were gone, but not all of the hostility toward race mixing. These he disregarded because, after all, they got in the way of a good time.

Some of his best times, mine as well, were at the weekly teen dances on Empire Way. On Friday nights, live music shook the walls of an old bowling alley, recently converted into a community center. The crowd, mostly Filipino and black, always included a handful of white girls. They stood against the walls in the dimly lit building, their pale skin and high bouffants shining like beacons in the dark.

Rico always showed up at the dances alone, resplendent in his tight black slacks, matching black jacket, and felt hat with a narrow, "stingy" brim. He wore pointed Italian boots and a pink shirt with a high collar pressed to a sharp thin edge. All that was missing was the Cadillac, which he wanted but couldn't come close to affording. So he arrived by bus, riding it like a prince of public transportation. I knew he didn't have a car, but it made no difference to the young women he left with even if they had to pay their own fare.

Rico figured he was doing them a favor. They were in it, he said, for the danger.

The bands, always black, carried a horn section in addition to two guitarists and a drummer. The extra members shrank each musician's share of the profit, which wasn't much to start with. But no matter. This was black music, not white, and the horns made it raw and powerful, something white bands never could do.

Rico loved the horns and the sweating black angels who played them. The brass was his rhythm and blues herald and once it kicked in, he'd scan the room and wordlessly choose his partner, usually a semi-lovely blonde. There were never any words, none were needed, just a nod in the general direction of the dance floor.

Inevitably, she'd follow because she knew who Rico was and understood the rules. Out on the floor she'd move and match the rhythm, sometimes well, as white girls trying to pass for something else were often able to do. But it was Rico's show, and he was its dark star.

If the music was slow, Rico would hold her tight and softly sing the lyrics of lost or impossible love. With the horns setting the mournful mood, he'd roll her rhythmically with his thigh between her legs; using it like a rudder, he'd guide her inches off the floor as he leaned back. I told him once that I could always tell his dance partners; they walked funny, like they'd spent the day on horseback.

Rico changed with the song. To an upbeat tempo he'd skate across the hall, gliding on one leg like James Brown, never a single pomaded hair ever out of place. Then he'd stop suddenly, do the splits from which he'd rise to continue his journey to the other side. He defied gravity, just like James.

And just like James, his most obvious talents weren't suited for college. He had other skills, other deep potentials, but by the time public school was through with him, I know he wasn't sure what they were, or even that they were.

Before Rico left for the Marines, we had a chance to talk one last time. I'd heard a rumor he'd enlisted and had to find out. I knew where to look too—the Cherry Street, a small boxing gym downtown. He was always honing skills he knew would be useful outside the ring. Although he'd fought just a couple of amateur fights, the old guys said he had "pro" written across the knuckles of both hands.

He was there when I walked in, sparring a scared looking Mexican kid. I arrived just in time to see him throw a perfectly timed right hand counter at his foe's head that, even with thick headgear and fat sparring gloves, managed to knock him hard against the ropes. It was the kind of punch that loosens your eyeballs and rolls them under your brain. It was even more devastating because Rico threw it just as the Mexican was leaning into his own jab, thus doubling the impact.

Rico, the old men said, was a natural counterpuncher. It's a rare gift that allowed him to attack when he sensed an opponent's offensive move. Rico had just displayed his talent; the sound of the punch, his perfect form, the sharp backward snap of the Mexican's head, all testified to it. This quick sequence of events, witnessed by myself and the small circle of Cherry Street regulars, drew our collective "ooh."

We knew an assassin was at work and like a good craftsman, Rico knew his work wasn't done. Seeing the Mexican draped helplessly against the ropes with his hands down was too good an invitation to resist. He almost skipped like a schoolgirl to close the distance between him and his prey, holding his right hand back a bit more than usual.

He had enough torque in his right to launch his victim on a straight trajectory, like one of Henry Aaron's line drives, to some southern point where Spanish was spoken. I knew it, and evidently Tommy did too.

Tommy, a part-time manager, also ran the Cherry Street. He was once a decent pro, but it must have been years ago. Rico always pointed out Tommy's ample belly and explained that he boxed before the discovery of electricity and pan fried pork chops laced heavily with garlic.

I was surprised that the old manager, despite his girth, was nimble enough to scramble into the ring and slide like a fat snake on his gut. He was vainly trying to beat Rico to his launching spot.

The old man knew he was too late, but yelled anyway. "Stop," he screamed from his prone position as the right hand rocket took off.

"Goddamnit," Tommy muttered from the canvas. The Mexican's torso sagged deep into the ropes, which strained before flinging him face forward.

He was out before he hit and landed on his nose and lips, surely not his landing gear of choice, around which small pools of blood started to form. At the side of his face lay his mouthpiece, jarred loose by the impact.

Tommy was livid as he turned to look at the prostrate body; his assistants, armed with smelling salts and towels were now entering the ring. The old man rose, positioning himself close to Rico and in front of him.

"Get outta here," he screamed as he pumped his stubby arms against his sides. With each hit, his heavy tits shook more than a stripper's. I giggled; he looked like he was trying to fly.

"You got it," Rico said calmly as he turned to go.

"And don't come back," Tommy added.

"Got that, too." Rico spoke calmly as he crawled between the ropes. He paused, one leg in the ring the other out, and turned toward Tommy.

"Too much garlic in them last chops," Rico said. "Smell like a gypsy queen."

"You're outta here," Tommy screamed, hurt by the truth.

Rico started to walk toward the dressing room. "Startin' to look like one too, fatso," he said without looking back but loud enough to be heard.

It wasn't the first time Tommy had yelled at Rico for losing control and fighting instead of sparring. But I thought this might really be it—not because Tommy wouldn't take him back, a fight manager almost never turns away a potential moneymaker and Tommy loved my friend's talent more than porkchops—but because Rico knew it was over and wanted to leave with a bang. That was his way.

I wondered what he'd say as I followed him back to the dressing room. I opened the door slowly and saw him in the dim light sitting on a stool, slumped in front of his locker. The cool air collided with the heat from his body creating steam that covered him like morning fog. It was a little eerie. I stood by the door, waiting for him to turn and speak or otherwise signal a return to more familiar terrain.

Finally, he looked over his shoulder and nodded at me. It wasn't much of a sign, but it would do for the moment.

"Goin' up in smoke, man," I said, trying to sound calm.

Rico looked at himself. He chuckled. "Sure 'nough."

"What happened?"

"Fucker uppercut me," he explained. "But that pig, Tommy, didn't do shit. He knows the rules for sparring. Break clean, no cheap shots."

"Nailed me good, too," he said angrily, pointing to a discolored spot on his neck. "Wanted a fight, so he got one. Stapled his face to the floor."

I nodded while Rico laughed at the recent memory of the prostrate Mexican.

At that point I felt comfortable enough to raise the question that brought me to the gym in the first place.

"I heard, man," I said quietly. "True story?"

He didn't answer.

"Your mom called mine and she don't want you to. . . ."

He interrupted me and stared at the floor as he spoke. "Can't help it," he said. "Got nothin' goin' here."

It was the answer I didn't want. I glanced around the room, searching for a spot to sit. I felt heavy, like a bunch of men, each the size of Buddha, had jumped on my back. Spotting a bench across the room, I walked toward it.

"Damn," I said to myself as I sat and buried my face in my hands. The draft had already claimed more young Filipinos from our neighborhood than I cared to count. Blacks, too. A few had enlisted. I regarded military service as inevitable; we all did. In that sense we were like our fathers and uncles who fought in Europe or in the Pacific and, if they were lifers as many Filipinos were, in Korea, too. The government would call, and we would go. It was as simple as that.

We vaguely hated Communism, although we couldn't tell Groucho Marx from Karl. I didn't learn until much later that poor boys always carried the flag in dangerous places for powerful, arrogant, and profoundly foolish old white men. But that was later.

At sixteen, all I knew was that our time was coming. I just wanted it postponed, when Rico and I could do it together.

"Had to, Buddy," he said, using my nickname and interrupting my morose reverie. "Got no school, got no job. Ain't colored, so ain't got no African thing."

"What we got?" Rico asked, referring to Filipinos in general and himself in particular. He was that way sometimes when he talked about his future, one he was sure he didn't have. Rico stared at me straight and hard.

I scratched my head and scrambled. I had to throw a curve and back him off.

"White girls," I finally said. "Especially blondes, tall long legged ones."

His laugh finally broke the momentum that was building to an uncomfortable point.

"Yeah," he laughed. "Devils. But I love 'em. Most bloods don't touch 'em now, you know, with that black power stuff and all, except maybe Sammy Davis."

He smirked. "Leaves more for me."

At that point I was confident enough to try to turn it serious again. "Rico, don't go," I said quietly. "There's ways, you know, deferments. White guys do it all the time. Like marriage. . . ."

He shook his head and looked at me like I was the Mexican kid on the canvas.

"College," I said, trying again. I knew I was grasping and I knew he did, too.

He rolled his eyes in confirmation. "Yeah," he said. "Like I'm a perfect candidate."

I was making no points and getting a little desperate. "Your mom," I said finally.

That hit the spot and forced him to pause before speaking.

"Don't play that, man," he said finally. "I love her, but I'm eighteen, I signed, and I'm gone. Marines own my butt now, not mama."

That ended it. I knew the matter was closed before I had a chance to open it. The Buddhas got heavier and I sagged a bit more.

Rico sensed this and tried his best to cheer me up.

"Hey man, every Flip wants a gunfight," he said with bravado. "You know, our heroic but futile tradition. Bataan and all. More stuff to impress the ladies with and tell the kids."

His attempt to cheer me didn't work. Undeterred he tried another route.

"I thought about leavin' and what I'd leave you." Rico spoke solemnly as he reached into his training bag. He found what he was looking for and handed it to me; it was a small black address book.

I looked at the small book and reached to take it.

"What's this?" I asked dully.

Rico feigned surprise. "You raised in a cave or what? It's an address book, Gomer, full of white girls, 'specially blondies. Ain't gonna need it now. Gettin' me a new one anyway, full of Vietnamese writin' and Vietnamese names."

"I'm changin' my taste," he said, hands shaking in imitation of a drum roll. "Expandin' horizons. Goin' like Columbus where no Flip's ever been. . . ."

Trash alert. It would soon be coming heavy, and I didn't want to hear it.

"Damn, man, all right, OK," I said sharply.

He seemed to notice my irritation, or at least that's what I thought. "I've had this book a long, long time," he said. Rico sounded serious, but it was hard to tell. But going to war was no trifling matter, so, like a trout rising to a fisherman's fly, I gave him the benefit of the doubt.

I was wrong.

"Got it years ago," he said with the same solemn tone that lured me quicker to the bait.

My silence told Rico I was hooked. He paused dramatically before reeling me in.

"Before my first shorthair," he said in a near whisper.

Deadpan, he continued. "What the hell," he said as he shrugged his shoulders, "a boy's gotta dream."

I couldn't help smiling despite my growing irritation and sense of impending loss. He didn't miss a step.

"That book there," he said before repeating himself for emphasis. "That book there even got a name."

It was too late. It was Rico's dialogue, just like it was always his dance. My role was just to come along.

"What is it, man?" I asked with a sigh.

" 'Hos I Know,' " he said.

Rico studied me, searching for a sign of reaction. I didn't give him one; for me the moment was too serious.

"Oh," I said flatly. "So, this is it?"

I heard myself speak the words creating the accusation. I'd miss him, which was all the more reason to keep the tone even because in our neighborhood, emotion was for sissies and not to be shown, ever, even to friends. I thought I'd succeeded, too.

I guess I didn't.

"Hey," Rico said, "it ain't forever." His voice was softer. I studied him; this time he wasn't setting me up.

"Man, at least come by tonight," I said hopefully. "My folks, dinner, you know, a righteous goodbye."

"Can't."

I knew that for Rico "can't" meant "can't," never "maybe." I pressed him, though, because there was nothing to lose. I shot both barrels, or tried to.

"The folks, man, they. . . ."

"Can't." His tone was firmer and ended any further appeal to my parents' affection. Rico looked at me and didn't speak until he was convinced I got the message.

"Look," he said finally, "got some time before reportin' and I'm gettin' outta town, maybe Frisco. Ain't never been there and I'd like to go, you know, like Cookie said he'd do."

Cookie was our friend, a sweet young black kid we grew up with. Like Rico and me, and everyone else in the neighborhood, he was poor and just muddling through.

All he talked about once he figured out his penis wasn't just for aiming at a pot was getting laid. Unlike Rico, he didn't care much about race—a fact attested to by his multi-colored children and their angry mono-colored grandparents who universally threatened to harm him. He placed more importance on a girl's attitude; enthusiasm counted. His other concerns were finding more eligibles and safer places to hide.

Cookie knew Seattle was too small; he kept bumping into relatives of his lovers who wanted to kill him. The last, the brother of a Chinese girl, almost did, shooting at him with a large caliber semi-automatic but missing. His frustrated assailant shouted at the fleeing Cookie that the next time he'd turn him into a barbecue slab and hang him from a hook.

The image of his glazed flank on display in the front window of a Chinatown restaurant frightened him, and he decided it was time to go. Cookie had to figure out where and thought he'd found heaven when he read about San Francisco and its sexual and political revolution.

I last saw Cookie at his house. He'd called to say he was leaving town. He'd grown his hair out and I listened while he recited a litany of black power tenets.

"You an African, man," Cookie said to me as I walked through the door.

"Nah, man," I said. "Got it wrong, blood. I dance like one, but you the African."

"Really, Buddy, really," Cookie said sounding earnest. "Listened to this talk show last night. Had this blood, a professor from California. He says life started in Africa; that makes us Africans."

"That include LBJ?" I asked.

"Guess so," he said.

"Shit," I said. "Pay money to see him dance."

"Shit," he replied. "Pay money not to."

Knowing Cookie, I figured he embraced only those parts of the emerging black creed that suited him. After we agreed I wasn't an African, he confirmed my suspicion. He said he was going to San Francisco to surrender himself to a commune full of middle class hippie girls.

"I'm promotin' social justice, man," he said smugly.

Somehow, I'd never pictured Cookie as the chosen vehicle for social progress. "Sure," I said with undisguised cynicism.

"Hey, man," he said with a shrug. "We ain't rich white boys. Poor folk gets over any way we can. You know that."

Cookie was about to leave before his draft notice came. He never got over Vietnam, dying there, or reached San Francisco, either.

Rico didn't want to make the same mistake. Whatever would happen in the Marines, well, that would happen. In the days left he could call his own, I knew he'd be going to Frisco. It was a good reason, maybe the best, so I backed off and let the matter drop.

He must have known I'd surrendered, and that giving up wasn't easy.

"Look," he said softly, "it's hard, 'specially cuz you and me are like this." He clenched his fist to illustrate. "Tight like brothers."

Sadly I glanced at him and nodded agreement.

"Guess this is it," I said as I extended my hand. "Better get goin'."

He gripped it hard and pulled me to him. We hugged awkwardly.

"Look," he said after releasing me, "you're smart and you're goin' to Catholic school. If the shit's still goin' a year from now, get your butt in college. At least you can cut a deal and be an officer with a safe job and a desk. Don't do like I'm about to and go put yourself in a box."

He was then silent for minute, maybe more, staring at the floor and breathing heavily. When he finally spoke I was surprised and a bit unnerved by what I thought was the tone of his voice and his choice of words.

"Damn," he muttered.

"Damn," he said again as he looked at me. "We're like brothers, you know, but we're different cuz you got choices here and I don't. Only choice for me's a door to a war zone and hope that if I survive that, then maybe it gets better."

He paused before speaking again.

"Buddy," he added bitterly, "you got hope without even havin' to leave town."

I wasn't sure if his anger was directed at me or his situation.

"Rico," I said while reaching desperately for something to say. "Man, I . . ."

"Better leave, man," he said cutting me off. "We're cool, but I just gotta sort it out."

Staring at him, I tried to understand the new face of an old friend. I froze and stayed seated because I couldn't accept what I'd just heard.

He stared back. "Man, you understand English?"

I did. This time his anger was clear. Instinctively I rose and took the first steps of a backward shuffle toward the door. I knew that tone, having heard it directed at scores of childhood enemies, but never before at me.

As I retreated I didn't take my eyes off him and, to this day, I'm not sure if it was because of fear for what he might do, or love for a friend I may never see again. Opening the door, I lingered to look and saw him through the dim light, slouched forward, head bowed.

I took that picture and folded it into a seam of eternal memory as I turned toward the exit. I knew I'd think about it, not just that night or the next, but for a long time to come.

I Would Remember

Carlos Bulosan

I first saw death when I was a small boy in the little village where I was born. It was a cool summer night and the sky was as clear as day and the ripening rice fields were golden in the moonlight. I remember that I was looking out the window and listening to the sweet mating calls of wild birds in the tall trees nearby when I heard my mother scream from the dark corner of the room where she had been lying for several days because she was big with child. I ran to her to see what was going on, but my grandmother darted from somewhere in the faint candlelight and held me close to the warm folds of her cotton skirt.

My mother was writhing and kicking frantically at the old woman

CARLOS BULOSAN, self-taught Filipino writer and union activist, was born in the Philippines in 1913 and became the foremost chronicler of the Filipino/Filipino American struggle. He arrived in Seattle in 1930 and, until his death in 1956, Bulosan wrote in many literary genres. His best-known work is his autobiographical novel, *America Is in the Heart*, and *The Laughter of My Father*. Much of his fiction was published in the 1940s in *The New Yorker*, as well as *Harper's Bazaar*, *Arizona Quarterly*, and most recently in a 1979 issue of *Amerasia Journal* devoted to his life and writings.

who was attending her, but when the child was finally delivered and cleaned I saw that my mother was frothing at the mouth and slowly becoming still. She opened her eyes and tried to look for me in the semi-darkness, as though she had something important to tell me. Then she closed her eyes and lay very still.

My grandmother took me to the field at the back of our house and we sat silently under the bending stalks of rice for hours and once, when I looked up to push away the heavy grain that was tickling my neck, I saw the fleeting shadow of a small bird across the sky followed by a big bat. The small bird disappeared in the periphery of moonlight and darkness, shrieking fiercely when the bat caught up with it somewhere there beyond the range of my vision. Then I thought of my mother who had just died and my little brother who was born to take her place, but my thoughts of him created a terror inside me and when my grandmother urged me to go back to the house I burst into tears and clutched desperately at two huge stalks of rice so that she could not pull me away. My father came to the field then and carried me gently in his arms, and I clung tightly to him as though he alone could assuage my grief and protect me from all the world.

I could not understand why my mother had to die. I could not understand why my brother had to live. I was fearful of the motives of the living and the meaning of their presence on the earth. And I felt that my little brother, because he had brought upon my life a terrorizing grief, would be a stranger to me forever and ever. It was my first encounter with death; so great was its impress on my thinking that for years I could not forget my mother's pitiful cries as she lay dying.

My second encounter with death happened when I was ten years old. My father and I were plowing in the month of May. It was raining hard that day and our only working carabao was tired and balked at moving. This animal and I grew up together like brothers; he was my constant companion in the fields and on the hillsides at the edge of our village when the rice was growing.

My father, who was a kind and gentle man, started beating him with sudden fury. I remember that there was a frightening thunderclap somewhere in the world, and I looked up suddenly toward the eastern sky and saw a wide arc of vanishing rainbow. It was then that my father started beating our carabao mercilessly. The animal jumped from the mud and ran furiously across the field, leaving the wooden plow stuck into the trunk of a large dead tree. My father unsheathed his sharp bolo and raced after him, the thin blade of the steel weapon gleaming in the slanting rain. At the edge of a deep pit where we burned felled trees and huge roots, the carabao stopped and looked back; but, sensing the anger of my father, he plunged headlong into the pit. I could not move for a moment; then I started running madly toward the pit.

My father climbed down the hole and looked at the carabao with tears in his eyes. I do not know if they were tears of sadness or of repressed fury. But when I had climbed down after him, I saw big beads of sweat rolling down his forehead, mingling with his tears and soaking his already wet ragged farmer's clothes. The carabao had broken all his legs and he was trembling and twisting in the bottom of the pit. When my father raised the bolo in his hands to strike at the animal, I turned away and pressed my face in the soft embankment. Then I heard his hacking at the animal, grunting and cursing in the heavy rain.

When I looked again the animal's head was completely severed from the body, and warm blood was flowing from the trunk and making a red pool under our feet. I wanted to strike my father, but instead, fearing and loving him, I climbed out of the pit quickly and ran through the blinding rain to our house.

Twice now I had witnessed violent deaths. I came across death again some years afterward on a boat when, on my way to America, I befriended a fellow passenger of my age named Marco.

He was an uneducated peasant boy from the northern part of our island who wanted to earn a little money in the new land and return to his village. It seemed there was a girl waiting for him when he came back, and although she was also poor and uneducated, Marco found happiness in her small brown face and simple ways. He showed me a faded picture of her and ten dollars he had saved up to have it enlarged when we arrived in the new land.

Marco had a way of throwing back his head and laughing loudly, the way peasants do in that part of the island. But he was quick and sensitive; anger would suddenly appear in his dark face, then fear, and then laughter again; and sometimes all these emotions would simultaneously appear in his eyes, his mouth, his whole face. Yet he was sincere and honest in whatever he did or said to me.

I got seasick the moment we left Manila, and Marco started hiding oranges and apples in his suitcase for me. Fruits were the only things I could eat, so in the dead of night when the other passengers were stirring in their bunks and peering through the dark to see what was going on, I sat up. Suddenly there was a scream and someone shouted for the light. I ran to the corner and clicked the switch and when the room was flooded with light, I saw Marco lying on the floor and bleeding from several knife wounds on his body. I knelt beside him, but for a moment only, because he held my hands tightly and died. I looked at the people around me and then asked them to help me carry the body to a more comfortable place. When the steward came down to make an inventory of Marco's suitcase, the ten dollars was gone. We shipped back the suitcase, but I kept the picture of the girl.

I arrived in America when thousands of people were waiting in line for a piece of bread. I kept on moving from town to town, from one filthy job to another, and then many years were gone. I even lost the girl's picture and for a while forgot Marco and my village.

I met Crispin in Seattle in the coldest winter of my life. He had just arrived in the city from somewhere in the east and he had no place to stay. I took him to my room and for days we slept together, eating what we could buy with the few cents that we begged in gambling houses from night to night. Crispin had drifted most of his life and he could tell me about other cities. He was very gentle and there was something luminous about him, like the strange light that flashes in my mind when I sometimes think of the hills of home. He had been educated and he recited poetry with a sad voice that made me cry. He always spoke of goodness and beauty in the world.

It was a new experience and the years of loneliness and fear were shadowed by the grace of his hands and the deep melancholy of his eyes. But the gambling houses were closed toward the end of that winter and we could not beg anymore from the gamblers because they were also starving. Crispin and I used to walk in the snow for hours looking for nothing, waiting for the cold night to fall, hoping for the warm sun to come out of the dark sky. And then one night when we had not eaten for five days, I got out of bed and ate several pages of an old newspaper by soaking them in a can of water from the faucet in our room. Choking tears came out of my eyes, but the deep pain in my head burst wide open and blood came out of my nose. I finally went to sleep from utter exhaustion, but when I woke up again, Crispin was dead.

Yes, it was true. He was dead. He had not even contemplated death. Men like Crispin who had poetry in their soul come silently into the world and live quietly down the years, and yet when they are gone no moon in the sky is lucid enough to compare with the light they shed when they are among the living.

After nearly a decade of wandering and rootlessness, I lost another good friend who had guided me in times of helplessness. I was in California in a small agricultural community. I lived in a big bunkhouse of thirty farm workers with Leroy, who was a stranger to me in many ways because he was always talking about unions and unity. But he had a way of explaining the meanings of words in utter simplicity, like "work," which he translated into "power," and "power" into "security." I was drawn to him because I felt that he had lived in many places where the courage of men was tested with the cruelest weapons conceivable.

One evening I was eating with the others when several men came into our bunkhouse and grabbed Leroy from the table and dragged him outside. He had been just about to swallow a ball of rice when the men burst into the place and struck Leroy viciously on the neck with thick leather thongs. He fell on the floor and coughed up the ball of rice. Before Leroy realized what was happening to him, a big man came toward him from the darkness with a rope in his left hand and a shining shotgun in the other. He tied the rope around Leroy's neck while the other men pointed their guns at us, and when they had taken him outside, where he began screaming like a pig about to be butchered, two men stayed at the door with their aimed guns. There was some scuffling outside, then silence, and then the two men slowly withdrew with their guns, and there was a whispering sound of running feet on the newly cut grass in the yard and then the smooth purring of cars speeding away toward the highway and then there was silence again.

We rushed outside all at once, stumbling against each other. And there hanging on a tall eucalyptus tree, naked and shining in the pale light of the April moon, Leroy was swinging like a toy balloon. We cut him down and put him on the grass, but he died the moment we reached him. His genitals were cut and there was a deep knife wound in his chest. His left eye was gone and his tongue was sliced into tiny shreds. There was a wide gash across his belly and his entrails plopped out and spread on the cool grass.

That is how they killed Leroy. When I saw his cruelly tortured body, I thought of my father and the decapitated carabao and the warm blood flowing under our bare feet. And I knew that all my life I would remember Leroy and all the things he taught me about living.

Melpomene Tragedy

Theresa Hak Kyung Cha

She could be seen sitting in the first few rows. She would be sitting in the first few rows. Closer the better. The more. Better to eliminate presences of others surrounding better view away from that which is left behind far away back behind more for closer view more and more face to face until nothing else sees only this view singular. All dim, gently, slowly until in the dark, the absolute darkness the shadows fade.

She is stretched out as far as the seat allows until her neck rests on the back of the seat. She pulls her coat just below her chin enveloped

THERESA HAK KYUNG CHA, multimedia artist and author of *DICTEE*, was born in Pusan, Korea, in 1951. At the time of her tragic death in 1982, Cha had been working on several projects, including a film and a book. In 1992–93, a retrospective of her video, film, and textual work was exhibited at the Whitney Museum in New York. *DICTEE* has deeply influenced the works of Korean and other Asian American women writers and visual artists.

in one mass before the moving shades, flickering light through the empty window, length of the gardens the trees in perfect a symmetry.

The correct time beyond the windows the correct season the correct forecast. Beyond the empty the correct setting, immobile. Placid. Extreme stillness. Misplaces nothing. Nothing equivalent. Irreplaceable. Not before. Not after.

The submission is complete. Relinquishes even the vision to immobility. Abandons all protests to that which will appear to the sight. About to appear. Forecast. Break. Break, by all means. The illusion that the act of viewing is to make alteration of the visible. The expulsion is immediate. Not one second is lost to the replication of the totality. Total severance of the seen. Incision.

April 19
Seoul, Korea

Dear Mother,

4. 19. Four Nineteen, April 19th, eighteen years later. Nothing has changed, we are at a standstill. I speak in another tongue now, a second tongue a foreign tongue. All this time we have been away. But nothing has changed. A stand still.

It is not 6. 25. Six twenty five. June 25th 1950. Not today. Not this day. There are no bombs as you had described them. They do not fall, their shiny brown metallic backs like insects one by one after another.

The population standing before North standing before South for every bird that migrates North for Spring and South for Winter becomes a metaphor for the longing of return. Destination. Homeland.

No woman with child lifting sand bags barriers, all during the night for the battles to come.

There is no destination other than towards yet another refuge from yet another war. Many generations pass and many deceptions in the sequence in the chronology towards the destination.

You knew it would not be in vain. The thirty six years of exile. Thirty six years multiplied by three hundred and sixty five days. That one day your country would be your own. This day did finally come. The Japanese were defeated in the world war and were making their descent back to their country. As soon as you heard, you followed South. You carried not a single piece, not a photograph, nothing to evoke your memory, abandoned all to see your nation freed.

From another epic another history. From the missing narrative. From the multitude of narratives. Missing. From the chronicles. For another telling for other recitations.

Our destination is fixed on the perpetual motion of search. Fixed in its perpetual exile. Here at my return in eighteen years, the war is not ended. We fight the same war. We are inside the same struggle seeking the same destination. We are severed in Two by an abstract enemy an invisible enemy under the title of liberators who have conveniently named the severance, Civil War. Cold War. Stalemate.

I am in the same crowd, the same coup, the same revolt, nothing has changed. I am inside the demonstration I am locked inside the crowd and carried in its movement. The voices ring shout one voice then many voices they are waves they echo I am moving in the direction the only one direction with the voices the only direction. The other movement towards us it increases steadily their direction their only direction our mutual destination towards the other against the other. Move.

I feel the tightening of the crowd body to body now the voices rising thicker I hear the break the single motion tearing the break left of me right of me the silence of the other direction advance before . . . They are breaking now, their sounds, not new, you have heard them, so familiar to you now could you ever forget them not in your dreams, the consequences of the sound the breaking. The air is made visible with smoke it grows spreads without control we are hidden inside the whiteness the greyness reduced to parts, reduced to separation. Inside an arm lifts above the head in deliberate gesture and disappears into the thick white from which slowly the legs of another bent at the knee hit the ground the entire body on its left side. The stinging, it slices the air it enters thus I lose direction the sky is a haze running the streets emptied I fell no one saw me I walk. Anywhere. In tears the air stagnant continues to sting I am crying the sky remnant the gas smoke absorbed the sky I am crying. The streets covered with chipped bricks and debris. Because. I see the frequent pairs of shoes thrown sometimes a single pair among the rocks they had carried. Because. I cry wail torn shirt lying I step among them. No trace of them. Except for the blood. Because. Step among them the blood that will not erase with the rain on the pavement that was walked upon like the stones where they fell had fallen. Because. Remain dark the stains not wash away. Because. I follow the crying crowd their voices among them their singing their voices unceasing the empty street.

There is no surrendering you are chosen to fail to be martyred to shed blood to be set an example one who has defied one who has chosen to defy and was to be set an example to be martyred an animal useless betrayer to the cause to the welfare to peace to harmony to progress.

It is 1962 eighteen years ago same month same day all over again. I am eleven years old. Running to the front door, Mother, you are holding my older brother pleading with him not to go out to the demonstration. You are threatening him, you are begging to him. He has on his school uniform, as all the other students representing their schools in the demonstration. You are pulling at him you stand before the door. He argues with you he pushes you away. You use all your force, all that you have. He is prepared to join the student demonstration outside. You can hear the gun shots. They are directed at anyone.

Coming home from school there are cries in all the streets. The mounting of shouts from every direction from the crowds arm in arm. The students. I saw them, older than us, men and women held to each other. They walk into the *others* who wait in *their* uniforms. Their shouts reach a crescendo as they approach nearer to the *other side*. Cries resisting cries to move forward. Orders, permission to use force against the students, have been dispatched. To be caught and beaten with sticks, and for others, shot, remassed, and carted off. They fall they bleed they die. They are thrown into gas into the crowd to be squelched. The police the soldiers anonymous they duplicate themselves, multiply in number invincible they execute their role. Further than their home further than their mother father their brother sister further than their children is the execution of their role their given identity further than their own line of blood.

You do not want to lose him, my brother, to be killed as the many others by now, already, you say you understand, you plead all the same they are killing any every one. You withstand his strength you call me to run to Uncle's house and call the tutor. Run. Run hard. Out the gate. Turn the corner. All down hill to reach Uncle's house. I know the two German shepherd dogs would be guarding one at each side, chained to their house they drag behind them barking. I must brave them, close my eyes and run between them. I call the tutor from the yard, above the sounds of the dogs barking. Several students look out of the windows. They are in hiding from the street, from their homes where they are being searched for. We run back to the house the tutor is ahead of me, when I enter the house the tutor is standing in front of him. You cannot go out he says you cannot join the D-e-m-o. *De. Mo.* A word, two sounds. Are you insane the tutor tells him they are killing any student in uniform. Anybody. What will you defend yourself with he asks. You, my brother, you protest your cause, you say you are willing to die. Dying is part of it. If it must be. He hits you. The tutor slaps you and your face turns red you stand silently against the door your head falls. My brother. You are all the rest all the others are you. You fell you died you gave your life. That day. It rained. It rained for several days. It rained more and more times. After it was all over. You were heard. Your victory mixed with rain falling from the sky for many days afterwards. I heard that the rain does not erase the blood fallen on the ground. I heard from the adults, the blood stains still. Year after year it rained. The stone pavement stained where you fell still remains dark.

Eighteen years pass. I am here for the first time in eighteen years, Mother. We left here in this memory still fresh, still new. I speak another tongue, a second tongue. This is how distant I am. From then. From that time. They take me back they have taken me back so precisely now exact to the hour to the day to the season in the smoke mist in the drizzle I turn the corner and there is no one. No one facing me. The street is rubble. I put my palm on my eyes to rub them, then I let them cry freely. Two school children with their book bags appear from nowhere with their arms around each other. Their white kerchief, their white shirt uniform, into a white residue of gas, crying.

I pass a second curve on the road. You soldiers appear in green. Always the green uniforms the patches of camouflage. Trees camouflage your green trucks you blend with nature the trees hide you you cannot be seen behind the guns no one sees you they have hidden you. You sit you recline on the earth next to the buses you wait hours days making visible your presence. Waiting for the false move that will conduct you to mobility to action. There is but one move, the only one and it will be false. It will be absolute. Their mistake. Your boredom waiting would not have been in vain. They will move they will have to move and you will move on them. Among them. You stand on your tanks your legs spread apart how many degrees exactly your hand on your rifle. Rifle to ground the same angle as your right leg. You wear a beret in the 90 degree sun there is no shade at the main gate you are fixed you cannot move you dare not move. You are your post you are your vow in nomine patris you work your post you are your nation defending your country from subversive infiltration from your own countrymen. Your skin scorched as dark as your uniform as you stand you don't hear. You hear nothing. You hear no one. You are hidden you see only the prey they do not see you they cannot. You who are hidden you who move in the crowds as you would in the trees you who move inside them you close your eyes to the piercing the breaking the flooding pools bath their shadow memory as they fade from you your own blood your own flesh as tides ebb, through you through and through.

> You are this
> close to this much
> close to it.
> Extend arms apart just so, that much. Open
> the thumb and the index finger just so.
> the thumb and the index finger just so.
> That much
> you want to kill the time that is oppression itself.
> Time that delivers not. Not you, not from its
> expanse, without dimension, defined not by its
> limits. Airless, thin, not a thought rising even
> that there are things to be forgotten. Effortless. It
> should be effortless. Effort less ly
> the closer it is the closer to it. Away and against
> time ing. A step forward from back. Backing
> out. Backing off. Off periphery extended. From

imaginary to bordering on division. At least
somewhere in numerals in relation to the
equator, at least all the maps have them at least
walls are built between them at least the militia
uniforms and guns are in abeyance of them.
Imaginary borders. Un imaginable boundaries.

Suffice more than that. SHE opposes Her.
SHE against her.
More than that. Refuses to become discard
decomposed oblivion.
From its memory dust escapes the particles still
material still respiration move. Dead air stagnant
water still exhales mist. Pure hazard igniting flaming
itself with the slightest of friction like firefly. The loss
that should burn. Not burn, illuminate. Illuminate by
losing. Lighten by loss.
Yet it loses not.

Her name. First the whole name. Then syllable by syllable counting
each inside the mouth. Make them rise they rise repeatedly without
ever making visible lips never open to utter them.

Mere names only names without the image not *hers*
hers alone not the whole of *her* and even the image
would not be the entire
her fraction *her* invalid that inhabits that rise
voluntarily like flint
pure hazard dead substance to fire.

Others anonymous *her* detachments take her place. Anonymous
against *her*. Suffice that should be nation against nation suffice that
should have been divided into two which once was whole. Suffice that
should diminish human breaths only too quickly. Suffice Melpomene.
Nation against nation multiplied nations against nations against themselves. Own. Repels her rejects her expels her from *her* own. Her own

is, in, of, through, all others, *hers.* Her own who is offspring and mother, Demeter and Sibyl.

Violation of *her* by giving name to the betrayal, all possible names, interchangeable names, to remedy, to justify the violation. Of *her*. Own. Unbegotten. Name. Name only. Name without substance. The everlasting, Forever. Without end.

Deceptions all the while. No devils here. Nor gods. Labyrinth of deceptions. No enduring time. Self-devouring. Devouring itself. Perishing all the while. Insect that eats its own mate.

Suffice Melpomene, arrest the screen en-trance flickering hue from behind cast shadow silhouette from back not visible. Like ice. Metal. Glass. Mirror. Receives none admits none.

Arrest the machine that purports to employ democracy but rather causes the successive refraction of *her* none other than her own. Suffice Melpomene, to exorcize from this mouth the name the words the memory of severance through this act by this very act to utter one, *Her* once, Her to utter at once, *She* without the separate act of uttering.

The Chinese in Haifa

Jeffery Paul Chan

Bill dreamed he heard the cry of starving children in Asia bundled together in a strangely familiar school yard. They pressed up tightly against a Cyclone fence and they were dressed in quilted black uniforms that reached down to the ground with wide sleeves they used for handkerchiefs dabbling at their flat brown noses, a mosaic of fingers and faces reaching toward him through the squares of wire. Their gaping figures settled into the grain of the vestibule door of his grandfather's house. It was solid oak with cleverly fashioned brass mullions molded to the likeness of Taoist household deities, blending wheat chaff and shoots of new rice into the bodies of farm animals, with the toothless smile of Hotai and a border of tiny lion dogs snatching at tails and paws or locked jaw to jaw in a faceless struggle. The frieze was grimy with age and a narrow green cuticle outlined the hole where the brass met the wood and where the clear lacquer had begun to flake and crack. The door swung back and instead of his children he saw

JEFFERY PAUL CHAN, born in 1942, is a professor of Asian American studies/English at San Francisco State University. He is coeditor of *Aiiieeeee!* and *The Big AIIIEEEEE!*

what might have been the fleeting figure of his wife driving a line of coolies down a dark hallway. Take everything, take everything, she screamed. Then his father appeared, oversized on a stretch of bright green fairway. He was wearing his powder blue slacks and his favorite alpaca sweater, white with dark blue piping up the sleeves. Bill caught sight of a golf ball nestled in a clump of dandelions. His father was intent on the ball, lining up a second shot to the green. Bill felt apprehension tighten his throat. His hands trembled as his father suddenly relaxed his pose. He looked over his shoulder, straight into Bill's eyes. He winked and casually pushed the ball clear of the weeds. The ball exposed was incandescent, each dimple seemed to catch fire until it shone brilliant white and the glare made Bill turn away but he could not escape it because he was not there.

The movers finally managed to wedge their van under the carport roof. At first Bill Wong kept to his study. He heard his wife out on the driveway and avoided her, avoided the squabble she'd promised when she phoned the night before from "The Chickencoop," his name for his sister-in-law's duplex in Chinatown. Last night on the phone he heard the television hissing the news and there was the brittle sizzling of a wok in the kitchen. His wife was calling from the living room. He suspected the conversation was being overheard. He pictured his sister-in-law, her husband, the oldest daughter with her hand over her mouth, all perched around the extension, three monkeys listening intently. He politely inquired about the children who now lived in Hong Kong with their grandmother. They were happy. "Of course they're happy," she snapped. "They like their grandma." Her sister was happy to get the furniture, the linen, the dishes. Bill resisted the urge to ask where in the hell she would put it. But she read his mind. "You got the house. I get everything else tomorrow, Bill, everything." The emphasis was like everything else in their marriage, awkward, unnecessary. Would the kids drop him a postcard? There was a pause, then his sister-in-law answered from the kitchen.

"Bill? This is Mamie," she said abruptly. Now Bill was sure her husband was listening, too. His wife fumbled with the receiver in the living room, then hung up.

"Goddamn it, put Alice back on the phone." He tried to sound testy, but it came out like a whine. All of Alice's family could read his mind.

"I'm still here," Mamie said.

"That's swell."

"Now, Bill. Alice and us think it's better if the kids don't think about you for a while," she began.

"Mamie, this is none of your goddamned . . . oh, shit . . ." How in the hell would they accomplish that? Horrible Chinese tortures? A water cure? Prefrontal lobotomy?

"You know they're learning to write Chinese? By Christmas, they can write to you in Chinese."

Her twisted optimism and the smell of bait rising from her unctuous tones made him sick. "Gee, that's terrific, Mamie. How am I supposed to read it?"

"Now don't you be selfish, Bill. You let your own ignorance rob your kids of their heritage. That's your way."

"Terrific, Mamie," he said, letting his voice drop to a whisper.

"What did you say? What, Bill?" he heard as he slammed the receiver against the wall. It had bounced on the linoleum twice, then swung by the cord, emitting shrill angry squeals.

There was nothing left to hear. The following day he sat in the shade by the side of the house sipping from the hose and smelling bay leaves. He watched his wife with the toaster under her arm struggle down the steep driveway to her car. She had come in the company of the moving men. Mamie had her kids to look after.

Her atrocious green knit dress was tight around the sleeves and her arms looked creased and damp with sweat. She'd gained some weight in the few months since the divorce. She looked vulnerable. She avoided seeing him, and she left before the van finally rolled down the hill at dusk, followed by a pack of neighborhood dogs that barked and snapped. The engine exploded as the muffler tore against the pavement. He watched the truck make its way down the narrow road. Then there was nothing left to see.

The lights of his neighbor's garage beamed through the tangle of ivy that had begun to climb the window of his study. He smiled at his reflection. "Let's get stoned," he invited himself. He yanked his desk drawer open, found the dope, and rolled a joint. Without thinking, he looked over his shoulder, then examined his reflection again. Paranoia, he thought. No one here to tell him not to smoke, no children around to be corrupted. He studied himself, one eyebrow raised, peering out from a frame of ivy. He swept the stray crumbs of pot from his desk blotter into a plastic bag, then tucked the cigarette papers and bag into a manila envelope marked "interdepartmental mail," snapped a rubber band around it, and set the package into his filing cabinet under "D" for dope. He ignored the papers he was supposed to correct, neatly stacked on his desk. The top page was stained red where he had spilled wine the night before.

Alice had thrown everything that was his into the long narrow corridor behind the laundry room. She'd stuck it all into paper cartons, filled boxes with his books and clothes and jumbled them on top of one another, a precarious pile threatened with momentary collapse. But there was nothing unusual about the room's disorder. The cold and damp creeping through the unheated walls had already warped the unpainted pine bookshelf he had built after the collapse of his marriage. Overdue notices from the school library were sandwiched between pictures drawn by his daughter that curled out from his bulletin board with her name and date of execution. They were nearly a year old.

He clenched the joint tightly between his teeth, touched a match to the end without inhaling the flame, then filled his lungs with smoke. He felt petulant and self-indulgent. It was all clear. His wife was a vampire, and now she watched him from every dark window in the empty house. Soy sauce dribbled down her jaws. Now that he was starting to relax, settled down with his smoke, she wanted to make love. Afraid? There was nothing to be afraid of.

In the kitchen someone had taken a chicken pie out of the refrigerator and left it to thaw on the counter top. He pulled a chair from the study and sat at the back door, listening to the chicken pie drip into the sink and the sounds of the neighborhood settling into evening. He could still hear birds slapping against the curtain of eucalyptus trees in the grove at the bottom of the driveway. The night had turned cold and a thick cloud cover erased the last lights in the sky. He finished his smoke, pinched the last ember between his fingers, then swallowed the roach. Supper. The taste of ash and paper, the alfalfa smell of it all, shut his lips against a mouthful of saliva he could feel welling up from his throat. But there was no place to spit. He stripped his shirt off and washed and drank from the garden hose. "God in heaven, I'm free," he said. His voice was tentative and hoarse. He went back in the house and fell asleep on the carpet in the empty living room.

The morning sun had just broken over the ridge of hills, burning away the fog trapped in the crown of redwood trees behind the house. Bill finished his shower, then dripped water down the hall to the linen closet where he discovered she had taken every towel from the shelves. He remembered her words. "Everything. Everything." He rubbed himself dry with an old sweatshirt he found in a bag of garbage in the kitchen that smelled of rotting chicken pie. Peering out the window at the trees, he wondered what time it was. She had taken the clock radio that always rested on the kitchen table. The table was gone, for that matter. He walked into the living room and kicked the front door open. The warm, steamy air began to condense on the windows near the floor, and he drew a stick figure with his big toe on a frosted pane of glass. He heard someone crunching up the path. The hair on his legs rose in the chill and he remembered he was naked. He wrapped the still damp sweatshirt around his waist.

Herb Goldberg carried a thermos bottle in his hand and the morning paper tucked under his arm. The sleeves of his old work shirt were wet from the heavy dew on the shrubs and his hands and fingers were white with cold. He had a transistor radio stuck in his shirt pocket with the earphone plugged into his ear so that he looked like he was wearing a hearing aid. He clumped heavily up the stairs, slapped the paper and thermos down on the porch rail, and pulled two coffee mugs from his back pockets. They looked at one another for a moment before Herb broke into an embarrassed grin, his wide walrus mustache twitching with what looked like dried toothpaste at the ends.

"Listen," he said. "My mother started at five-thirty this morning making blintzes 'cause she's flying to Haifa today, the Japs just bombed an Israeli airliner in Rome, and I just left the kids at the Hauptmanns. Let's get the hell out of here and go fishing." He walked past Bill to eye the empty living room. "Oh, man," he shouted. "Alice took everything, huh?"

"Morning, Herb." Bill opened the thermos and filled both cups. "Hey, the coffee smells fine. Thanks."

"That, my friend, is genuine Kenya Blue. Real coffee! None of this MJB crap. Ethel was in the city yesterday picking up my mom at the airport." Herb stepped out on the porch and took his mug in both hands, blowing a cloud of steam. "She saw Alice and the moving van yesterday afternoon and she guessed you didn't have a coffeepot anymore."

"Listen, I had to towel off with a roll of toilet paper!" Bill laughed and ran his hand through his hair, rubbing his damp scalp. "What time is it anyway? It must be early because I'm still out of my mind. Kenya Blue sounds like something I smoked last night."

Herb held his hand up, signaling Bill to be quiet. "Goddamn Japs," he whispered. "Good God in heaven, did you hear that?"

Bill put one finger in his ear. "No."

"I been following it on the news," he said. "Three Japanese terrorists opened up on passengers getting on an Israeli jetliner in Rome. Machine guns and hand grenades. Can you imagine that! And here my mother's going to Israel today. Christ on his ever lovin' crutch! What in the hell do the Japs have against us?"

Bill was confused. "Japanese disguised as Arab guerrillas?" He tried not to smile. "To do in your mother?"

"No, no. They were Japs, dressed like Japs," Herb said bitterly.

Bill wanted nothing to do with the conversation they were having. If Herb wanted to rage about Japs, that was his business. "Listen, thank Ethel for me. The coffee and all, that's very thoughtful."

Herb removed the plug from his ear and coiled the wire into his pocket. "Thank her yourself. I think she's all hot to find you a nice Jewish girl."

"What, are you inviting me home to meet your sister?"

Herb waggled a finger in his face. "My *mother*," he said. Bill sat back on an aluminum garden chair and stuck his feet out over the railing. The coffee cut through the hangover and he squinted in the sunlight, looking over the wet trees and the ribbon of road that led out of the canyon to the town that sat by the freeway that went to the city where his wife, his children, and the Chinese were forever distant strangers. His feet were cold, his toes were numb. He pushed the chair back, tipping. Herb grabbed his naked shoulder from behind and Bill nearly fell over backward.

"Yeah, Wong, I'm inviting you to lunch if you can catch it. There's a low tide at nine we can make." He caught the chair and held it, threatening Bill.

"How can I refuse?"

Herb set him upright. "All right. You see? I saved your life again. I should adopt you since you obviously don't know how to take care of yourself." He laughed, pointing into the empty house. "Today's agenda calls for rock fishing till noon."

"You sure you want me in the house with your mother around? I don't want her to get the idea that I might be a terrorist in disguise." The sweatshirt had slipped off, and he hoped Ethel wasn't looking out from the garage.

"Nahh. You're no Jap." Herb grinned. "You're a Chinaman. I explained that all to you already. Go on now and get your pants."

Bill dressed quickly, and together they walked across the hill to Herb's house. He saw Ethel peering from the kitchen window and he waved. Herb continued to rave about the Japs as they tied his long bamboo fishing poles to the side of the car. Ethel appeared, wiping her hands on her apron.

"Good morning, Bill."

"Morning, Ethel."

"Herb," she said.

Herb answered, "Good morning, Ethel."

"Please take out the garbage before you leave."

"Where's Mama?" he said, turning toward the kitchen.

"She went back to bed. Don't make so much noise." She turned to look at Bill as he wrapped twine around the aerial to hold the fishing poles. "Did you hear what time we had to get up this morning?"

"Yes, I heard." Bill looked at her face. She wasn't wearing any make-up. She had that clean, well-scrubbed, early in the morning look she wore after the kids had gone to school when the three of them would have coffee in their kitchen before he drove Herb to the bus stop on his way to class. "I am a Japanese terrorist this morning. I fell asleep on the rug last night and my back hurts. It's awful. I want to shoot up an airport and scream at people in Japanese."

"Well, you do look a little awful," she offered, teasing.

"Just put your finger there." He indicated a knot he wanted held down.

"Catch something we can eat for lunch and we'll cook it Chinese style."

She stood next to him, her finger on the twine. With her other hand she massaged his back. "Sure. Ahhh. Sure." Bill tensed and glanced back at her. She smiled coyly.

"Does the little terrorist want me to walk on his back?"

A short blast from the horn startled him, and he saw Herb behind the wheel. He leaned over and remonstrated, "She's too small, Wong. Throw her back and we'll catch a bigger one."

"Yes, boss," he said.

Bill stood up on the gray knuckle of rock. His tennis shoes were frictionless along the face of the tide pool. He stepped where the water was shallowest and barely touched the green slime of algae surrounding every foothold. Tiny crabs skipped and fell before him off the rocks and skittered like gravel into the water before his feet slipped past them. Every rock seemed to be covered with crabs. The sound of the breakers steadied in his ears like his own breathing, like meditation. He lit a cigarette while his hands were still dry enough to strike a match. The imperceptible movement of the tide washed over the rock he stood on and he could feel water seep into his shoes. His feet felt warm and scummy. He slipped along a carpet of purple seaweed knee deep into the water and made his way along a submerged granite shelf, groping with the tip of his pole behind a ribbon of kelp into a long, deep fissure. He pulled back a fraction to let the hook dangle without getting tangled around the pole. Something nibbled at his bait, a slight bump and a nudge. It reminded him of his wife making love. "Come out, Alice," he crooned.

And whether it was the excitement of the catch or the weary energy he drew from the roach digesting in his stomach from the night before, he knew for certain it was his wife tucked warily in the dark crack, guarding his children from him, her arms and legs wedged against the tight walls of her watery cave. Come out, Alice, he sang, come on out of there. He eased the tip of his pole in another inch.

Why do you waste your time fishing for that stuff, she used to say. I can buy it for you cheap. For a dollar in Chinatown, she used to say.

He shortened his grip and with both hands set the hook with a quick jerk, and he had her, he had this fish passing for his wife. He felt a violent current of energy running the length of the fishing pole. Whatever it was, it was big. He looked behind him, judging the distance to the beach. The water was too deep to wade straight across, so he edged around the pool to the last visible foothold and stood out of the water. He jammed both feet tight against a clump of mussel shell, trying to steady himself. His pants pockets poured sea water down his legs. He braced himself, then pulled hard, wrenching the fish from its hiding place. She pushed off from the shallow bottom, nearly jerking the pole out of his hand. The weight of her snapped at the short line, snapped the tip of his pole back and forth, and he felt his shoes scrape against the sharp edges of the shells, then pull away. He landed on both feet in water up to his waist. Now the violence was real for him. Too real. The fish pushed off from the shallow bottom and jumped clear of the water. The pole slipped from his hands and hit him. He stepped backward, green water and kelp and foam splashing in his face, his feet slipping on the rocky bottom. His feet came out from under him and he landed hard on the dry gravel. The pole lay between his legs. The fish on the end of it panted in the brackish puddle.

To hell with her, he didn't want her any more. The hook must have passed through the roof of her mouth. Blood flooded the white of one bulging eyeball. He stood up and kicked the pole into the water. "Hey, that's my pole!" Herb shouted from behind him. "And that's our lunch!" His soaking pants had nearly fallen off, and sea water stung the cuts on his hands and arms. He sat on a piece of driftwood and watched the fish twist over slowly, propped up by a hard ridge of bone on the top of its head, and he could see the flesh on its belly was a bright blue. Die, Alice, he thought to himself. The tail swept back and forth in a mimicry of agony, its gill plates snapped open and shut forcing air through its lungs and strangling it. Red fiddler crabs scurried around the fish, plucking delicately at the fins. Again it rolled over, its face impaled on the hook, the barb gleaming out of its one bloodshot eye. There was an impish expression on its face. A smile suggested by its thick purple lips, the fishing line pulling up against the mouth, became a sneer that belonged to his wife, his ex-wife. She seemed pleased. Why not? She'd just eaten.

Herb appeared on the bluff directly behind him and he laughed with excitement. "That damn thing must weigh ten pounds! Man, it sure is ugly, Wong!" Bill looked up at him and waved. He remembered now that the fish was for Ethel. They would cook it, Chinese style. He laughed to himself.

"That's my wife you're talking about."

Herb came leaping down from the rocks. "What did you say?"

"That's a capizone. Not known for their beauty." Bill took the end of the pole and heaved it out of the water, letting the fish roll in the dirt.

Herb was out on the patio picking coriander for the fish and Bill and Ethel were cooking in the kitchen. Bill watched him wander past the straw flowers Ethel had gathered on the windowsill just over the sink, pinpoints of startling amethyst and ruby in smoke glass bottles. Tiny ceramic miniatures of farm animals Ethel bought in Chinatown pastured around a can of cleanser. Ethel padded barefoot across the kitchen floor and dipped hot oil over the fish laid on a bed of bean cake. "I hope I'm doing this right," she said.

"What we need is a piece of window screen stretched across some sort of frame. That way you wouldn't waste so much oil." He took the spoon from her hand.

"Did you cook for Alice?"

"Sure. I cooked. I even made a screen for frying the fish."

"But she took it." Ethel cocked her head, catching his words as they fell. "Everything," they said simultaneously. "Alice took everything!" They laughed.

The kitchen was redolent of garlic and ginger. The fish sent up clouds of thick steam as the oil crisped its flesh, drawing blisters of juice where the body had split apart.

"Careful!" Bill caught her by the shoulder as the oil exploded, sending a hot shower down around her legs. She danced back a pace from the stove.

"Ooh, I think I got the oil too hot."

"That's all right, but you better stand out of the way." Her eyes are positively green, he thought, they seem to change color in the sunlight coming through the open door.

"I saw the moving people yesterday. Was that the refrigerator going down the driveway?" She balanced her head against her hand, a finger stuck in her mouth, gnawing on her wedding ring.

"I went into the kitchen after everybody was gone," Bill said, "and found my frozen dinner in the sink. It was so sad, my dinner, all thawed out and starting to smell."

"Poor baby. You can put all the frozen dinners you want in our freezer, and we'll even give you a key for your very own." She heaped green onions and tomatoes on a chopping board. As she brushed past him he caught the aroma of lilac and garlic and something else like home permanent solution in her hair, her tight blonde curls turning limp and feathery in the humid kitchen. She wore one of Herb's old shirts with the tails wrapped around her waist. When she held herself to attention slicing tomatoes at the counter, he marveled at her legs, tanned to the ankles. Her faded denims were cut off and rolled up to where the pockets stuck out around her thighs like the uncreased tabs on a paper doll. Her toenails were brushed with blue polish.

Herb appeared at the kitchen door just as a covey of jets from the Naval Air Station laid a vapor trail across the sky. A clap of thunder rattled the dishes and silverware on the table. He stood there clutching the coriander wetly in one hand and watched the planes disappear.

"Leave the door open, Herbie. I don't want the smoke to settle into the walls." She smiled warmly at Bill, a guileless and direct smile that made him conscious of his eyes lowering to her knees, to her bare brown feet. "You must be starving to death," still a lax affectionate smile, a lopsided complexity as she rubbed the corners of her eyes tearing in the clouds of oily smoke.

He looked at Herb. "I think it's done."

Herb settled into his chair. "Where's Mama? Still asleep?" He put a stalk of green onion in his mouth and clipped the stems from the coriander with a pair of scissors. Bill swung the plate to the table with a flourish of Ethel's pot holder. Herb deliberately sprinkled the leaves of coriander over the steaming fish, and they all sat back in their chairs. It was a moment of respect reserved for some unspoken grace. Ethel whispered, "I think she's still asleep."

"Let her sleep then. Look," he said with mock awe. "Look at it." All three groaned loudly, Herb beating on the table with his fork. "Let's eat it!"

Ethel started spooning fish onto Bill's plate. "Herbie, are you sure you want to drive her to the airport? You know you're going to hit all that weekend traffic."

"Sure, sure. It's me or you, and I'd rather it be me. You're the mommy. You can have the kids when they get home. That's why we have a successful marriage, Bill. Sharing and caring."

Bill waited until Ethel was settled into her chair. Then he said, "You can't sit down yet. Give me a fish eye."

Herb looked around the table, then went to the refrigerator for horseradish. Ethel leaned back and maneuvered a gallon of wine over her head from the counter to the table and filled their glasses, spilling as much as she poured. "No, no," she said. "The eyes are for Mama Herbberg."

Their knees touched under the table. Bill was sure it was an accident, as sure as he knew there were bony ridges just beneath her kneecaps. He could almost feel them. He finished his wine. "More, please," he said, holding out his glass.

"I think all this hijacking nonsense is ridiculous. You know your sister had her handbag searched in Los Angeles when she took Mama to the airport." She bit into a tomato wedge and the juice ran down her chin.

Herb spooned horseradish over his fish. "It wasn't a hijacking. They didn't even ask for anything, no demands, nothing, just opened up with their Soviet," stressing the word *Soviet*, "machine guns, and blasted away. One's still alive. I hope they castrate the bastard so he doesn't breed any more like him. Fire with fire."

Ethel brought her eyebrows together and took a sip of wine. "That would be a bucket of cold water."

Bill stood up as Herb's mother suddenly appeared in the kitchen. She was tall like her son, the same dark brown hair and dark eyes, slightly puffed with sleep, glazed, framed with waxy mascara. "So. When do we leave?" she said excitedly.

"Mama, you should have slept longer," Herb said as he leaned across the table to kiss her cheek.

"I can sleep on the plane." She turned her head to accept the kiss, reaching at the same time to take Bill's hand. "You must be Bill. My son and daughter say nice things about you."

"How do you do," Bill began, but her smile suddenly vanished. She stood awkwardly over the table, Bill's hand in her own, and sniffed at what she saw in front of her. She completed the smile, let go of his hand, and picked at the fish with a teaspoon. "Very tasty, dear, but you know it's not nice to look at the whole thing. It looks right up at you."

They all stared down at it. The eyes were a solid milky white. A clove of garlic protruded from its mouth and Ethel pushed it back, giggling.

"Is it fresh?" she demanded.

"Bill caught it this morning, Mama," Herb told her.

"Where?" she inquired suspiciously.

"In the ocean, Mama, in the ocean. We went fishing this morning, after you went back to sleep."

She prowled around the kitchen replacing dishes. She snatched a dishtowel from the back of Herb's chair and put it through the handle of the dishwasher, then took a sponge and wiped up spilled oil from the counter top. "Where are the children now, Ethel?"

"Mrs. Hauptmann's got them, Mama. She gives them their lunch today." Ethel delicately removed a bone from between her lips. "They don't like fish either."

"So who can blame them?" She began laughing at herself, caught Bill's eye and stopped. "All right, food is food. Is this the way the Chinese cook fish, Bill?" He nodded. She heaved a sigh. "Bill, you just have to put up with me. I have to know everything, don't I, Herbie?"

"Herb said you made blintzes this morning, Mrs. Goldberg."

"You like blintzes? Ethel, you give Bill some blintzes from out of the freezer."

"I love blintzes," Bill said.

She sat down between Herb and Ethel and motioned to Bill. "Eat." She was too excited to eat. "You have that house with the steep driveway right next door? You must get a lot of sun up there. You have a garden?"

Bill nodded through an exchange of questions and a barrage of small talk. Now and again he caught Ethel smiling. She began to imitate his every nod. When he folded his arms, she folded hers. Mrs. Goldberg explained that she would fly to Tel Aviv, then to Haifa. Her niece had married an Israeli engineer. Bill poured wine for her, and she allowed for a second glass, then a third. She described an enormous family as she talked, and she reached out with her hands to touch her son. She held his hand to her cheek, and rapped the knuckles of her other hand on the table for luck. "We have big families," she said with a great deal of satisfaction. She reached for Ethel and patted her on the arm. "You must know about big families, Bill. The Chinese always have big families, like Jews. Herbie and Ethel are waiting for what I don't know. Two beautiful children, but just two. Did you come from a big family, Bill?"

"No," Bill said. "I was an only child."

"You know, I can tell. You don't know how to talk through an old lady. You're too quiet. That's a good thing sometimes, but sometimes a good thing is too much."

"My mother had a large family."

"Yes?" she said. "How many?"

"Nine."

"Nine? Nine is a good size. We had eleven, but one died."

"Who, Mama?" Herb carried his plate to the sink.

"I had a sister and she died of pneumonia when she was four. She was Miriam. I was only five, but I remember her."

"My mother had a sister who died when she was young," Bill confided.

"Yes?" She beamed across the remains of the fish. "There, you see?"

Bill thought it was a strange issue to make an alliance from. But he was drawn to her, hostile, then open, testy like a peacock and at once glorious. "But I never heard them speak of her," he offered. "I saw her picture once in a photo album my uncle kept."

"But that's the way. They had nine to take care of, your grandparents."

"Yes," he said.

"That's what families are for," she said.

"What are they for?"

"So when you lose one, you have more."

"Wouldn't it be the same if you never had one, never started?"

"Started what? Everybody's got a family. What do you mean? You come from one family, you make another."

Bill didn't know whether to laugh or not. He was confused. Maybe she was drunk.

"Now you, Bill, you're not young but you're not old, either. When you're as old as me, maybe you want to sit in one place. Stand still, maybe. Maybe. Me, I don't want to wait around to die."

Ethel was at the sink listening to them talk. "Mama's got one foot in the grave."

"No! That's a bad joke! I'm not dying, not yet! I'm only being practical. Who wants me to die on them? Who wants to walk into my room and find me home, but not home. It would kill my friends, I mean, they're not chickens. So I keep moving. Maybe I'll go in the airplane or someplace maybe where they can send a body home, but they pack me up. It's easier. I fall down and maybe I won't scare somebody to death. I don't know. Maybe you're right. If you never start—how can that be? Everybody has family." She stopped abruptly. Finishing the rest of her wine, she started to laugh. "You made me talk and I don't even know what I'm talking about, Bill."

Herb roused himself from the half-sleep he had fallen into while his mother was talking, and got up from the table. "It's about time. Let's get your luggage, Mama."

Bill rose, smiling. He steadied himself on the table. He began, "I'm glad we got drunk together."

But she put her hands to his lips. She leaned across the table and whispered in his ear. "Who would have me," she hissed, "who wants an old lady around the house after a few days?"

"Come live with me, Mama," Bill said softly.

She stood back and smiled at him. "You should have children, Bill."

And before he could reply, Herb lied. "Bill's a confirmed bachelor, Mama."

"Well, not confirmed," Bill said.

She nodded as if she understood. She straightened herself up and began to talk energetically. "I stick my nose into everybody's business. But I'm a great-grandmother once over so it's forgivable. You'll pardon me, but I'm sure your mama would say the same thing. You should marry, have children." She indicated Herb and Ethel with a wave of her hand. "Have a big family. My speech is over." She laughed, and Bill heard a faint edge of contempt in her laughter.

Ethel winked at Bill from over her shoulder. "Maybe you can find Bill a nice Jewish girl, Mama, in Haifa."

"Are there Chinese in Haifa?" Herb asked.

"The Jews and the Chinese," she said, standing in the middle of the room and weaving her eyes back and forth from her son to his wife, "they're the same." She walked to the door and Herb followed. "You know there are Jews in China, there must be Chinese in Haifa. It's all the same, even in Los Angeles." She went out the door.

They stood in the garage together while Herb put her suitcases in the trunk and started the car. Mrs. Goldberg gave Ethel a long hug, then walked up to Bill. "You have a safe journey Mrs. Goldberg. I'm glad to have met you."

"So polite you are." She shook his hand. "I was glad to meet you, too. You're too quiet, though." Then, loudly over the noise of the car, she said, "Ethel, you get him married. You get married before I come back."

He nodded.

"Drive carefully, Herbie," Ethel shouted as the car backed slowly out of the garage. She waved as the station wagon turned the corner and disappeared.

Ethel breathed a sigh of relief. They stood together in the driveway. A riot of fuchsias hung from the redwood baskets suspended over their heads. The sound of bees flew around their ears. "Thank you, Ethel. Lunch was fine."

"Oh, Bill." She stretched her arms and yawned deliberately in his face. "Mama's right, you're so polite." She crossed over the driveway, tracing little dance steps on the concrete. Then, setting her foot on a tricycle, she pushed off up the path littered with empty paint cans and discarded lumber that connected their houses, coasting to a stop against some loose cinder blocks scattered in the weeds. She looked over her shoulder at him. "Bet you can't catch me," she shouted.

Bill felt such irony in the confession he made to himself as he slowly followed her through the trees. He probably couldn't catch her. His feet struck the hard pan and he nearly stumbled over the exposed roots of creosote bushes that held the hill together during the long wet winters he would spend in his empty house, alone with his neighbor's wife. He found his footing in the eroded path the rain cut in the earth. He gathered his energies together and took the hill at a jog. He could see Ethel's head, just visible beyond his driveway. He followed her path, marked by a cloud of fine yellow dust that hung in his face and caught in his nose and throat.

She was standing on the porch pouring herself a cup of coffee from the thermos he'd forgotten to return. He stood for a moment at the bottom of the stairs, catching his breath. She saw him, smiled, then wandered uncertainly through the open doorway. He found her in the living room, her back to him, staring at the blank walls. She refused to turn around even as he wrapped his arms around her from behind.

"Got ya!" he said, his tone a shade too jovial. Herb's shirt was already unbuttoned. He untied the shirt tails and gently kissed the nape of her neck.

"You didn't chase me," she complained in a whisper as his hands covered both of her breasts.

Bill spent the rest of the evening in his study. He had thrown the window open to let the stale air escape, and he heard the Goldberg children's noisy return just before nightfall. He watched the lights of Herb's station wagon as it pulled up the road a few minutes later, saw the momentary red afterglow of the brake lights, heard the engine sputter to a stop and the garage door slide shut. His hands went searching through his desk drawer and found a nail clipper. He pared methodically at his fingernails, scraping bits of dry fish scale from under the cuticles. He licked his thumb and tasted the salty wrinkles that lined the back of his hands. Tiny cracks appeared where he'd cut himself on the rocks, and they stung as he scratched away the dried skin.

It was cold now, and he closed the window. A few shreds of ivy caught in it and hung inside the frame. He could see fog gathering along the lowest ridges of the hillside, caught in the brittle blue glare of a street lamp. He pulled the filing cabinet open, shook out some dope, and rolled a joint, carefully brushing the stems and seeds into an ashtray. He snapped his desk light on and lit the joint, the smoke easing down his throat and filling his lungs. He held his breath for a moment, then blew a white cloud billowing around the lamp. There was an initial disappointment, a change that he could taste as chemistry blunting his mind, the acrid combustion of cigarette paper and spit. But suddenly the taste was gone. His mouth was dry. A premonition that Ethel was looking over his shoulder made him glance into the darkened window to catch her reflection behind him. But he was alone. His hand held the burning joint in front of his mouth, the smoke curling undisturbed across his face. A vague collection of swarthy Japanese in mufti crowding around Herb's station wagon at the airport grew in his mind's eye.

Falling Free

Diana Chang

L et it go, let it go. This is peace. I am what I am now, one with this house I spend my hours in—its lines which travel past corners my only distances. My worn chair reflected in the window is ghosted before my time. Such whiteness I face from wall to wall. White is the color of mourning where Ying has gone, the awesome color which is absence, is purity, is outward-boundness, a flight of the pale body into pitch blackness.

Our son-in-law looks tribal or like a gypsy with green eyes shaded by thick straight lashes. He's part Welsh, part Portuguese. Ying, my husband, said, "I'm of two minds regarding miscegenation. You think it's a simple matter? I'm a liberal, however, a liberal," he repeated, his foot tapping.

"Mimi," I said, "is of one mind." She wanted that gypsy-like assistant professor, and he desired her, our fine-boned daughter.

DIANA CHANG's novel, *The Frontiers of Love*, was the first novel published by an American-born Chinese American. Her poetry and fiction have been published and anthologized widely; *Earth Water Light* is her most recent chapbook. She is also a painter and has taught creative writing at Barnard College.

I'm almost color blind now. At any rate, green and blue I find hard to distinguish in the evening. The world in shrinking imploded into our grandchild's face and body. I can't take my eyes off him. I lean too close, I'm sure, absorbing his features, their mixed aspects, raceless or twice bred, as they slip into combinations surprising and new.

Let it go. I'm of my years airing themselves in my breath. I should not have written Timothy. I passed commonsense over to him to employ—which he'll do. He shall. He won't get in touch with me.

How long is it that I've been the sensible one? If we count it from when we met—decades, only decades. By writing Timothy, Ying's colleague, I handed over commonsense. All I want is aloneness now, the choreography of meals, the pruning of plants, a walk to the corner, the easement of lying in bed, my form stretched out before me to look down at, as though I've already left it behind.

I *will* Timothy not to call. Anyway, I won't let him leave Boston.

All of us are Chinese some of the time, I say. But I'm not certain what I mean. Other times, I'm a Calvinist, familiar with dimity and yokes. My favorite summer dress is Danish, my gold ring Greek, my face cream French, my daydreams I can't place. For someone so unsure of who I am, from time to time I have such definite statements to make. My thoughts are reckless, braver than Ying's. Yet, for decades, I ignored Timothy, ignored even the thoughts I refused to think. *That* is Chinese.

The phone rings. It has a cutting edge. I look at it. One. Two. Three. I once had a cat who stared at phones when they rang. Now I stare, too. Four. It stops, leaving the house emptier. Fragrances have leaned against me. There's so much speech in silent things.

For a long time, I was young. Spaces happen now which I can't fill. I'm often away from myself. The past tense can bury me like a landslide. The past tense is the most populated country of the countries I've lived in. Friends have gone. Mimi, our daughter, has died. There was no one for Ying to stay in the States for, except me.

He writes twice a month. He sounds more and more Chinese. It's life which will divorce me. It'll leave me behind, receding.

Timothy.

It's too late. His name's just a reflex. I no longer secrete longing. I'm beached; and the moon's a dead pebble. My dry hands seek my dry cheek. My clocks move but return to the same hour twice a day, on time. I'm noticing in new, dry-eyed ways. As for my age, I'll never catch up with Ying's, which puts me ahead like daylight saving. I'm months and months younger, enough months to count as years, and I always rubbed it in. "You're getting on!" I declared thirty years ago. "It's too bad!"

Ying said in St. Croix, "Compared to these people you look like an eleven-year-old."

I was forty-seven and he fifty-three then and, made self-conscious, I tugged at my bikini. "It's all that butter and sides of beef and hard liquor they stow away," I said. "And have stowed away since Druid times. They can't help it, you know."

They. Americans were they. German tourists, Swedish ones. But so were Chinese. "Look," Ying said, "they have to catch up with technology." He was worrying over mainland China. "They're of nowhere."

"From nowhere," I corrected him.

"With all its ills," he went on, "they can't bypass industrialization. Mao will learn the hard way, mark my words."

Ying's part of that "they" now. I'm now from nowhere, no longer part of a "we." Interesting. I'm only I, I am. I still am, however. So far and meanwhile. Till I leave even me.

Timothy's last name is Ayres. Scottish. I'll explain to him I was having one of my lapses when I wrote that letter.

I try not to think of China because its fate hurts so. The other side of everywhere, of everyone, living and unlived, forced to try to catch up with—to keep pace with—imperfections of driven, self-searching barbarians.

I have to save my eyes. But what for? I don't watch television any more and don't miss it. My desk, my sofa, the refrigerator, the radio are islands in a sea of floor. I take beads on distances before embarking toward the letters, cushions, eggs, music—the other soul in this house.

Impossible lamp. I turned you off at four this morning. Full of yourself, you snap back on! There's a break in the shrubbery which is lined up with an aisle between a neighbor's trees. Through it, dawn rises like water filling a bathtub.

I'm to soak myself because of the insistence in my thigh and back. Perhaps camel's humps are trying to grow out of me, repositories of memory which won't lie down, go away. My hands seek out past days to knead, to work out their ache.

When I was in the hospital, I heard him say, "No heroic measures." I believe Dr. Walsh was talking to my grandson. "At her age, you understand." And then the two lads at the foot of my bed traveled away on platforms until I could no longer hear them.

When Dr. Walsh reappeared suddenly, I scrabbled at the sheets, swung my legs, moved toward him. It was as though my skirts were tied at the bottom.

"Mrs. Kuo! You do my heart good," he declared, plunging toward me.

"Nothing's wrong with mine," I said. "I'm strong. Don't think I'm on my last legs."

He carried me, put me back to bed as though, as though I were the child. Determination returned to me. Like the lamp, I snapped back on. And you see, I'm here at home again, the two of me—the me and the you. It comes of talking to oneself; however, which one of us would stop me? We laugh together. You tell me who's to stop us. I've never been freer. I think anything I like, do as I please. I'm as single as I was at nine, a sweet age. My mind is clear and could shine.

I stare at the telephone. One; two; three? Yes, four; five. It rings on, disappoints me. Bitter, yet I am also relieved.

Probably my neighbor, a strong woman, across the street and half a block down. She's short of cash, so helps out with storm windows, mowing, raking.

I'm looking at albums she took down from the attic for me, my nose a couple of inches from faces. "See," I say to you, "that was when Timothy arrived in a convertible, his scarf looped around his neck." Timothy, our guest, was Ying's colleague; both of them involved with Venus scrutinized from Yerkes Observatory, tracking gases and speeding light. They dealt with infinity, seemed to wonder at nothing. My physicist husband, Ying, was sure of me, while Timothy, married often, waited.

If only I knew I could stay in touch with myself forever.

The camera is a gun shooting down moments. I take in small people, tiny views I don't remember from where: outside Athens, on a French canal? Is that lake Swiss or in Hangchow, the honeymoon city, the sheen of one sky continuing into the next?

I expel exasperation. I will not have it. Buds, nodes, appear on my knuckles, rosaries to tell. You and I laugh. It's the beads have things to tell, not I. My neck feels yoked by an influence I'm to serve. Mimi, our daughter, was swayed by a rare disease of the blood when she was thirty-three, four months and seven days. Winston, our grandson, Ying and I brought up mostly, though his gypsy-like father would claim otherwise.

Simply because it rings, must I answer it? It yelps, so willful. You see, you're withdrawing, I point out to myself. But this is peace! I'm what I am now. My ledges, plants, cant of roof upraised. I'll leave through the skylight, God sucking me upward through his straw. I rather like that thought, I must say, vain, as usual. He'll vacuum me up, aspirate me. For once, I'll be his aspiration, momentarily in the light and years of galaxies. Ying could never get used to my most natural thoughts. After fifty-five years here, he had to go all the way to China to get away from me. That's my next-to-final thought about him. There's always more to think, have no fear. The life of radioactivity is forever. The life of death is everlasting. I've been married over fifty years, years made contingent by Ying's need to go home.

I'm sorry I wrote that letter. I simply won't answer the phone for a week. I'm content, after all.

He stepped out of the convertible, rather tall; I remember being nonplussed, as though his height put me in a quandary. Sitting, Timothy folded into another man. As he approached us, Ying standing next to me, the scarf around his neck slipped out of its loop. He picked it up and, as Ying introduced us, Timothy flung it over my head like a skipping rope, flicking one end through the other. The fringe, though almost weightless, prickled. We smiled at one another slowly, as if remembering, though we'd never met before.

"It's yours," Timothy talking, I recognized, to fill stopped time I knew we both heard. "It suits you. Besides, Ying, I forgot to bring a present. You know me. So this is your pearl of the Orient."

"For Pete's sake, come in," Ying answered, taking Tim's arm. Ying was American that day. "You're full of baloney, come what may." Sometimes he sounded like a Rotarian, but a xerox of one, though he didn't know it then or now.

"Leave May out of it," Tim retorted, referring to his wife who was suing him for the first of what turned out to be their two divorces. That day we were only writing our stories or reading one another's, while now our lives have become knowledge of endings. I feel I know nothing; yet I also know volumes to be remaindered. One comes to the end of mysteries generating themselves; to the end of wanting. It's a thought. Yes. I'll leave off everything except this containment, this management of myself in my home.

I wound it around my neck twice so it wouldn't slip off. Its silk is the color of moonlight on a pond, a blond presence, the color of sheen.

Friends call; visit; take me for rides. Miriam across the street goes marketing with me. There're plenty of people left. More than enough.

I'm the center. I stand in the middle which, according to the Chinese, is the fifth direction. Ying who often sounded like a Rotarian when it suited him here, is now Peking man, imagine. I'm the center, a Chinese direction. He needn't think I'm so American yet!

In a section of plate glass the length of a building, I saw a woman hurrying along. Her knees raised themselves to climb but the sidewalk was level. Her stepping was hurried, stiff, floating. I gasped; she, too.

"That's you!" I said to me. I—who used to move like a dress hung on a hanger loose in the wind.

The woman's hair was as silver as anyone's here. That's why I didn't grasp who she was. So, finally, she resembled the rest, weathered silver like any Caucasian. Hers was a new gait, a new identity. At the corner, she and I put hands out for support on rear fenders of cars. "You're me," I said to her. "You're me," she said back. What I saw mirrored before me was also everything behind me.

Polarity, space, time. Ying and I reflected on such matters. "You, of course, in your way," he never neglected to add, which in the long run never did match his.

"You must remember you have lapses," Dr. Walsh said in his grown-up manner. "You mustn't go out any more without a companion. And I forbid you to drive."

The mind is punishing the body, denying it in exactly the way I would. The mind simply absents itself, rehearsing for the eviction of evictions. And the tenement lets in the sky even below the stairs. I sometimes feel like mesh dissolving into light. I almost died in the crash, which was my fault.

So busy; busy; so busy. In this house, I put out my palms to stroke the flanks of time. At last I have time. It lies at my feet like rugs; hangs in mid-air unsupported. By staring down time, I still it. I need no one—finally!

So busy, busy, busy! I was interviewed; won awards for my designs. I turned out costumes for *Kismets, Kings and I's,* and Rattigans, too. Ying Y. Kuo, the young physicist, was backstage when a relative of his was in *The King and I.* He picked me up off the floor when a bolt hit me out of the blue. It was heavy metallic fabric and knocked the breath out of me, so I didn't notice that he fell in love on the spot. "I was the one hit," he told me, laughing abruptly, astonished.

"Really?"

"Definitely."

He saw and he loved. "I was the one hit," he said many times, astonished.

"You felt hit?" I asked.

"Definitely."

Timothy said, "Admit to it. Just admit to it and I'll leave you alone."

I never admitted to it. I never said to him, "I saw and loved." Timothy admitted to it all, over the years, during which he married two or three or however many times. He signed notes slipped into my hand at parties, at a lunch or two: "Perpetually, comma, perpetually, Tim."

I said to him, "Sure. You'll always be perpetually Timothy Ayres."

"You're a coward," he said.

"I'm married. I've a daughter. I love Ying Y. Kuo, who happens to be my husband."

"All three are true," he answered. "But something more is also true."

"You're just another star-gazer," I told him. Ludicrous. Transcendent. Intrepid; wild with themselves, with grace. Shamelessness a part of their genius.

The Chinese are matter-of-fact. Didactic. Categorical. Yes. There are ways to be; and they know those ways. They do. These Westerners. What keeps them together, I wonder? So selfish, so soulful. I'm a canal with locks. Timothy the open sea, his stole of silk streaming on the wind of the cosmos. Women threw him out of their beds; he abandoned ship and struck out alone, not once, not twice. I stayed happy with Ying, together we weathered Mimi's illness and death. I saw that that was the meaning of marriage. Any Chinese would agree. I even agree with myself.

For decades I longed. It was like a disease of the blood, which took Mimi away. Heart and womb, the one over the other, waited. I laughed at myself. At Palo Alto, Ying was promoted over him. It was a sign from outer space.

Timothy left Palo Alto. We lost track of him for three years. He sent cards with no return address from Paris, Buenos Aires, Baltimore. A book came out. For a season he was famous in celestial circles. I took that as a sign, too. He belonged now to his success. Thank my lucky stars.

This house is in a state of sleep. The porch snores softly. I wake into its dream daily.

The phone rings four, five, six times. I'm disappointed when it doesn't ring; disappointed when it rings too often. On the first ring, I jumped to turn off the alarm. But you're awake. It's not the clock. I'm awake like a cat or a dog, unknowing. Is that armchair wondering where Ying's gone? "China, China!" I cry out. "He's gone to a different condition, you fool," I tell the head rest. "Make no mistake. The Chinese *can* go home again." But it's given me a turn, I can tell you.

Winston, his Eurasian brow furrowed, his exasperation unconcealed, said, "I thought Chinese women were cooperative." My grandson didn't use the words, "docile," "passive." He knows better than that. "Why the hell can't you see you should be in a home? With people. You'll be taken care of. Don't you want to be safe, happy? Grandpa had no business splitting—at his age. At yours. And he was always grinding the Chinese ax of propriety. How would this look! How would that look! As though anyone's wasting a glance. You want to know what it is? It's unseemly—his favorite word. A disgrace. Abandoning you. I'm getting you into a home, I don't care what."

I banged my fist on his arm. "I like it here. This *is* my home. As he said, what would I be doing in Peking. I don't blame Gramps one bit."

"Gramps," Winston repeated. "This bi-cultural, sitting on the cusp, oh so Westernized, mixed up family! And it isn't Peking. It's Beijing, and if we don't practise, we'll never catch on to this new spelling. Tell me straight—is it Chinese to abandon your wife when she's as old as the century?"

"Here they abandon earlier. You're the one bringing up this ethnic stuff. You true blue Chinese-American Eurasian. I used to think I belonged nowhere. But not so. I belong everywhere, anywhere, even on Maple Lane in Westchester. And I'm only seventy-nine. Try to get my age straight."

He guffawed in the agony of a twenty-seven-year-old and stopped himself in time from slapping my back. He could have broken me in two, which may be my natural condition, come to think of it.

"Winston," I said to him, "I stopped thinking in Chinese when I was just about your age. Chinese is another syndrome. But what would you know about it." I leaned too close, intrigued with his features.

"Suppose you fall and can't get to the phone."

"I'm not saying you're wrong. But Gramps is right, too. He's being Chinese. You know how they are about family. Hopeless cases."

"You're something else," Winston said. His body movements are like James Dean's or Alan Ladd's, but though his hair is brown he has Shantung bones. I remember the day he arrived in American— purplish-red and kicking out of Mimi at Doctors Hospital, the mayor oblivious a couple of blocks away of still another "Oriental" who'd slipped over a border. I laugh. How Chinese of me to claim him as Chinese when he's half Caucasian.

I'm at the border. This grayness may not be dusk, but a dawning. Remember that, I order myself, the thought already gone.

Mimi died on an operating table twenty years ago. How old would she be now? While I remained her horizon, she would have been becoming my past ages. My son-in-law remarried so he's no longer my son-in-law. So he, too, left. Or am I confused? No, Lewis moved back to Indianapolis. Winston, some sort of junior curator, is with a museum in Los Angeles. He makes appearances and vanishes as though I rub whatever makes genies come and go.

He wants me in an old-age home. Without a daughter how can I know my age? Since Mimi died, I've felt ageless. Periodically, Winston gives up on me. I annoy young people more and more.

The phone. I count: one, two, three, four and so forth. It's beautiful to be alone here on the sofa. I shall not answer the phone all day; I will not. This is enough. Once a week my neighbor takes me marketing. She describes new ways of making jello. I marvel at her kindness. We have supper out, my treat, and feel girlish about it. Friends take me to the movies once, twice a month, and I sit down front. What more do I want? The window sills are strands, the bush outside the kitchen is all I need of parks, and as for flowers, my thickened knuckles smart with feverish buds. I put my hand before my face, press against time's haunch. Time has volume here.

•

Before departing, Ying said, "I'm thinking of you alone here. Though the financial arrangements are secure, more than secure. Winston's a man now, too, and will look out for you."

"From California," I didn't put in, for there are telephones in this country. It's not the Australian outback, unconscious next to insomniac cities.

I said instead, "I want you to stay, but . . ." I reassured him, "you must go. I do understand."

"I am Chinese," he said.

"No need to say," I said in Chinese, as if losing my bearings.

He said, "A man must die in his native land."

"You talk," I declared, "as if winding up a speech at a banquet." My remark was of the sort which always derailed his trend of thought. Not that my comment was so American, but that his rock bottom mode is Chinese, and he feels defined by the use of maxims.

I continued, "Die! All this talk about dying! You're only eighty-two." We didn't smile. That was three years ago when the detente was well-established, and his brother who had been imprisoned in a windowless closet under the stairs of a school building by seventeen-year-old Red Guards, asked him to visit. And to stay. By letter, he'd instructed them to ask him, I didn't let on I knew. His letter had said, "It will be easier on my wife, if you and Erjieh demand that I return. Suddenly, I'm overwhelmingly homesick, a sign, perhaps, that my time is short."

"You won't be able to adjust," he said to me. "You're too advanced in years, even if you are appropriately younger than I, and too used to comforts, luxuries. Where do you suppose you can get sauna treatments? Is your arthritis getting any better? How can I ask you to make such sacrifices at your age? I can't be so unreasonable, can I?"

Enough. Enough. In one breath, he asked so many questions.

He had another one. "They'll find you so foreign, don't you agree?"

I've taught myself to need no one. Long since, long since. The moon's no longer pulling at my blood. Long since.

"My native land," he said. "Fatherland." Words, phrases turned in the manner of a cadenza, the mind braking the way an ice skater does after a flourish, making himself into an exclamation point. "It's a proper goal, a fitting conclusion to my life, my career. I can bring something to China, too, as a physicist emeritus, above politics, beyond self-interest."

I remembered myself, a girl, riding through China, provinces slipping through the loop of the train.

Timothy's convertible waited outside. We proceeded indoors to our living room. Or was that when we had our first apartment in even earlier days? A tree grew through our second-floor deck. Was my hair long then, heavy as liquid coal, glinting maroon in the sunlight, or was it cropped short again? The first time its bob made me the talk of Shanghai, when I was fourteen, and here, too, a little later. My father, a magistrate educated in France, was weak in my hands, so I was told by those who found me spoiled, oh spoiled rotten. But I wasn't ruined then. It's now that I am, that things could be described as spoiled. Timothy was spoiled, too, leading directly to his being single today after three wives. Two did die of natural causes, it's perfectly true, one of them May—just before their third time together. He's irresistible, to hear everyone tell it, though I've never been fooled. I'm not Chinese for nothing. But he is also intelligent and far-sighted, focussed on the horizon when most of us don't look past sills.

The four of us were at the Princeton Club. Ying was greeting someone half a room away.

Timothy was looking at him, while he said to me, "Have you ever heard me? Answer me!"

I told him, "I'm all ears, all ears, but no heart." I felt nothing at all for him, for his second wife coming down the hall from fixing her hair. Tall and single minded about being his wife, she was perfect for him, as Ying'd been the one to observe.

Through his teeth, Timothy repeated, "Remember how I feel."

I did; I do. I remember how we felt.

"Leave me alone!" I cried. Like a mirage in the Gobi desert in August, his wife shimmered toward us . . . a trick of my eyes, I suppose.

"I never will," he said, angrier at himself than at me.

"You want to wreck my life. I hate you."

"Never."

As a last resort, I said, "I am *Chinese.*"

"And cruel," he retorted, the patient one.

But he was cruel, too, his presence a hardship.

"You're so foreign!" I exclaimed, in disgust or in despair?

Oh, the phone. I count. I turn away, go to the front door, open it. It's rained. The lawn is Ireland, the flagstones like ancient Chinese mirrors before glass came into being. Freshness rushes into the house like a young athlete, wholesome, muscular. Knocked back, I lean against the door. The athlete reaches the bedroom, bounds up the stairs I no longer use. I then step back with extraneous motions and close out the glare, the universal air. What was I doing just now? Mail falls out of my hand. That's it, I'd picked up the mail left on the doormat, a special concession of the postwoman to save me a trip down the driveway in bad weather. I bend in stages, pick up all of it a second time and, hand on hip, straighten up inch by inch to go to the desk.

No letters from anyone I know this time. Most are away. Migratory. I've lived out a century of refugees, and tourists. I, too, am waiting for exit papers. I laugh at myself laughing. In the hospital they gave me quarts of someone's blood, lymph and elixirs of values not my own. Perhaps her name is Jane Smith. The tree I crashed into should have shared my semi-private room, hooked up to plant foods. Poor traumatized being, it doesn't climb aboard planes, leave and write me love's rationalizations. I'm sorry I hurt you, tree. Thank you for stopping me half dead in my tracks. I might have crashed into anti-matter instead.

"These Americans," Ying has said. "Those Chinese." I, too, have uttered these and those words. We would have been rendered speechless otherwise. Ying said, "Timothy doesn't marry for good. We Chinese are taught to love once, deeply and faithfully."

"Divorce isn't easy for anyone, including them," I put in. "That he remarries the same girl makes him nice, don't you think?"

"You always generalize from too little."

He was right and for all his star-gazing was more down to earth.

"We marry as much for the sake of the institution as for ourselves," I said, surprising myself. "We serve the institution. They marry for the sake of one another and of themselves."

"Another aspect of individualism again."

"Why don't you say what you think?"

"Selfishness," he said. "Shamelessness, too. They don't care what anyone thinks."

"I'm so glad you'll never divorce me," I said.

"I have no reason to."

He was right. I gave him no reason to go home. And we're not divorced. It's Timothy who ended up with no one. Serves him right. It's Timothy who's alone.

And I.

We Chinese are rational. It's good to know, to bank on.

At the supermarket yesterday, I said to Miriam, "These people look familiar."

She misunderstood. "Uhn-uhn . . . your eyes," she said. "Hold onto me."

Americans look familiar now. After all, I did go to college here. My name was Kiki Lee before it became Kiki Kuo. Kiki Kuo. People calling me have sounded like crickets all these years, all because my father studied at the Sorbonne, and thought Kiki sounded Chinese. After Ying dies, will he still be Chinese? I feel neither Chinese nor not Chinese. I feel incredulous, living here on Maple Lane.

It's Timothy Ayres who's making me carry on like this. You see, if you marry your own kind you don't have to engage in so much realizing.

I have some tea. I neaten up the counters. It's ten-thirty. I take off my silk crepe robe, designed for a production of the *Mikado*. I dress well all of the time now, no longer saving things for better occasions. I throw the robe to a chair. It slips off, but I leave it. The sleeve is snagged in several places by the chair's unrepaired arm. I will never wear out my clothes accumulated over the years. I keep three diamond rings on my left hand at all times, and wear seven bracelets and five fine gold chains. Other things are in the safe deposit for Winston's future wife. I will love her sight unseen. I love her already, whoever she may be.

The phone. One, two, three; yes, of course, four, and so on. I suppose I'll have to call my neighbor so she doesn't worry. I don't need anyone! I wash my neck and arms gingerly as if water were scarce. I don't take off the bracelets and necklaces. I put on my lacy nightgown, plait my hair, perfume my shoulders. It's a bit macabre, I agree.

I ease myself into bed, pull the comforter up to my chin. Ah. It's good to lie down. I feel capable, lying down, the way young people feel standing and ready to go.

In sleep I am ready to go. It's only a longer lapse in my day. I don't sleep so much as I swoon, aware of time passing and refusing to pass, of time hanging like curtains of snow. White is the color of mourning in China. In the dark I stare down time, as though I could win against it. I fall asleep, I suppose. I dream of a white face at the whitening window.

The ring jangles through me. I am fully awake. Two. Three rings. Then silence. Only three rings! My eyes widen. I am robbed clean of any thoughts to think. I begin to count slowly, as I told Timothy I would. . . . and fifty-five, and fifty-six, and fifty-seven and fifty-eight and fifty-nine. Sixty. The phone begins to ring again. I am breathing with my lips parted. My mouth is dry, but my mind is a fair day on a plateau.

My letter had said, precisely, "If you are still there for me, phone me from Boston. I'm not what I used to be, so ring three times. Then hang up and, a minute later, ring again. That way I'll have time to get to the phone."

Lying on my side, I reach out. My thin braid is caught under my back. I jerk at it. I pick up the receiver.

"What an hour to call," I declare. "You're so inconsiderate!"

In such a rush he doesn't hear me, he says what he has to say, "I've been in the hospital—nothing serious. Just got your letter last night." He sounds as if he's been running. "How are you?"

Leaning on an elbow, I take in his voice.

"I wanted to wake you up," he says, and hears himself. A pause. "Finally."

I laugh, throw back my head and lie flat listening.

"I'm not in great shape," he says. "I hope you're good and rickety, too."

"Worse than that."

He sighs. "Wasted."

"You threw yourself away on too many women."

"Wasted years." Voices don't change any. He sounds the way he did at the beginning.

"I've been playing dead," I say. Where do the words come from? I didn't know I'd been playing dead. "I thought it'd be easier. Isn't that turned around though?"

"Did you worry I wouldn't call?"

"No, not at all." I remember he said I was cruel. "Yes," I say.

And so we continue. What was once so hard is now so easy. We're beyond differences, situations, exempt at our age from most things, even regret. And he's agreeing to everything. That he rent an apartment nearby for now. That we take each day as it comes, staring down time together.

Fragments of conversations we've had, the scarf the color of moonlight, postcards from Brussels and Baltimore, I possess in this montage, time not a corridor but a meadow surrounding a center, a maypole rippling with ribbons. I can blossom; I can attract bees.

I'm a woman in a lacy gown, making my own way. I shall put up my silver hair for an old man to take down.

"I'm well past longing," I say into the phone, stretching an arm above my head.

I've summoned him, haven't I, to the task of our prevailing?

Natives

Fiona Cheong

I say you have blue eyes. You say, for me to tell you what it means. You sit there, contemplative, your hands on the tabletop, inches away from mine and all I would have to do I could stretch my fingers, trace a line transparent across your knuckles where they rest, where you sit. Sunlight masking your gaze, makes your eyes unreal, blue to greenish blue like seawater, or shells greenish blue that people now wear for earrings. I wonder can you hear me. That morning we woke up in different places, each at four o'clock—could it be that long ago, and do you remember the night before? We drank wine in your kitchen. Near midnight you took me home. I stepped out of your car into cold snow swept like cream against the sidewalk edge. You waited to watch me find my key. That night there were no stars, just sky that

FIONA CHEONG's first novel was *The Scent of the Gods*. The story "Natives" is excerpted from a novel-in-progress. "I was born in Singapore in 1961. My father sold life insurance. My mother was a primary-school teacher, who taught art and English. They are both presently retired, and living in Singapore. I came to the United States when I was eighteen to attend college. . . . At the moment, I teach writing at Howard University. . . ."

glowed without light from the rooftops to the trees on the other side. And the road was wider. It was quiet and wild. There might have been a moon, and my cousins hiding in trees waiting to jump out, Grandpa's ghost breathing wind from underneath the stairs and a room with a locked door where we were not allowed to go—we, my brother Matthew and I, back there in years far away from here. (We lived there in a semi-detached house. It was made of brick, painted grey and yellow, and stood on a street with other semi-detached houses and flexible metal fences fraught with hibiscus on the inside, and iron gates. Grandpa came to live with us when I was five. He was sick and old. Mama prepared a bed for him in the room underneath the stairs. It was a warm dark room with a table lamp, a night stand, a big armchair. My father and his younger brother, Uncle Philip, carried the blue baby dresser down from Matthew's room and Mama unpacked Grandpa's clothes for him. She put Grandpa's statue of Our Lady on the dresser and told my father to knock a nail in the wall. Then Uncle Philip took Matthew and me outside and told us to get into the car. We went to the flower shop and bought Golden Showers and when we got back there was a nail in the wall and Mama was hanging a crucifix on it.) There might have been a moon, that morning you and I woke up at four o'clock. It was cold. It was snowing. The bridge over Crescent's Creek was iced and the wheels of trucks sounded hollow over hard grey steel. We met that morning, half-past six on the third floor. You asked what was I doing there so early. I said, "I woke up at four o'clock." You looked at me, then said, so did you. I pretended it was nothing. Coincidence. An accident. You bent to drink from the water fountain, one hand in your jacket pocket. Then you said, you wanted to know why we both woke up at four o'clock. You were looking straight at me so I smiled. But you kept looking at me and then I had to look away.

Now here you sit, contemplating distance. Is there not always distance between people? Always silence. But can you hear the music, the jukebox playing *Stay . . . just a little bit longer.* Its rhythm swings, once, twice, off the windowglass. Intangible, it shatters sunlight without trace. See the window, arched and stained. It hangs there as if this were a church. This is not a church, I hear you say. You insist: look at these rows of picnic tables, these benches attached to them. So I look, hearing the people and their voices and the music rocking all. You, walking through them minutes ago, cut through them like rain. Only rain can shake sounds when sounds collapse feverish becoming one long hum, shake the way a sudden drizzle could shake the damp and heavy stillness of tropical afternoons, where sounds once melted colorless in the heat and only the rain could shake them apart, make them distinct again, separate grass from grasshopper swinging blade to blade, leaf from leaf in the sugarcane, poised nearby the smooth boned shape of my brother's foot. (We were in the other place then, where we lived, in a semi-detached house painted grey and yellow. The hibiscus hedge was thick and green. It flowered throughout the year and the flowers were big. They had warped rosy petals. Between our house and the hedge we had grass, not a garden, and not neat enough for a lawn. A papaya tree, we had that. Our papaya tree stood in the center of the grass. In the corner to its right there was a swing. My father bought that swing for me when I scored highest on the exams in 1969. I was in Primary 2A that year. My best friend was Jasmine who lived next door. Jasmine and I went to the same school and the schoolbus picked us up together. During P.E. we changed our clothes together. In the evening she would come over and sit on my swing and sometimes when she came over I was still doing my homework and she would sit on the swing by herself. But I made Matthew ask my permission whenever he wanted to sit on it, and that made him angry.)

Can you hear me—how did you find me here?

Your hands move, unfold from each other like doors—small hands, fair-skinned, you. Come from some place West, I heard you say, one afternoon before the cold began to settle in. Remember the meeting, called in this country an orientation meeting. *Orientation*: a noun constructed from the verb *to orient*. *To orient: to familiarize; to set in any definite position with reference to the points of the compass.* We were to be oriented, you and I, in that room where people told their names. When the fair-skinned ones told their names I tried to look at them but many of them were blue-eyed and they sat there straight like conquering heroes and I became frightened. Silly, do you think. Primitive. But would you say *Primitive*? Perhaps I confuse you with another, past friend, lover. But that was why I could not see you. Sometime between three and four o'clock I saw a huge window in the right wall, where the sun came flooding through, and a blaze lit up the marble floor surrounded by us in the circle we had been asked to make earlier walking into the room. Understand this: the sight of Anglo-Americans was not new to me. (Mama brought me here thirteen years ago. She wanted me to go to American school, learn American science. It was I who decided to stay on.) But something in that moment, in that room, had to do with turning twenty-three, no longer seventeen. Twenty-three was old enough to see the people kept, that we have known, empty spaces where we still move in the past. So this was what I did: At that moment in that room, I looked away, outside the window. Outside stood a healthy dogwood tree, its late-summer leaves shimmering in light. From where I sat, I could see the trunk slanting half the window. The rest of the window held sun from a blue sky. Understand this also: Asian children know all about Europeans. Perhaps you think this knowing blinds the children. One speaks of not seeing the forest for the trees—it is not easy sometimes to know which is the forest, which, the trees.

It was much later when I saw you. Autumn had arrived. I met you on the curb waiting to cross the road. We crossed together and then had to walk up the slope. It had rained during the night. The grass was soft. When you slipped and fell away I caught your wrist and pulled you up and you came up laughing. But the wet earth left a stain on the right knee of your pants like a bruise.

Was that the Autumn you bought the piano?

(Jasmine took piano lessons—from the old man who came to her house on Saturdays. I never did. But other things we did the same, even grew the same. When we were nine, we outgrew Mary, Karen, Luke and Jonathan, outgrew them all. One Saturday before the old man came, we six were talking outside Jasmine's gate and Matthew came running out of our house to say that Mama had just told him that in a few years he would grow taller than Jasmine and me because he was a boy. Jasmine looked at him, then threw her head back laughing. "You'll never catch up," she said. "Anna and I are going to grow taller and taller, as tall as the trees." She was leaning on the gate when she said that, pressing her face on the iron squares. Then she let go and stood back and I could see the marks of the squares on her face before the blood rushed back and the lines disappeared.)

Please stay. Where are you going? Nowhere, you say. But you turn to the window. Tell me again you're not going anywhere. I follow your gaze, trying to follow you—to slopes outside these panes of leaded glass. Late winter slopes. There they fall, patterns of slants and melting light, where the sun-angled ground leaves ivy and brick of ancient libraries to fall, tumble open to Northern snow that now sprawls broken in patches with cold grass and scratchy trees. The libraries seem blind, their windows tall rectangles staring darkly into wind.

See behind the clock tower, the sun shoots gold like a coin when we held a torch to it in the dark, that year Jasmine and I woke up to cut the apple in half and look in the mirror to see the faces of our future husbands. We were eleven, then. The kitchen when we stepped into it was soft with moonlight. When I took the knife out of the drawer, it shone silver and slim. Jasmine stood leaning against the counter by the sink. She rolled a green apple up and down the cutting board. I gave her the knife. She took it without looking up. I wedged a hand mirror between the cutting board and the counter wall behind. It was Mama's hand mirror, smooth and oval like a face, with a dark red edge. I pulled Matthew's torch out of my pajama pocket and clicked it on. Mama's hand mirror lit up. Jasmine balanced the knife steadily on the crest of the apple and I said, "Careful." She did not look up. "Jas," I said, "maybe we better not." She lifted the knife, turned the apple around with her other hand, adjusting it, as if there was a right way to cut the apple and a wrong way. I gripped the edge of the counter. It was a cool white Formica counter, looking grey in the moonlight. Jasmine lowered the knife again. When the living room clock chimed for midnight she slid the blade into the apple, then dragged it back and forth with soft sawing sounds. I heard it hit the board. I saw the two halves rocking neatly on the wood. When they stopped, they became so still and pale and perfect, they seemed to have been there forever, as if before I gave Jasmine the knife, before we even came down the stairs, they were already there, split in two, side by side on the cutting board. We were supposed to look in the mirror when the apple broke but I did not do it. Only Jasmine looked. Or she told me she looked. We did not talk about it until we were back upstairs. Then I asked her if she saw anything but Jasmine just lay quietly next to me and stared straight up at the ceiling. "You didn't look, either," I said. After a while she said, "Yes, I did." She said it very softly. After that, she would never talk about it again.

I have yet to grow used to your evenings. Your winter darkness comes so fast, so sudden. Jasmine never liked evenings. She would call me over and we would do things until the night arrived. The night itself was all right. It was the twilight she couldn't bear, I think, the in-between time. Evenings were slow where we grew up, you see, so slow a child could sit in them and watch the grownups come home, watch all the grownups come home, one by one, watch them drive around the corner where they would slow down expecting to see children playing on the road, watch them park their cars, swing open doors, step out, close doors, turn keys. They would wave walking to their own gates, reach inside, slide the latch, open gates, step inside, close gates, then let each latch slide back. All of these movements a child could watch because the evenings were so slow, so full of time, in-between time, which Jasmine couldn't bear.

Here evenings come different. Years here come different. You have seasons. Winter, spring, summer, fall, I've learned to say, to know your seasons' sounds. It was like learning the Alphabet, learning that September comes windy. When I was seventeen, in September a street lamp hummed white buzz. I stood beneath it, heard nearby the leaves of a tree caressing stone, saw above the tree, the Southern Cross lay pinned to the flapping dark. Winter, spring, summer, fall, I tried to say, but another night, a distant night, began to move, and then was rapidly coming close, when my father took me outside and Matthew followed us and then Jasmine came out of her house and there we all were, standing by the swing, the papaya tree behind us, underneath the Cross in that other place.

Can you hear me?

It is from that place I speak, you know, though I speak to you—

there, where you have never been, where you cannot go, like the place in you where I cannot go and you run there only to outrun me, when my silence makes you mad—from there I say, you have blue eyes, from there I see. And what does it mean, some of it you know and I could repeat what you know, say, remember the Europeans. And this: Columbus invaded America in 1492. And this, too: In 1621 the Dutch West India Company invaded Africa. But here, back to where it began: 1254. A man was born in 1254. You learned his name when you were very young.

You get the picture. You teach this picture, constructing it with words in air and chalk. I have seen your words, heard your voice in the classroom—I was passing by—and your students' voices unwary of your quiet intent to make them political. You want to begin revolutions in their lives. You want to try—to undo crimes.

They cannot be undone.

You want to say yes, they can. *They can.*

Not by you.

Tell me.

Father Ignatius, the handsome priest, who was very kind. He was only twenty-two years old when he came to us from Rome. I could begin with him. Or with the old nun, who wore dark glasses and a black habit, the cloth of Orders in foreign countries. She lived in a room in the back of the convent, and never came outside, except to go to the shops. She rang the church bells. Or I could say, Mama. Mama was pretty. Old people used to stop us on the street, to tell Mama she was pretty, that she had an ancient face. I would stand by waiting, smelling Mama's dress, and did not understand: An ancient face, was that good or bad? Mama would smile politely, say thank you. The old people would stay with us awhile, and talk to Mama and Mama would talk to them—women's voices high above me broke the silent heat—I hear them still on summer nights, summer nights your season that comes closest to the tropics, mine, where, warm and humid, leaves rustled unseen in the dark. I hear them, know now what the old people meant. There was an illness in our country. The good kind well-meaning surgeons were grafting sanitized European eyelids onto misguided, misinformed Chinese women.

Mama lived unscarred.

I would like to remember her that way. I would like not to tell you, have to tell you, that it began that year that I was seven—but Matthew was only six, and in the afternoon he said to come and help him build a card-house on the floor. We took the cards out of the kitchen drawer where my father kept them—my father played Black Jack—we built our house till it was halfway up. Then Mama came into the room with a rotan in her hand—a long slim bamboo cane with a looped handle —whipping cane. She made us take off all our clothes. What happened afterwards had nothing to do with us. And now I think Mama did not know that.

My Uncle Philip came home early that day. It was his last day with us. He was leaving for Australia the next morning, to take charge of a new branch that the life insurance company he worked for was opening. I could hear his keys rattling outside the bedroom. He was trying to unlock the door. The door swung back so hard when he opened it, it slammed against the wall. Matthew and I watched it swing forward again. We heard Mama start to cry. She sat down on the floor, and when Uncle Philip walked past her, she tried to touch his trousers.

The sun was tilting on the floor when Uncle Philip came to us. We saw him pass through the light like a ghost. He stopped at the wall where we were, and when he knelt down and picked me up, his arms were shaking. He carried me downstairs and out the front door, and when we passed the papaya tree I counted three sparrows on the branches and then we were outside the gates. He put me in his car and when he closed the car-door from outside, he tested it to see that it was locked.

Then he went back into the house, for Matthew.

Five o'clock. You watch the light wash clear off mirrors on passing cars below the slope, the road with its edges lined on iron posts and chains, home-going the sounds from there.

Tell me.

Tell you: Once I dreamt a dead boy sitting in a garden. He sat straight on a stone bench, his head leaning forward just a bit. It was dark in the garden and the trees whispered the dead boy's voice in a warm wind, telling us not to bury the dead because they were not really dead. Mama was in the garden, too, and when she heard the dead boy's voice in the warm wind she said, Make the sign of the cross on him, his soul is restless. Do what I tell you, Anna. I moved closer to the dead boy. In the name of the Father, I touched his forehead. And of the Son, I touched his chest. When his eyes started to open, I tried to call Mama but only the warm wind answered, scratching the dead boy's voice into the trees like ash.

The second night I dreamt a wedding, dreamt a long dark hall where walls flickered from candles, and silent people walked in crowds up and down the floor. The people had no faces. Their heads were masses of black hair framing skin as smooth as children's skulls. I was the bride. There was no bridegroom. The silent people walked and passed me one way and then the other, one way, and then the other, until their bodies flowed, and the room was all movement and shadowed light, and the movement was like the flight of great flocks of birds. Mama was following me around the floor, nagging at me to let the surgeon cut my eyes, to let him sew the double eyelids before my skin became too old, became soft like smelly wet leaves under trees. Make bigger eyes, she said. You have long eyelashes but people cannot see them because your eyes are too small. Make bigger eyes and you will be pretty. We moved together near the walls, our feet warm with the heat of candles.

The third night I dreamt Jasmine and me lying outside on the grass, and the figure of a man standing across the road. He was tall and thin and wore a dark raincoat and a dark hat. The streetlamp lit the pavement behind him, making a pool of cement milk-soft. The man himself stood in shadows, his presence strong in the night like the smell of an animal dying. He was watching us. I could hear Jasmine breathing sleep beside me like a song that Sister Angelica used to sing to us in Kindergarten, something low and sweet on her guitar, and shy as the sound of wind-chimes. And I whispered, "Jasmine," but she did not wake up. I grabbed her shoulders and shook her. The man stepped off the pavement onto the road. He started to walk, his shape coming closer and closer. Jasmine was still asleep. I could not wake her.

The man stepped onto the grass.

I got out of bed and walked to the window and there she stood. She was downstairs on the grass, wearing pale blue pajamas and carrying a candle. It was that December we saw the fortune-teller. Rain hung in the air, a warm breath. Jasmine stood, steady on the grass, and looked up at my window. I waved to her. She waved back. When she turned and walked into her house, I saw her candle make paths through river water green with reeds.

I could begin with you. You are the difficult place. Recall October, when days came thick with sun and falling leaves, and the wind traced our shadows on pebbled ground. You moving beside me moved like Jasmine, smelled like Jasmine. Smell of leaves just starting to decompose, smell of warm old earth. We scattered gravel with our feet, kicked loose stones free, watched them roll off the road's edge. They dropped scattering down the hillside, all the stones white and smooth like pieces of light. You showed me where to leave the road, to walk down to the river, on a path of bare earth washed clear of grass, between trees that leaned. The trees leaned out of slanting ground. I marked where the river marked the bottom, and water bent its way transparent blue. You looking too, said, the river was shaped like the small of someone's back. You raised your hand, curved the air with your palm, curved a black night shadow—sheets where someone under the sheets lay sleeping. I saw the form return the child, your hand raised to the sharp leaf light cast in gold, and sun splinters that fell, fell caught among the trees. I wanted then to catch your hand, in mid-air to close palm over palm, dare to do it, to be brave as children cupping palms for water.

Hasn't anyone taught you how to ask?

Water's edge, the wet ground where we stopped, and watched men fishing on the opposite bank. They wore red jackets, soft grey hats, and held thin lines angled to cold sunlight. There I saw wind touch your ears soft as midnight, and children on the hill behind you—there were five. They carried sleds. They climbed that hill like soldiers, pink, blue and green. What did you see? Did you hear them laugh against the sky already winter there, though autumn here. The hill had snow, rose against you, bright with its children. On its crest some of the trees were already bare, white trunks dipped in shallow ankled snow. I looked past you, above you, saw leafless branches sprawled to split the sky.

That day you played the piano. On your bed I sat crosslegged, sat as taught to do by nuns long dead. Mid-afternoon the sun outside your shadeless window I said to you, Get some shades. You smiled, said it was all right when there was more light outside than inside. What about at night, I said. You said, leave the lights off, then reminded me that I liked the dark anyway.

Did I like the dark? At suppertime the sense of you moving about the room, I liked, so said turn off the lights. You brought candles to the table. Winter afternoon darkened, chilled. The sky through branches that shivered in wind I watched, till you ready for me said I ought to see that tree in summer the leaves made the kitchen look another place. In wind the branches you called me from, drew me from closing sky black. Your candles on the table dripped wax I peeled warm from white cloth. Leave it, you said. And when you saw I could not stop, you reached to hold my hands, and warmed them in yours.

In dark you carried candles into another room, said, Come with me, and I went.

Moon

from Chinese American Revenge Tales

Marilyn Chin

Moon was a little fat Chinese girl. She had a big, yellow face befitting her name. She was sad and lonely as were all little fat Chinese girls in 1991, and she had a strange, insatiable desire for a pair of trashy blonde twins named Smith (no accounting for taste, of course). Every night she would wander on the beach in search of them, hoping to espy them taking a joyride around Pacific Beach in their rebuilt sky-blue convertible Impala: their long blond hair swept backward like horses' manes, their faces obscenely sunburnt, resembling ripe halves of peaches.

One chilly September evening the boys stopped to make a campfire on the beach; and Moon, feeling quite full and confident that day, descended upon them, waddling so fat, so round and shiny with sea-spray. She offered them chocolate Macadamia nut clusters and began

MARILYN CHIN is a poet and tale writer. She was born in Hong Kong and raised in Portland, Oregon. Her first book, *Dwarf Bamboo*, was published in 1987. She has received numerous awards and teaches creative writing at San Diego State University. "Moon" is from a series of naughty stories tentatively titled *Chinese American Revenge Tales*.

to sing, strumming a tiny lute-like instrument her grandmother sent her from China. She began singing in an ancient falsetto a baleful song about exiled geese winging across the horizon, about the waxing and waning of stormy seas, about children lost into the unknown depths of the new kingdom.

The boys were born and raised in "the valley" and were very unsophisticated. They were also functional illiterates and were held back twice in the fifth grade—and there was no way that they could have understood the complexities of her song. They huddled in that sporting male way and whispered surreptitiously, speaking in very short sentences between grunts or long, run-on sentences with ambiguous antecedents, so that Moon was not quite sure whether she was the subject of their discussion. Finally, the boys offered to give fat Moon a ride in their stainless steel canoe they got for Christmas (we know, of course, that they were up to trouble; you don't think that their hospitality was sincere, do you?).

Moon graciously accepted their invitation. Actually, she was elated given the bad state of her social life; she hadn't had a date for centuries. So the two boys paddled, one fore, one aft with fat Moon in the middle. Moon was so happy that she started strumming her lute and singing the song of Hiawatha (don't ask me why, this was what she felt like singing). Suddenly, the boys started rocking the boat forcefully—forward and backward making wild horsey sounds until the boat flipped over, fat Moon, lute and all.

The boys laughed and taunted Moon to reappear from the rough water. When she didn't surface after a few minutes, it suddenly occurred to them that she was drowning; they watched in bemusement while the last of her yellow forehead bled into the waves. Finally, they dove in and dragged her heavy body back into the boat, which was quite a feat for she was twice as heavy wet than dry—and she was now tangled in sea flora.

When they finally docked, Moon discovered that the boys saved her only to humiliate her. It appeared that they wanted a reward for saving her life . . . a blood-debt, if you will. In this material world—goods are bartered for goods—and actions however heroic or well-intentioned in appearance are never clearly separated from services rendered. And in the American ledger, all services must be paid for in the end; and all contracts must be signed at closing bearing each participant's legal signature. Thus, the boys ripped off Moon's dress and took turns pissing all over her round face and belly saying, "So, it's true, it's true that your cunts are really slanted. Slant-eyed cunt! Did you really think that we had any interest in you?"

After the boys finished their vile act, they left Moon on the wharf without a stitch on, glowing with yellow piss. And she cried, wailed all the way home on her bicycle. Imagine a little fat Chinese girl, naked, pedalling, wailing.

When Moon got home her mother called her a slut. Her father went on and on about the Sino-Japanese war and about the starving girl-children in Kuangtung—and look, what are you doing with your youth and new prosperity, wailing, carrying on, just because some trashy white boys rejected you. Have you no shame? Your cousin the sun matriculated Harvard, your brothers the stars all became engineers. . . . Where are the I. M. Peis and Yo Yo Mas of your generation?—They sent her to bed without supper that night as a reminder that self-sacrifice is the most profound virtue of the Chinese people.

Up in her room Moon brooded and swore on a stack of Bibles that she would seek revenge for this terrible incident—and that if she were to die today she would come back to earth as an angry ghost to haunt those motherfuckers. With this in mind, Moon swallowed a whole bottle of sleeping pills only to cough them back up ten minutes later. Obviously, they didn't kill her. However, those ten minutes of retching must have prevented oxygen from entering her brain and left her deranged for at least a month after this episode (hey, I'm no doctor, just a story-teller, take my diagnosis with caution, please). Overnight, she became a homicidal maniac. A foul plague would shroud all of southern California, which, curiously, infected only blonde men (both natural and peroxided types, those slightly hennaed would be spared).

For thirty days and thirty nights Moon scoured the seaside, howling, windswept—in search of blonde victims. They would drown on their surfboards, or collapse while polishing their cars. . . . They would suffocate in their sleep next to their wives and lovers. Some died leaving a long trail of excrement, because whatever pursued them was so terrible that it literally scared the shit out of them. And not since Herod had we seen such a devastating assault on male children.

On the thirty-first night, the horror subsided. Moon finally found the Smith boys cruising in their sky-blue convertible Impala. They were driving south on the scenic coast route between San Clemente and Del Mar when she plunged down on them, her light was so powerful and bright that the boys were momentarily blinded and swerved into a canyon. Their car turned over twelve times. They were decapitated—the coroner said, so cleanly as if a surgeon had done the job with a laser.

Moon grew up, lost weight and became a famous singer, which proves that there is no justice in the universe, or that indeed, there is justice. Your interpretation of this denouement mostly depends on your race, creed, hair color, social and economic class and political proclivities—and whether or not you are a feminist revisionist and have a habit of cheering for the underdog. What is the moral of the story? Well, it's a tale of revenge, obviously, written from a Chinese American girl's perspective. My intentions are to veer you away from teasing and humiliating little chubby Chinese girls like myself. And that one wanton act of humiliation you perpetuated on the fore or aft of that boat of my arrival—may be one humiliating act too many. For although we are friendly neighbors, you don't really know me. You don't know the depth of my humiliation. And you don't know what I can do. You don't know what is beneath my doing.

No Sayang Lost

Lawrence Chua

Paul:

Where's your bit of rice? I wasn't supposed to be walking into the women's bathroom and they were clearly surprised when they saw me. My boyfriend was sitting on the sink, his milky cheeks flushed. The woman who posed the question regarded her drink for a full moment before slurring, I'm so glad you're white and polished and not all brown and fried. It triggered the expected laughter. I smiled, so everyone else in the room would not perceive me as over sensitive to these kinds of things, and walked away. At home my boyfriend asked me to urinate on him, and all the while I stood over this man, drenching him, I couldn't help but wonder if this wasn't inspired by some misplaced need to apologize.

LAWRENCE CHUA is a writer and director. The managing editor of *Bomb* magazine, he also contributes to *Crossroads*, a weekly newsmagazine on National Public Radio. His writing has appeared in *Rolling Stone*, *The Village Voice*, *The New York Times*, *Premiere*, *Transition*, *Flash Art*, the *Los Angeles Times*, the *Chicago Tribune*, *W*, *Interview*, *Vibe*, and *Artforum*. He is also co-producer of "Radio Bandung," a weekly radio newsmagazine.

Virapong:

His body in recline is formed by one brush stroke of gold ink. An orchestration of ligament rendered to give the appearance of ease. He has a boxer's face with a flattened nose and dim, petty eyes. His most lucrative feature, though, is his foot long cock as thick as my wrist. I can't stop thinking about him. I've already travelled twice around the world on his cheeks, imagined the universe spread over his skin, his mouth covering me like a cloud. I push my nose into the back of his neck where the hair is shaved to velour. There are exactly two hairs growing from his armpit that smells of sweat and cheap soap. The first night I watch him play with the revolving doors at a nightclub. Later, he buys me a rose, puts his hand up to my ear as if to tell me a secret but kisses me instead. The next week, he slips a silver ring on my finger. I like the way he gets all possessive around other guys and calls me his little monster, even though we're the same height, the same age, the same skin color. I live with his family now, and early in the morning, we fool around in the basement before his father wakes up. I still get restless when he leaves me at night to go to work. It's becoming quite apparent that he adores being the whore with the hardon of gold, but he's becoming more selective in who he allows to regard him. They don't let white men into the places where he works. That kind of lust is entertained elsewhere.

Jerry:

I let him take my hand, wiggle his thumb in my palm. We exchange drinks and I smoke half a cigarette from between his thick fingers. He puts my head on his chest. His cool skin is thumping underneath his shirt. His family just came here from the capital and he's lonely. He wants to travel. I hear him tell our friend he wants someone to take care of him, to pay the fare as far as Singapore. I hear him say this, but he doesn't specify the gender. He never brings it up when he drives by at 5 A.M. to take me for a spin on the beach, where, in the glow of pre-dawn, we talk, kiss, and grope distractedly, each too tired to fulfill what we've started. He has tiny nipples that taste like starfish. I like the feel of his broad tongue in my mouth. When he talks, I look at his manicured hair, shiny with oil. If I don't leave tomorrow, I'll call you, I promise.

Joe:

You make me nervous. I've been wanting your bones for nearly a year, since I first saw you next to that Harvard chink with a profile like Bart Simpson. Now, sitting next to you, I can barely speak. There is some gap between us I can't bridge. Solidarity is the moment our heads touch the back of the couch at the same time and I can see the light growth of hair dusting your cheekbones. I'm thinking of your inner thigh rubbing against my lips, of the pattern the hairs might form growing down there. I'm wondering how you taste and I want to tell you that I think I love you, but instead it comes out as "I love your shirt," or maybe, in a more intimate moment, "I love the way you smell." "*Manis*, don't sleep with the enemy," you told me. That was before I felt your muted dick in my hand. I sense that your own desire is defined more by a sense of fair play. You've become bored, like me, of the specifics of vanilla poetry we grew up with and now you know, somewhere, it would be somehow more valid to have a boyfriend who looks more like you. But you still haven't made the leap between conscience and consciousness. Call me when you've worked it out.

Dragon Seed

Kiana Davenport

I confess to remembering. I confess to a morning, I was fifteen, when I realized cousin Jen was dying. Her gestures had slowed, her kimono sleeve dragged through the guava jam at breakfast. Lupus had been in her for ten years and now at twenty-five, she fought her pain with drops and puffs, giving her beauty an eerie detachment.

She was mix-marriage mongrel like most of us, mother Hawaiian, father Chinese, but her carriage, her vowels were pureblood, her fine skin "one-pound powder" pale. Even her feet were tiny, a footbinder's dream. By thirty, Jen looked frightful. The butterfly rash, sign of the wolf, had settled on her face, her hair was a prodigy of white spiders.

The day she died, the Catholic priest refused her Extreme Unction because of her "appetite for filth." Wu flung himself across her corpse and wailed. He was a neighbor boy, pureblood Chinese, my age but older, that is, older appetites. The first time he saw Jen, he was nine years old, and lay down at her feet. As Lupus settled in her joints, Wu

KIANA DAVENPORT, of Hawaiian descent, is the author of A *Desperate Season*, *The Power Eaters*, and *Wild Spenders*. She is currently working on a collection of stories entitled *Pacific Woman*. "Dragon Seed" is excerpted from her novel-in-progress, *Shark Dialogues*.

became her knight, her mounted archer, riding out to slay the dragon, bringing her its Seed.

After she died, we clung together, Wu and I, because it seemed all life had ended. After Jen it was only epilogue. Great literature, music, Albinoni and Bach, things deeply foreign to our family, had kept Jen afloat in her sea of pain, and on humid sleepless nights she had charted my escape to worlds beyond our island life. I would sit smelling her books while she read aloud, and through them smell printing presses, perfumed sleeves of poets in time zones far away from palms, incessant palms. I wanted that life. Jen had said she would help me get it. Now Wu and I sat on decaying wharfs, bereft, watching dead housepets float down the Ala Wai Canal.

"I got to leave Honolulu, or die," he said.

"I'm going too," I vowed.

Eventually he made the break, I only did in dreams. We were working our way through university then, Wu dissecting frogs for the biology department, while I sliced pineapples for Dole. Some nights when we met by the Ala Wai, my arms were covered with pineapple sores, and Wu was sick from the smell of formaldehyde. Some nights we just broke down and wept.

One day he led me down to Chinatown, dark pocket of downtown Honolulu. Behind honky-tonk saloons and bar-girls, old men gambled at fan-tan and mah-jongg. Midst hidden chimes, burning joss, smell of salt fish, ginger, jook, ancient addicts clung to tenement walls like starfish; we watched them siphon by. I knew where we were going. I wanted to.

For years I had spied, watching Jen puff her little pipe. As Lupus grew worse, she laid the pipe down, started putting drops of laudanum in her tea. One day when pain was total, her joints hugely swollen, fingers swirling arthritically, Jen had put the tea aside, and drank the laudanum straight.

Now, stopping in a greasy alley, Wu knocked on a door. In Chinese, someone asked his name.

"One Wu," he whispered. "One *pake-brudda*." Chinese-friend.

They asked who was with him. He answered again. "One *wahine*." Local girl.

A tiny man in black pajamas opened the door, face violent, body rigid, like a loaded pistol. Wu thrust a wad of bills at him. He counted them and bowed, then led us through steamy, crowded rooms, families brooding over plates of food on oilcloth. Each family froze at our passing, chopsticks poised like antennae of large, alert insects. An old woman waved, a prawn collapsed between her teeth, tentacles whiskering her smile.

Through a sudden courtyard, a slum of orchids, then we entered darkness, a room maybe thirty feet long. Mounting each wall to the ceiling were rows of bunks with bare mattresses and pillows. Some of the bunks were occupied; I could tell by the eerie glow. I was seized with such terror then, my knees went.

Wu held me up, smiling at our host. "This one uptight *wahine*. She be okay when puff da Seed." He gave him extra bills for sheets, and with his hand warm on my hip, led me to a bunk.

"I don't think I can," I whispered.

"Try," Wu said, "It make everything kind."

His voice was odd, like his lungs were already hungry and waiting. I sat on a bottom bunk, feeling the skin jump off my face. Wu dragged a mattress from another bunk and lay down at my feet, then reached up touching my cheek, feeling the pulse of terror. The tiny man gave us two bamboo pipes, small porcelain oil lamps with smoky flames, and two balls of brown gum the size of playing marbles. Wu pressed the gum into the pipes, inhaled, helped me inhale, got them melted and going over flames.

"Give me your hand," I begged. I was so afraid of dying. Then his fist was a warm, steady mass in my palm.

We lay on our sides, puffing, and someone moaned above us in a dream. Soon the gum had burned away and Wu blew out the lamps. The sweet smoke clotted my lungs and I wanted to be sick. I tried to say this. To open my eyes. Form. The. Words. But I was massively adrift. Somewhere in the Gobi, a Mongol milked a singing horse. Caravans approached. Someone quietly removed my skin.

"Wu!" His hand was still in mine, I felt its weight. It could have been a dog's paw, a grenade.

He answered, and his voice was very close, and very far away. "This how we do it . . . this how we part da walls . . ."

They got to know us in that alley, and after a while my nausea went away. One night on those bunks, Wu came at me, slick and amber. Our bodies drugged, hi-jacked, indifferent as assassins. Outside, we were like wild dogs, snapping at life, running in circles. Only Chinatown calmed us down. Wu stole vases from his parents' house, fans and bowls from mine, things we could pawn. Shoplifting at McInerney's and Taneguchi's, returning the goods for cash, we ran to our alley and dreamed.

He promised we'd never grow addicted. If we respected Dragon Seed, it would respect us. And yet . . . and yet . . . one day in class at university I moaned. I looked across the room at Wu. He was staring right through me, lips curled back, like he would bark out loud. I left Dole Pineapple for a *saimin* stand. Wu found work at a laundry, both jobs two minutes from our alley.

"Filth!" my mother cried. "You going turn out just like Jen."

I couldn't answer, knowing my sour breath would convict me. Nothing helped. Not garlic. Not myrrh and golden seal. When Wu and I ran out of money, we jackaled old men combing three-whisker chins in moonlight, or drunken tourists. I'd stroke my hips, dazzle them, Wu would come up from behind.

One night in rich Auntie Rachel's house, I saw a book of jade-pages thin as eyelids, gold-lettered, breathed on by an Empress, even faint Empress fingerprints. Priceless, museum-quality. I thought it was just another bauble with which Uncle Hiro, a *Yakuza*, kept his wife in thrall. I took it to a jade shop on Kalakaua Avenue. Horrified, the owner called the cops. Auntie Rachel said if I came near her house again, she'd cut my eyes out, keep me on a leash. Wu laughed, said I had no gift for theft, that one must only take what people were ashamed of, so they would not report it.

Now, our host in black pajamas greeted Wu and me like family, eyes plump with the never-to-be-said, that we had reached the point at which Dragon Seed ceases to be kind, the point at which its motionless speed addicts to you. We lost interest in other humans. Our speech slowed, like those who have lived for long periods with animals. We sat like Ice Age artifacts waiting for the hour of small gestures, the lighting of a pipe.

Somehow, I managed classes, exams, great spurts of academic passion. Term papers written overnight. I think of the ease with which Wu discarded university. Expelled for stealing lab equipment. The ease with which he discarded me.

One night he threw his pipe across the floor. "So fuckin' amateur, this nineteenth century shit! You know what they selling in da street?"

Next day he brought me black, bitter leaves. "Make tea each time before we puff. Break da habit. So you don't want to puff no more."

Three weeks later, he enlisted. In two months he was in Army basic training, California. The night before he left, he talked of Jen.

"Yeah, sure! I was her runner, picking up her Seed. She want company, teach me how to smoke, teach me *everything*. Thirteen, I was her lover! Just a kid."

When he was sent to Vietnam, I didn't grieve, I lacked awe for anything. But there were nights when I could feel my nerve-ends begging, each nerve a gaping mouth, nights when I wanted that smoke licking at my lungs. It was a feeling deeper than need, deeper than the human condition; I seemed to back-flip through my soul. I went to Chinatown alone, I smelled the smells. Walls hung with mildew. Mattresses of living yeast. Whose lips had touched this pipe?

Maybe it was the bitter leaves Wu had given me: Seed made me deathly ill. After that, even the memory of clicking mah-jongg tiles in that alley made me retch. Or was I retching for the lack of it? Acupuncture and Wu's herbs curbed the awful insomnia, the gut-grinding weeks of what my family called withdrawal. Slowly recovering, I turned my appetite back to books. Senior year on Dean's List.

I still carry teeth impressions in my arm from the day the Army chaplain pulled into our yard, and told us Wu was MIA. I knew he was dead. One syllable hacked from my lips. I never cried, never spoke his name. I ran. Up and down the mountains, across lava shelves, pounding empty beaches every night. He had touched parts of me no other man would ever know, done things I didn't have a name for, kept me slick, circuits lit, terribly alert. I had loved him the way we love unspeakable perversions, the ones that don't let go.

Physically purged now, I could die: the Catholic priest would give me absolution. But part of me still hungered for that filth. Maybe the hunger was a requiem for Wu. Maybe I was trying to outrun it, foolish girl, like outrunning radiation. Finally I said goodbye to him, carrying a paper lantern to the sea, watching a small ribbon of softly glowing light float on the tide, taking his soul home to the Buddhist Paradise.

Graduation day, in gown and mortarboard, I almost wept, my wrists and knees so swollen. And it began, Jen's legacy. Do not believe what poets say; suffering does *not* bring wisdom. It brings stupidity, grinds you into powder. Day after day, hour after hour, Lupus flared, wracked me, wrung me dry with fever. Medication made me worse. Aunties fed me licorice root, grated soapstone, scallion hearts, which cut the fever. But things inside came up in acid broth, taking enamel from my teeth.

Weeks of pain, then it deserted me. One night, like that! it went. I ran outside in circles, pulled wings from a hundred fire-flies, hung their bellies in my hair. I climbed great organ-pipe roots of the banyan that Jen had said reminded her of Bach, and sang all night, a woman blinking off and on. Aunties warned Lupus would return, that it was in me now, forever. Mother cursed them, said she would eat their bones.

I made such plans. See the world, Statue of Liberty (maybe see the *real* New York, urban cowboys twirling human skin lassoes), see the Louvre, the Hermitage, Kyoto. Ride a *cyclo-pousse* in Chiang Mai. I would see and know all such extremes, then come home and teach, guide young minds, as Jen had guided me.

Graduation *Luau*—eight treasure wintermelon soup, pigeon filled with lotus bulbs, *mahi mahi*, pig and *poi*. Real Chinese Hawaiian feast. Uncles and aunties built a small pyramid of envelopes of money for my Good-Health Circling-the-World Graduation Tour. Wearing *leis* of seven different orchids, I bit down on a pigeon heart . . . and it was Wu's. I felt his pulse, he was somewhere in the world.

Sure enough, the Army brought him home. Shot-up foot, months in military rehab. Now, coming at me in a slow, postmortem glide. He pulled off aviator shades, his face starved and gray, eyes eerie, brighter than his medals. I went down on my knees. After weeks of family celebrations, local-hero TV interviews, one day he drew me into the shadows, down a path of crushed plumerias.

"Hey, Ming, want go to Chinatown? Old time's sake?"

I would have crawled through fire.

The same alley limned with bok choy, same little, loaded-pistol man. Lying on the same old bunks with pipes lit, waiting for nausea that never came. Waiting for him to touch me. He smiled, rolling up his sleeves. On his arms, snail-track tattoos.

"Oh, Wu." I touched the tracks, trying to erase them.

"This how I do it now," he whispered. "This how I part da walls."

In Vietnam, they'd kept him far from combat; he looked too much like the enemy. His orders were decoding, Chinese-speaking Wu. Bored, wanting to see real combat, one day he talked his way aboard a recon plane, shot down somewhere outside Hoi An. For days he lay hidden in a paddy; maybe the rice-mud helped him, kept his shot-up foot from turning green. Every day, he said, he watched this little mama-san sitting in the sun, polishing her new metal legs.

"She walk like Tin Man in Judy Garland movie! But oh, so proud."

When the Army finally tracked him, and Medevac'ed him out, the escort bomber blew her legs, and all of her, away. And took her village, too. Old mama-san was Cong. Her face, those metal legs, kept leaking through his sedatives and morphine. For weeks Wu couldn't close his eyes, just lay there in his leg-cast, shrieking. An orderly took pity on him, shot him up with heavy stuff. The heaviest.

Maybe his tales from the paddies were tall tales. Maybe Wu had started shooting smack on R&R, with some child-whore in Bangkok. Maybe he was priming me.

"Dragon Seed so small-time. Next time your joints hurt, I'll take you where you don't feel nothin'!" He put his hand on me. "Ah, Ming, skin soft as dew on ginger."

My circuits lit, terribly alert. His slick, perfect entry.

After that, he courted me, knowing lupus would return, knowing the sickness was a dancer that waltzes off, masquerades, then peeks from behind a fan. Eventually, Wu grew impatient, desperate to show me the void, but I couldn't do it, couldn't make that leap from pipe to needle without the craven need. Some nights I watched him nodding out, wondering who I could blame it on. Jen? The war? Or was it just the sum of living? Binge, purge. Binge, purge. Until we're nothing, eyes on stalks.

Wu grew more impatient, I could lose him in a minute. If Lupus was my only hold on him, I tightened the embrace, started praying for another flare up—hideously swollen joints, bone-shattering fatigue, the wolf mark leaping on my face. I prayed for so much pain I'd beg him, *Do it. With the needle. Hook me. Like a fish.* Then we'd be unsuited for anyone but each other.

We waited, two people on a platform, looking down the track. Lupus would return, but in its own dreadful time. We waited.

One night in Chinatown, Wu put his hand on me, and whispered in my hair. "Ah, Ming . . . it cost so much to live."

I moaned, drifted back to dreams, cradling my pipe, inside it, dark, exhausted little mummy.

Now, I imagine Wu that night, sliding from my bunk, dragging his small kit, dragging his extinction. Alcohol, lighter, spoon, cotton, rubber cord, syringe, an arsenal in moonlight. At dawn, I found him curled up like a child. He seemed no bigger than my fist.

Eucalyptus

Hisaye Yamamoto DeSoto

Laurel and I have stayed in touch over the years, both of us more or less back in business, exchanging yearly cards and such. One day she even drives over for dinner—rice and chicken teriyaki—during which I ask if she heard from Mary of Van Nuys. I recall them getting along famously, Laurel admiring Mary's wry matter-of-factness. There isn't a city in the country you could name where Mary hasn't once lived—St. Louis, Wichita, places like that. When we line up for our medication, Mary always gets Metamucil along with her pills.

Laurel flabbergasts me by answering, "Toki, you're the only one I remember." How can this be? I can summon up so many faces, wondering to this day about their gnawing concerns. True, our cots are next to each other, and I always make it a point to seek her out because she seems perfectly fine to me. The urgent advice of my husband Saul, a pretty shrewd fellow, is to stick with the ones that are just about to

HISAYE YAMAMOTO DESOTO was born in Redondo Beach, California, in 1921. Her acclaimed collection of essays and stories, 17 *Syllables and Other Stories*, is now in its third edition.

go home, to get in on the secret of getting well. The only trouble is that everybody else in this place seems okay to me; I feel like the only sick one.

So, those hot July days on the broad patio, Laurel and I usually share the shade of the same bright-striped canvas swing. We light endless cigarettes, weave colored yarn onto plastic baskets, call it occupational therapy. We wait for our names to be called if it's our day to see the psychiatrist. When that horrible sensation of psychic imbalance overwhelms me, when I become Munch's anguished, O-mouthed woman at this end of the bridge, I lift my eyes towards the eucalyptus trees towering over the terraces behind the mansion, silently praying, O God above the eucalyptus trees . . . help me, heal me, make me whole. . . .

So when Laurel says she doesn't remember Mary, whose sweet, weatherbeaten face I would recognize anywhere in the world, it throws me for a loop. Then a possible explanation occurs to me: Laurel, impatient to get back to the land of the living, opts to stay on for electro-shock while I, willy-nilly, venture back uneasily to my place with my husband and children. Perhaps it is the electro-shock that has erased the memory of all the other women. There is a college student here who has undergone electro-shock and complains about the results. Her bed in the dormitory is surrounded by piles of books which she seems to be reading all at one time. Once I overhear her crying out to her visiting parents, "How would you like it if you lost your whole memory?"

This might be the cause of Laurel's forgetfulness. The treatment doesn't seem to hasten her discharge. After she gets back to her apartment and a less demanding job—part of her condition seems to be the result of stress at the workplace, where a superior without let-up demanded perfection. We keep tabs on one another by phone. "So how are you doing?" I ask. "Oh, you know," she says, "Comme ci, comme ça," which is exactly my condition.

There are others getting electro-shock, the idea of which terrifies me. One morning at the medicine counter, the nurse doesn't hand me my tiny fluted paper cup of the usual medications. "You don't get any today—you're scheduled for electro-shock."

My hair stands on end. "Nobody told me about it," I protest.

"Here's your name on the list," she says, turning the paper around so I can see for myself. "There. Amparo Martinez."

What a relief, "That's not me. I'm Toki Gonzales." Amparo's the only other Hispanic name in the place. I can't help an inward epithet about white people. Amparo, she's the one who's been weeping ever since she got here. When her bewildered husband, small and mild-mannered, tries to comfort her during his visits, she answers in wails and sobs. True, neither of them look stereotypically Hispanic, but neither do I, being Japanese and having acquired my surname through marriage.

Most of the staff and patients are white. But there is a sprinkling of us others. When I first get here, a young Chinese couple attend to me. It seems to be the middle of the night, and I undress and lie down on the examining table so they can attach any number of gadgets and wires to my body, which they hook up to machines. Are they husband and wife? Brother and sister? They go about their monitoring job efficiently, saying little. My rib cage reminds me of an old washboard. I've lost a lot of weight from not being able to eat. Solid food won't go down at all, so I've only had a few sips of milk in recent days.

The occupational therapist is also Chinese. She's usually in her office, so her assistant, a tall, young black girl from Minnesota, is the one seeing to our activities. She drags us to the terrace out back to play tetherball. I'm surprised to find myself enjoying it. She also comes out to the patio to check our handiwork on the plastic baskets. Arts and crafts are not my forte. My yarn work is pretty basic and mangy compared with the meticulous, imaginative productions of some of the others. It takes me forever to finish one, because I have to undo a lot of it and start all over again.

Then there's Phyllis, ah, Phyllis. We all flock around her when she's on duty. She is tender loving care in person. She sits with us and chats as though she has all the time in the world. She gives us a no-fail method for fixing corn-on-the-cob, for instance. When, after a day or two, I finally decide to take a shower, I ask her to stand by outside the stall because I'm still afraid to be enclosed by myself, afraid I'll go berserk. She obliges, like it's the most natural thing in the world. When one of the women curses a mite too much for Phyllis' taste, she takes her into the washroom and cleans her mouth out with soap, while we gather around and watch. The offender takes it in good humor, too. Phyllis is black and the only person on the staff we'd all do anything for.

The only black patient comes and goes twice during my stay of a month or so. The young woman is obviously distraught on both occasions, and her husband equally so. He does not really want her to be admitted, it appears; he wants her home where she belongs. But he doesn't know what to do with her at home, either. An auto accident has left her in this tortured state. No physical scars, but the psychic ones incapacitate her. The husband is not alone; men tend to respond to this kind of emergency with impatience and anger. They have been on the receiving end of care so long, taking for granted all the work that goes into a smooth-running household, that they cannot seem to grasp that they will just have to do without for awhile.

Later in the day I meet Amparo in the corridor. She's no longer crying, for the first time, but she doesn't seem to know where she is. I guide her to the other dormitory and help her find her bed. But she doesn't need any help after her second treatment the following week. She is suddenly transformed into another woman entirely, engaging in sprightly conversation, even clasping her hands in joy over the gain of a pound or two when we all go in for our weighing.

The shock treatment also works miracles for Anna, the tall blonde European who sits alone at the card table playing endless solitaire. After one treatment—the patient is first anesthetized here before the current is applied—she comes to life, bringing out her art supplies, large sheets of thick, grainy white paper and charcoal sticks. Nothing will do but I must sit for her; she has never drawn a Japanese before. However, as I oblige because I have nothing much else to do, I am alarmed to note that when the intercom comes on with its static buzz, she almost leaps out of her skin, as though the electrical residue in her is responding to the electricity in the speaker up there on the wall. She continues her quick sketching after each interruption, making no mention of this reaction. She says this is her second episode of depression, her first coming some years ago after the death of her brilliant husband. After a day or two, she is gone. The word is that "she came back too fast." After a short absence, she is back among us, a charming and witty conversationalist as she resumes her sketches in the "booby hatch," which is what she calls Hilltop House.

Amparo and Anna are not the only unforgettable people. There is a gorgeous young woman who goes out every weekday to a job, her face carefully made up and her head wrapped in a turban. It seems she cannot be trusted with scissors; she has a compulsion to cut off all her hair. Her latest barbering results when she borrows shears from a woman who keeps them to cut the yarn for her baskets. "I didn't know," the woman says. "When she asked to borrow them, I just handed them to her, like I would anybody else." The owner of the scissors seems hale and hearty to me; the only possible clue to her being here is when I overhear her saying, with rapture, "I just love pills!" As for the shorn beauty, the story is that her father had his heart set on a son instead of a daughter.

There is another well-dressed woman who comes out to the patio every morning and works a crossword puzzle. "I do it to make sure I'm not crazy," she says. But her wardrobe causes another young woman some distress, "That's why I'm sick, because I can't afford pretty clothes." We doubt her, but we do not plumb much more. She and her husband are from Kansas. He comes to take her back home, to Menninger's.

Hilda is a plumpish woman who reads omnivorously. If she is not ensconced in one of the easy chairs in the spacious living room with a heavy tome in her lap (one seems to be the history of France), she is walking around with a couple more. I can't help noticing her in the dining room because her enjoyment of food is obvious. She grabs a couple pieces of dessert for herself before she sits down with the others at her table. Some months later, when I return for a group therapy session or two, I encounter her there looking emaciated. "She's been fasting," someone explains. "She says she doesn't deserve to eat." Another woman's arms are purple-raw. She has scratched them till they bleed. "I have blasphemed against the Holy Ghost," she says, "I have committed the unforgivable sin." We get to a Bible to check the passage, but she is not specific about the manner in which she has blasphemed. Someone brings up Saul who persecuted Jews, but who later became Paul the Christian missionary. Would she not say that if anyone had blasphemed, Saul surely had? Yet he was forgiven, even chosen to spread the Word. But she refuses to accept this premise. She is Catholic, and one Sunday her family comes to take her to Mass, and she agrees to go.

This one has come here after the birth of a son. "I hate him," she says. "Everything would be all right if he would just go away." She already has a little daughter whom she loves dearly. There is a lovely young Britisher whom I meet in the library. We both have been unable to read. All the books look too demanding. She has dark hair cut short like a black cap and her eyes have a brooding look. She has bandages on both wrists. I find what looks like an easy book to read, by Henry Van Dyke, something about the three wise men. She lounges in a chair and gently answers questions in her clipped speech. We both agree we're smoking too much. Later, out on the patio, she has visitors. Her husband, a musician in a black combo, has brought fellow band members along to cheer her up, and there is much laughter as they converse.

One husband is indignant when he finds out that we can help out in the kitchen washing pots or whatever, as part of our therapy. "We're paying good money here—why should you have to wash dishes? That's ridiculous!" His wife has a semi-private room. She recalls that her mother attempted suicide once, after which she followed her mother around wherever she went. In her gentle voice, she tells us that she doesn't want to live any longer, but that she is afraid to die.

One day there is an intercom announcement about some of the patients going down to a nearby restaurant for lunch and coming back tiddly. We are reminded that drinking is strictly forbidden. I suspect my roommate to the right in the dormitory, the older woman who doesn't seem to belong here—there's nothing wrong with her that I can see. Probably she's here because of booze.

When I first get to Hilltop House, I am frightened by what might lay in store. In the dining room that night, I am seized with vertigo. The food on my plate, which I cannot eat, is a blur. I stare at the blur and am certain that this time, I am going over the edge into darkness from which I will never come back.

Somehow I am out on the patio in the warm evening air. A small group of young women, younger anyway than my 38 sit here and there about me. I hear their voices through my fog of sustained agony, and I cannot believe what I am hearing. They are like grizzled veterans of the emotional wars. They gaily accuse each other of having had to wear diapers back there at the county facility they've been transferred from. I dimly sense that they are, each and every one of them, interrupted suicides.

This is where Phyllis first appears. I hear one of the girls ask her, "Don't you think he'll leave his wife and marry me?" And Phyllis shakes her head, "I wouldn't count on it."

The first hint that maybe I will get over this thing comes when the head psychiatrist interviews me. He diagnoses it as "anxiety." It feels good to have a definite name for it. He says others have been helped here.

The doctor in charge of my case is on the quiet side, bespectacled, and I blurt out everything in my life that I can think of that could possibly be a clue to my problem. One day we discuss a current magazine article about psychiatry. So how do I feel about the psychiatry I'm having, he asks. "I guess you're the ideal psychiatrist," I say, "bland, colorless, nonintrusive, but expertly guiding the patient."

At my next appointment, he's smoking a long cigar.

Another time I tell him about a friend up north to whom I've mentioned my illness. "Let me tell you about MY operation," the friend has written; it seems he has been suffering all along. "He's Jewish," I remember the yarmulke, "very devout." Such a slight movement backwards in his chair so I barely notice, as I go on, "God doesn't seem to sustain him, either." Afterwards, I remember. The instinctive recoil— ah, I did not mean; he must be—inadvertently have I caused the doctor pain?

As I grope my way towards health, I realize I am learning things. "I lost my girlish laughter" is a phrase now with new meaning, as is "The Age of Anxiety." Finally, too, I understand: "If the salt hath lost his savour, wherewith shall it be salted?"

The doctor gives me a sentence to live by, "There is nothing in daily life that is insurmountable." Even though I think to myself, it's not daily life; it's the accrual.

I tell him of days gone by when my heart almost burst with the joy of being alive, when even the dog crud along the sidewalk seemed right and proper. He suggests that perhaps I could learn to scale down this romanticism, that perhaps then I need not descend to feelings so low, reduced to a quivering mass of protoplasm by my "fear of responsibility." But I do see little ways in which I am getting better. The freeway noises no longer prevent my sleep. I am able to down food, even enjoy the chocolate cake baked by the rather hefty cook (she says she climbs the steep hill each day but cannot lose a pound). I even sit down at the grand piano in the living room and tinkle out the few bars I remember of "Für Elise."

Still, when I leave, I don't feel ready. I understand now why Molly, another patient, sneaks off without a word to anyone. She probably doesn't see that much improvement and is just going home to give it a try.

There has been a study of neurotics that is something to ponder. The Eysenck Study, it is called, and it says that in patients undergoing psychoanalysis, there is a 44% improvement rate, in those undergoing psychotherapy, a 64% improvement rate. But there is a 72% improvement rate in those who receive no treatment whatsoever. What is one to make of such statistics?

It is good to be home and to have the children back. First, kind relatives and friends take them in, obliging me forever. When it looks like I might be awhile, friends arrange for the boy to go to the Japanese Children's Home. He loves it there because there is sushi every day— his favorite food. And the kids there are taken to a pool for swimming lessons. The girls, still babies, go to a foster home. The lady there loves babies and her three children, including an adopted half-Japanese daughter, are all in school now, so she has decided to care for other people's children. Her husband's work keeps him away from home a lot. But Saul is agitated by the children's absence and annoys the lady by calling constantly.

It takes me a couple of years before I finally have a really pleasant day. Meanwhile I return to Hilltop House for some group therapy meetings. One day when I arrive, Phyllis takes me aside and asks me to speak to a Korean woman who has just arrived. So I find in her another woman who, after an extremely difficult delivery, cannot accept her newborn son. She tells me of her symptoms, which are much like mine in the beginning, and I am able to assure her that she is going to be all right.

Hilltop House also phones when another Asian patient turns up. So I call her and learn that she is from Japan. I have to rummage in the back of my mind for words that I haven't used in years, but manage to get the information that she and her brother have come to this country together. They are getting on well until her brother falls in love with and marries a white girl. Whether from feelings of abandonment or not, she decides to kill herself. But she is fine, she tells me, she has already finished a whole slew of baskets. She certainly sounds chipper enough.

However, when I get over to the House the next time and inquire about her, she is gone. She has been transferred to a facility for more serious cases. "She sounded fine when we talked on the phone," I protest. "Some do that," I'm told. "They hide their real feelings and they're thinking of ways to do themselves in."

I remember one who is discharged and goes home. The news we get the next day is that she is dead. We are pretty subdued for the next few days. I don't know whether the group therapy helps or not. As we are partway through one session, the psychiatrist observes, "I know why everyone is so depressed." He says it is because he is going to be away for a couple of weeks. When he leaves the room, most of us express surprise. We had no idea he was going to be absent. This is the same doctor who lays down the dictum, "All depression is anger turned inwards." Which reminds me that I have heard it said that it is obvious in medical school which students are going to take up psychiatry.

Unwanted sons, intransigent married lovers, husbands and sons who treat us like dirt, father who wanted a son instead—this aggregate of female woe, are we all here because of what men do or don't? No, it is not that simple. Probably there are men in like places whose vulnerabilities stem from dealings with mothers, wives, women friends? Where do the roots of our malaise lie buried? In the ways we are nurtured or not nurtured? Or further back, when the first mother received news of her firstborn refusing to keep his only brother?

The echo of her howl comes to us without diminution across the tumult of the ages.

The Bread of Salt

from *Mindoro and Beyond: Twenty-one Stories*

N. V. M. Gonzalez

Usually I was in bed by ten and up by five and thus was ready for one more day of my fourteenth year. Unless Grandmother had forgotten, the fifteen centavos for the baker down Progreso Street— and how I enjoyed jingling those coins in my pocket!—would be in the empty fruit-jar in the cupboard. I would remember then that rolls were what Grandmother wanted because recently she had lost three molars. For young people like my cousins and myself, she had always said that the kind called *pan de sal* ought to be quite all right.

The bread of salt! How did it get that name? From where did its flavor come; through what secret action of flour and yeast? At the risk

N. V. M. GONZALEZ was born in the Philippines in 1915 and grew up in the province of Mindoro. His novels and story collections include *The Winds of April, Seven Hills Away, Children of the Ash-Covered Loam and Other Stories, The Bamboo Dancers,* and *Mindoro and Beyond.* An autobiography, *Kalutang: A Filipino in the World,* a collection of critical essays, *The Father and the Maid,* and a retrospective collection of his short stories, *The Bread of Salt and Other Stories,* were recently published. A distinguished scholar, teacher and critic, he is Emeritus Professor of English, California State University, Hayward, and lives in Hayward, California.

of being jostled from the counter by other early buyers, I would push my way into the shop so that I might watch the men who, stripped to the waist, worked their long flat wooden spades in and out of the glowing maw of the oven. Why did the bread come nut-brown and the size of my little fist? And why did it have a pair of lips convulsed into a painful frown? In the half-light of the street, and hurrying, the paper bag pressed to my chest, I felt my curiosity a little gratified by the oven-fresh warmth of the bread I was proudly bringing home for breakfast.

Well I knew how Grandmother would not mind if I nibbled away at one piece; perhaps, I might even eat two, to be charged later against my share at the table. But that would be betraying a trust; and so, indeed, I kept my purchase intact. To guard it from harm, I watched my steps and avoided the dark street corners.

For my reward, I had only to look in the direction of the seawall and the fifty yards or so of riverbed beyond it, where an old Spaniard's house stood. At low tide, when the bed was dry and the rocks glinted with broken bottles, the stone fence of the Spaniard's compound set off the house as if it were a castle. Sunrise brought a wash of silver upon the roof of the laundry and garden sheds which had been built low and close to the fence. On dull mornings the light dripped from the bamboo screen which covered the veranda and hung some four or five yards from the ground. Unless it was August, when the damp northeast monsoon had to be kept away from the rooms, three servants raised the screen promptly at six-thirty until it was completely hidden under the veranda eaves. From the sound of the pulleys I knew it was time to set out for school.

It was in his service, as a coconut plantation overseer, that Grandfather had spent the last thirty years of his life. Grandmother had been widowed three years now. I often wondered whether I was being depended upon to spend the years ahead in the service of this great house. One day I learned that Aida, a classmate in high school, was the old Spaniard's niece. All my doubts disappeared. It was as if before his death, Grandfather had spoken to me about her, concealing the seriousness of the matter by putting it over as a joke. If now I kept true to the virtues, she would step out of her bedroom ostensibly to say Good Morning to her uncle. Her real purpose, I knew, was to reveal thus her assent to my desire.

On quiet mornings I imagined the patter of her shoes upon the wooden veranda floor as a further sign, and I would hurry off to school, taking the route she had fixed for me past the post office, the town plaza and the church, the health center east of the plaza, and at last the school grounds. I asked myself whether I would try to walk with her and decided it would be the height of rudeness. Enough that in her blue skirt and white middy she would be half a block ahead and, from that distance, perhaps throw a glance in my direction, to bestow upon my heart a deserved and abundant blessing. I believed it was but right that in some such way as this her mission in my life was disguised.

Her name, I was to learn many years later, was a convenient mnemonic for the qualities to which argument might aspire. But in those days it was a living voice. "Oh that you might be worthy of uttering me," it said. And how I endeavored to build my body so that I might live long to honor her. With every victory at singles at the handball court—the game was then the craze at school—I could feel my body glow in the sun as though it had instantly been cast in bronze. I guarded my mind and did not let my wits go astray. In my class I would not allow a lesson to pass unmastered. Our English teacher could put no question before us that did not have a ready answer in my head. One day he read Robert Louis Stevenson's *The Sire de Maletroit's Door*, and we were so enthralled that our breaths trembled. I knew then that somewhere, sometime in the not too improbable future, a benign old man with a lantern in his hand would also detain me in a secret room and there daybreak would find me thrilled by the sudden certainty that I had won Aida's hand.

It was perhaps on my violin that her name wrought such a tender spell. Maestro Antonino remarked the dexterity of my stubby fingers. Quickly I raced through Alard—until I had all but committed two thirds of the book to memory. My short brown arm learned at last to draw the bow with grace. Sometimes when practising my scales in the early evening, I wondered if the sea wind carrying the straggling notes across the pebbled river did not transform them into a Schubert's *Serenade*.

At last Mr. Custodio, who was in charge of our school orchestra, became aware of my progress. He moved me from second to first violin. During the Thanksgiving Day program he bade me render a number complete with pizzicati and harmonics.

"Another Vallejo! Our own Albert Spalding!" I heard from the front row.

Aida, I thought, would be in the audience. I looked around quickly but could not see her. As I retired to my place in the orchestra I heard Pete Saez, the trombone player, call my name.

"You must join *my* band," he said. "Look, we'll have many engagements soon. It'll be vacation time."

Pete pressed my arm. He had for some time now been asking me to join the Minviluz Orchestra, his private band. All I had been able to tell him was that I had my school work to mind. He was twenty-two. I was perhaps too young to be going around with him. He earned his school fees and supported his mother hiring out his band at least three or four times a month. He now said:

"Tomorrow we play at a Chinaman's funeral. Four to six in the afternoon. In the evening, Judge Roldan's silver wedding anniversary. Sunday, the municipal dance."

My head began to whirl. On the stage, in front of us, the Principal had begun a speech about America. Nothing he could say about the Pilgrim Fathers and the American custom of feasting on turkey seemed interesting. I thought of the money I would earn. For several days now I had but one wish, to buy a box of linen stationery. At night when the house was quiet I would fill the sheets with words that would tell Aida how much I adored her. One of these mornings, perhaps before school closed for the holidays, I would borrow her algebra book and there upon a good pageful of equations, there I would slip my message, tenderly pressing the leaves of the book. She would perhaps never write back. Neither by post nor by hand would a reply reach me. But no matter; it would be a silence full of voices.

That night I dreamed I had returned from a tour of the world's music centers; the newspapers of Manila had been generous with praise. I saw my picture on the cover of a magazine. A writer had described how many years ago I used to trudge the streets of Buenavista with my violin in a battered black cardboard case. In New York, he reported, a millionaire had offered me a Stradivarius violin, with a card which bore the inscription: "In admiration of a genius your own people must surely be proud of." I dreamed I spent a week-end at the millionaire's country house by the Hudson. A young girl in a blue skirt and white middy clapped her lily-white hands and, her voice trembling, cried "Bravo!"

What people now observed at home was the diligence with which I attended to my violin lessons. My aunt, who had come from the farm to join her children for the holidays brought with her a maidservant, and to the poor girl was given the chore of taking the money to the baker's for rolls and pan de sal. I realized at once that it would be no longer becoming on my part to make these morning trips to the baker's. I could not thank my aunt enough.

I began to chafe on being given other errands. Suspecting my violin to be the excuse, my aunt remarked:

"What do you want to be a musician for? At parties, musicians always eat last."

Perhaps, I said to myself, she was thinking of a pack of dogs scrambling for scraps tossed over the fence by some careless kitchen maid. She was the sort you could depend on to say such vulgar things. For that reason, I thought, she ought not to be taken seriously at all.

But the remark hurt me. Although Grandmother had counseled me kindly to mind my work at school, I went again and again to Pete Saez's house for rehearsals.

She had demanded that I deposit with her my earnings; I had felt too weak to refuse. Secretly, I counted the money and decided not to ask for it until I had enough with which to buy a brooch. Why this time I wanted to give Aida a brooch, I didn't know. But I had set my heart on it. I searched the downtown shops. The Chinese clerks, seeing me so young, were annoyed when I inquired about prices.

At last the Christmas season began. I had not counted on Aida's leaving home, and remembering that her parents lived in Badajoz, my torment was almost unbearable. Not once had I tried to tell her of my love. My letters had remained unwritten, and the algebra book unborrowed. There was still the brooch to find, but I could not decide on the sort of brooch I really wanted. And the money, in any case, was in Grandmother's purse, which smelled of "Tiger Balm." I grew somewhat feverish as our class Christmas program drew near. Finally it came; it was a warm December afternoon. I decided to leave the room when our English teacher announced that members of the class might exchange gifts. I felt fortunate; Pete was at the door, beckoning to me. We walked out to the porch where, Pete said, he would tell me a secret.

It was about an *asalto* the next Sunday which the Buenavista Women's Club wished to give Don Esteban's daughters, Josefina and Alicia, who were arriving on the morning steamer from Manila. The spinsters were much loved by the ladies. Years ago, when they were younger, these ladies studied solfeggio with Josefina and the piano and harp with Alicia. As Pete told me all this, his lips ash-gray from practising all morning on his trombone, I saw in my mind the sisters in their silk dresses, shuffling off to church for the evening benediction. They were very devout, and the Buenavista ladies admired that. I had almost forgotten that they were twins and, despite their age, often dressed alike. In low-bosomed voile bodices and white summer hats, I remembered, the pair had attended Grandfather's funeral, at old Don Esteban's behest. I wondered how successful they had been in Manila during the past three years in the matter of finding suitable husbands.

"This party will be a complete surprise," Pete said, looking around the porch as if to swear me to secrecy. "They've hired our band."

I joined my classmates in the room, greeting everyone with a Merry Christmas jollier than that of the others. When I saw Aida in one corner unwrapping something two girls had given her, I found the boldness to greet her also.

"Merry Christmas," I said in English, as a hairbrush and a powder case emerged from the fancy wrapping. It seemed to me rather apt that such gifts went to her. Already several girls were gathered around Aida. Their eyes glowed with envy, it seemed to me, for those fair cheeks and the bobbed dark-brown hair which lineage had denied them.

I was too dumbstruck by my own meanness to hear exactly what Aida said in answer to my greeting. But I recovered shortly and asked:

"Will you be away during the vacation?"

"No, I'll be staying here," she said. When she added that her cousins were arriving and that a big party in their honor was being planned, I remarked:

"So you all know about it?" I felt I had to explain that the party was meant to be a surprise, an asalto.

And now it would be nothing of the kind, really. The women's club matrons would hustle about, disguising their scurrying around for cakes and candies as for some baptismal party or other. In the end, the Rivas sisters would outdo them. Boxes of meringues, bonbons, ladyfingers, and cinnamon buns that only the Swiss bakers in Manila could make were perhaps coming on the boat with them. I imagined a table glimmering with long-stemmed punch glasses; enthroned in that array would be a huge brick-red bowl of gleaming china with golden flowers round the brim. The local matrons, however hard they tried, however sincere their efforts, were bound to fail in their aspiration to rise to the level of Don Esteban's daughters. Perhaps, I thought, Aida knew all this. And that I should share in a foreknowledge of the matrons' hopes was a matter beyond love. Aida and I could laugh together with the gods.

At seven, on the appointed evening, our small band gathered quietly at the gate of old Don Esteban's house, and when the ladies arrived in their heavy shawls and trim *panuelos*, twittering with excitement, we were commanded to play the "Poet and Peasant" overture. As Pete directed the band, his eyes glowed with pride for his having been part of the big event. The multicolored lights that the old Spaniard's gardeners had strung along the vine-covered fence were switched on and the women remarked that Don Esteban's daughters might have made some preparations after all. Pete hid his face from the glare. If the women felt let down, they did not show it.

The overture shuffled along to its climax while five men in white shirts bore huge boxes of food into the house. I recognized one of the bakers in spite of the uniform. A chorus of confused greetings, and the women trooped into the house; and before we had settled in the *sala* to play "A Basket of Roses," the heavy damask curtains at the far end of the room were drawn and a long table richly spread was revealed under the chandeliers. I remembered that in our haste to be on hand for the asalto, Pete and I had discouraged the members of the band from taking their suppers.

"You've done us a great honor!" Josefina, the more buxom of the twins, greeted the ladies.

"Oh, but you have not allowed us to take you by surprise!" the ladies demurred in a chorus.

There were sighs and further protestations amid a rustle of skirts and the glitter of earrings. I saw Aida in a long, flowing white gown and wearing an arch of *sampaguita* flowers on her hair. At her command, two servants brought out a gleaming harp from the music room. Only the slightest scraping could be heard because the servants were barefoot. As Aida directed them to place the instrument near the seats we occupied, my heart leaped to my throat. Soon she was lost among the guests, and we played "The Dance of the Glowworms." I kept my eyes closed and held for as long as I could her radiant figure before me.

Alicia played on the harp and then in answer to the deafening applause, she offered an encore. Josefina sang afterward. Her voice, though a little husky, fetched enormous sighs. For her encore, she gave "The Last Rose of Summer"; and the song brought back snatches of the years gone by. Memories of solfeggio lessons eddied about us, as if there were rustling leaves scattering all over the hall. Don Esteban appeared. Earlier, he had greeted the crowd handsomely, twisting his mustache to hide a natural shyness before talkative women. He stayed long enough to listen to the harp again, whispering in his rapture: "Heavenly, heavenly. . . ."

By midnight the merrymaking lagged. We played while the party gathered around the great table at the end of the sala. My mind travelled across the seas to the distant cities I had dreamed about. The sisters sailed among the ladies like two great white liners amid a fleet of tugboats in a bay. Someone had thoughtfully remembered—and at last Pete Saez signalled to us to put our instruments away. We walked in single file across the hall, led by one of the barefoot servants.

Behind us a couple of hoarse sopranos sang "La Paloma" to the accompaniment of the harp, but I did not care to find out who they were. The sight of so much silver and china confused me. There was more food before us than I had ever imagined. I searched in my mind for the names of the dishes; and my ignorance appalled me. I wondered what had happened to the boxes of food that the Buenavista ladies had sent up earlier. In a silver bowl was something, I discovered, that appeared like whole egg yolks that had been dipped in honey and peppermint. The seven of us in the orchestra were all of one mind about the feast; and so, confident that I was with friends, I allowed my covetousness to have its way and not only stuffed my mouth with this and that confection but also wrapped up a quantity of those egg yolk things in several sheets of napkin paper. None of my companions had thought of doing the same, and it was with some pride that I slipped the packet under my shirt. There, I knew, it would not bulge.

"Have you eaten?"

I turned around. It was Aida. My bow tie seemed to tighten around my collar. I mumbled something I did not know what.

"If you wait a little while till they've all gone, I'll wrap up a big package for you," she added.

I brought a handkerchief to my mouth. I might have honored her solicitude adequately and even relieved myself of any embarrassments. I could not quite believe that she had seen me, and yet I was sure that she knew what I had done; and I felt all ardor for her gone from me entirely.

I walked away to the nearest door, praying that the damask curtains hide me in my shame. The door gave on to the veranda, where once my love had trod on sunbeams. Outside it was dark, and a faint wind was singing in the harbor.

With the napkin balled up in my hand, I flung out my arm to scatter the egg yolk things in the dark. I waited for the soft sound of their fall on the garden-shed roof. Instead I heard a spatter in the rising night-tide beyond the stone fence. Farther away glimmered the light from Grandmother's window, calling me home.

•

But the party broke up at one or thereabouts. We walked away with our instruments after the matrons were done with their interminable goodbyes. Then, to the tune of "Joy to the World," we pulled the Progreso Street shopkeepers out of their beds. The Chinese merchants were especially generous. When Pete divided our collection under a street lamp, there was already a little glow of daybreak.

He walked with me part of the way home. We stopped at the baker's when I told him that I wanted to buy with my own money some bread to eat on the way to Grandmother's house at the edge of the seawall. He laughed, thinking it strange that I should be hungry. We found ourselves alone at the counter; and we watched the bakery assistants at work until our bodies grew warm from the oven across the door. It was not quite five, and the bread was not yet ready.

Film Noir

excerpt from a novel-in-progress

Jessica Hagedorn

Marlon Rivera is watering his garden. The temperature has already climbed past the humid eighties and the sky is brown with smog. His fishnet tank top clings to him, soaked with sweat—but Marlon doesn't care. His feet streaked with mud, he flip-flops in his rubber thongs on the glistening grass. *Squish, squish.* He sprays with his garden hose—ferns, wild lilies, cactus, the roots of a jacaranda tree. Everything squishy, fluid, wet. He is happy. His hibiscus and roses are blooming in the heat—shades of red blazing on Marlon Rivera's amazing but tiny front lawn.

"Good morning, Senor Rivera." His neighbor, the famous dead director's wife Isabel L'Ange, addresses him with a clipped English accent. Peggy Ashcroft. Dame Edith Evans. The accents vary with her moods. A few days ago she was somewhere within the melodious regions of Brazil—all o's and swirling j's—and a purring, fake French Eartha Kitt. But then, she'd been drinking.

After several tries and muttered curses, she yanks her key out of the rusty lock on her door. She turns the door knob once to check it, lets out a deep breath. "Damn heat. My keys always get stuck—"

"Up so early?" Marlon Rivera smiles. She is one of his favorite people, an authentic grande dame, he likes to tell his friends. Very chichi.

She is deadpan, impassive, as usual. "At my age, sleep is a damn waste of time. You'll be home this morning? Keep an eye out for me, will you?" She and her husband had been robbed once, years ago, in their Spanish villa in the Valley. There were three men. Her pajama-clad, barefoot husband was made to lie on the cold tile floor with his hands tied behind his back. Their only daughter, who was four at the time, had a gun aimed at her head while Isabel led the other two men to a safe in the library that contained a lot of cash and Isabel's jewels. "It was such a cliche," she said to Marlon, "that safe. Hidden behind a mediocre impressionist painting! They knew exactly where to look —they had us all figured out."

And now, having outlived her husband and daughter, Isabel L'Ange lives next door, with five cats she calls "my children." All the windows to her modest cottage except for one are nailed shut. "An old woman like me," she'd say, without bitterness. "I'm easy prey."

On this muggy morning, with the sun trying in vain to burn through layers of shit in the sky, Isabel L'Ange is decked out in her uniform for facing the public—a well-worn, khaki safari pantsuit, expensive walking-shoes, and the frayed, yellowed, soft Panama hat which had once belonged to her husband, Fritz. Her wiry, white hair is pulled back in a ponytail; her skin still smooth and bronze, even without make-up. She is a former Forbidden City chorus girl and starlet. Part Chinese, Black, and Filipino. Her beauty awesome and upsetting in her youth. Anna May Wong and Dorothy Dandridge had been her rivals. Her career was short-lived, but her marriage to the legendary director guaranteed her an uneasy place in Hollywood history. "Those studio guys had no use for me—I was an uppity nigger, always shootin' off my big mouth," she said to Marlon the first time they got high together.

"You were amazing in *Harlem Rhapsody* . . ."

She looked bored. "Bullshit. I was a passable dancer, and a mediocre singer. I sleepwalked through most of those films. Thank god for Fritz."

"What about that bit in *Shanghai Deadly*? Pure sex! You and Mitchum practically burned up the screen—"

"Absolute bullshit."

It amused her that he had seen her movies. "You mean all four of them?" Isabel's laugh was light and airy, but her eyes remained flat and guarded. "You must be the only one—"

"No," Marlon said, "you were a popular star in Manila, believe it or not."

"I was a starlet, for godsake. Second banana."

"There were contests," Marlon said. "For the Isabel L'Ange of the Philippines. There was even a take-off made called *Manila Rhapsody*. My mother took me to see it twice. We were heartbroken when you got married and retired from the movies . . ."

Isabel L'Ange was silent, and Marlon wasn't sure if he'd offended her. "My mother . . ." he stammered. "My mother was . . . the most beautiful woman in the town of Paete, Laguna."

Marlon Rivera blinks.

Clutching her briefcase, Isabel L'Ange grimaces in pain as she limps towards the curb where her car is parked. "Where's your cane?" Marlon calls out to her. "You need a walking-stick—one of those elegant things with an ivory tip—"

She pretends not to hear him.

"Off to the lawyer's—" she tells him in today's lilting voice, though Marlon Rivera hasn't asked. Tomorrow, husky and growling. Tallulah Bankhead. "Join me for tea later?" She stares warily at Marlon with eyes that are a faded brown. She expects him to say no, even though they've been meeting every afternoon for tea ever since Marlon could remember.

"Love to," Marlon says.

It is their daily ritual, broken only when Marlon is on tour, dancing with road companies and choreographing the millionth run of *Flower Drum Song* or *West Side Story*, or playing the Yul Brynner part in a second-rate dinner theater production of *The King and I*. Tampa, Jacksonville, Orlando, Gainesville. He'd been to every stop in Florida, it seemed. The role is Marlon's current favorite—his only chance to play a lead. He refuses to wear a latex cap and even shaves his head. While four hundred senior citizens chew leathery prime rib and overcooked broccoli, Marlon bellows "Shall We Dance?" and hams it up. Most of the children in the cast are Filipino and call him "Tiyo" or Uncle. They join Marlon onstage for carefully choreographed bows. Their parents hover in the wings, inviting Marlon over for homecooked adobo dinners and introducing him to their older, virgin daughters and embarrassed, unmarried nieces. "Meet the king of show business," they'd say, "remember how wonderful? He was Chino in *West Side Story!*"

After the show, several members of the audience inevitably approach Marlon for an autograph. "You speak such good English!" a woman with bleached blond hair exclaims. She is about seventy years old and her face is painted like a doll's—pink cheeks and heart-shaped red lips, terrifying eyes glittering black with mascara. She shoves a notebook at Marlon and he thanks her in spite of himself, thanks everyone clustered around him backstage, peering, shoving, poking at him. He is still in full make-up and costume, and obligingly poses for snapshots with his fans.

Isabella Arabella. B-movie temptress and reclusive widow. Marlon Rivera's neighbor and fantasy mother. Isabellina the bankrupt martyr. "He blew all the money," she once said about her husband in a drunken confession. She hiccupped while she laughed. "All the fucking money."

Marlon watches the old woman as she slowly maneuvers herself into her dusty beige Honda. It seems an eternity, but she finally drives off, disappearing in a white film of heat.

"So this is Hollywood," his surly niece Raquel had said on her first visit.

"Yeah," Marlon said, "Victor Mature's my landlord, Troy Donahue rents my garage, and Anna May Wong lives next door."

"Anna May Wong's dead." Raquel was inspecting Marlon's altar in the living room.

"I'll show you Troy's motorcycle later if you want."

"Who's Troy Donahue?" The young man with Raquel asked.

They ignored him. Raquel made a gesture as if to pick up one of the black angel figurines on the altar, then changed her mind. "Tiyo Marlon, how long have you lived here?"

"I dunno. Long enough. Go ahead, pick it up."

"Ma has never lived in a place that long—"

"You mean since she came to America," Marlon corrected her. "She lived in your house in Manila for years—since after the war. All that wandering started after she and your father—"

"What's all this?" Raquel indicated the altar with her chin. A Pinoy habit, Marlon observed, pleased.

"Santo Niño from Cebu, a cross from Peru, hey it rhymes." Marlon went on: "La Virgen de Guadalupe from Mexico, another one from who knows where except I bought it in Manila . . . They told me it was from the diggings in Panay—overcharged me. . . . 'Antique,' DAW! You know they got factories in Cebu that turn these out . . . perfect antiques with broken noses! For the tourist market, siempre. I knew better, but I bought it anyway. The vendors were laughing behind my back. Tourist Pinoy!" He shrugged. "That's what I deserve, for being gone so long. . . . Isn't it ugly? Look at her hair. It's real. I love this ugly Virgin, I really do—"

Raquel made a face at the crying madonna. "Spooky."

"Our Lady of Bad Dreams," Marlon agreed.

"Are you lovers?" Marlon asked his niece. She was stretched out on his sofa, running her fingers through her short, magenta-streaked hair, yanking it upwards into terrifying, spiky clumps. The young man was out of earshot, on the phone in the next room.

"Sometimes." Then, after a moment's silence—"We're going to live in Malibu."

"Malibu? But you don't have any money."

Raquel blushed. "His buddy Jeffrey rents this wreck of a house on the highway—it's wonderful and awful, the termites have eaten away the foundation. I think the owner plans to tear it down in about a year, but meantime—"

"What does your mother think?"

She tried to seem casual. "My mother. My mother's pissed."

The young man loped into the living room. "I'm hungry, Rock."

"You're always hungry." She made no move to get up from where she was sitting.

"Let's go over to Danny's Diner."

Marlon wouldn't hear of it. "You'll stay right here. I'll cook up some of my famous adobo. Have you ever tried adobo?" He asked the young man.

"Rocky's mom made it once."

"Well, I'm sure it was good, but I'm the better cook. You haven't had the real thing until you've tried my adobo."

"The best," Raquel Rivera said.

"When you cook adobo, you gotta make sure there's plenty of black peppercorns and the right kind of vinegar. You gotta use plain white vinegar—nothing fancy, that's the key. Lots of it. And garlic—the more, the better. You got anything against pork?" Marlon studied the young man, tall and maybe a little too skinny, but pretty enough with that gold hoop in his ear. Elvis Chang, Marlon thought to himself, amused. Elvis Chang in the home of Marlon Rivera.

"Nah," the young man said. "I'm Chinese."

"Ahh." Marlon smiled. "Of course. How could I forget?" He winked at his niece, got up from where he was sitting, and sauntered off into the kitchen, the largest room in his stucco bungalow.

They watched him cook.

"What was it like . . ." The young man hesitated, suddenly shy.

"What 'it'?" Marlon was still smiling.

"*West Side Story*. Weren't you one of the original cast members?"

"Both the Broadway and movie version—isn't that so, Tiyo Marlon?" Raquel sat at the kitchen table and pulled out a cigarette from her leather jacket. "Mind if I smoke?"

"Yes," Marlon said, "and yes to your other question." He opened the refrigerator and pulled out a large plastic bowl. He dipped his finger in the marinade and licked it, making a face. "Needs more," he murmured to himself, pouring vinegar on the cubes of pork and beef mixed with chicken wings. "Hmmm . . ." He added a teaspoon of sugar then tasted it again, perplexed. "Have you seen the movie?" Marlon asked the young man. Raquel held the unlit cigarette in a disgruntled pose, not sure whether to defy her uncle.

"Yeah, on tv once. But Rocky says I should see it in the theater—"

"She's right. There's nothing like a big screen, especially for that opening sequence. Aerial shots of New York City—remember that?"

"Oh, yeah." The young man tried to look impressed.

"Stunning. And remember—the first fifteen minutes of the movie had absolutely no dialogue! Very innovative for its time, di ba? Only music and street dancing—" Marlon plugged in his always dependable, industrial-size, "I love to feed the world" Hitachi rice-cooker. "You like rice, I presume?" He was flirting, the young man was aware of that. It made him uncomfortable. Rocky's uncle was an attractive man. In spite of his graying hair, he still had the body of a twenty-year-old dancer. And his face, too. Hard, brown, smooth.

"That chick was no Puerto Rican," Elvis said.

Marlon gave him a mocking look. "You mean Miz Natalie Wood?" He paused. "And what about me? Did I pass for Puerto Rican?"

Elvis Chang shrugged, his face closing off and taking on the same sullen cast as Marlon's niece. They both sat there frowning at him.

"Ay, puta!"

Raquel looked up as her uncle cursed. "Bay leaves," Marlon Rivera hissed. "I forgot the bay leaves!"

Much later, after the dishes had been cleared and the young man had walked ahead in the darkness to warm up his battered pickup truck, Raquel lingered behind on Marlon's front steps. "I love your orchids," she said. "I'm not good at any of those things. Cooking. Gardening." She smoked her clove cigarette with studied gloom. Marlon gazed at her with affection. His niece was reinventing herself moment to moment, day by day. Los Angeles suited her.

"Is that boy one of your musicians?" Marlon asked, adding, "I liked him." Raquel nodded, and turned her head away to exhale perfumed smoke. "We've got a band," she said.

She didn't bother to say goodbye. Zipping up her leather jacket, she started down the flagstone steps then suddenly turned to address him. "He's got the most incredible tattoo," she whispered, her eyes shining with lust. "A dragon wrapped all around his belly . . . Do you know how that must've hurt?"

Isabella of Spain, Marlon calls her when he's high.

"What happened to that lover of yours? He was such a sweetie." The old woman is in good spirits today; the meeting with the lawyers must've went well. Her eyes are darting and alive, she sits with her back straight in spite of the pain.

He lies and says Stephen is in Mexico on an assignment. They are drinking rum and Coke in the garden. "Let's have tea at my place," Marlon had insisted. On days like this, Marlon couldn't stand being inside her cottage, with its carpets and furniture covered with cathair and lint, and the airless rooms reeking of piss.

"Oh yes," the old woman says with enthusiasm, "Let's!"

"Balthus! Gustav! Demian! Marmalade! Thelonius!" Isabel croons for her cats. "Mama's going next door for a bit," she informs the one-eyed Balthus, biggest and oldest of the neutered bunch. The others are out back, hunting rats and snakes in her weed-choked yard. Marlon hears them fight, a burst of screeching and howling in the distance.

She comes over with a bottle of Haitian 5-Star Barbancourt rum and a wrinkled lime that has obviously been in her refrigerator too long. Marlon supplies the Coke and the ice. They sit on Marlon's white lawn chairs, a white table between them. "Are you hungry?" But she's never hungry, and only eats when he cajoles her. "Just a little bit," he says, "otherwise you'll get drunk too fast." This always amuses her, and she allows him to serve up leftovers on a paper plate, delectable leftovers which she picks at to please him while she sips more rum and Coke. "Your food is too good," Isabel L'Ange admits, "but I couldn't care less."

"Eat."

"And that niece of yours? Let's see—" the old woman is being playful, "She must be in New York. Stephen is in Mexico and Rachel is in New York."

He doesn't respond. It is almost seven in the evening, but the sun refuses to set and there is still no breeze.

"Tell me again," she pleads, "about your mother choosing your name."

"I chose my name," Marlon reminds her, irritably. "After I saw *The Wild One*. My mother called me Epifánio Sebastián for two reasons—after the feast of the Epiphany, which was my birthday. And after her favorite saint—"

"Ahh yes," Isabel beams at him, "you told me once. Sebastián. She thought he was the most handsome." She has put on her bracelets for this special occasion. Heavy gold bracelets, with miniature charms dangling . . . A conch shell, a jade heart, a curved, coolie hat. A bicycle, an abacus, a pair of slippers. Isabel's face is glowing. The liquor has taken effect, softening her features. "You're very lucky," she says.

"I never thought so."

"But you are. To be born Catholic—it's quite a legacy, in spite of what you think . . . And I know what you think."

He says nothing, gazing at her with his angry little smile.

"That it is a burden. Some hideous burden that has been imposed upon you . . . and your people—" Isabel smiles back at him, then pours herself, this time, a glass of straight rum. They talk in shorthand. "*Our* people. Do you know I've never been to Manila? My mother's folks were from someplace called Samar. Beautiful name, isn't it? All I knew. Fritz was invited once, for one of those festivals. Back when . . . that woman. But I never wanted to go. That woman, I said. You can't. So he went alone." She giggles. "Had a ball, he said. Great parties, that woman. Not politically correct, I scolded him. Couldn't give a shit, dear Fritz. *To the people*." The smile pasted on her face, she toasts Marlon with her glass.

Now shy, now sad, she waits for him to speak. When the silence becomes unbearable and there is no more to drink, Isabel L'Ange makes a motion to leave. "I've talked too much, haven't I?"

The night is too young and there is no breeze. Should he go back inside and find . . . Stephen used to forget hiding bottles of tequila or rum way back behind the pots and pans stacked inside the kitchen cabinets. Weeks would go by, then Stephen would unearth some forgotten treasure. Should he bother looking? Marlon Rivera shrugs and makes a gesture with his hand. He is angry but not drunk enough yet. He collapses into himself and broods. Isabel sits back down. She stares at the street, unsure of what to do next; Marlon knows she is afraid of his rage, and this saddens him. "I'm okay," he says softly to her, "don't worry."

She is memorable in the fading light. The heavy lids of her almond-shaped eyes, her cheeks sunken with age. In profile, there are still elements of this and that. Marlon considers this and feels blessed.

Garbo in **Ninotchka**. *Sonia Braga in* **Dona Flor**. *Lena Horne in* **Cabin in the Sky**. *Dorothy Dandridge in* **Carmen Jones**. *And his favorite, The most beautiful and uncelebrated of them all, Anna May Wong. The laundryman's daughter. In her first. Was it* **Lotus**? *Or* **Jade**? **Jade Lotus Blossoms**? *Or that Dietrich movie whose title temporarily eludes him. Probably her best. A definite vehicle for Marlene, but Anna May stole the show.* **Shanghai**. *It was always* **Shanghai** *something.*

Afterbirth

Kimiko Hahn

In some societies women eat the placenta after that final stage: the expulsion of the afterbirth when the belly heaves a great sigh and lies on the pelvis like a nostalgic sack. The baby, clipped off from her past, dried and slapped into breath, then realizes our world not in the sense of thinking but becoming: the light becomes light. Warm becomes partial as the crescent moon. Sweet issues from this form. The woman eats the long-baked fruit of her uterus.

Rose missed something when she moved from the small town of her childhood to a city near water. Not the farms, though the smell of hay did become nostalgic. Not the Church of the Immaculate Conception bells down the street. Not her high school sweetheart. Maybe the Calico. A little her mother's *night night dear*, or Moonlight Magic, their favorite nailpolish. Her father was rarely home, he practically

KIMIKO HAHN, the daughter of two artists, grew up near New York City and now lives in Manhattan with her husband and their two daughters. She is the author of two collections of poetry, *Air Pocket* and *Earshot*. She currently teaches poetry at Sarah Lawrence College and Asian American literature at Yale University.

lived at the plant and smelled of industrial glue—not his fault. The smell of salt three blocks away, the taste of it even through storm windows, shrivelled her guts till she'd lie down in her furnished room and sob. Over the phone her father told her to go and see a movie. Air out.

When her sister's water broke at a Fire Dept. pot luck they'd been laughing about how male genitals come in diverse shapes, laughing till tears and snot hung from their angelic faces. A little water trickled down Hazel's leg. They knew. They knew within 24 hours an event would sever their frames of reference so they'd never feel quite the same closeness. And that their whole lives were a preparation for the loss the baby would bring, male or female.

Rose's two favorite exhibits at the Natural History are oceanic: the tidal pool section where you can see at eye level the starfish fastened onto rocks, barnacles fastened onto anything, animals resembling party blowers, baby crabs and anything else caught in that wealth. Then of course the life-size blue whale suspended from the ceiling so you can linger beneath her. Imagine being a calf to the world's largest animal, the female even larger than the male.

At 19 her sister had had an abortion and confided in Rose, then 15 years old. Hazel had spent the whole summer positioning herself to tell her parents. Finally, on the last day of their summer holiday she went to their room, informed them and felt the unexpected horror from her mother and tenderness from her dad. Back in her room, a joke from the afternoon made the two girls laugh till tears and snot hung from their angelic faces.

There's a myth about the placenta from an Asian country tucked against the continent and its classical influences. The women say it is a second infant who battles with the child for blood so one grows skull, bones and flesh while the other remains a great pulsating heart, longing for lips to suck on the mother's breast. The women bury the placenta deep in the ground away from wild dogs then plant orchids over it so the roots may reach the child's remains and lift its desire toward the clouds, beckoning rain for itself and its sibling who it forgives in its new existence, fragrant and ecstatic in its gift. Drought is blamed on the midwife who fails to perform the rite.

Monica hadn't been sure she was ready for a baby (child yes, but a baby?) but when she became pregnant she was pleased. Her body swelled like a flower just before it opens: greenish, delicate, insistent. By the third trimester her limbs looked like attachments and she began to feel less happy and more anxious to get to the pain and labor. The baby kicked a lot. (A boy?) Then stopped kicking. Tests showed it was okay. But two weeks later she demanded another test: "negative." The baby was negative. The obstetrician would have to induce labor. Could she go through it—deliver a dead baby and still be sane? Would the baby go to heaven and bond with the Angels?

Milwaukee, Boston, Los Angeles—wherever Hazel travelled she would find strong women she'd unconsciously drawn toward her not in desperation but in the habit of desperation for someone who could imitate men scratching their balls, compare cellulite or explain night terrors. Later she would discover her three-year-old's imaginary companion, sometimes "in high school," sometimes in her belly, kicking and trying to get born. She called her Cheechee.

There were nine chicks to begin with but a rat ate seven so by the time Eleanor took her children to see the Church's last two chicks they hid as best they could. The gardener gave her a paperbag and winked. She plopped one fuzzy one in and hurried home to raise it for a couple months in her apartment on cornmeal and grits. A few weeks later she pointed out how the tail feathers were about to unfurl.

And that bump on its head may be a male's comb. Soon a little red hedge did appear on its head. Still unsure she said wait to see if it lays eggs.

At the hospital Rose appeared with a potted gardenia and the chapstick her sister requested. The long labor, the hours of *whoo whoo whoo—hee hee hee* every three minutes dried Hazel's lips like a weekend in Phoenix with a new boyfriend. She smiled and tasted blood. Rose kissed her cheek and touched the pulsating baby's head at her sister's breast. The spent body, empty of child, full of milk, in no way resembled her own, a long-stemmed flower. Her body seemed sad in a way unlike her own sad body. Is it men who separate women from one another or children? Both? *Remember our vacation together two years ago?* Rose tried. A recollection of shells, magazines, aloe vera and women talking about women.

The people on an archipelago off Australia believe the placenta to be related to the jellyfish, the large ones that resemble plastic-encased intestines. Women must bathe in lagoon water each day of their pregnancy to "bleed in" the salts that nurture the baby and insist on the simultaneous growth of the placenta. Upon the twin birth of child and afterbirth the midwives ceremoniously return the placenta to the rich broth of the sea. Seawater is sprinkled on the baby and he or she is given the name of a seaweed, in memory of its origin.

On their vacation Rose had spoken of her love for father and Hazel for mother, not directly but in defending actions or inactions. They were collecting starfish a storm had churned up from below a shelf. They put several into a plastic cup: rough, slimy, still alive. Moving like a person dying in water. Like actors do. The hands and face toward the air as if a mother could reach down. Their legs flail slowly until their feet act more as anchors, silly anchors. And the last breath is water.

The two dried the starfish on the porch railing until stiffened. *Father treats us three like a private audience. Mother does nothing but ignore him.* They continued to argue until one was near tears then turned to something like the starfish. Delicate in death. Resourceful in life: cut in pieces they grow new limbs. But what do they eat? Can they see? What a simple method of procreation, cutting off a limb.

Midwives in a number of polar societies believe the placenta to be the gut of the bear, nourishing the unborn as the real one later nourishes and clothes with its great hulk of fur and flesh. The mass of afterbirth is placed beside the child then his cord is cut and he is wrapped in a steamy aura of cloth and breath. The eyes squint and blink. When the infant is sufficiently pink the placenta is laid outside for a cub to retrieve its orphaned tissue, to ready itself for the vision of hand and blade.

I didn't see the afterbirth. I even remember not looking though I asked my husband later and he said it looked *like a heart.* But how would he know? Whose heart had he seen? I decided to ask other women to see if it matched my image of a jellyfish, collapsed onto the sand, a glassy disk with scarlet arrows shooting out flowerlike to sting any curious or careless creature. I admit I was afraid to look, as if a vital organ had been expelled by accident.

From an outdoor cafe Rose watched a couple of medics walk by in their green outfits and recalled the resident pulling off his for her to examine his *heart.* Licking his balls as if they were right and left ventricles.

pla.cen.ta \ plə -ǝent-ə\ n [NL, fr. L, flat cake, fr. Gk plakount-, plakous, fr. plak plax, flat surface—more at PLEASE] 1 a : the vascular organ in mammals except monotremes and marsupials that unites the fetus to the maternal uterus and mediates its metabolic exchanges through a more or less intimate association of uterine mucosal with chorionic and usu. allantoic tissues b : an analogous organ in another animal 2 : a sporangium-bearing surface; esp. : the part of the carpel bearing ovules

What did the afterbirth look like? Like something from a tidal pool—wet, slippery, translucent, intelligent? Like a blimp slightly deflated after one of its slow surreal journeys over Manhattan? a puddle of lotion accidentally squirt onto the linoleum? the beef eyeball dissected in Bio 101? a gourmet aspic with flecks of carrots and pineapples? a lightbulb? did it look like a liver? a planet? And did it look hungry?

Now at Christmas dinner their parents' attention centers around Hazel's daughter. The two sisters are orphaned except by the extended complement. Each visit Hazel mistakenly calls her sister by her daughter's name, Mia. After dinner Rose and her husband disappear into the blue snow. The two women don't speak till some months later.

Turn dough onto lightly floured surface and knead until smooth and elastic, about ten minutes. Shape dough into ball and place in greased large bowl, turning over so that top of dough is greased. Cover with towel; let rise in warm place (80 to 85 F.), away from draft, until doubled, about one hour.

They don't speak for months. Folding her daughter's laundry Hazel thinks of the year her sister shared the apartment and lived in this room. She had hung clothes, scarves and bags on an abandoned window gate leaning against the wall. A futon was also covered by antique clothes. At night Rose would push the debris aside, a wave pushing up sand, shells, sea glass, then curl up in the crook, a cat in laundry, a child in the backseat of a car.

Anne and her daughter Annie read a child's gardening book that contained a cross section of a lily with its stamen, pollen, pistil, egg cells. They brought in a wilted Day Lily from a glass vase in the bedroom and sat in the kitchen dissecting it. The mother scooped up some eggs with the tip of the knife, a row small as taste buds, and rubbed them on Annie's finger. Greenish white. Almost translucent. She couldn't understand why they couldn't grow. Even after going over the part about the pollen.

Examining an old album the daughter wished her mother had had a white wedding gown. Wished she'd manicure her nails. Curl her hair. Wear stilettos.

At last Rose called to tell Hazel she'd passed her orals. The conversation became a synopsis of the exam—rare, marine plantlife such as *Pilina earli*, references to historic explorations such as the Tektite team of 1970, the consequences of six million barrels of oil across the Persian Gulf's water and sky—and how she finessed an answer using her research on the dangers of ecotourism. She talked so much Hazel felt she was submerged without a watch. She wondered if the professors felt a lack of air. They catalog seagrass for hours logged underwater but cannot carry on a conversation. Hazel thinks, *Still it's pretty good for a kid from the plains.*

July 5, 1990
I can't seem to finish Wittig. The progression is so non-linear I cannot hold onto the narrative thread. Even so I am constantly drawn back

to it for structural and poetic inspiration, for its rich collection of female imagery and feminist vision. Curious that a man translated it.

They made a date to bake cupcakes for Mia's birthday party. While the father took her to the park Hazel and Rose laid out the ingredients. One beat eggs and folded in mix while the other greased the tins. While the cupcakes baked the sisters sat on the fire escape sunning their legs and sipping iced coffee. They talked about how Hazel's friends were now all women with children and how Rose still really didn't have women friends. An hour later they solemnly began to decorate the cupcakes with sprinkles, coconut, nuts and kisses. When Hazel laughed loudly at her sister's cunt-like arrangements Rose stuffed a cake in her mouth; Hazel returned the favor. They laughed until cake and tears ran down their white t-shirts.

After the second daughter was born a son was out of the question. Her husband became resigned and Hazel, relieved. At home Mia pointed out the people in a hospital photo: Mama, Dada, Mia—and doodoo. The parents laughed till they cried.

Rose watched two men walk by with babies in strollers, one African American, the other of partial Asian descent. The babies wore lemon-colored pajamas, their hair jutting up like little bantams. They spit pacifiers onto the sidewalk, clucked and flapped their arms and legs for some tit until momentarily distracted by a man waist-deep in a hole vibrating with his jack-hammer. The fathers stopped to watch, too. Yoko, her classmate, remarked: men love to watch men working.

As promised Eleanor brought the bantam back to the Church yard, releasing it to its mother. Would she welcome this stranger? try to peck its eyes out? would she mistake it for a prospective mate? would their eggs have double yolks?

There's a myth found in several places along the Eastern coast of South America and Western coast of Africa. Linguistic differences alter emphasis but the basic story is that the placenta is a cake placed in the womb by the goddess of harvest (be it rice, potato, wheat, etc.). If the mother's blood passes through to the child it's a girl, if not the vagina closes, the clitoris and lips lengthen, the nipples and brain shrink—the child becomes a boy. The story is transmitted matrilineally.

The little girl hopped around, a signal for her mother to take her to the peepee tree just outside the playground. She pulled off her panties, held up her dress, stood with legs apart and urinated with such force that the stream shot out like a boy's. Her mother pulled the panties back on before the little girl raced back to her friends and the mother to hers.

The Water-Faucet Vision

Gish Jen

To protect my sister Mona and me from the pains—or, as they pronounced it, the "pins"—of life, my parents did their fighting in Shanghai dialect, which we didn't understand; and when my father one day pitched a brass vase through the kitchen window, my mother told us he had done it by accident.

"By accident?" said Mona.

My mother chopped the foot off a mushroom.

"By accident?" said Mona. "By *accident*?"

Later I tried to explain to her that she shouldn't have persisted like that, but it was hopeless.

"What's the matter with throwing things," she shrugged. "He was *mad*."

That was the difference between Mona and me: Fighting was just fighting to her. If she worried about anything, it was only that she

GISH JEN is a "writing mom." Her first novel, *Typical American*, was nominated for the National Book Critics' Circle Award. The recipient of a recent Guggenheim fellowship, she is currently at work on a second novel.

might turn out too short to become a ballerina, in which case she was going to be a piano player.

I, on the other hand, was going to be a martyr. I was in fifth grade then, and the hyperimaginative sort—the kind of girl who grows morbid in Catholic school, who longs to be chopped or frozen to death but then has nightmares about it from which she wakes up screaming and clutching a stuffed bear. It was not a bear that I clutched, though, but a string of three malachite beads that I had found in the marsh by the old aqueduct one day. Apparently once part of a necklace, they were each wonderfully striated and swirled, and slightly humped toward the center, like a jellyfish; so that if I squeezed one, it would slip smoothly away, with a grace that altogether enthralled and—on those dream-harrowed nights—soothed me, soothed me as nothing had before or has since. Not that I've lacked occasion for soothing: Though it's been four months since my mother died, there are still nights when sleep stands away from me, stiff as a well-paid sentry. But that is another story. Back then I had my malachite beads, and if I worried them long and patiently enough, I was sure to start feeling better, more awake, even a little special—imagining, as I liked to, that my nightmares were communications from the Almighty Himself, preparation for my painful destiny. Discussing them with Patty Creamer, who had also promised her life to God, I called them "almost visions"; and Patty, her mouth wadded with the three or four sticks of doublemint she always seemed to have going at once, said, "I bet you'll be doin' miracleth by seventh grade."

Miracles. Today Patty laughs to think she ever spent good time stewing on such matters, her attention having long turned to rugs, and artwork, and antique Japanese bureaus—things she believes in.

"A good bureau's more than just a bureau," she explained last time we had lunch. "It's a hedge against life. I tell you, if there's one thing I believe, it's that cheap stuff's just money out the window. Nice stuff, on the other hand—now that you can always cash out, if life gets rough. *That* you can count on."

In fifth grade, though, she counted on different things.

"You'll be doing miracles too," I told her, but she shook her shaggy head and looked doleful.

"Na' me," she chomped. "Buzzit's okay. The kin' things I like, prayers work okay on."

"Like?"

"Like you 'member that dreth I liked?"

She meant the yellow one, with the criss-cross straps.

"Well gueth what."

"Your mom got it for you."

She smiled. "And I only jutht prayed for it for a week," she said.

As for myself, though, I definitely wanted to be able to perform a wonder or two. Miracle-working! It was the carrot of carrots: It kept me doing my homework, taking the sacraments; it kept me mournfully on key in music hour, while my classmates hiccuped and squealed their carefree hearts away. Yet I couldn't have said what I wanted such powers *for*, exactly. That is, I thought of them the way one might think of, say, an ornamental sword—as a kind of collectible, which also happened to be a means of defense.

But then Patty's father walked out on her mother, and for the first time, there was a miracle I wanted to do. I wanted it so much I could see it: Mr. Creamer made into a spitball; Mr. Creamer shot through a straw into the sky; Mr. Creamer unrolled and re-plumped, plop back on Patty's doorstep. I would've cleaned out his mind and given him a shave en route. I would've given him a box of peanut fudge, tied up with a ribbon, to present to Patty with a kiss.

But instead all I could do was try to tell her he'd come back.

"He will not, he will not!" she sobbed. "He went on a boat to Rio Deniro. To Rio Deniro!"

I tried to offer her a stick of gum, but she wouldn't take it.

"He said he would rather look at water than at my mom's fat face. He said he would rather look at water than at me." Now she was really wailing, and holding her ribs so tightly that she almost seemed to be hurting herself—so tightly that just looking at her arms wound around her like snakes made my heart feel squeezed.

I patted her on the arm. A one-winged pigeon waddled by.

"He said I wasn't even his kid, he said I came from Uncle Johnny. He said I was garbage, just like my mom and Uncle Johnny. He said

I wasn't even his kid, he said I wasn't his Patty, he said I came from Uncle Johnny!"

"From your Uncle Johnny?" I said stupidly.

"From Uncle Johnny," she cried. "From Uncle Johnny!"

"He said that?" I said. Then, wanting to go on, to say *something*. I said, "Oh Patty, don't cry."

She kept crying.

I tried again. "Oh Patty, don't cry," I said. Then I said, "Your dad was a jerk anyway."

The pigeon produced a large runny dropping.

It was a good twenty minutes before Patty was calm enough for me just to run to the girls' room to get her some toilet paper; and by the time I came back she was sobbing again, saying "To Rio Deniro, to Rio Deniro" over and over again, as though the words had stuck in her and couldn't be gotten out. As we had missed the regular bus home and the late bus too, I had to leave her a second time to go call my mother, who was only mad until she heard what had happened. Then she came and picked us up, and bought us each a fudgsicle.

Some days later, Patty and I started a program to work on getting her father home. It was a serious business. We said extra prayers, and lit votive candles; I tied my malachite beads to my uniform belt, fondling them as though they were a rosary, I a nun. We even took to walking about the school halls with our hands folded—a sight so ludicrous that our wheeze of a principal personally took us aside one day.

"I must tell you," she said, using her nose as a speaking tube, "that there is really no need for such peee-ity."

But we persisted, promising to marry God and praying to every saint we could think of. We gave up gum, then gum and slim jims both, then gum and slim jims and ice cream—and when even that didn't work, we started on more innovative things. The first was looking at flowers. We held our hands beside our eyes like blinders as we hurried by the violets by the flagpole, the window box full of tulips outside the nurse's office. Next it was looking at boys: Patty gave up angel-eyed Jamie Halloran and I, gymnastic Anthony Rossi. It was hard, but in the end our efforts paid off. Mr. Creamer came back a month later, and though he brought with him nothing but dysentery, he was at least too sick to have all that much to say.

Then, in the course of a fight with my father, my mother somehow fell out of their bedroom window.

Recently—thinking a mountain vacation might cheer me—I sublet my apartment to a handsome but somber newlywed couple, who turned out to be every bit as responsible as I'd hoped. They cleaned out even the eggshell chips I'd sprinkled around the base of my plants as fertilizer, leaving behind only a shiny silverplate cake server and a list of their hopes and goals for the summer. The list, tacked precariously to the back of the kitchen door, began with a fervent appeal to God to help them get their wedding thank-yous written in three weeks or less. (You could see they had originally written "two weeks" but scratched it out—no miracles being demanded here.) It went on:

> *Please help us, Almighty Father in Heaven Above, to get Ann a teaching job within a half-hour drive of here in a nice neighborhood.*
>
> *Please help us, Almighty Father in Heaven Above, to get John a job doing anything where he won't strain his back and that is within a half-hour drive of here.*
>
> *Please help us, Almighty Father in Heaven Above, to get us a car.*
>
> *Please help us, A.F. in H.A., to learn French.*
>
> *Please help us, A.F. in H.A., to find seven dinner recipes that cost less than 60 cents a serving and can be made in a half-hour. And that don't have tomatoes, since You in Your Heavenly Wisdom made John allergic.*
>
> *Please help us, A.F. in H.A., to avoid books in this apartment such as You in Your Heavenly Wisdom allowed John, for Your Heavenly Reasons, to find three nights ago (June 2nd).*

Et cetera. In the left hand margin they kept score of how they had fared with their requests, and it was heartening to see that nearly all of them were marked "Yes! Praise the Lord" (sometimes shortened to PTL), with the sole exception of learning French, which was mysteriously marked "No! PTL to the Highest."

That note touched me. Strange and familiar both, it seemed like it had been written by some cousin of mine—some cousin who had stayed home to grow up, say, while I went abroad and learned what I had to, though the learning was painful. This, of course, is just a manner of speaking; in fact I did my growing up at home, like anybody else.

But the learning *was* painful: I never knew exactly how it happened that my mother went hurdling through the air that night years ago, only that the wind had been chopping at the house, and that the argument had started about the state of the roof. Someone had been up to fix it the year before, but it wasn't a roofer, it was some man my father had insisted could do just as good a job for a quarter of the price. And maybe he could have, had he not somehow managed to step through a knot in the wood under the shingles and break his uninsured ankle. Now the shingles were coming loose again, and the attic insulation was mildewing besides, and my father was wanting to sell the house altogether, which he said my mother had wanted to buy so she could send pictures of it home to her family in China.

"The Americans have a saying," he said. "They saying, 'You have to keep up with Jones family.' I'm saying if Jones family in Shanghai, you can send any picture you want, *an-y* picture. Go take picture of those rich guys' house. You want to act like rich guys, right? Go take picture of those rich guys' house."

At that point my mother sent Mona and me to wash up, and started speaking Shanghaiese. They argued for some time in the kitchen, while we listened from the top of the stairs, our faces wedged between the bumpy Spanish scrolls of the wrought iron railing. First my mother ranted, then my father, then they both ranted at once until finally there was a thump, followed by a long quiet.

"Do you think they're kissing now?" said Mona. "I bet they're kissing, like this." She pursed her lips like a fish and was about to put them to the railing when we heard my mother locking the back door. We hightailed it into bed; my parents creaked up the stairs. Everything at that point seemed fine. Once in their bedroom, though, they started up again, first softly, then louder and louder, until my mother turned on a radio to try to disguise the noise. A door slammed; they began shouting at one another; another door slammed; a shoe or something banged the wall behind Mona's bed.

"How're we supposed to *sleep?*" said Mona, sitting up.

There was another thud, more yelling in Shanghaiese, and then my mother's voice pierced the wall, in English. "So what you want I should do? Go to work like Theresa Lee?"

My father rumbled something back.

"You think you're big shot because you have job, right? You're big shot, but you never get promotion, you never get raise. All I do is spend money, right? So what do you do, you tell me. So what do you do!"

Something hit the floor so hard that our room shook.

"So kill me," screamed my mother. "You know what you are? You are failure. Failure! You are failure!"

Then there was a sudden, terrific, bursting crash—and after it, as if on a bungled cue, the serene blare of an a cappella soprano, picking her way down a scale.

By the time Mona and I knew to look out the window, a neighbor's pet beagle was already on the scene, sniffing and barking at my mother's body, his tail crazy with excitement; then he was barking at my stunned and trembling father, at the shrieking ambulance, the police, at crying Mona in her bunny-footed pajamas, and at me, barefoot in the cold grass, squeezing her shoulder with one hand and clutching my malachite beads with the other.

My mother wasn't dead, only unconscious, the paramedics figured that out right away, but there was blood everywhere, and though they were reassuring about her head wounds as they strapped her to the stretcher, commenting also on how small she was, how delicate, how light, my father kept saying, "I killed her, I killed her" as the ambulance screeched and screeched headlong, forever, to the hospital. I was afraid to touch her, and glad of the metal rail between us, even though its sturdiness made her seem even frailer than she was; I wished she was bigger, somehow, and noticed, with a pang, that the new red slippers we had given her for Mother's Day had been lost somewhere along the way. How much she seemed to be leaving behind, as we careened along—still not there, still not there—Mona and Dad and the medic and I taking up the whole ambulance, all the room, so there was no room for anything else; no room even for my mother's real self, the one who should have been pinching the color back to my father's grey face, the one who should have been calming Mona's cowlick—the one who should have been bending over us, to help us to be strong, to help us get through, even as we bent over her.

Then suddenly we were there, the glowing square of the emergency room entrance opening like the gates of heaven; and immediately the talk of miracles began. Alive, a miracle. No bones broken, a miracle. A miracle that the hemlocks cushioned her fall, a miracle that they hadn't been trimmed in a year and a half. It was a miracle that all that blood, the blood that had seemed that night to be everywhere, was from one shard of glass, a single shard, can you imagine, and as for the gash in her head, the scar would be covered by hair. The next day my mother cheerfully described just how she would part it so that nothing would show at all.

"You're a lucky duck-duck," agreed Mona, helping herself, with a little *pirouette*, to the cherry atop my mother's chocolate pudding.

That wasn't enough for me, though. I was relieved, yes, but what I wanted by then was a real miracle, not for her simply to have survived but for the whole thing never to have happened—for my mother's head never to had to been shaved and bandaged like that, for her high, proud forehead to never have been swollen down over her eyes, for her face and neck and hands never to have been painted so many shades of blue-black, and violet, and chartreuse. I still want those things—for my parents not to have had to live with this affair like a prickle-bush between them, for my father to have been able to look my mother in her swollen eyes and curse the madman, the monster that could have dared done this to the woman he loved. I wanted to be able to touch my mother without shuddering, to be able to console my father, to be able to get that crash out of my head, the sound of that soprano—so many things that I didn't know how to pray for them, that I wouldn't have known where to start even if I had the power to work miracles, right there, right then.

A week later, when my mother was home, and her head beginning to bristle with new hairs, I lost my malachite beads. I had been carrying them in a white cloth pouch that Patty had given me, and was swinging the pouch on my pinky on my way home from school, when I swung just a bit too hard, and it went sailing in a long arc through the air, whooshing like a perfectly thrown basketball through one of the holes of a nearby sewer. There was no chance of fishing it out: I looked and looked, crouching on the sticky pavement until the asphalt had crazed the skin of my hands and knees, but all I could discern was an evil-smelling musk, glassy and smug and impenetrable.

My loss didn't quite hit me until I was home, but then it produced an agony all out of proportion to my string of pretty beads. I hadn't cried at all during my mother's accident, and now I was crying all afternoon, all through dinner, and then after dinner too, crying past the point where I knew what I was crying for, wishing dimly that I had my beads to hold, wishing dimly that I could pray but refusing, refusing, I didn't know why, until I finally fell into an exhausted sleep on the couch, where my parents left me for the night—glad, no doubt, that one of the more tedious of my childhood crises seemed to be finally winding off the reel of life, onto the reel of memory. They covered me, and somehow grew a pillow under my head, and, with uncharacteristic disregard for the living-room rug, left some milk and pecan sandies on the coffee table, in case I woke up hungry. Their thoughtfulness was prescient: I did wake up in the early part of the night; and it was then, amid the unfamiliar sounds and shadows of the living room, that I had what I was sure was a true vision.

Even now what I saw retains an odd clarity: the requisite strange light flooding the room, first orange, and then a bright yellow-green, then a crackling bright burst like a Roman candle going off near the piano. There was a distinct smell of coffee, and a long silence. The room seemed to be getting colder. Nothing. A creak; the light starting to wane, then waxing again, brilliant pink now. Still nothing. Then, as the pink started to go a little purple, a perfectly normal middle-aged man's voice, speaking something very like pig latin, told me quietly not to despair, not to despair, my beads would be returned to me.

That was all. I sat a moment in the dark, then turned on the light, gobbled down the cookies—and in a happy flash understood I was so good, really, so near to being a saint that my malachite beads would come back through the town water system. All I had to do was turn on all the faucets in the house, which I did, one by one, stealing quietly into the bathroom and kitchen and basement. The old spigot by the washing machine was too gunked up to be coaxed very far open, but that didn't matter. The water didn't have to be full blast, I understood that. Then I gathered together my pillow and blanket and trundled up to my bed to sleep.

By the time I woke up in the morning I knew that my beads hadn't shown up, but when I knew it for certain, I was still disappointed; and as if that weren't enough, I had to face my parents and sister, who were all abuzz with the mystery of the faucets. Not knowing what else to do, I, like a puddlebrain, told them the truth. The results were predictably painful.

"Callie had a *vision*," Mona told everyone at the bus stop. "A vision with lights, and sinks in it!"

Sinks, visions. I got it all day, from my parents, from my classmates, even some sixth and seventh graders. Someone drew a cartoon of me with a halo over my head in one of the girls' room stalls; Anthony Rossi made gurgling noises as he walked on his hands at recess. Only Patty tried not to laugh, though even she was something less than unalloyed understanding.

"I don't think miracles are thupposed to happen in *thewers*," she said.

Such was the end of my saintly ambitions. It wasn't the end of all holiness; the ideas of purity and goodness still tippled my brain, and over the years I came slowly to grasp of what grit true faith was made. Last night, though, when my father called to say that he couldn't go on living in our old house, that he was going to move to a smaller place, another place, maybe a condo—he didn't know how, or where—I found myself still wistful for the time religion seemed all I wanted it to be. Back then the world was a place that could be set right: One had only to direct the hand of the Almighty and say, just here, Lord, we hurt here—and here, and here, and here.

excerpt from *The Floating World*

Cynthia Kadohata

1.

My grandmother has always been my tormentor. My mother said she'd been a young woman of spirit; but she was an old woman of fire. In her day it had been considered scandalous for young Japanese women to smoke, but she smoked cigars. Once, when she got especially angry, she took a piece of damp cosmetic cotton and placed it on my ankle so I would hear the sizzle of cotton and think it was skin burning. Later *she* cried. Of the four of us kids, I thought she liked me least. My mother said she didn't dislike me but just expected more of me because I was the oldest.

My grandmother surprised my family by dying one night in a motel in California. Neither of my three brothers liked her any more than I did, and none of us cried at the funeral. My grandmother used to box our ears whenever she pleased, and liked to predict ghastly futures for all of us. We traveled a great deal, and sometimes in the car she talked

CYNTHIA KADOHATA is the author of two novels, *The Floating World* and *In the Heart of the Valley of Love*. She was born in Chicago and now lives in Los Angeles. Her stories have appeared in *The New Yorker*, *Grand Street*, and *The Pennsylvania Review*.

on and on, until even my mother became annoyed and told her to keep it *down*, just as if she were one of us kids. When she got mad she cursed me. "May you grow hair on your nose!" she would say, and I would run to check a mirror.

Her name was Hisae Fujiitano, a name sort of partway between mine and those of my ancestors. You can trace some of the changes in my family through the changes in our names. In 1875, for the first time, the parents of all my great-grandparents took family names: Yanagita, Osaka (my father's name), Nambu, Takeda, and four Satōs. Before the 1870s, most commoners in Japan were not allowed family names. When the names finally were allowed, sometimes everybody in a village was ordered to take the same one: thus the four Satōs. My mother's mother was born Satō Hisae in a village of Satōs. But though Hisae was her given name, my great-grandparents called her Shimeko, which isn't a real name. "Shimeru" means "to close." They called her Shimeko because she was their eighth child and they hoped that from then on my great-grandmother's womb would be closed.

When Hisae's family came to the United States, her father changed their name to go with their new life. The new name was Fujiitano. Fujii had been the richest man my great-grandfather had ever known, and Itano the happiest. Years later, in Hawaii at the start of World War II, the local school made my grandparents change their children's first names before they could enroll. Satoru, Yukiko, Mariko, Haruko, and Sadamu became Roger, Lily, Laura, Ann, and Roy. Today their original names are just shadows following them. My brothers and I all have American names: Benjamin Todd, Walker Roy, Peter Edward, and me, Olivia Ann.

Before my grandmother died, she told me everything about herself. Sometimes, sitting next to me, she might suddenly grab my hair and pull me over to tell me one more fact about herself: how she had never seen a book until she was twelve, or how she had never cut her long, long hair. She lived with us after her third husband died. But my brothers and I were way ahead of her. Right before she moved in, we gave her a neck chain with a bell attached so we would always hear her approaching and could hide before she reached us. We bought her the bell one Christmas, and she always wore it.

My grandmother liked to tell us about herself during evenings while we all sat talking in front of the motels or houses we stayed at. We were traveling then in what she called ukiyo, the floating world. The floating world was the gas station attendants, restaurants, and jobs we depended on, the motel towns floating in the middle of fields and mountains. In old Japan, ukiyo meant the districts full of brothels, teahouses, and public baths, but it also referred to change and the pleasures and loneliness change brings. For a long time, I never exactly thought of us as part of any of that, though. We were stable, traveling through an unstable world while my father looked for jobs.

It seemed as if we were always the only family at the motels we stayed at, and the proprietors often gave my brothers and me candy, matches, or gum. We saved most of what we got, and sometimes as my grandmother told stories we would make trades with each other: matches for gum, candy for matches. I had a special piece of chocolate that I'd had for three years and would never trade. Sometimes I licked it, for luck.

My grandmother owned a valise in which she carried all her possessions, but the stories she told were also possessions. The stories were fantastic, yet I believed them. She said that when she was young fireflies had invaded her town, so the whole town was lighted even during the nighttime. She said she had been told that the summer she was born, strange clouds passed through the sky. Every night for seven nights, a different cloud. The clouds all had a strange glow, as if someone had taken the moon and stretched it into a cloud shape. Those seven moon-clouds, she said, had been a lucky omen. As she spoke, she always gestured a great deal, so the background to her stories would be the soft tinkling of the bell we had bought her.

She did most of the talking, but once in a while one of my parents spoke up to amplify or to make their own, new contributions. Other times, my parents might gently indicate that she should stop talking because it was our bedtime, or because they did not approve of the subject. No matter—if she wanted to tell me something she would seek me out later. She would run after me, shouting her facts: I had a white dog! I broke my leg three times! My first husband and I had sex in a public bathroom!

Sometimes my father did seasonal farming work and my mother helped out, but mostly he found work as a body-and-fender man or a carpenter. We sometimes traveled in the Pacific states with one or two other young Japanese families, heading for jobs the fathers had heard of. We moved often for three reasons. One was bad luck—the businesses my father worked for happened to go under, or the next job we headed to evaporated while we were in transit. Also, it could be hard even into the fifties and sixties for Japanese to get good jobs. Nothing was ever quite the position my father felt he deserved. The third reason was that my parents were dissatisfied with their marriage, and, somehow, moving seemed to give vent to that dissatisfaction. It was always hard to leave our homes, but once we started traveling, a part of me loved that life. All the packing and moving was especially hard on my parents, but I think even they enjoyed some of the long drives—at least, they did when my grandmother was quiet. I remember how fine it was to drive through the passage of light from morning to noon to night.

What I learned, traveling in Oregon, Wyoming, California, and Washington, was that my first grandfather had drowned off the coast of Honolulu. My third, I knew, had died of old age. My grandmother said she was still married when she met her third husband. She had been trying to fix him up with a woman from Japan, but he decided he wanted to marry her instead. He begged her to leave her second husband, and she couldn't resist his begging.

"You couldn't resist because you loved him so much?" I said. "You couldn't resist because he was so handsome?"

"I couldn't resist because his begging was like buzzing in my ears," she said. "I had to make it stop." She hit one of her ears as if to stop some buzzing.

Actually, it was my mother, one evening when we were in northern California, who told me her father had drowned. We were staying at a place someone had lent us while my father had a temporary job helping a friend build a farmhouse. When he finished with this job, we would be on our way to Arkansas, where my father was going to buy into a garage another friend of his owned. "It'll be the first time I've ever owned anything big," he said. "A car don't count."

I was sitting on the porch with my mother and brothers. My father had already gone inside to take a shower and go to bed, and my grandmother was napping.

"Olivia, go get Obāsan," said my mother. "It's pretty out here. She should see." Two Japanese words for "grandmother" are "obāsan" and "obāchan." You call your grandmother Obāsan if you're not close to her, Obāchan if you are. I think my mother would have liked for us to call our grandmother Obāchan, but we never did. We called her Obāsan. My father wanted us to call her Grandma—more American.

Ben and Walker looked at me. We took daily turns dealing with Obāsan. Ben was eight, four years younger than I; Walker was seven; and Peter, two. Ben was the opposite of Walker, outgoing and talkative where Walker was quiet and brooding. I was sort of outgoing and quiet both, depending.

"I think it's Ben's turn," I said.

His jaw dropped in outrage. "No. Remember, I gave you gum and you said you would take my turn."

He was right—I had the gum in my mouth. I tried to swallow it and almost choked. So I went inside. The house was one room. The light was very low, barely good enough to read in, and the room was smoky from my grandmother's cigars.

"What do you want?" said Obāsan.

She took an ominous step toward me with her cigar and I got scared and ran. When I got outside and saw my mother, I remembered she'd wanted me to get my grandmother. So I turned around and shouted as loudly as I could, "Mom wants you!" When I saw her at the door I turned to my mother, who was standing right next to me. "She's coming," I said.

"Goodness," said my mother.

My grandmother sat outside with us, and after a while, when I'd decided she was in a good mood, I asked her whether she'd cried for weeks after her first and third husbands died.

"Does a slave cry when the master dies?"

"It depends," I said. "Did you love any of your husbands?"

She paused, and I could see that she had loved one of them. But she didn't say so. She said, "I loved all of them in a way, and none of them in a way."

"So why get married?"

"Because they asked." I knew that Japanese women were nothing without husbands, and she probably had not wanted to be nothing.

"I remember the day my father drowned," said my mother. We always got extra quiet when my mother spoke. This was the first I'd heard of any drowning. My mother rarely initiated small talk, and usually when she spoke she had something she especially wanted to say. She had an elegant, lush face, and always had about her a slight air of being disoriented, as if she could not quite remember how she came to be wherever she was. I think sometimes people interpreted that disoriented air as aloofness. "When I found out what had happened to him, I went outside and wandered around for hours, and I found a wooden rose in a field. It had the look, texture, and strength of a piece of carved wood, but it was a real flower. It was alive. I've never found a reference to a wooden rose in books on flowers, but I'm sure it existed. I remember thinking it was impossible, just like my father's death was impossible. For a few hours, I was in another realm, and impossible things happened."

The house my father had been working on sat way in the distance. The family would be moving there the following week. Fireflies hovered around the house, but they weren't the fireflies of my grandmother's childhood invasion. They blinked like Christmas lights. They made the house seem enchanted. I thought how lucky some children would be to live in a place like that.

My grandmother pushed my head down suddenly so that the side of my face was pressed against the concrete porch. "Be careful you never marry anyone who's going to die young," she said.

I tried to say okay, but my mouth was being squished by her hand, so I said, "Uh-keh."

She let me go and wiped her nose with the back of her hand. I sat up and saw my big wad of gum sitting on the porch. I dusted it off, plunked it into my mouth, and blew a big bubble to show my grandmother she didn't bother me. In truth, I was shaking inside. But anyway I thought I had found out something I'd wanted to know—it was her first husband she'd loved. I liked finding out things about her. I just wished it weren't such hard work.

•

IN THE MORNINGS, Obāsan always took my brothers and me for walks, but in the evenings she liked to go for drives. I always went with her, because my mother made me, "just in case something happens," she said. My brothers were too young to go, and my mother and father were always too tired. When I wanted to go somewhere at night, my parents asked my grandmother to accompany me—just in case. So my life intertwined with my grandmother's.

That night, we went for one of her drives in my father's gray, whale-shaped car. She was so tiny she had to sit on two pillows, way forward on the seat. One good thing about her drives was that I was always seeing something surprising—a pet camel in someone's backyard, or a set of elderly men triplets, dressed the same way down to their canes. I liked downtowns the best, the way the neon and shadows cut into each other when the streets were empty. Whenever we waited at a stop sign or traffic light, my grandmother clicked her arthritic knee— it sounded as if she were clicking her toenails against something. I had no idea what Obāsan saw that she liked, or what she got out of those drives. Sometimes she tricked me into not hating her. She gave me change to buy candy, or she let me drive for a couple of minutes. But pretty soon she would be the same again—cruel, name-calling, quick-tempered.

After we'd driven in circles for a while, she said she needed to use the bathroom, and she left me to sit in the car while she walked off into the darkness. We were not far from where we were staying, and I spotted a man who owned a nearby farm walking toward the car. I hadn't met him, but my mother had pointed him out before. He was easy to recognize, tall, with only one eyebrow, big and black like an extra eye. He was drinking from a paper cup, and I went out to call him—maybe he would let me have a sip of whatever he was drinking.

I liked to talk to strangers. My parents were proud of the way I talked. "If you couldn't see her, you wouldn't even know she was Japanese," they would say. When I spoke with outsiders I was showing off, but they never understood this. I was trying to impress them, to make them like me. But at the same time I was always taunting them. See, I can talk like you, I was trying to say, it's not so hard. My grandmother didn't like that I wanted to impress them, but she liked the taunting part. "Smile at them," she would say. "Hakujin don't know when a smile is an insult." Hakujin were white people. She always said her experience showed that if you hated white people, they would just hate you back, and nothing would change in the world; and if you didn't hate them after the way they treated you, you would end up hating yourself, and nothing would change that way, either. So it was no good to hate them, and it was no good not to hate them. So nothing changed.

"Hi," I said to the man who owned the farm. He didn't answer, so I went on. "What are you drinking?"

"Coffee."

"Oh." He sat down on the hood of the car and crossed his legs. I climbed on the hood and sat next to him.

He swept his hand toward the landscape. "Where do you locate your expertise in this world?" he said.

"Excuse me?" There was something strange about him, besides the way he talked, but I couldn't put my finger on what it was. I peeked into his cup to see how much was left: not much.

He told me he used to teach at a university, and his question simply meant "Who are you?" I didn't think they would let someone who talked the way he did teach at a university, but of course that was before I ever went to college.

"How come you stopped teaching?"

"Because I killed someone."

I thought he meant in a car accident or something, and I started to say "I'm sorry," but I stopped myself. Another car drove by, illuminating his face, and I saw what was so strange about him. He wasn't who I thought he was, not the farmer at all. I saw angles on his face where I thought there had been slopes, and he had a flesh-colored bandage, partly hidden by hair, over one of his eyebrows.

"You have two eyebrows!" I said. "You're no farmer."

He paused, I see now because he didn't know what I was talking about. But I thought I had stunned him with truth.

I stood straight; then he did, too. The way he moved, so relaxed, it seemed he moved slowly, but really the movement had been swift. I climbed casually back on the car, and he sat down again, too.

"I have to get going in a sec," I said, faking a yawn. I thought things over. I wasn't scared exactly. I figured maybe Obāsan had somehow arranged all this to scare me. Then I remembered what my mother had said about the wooden rose, and I felt as if maybe I was in that other realm now, and I could get hurt. I stood up, and the man did, too. He really was big—and he seemed to have grown in the last few minutes. Whereas before I thought I'd reached his chest, I now reached his waist. All of a sudden he tilted his head, listening. Then I heard it, too, the tinkling of a bell, getting closer behind us.

We both turned to look, and my grandmother walked up and stopped a few feet from the other side of the car. Maybe my demeanor told her something, because she seemed to sense my fear. She smiled her widest smile at the man. She didn't smile often, and if you saw her you would know why. Her smile made her look as if she had a stomachache. Though we were staring straight at her, she announced shrilly, "I'm back." She and the man looked at each other for a long minute, and then she leaned over, still smiling, and picked up a stick from the ground. She came forward, waving the stick and repeating shrilly, "I'm back. I'm back. I'm back."

The man left then. He walked the way he'd stood up before, an illusory slow motion, but really he moved very quickly. I watched him get smaller and smaller as he walked away.

"That man was going to kill me."

"I should have let him."

We got in the car. I thought the only reason she'd scared the man away was so my mother wouldn't get angry with her if something happened to me. I was sick of her meanness, her insults, her hatred. I decided not to speak to her again for as long as I could, maybe a week, or even two. And if she wanted to go for a ride I would refuse to go.

She drove as usual, with lots of stops and jerks. She didn't speak, either. Once, maybe when she thought I wasn't looking, she glanced at her hand, and I saw several deep indentations and a thin cut on her palm. She gave me a sharp look. "Mind your own business, nosy girl," she said. It took me a moment to realize what had happened—she'd been squeezing the stick so hard it cut into her hand. I bet she would have killed that man had he tried to hurt me.

•

LATER, IN BED, I was the last one up, as usual. Ben and Walker, covered by sheets, were white humps on the floor, and Peter slept in a crib we'd borrowed. My parents, lying unusually close together, looked like one larger person. My grandmother was on her side, her sheet hanging off the bed, one of her breasts hanging out of her night-gown. Her breast was smooth and white, in contrast to her ravaged, red face. I pressed my fingers over my nipples and ran the fingers up my chest and neck and face—the same smooth skin all over. It was hard for me to picture how a baby girl whose birth had been marked by seven moons floating across the summer sky had come to be in this house, and had come to be the person she was—unhappy, cruel, the nemesis of her grandchildren. I tried to imagine this happening. But there were windows all over, and the wind passed over me, back and forth, back and forth, until it seemed, at the time, that I had more important things to imagine.

2.

Sometimes as I lay awake in bed I made up fantasies. I imagined something awful, like my parents getting killed, or that I was a grown up and a man I loved died. At the end of my fantasy my stomach would hurt or I would cry. The point of these fantasies was to make my stomach hurt. When I was little my parents had to take me to the doctor because I got ulcers.

Other times, I thought about things that had already happened, moments or days or years ago. A gargoyle on the front door of this house reminded me of a house with a gargoyle I lived in a couple of years earlier.

MY PARENTS WERE BROKE and having marriage problems, and two of my brothers and I went to stay with a foster parent in Nebraska. His name was Isamu, and my father knew him from a farm they'd both worked on in California. He was a little crazy, in my opinion, but my father trusted him.

Peter, who'd just been born, went to stay with one of my mother's sisters. Ben, Walker, and I couldn't stay with any of my mother's four brothers and sisters, because they already had twenty-seven children among them. And my parents didn't want us to stay with Obāsan, supposedly because her third husband had just died. I think the real reason was that my grandmother, seventy-three, was consumed with an affair, and my parents thought this might be a bad influence on us. I was all for her having an affair, because if she did she might get married again. If she didn't get married, I feared she would come to live with us eventually. That's what happened—her boyfriend passed away later that year.

Ben, Walker, and I were well behaved in our way, and Isamu hardly ever lost his temper. The only time he got truly mad was at the end of our first week, when he decided we should no longer take baths together.

My brothers and I used to take bubble baths with Tide detergent. We could make bubble forts three feet high. The night we got in trouble, Ben had just climbed into the water—Walker and I were already in the tub—when I noticed that some veins or something on Ben's bottom seemed to spell the word "hello."

"Holy smokes, it's a miracle," I said. "Lean over."

Walker and I were marveling over him when Isamu came in and got really quite alarmed. He hauled us out of the tub and chased us naked from the bathroom. "What are you up to? Are you mad?" he said.

"It's a miracle!" Ben cried as we slipped through the halls. We didn't get to rinse off all night. Later I passed the boys' room and saw Ben, his pants pulled down, trying to view himself in a hand-held mirror. He kept turning slightly to get a better view, but it was a hopeless task. Since I was the oldest, I was the only one who got punished. I had to write "I will be clean and decent" five thousand times. It took me more than a week, and toward the end I used Band-Aids to keep my fingers from blistering.

Isamu's house was eccentric but homey. I liked the kitchen tapestry with the state motto, "Equality Before the Law," but didn't like the stuffed squirrel beneath it. Besides his gargoyle, he owned a couple of other items with faces. A flower vase was shaped like a bunch of broccoli, with eyes near the handles, and two purple glass turtles grinned wildly from a living room bureau.

Isamu had a daughter he was besotted with. Once, she was supposed to come visit by train. We drove thirty miles to the station, but the train was ten hours late. My brothers took naps, but I stayed up, thinking and daydreaming. I dreamed my parents were never coming back. My stomach started to hurt so much I had to stop thinking. Isamu talked about his daughter, what a princess she was, how generous and smart. The wind outside the car knocked over the surrounding weeds, first one way, then the other. The train came, and his daughter wasn't on it. When we got home and called, she explained she'd decided to come another time and had completely forgotten to phone.

We all went outside to sit in back. Isamu turned to us, his eyes ugly and cruel. We froze. He said his daughter was a slut. I didn't know what that meant, but I knew it was awful. Walker's feet had been making scraping sounds in some dry leaves, but the sound stopped abruptly. My brothers and I held hands. I wondered what my parents were doing at that moment, and then I started to worry about Peter, as well. Sometimes my mother let me give him his bath. He had extremely sensitive ears, and if you got even a little water in them he would be in pain for hours. I worried all night, even in bed, that my aunt might not be washing his ears carefully enough.

OBĀSAN WAS MUMBLING IN HER SLEEP, but in Japanese, a curse I couldn't quite understand. I figured she must have been dreaming about me.

NEITHER MY PARENTS nor Ben and Walker like to talk much about those days, and one of the few concrete reminders I have of my time in Nebraska is a photograph of my brothers that Isamu took when we first moved in. In the picture they're standing on a crate you can't see, their black tops barely lifted above the surrounding mass of yellow. I'm in the picture, too; if you look closely you can see my hand reaching up between two wheat stalks. Ben used to tease that it was his favorite picture of me.

Once we got used to the place, I started to like my days at Isamu's. They were a brief peaceful pause before Obāsan moved in with my family.

Isamu didn't have many friends. There were no other Japanese in town, and I guess he didn't feel he had much in common with most of the people around. To keep himself busy, he kept a constantly long list of chores for himself. Once, he spent all afternoon choosing an address book. He liked my penmanship and wanted me to write in the names. First he had to decide whom to write down. "Let's see . . . my daughter, my nephew, and my nephew's daughter," he said. "She has her own phone. I think they spoil her."

"What about your gin rummy friends?" He played once a week.

"I don't call them that much. I never write them."

"Didn't you say you had a cousin in Omaha?"

"Oh, right, my cousin. Now how many is that?"

"Four."

He thought awhile. "Okay, write down my gin rummy friends." So he had seven people in his phone book.

The next day his chore was planting a tree. There were about forty trees in the backyard, planted individually on succeeding anniversaries of the day he married his late wife. He still kept this up, though Meg had been gone for eleven years. "Habit," he said. "Anyway, I need the exercise." I watched him dragging the sapling. Stopping, sweating, stopping, sweating. I feared he might faint.

Several months later, our parents came for us on a freezing winter afternoon. They looked slightly different, in that indefinable way people you haven't seen for a while look slightly different. After a few minutes I started to feel shy with them. When we'd first spotted their car coming, we'd been in the front yard, building in the snow with Isamu. Ben saw the car first, and went tearing down the road, screaming and yelling. Then we stopped making noise so we could concentrate better on running our fastest. We were almost to the car when I stopped suddenly. My brothers passed me. I turned around. Isamu looked forlorn, standing alone in all that snow. "Don't leave!" he said. No one else seemed to hear him, or maybe I just imagined it. Then my mother was twirling me through the air, and I thought I would swoon.

After supper my family drove off. We were going to California to pick up Peter. I liked to stick my head out the window, and my mother always gave me permission to open the window for five minutes, no matter how cold it was. I felt the frigid air hit my face. It was dark out. When the plains were white that way, I always had difficulty making out where the earth ended; it was as if the ground simply curled upward. When it was still dark out each morning on the way to our school bus, I used to look at the lighted farmhouses and imagine how cities must be, with lighted houses piled on lighted houses. That's the way I imagined apartments, farmhouse on farmhouse into the sky. In the night I could picture it without even closing my eyes.

I looked at the farmhouses on the ceiling of the house we were staying at. My grandmother's snoring filled the room. She sounded like an elephant with a breathing problem, but we were used to it.

3.

Sometimes Obāsan slept for hours and hours, until we thought she was sick, while other times she required no sleep at all. Though she and I had returned late the night before, she woke my brothers and me at six, as usual, for our morning hike. We always had to go with her, unless we weren't feeling well. But I didn't mind. Some days, the people we met on those mornings would be the only people I talked to besides my family and whatever family we were traveling with. Those walks were some of my favorite times growing up.

It was still dark gray out. She wanted to take a long walk. My father's job wouldn't be finished until evening, and we had nothing to do all day. We put Peter into a stroller and headed off through a sloping field and some orchards. Peter was used to bumping along. He could sleep through anything. A fine mist broke up our view, as if each drop of mist were a dot of paint. The mist sprayed coolly on our cheeks as we walked through the field, and the long misted grass brushed our ankles. I could feel the blood flowing to my face as I tried to keep up with Obāsan, who always walked briskly.

We saw some kids outside a farm. They'd probably be going to school later. "What's today?" said Walker.

"Wednesday."

"Wednesday." He didn't say anything else. Walker hardly ever talked, except to repeat something just said. Sometimes we called him Echo.

Obāsan had a cigar and stopped to blow smoke rings into the air. The sky, white-gray, showed through the rings.

"Will you smoke when you get older?" Ben asked me.

"I'll never smoke. I want to be the opposite of Obāsan. Anything she does, I never will."

"She eats," said Ben. "And you have to eat." He crossed his eyes at me.

I chased him through the grass, but he stopped abruptly and knelt, and I fell over him. I rolled, just for fun, through the damp field. When I got dizzily to my feet, my grandmother and brothers were watching me. With them stood an old man. That is, his face didn't appear old, but he had wispy white hair that stood on end, seeming to move and fly of its own accord, like something alive. He'd appeared out of nowhere—all around us were fields. I sort of salivated inside whenever I met someone new. I was nosy, and I thought new people might tell me interesting things.

Obāsan didn't speak. There was something imperial about the way she held herself, the way she ignored the man. She appeared to be looking through him, at the sky and the fields. I could see she wasn't going to speak, so I told the man I hoped we weren't trespassing.

He chewed on something and glanced over the beautiful misted fields. The fields were full of varied greens. They were his fields, I felt sure. "Maybe you're trespassing," he said. I felt a brief fear, probably just left over from the night before.

"Sorry."

He chewed some more. The wind blew at his hair. I thought the wispy strands might fly away. "But maybe you're not," he said.

Obāsan continued to gaze through him. "We'll go now," I said. We turned and began to leave. I noticed Obāsan's cigar was gone. I noticed something burning a hole in her pocket. Obāsan, so brave last night, was scared of this man. She was scared of what he might think of her cigar.

"Hey," the man called, and we turned around. "I'll sell you some apples cheap."

Everyone looked at me expectantly. "What kind of apples?"

"What kind do you want?"

"Well, are they good?"

"The best."

The hole in my grandmother's pocket had stopped smoking.

We went with the man to buy some apples. Men had come out to work some of the fields. The men touched their hats when they said "Good morning" to me and my grandmother, and I felt very grown up.

"Where are you all from?" said the man.

"Here and there." My grandmother had told me once never to tell people where I came from or what my name was.

He nodded at her. "She speak English?"

I considered this question. Maybe she didn't want me to tell. "I'm not sure," I said, stupidly.

Behind a barn sat several bushels, a couple of them filled with large golden delicious apples, sunbursts of pale rose and green on the rich yellow skins. We pooled our money—Obāsan had most—and bought two dozen apples. My grandmother owned a magic purse that never emptied, though she didn't work and had never made much money. She always had a couple of dollars.

"You know how to pick good apples?" said the man.

"Color?" said Ben.

"Nope."

"Smell?"

"Nope." He paused before saying with mock impatience, "Do you want me to tell you or not?" He paused again, throwing an apple into the air. Finally he said triumphantly: "Sound." He squeezed and rubbed the apple between his large hands until it squeaked. "Good one," he said. "It sings. Never buy an apple unless it sings." He added hurriedly, "Of course the ones you just bought are all good." He rubbed and rubbed, making three distinct notes, enough for "Mary Had a Little Lamb" and another song I didn't recognize, and he moved his head in time with the music, his hair following the movement of his head. We also tried to play the apples, but ours sounded like tiny sick cows.

We headed back without the man. I felt very happy, almost elated, for no real reason, just for the way the morning had started. The workers in the fields stopped again to touch their hats.

"Hey!"

We turned around, saw the man standing in the distant mist.

"Someday you teach your kids that apple trick!" he called. He tapped at the space above his head as if he wore a hat, and then walked off with his dancing hair, and with his singing apple still in hand.

He'd given us no bags, so we had trouble carrying the apples. Obā-san walked way ahead with Peter. We kept dropping the apples, but soon we were having so much fun chasing after the falling fruit that we began to drop it deliberately. As I chased a stray apple, I saw Obā-san stop walking, and I thought she wanted to scold us. But she was staring out over the fields, the way you might stare at someone who is leaving you. She had worked on a celery farm a few seasons, and I wondered whether she was remembering that. Today when I think back on how she looked, I believe she knew then she would die soon. I bit into an apple, and she turned to glare at me. My brothers had run way ahead with the stroller. "Give me that apple." She walked toward me. "Don't eat that."

"How come?"

"It's dirty."

Every time she took a step toward me I took a step back. Sometimes I ran from her, but I never ran hard. I didn't want her to catch and hit me, but I didn't want to lose her, either. It was our responsibility to keep an eye on each other. I continued eating my apple but rolled up the rest of the fruit in my skirt and hurried home, making sure never to lose sight of Obāsan. By the time we got to the house, her face was all evil and anger. I felt scared now, so I ran inside, chained the door, and sat on the bed to finish the apple. I jumped when the door jerked partway open, stopped by the chain. One of Obāsan's eyes peered in. If I squinted, she looked like a Cyclops. I chomped into a new apple, still staring at her. She reached her hand in, jiggling the chain while my heart pounded, but she couldn't open the door. She cajoled, she bribed, she threw kisses. She jangled her purse, suddenly full of coins. "Livvie, my sweet, I have to use the bathroom," she said. But I knew she was lying. I could have closed the door or hidden from sight, and my body jerked with the impulse to get up. Instead I bit into my third apple and felt mesmerized by my grandmother's face.

"I can't open it," I said. "You'll hit me."

She stood there, her arthritic knee clicking. Finally she left, and I didn't hear any clicking or tinkling or muttering. I sneaked to the door and slowly opened it. She was sitting on a little bench on the porch. She had a peaceable look on her face. I went to put the remaining apples next to her and sat on a stair. The mist had risen, covering the sky with gray lace. Something pounded across my ear, knocking me over. "Why did you give that man my money?" Obāsan said.

WHEN MY FATHER FINISHED WORK that evening, we started driving immediately. We were going to visit with relatives in Los Angeles, then head to Arkansas. The Shibatas, a family we'd met that week, were traveling with us to L.A. We stopped for the night at a small motel. That was a long time ago—the motel cost two dollars a night. It had a lighted pink vacancy sign, and another sign reading Cal-Inn. The view was lovely: almond groves made jagged black lines on the horizon, and I thought I smelled almonds in the air. After supper, everyone sat on the curb outside the motel. There were only two cars besides ours and the Shibatas' in the parking lot. My brothers and I and the Shibata children played strings, cards, and jan ken po—the Japanese version of paper-scissors-rock. Then we sat briefly bored, scraping and rapping our bare feet restlessly on the parking lot concrete.

Susie Shibata and I got up to sing for everyone. We did a little dance. I sang more on key, yet her voice held more sweetness, so I sat back and listened. I was singing softly along when Obāsan pushed me from my place at the curb—she'd been sitting behind me, I suppose. Ordinarily I wouldn't have felt indignant, because it had always been a rule that we either must offer our elders our seats or expect to be forcibly removed. But Obāsan had pushed me especially hard this time. And she'd been mean to me while we were cooped up in the car all day. Several times she'd boxed the side of my head and told me to quiet down.

"You made me scrape my knee," I said. I held up my knee, my foot dangling in the air. "See the blood? You're in my seat, and please move now."

"What did you say?" she said. She rubbed her fingers together. I could just hear the dry skin scraping.

She reached out and grabbed my wrist, but I tried to pull it away and run. She held fast, though. I wouldn't have thought she was so strong, but I couldn't get away. We called her Pincher Obāsan behind her back. One of her methods of punishment was to smile as if she loved you with her full heart, all the while squeezing you inside the wrist. You were supposed to smile back as best you could. We had a funny picture of Ben getting pinched. With that smile, he looked like a lunatic. Now I opened my lips, pressed my teeth hard together, and tried to keep my eyes opened wide. Obāsan smiled easily back at me as she pinched. The lighting made her gums look brown, and I knew her top teeth were dentures. I was determined to outsmile her. Once, when she'd got mad at Ben and pinched him for something like fifteen minutes, he outsmiled her, and finally she broke down, patted his head, and gave him a nickel. I would make her give me a nickel, too. But she didn't stop, and after a while I felt my pulse between her fingers. I thought a vein would burst, or my skin might fall off in her hands.

"You've got the record!" encouraged Ben. Meaning it had been more than fifteen minutes.

Obāsan seemed to pinch more tightly. "All right!" I said. She let go, and I went off to sit by myself. My mother came over and ran her hand across my head. When I felt I could talk without crying, I said, "Mom, I was just sitting there. She pushed me. You saw."

"She's old," said my mother. "But I'll tell her not to be so hard on you. Okay?"

"She's evil," I said. "When she smiles I see she's a devil." I sucked on my wrist.

My mother laughed. "Oh, you never even knew her during her pinching prime. I could tell you stories."

"Obāsan pinching stories!" I said. "That's the last thing I want to hear."

My father rose to go in, as did Mr. Shibata. "Seven o'clock?" said my dad. Mr. Shibata nodded. Seven was when we would start out the next day. Before he went in, my father knelt beside me and my mother. "How'd you like to sit in front with us tomorrow?"

"Okay."

"You can have the window if you want or the middle if you want," said my mother.

"Thank you," I said. But I wasn't appeased.

My father went in. My mother followed with Peter, and I followed her. I didn't want to sit outside with Obāsan.

My mother sat on the bed and leafed through a book about presidents' wives. She admired presidents' wives and liked to know what they ate and wore, liked to know the odd fact that made them human. For instance, she liked knowing that Andrew Jackson's wife married him mistakenly, thinking she'd obtained a divorce from her first husband, or knowing that Mrs. Polk, who was very religious, prohibited liquor and dancing in the White House—"No wonder the Polks had no children," she would say. She'd probably inherited her interest in first ladies from Obāsan, who used to revere the Japanese emperor and his wife. "The emperor was a moron," Obāsan once said, "but he was still the emperor."

My grandmother came inside; I went out.

It was always a relief when she went in for the evening, but it felt especially wonderful that night. My brothers and I played tag back of the motel, and later we peeked into the rooms of strangers, but saw nothing. When we'd finished playing, only Mrs. Shibata and Susie still sat on the curb.

Though Obāsan always went inside early, she usually came to the door when a car approached the motel office. "Get in. What will people think, with Japanese hanging around like hoodlums at night?" We would all go in, watch until the car had left, then wander out, continuing this wandering in and out until time for bed. But tonight a car drove up and I waited expectantly for Obāsan's voice. When it didn't come I figured she'd gone to sleep, and I turned around, idly, to glance through the open door. I was really quite shocked to see my grandmother, looking cadaverous in the neon, standing in the doorway silently watching the car. She came out and sat with us briefly, an event unprecedented at that hour. She talked of her life. "My memories are a string of pearls and rocks," she said. I thought that was a line she'd memorized to say to us, but then she stretched her bony hands through the air, so for a moment I seemed to see the glitter of the string extended over the concrete lot. But the next moment she turned to me in one of her furies. "*I* don't know," she cried. But I didn't know what she was talking about. It was like the night Isamu got upset because his daughter had failed him. With all the older people I knew, even my parents, I occasionally saw that fierce expression as they exclaimed over something that had happened years ago, losses in a time and place as far removed from my twelve-year-old mind as the dates in a schoolbook.

Later I lay on the floor under the sheets. My wrist still hurt. I couldn't sleep. I watched as my grandmother walked to the bathroom. Obāsan was in there for a long time, and after a while I started to hear noises like coughing. I got up and knocked on the bathroom door, but Obāsan didn't answer.

The door was unlocked, though. Obāsan lay in her housedress on a towel she must have placed on the floor. Though I know now it was just my imagination, at the time I thought she seemed to have been expecting me. She was already not of this world, and she spoke with a fury unnatural even for her. "You! Get your mother," she said. It was a hiss, a rasp, and a cracked whisper all at once. I felt cold, as if there were ghosts in the room. But it was my own body, making me cold in the warm night. I reached back to close the door and turned to watch her again.

"Get your mother," Obāsan said. Still with fury but, now, something else, too. The hint of a "please" in her voice.

I saw in the mirror that I was crying and shaking. I had hated my grandmother for so long.

"Get your mother." This time Obāsan sounded desperate, pleading.

She said it two more times, once with draining hope and the last time peacefully. "Get your mother," she said, with calm, peaceful resignation. She closed her eyes and I left. I got under the sheets again. Dim light shone through the sheet over my head, a glow like very early morning. Sometimes, when I couldn't quite place what I was feeling, I would search through my body, from my toes up to my calves, between my legs, and on up to my head. Now my stomach hurt. I thought I heard noise from the bathroom. Obāsan was ready to die, I thought. And then I felt very sleepy.

When I next woke, Walker had just found Obāsan dead on the bathroom floor. He clung to me as we stood at the door. My mother stood over her mother, horrified. My father was grim.

"She made me kill her!" I said.

"She made me kill her!" Walker echoed.

My parents just thought I was crazy with grief.

We sent Obāsan's body to Wilcox, California, which was where her third husband was buried, and drove there for the funeral. As I watched the casket buried, I felt surrounded by a cool, choking swirl of air that made me cough up phlegm and made my eyes smart and water, and I knew that Obāsan was there. But the coldness went away, and it never returned. I looked toward the sky, to see whether my grandmother's ghost might be heading heavenward. "No, she must have gone down there," I said, pointing with my thumb toward the ground. I automatically braced myself for the ear boxing I always got when I said something I knew I shouldn't say; but there would be no more of that. I placed a bouquet of red plastic flowers on the gravestone.

Peter pointed at the flowers. "Obāsan?" he said—as if the whole of her life had been distilled into the flash of color in the gray cemetery.

We headed for Los Angeles to visit relatives. On the drive down we had some of Obāsan's riches—enameled boxes, painted fans, and old journals filled with graceful Japanese writing. We had her purse, empty now, and a picture of her as a striking woman in her twenties. As we drove, I played the last time I'd talked to her over and over in my mind, changing the end so that in my fantasies I went to get my parents for help. But when I emerged from my fantasy and thought about how evil I had been, I got a feeling I get sometimes even today, that there are things I am scared to know. My mother had cut off her mother's long braid and given one strand each to Ben, Walker, and me. The strands were black at one end and white at the other. I tied a string around mine and folded it into one of the enameled boxes. All the windows in the car were open. It was early evening, and we were halfway between Wilcox and Los Angeles. I stuck my head out the window. I was free. But I didn't feel free.

Twisters and Shouters

from *Tripmaster Monkey: His Fake Book*

Maxine Hong Kingston

In the Tenderloin, depressed and unemployed, the jobless Wittman Ah Sing felt a kind of bad freedom. Agoraphobic on Market Street, ha ha. There was nowhere he had to be, and nobody waiting to hear what happened to him today. Fired. Aware of Emptiness now. Ha ha. A storm will blow from the ocean or down from the mountains, and knock the set of the City down. If you dart quick enough behind the stores, you'll see that they are stage flats propped up. On the other side of them is ocean forever, and the great Valley between the Coast Range and the Sierras. Is that snow on Mt. Shasta?

And what for had they set up Market Street? To light up the dark jut of land into the dark sea. To bisect the City diagonally with a swath of lights. We are visible. See us? We're here. Here we are.

MAXINE HONG KINGSTON was born in Stockton, California, and educated at the University of California, Berkeley, where she is now teaching. She is the author of several extraordinary works: *The Woman Warrior: Memoirs of a Girlhood Among Ghosts* (winner of the National Book Critics' Circle Award for nonfiction), *China Men* (winner of the National Book Award for nonfiction), and her latest novel, *Tripmaster Monkey: His Fake Book*.

What else this street is for is to give suggestions as to what to do with oneself. What to do. What to buy. How to make a living. What to eat. Unappetizing. The street was full of schemes: FIRE SALE. LOANS. OLD GOLD. GUNS NEW AND USED. BOUGHT AND SOLD. GOING OUT OF BUSINESS. OUR PAIN YOUR GAIN. Food. Fast-food joints. Buy raw, sell cooked. If he got a-hold of food, he'd just eat it, not sell it. But we're supposed to sell that food in order to buy, cook, and eat omnivorously. If you're the more imaginative type, go to the mud flats, collect driftwood, build yourself a cart or a stand, sell umbrellas on rainy and foggy days, sell flowers, sell fast portable hot dogs, tacos, caramel corn, ice-cream sandwiches, hamburgers. Daedalate the line-up from cow to mouth, and fill up your life. If a human being did not have to eat every day, three times a day, ninety percent of life would be solved.

Clothes are no problem. He'd found his Wembley tie on a branch of a potted plant in front of the Durant Hotel, and an Eastern school tie hanging on a bush on Nob Hill. Coats are left on fences and wrist-watches inside of shoes at the beach.

Musicians have a hard time of it. Sax players and guitarists and a bass player have left their instruments in pawnshops; they're away perhaps forever, trying to make money, and to eat. A lot of hocked jewelry sits in the windows overnight; the real diamonds, they keep in the twirling-lock safe. These cellos and jewels belonged to people who for a while appreciated more than food. The nature of human beings is also that they buy t.v.s, coffee tables, nightstands, sofas, daddy arm-chairs for dressing the set of their life dramas.

Market Street is not an avenue or a boulevard or a champs that sweeps through arches of triumph. Tangles of cables on the ground and in the air, open manholes, construction for years. Buses and cars trying to get around one another, not falling into trenches, and not catching tires in or sliding on tracks, lanes taken up by double and triple parking. Pedestrians stranded on traffic islands. How am I to be a boulevardier on Market Street? I am not a boulevardier; I am a bum-how, I am a fleaman.

Now what? Where does a fleaman go for the rest of the evening, the rest of his adult life? The sets haven't started at the Black Hawk, but no more spending extravagant money on music. Music should be overflowing everywhere. It's time to find out how much free music there is. And no hanging out at the Albatross anymore, taken over by scary Spades. To feel the green earth underfoot, he could walk on the green Marina, look at the moon over the sea, and perhaps a second moon in the sea. Keep track of moonphases; are you going through changes in sync with werewolves? But something about that nightlight on the grass that looked sick, like the Green Eye Hospital. *I saw: Hospitals.* No walk in the Palace of the Legion of Honor either, not to be by himself in that huge dark; better to have a companion, and impress her at high noon, Wittman Ah Sing as Hercules chained to the columns and pulling them down, while shouting Shakespeare. If he went to Playland at the Beach, he would get freaked out by Sal, The Laughing Lady setting off the laughing gulls. Haaw. Haaaw. Haaaaw. He had yet to walk across the Golden Gate at night, but did not just then feel like being suspended in the open cold above the Bay; the breath of the cars would not be warm enough. Continue, then, along Market.

No boulevardiers here. Who's here? Who are my familiars? Here I am among my familiars, yeah, like we're Kerouac's people, tripping along the street.

> *Soldiers, sailors,*
> *the panhandlers and drifters,*
> *[no] zoot suiters, the hoodlums,*
> *the young men who washed dishes in cafeterias*
> *   from coast to coast,*
> *the hitchhikers, the hustlers, the drunks,*
> *the battered lonely young Negroes,*
> *the twinkling little Chinese,*
> *the dark Puerto Ricans [and braceros and pachucos]*
> *and the varieties of dungareed Young Americans*
> *   in leather jackets*
> *   who were seamen and mechanics and garagemen*
> *   everywhere . . .*
> *The same girls who walked in rhythmic pairs,*
> *the occasional whore in purple pumps and red raincoat*

whose passage down these sidewalks was always
so sensational,
the sudden garish sight of some incredible homosexual
flouncing by with an effeminate shriek of
general greeting to everyone, anyone:
"I'm just so knocked out and you all know it,
you mad things!"
—and vanishing in a flaunt of hips . . .

Well, no such red-and-purple whore or resplendent homosexual. Might as well expect a taxi door to open and out step a geisha in autumn kimono, her face painted white with tippy red lips and smudge-moth eyebrows, white tabi feet winking her out of sight on an assignation in the floating demimonde.

Shit. The "twinkling little Chinese" must be none other than himself. "Twinkling"?! "Little"?! Shit. Bumkicked again. If King Kerouac, King of the Beats, were walking here tonight, he'd see Wittman and think, "Twinkling little Chinese." Refute "little." Gainsay "twinkling." A man does not twinkle. A man with balls is not little. As a matter of fact, Kerouac didn't get "Chinese" right either. Big football player white all-American jock Kerouac. Jock Kerouac. I call into question your naming of me. I trust your sight no more. You tell people by their jobs. And by their race. And the wrong race at that. If Ah Sing were to run into Kerouac—grab him by the lapels of his lumberjack shirt. Pull him up on his toes. Listen here, you twinkling little Canuck. What do you know, Kerouac? What do you know? You don't know shit. I'm the American here. I'm the American walking here. Fuck Kerouac and his American road anyway. Et tu, Kerouac. Aiya, even you. Just for that, I showed you, I grew to six feet. May still be growing.

Like headlines, the movie marquees seemed to give titles to what was going down—MONDO CANE, THE TRIAL, LORD OF THE FLIES, DR. NO, MANCHURIAN CANDIDATE, HOW THE WEST WAS WON. Now, if there is one thing that makes life bearable, it's the movies. Let them show a movie once a week, and Wittman can take anything, live anywhere—jail, a totalitarian socialist country, the Army. Not educational films but big-bucks full-production-values American glitz movies.

WEST SIDE STORY. The biggest reddest block caps told him to go see *West Side Story*, which had returned from the sixth International Film Festival at Cannes. The girl in the ornate ticket booth said that he was on time, so he bought a ticket and went into the Fox. Inhaling the smell of the popcorn and the carpet, he felt happy. In the middle seat a screen-and-a-half's width away from the front, he continued happy. In the breast pocket of his Brooks Brothers suit, on a page margin, Malte Laurids Brigge: *This which towered before me, with its shadows ordered in the semblance of a face, with the darkness gathered in the mouth of its centre, bounded, up there, by the symmetrically curling hairdos of the cornice; this was the strong, all-covering antique mask, behind which the world condensed into a face. Here, in this great in-curved amphitheatre of seats, there reigned a life of expectancy, void, absorbent: all happening was yonder: gods and destiny; and thence (when one looks, up high) came lightly, over the wall's rim: the eternal entry of the heavens.* Then a thunder-clapping pleasure—the movie started with simultaneous blasts of Technicolor and horns.

"When you're a Jet, you're a Jet all the way from your first cigarette to your last dying day." Oh, yes, that's me, that's me, a-crouching and a-leaping, fight-dancing through the city, fingers snapping, tricky feet attacking and backing up and attacking, the gang altogether turning and pouncing—monkey kung fu. "You got brothers around . . . You're never disconnected . . . You're well protected."

Oh, yes, all the dances in all the wide and lonely gyms of our ad-olescence should have been like this. Us guys against one wall and you girls across the basketball court and along the opposite wall ought to have come bursting out at one another in two co-operating teams. The girls, led by Rita Moreno, high-kicking and lifting their skirts and many petticoats. "I like to be in America. Everything free in America."

And Tony meets Natalie Wood, and asks her to dance, and falls in love at first sight with her. Me too. "I just met a girl named Maria." And I'm in love with her too. Though her brother and her boyfriend belong to the Sharks, I love her like a religion.

In this world without balconies, climb a fire escape to court the city girl. And no sooner kiss her but have to part. "There's a place for us." Our monkey finds himself crying. Stop it. Look, identify with Chino, the reject. "Stick to your own kind." What kind of people are Tony and Maria anyway, both with black wavy hair, and looking more like each other than anybody else on or off the screen? They are on the same mafioso side, Natalie Wood as dark as a star can be. "Make of our hands one hand, make of our hearts one heart, make of our lives one life, day after day, one life." (Wittman had been to a wedding, he was best man, where his college friends had sung that song as part of the ceremony. The bride was Protestant and the groom was agnostic.)

The Jets are an Italian gang? But what about jet black? Like the Fillmore, the Western Addition. Black. Only they don't hire and cast Blacks, so Russ Tamblyn, as Riff the gangleader with kinky hair, indicates Blackness, right? (Like Leslie Caron with her wide mouth as Mardou Fox in *The Subterraneans* is supposed to be Black. George Peppard as Jack Kerouac, also as Holly Golightly's boyfriend in *Breakfast at Tiffany's*. Mickey Rooney with an eye job and glasses as Holly's jap landlord, speaking snuffling bucktoof patois.) The leader of the Sharks is Bernardo, Maria's brother, played by George Chakiris. Greek Danish Puerto Ricans of the East Coast. This is Back East, where they worry about Puerto Rican gangs, who are Black and white and blond. Don't the rest of the audience get Sharks and Jets mixed up in the fight-dancing? They should have hired dark actors for one side or the other. But not a face up there was darker than Pancake #11. Come on. Since when? A white-boy gang? Two white-boy gangs. White boys don't need a gang because they own the country. They go about the country individually and confidently, and not on the lookout for whom to ally with. "You got brothers around; you're a family man . . . We're gonna beat every last buggin gang on the whole buggin street." They mean they can beat kung fu tongs, who invented fight-dancing, and they can beat the dancing Black boxers, who fight solo.

Wittman got up and moved to a seat two rows forward, on the aisle, near the exit, but entered the movie no deeper, looking up at the squished faces. Can't get sucked in anymore. He went up to the balcony, smoked, nobody telling him to put out his smoke, and watched Tony talk to Doc, this lovable old *Jewish* candy-store guy—get it?—this movie is not prejudiced. Some of the Italians are good guys, Tony is reformed, and some are bad guys; the bad guys, see, are bad for reasons other than innateness. Wittman got up again and climbed to the back of the balcony. He would walk out except that he was too cheap to leave in the middle of movies. There weren't very many people in the audience, and they were spread out singly with rows of empty seats around each one, alone at the movies on Friday night with no place else to go. "The world is just an address. . . ." So, white guys, lonely also, borrow movie stars' faces, movie stars having inhabitable faces, and pretend to be out with Natalie, and to have a gang.

Chino does not disappear de-balled from the picture. He hunts Tony down and shoots him dead. Maria/Natalie kneels beside his body, and sings with tears in her eyes. "One hand, one heart, only death will part us now." Gangboys look on through the cyclone fence. She throws away the gun, which hits the cement but doesn't go off. "Te adoro, Anton," she says foreignly. Some Sharks, some Jets, biersmen, in rue, bear the dead away. The end.

Where are you, Bugs Bunny? We need you, Mr. Wabbit in Wed.

Wittman came out of the theater to the natural world that moves at a medium rate with no jump cuts to the interesting parts. Headache. Bad for the head to dream at the wrong time of day. The day gone. Should have cut out—the only human being in the world to walk out on *West Side Story*—too late. He'd stayed, and let the goddamn movies ruin his life.

Well, here was First Street, and the Terminal. The end of the City. The end of the week. Maws—gaps and gapes—continuing to open. But Wittman did too have a place to go, he'd been invited to a party, which he'd meant to turn down. He entered the Terminal, which is surrounded by a concrete whirlpool for the buses to turn around on spirals of ramps. Not earth dirt but like cement dirt covered everything, rush-hour feet scuffing up lime, noses and mouths inhaling lime rubbings. A last flower stand by the main entrance—chrysanthemums. And a bake shop with birthday cakes. A couple of people were eating creampuffs as they hurried along. People eat here, with the smell of urinal cakes issuing from johns. They buy hot dogs at one end of the Terminal and finish eating on their way through. They buy gifts at the last moment. Wittman bought two packs of Pall Malls in preparation for the rest of the weekend. No loiterers doing anything freaky. Keep it moving. Everybody's got a place to go tonight. Wittman bought a ticket for the Oakland-Berkeley border, and rode up the escalator to the lanes of buses. The people on traffic islands waited along safety railings. Birds beak-dived from the steel rafters to land precisely at a crumb between grill bars. The pigeons and sparrows were greyish and the cheeks of men were also grey. Pigeon dust. Pigeons fan our breathing air with pigeon dander.

Wittman was one of the first passengers to board, and chose the aisle seat behind the driver. He threw his coat on the window seat to discourage company, stuck his long legs out diagonally, and put on his metaphor glasses and looked out the window.

Up into the bus clambered this very plain girl, who lifted her leg in such an ungainly manner that anybody could see up her skirt to thighs, but who'd be interested in looking? She was carrying string bags of books and greasy butcher-paper bundles and pastry boxes. He wished she weren't Chinese, the kind who works hard and doesn't fix herself up. She, of course, stood beside him until he moved his coat and let her bump her bags across him and sit herself down to ride. This girl and her roast duck will ride beside him all the way across the San Francisco–Oakland Bay Bridge. She must have figured he was saving this seat for her, fellow ethnick.

The bus went up the turnaround ramp and over a feeder ramp, this girl working away at opening her window—got it open when they passed the Hills Brothers factory, where the long tall Hindu in the white turban and yellow gown stood quaffing his coffee. The smell of the roasting coffee made promises of comfort. Then they were on the bridge, not the bridge for suicides, and journeying through the dark. The eastbound traffic takes the bottom deck, which may as well be a tunnel. You can see lights between the railings and the top deck, and thereby identify the shores, the hills, islands, highways, the other bridge.

"Going to Oakland?" asked the girl. She said "Oak Lun."

"Haw," he grunted, a tough old China Man. If he were Japanese, he could have said, "Ee, chotto." Like "Thataway for a spell." Not impolite. None of your business, ma'am.

"I'm in the City Fridays to work," she said. "Tuesdays and Thursdays, I'm taking a night course at Cal Extension, over by the metal overpass on Laguna Street. There's the bar and the traffic light on the corner? Nobody goes into or comes out of that bar. I stand there at that corner all by myself, obeying the traffic light. There aren't any cars. It's sort of lonely going to college. What for you go City?" He didn't answer. Does she notice that he isn't the forthcoming outgoing type? "On business, huh?" Suggesting an answer for him.

"Yeah. Business."

"I signed up for psychology," she said, as if he'd conversably asked. "But I looked up love in tables of contents and indexes, and do you know love isn't in psychology books? So I signed up for philosophy, but I'm getting disappointed. I thought we were going to learn about good and evil, human nature, how to be good. You know. What God is like. You know. How to live. But we're learning about P plus Q arrows R or S. What's that, haw? I work all day, and commute for two hours, and what do I get? P plus Q arrows R."

She ought to be interesting, going right to what's important. The trouble with most people is that they don't think about the meaning of life. And here's this girl trying for heart truth. She may even have important new information. So how come she's boring? She's annoying him. Because she's presumptuous. Nosiness must be a Chinese racial trait. She was supposing, in the first place, that he was Chinese, and therefore, he has to hear her out. Care how she's getting along. She's reporting to him as to how one of our kind is faring. And she has a subtext: I am intelligent. I am educated. Why don't you ask me out? He took a side-eye look at her flat profile. She would look worse with her glasses off. Her mouse-brown hair was pulled tight against her head and up into a flat knot on top, hairpins showing, crisscrossing. (Do Jews look down on men who use bobby pins to hold their yarmulkes on?) A person has to have a perfect profile to wear her hair like that. She was wearing a short brownish jacket and her bony wrists stuck out of the sleeves. A thin springtime skirt. She's poor. Loafers with striped socks. Flat shoes, flat chest, flat hair, flat face, flat color. A smell like hot restaurant air that blows into alleys must be coming off her. Char sui? Fire duck? Traveling with food, unto this generation.

Yeah, the lot of us riding the Greyhound out of Fresno and Watson-ville and Gardena and Lompoc to college—even Stanford—guys *named* Stanford—with mama food and grandma food in the overhead rack and under the seat. Pretending the smell was coming off some-body else's luggage. And here was this girl, a night-school girl, a Con-tinuing Ed girl, crossing the Bay, bringing a fire duck weekend treat from Big City Chinatown to her aging parents.

"Do you know my cousin Annette Ah Tye?" she asked. "She's from Oak Lun."

"No," he said.

"How about Susan Lew? Oh, come on. Susie Lew. Robert Lew. Do you know Fanny them? Fanny, Bobby, Chance Ong, Uncle Louis. I'm related to Fanny them."

"No, I don't know them," said Wittman, who would not be bad-gered into saying, "Oh, yeah, Susan them. I'm related by marriage to her cousin from Walnut Creek."

"I'm thinking of dropping philosophy," she said. "Or do you think the prof is working up to the best part?"

"I don't know what you say," said Wittman. *Know* like *no*, like *brain*. "I major in engineer."

"Where do you study engineering?"

"Ha-ah." He made a noise like a samurai doing a me-ay, or an old Chinese guy who smokes too much.

"You ought to develop yourself," she said. "Not only mentally but physically, spiritually, and socially." What nerve. Chinese have a lot of nerve. Going to extension classes was her college adventure. Let's us who wear intellectual's glasses talk smart to each other. "You may be developing yourself mentally," she said. "But you know what's wrong with Chinese boys? All you do is study, but there's more to life than that. You need to be well rounded. Go out for sports. Go out on dates. Those are just two suggestions. You have to think up other activities on your own. You can't go by rote and succeed, as in engineering school. You want a deep life, don't you? That's what's wrong with Chinese boys. Shallow lives."

What Wittman ought to say at this point was, "Just because none of us asks you out doesn't mean we don't go out with girls." Instead, to be kind, he said, "I not Chinese. I Japanese boy. I hate being taken for a chinaman. Now, which of my features is it that you find peculiarly Chinese? Go on. I'm interested."

"Don't say chinaman," she said.

Oh, god. O Central Casting, who do you have for me now? And what is this role that is mine? Confederates who have an interest in race: the Ku Klux Klan, Lester Maddox, fraternity guys, Governor Faubus, Governor Wallace, Nazis—stupid people on his level. The dumb part of himself that eats Fritos and goes to movies was avidly interested in race, a topic unworthy of a great mind. Low-karma shit. Babytalk. Stuck at A,B,C. Can't get to Q. Crybaby. Race—a stupid soul-narrowing topic, like women's rights, like sociology, easy for low-I.Q. people to feel like they're thinking. Stunted and runted at a low level of inquiry, stuck at worm. All right, then, his grade-point average was low (because of doing too many life things), he's the only Chinese American of his generation not in grad school, he'll shovel shit.

"It's the nose, isn't it, that's a chinaman nose?" he asked this flatnosed girl. "Or my big Shinajin eyes? Oh, I know. I know. Legs. You noticed my Chinese legs." He started to pull up a pants leg. "I'm lean in the calf. Most Japanese are meaty in the calf by nature, made for wading in rice paddies. Or it's just girls who have daikon legs? How about you? You got daikon legs?"

She was holding her skirt down, moving her legs aside, not much room among her packages. Giggling. Too bad she was not offended. Modern youth in flirtation. "You Japanese know how to have a social life much better than Chinese," she said. "At least you Japanese boys take your girls out. You have a social life."

Oh, come on. Don't say "your girls." Don't say "social life." Don't say "boys." Or "prof." Those Continuing Ed teachers are on a nontenure, non-promotional track. Below lecturers. Don't say "Chinese." Don't say "Japanese."

"You know why Chinese boys don't go out?" she asked, confiding some more. Why? What's the punchline? He ought to kill her with his bare hands, but waited to hear just why Chinese boys stay home studying and masturbating. You could hear her telling on us to some infatuated sinophile. Here it comes, the real skinny. "Because no matter how dumb-soo, every last short boy unable to get a date in high school or at college can go to Hong Kong and bring back a beautiful woman. Chinese boys don't bother to learn how to socialize. It's not fair. Can you imagine a girl going to China looking for a husband? What would they say about her? Have you ever heard of a Japanese girl sending for a picture groom?"

"No," he said.

"And if Chinese boys don't learn to date, and there are millions of wives waiting to be picked out, then what becomes of girls like me, haw?"

Oh, no, never to be married but to a girl like this one. Montgomery Clift married to Shelley Winters in *A Place in the Sun*. Never Elizabeth Taylor.

"You shouldn't go to China to pick up a guy anyway," he said. "Don't truck with foreigners. They'll marry you for your American money, and a green card. They'll say and do anything for a green card and money. Don't be fooled. They'll dump you once they get over here."

Another plan for her or for anybody might be to go to a country where your type is their ideal of physical beauty. For example, he himself would go over big in Scandinavia. But where would her type look good? Probably the U.S.A. is already her best bet. There's always white guys from Minnesota and Michigan looking for geisha girls.

"No, they won't," she said. "They'd be grateful. They're grateful and faithful forever. I'm not going to China. People can't just go to China. I was talking hypothetically." Oh, sure, she's so attractive.

"Last weekend, I went to a church dance," she said, letting him know she's with it. "I went with my girlfriends. We go to dances without a date for to meet new boys. All the people who attended the dance were Chinese. How is that? I mean, it's not even an all-Chinese church. The same thing happens at college dances. Posters on campuses say 'Spring Formal,' but everyone knows it's a Chinese-only dance. How do they know? Okay, Chinese know. They know. But how does everybody else know not to come? Is it like that with you Japanese?"

"I don't go to dances." Don't say "they."

"You ought to socialize. I guess the church gave the dance so we could meet one another. It's a church maneuver, see?, to give us something beneficial. We'd come to their buildings for English lessons, dances, pot luck, and pretty soon, we're staying for the services. Anyway, there was a chaperone at this dance who was a white acquaintance of mine from high school. We're the same age, but he was acting like an adult supervisor of children. We used to talk with each other at school, but at this dance, of course, he wouldn't ask me to dance."

"What for you want to dance with him? Oh. Oh, I get it. I know you. I know who you are. You're Pocahontas. That's who you are. Aren't you? Pocahontas. I should have recognized you from your long crane neck."

"No, my name is Judy. Judy Louis." She continued telling him more stuff about her life. On and on. Hadn't recognized her for a talker until too late. Strange moving lights, maybe airplanes, maybe satellites, were traveling through the air. The high stationary lights were warnings, the tops of hills. It seemed a long ride; this voice kept going on beside his ear. He looked at the girl again, and she looked blue-black in the dark. He blinked, and saw sitting beside him a blue boar. Yes, glints of light on bluish dagger tusks. Little shining eyes. Not an illusion because the details were very sharp. Straight black bristly eyelashes. A trick of the dark? But it was lasting. Eyes and ivory tusks gleaming black and silver. Like black ocean with star plankton and black sky with stars. And the mouth moving, opening and closing in speech, and a blue-red tongue showing between silver teeth, and two ivory sword tusks. He leaned back in his seat, tried forward, and she remained a blue boar. (You might make a joke about it, you know. "Boar" and "bore.") He couldn't see where her face left off from her hair and the dark. He made no ado about this hallucination, acted as if she were a normal girl. Concentrated hard to hear what she was saying. "You're putting me on, aren't you?" she was saying.

"What you mean?"

"You're not really Japanese. You're *Chinese*. Japanese have good manners." Her piggy eyes squinted at him. He wanted to touch her, but she would think he was making a pass. But, surely, he could try touching a tusk, because the tusks can't actually be there. "And you look Chinese. Big bones. Long face. Sort of messy."

"Listen here. I'm not going to ask you out, so quit hinting around, okay?"

"What?! Me go out with you? I not hinting around. I wouldn't go out with you if you ask me. You not my type. Haw."

"What type is that? Missionaries? Missionaries your type? You know where you ought to go for your type? I know the place for you. In New York, there's a nightclub for haoles and orientals to pick each other up. It's like a gay bar, that is, not your average straight thing. Sick. Girls such as yourself go there looking for an all-American boy to assimilate with, and vice versa. You can play Madame Butterfly or the Dragon Lady and find yourself a vet who's remembering Seoul or Pearl Harbor or Pusan or Occupied Japan. All kinds of Somerset Maugham combinations you hardly want to know about. Pseudo psycho lesbo sappho weirdo hetero homo combos."

"You the one sick. Look who's sick. Don't call me sick. You sick." The blue boar had eyebrows, and they were screwed together in perplexity. "*If* you are a Japanese, you shouldn't go out with a Chinese girl anyway, and I wouldn't go out with you. Japanese males work too hard. Chinese males dream too much, and fly up in the air. The Chinese female is down-to-earth, and makes her man work. When a Japanese man marries a Chinese woman, which does not happen often, it's tragic. They would never relax and have fun. A Japanese man needs a girl who will help him loosen up, and a Chinese man needs a girl who will help him settle down. Chinese man, Chinese woman stay together. I'm going to do a study of that if I go into psych."

"Don't say 'tragic.' You want the address of that place where keto hakujin meet shinajin and nihonjin? Look, I'm just helping you out with your social life."

His talking to her, and her speaking, did not dispel her blueness or her boarness. The lips moved, the tusks flashed. He wanted her to talk some more so he could look closely at her. What was causing this effect? The other people on the bus had not turned into animals.

"Help *yourself* out with your *own* social life. Why *don't* you ask me out on a date? Haw?" The boar lips parted smiling. "Because you are scared." "Sked," she pronounced it. "You been thinking about it this whole trip, but you sked." Don't say "date."

"No, I'm not." You're homely. He can't say that. She functions like she's as good-looking as the next person, and he's not going to be the one to disabuse her.

This guise, though, is not plain. A magnificent creature. The voice that was coming out of it was the plain girl's. She must be sitting next to him engulfed in a mirage.

He touched her on a tusk, and it was there, all right. It did not fade into a strip of metal that was the window frame. The narrow eyes looked at him in surprise. "Hey, cut it out," she said, pushing his hand away from her mouth with a gentle cloven hoof. She giggled, and he backed away as far over by the aisle as he could back. What he had touched was harder than flesh. Bony. Solid. Therefore, real, huh? She giggled again. It is pretty funny to have somebody touching you on the teeth. Warm teeth.

"What was that for? Why did you do that?" she said. "Why you touch my teeth? That isn't the way to ask for a date."

"I'm not asking you for a date. I do not want to date you."

"Well, I understand. You don't like aggressive girls. Most guys can't take aggressive girls. I'm very aggressive." She'll never admit to homeliness. "Aggressive girls are especially bad for Japanese boys."

"Lay off my race," he said. "Cool it." Which was what he should have said in the first place. She went quiet. Sat there. But did not change back. The bus went on for a long time in the dark. And whenever he glanced her way, there beside him was the blue-black boar. Gleaming.

"Hey," he said, tapping her on the shoulder. Boar skin feels like corduroy. She cocked a flap of silky ear toward him. "See these people on the bus? They all look human, don't they? They look like humans but they're not."

"They are too," she said.

"Let me warn you." He looked behind him, and behind her. "Some of them only appear to be human." What he was saying even sent shivers up his own back. "There are non-humans in disguise as men and women amongst us."

"Do you see them everywhere, or only on this bus?"

"On this bus, maybe a few other places. I'm surprised you haven't noticed. Well, some of them have gotten the disguise down very well.

But there's usually a slip-up that gives them away. Do you want me to tell you some signs to watch out for?"

The boar's great blue-black head nodded.

"You've seen 'The Twilight Zone' on t.v., haven't you? Have you noticed that Rod Serling doesn't have an upper lip?" He demonstrated, pressing his upper lip against his teeth. "That's a characteristic sign of the werewolf." The glittery eyes of the boar opened wider, surprised. "Their hands are different from ours. They wear gloves. Walt Disney draws them accurately. And Walter Lantz does too. Goofy wears gloves, but not Pluto. Goofy is a dog, and Pluto is a dog, but Pluto is a real dog. Mickey and Minnie, Donald and the nephews, Unca Scrooge—and Yosemite Sam—never take their gloves off. Minnie and Daisy wash dishes with their gloves on. You see women in church with those same little white gloves, huh? They are often going to church. There are more of these werewomen in San Francisco than in other cities."

"What do they want? What are they doing here?"

"You tell me. I think they're here because they belong here. That's just the way the world is. There's all kinds. There are cataclysms and luck that they probably manipulate. But there's different kinds of them too, you know; they don't get along with one another. It's not like they're all together in a conspiracy against our kind."

"Aiya-a-ah, nay gum sai nay, a-a-ah," said the creature—the Pig Woman—beside him. "Mo gum sai nay, la ma-a-ah." Such a kind voice, such a loving-kind voice, so soothing, so sorry for him, telling him to let go of the old superstitious ways.

At last, the bus shot out of the tunnel-like bridge. Under the bright lights, she turned back into a tan-and-grey drab of a girl again. Wittman got himself to his feet, rode standing up, and the bus reached the intersection of College and Alcatraz. Here's where I get off.

"Goodbye," she said. "Let's talk again. It will make our commute more interesting." She was not admitting to having weirdly become Pig Woman.

He said, "Huh." Samurai.

Joy Kogawa

Blind alleys, culs-de-sac, no-trespassing signs. What remains for me of the two years following Uncle's death is a desperation of dead ends in my efforts to reach Stephen.

I'm still teaching school at Cecil and go back to see Obasan in Granton about once a month. Her health is deteriorating steadily. At times it feels criminal to leave her alone and I ask her repeatedly to come and stay with me, but she will not. Her house, she says, needs care. So also does she. Her short-term memory is almost gone.

"What reason? Forgotten," she says with a chuckle when she catches herself wondering what she started out to do. After supper one night, she can't remember that she has just eaten. All her old pots are ruined, blackened and burnt. The sturdy old rice pot as well. I take a chisel and hammer to it one Saturday night to try to budge the burnt prunes which are one soldered mass of coal lumps. The next week she

JOY KOGAWA was born in Vancouver, Canada, and now lives in Toronto. She is the author of several books of poetry and children's fiction. Her novel *Obasan* received an American Book Award. Her most recent novel, *Itsuka*, is excerpted here.

searches so persistently for the old pot that I dig it out of the garbage and give it back to her. The kitchen, her queendom, is finally crumbling from her control and turning into a minefield of taps and stove knobs and freezing pipes needing to be constantly checked. It's not a situation that can continue.

I go and sit on the square wooden cistern cover outside the kitchen door and think about what to do. The box is a humble throne in a new springtime of weeds—purple-flowered thistles, crabgrass, a few carrot fronds with rat-tail roots. Uncle's world has become a scratch patch.

The rage within begins its slow emergence that winter as I drive back and forth through the early blizzards and the freezing snow. The night of the freak storm, I'm trapped in a snowdrift for five hours and finally get to Granton at 2:00 a.m., after inching along in a convoy of cars trailing a snowplow. Obasan is asleep and there is water all over the kitchen floor from a tap that has been left on to keep the pipes from freezing. She forgot to unplug the drain. We need help. I drive her back with me to Cecil. She wants to return the next day.

Two weekends after this, I arrive to find the kitchen sink overflowing again and Obasan asleep in a lukewarm bathtub. I carry, drag, her unresponsive body the few shuffling steps to her bed.

All that wind-reaping Alberta winter, I drive over the squealing snow, from Cecil to Granton, then back to Cecil, stumbling into my unmade bed in the early still-dark morning. Then, groggy at 9:00 a.m., I sleep-walk into the classroom to face the upturned faces of the children with their thousand unanswerable questions.

One weekend before Christmas I drive home to find there's been a power failure. The furnace is out. The water pipes have burst under the sink and flooded the cupboard. I find Obasan squatting with soggy cardboard cartons of food, jelly powders, salt and cereals piled on a stool while the water seeps over the floor and under the stove to a low spot from where it drips into the dirt cellar below.

It's idiocy working with her in the house that weekend. Hank drops by with the milk and stays to fix the pipes. "This ol' house gettin' ready to meet the saint eh?" he says, giving his head a quick shake.

"Guess so."

Obasan is salvaging the unsalvageable. Nothing is ever to be discarded. Plastic bleach bottles are waste paper baskets and plant trays. Mandarin orange boxes are covered stools. Even the hems of her slacks are not cut but are rolled under till they form a heavy clump of cloth at her ankles. There seems to be an inability to let go. Or a sense that usefulness is inherent in all matter. Perhaps it's also a type of tenderness, a treasuring of every tentative little thing. Unlike Pastor Jim, she does not divide the world into the saved and the lost.

The cold she catches that weekend will not let her go and develops into pneumonia.

"She's a very sick lady," the doctor says.

As I drive her to the hospital in Lethbridge, I'm unaware that she has begun her long last haul. I take ten days off and call Aunt Emily, who flies down noisily that week and charges down the hospital corridor with questions as we make our way to Room 212.

Obasan is a small rag-doll shape in the all-white room. In the next bed a barely conscious woman who looks a hundred years old lies gray and heaving in a tent of steam. A breathing machine.

"Kusuri," Obasan says absently in greeting. "Medicine." She gestures around her head and indicates the woman beside her.

Aunt Emily hesitates in her stride, then, leaning over, she cups her mouth to Obasan's ear. "Emily yo," she shouts. "It's Emily here."

"O," Obasan says, shifting her head and staring up. "Emiri-san?" She reaches out and pats Aunt Emily's arm. Obasan's slight smile is that of a small child's faint hope. "Emiri-san?"

A heavy-set nurse comes in with a basin and Aunt Emily immediately begins a barrage of more questions. What, she wants to know immediately, are all the facts? Will Obasan be here long? Is there anything serious?

"You'll have to speak to the doctor," the nurse answers in a not unkindly tone.

"You must be able to tell me something," Aunt Emily says impatiently, emphasizing the "something" with a lift of both hands.

The old woman in the next bed lets out a low moan, a sound of utter weariness. The nurse reaches into the steam tent and feels for the old woman's pulse. "We're doing what we can here," she says sharply.

"I'm not being critical. I just need to know," Aunt Emily replies even more sharply.

I'm glad Obasan is deaf and can be spared the distress of their unseemly aggression.

Back home, Aunt Emily's exasperation overflows again when I suggest I might quit teaching to care for Obasan. "And just what do you think you'll do all day?" She waves her arms in the crowded kitchen and her knuckles knock against the fly swatters that hang beside the stove, setting them dancing. "You'll get mind rot. You'll become a TV addict."

The old black and white TV is in a constant twilight zone of flickering shadows and suits Aunt Emily's definition of my life on the prairies. Her solution to all our problems is that Obasan and I should move to Toronto. But I know Obasan cannot be moved from her little house.

"We'll think about it when she's better," I say, though I can't see how our moving to Toronto will help anything. Aunt Emily leaves the next day for a speaking engagement in Vancouver.

The doctor is not optimistic when I speak with him the following week. He says she is no longer capable of living on her own and the best thing would be to place her in a nursing home. It's unthinkable.

I call for Stephen. "It's an emergency. Please ask him to call me." I leave three messages and finally hear from him the following week. He's about to go on tour again, he says, and cannot help.

"But what'll I do?" I ask. "Can't you postpone the tour?"

I can't tell from the low monotone of his voice what he's feeling. "You should listen to the doctor," he says.

"You mean put her in a home? That's murder."

There's a long sigh at the other end. "You can't take care of her," he says. "I can't. There's nothing I can do. Nothing."

"What do you mean—nothing?" I grip the receiver tightly to my ear and can feel the sand in my throat. "What do you mean?"

After three weeks Obasan is released to my care. I arrange for two neighboring women, plus Hank and a visiting nurse, to check on her. In late winter, I decide she has to come to be with me in Cecil. It's like caring for a baby. I pack her patched underclothes, nemaki, housecoats, sweaters, her chocolate box of photographs, magnifying glass, big-print Bible, her royal family scrapbook.

The penultimate crisis begins in the spring of 1974, a year and a half after Uncle's death. I come home from school to find the apartment door open and Obasan lying on the wet prickly brown grass in the backyard. She's in the hospital for days in a barely responsive state. The old doctor at the Cecil hospital says he doesn't know what's wrong. "At her age, who knows?" he says. After two weeks, the crisis is over. The doctor says she seems to have stabilized and perhaps could go on indefinitely.

She can hardly hear at all now. She's incontinent. Like an infant's, the reflexes of her mouth function when a spoon is placed to her lips. Her lungs have survived another battle. Her mind has all but lost the war. She's moved to a chronic care room where three others are also in a twilight of staring, mouths open, life seeping downhill through the granular bed of sleep.

I begin another barrage of calls to Stephen.

"I have to sell the house. I need you. What should I do with Grandpa's tools? What about your music books?" His only response is a heavy sigh at the other end of the long-distance line.

I work feverishly through the following weekends, digging through the collected memories of the Nakanes and Katos of Granton, Slocan and Vancouver. Of that once-upon-a-time clan, all that remains is one aged aunt, in a small-town prairie hospital, another childless aunt in Toronto, one successful brother and me, spinster schoolteacher.

So much happens in a lifetime. Wars come and go. People die. Families disappear. Even the living grow faint as memories.

Obasan, of course, has kept everything—Stephen's first crystal radio, which he made when we were moved to Granton, and my red, white and blue ball, my Mickey Mouse, paper dolls, coloring books, broken wax crayons and pencil stubs. There are some Big Little Books and a collection of bubble-gum cards. I alternate between frenzied packing, discarding and fits of weeping. Obasan has spent her lifetime treasuring these things that I am now throwing away. I tackle the photographs, letters, the portrait of Miss Best, Stephen's home-made musical instruments—the thrumming rubber-band box, the pieces of elastic as brittle as bits of dried spaghetti—our old boots—Uncle's, Obasan's, Stephen's, mine—the rice tins in the cellar full of seeds from

Uncle's last harvesting. I'm an undertaker disemboweling and embalming a still breathing body, removing heart, limbs, life blood, all the arteries, memories that keep one connected to the world, transforming this comatose little family into a corpse. We have entered the garbage-dump stage of life and I'm rototilling it all—rags, plastic dishes, frayed curtains, a growing heap of plastic bags. When the garbage collector carts away the mound of black bags, I can feel the muscles and bones, the last connective tissues, strain and snap. The new owners of the house bulldoze it. Our shack of memories disappears. I should not have let that happen. I forgot to take out Uncle's home-made furniture.

Obasan deteriorates slowly. She alternates between wanting to return to her non-existent house and wanting release altogether. She mourns her absence from her house. I mourn her mourning. We never speak of it. She seems to be seeking a sign, some messenger to tell her she is permitted to go.

There are days when I don't know where in her mind she has gone. Days when I think it has to be the end. Days when I think it will never end. Days when I ache for her release, from the morning, noon and night, eating, breathing, defecating body. I blame myself for the murder of her house. I blame Aunt Emily and Stephen for abandoning us. I blame the universe for the scheme of life.

On August 16, 1974, her skin is the color of ashes. She looks as though she has reached the final barrier. But the next day she's back again, waiting in her wheelchair, patient and silent and deaf, her tapered fingers at peace entwined in her lap, then half lifted in some vaguely remembered language of service.

Some nights I leave her convinced she cannot survive till morning, then the next day the crisis is past and she's back, conscious again, her fork dividing the hospital food, taking a portion for herself, then tapping the edge of her plate with her still graceful fingers in a gesture of offering. She cannot survive without offering. Those hands remain, even after decades of drudgery, the delicate precise hands of a koto player, plucking the strings. They are lost now in the snowy world of white sheets. Even in her last days, her hands, confused in the air, still tremble to serve.

I sit beside her, silent as well, not wanting to shout in the hospital. I bring her boiled eggs to peel or peas to unpod. And we are there together, our hands speaking of the kitchen queendom and the past. Our language is gestures, the nodding and shaking of heads, the shrugging of shoulders. A pat on the side of the bed is a request for me to sit. A slight wave means "no." In her cluttered little domain she was once servant and queen. She is now a prisoner, a captive of an orderly, efficient, cold, inevitable ending.

One evening I arrive to find Obasan cannot recognize me. The story I piece together is that she went wandering sometime in the middle of the night. She was found around 2:00 a.m. in a room down the hall, holding her walker and peering at a young man. No one could understand what she was trying to do or say.

There is little mercy in some institutions. You are permitted one mistake. She's tied down in her wheelchair and in her bed.

During a snowfall in early October, she asks if it's Christmas. Her throat, unused to the effort of speech, sounds like a shortwave radio —a brief rasp, her throat clearing static through her dry round mouth.

"Ima Christmasu?" I'm able to make out. "Is it Christmas now?"

I shake my head and put the spoonful of soup to her lips. She moves my arm away, then waves her hand up and down to indicate the snow pelting past the window.

"Ima Christmasu?" she repeats. "Ima Merry Christmasu time?"

She's so insistent, I finally give in and nod agreement. It's Christmas in October. She's content. She repeats the statement once more to solidify the fact. "Ima Merry Christmasu time."

Then, looking intently at my face and tapping my wrist for emphasis, she says loudly, "Steebun wa Merry Christmasu time ni kuru?" She's being as conversational as she can be but it's an excessive plea. An extremity of asking. "Will Stephen come at Merry Christmas time?" She has not once in all her days directly requested anything.

I lie. I say through the nodding of my head that Stephen will arrive. With all my heart I will it to be so—the snow a sign of Christmas and Christmas a time for Stephen's visit.

She lies back against her pillow and settles down. She is content. She has said more than enough.

I have no idea of Obasan's capacity to trust. And even less of Stephen's capacity to stay away. Beethoven, they say, was a deaf musician. No musician could be more deaf than Stephen. My brother has no time to participate in a small prairie dying.

"Steebun wa?"

"Europpa."

It's Stephen from whom I have learned most how not to be. He would not stay. I learned not to leave. He would not submit. I learned not to rage. At least not in the usual ways. It's Stephen who's been entrusted with the family's hopes and dreams and it's he in the end who is needed at the hospital more than me. His absence is unendurable.

Life's final passage is not as neat as it is often portrayed. In movies, there's a last little sigh, a turning of the head, then a fluttering and weeping of mourners. But my dear aunt's departure is an indecisive journey. She attempts to leave, attempts to stay. She keeps stepping back from the gate.

I call and call Stephen for her sake. I travel down all the avenues, the tunnels, all the paths I can imagine in my towards-him way, seeking the right time, the right word to reach him.

"She needs you, Stephen."

I write. I phone. I try approaching through friends, through strangers. I beg. I weep. Once I scream.

Stephen. Stephen.

Where into the wide world is he compelled to flee? I search throughout the cities of the world, calling for him in concert halls, in hotels. I run from echo to echo, looking for him, the one who leaves, the seeker of garlands. What demon sends me clawing through the night to my brother, my mother, my loved ones in their caves in their graves in the valley of dry bones singing the songs of childhood?

Stephen, I seek you diligently, and find a world of shovels overturning a soil full of dreams, half-dreams and sand, in a land of shadows. You seek to fashion a house of music where love can always live. But in all that labor, you only unearth for us our longing, our hands, mine and Obasan's, clutching at absences.

Most of the time when I call, he is in another country.

"Allo Naomi? I'm soree. Ee is not 'eer. Yes, I will tell 'eem you called."

Each time I think I cannot forgive him. But I do, over and over until gradually I reach out less, and then finally not at all.

"I can't come right now."

"When then?"

"I just can't right now. Don't lay your guilt trip on me."

During this year, a new heaviness forms and starts to grow. A harder, more solid shape. Anger. I begin to want him to know the hurt. I can feel the want. Then even that gives way. When my love for him is bludgeoned, a solid emptiness takes shape. A dry weeping, a form of gangrene, sets in.

What I feel some days is that unless that hard hollow is surgically removed, it will grow and overtake my very life. Maybe it's already done so. Perhaps if I had borne children I would have had no time to construct this deformity which I still bear. I'm reminded of a gory article Aunt Emily was reading in which a woman from San Francisco was poisoned from inside by an incompletely aborted fetus. There's a surgeon needed. There's a time for scalpels.

"The truth," Aunt Emily says, sounding uncomfortably like Pastor Jim and quoting a higher source than herself, "the truth will make you free. If you know what Stephen's truths are, you'll stop blaming him."

Aunt Emily is a minor surgeon of the soul, but her operations on me have not been successful. She herself bears no Stephen-shaped scars.

"Trouble with you, Nomi," she said once, glaring up at me over her reading glasses, "trouble is, you're too much of an accountant. One up for you, you wrote him a letter. One down for him, he never replied. Life's not like that."

I know she's right. It's not the accountant who makes the world go round. She must have sent me fifty letters to my one or two replies. Her answer to problems is to be busy. It works for her.

"Find someone else to help," she writes one time from Mexico.

"Call Mrs. Makino. Or ask a stranger. Every tenth stranger is an angel. And don't worry if you don't believe in angels. Just rely on them."

The advice is useless. No kindly, well-intentioned friend, stranger or available angel can fill in for Stephen, absent stepson, absent brother. I can feel the shape of our memories together evaporating from that huge room in my heart where he used to live.

Sometimes I sit by Obasan's bedside and plead with her spirit to release us both. Sometimes I rage at the skies. She is waiting, I believe, to say goodbye to Stephen. She is waiting for him to finish his tours. It seems at times that she can will herself to wait forever and she will outlast us all.

When Stephen was in high school, he tried to make a metronome out of a toy electric motor, but its tick was erratic. I think of it sometimes, watching the uneven pulse in Obasan's neck, her life in limbo, marking time, waiting for Death to arrive, to release her finally from the interminable toil and bondage of breath.

"Merry Christmasu ni. . . ." It feels like the water-drip torture, her mouth forming the same words, over and over, night unto night. I can hardly see the point of the barely awake, breathing, heaving effort. Where into the scheme of things does this joylessness fit?

Nakayama-sensei visits us several times. He cups his hands to her ear and sings hymns so loudly that some old men in the corridor come by and stand at the doorway, listening. "Good day," they nod. At times I think I see Obasan's mouth moving as if she's trying to sing along.

"Toh toki waga toh mo. . . ." My precious friend. . . .

The spring day Stephen returns to Montreal from his European tour, she sits up in bed for the first time in months and requests food. She drinks some soup. All day, she is alert, agitated, intent.

"Steebun. Rippa. Rippa," she says once clearly. "Stephen. Wonderful. Wonderful."

I try to stand in.

The phone call at 5:00 a.m. the next morning says she died at 3:30. I lie in bed and find her spirit everywhere—in the arrangements of the flowers above my head—one yellow blossoming and two green buds. It's as if she's telling me that death is the flowering and that we, the living, are not yet in bloom.

Her last act of service was to wait for Stephen in order to praise him. An extreme and extravagant gesture. In the end, he did not hear. Obasan, who devoted all her days to our remnant family and especially to Stephen, did not deserve that long last loneliness.

The Connoisseur of Chaos

> And of ourselves and of our origins
> In ghostlier demarcations, keener sounds.
>
> —Wallace Stevens

Mao Zedong had been in this library before, maybe seventy-one years ago exactly, here, looking at the same history books that he was to have shelved yesterday, not reading them but knowing what they promise for his imagination, looking out the dusty window to the sun setting on farmers seeding in the fields in another March or this March or not March at all, but April or May in 1918. That same night or another night, he may well have dreamed that soldiers were beating down his door as his friends gathered theory and strategy in secrecy, but woke up before they had a chance to bust through to a darkened room and see him sitting upright in bed and sweating and reaching for a cigarette like his namesake, but at least knowing from the shape of his cassette player against the window that this is now his room in

ALEX KUO's fiction has appeared in numerous magazines and anthologies. His most recent book is *Changing the River*, a collection of poems. The recipient of a National Endowment for the Arts fiction fellowship, he was *changchuned* to China in 1991–92 as a Fulbright scholar; there, in four winter months, he completed two novels, *Cold War* and *Point Blank*. He was born in Boston and schooled in Illinois and Iowa, and currently resides in Moscow, Idaho.

1989, and it is March, the planning meeting safely over, and the blood-soaked fields he saw from the library window zoned out in the last forty years of Beijing's annexation. Be cautious of involving the workers in your arrangements, someone had warned, it can easily end up in chaos, or worse.

After holding out for several weeks against an equally stubborn central committee, the students were beginning to get impatient and anxious. Mao was the first to get off the Boeing 747 in San Francisco, where a crowd of mainlander well-wishers, friends of the movement and reporters had gathered to greet him. He tucked in his shirt and gave a speech. Tiananmen Square was almost completely jammed with people, but somehow food had managed to get in and people out to the airport safely, the traffic-controlling students magically opening instant lanes for the occasional ambulance needed by an aspiring dissident.

Mao's girlfriend tugged at his sleeves while he was being interviewed on CNN. He must get out, disperse the crowd now, there will be trouble. At breakfast on June 3, her highly-placed father had instructed her not to go to the square anymore, that she and her Uygar boyfriend must stay away. The urgency in his voice convinced her, but Mao would not listen to her, that short irreversible step between imagination and memory. As the coordinator of the information center he could not leave, he had to stay to wrangle with rumors, examine the sources of disinformation, and disseminate the occasional news releases to the salivating international press gathered here for Gorbachev's visit. After he gave another speech into a VOA microphone, a girl yelled into the gathering twilight, "Mao Zedong! I love you!" And he replied "Me too, I love myself too!," somewhere between his personal act of survival and uncontrollable public weeping. At the main terminal a FAXed message waited for him: Congratulations on your Nieman scholarship at Harvard. Count on me for support. Best regards, Edward Kennedy. Already in the visible distance the PLA was gathering in numbers, but the students were convinced that this was not Hungary, that this was an army of the people's liberation, that the soldiers were on their side. Somewhere in there Mao attended a few classes, but it must have been in Cambridge a few weeks later because one morning a prompted message appeared on his computer screen: YOU ARE DRINKING THE BLOOD OF THE STUDENTS.

Some students from an engineering university were operating a portable generator to help Mao's lap-top computer keep track of the accumulating information that was beginning to arrive faster than the Kentucky Fried Chicken donated by interested downtown merchants. Sometime in here he found a Chinese restaurant in Boston, and after ducking a 7.62 bullet between the lions at Tiananmen Square more than half a century ago, he almost took it again from a Chinese waiter's meat cleaver for not leaving a tip in his attempt to break from his country's past, its corruption, nepotism, the hopelessness of opium, the right indistinguishable from the left, the absence of dreams. Events were accelerating beyond the organizers' anticipation, and with the whole world watching, it was becoming almost impossible now to distinguish between rumor and lore, just as it was for countless previous generations. Next it was lunch with Marlon Brando at Taos and later dinner with Andrei Sakharov in Boston before establishing a computer information network for the movement at Brandeis.

At the moment when he was paying the least attention after several sleepless days and nights, the sound of firecrackers popping off to the south of the square where the workers had gathered in great numbers astonished Mao, but he was not surprised, until he recognized it as the short and rapid, keener bursts of automatic gunfire. Mao's computer hit the concrete under the tent, and amidst the screaming and stench of smoke and popping of exploding bodies, several questions floated into the air: ABORT? IGNORE? RETRY? ESCAPE? For a moment he thought about changing his life now and removing his name from history, in the name of the father.

Safe

Cherylene Lee

My brother sets himself on fire every summer. He's not a pyro-maniac and it's not a political statement. He does it in front of people at Worlds of Water, U.S.A. My brother is a flame diver—a stuntman on a high diving platform who douses himself in flammable liquid, has someone light a torch to him, then launches himself into a cool blue pool, toes pointed, form correct—though that is hard to make out through all the flame and smoke. He says the crowds go wild because they feel afraid. He makes them feel safe.

Safe. That is the most important consideration for our family. Per-haps there is a Chinese gene encoded with a protein for caution. Or

CHERYLENE LEE is a prize-winning fiction writer, playwright, and poet whose works have been anthologized in *The Southern California Anthology 1985*, *Sister Stew*, and Lawrence Yep's *American Dragons*, among other collections. Her plays have been pre-sented at numerous venues, including East West Players and the Mark Taper Forum in Los Angeles, the Pan Asian Repertory in New York, the Kumu Kahua in Honolulu, and the Group Theater in Seattle.

perhaps it's because my father's tailor shop is not doing so well or because of my mother's blindness. Perhaps it's because my mother and father married late in life and weren't sure how to protect their children.

We try to take precautions. My mother won't go out at night for fear of what the darkness holds. She doesn't like me to take a shower after dinner for fear I might get a cramp and somehow drown in the shower's spray. She doesn't like me to walk home from school alone, nor does she like me to walk home with boys. She'd rather I walked home with girls, at least three for maximum protection so one can always run for help. I've tried to explain to her, I like walking alone, it's not always possible to walk in female threes, I don't even have that many girlfriends. "You have to watch out at your age, you can't be too safe," she warns, "but don't hang around with the fast ones."

My father is just as bad. He's so afraid someone will dent his car, he won't park in a lot that doesn't have two spaces side by side for his ten-year-old station wagon. He refuses to go into a grocery store if he could be the first or last customer—"That's when robbers are most likely to come." He won't eat in restaurants without first wiping the chopsticks, rice bowl, tea cup, or plate, silverware, and glass—"So many germs everywhere." He has more locks and alarms on his tailor shop door than the bank that's two doors down. It takes him ten minutes to open them up each day, turn off the alarms, before calling my mother to let her know that he has arrived safely.

We live in San Francisco—a city with its share of dangers though my parents have done their best to shield my brother and me from having to face most of them. More than from just physical harm, they've tried to protect us from loss—loss of face, loss of happiness, loss of innocence. So far we have been protected by their constant vigilance. Not that I have been sheltered so much I can't go places on my own or do things without my parents' consent, but their warnings, cautions, and dire predictions have had an effect. While I have always felt safe and have never wanted for anything, neither can I say that I've ever wanted at all. I have never been in danger, never known a need for risk. That's why I was so shocked when my brother announced he wanted to become a flame diver.

It isn't as risky as it seems, at least according to my brother who claims he could do the dive in his sleep. He wears a special flame-retardant suit. It protects him head to foot from the flames that consume him three times a day, six days a week, three months of the year. His summer job—his only job—hasn't changed him much except that he has no facial hair. The suit shields him from burns, but the wind sometimes blows flames under his protective helmet, singeing the hair off his face. The first summer he started doing this work, it took me awhile to recognize what was different about him when he sat down to dinner. He had no eyebrows, no eye lashes, just eyes, big brown eyes that seemed too large for the rest of his face. Since then he's taken to drawing in eyebrows with an eyebrow pencil because he doesn't want people to worry. Otherwise he's normal, though for a while I admit I was afraid of my brother. Who was this guy who grew up with me and suddenly became a flame diver? I thought maybe he would turn into some awful monster with scarred flesh and a swollen head from the fire and adulation. But my brother remains the same—shy, soft-spoken, introverted. Maybe he's happier these days or maybe I just think that because I am relieved. After hearing so much about danger, all he's lost are his eyebrows.

I've never seen my brother actually do his stunt though our father has many pictures of his dives hanging on the walls of his tailor shop. My brother won't let any of us watch him. He thinks we'll jinx him and we don't want to do that. He hasn't let us watch him since a high school diving meet three years ago when he made the varsity swim team. On his final and hardest dive of that meet, his foot slipped during his preparation jump causing him to start his backward twist out of control and his head to nick the edge of the platform. Our mother, already nearly blind, became hysterical even before the blood began oozing up in the water. By instinct she started screaming, "My boy, my boy!" the instant his head made contact, before anyone else knew something was wrong. Her screams echoed like a wailing gull inside the indoor swim gym. Luckily my brother wasn't badly hurt, ten stitches closed him up, but he was so embarrassed by our mother's shrieking that he asked us not to attend anymore, our presence brought him bad luck. That's why we all stay away now and only look at the pictures of his dives after he's already done them. When we know he's safe.

According to my mother, her eyesight started going bad because my father's eyes wandered. Years ago, when his tailor shop was in Chinatown, his clients were mostly women. He made cheongsams, the tight-fitting Chinese dresses the girls in the Miss Chinatown contest wear. He also did special occasion clothes, Chinese jackets, western-style wedding dresses, men's suits and such, but his busiest time of the year used to be the months before Chinese New Year when the Miss Chinatown contest was held. He would carefully take the measurements of each eager contestant, help her choose material that brought out her best coloring—mostly variations on fire-engine red—and cut the gowns so that they showed off each girl to her best advantage. My mother used to help my father by doing the embroidery on the dresses. Dragons and phoenixes were her favorite and my mother's embroidery was beautiful, small stitches of metallic thread, so fine they looked like brush strokes. She never needed a pattern, the dragons and phoenixes appeared in her head, she saw their outlines, their wings outstretched, their images flying on satin or silk which guided her hands as if by magic.

Her embroidery made my father's work much sought after, but one day she claimed her husband of 12 years was taking too much time getting the measurements of a young girl. His hands lingered a bit too long over the tape encircling her hips. After that my mother refused to do any more embroidery. She said her eyesight was failing, though she saw with bitter sharpness all the times my father's eyes seem to pause over a young girl's figure. My mother refused to see a doctor. She claimed her vision was a gift of the gods, just like her dragons and phoenixes, and my father must be up to something very bad to make it become so blurry. She became so enraged at women entering the shop, she insisted on taking their measurements herself, though indeed her eyesight was very poor and she often mistook the numbers on the tape causing much grief during the fitting sessions. Without her special embroidery and because of her mistaken measurements, my father's business suffered. He became just another tailor, his prices were considered high, his patterns a bit old-fashioned. My father decided to move his shop away from Chinatown, to a neighborhood where he would have more men for clients, not young girls seeking the Miss Chinatown crown, and thereby give my mother some peace.

But the neighborhood he chose did not give them peace. The taquerias and salsa music, the easy gatherings of young men at street corners, the rapid Spanish spoken in shops made both my father and mother feel out of place. My mother stopped going to work with my father and preferred to stay at home. She spent her time making "frogs"—Chinese buttons of thin braid twisted into three circles forming the bulges of a frog's head and eyes. She didn't have to see in order to make these buttons, she could feel her way along. She knew by instinct the exact place where stitches were needed to hold the button's shape. But Chinese buttons were not popular items in my father's new location. My parents' caution toward the outside world increased with my father's diminishing income. Only the family home felt safe to them and this is what they tried to impart to both my brother and me.

Of course my parents didn't want my brother to become a flame diver. They didn't even want him to join the swim team in high school—"too many accidents happen in pools"—but my brother didn't tell them he joined until after he'd already done it. I helped him forge our parents' signatures on the school release form, as he had done for me whenever I cut class. He didn't tell them the truth until after his first competition when he won first place for the platform swan dive. That gave them something to brag about and brag my father did. None of his customers could ever leave his shop without some comment on the first-place ribbon hanging on my father's wall. Our parents didn't like that my brother had gone behind their backs —my father never mentioned that part or my role in the conspiracy —but their pride in my brother's accomplishment did mollify some of their fear. I suppose the possibility of a college scholarship also helped. My father couldn't afford to send my brother to college—he'd used his life savings moving his shop—and since my brother wasn't too academic, his talent for diving, risky as it was, seemed the best path toward the safety of college. My father thought my brother would get a diving scholarship, learn a risk-free well-paying profession, give up his high diving ways after graduation, and live a safe life ever after.

My brother didn't get a scholarship. Although he had a spectacular swan dive, he couldn't seem to master any other. Something happened to his orientation when he tried to perform twists and somersaults. Maybe that time he hit his head made him fearful of hitting the platform again. He couldn't seem to get the spin of going head over heels quite right. When he tried a half twist or a backward gainer, his body went over too far or sometimes not far enough. He suffered spectacular belly flops. He was such a perfectionist though, he practiced diving for hours, but usually only his favorite one—the elegant and beautiful swan dive. A repertory of one dive wasn't enough to impress college recruiters, who thought my brother odd in his singular passion for swan dives. He was looked at and passed over many times during his senior year. Our parents were crushed that my brother wasn't asked to try out for any college team, but my brother didn't seem to mind. He told me one night he thought he could perform swan dives for a living.

"Look at these guys," he showed me a magazine that advertised tours to Mexico displaying muscular men in skimpy bathing suits diving off impossibly high cliffs. "Nothing but swan dives. People pay to see this."

"But you're not Mexican. And those cliffs are so high."

"It doesn't matter, I'm not going to do cliffs. There are other ways to make dives exciting. Look at this." He pulled out another magazine showing tours to Puerto Rico. This ad pictured tourists outside a fancy hotel looking entranced at the sight of a man, encased in flames, diving into a deep blue pool. The tourists clutched at their drinks, their mouths and eyes open in amazement. The caption read: "Thrills everywhere, with comfort you can't compare. Come to the island that has it all—Puerto Rico."

"This is more what I had in mind."

"Puerto Rico?"

"No I'm going to become a flame diver. I can do it better than this guy. Look, he's not even vertical going in."

"But how can you, where can you—" I could hardly ask a question. None of us had ever been out of the state, let alone leave home for such far off lands as Mexico or unimaginably, Puerto Rico.

"I can do it here."

"We don't have a swimming pool."

"God you're so dumb. I'm talking about Worlds of Water, U.S.A. It's only 30 miles from here. It's the perfect place. People are tired of watching animals do tricks for them. They feel guilty about it. They would rather see a man on fire than dolphins going through flaming hoops."

"Wait till mom and dad hear this." I could already imagine their torrents of protests. They hated candles on birthday cakes, their fear of fire was so great.

"They'll come around," my brother assured me. "It's what I want to do."

When I was thirteen, my mother asked for her embroidery basket to see if I possessed her talent. She sat me down with scraps of cloth, a packet of needles, and spools of thread though her eyesight was so poor by then, she could no longer thread the needles. She told me to close my eyes and picture a mighty dragon. She told me to feel its power, feel the flames shooting from the mouth. "Let this image guide your hands, the needle will follow the flames."

I closed my eyes and tried to see her dragon. I tried to feel its heat and let the needle follow. But I was constantly pricking myself, the thread tangled, the cloth bunched up. When I looked at my clumsy stitches all I saw were chicken scratches, uneven threads, unraveling patterns, my mother's nerves frayed at the edge. I had no dragons and phoenixes in me. My mother told me to go wash my hands and be careful putting away the scissors. She knew I hadn't inherited her gift, but she protected me just the same. She said such embroidery was not in fashion, not important anymore. We never tried again.

"I didn't raise my son to perform silly tricks for strangers," was my father's first reaction. "You are not a trained animal."

"I'm not a caged one either," I'd never heard my brother use that tone, especially in front of our father. "I can do it, dad. I've been practicing diving for years."

"High school meets, this is different."

"What's wrong with going to city college?" mother asked. "You can learn a trade, meet a nice girl. Who will you meet at this water world? Nobody there but fish."

"Ma, I have learned a trade. I know how to dive."

"Trying to kill yourself is no way for my son to make a living."

"Diving isn't trying to kill myself, dad. It feels like flying to me."

"Didn't you hear how many people were killed in that plane crash over Mexico? Flying isn't safe anymore." Our mother knew how to change the subject.

"I'm talking about diving, Ma. Swan dives."

"So why do you have to set yourself on fire?"

"Because I need a gimmick to make it look exciting. Dangerous."

There it was—the D-word. They'll never go for it, I thought. How could he expect their support when he played on their worst fears? I felt sorry for my brother then. All his diving dreams and he had to choose the wrong word.

"But it only has to look dangerous, dad. Really it's very safe."

I don't think my father was always so cautious. He was quite the gambler once. He used to go to weekly poker games in Chinatown before he moved his shop. He used to talk about opening a factory or a specialty store featuring mom's embroidery. But that was before the trouble began, before she started accusing him.

When I look at my father now, sighing as he hems a pair of trousers, replaces a zipper, or watches my mother making her buttons, I don't think he ever had a wandering eye. I think my mother must have made it up because her vision was blurred. I think she was afraid without her embroidery, my father would no longer need her. She thought he would find a younger woman, leave her with two children, middle-aged, blind, and alone.

But that never happened. I think my father felt embarrassed that he had no dragon in his head. My mother was the one with the gift. She had the visions that spread to his cloth. She had the instinct that knew just how to hold buttons and things together. He was afraid he would lose her. They didn't know how to reassure themselves, so they moved the shop to a new location and tried to shield my brother and me from further loss in a dangerous world.

Three nights after my brother made his announcement that he was going to become a flame diver, my father brought home this special material—something like rubber only more flexible—and spent hours gluing it together with a special flame retardant glue. He placed a glued piece over our kitchen stove testing to see if it melted, putting his hand on the burner to see how hot it grew. He timed how long it took before the material grew too hot for his hand. He glued squares of it together to see if he could take more heat. My mother insisted my father not risk his sewing hands and stuck her own into the makeshift glove holding it over the gas flame, turning the stove to high, staring with unseeing eyes at the blue circle of heat, patiently daring it to burn her. My parents experimented for a month with different materials, different glues, different thicknesses, different flames before deciding a suit could indeed be made that would protect their flesh and blood. Engulfed by my brother's passion, only they could make him safe.

I haven't told my parents yet, not even my brother though maybe he would understand. I see a man after school. He lives two blocks from the school and I go to his house everyday before I walk home alone. He is an older white man, not as old as my father. He called to me from his window one day as I was walking home and asked if I could bring in his paper and check his mail box for him. When I brought in his paper and mail, he was very polite and apologized for troubling me, but he couldn't get out of bed. He asked if I had a few minutes and would I mind reading something to him, he wanted to hear another voice. He asked me to read Ann Landers' column. I think he was very lonely. I read to him and he thanked me and that's how it began. Now I read to him for 15 minutes everyday, sometimes things from the newspaper, sometimes things from magazines, mostly magazines about sex that he gets delivered in the mail. The magazines are the type my parents would never approve of me reading. I sit at the foot of his bed and read and he listens to me with closed eyes. Sometimes his body tenses and I see sweat break out on his forehead. He listens so intently, I feel heat coming off his body. He's always very polite to me. He says that I am a gift. He says that when he hears my voice, it helps him to feel alive.

My brother tells me what a rush it is to be a sponge for everyone's fear. To be so focused on what he does, he only hears his own heartbeat. He's vaguely aware of the ladder he climbs to the platform hanging above the pool. He doesn't hear the roll of the drum, he doesn't hear his name announced, he doesn't hear the height of the platform called out, he doesn't see the water. Encased in his protective suit, glued with familial pride, he feels which way the wind blows by the way it buffets his body. He tells me the exact routine. The number of deep breaths he takes, the number of sprays of butane needed to coat him from head to foot, the sound of the torch which explodes with a roar, the moment he holds his flaming hands outstretched before closing his eyes and flying. He tells me he opens his eyes at the peak of his arch—a dragon sailing through pure blue silk before tucking his head and splashing into the satin smooth mouth of the pool.

And I have imagined the crowd's awe building up with the flames, the tightening nerves with the drum roll, the fearful split second of silence, the collective breath for this human torch against blue sky, the lesser sun god, this crazy kid. And then I've imagined the plunge, a blurred arch of orange and smoke, a curve straightening to a lightning shaft, a sizzling hiss as he breaks the water, the cheers welling up like ocean waves sweeping aside stunned silence. I imagine when my brother surfaces and swims to the side of the pool, the audience sees a phoenix rising, their fears melt, the smiles grow, the celebration is complete. And as he doffs his helmet, waving his arms and smiling broadly, he reassures the crowd that all is well, nothing bad has happened, no loss has occurred. He dove through fire and survived. He lives to dive again. Everything is normal.

Geography One

Russell Leong

Spring rains appeared as the month ended, heightening the tropical humidity that enabled me to sleep at night with only a thin covering. Still waking up alone in the small hours before dawn, as I had been doing all month, I decided to leave Los Angeles for a day.

In empty cans scattered about my backyard mosquitoes began to deposit larvae in the tepid rainwater that had collected. Let them breed. I bought twenty tins of tuna fish from the Thrifty's Drugstore because they were fifty cents each. It was the easiest way to eat. I had pared my living habits down, not giving much thought to preparing any food outside of canned. Sometimes I left remainders for the neighborhood cats to eat in the yard. Even the *Times* was stacked haphaz-

RUSSELL LEONG moves to the mallet of the wooden fish drum. A writer, editor, and filmmaker, he was a member of the original Kearny Street Asian American Writers Workshop in San Francisco. His fiction and poetry appear in the first *Aiiieeeee!* anthology; *Tricycle: The Buddhist Review*; *ZYZZYVA*; and *The Open Boat: Poems from Asian America,* among other collections. His book of poetry, *In the Country of Dreams and Dust,* was published in 1993.

ardly on the steps; I did not bother to unfold the soggy pages or read the news.

In advance, I checked my car's highway map of Orange County, the region south between Los Angeles and San Diego. Fifty miles one way meant a daily commute for some people; for me, it was a rare journey, a hundred miles roundtrip. But I had never driven that many miles out of Los Angeles and recalled only the cross streets—Brookhaven and Katella—in Little Saigon. No address or phone number. Though Lạc Hải and I had been to the temple twice, at the time I did not pay attention to the route. Today I would search alone.

On the way home from work the night before, I stopped by the Thai market in Hollywood and bought two large boxes of dried Chinese noodles for the *sifu* of the temple. The market had escaped the burning of the riots last month, but the block still held the acrid smell of other charred buildings, an odor intensified by the May rains. I had withdrawn two ten-dollar bills from my wallet and placed them in a white envelope, scribbling my name and Hai's on the flap. The twin bills symbolized a kind of symmetry that I had hoped to achieve in my life. I placed a small framed photo he'd given me of himself into the shopping bag and put everything in my car trunk.

I needed to return to the place where I had felt home, a stranger among fellow strangers. If Vietnamese had been refugees to America when they first arrived, I was ironically in this position now, a refugee to that house that served as temple, shelter and garden for the Buddhist monk.

The Interstate Five funneled my car smoothly past working class industrial towns—Montebello, Commerce, Downey, Norwalk—southeast of downtown Los Angeles. The morning was warm, smudged with brown haze at the horizon. Sweat soaked my shirt. Billboard mirages of Las Vegas casino shows in the desert and sleek Japanese automobiles glittered between real palm trees and poplars. I held my speed at seventy miles an hour as my eyes focused on the road signs ahead. Santa Fe Springs. Anaheim. La Palma. I drove on. The freeway sign said "Twenty-two, Garden Grove Freeway Connector," which would lead me west to Little Saigon.

•

Housing on these suburban streets—Magnolia, Euclid, Beach—was arranged without regard for pedestrian life: one side of the street had fifteen-foot concrete sound barriers which backed middle class housing developments. Directly across from them on the same street, older, single family dwellings from the 1950s and '60s—the kind built on concrete slabs—faced the blank walls. Newer developments, built cheaply of beige stucco, segregated themselves from the older houses.

Finally, Brookhaven. My eyes searched its length for the simple tract house which served as the temple. The lush oriental arrangement of rose bushes, aloes, peach trees, sago palms, and the plaster statue of Kwan-yin—goddess of mercy—fronted the house. I stopped the car, took the shopping bag from the trunk and walked across the street. A single pair of men's black shoes was on the steps, not the usual dozen pair of shoes. The door was shut. I knocked once, then again. The window curtains were drawn. A black umbrella leaned against a windowsill. Hung outside the door was a talisman made of old Chinese copper coins laced up with red cotton string in the shape of a sword. No answer. Ten o'clock. Maybe the *sifu* was still asleep or out for the morning.

I resigned myself to waiting. The *sifu* had cut the flowering bodhi tree down to almost half of its original size. He said that the roots could spread under and beyond the house; in Vietnam they grew to gigantic dimensions. The smell of the roses he tended permeated the air. I paced up and down the narrow entrance way.

I rapped on the door again. Silence. In my anxious walking back and forth, I counted forty-five steps across the width of the house lot. A dirty blue Pontiac stopped beside me. An Asian man about my size got out, walked up to the temple door and knocked. Turning toward me, he asked in Vietnamese if anyone was home. I answered in English. He smiled.

"I'm in trouble. I need three dollars for gas." I gave him three rumpled bills.

"Thanks," he said, stuffing them into his shirtpocket. "I haven't been here in years. When I first came to this country ten years ago, I visited the temple. I promised Buddha that if the boat made it to Thailand, and if I ever got to America, that's what I would do. *Sifu* was kind, and rented me a room until I could settle down."

When I didn't respond, he continued.

"I'm a welder, but I got laid off yesterday. Maybe my wife will leave me because I took her forty dollars last night to the Bicycle Club. I lost it all. I can't stop gambling."

He sat himself down on a rock under one of the two peach trees at the entryway. "Here, sit down." He motioned with his hand. "It's cooler in the shade." I sat next to him on the other flat rock, absorbed by the droning of bees and passing automobiles.

"Those monks sleep late sometimes. They study old books at night," he said.

"Maybe he went shopping for food."

"If you see the monk, tell him I came by. I'll come back later."

He stood up. We shook hands and he hurried off without telling me his name.

After waiting two hours I got into my car and drove around the block to the corner shopping mall. Lạc Hai and I had walked through here the last time we visited the temple together. He bought yellow mums and gladiolas from the florist for the temple altar.

I returned to the temple but the door was still shut. I left the two boxes of noodles at the step. Should I leave the envelope with the money in the mailbox, in the plastic bag with the noodles, or slip it under the door? I decided that the door was safest, but retrieved the framed photograph of Hai from the bag.

The sun's glare obscured the image of Hai pressed behind the glass: the small petulant mouth and dark eyes set obliquely into the pale face that I remembered. On the surface of the finger-smudged glass, I could sense my own features reflected.

The rains had swollen the door tight and there was barely space underneath. I nudged the envelope in. Barking from behind the door—Phúc, the temple dog. He tugged at the envelope and it disappeared under the door for good. I hoped he would give it to his master. "Phúc, Phúc," I shouted. Perhaps he would recognize my voice.

Once more I drove off. I was hungry. At a Chinese-Vietnamese cafe I ate all of the squid and vegetable lunch plate. Returning to the temple, I saw that the package of noodles was still propped against the door. The man who had gambled away his luck and money had not come back. I would return to Los Angeles.

The night you left me you avoided my eyes. With my right index finger, I trace the printed image of the pink lotus framed in yellow: *Trà Mạn Sen*, Lotus Tea / 100 grams or 3.5 ounces. Red cardboard box, now emptied. I stir the last of the green leaves into a cup of hot water. The monk, I recall, had served us such a tea at the temple. But that evening we did not drink anything.

Now my throat is dry, as are my eyes. I refuse to cry over this common affair between men. *Junze zi jiao dan ru shui*—between gentlemen, friendship is transparent as water. That's about all I remembered from studying Chinese and that adage came in handy now.

More clarity: tacked on my kitchen wall, a torn newspaper clipping. On the paper, words by Aung San Suu Kyi, the Burmese leader under house arrest for her political speeches. She had written about coolness which lies beneath the shade of trees, of teachers, and of Buddha's teaching. I had cut the article out of the *L.A. Times*. I was not Buddhist, but I was moved because she had spoken her thoughts to thousands of people, whereas I have no one to speak to now.

I lock and unlock my hands, from fist to open palm, tracing the fate lines without caring whether they meant anything. Rub each fingertip. The tea is not strong enough, its bitterness turning to sweet aftertaste on the tongue. On the kitchen sideboard the bottle of *Crown Royal*, which a friend had given us for Tết, the lunar New Year. I uncap it, sniffing up the fumes, but recap the bottle.

I want to see you, Lạc Hai, your face clearly in my eyes. For I am a Chinese man from America, left dry by a man of water who was born in the delta between the Red and Black rivers.

Why were you born? Where did you come from? I'm standing in the kitchen, I realize, staring at the fissured plaster walls. At you. Offspring of Lạc Long Quân and Âu Cỏ, who between them according to legend produced one hundred eggs. Fifty of their children returned with their father to the seacoast; the others remained in the mountains with their mother. Those who went to the seas and the deltas became the Vietnamese.

So goes the tale. And thousands of years later you were born, Hai. How you came to America is your own story to tell. But how we met is mine. You thought you had the last word. No. My story is the last word since you will never say "yes" to me.

Blue outdoor floodlights spot the palm trees and bougainvillea, linger on Spanish roof tiles and French doors which link the hillside deck to the garden. The literal truth comes out in cliches: Hollywood Hills, circa 1920s neo-Italianate stucco mansionette. The living room was dressed for parties: gilded Indonesian wood carvings on plexiglass bases; stuffed white couches. A hundred decorative Asian men—Thai, Chinese, Filipino, Japanese, Vietnamese—were dancing on the hardwood floor, together with voracious Anglos who never looked as youthful as the Asians, even if they were younger. Double platters of fried chicken, lumpia, chow mein, lots of rice and American pies: peach, apple, cherry. International oriental buffet. Two cut-glass punchbowls overflowed with sangria and citrus rinds.

You were a gypsy, floating about the room, a red bandana around your shining brow, one silver earring, and a vest of dark leather. You never threw me a glance, but I followed your cheekbones and lips with my eyes as desire caught at my throat. Three days later, I telephoned you.

That's how it started, this encounter, an excursion that would convey my body and spirit through channels I had not foreseen.

The black Toyota pickup hurtles through the smog-white afternoon, heading south on the Interstate Five toward Little Saigon. You drive fast, sunglasses framing the bridge of your nose, hands cleanly maneuvering the stickshift with long fingers. Following the curve of the freeway, you tell me how you've traveled the roads of the world and ended up here.

Ten years ago, at eighteen, you went from Buddhist temple to temple seeking the peace of mind that each monastary promised. You shaved your head. You meditated on your knees. You talked past midnight with your teachers, wore out pair after pair of sandals strolling the muddy fields of Taiwan, Thailand, Japan, France. Skinny chickens, heat and cold, and thick-walled buildings were the same in every country. Bare floors. Old books. A few compassionate monks. Most of them, who just followed rituals without risking heart or mind, disappointed you in the end.

You observed their teachings well enough, but could not quell other desires. That desire which still causes your body temperature to rise in fever. But neither meditation nor lovemaking could contain or release this heat, for your pleasure walks the same path as your pain.

"Just friends for today," you tell me. "Tomorrow is less certain than the past."

Traveling a route you know by heart, you seek the pure sky of a childhood that was never yours. From dawn until dusk, your sky was fractured with rockets and fragments of fusclage. For your wartime hunger, Catholic orphanage nuns beat you with bamboo canes, bruising your child's skin.

A stranger to your history, I am neither father, brother nor lover. In the truck I touch your thigh. But you draw back, not trusting me or anyone else who touches you.

Exit Little Saigon: we swerve past the green enameled sign onto Bolsa, a boulevard crammed with two-storied strip malls—Vietnamese bakeries, banks, beauty parlors, stationery stores, coffeeshops, bookstores. Snack on sweet rice cakes and drink iced concoctions of brown sugar, red dates and seaweed. You drink and look away. I would have talked with you in a new language for me: Vietnamese. Now silence runs deeper between us.

You wanted to stop at the temple to visit your *sifu*, with whom you had studied for several months. First we buy flowers for the altar, pink, yellow and white mums. Inside the truck, I bring the large bouquet to my face. The petals darken into fingers that gesture with a sudden life of their own, settling upon my eyelids and lips.

The conversation between you and the monk was all yours. You sat across from each other in a corner of the room. The *sifu* did not look directly at you and not to me at all. But I stole a look at him— at his face tanned from gardening and at his clean-shaven head and nape. Then I bowed by the altar and left the room, exiting the side door to the backyard. It was a derelict space which backdropped the temple, painted yellow and trimmed at the roof, eaves and windows in red. For Vietnamese, as for Chinese, these colors must be auspicious.

The yard was large for a tract home's. The diving board on which I sat overhung the edge of the swimming pool drained of its water. A concrete kidney-shaped grave was swollen with the legs of odd chairs, cracked tables and a hundred aloe plants in black plastic tubs.

Somewhere inside the temple the monk was chanting. His sutras seemed to unlock doors, lift windows and solid walls, sweeping past wooden eaves of the western house and alighting upon the aloes in the yard.

I sat in the midst of the debris, discarding another layer of my life. Last week a friend told me that seven of his buddies had died of AIDS. No one wanted to know. In Asian families, you just slowly disappeared. Your family rented a small room for you. They fed you lunch. Dinner. Rice, fish, vegetables.

At my feet aloes thrust green spikes upwards from black dirt, promised to heal wounds and burns, to restore the skin's luster. From this ground pure light would surely arise over suburban roofs and power lines, illuminating the path of green aloes by which I would return to the house.

Inside the temple kitchen the monk was already cutting cabbages on the nicked formica table for supper. I found myself alone with him. You were gone to some other part of the house. Sound of sink water running down the drain.

From eastern deserts Santa Ana winds blow inwards to Los Angeles. Sand submerges my feet and ankles, then rises and fills my eyes. The wind plays tricks. I am alone in bed listening to it. Noises of branches and leaves rush against each other as arms and legs brush over mine. Burying me. My body is bloated with chrysanthemum leaves—a Mexican birthday pinata—waiting for children to break it open with sticks. What will fall out? Flowers float on the *Cửu Long*—Mekong. Do white petals heed death or life? I do not know. Santa Ana winds blow through cheap condominium walls in the City of Angels, currents which sap the vines of my desire.

Dry throat, the night after you left. Fifth gin and tonic. I am at The Bar drowning in the shadows of Asian men half my age who gyrate on the dance floor. A white man standing beside me named Doug or Eddy is talking. I listen, laugh, but do not turn my face to him. I wait for you to walk in with a new friend, for you both to cast insinuating glances, like violets, at this roomful of men. Only after I have seen this with my own eyes, will I leave. Dark petals unfurl, mocking me. Maybe it is the gin and tonic. I take black coffee, and after that, another gin.

I probably look younger than my thirty-seven years, in a white nylon windbreaker, snug levis, black sneakers. Yet I detest the remnants of youth on myself.

In the photograph, Hai, you were wearing a long-sleeved shirt that covered your arms, but it was not your concealed body or veiled spirit that most intrigued me. It was your journey that directed my imagination, as I had never ventured outside the country of my birth.

China was a mental atlas of winding rivers and mountain ranges; Vietnam was still farther away in space and time. Beyond the black and white images of soldiers, helicopters and villages captured on my television screen, that southern land was once the impassioned object of an anti-war demonstration that I had joined twenty years ago.

My stomach turns, entrails holding in rancid water, petals, leaves. The churning of Santa Ana air gathers momentum, drowning out the D.J.

If I make it home sober tomorrow morning, the sky should clear from the wind. The bartender does not want to pour me another drink. I insist.

"I'll give you a flower," I tell him. "Have you heard of "Flowers of Evil"? By a French poet. But I forget his name tonight."

The bar man relents.

Around me, floors begin to crack and sway. Chrysanthemums fall apart, their ravaged petals plucking up stray insects. Even hands to my ears cannot shut out the wind. Stop.

The television blazes. We live in the heat of the desert, in jerry-built towns of plastic pipe and drywall. I long for waters past.

In the tenth century, Ngô Quyền defeated a Chinese armada in the Bach Dang river. He ordered huge timbers tipped with iron to be buried in the tidal shallows. At high tide these were hidden, and when Chinese troopships appeared, lighter Vietnamese boats went out to meet them. Submerged timbers skewered the Chinese hulls. Then Vietnamese boats, their prows painted with lucky eyes, swiftly advanced and burned the Chinese ships.

Reaching the alluvial plains, between the brows of the Red and Black rivers, you can see the features of the land. Your face is flushed, sweating. Heat rises from your chest and belly. I press a cool white towel on you. More cold tea. You fall asleep in my arms. Maybe a fever, via these erratic winds, has seeped into your nostrils.

You get a haircut. It's almost like being home—mirrors and bicycles casually propped up below the banyan trees, and men, young and old, having a haircut and a shave. Only in Little Saigon your haircut is indoors under cool fluorescent lights. But the same extended conversations, the same jokes. Your hair falls to the floor in dark wisps and you flirt with the Amerasian haircutter. You feel almost home, but not quite. Even at my apartment, settled on the black leather and chrome couch with your Vietnamese martial arts novels and cassette tapes, you're awkward with my domesticity—your long legs angled out in borrowed cut-off sweatpants.

When we go out to eat with friends you joke in Vietnamese. The most I can do is utter the dishes in Chinese syllables. But that is not enough. Your accent betrays a thousand uprisings: revolts against forebearers and foreigners; against the Chinese, French, Japanese, Americans. When we get home one night you had not spoken with me at all: English disappeared from your vocabulary. I ask what's wrong. You turn your head away from mine on the pillow, muttering: "If you want soap opera dialogue then just turn on the TV okay?"

"No soap opera—Chinese opera. How about 'Taking Tiger Mountain by Strategy'?" I laugh, deflecting your sarcasm. "Don't forget I'm still Chinese."

"How would you know anything about taking? You never had your home taken away like I did. By Communists. In Saigon my stepfather had a three story house, with a small ballroom on the top floor. A balcony, with blue tiles, that we danced or slept on during the summer . . ."

Not wanting to hear the same story again, yet still wanting you, I smother your face with the coverlet and crawl quickly beneath it, bringing my face to your belly and pressing my lips farther down. I take you in my mouth until all I can hear is your breathing. Your body tosses and turns. Wordless. You come without touching me, your hands slackened against the pillow. So your silence is against me, a being who is both American and Chinese.

In the morning, I shave the shadow off my face. With the same razor that a man or a woman who decides to take Buddhist vows might use. A clean blade which bares the heads of those who seek Gautama wherever they may find themselves—Los Angeles, Canton, Saigon.

I learned that Vietnam lies in one time zone. That's all I remembered from Geography One, Junior High School, about Vietnam.

We lie awake. You speak to me across one zone, and I speak to you in another. Your thoughts turn away earlier or my words tumble out later. Or, just the reverse. Time zones which divide us.

Whenever you are alone you drive to Redondo beach and watch the water. Hai: the name for "water" which is your real name. Water which takes you back to the plains between the Red and Black rivers. One day you asked me the English name of the *mai* tree, with small yellow blossoms, which opens during Tết. I did not know the English name.

•

On the kitchen table: the green plate from which you ate, the cup from which you drank. You may not return, but I leave them anyway, as I leave your sandals at the door.

I fall deeper into sleep under which everything becomes transparent. My hands search for mineral places we had crossed together once. Your eyes travel farther back, to limestone hills above the river, dredging up timbers tipped with shining iron. Buried in river water. Hidden at high tide. Timber after timber, a forest of weapons. I stare at the deceptive calmness of the water.

I drop the teacup on the kitchen floor. It does not shatter, but remains whole. The cup holds departed kin, a spirit which wants to stay here. Neither libations nor liaisons could free me of it. Nonsense. Superstition. I am a college-educated Chinese American after all, raised in Queens, New York, by way of Connecticut, Seattle, and finally, Los Angeles.

Wash the night away. Rinse the plates and cups. Put them away, less the one in hand. Leaves, dark as sand or seeds, cleave to the bottom of my cup.

A truck lumbered past me, forcing me to steer my compact car against the next lane divider. Soon the glassy towers of downtown insurance and banking companies thrust their heads through the smog. The drive back up was faster than the ride down. I reached Hollywood where it was still the middle of the afternoon. I went to the Holiday Gym, a pink exercise palace with pop music piped in from dawn to dusk. In the mid-afternoon it was almost deserted. Methodically, on the chrome and red vinyl-padded machines, I crossed from one to the other, flexing back and biceps, doing situps and leg lifts to bury the time.

Though I had not seen the *sifu* I felt relieved even to have located the temple again. The steel-chromed bars rose up and down in front of my eyes. Sweat lined my face. I was imprisoned in my exertion of choice. I needed to sweat, whether it was under the sun or induced within this air-cooled environment. A few middle-aged Korean women with rubber headcaps were swimming in the lap pool. Their pale heads and shoulders, bobbing up and down in the green water, took on the androgynous cast of fleshy sea creatures.

After showering, I went home, opened a can of tuna fish and a can of cream of mushroom soup, and poured all of it over leftover rice. The kitchen clock read 5:30 P.M. Dead heat of traffic. I could wait. Maybe I would drive back to the temple tonight. Rewrapping the picture of Hai in white paper, I put it beside the door, intending to bring it back with me.

Night on the Interstate Five released the day's torpor: automobile headlights turned upon each other, thousands of metallic bodies feeding heat and carbon exhaust to the hungry darkness. I drove slowly, yielding to the cars already in front of me. I reached the Garden Grove freeway which connected to Little Saigon, but the sign said "West Connector Lane Closed." Darkness. So I got off the East exit, opposite to where I wanted to go. The faceless buildings of a vast suburban shopping mall in the City of Orange surrounded me; it was fifteen minutes before I realized I was traveling in a circle, around the perimeter of the shopping center's department stores, now closed. I continued driving down the empty streets.

Irritated, I did not think to stop the car and check my map. Instead my eyes searched for Vietnamese shop signs, oriental mini-malls and people. The pedestrians on the sidewalk had dark hair and were not tall. I squinted at them, hoping they were Asian. More auto body shops, Taco food signs and liquor stores. This was not Little Saigon, but a Latino barrio, part of Anaheim or Santa Ana.

I stopped at a red light and rolled down my window, catching the attention of the Asian driver in a grey Nissan sedan beside my car. "Bolsa," I yelled, the main street of Little Saigon. He pointed his finger in the opposite direction. I thanked him, and made a U-turn at the next light. Residential blocks had the same concrete barriers that confounded my vision and direction. Looking for a gas station not yet closed, I found one. The Pakistani said, "Drive down for a couple of miles, you will pass Euclid, then Brookhaven and make a right."

I tanked up two dollars of gas in case I got lost. Almost eight-thirty.

The temple might be shut for the night or the *sifu* already asleep. Following the gas attendant's directions, I found Brookhaven and turned right. I pulled my car up near the next door to the temple and got out. As I approached the door, the one light shining in a back window suddenly turned dark. I knocked softly. In an instant, the window lit up again. The door opened.

An unfamiliar face peered out. In the porch light I did not know whether the smooth face was a man's or a woman's. The person greeted me in Vietnamese. In the back room, I could see the *sifu* adjusting his robe.

"*Sifu*," I called.

He asked me to come in and sit and introduced me to his assistant. Under the dim light, the young man looked all of fifteen, but must have been at least ten years older. *Sifu* explained that they had been separated twenty years by the war, but had run into each other in Los Angeles. As a child, the young man had lived next door to the monk's house south of Saigon. After the youth arrived in the U.S., he attended a year of junior college but had to drop out. He ended up here at the temple.

I hung my head, apologized for the late hour, and hoped that I had not disturbed them. I explained that I had come in the morning, but that the temple door was locked. The *sifu* said, "Oh, I thought it was some traveling monks who had dropped by to visit and left us those boxes of noodles."

I unwrapped the photo and showed it to the monk. With a look of consternation, he handed it back to me. Glancing away from me, he focused his eyes past the carved brass candlesticks and fruit-laden platters, to a point beyond the image of the gold-leafed Shakyamuni Buddha that occupied the center place on the altar table.

In English, he said: "You need not say more." Switching to Vietnamese, he paused between sentences to allow his assistant to translate:

"A bird wants more than it can eat, so it flies into the trap; a fish wants more than it can eat, so it catches the hook. You must know when you have enough." He pointed to the curtained windows.

"There, in the daytime, can you see the two trees at the entrance to this temple? When birds alight on the leaves, the trees do not show happiness. When the birds fly away, the trees do not reveal sadness. You must be like these two trees, neither happy nor sad, at the birds' comings and goings."

The room enveloped the three of us, our knees and feet touching the felt carpet.

"For being born is unhappiness, as being sick is unhappiness, as old age or dying is also unhappiness. But still another form of unhappiness is happiness itself."

I could feel my hands go warm, and pressed my palms onto the carpet beneath my legs. It was ten minutes, if that much. The *sifu*'s words resounded, as sound does, in the spaces within me.

"Now, go home and sleep."

I thrust the framed photograph of Lạc Hai into his hands. "He does not belong to me," I said.

I stood up and thanked his assistant for helping. As I reached the door, the terrier, Phúc, barked at me, wagging his tail. I looked back at the monk, about to ask if the dog had retrieved the envelope with the money, but *sifu* nodded his head in the affirmative even before my asking.

"Next time you come," he said, "we'll cook some of the noodles for you."

I brought my palms together, bowed, and backed out of the doorway. Someone switched off the porchlight. My shoes were dampened with night dew and I put them on in the dark.

Black Korea

Walter Lew

Or your little chop-suey ass will be a target . . .

—Ice Cube

Last summer, four black cops arrested me because I was "dat chinese man." You want proof? Get me the money I need for a lawyer—I'll pay you back extra after I win.

We do win.

•

EPISODE: After an afternoon of collecting quotations, diagrams, and photos for an essay on *DICTEE* (the masterpiece by a Korean American murdered by a security guard in SoHo), a night in the Library of Congress's basement video dungeon, two of First District's finest holding cages, and Central Cell Block.

For being "dat chinese man."

WALTER LEW is a poet, documentary producer, translator of Korean literature, and multimedia artist. He has been published in *New Worlds of Literature* and *Breaking Silence: An Anthology of Contemporary Asian American Poets. DIKTE for DICTEE,* Lew's book-length "critical collage" about the late Theresa Hak Kyung Cha's work, was published in Korea in 1992. He is co-editing a forthcoming anthology of Asian American writing.

IN THE BASEMENT OF THE LIBRARY OF CONGRESS: Sat for two hours while Mudbrain and crew tried to figure out forms and sign their names. "Do they want our weight or his?" "I don't know—that's a tough one. You better go ask the captain." Don't they have to read me Miranda rights or something? What are one's rights when there's no witness but four empowered gook-grillers? Twenty more minutes pass.

"Do we put in his birthdate or ours?"

"I don't know. That's a tough one."

"I guess I'll go ask the captain. Man, these are tough."

Then it's time for handcuffs and hauling me again for the ride to First District. Young admirer driving the cruiser coos to Mudbrain, "Jeez, I didn't know you had it in you." Badge no. 31 *thirty-one, thirty-one, 7 p.m.* I repeat like a mantra. His name, too—Not mine.

AT FIRST DISTRICT: Crew congratulates itself, "This is good—it sets a precedent." Denied release on citation by Metro PD because "You mean dat chinese man? He hasn't been in the country long enough," despite my documents, sister, and a *Business Week* reporter saying I was born & raised in Baltimore, 60 miles away, despite my Bawl'mer English. "Do we put in his birthplace or our birthplace?" Aint Chinee, you shitheads, r u F.O.B. from the congo?

No ancestral pine and guardian-graced hillock in Baltimore, 200 ri away, quaked at all this. Sleep, grandfathers grandmothers: I know you sigh already from your own history.

TWO HOURS LATER, STILL AT FIRST DISTRICT: Mudbrain and his fat crew shuffle out of station, smiling, assuring my sister and journalist friend (family name: Hong) that I will be free in minutes. Just working for the public goode, ma'am. *They have a dream! They have a dreee-*

am! That from a gook corpse on the proud flank of Capitol Hill, even morons can one day feast in the glad tidings of proMOtion and like the permed asshole with the citizen's achievement awards covering his left tit who got a hard-on-all-ovah-his-body whenever he pushed me around ("Stand behind me and put your thUMB out") *even the lowly He and All the Righteous Rest may rejoice as they trample over fallen yellars and ba-baloneyans, always holding high the colors of our world-champion Killah-nation in the cause of of . . . Liberty and Freedom for All . . . No, I mean the* NEW WORD ODOR! *Hail to the . . . I have* SEEN *the gLory of the*

Now solely Metro PD's meat, yours Truly, Lew.

Half-nelsoned and shoved away from my sister pleading beyond the door that my rights be honored. Hong notes down names and badge numbers. Dried blood-smears all over the cell's lemon brick.

FOLLOW THE YELLOW BRICK WALL: *DICTEE,* I remember your second image: last wishes carved in the wall of a mine by starving Korean slave children (All for the goode of Japan, ma'am.): *Omŏni pogoship'ŏ Pae-ga kop'ayo Kohyang-e kagŏship'ta* I look down at the steel bench and, after idly glancing along the scattered initials and dates there, discern in the dim fluorescent light that, near the middle, a few *Korean* letters have also been scratched into it. After fifteen minutes of staring and studying, I still cannot make them form a complete word. First syllable: *Mu,* probably meaning "non-", "with-out-", "not", or maybe it's the *mu* of "soldier, weapon, martial." Then a *ch* and *n,* but there are no vowels in between to make a full syllable. I conjecture that, since one cannot have anything in the cell except the minimum of clothing—even my shoelaces have been confiscated—maybe police came at that point and took the stylus or the prisoner away.

Mu ch n

•

OFF TO CENTRAL CELL BLOCK: The whole airless paddy wagon to myself, wire tight around the wrists, doubled through my beltloops, marking more flesh each time we bounce through a rut and I'm bumped around on the metal plank, window so small and dull I don't know where the hell I am, back-and-forth around the city cuz brain-child forgot my papers.

"You're spending the night here in CCB, no matter what you say." Three hours to frisk, photograph, and fingerprint me for the third time (I think—I've lost track), tortured by "Married with Children" and Arnold S.'s "Commando" on the one-finger-typing officer's tube, though I enjoy the scene where Arnoould's high-heeled sidekick blasts open a paddywagon with an anti-tank bazooka.

Some Latino and Black youngsters I'm being processed with complain about their treatment.

"So sue us, go ahead and sue the whole fuckin department," the sandwich munching officer grins. "Do you know how HIGH the stack of cases waiting to be heard is?"

He lifts his free hand about four feet above the desk. (Me? I just want his fuckin sandwich.)

"Yeah, maybe you'll get heard 2 or 3 years from now. And you'd better have a good LAWYER too! We're the Federal government!"

Here we go. Just like a Bronson film. Big beautiful belaying pin switches to open and shut cages from a distance, brass showing through where the paint's chipped.

"Officer, put him in here with me, I'm LONEsome."

"Sorry, I don't assign the cells."

Mine is number 22, Jim Palmer's old number! The officer performs his most helpful service of the day: passing single cigarettes back and forth like lacing up a high-top as he walks along between the two rows of cages, 25 cents each.

IN CELL 22: To my surprise, I find my brothers of this evening in the many-throated, constantly thrusting and sighing conversation rolling like a wave up and down between the cages. A red bandanna'd gang member ("He's a SCHOLAR!") asks me into their banter, and I quickly conjoin my own solos of sympathetic cluck. They laugh and I laugh: we share our stories of false apprehending.

After a cup of Hi-C (orange color) for dinner, I lay down on a perforated metal frame (my bunk) in water and cigarette ash. For a night of conjuring poems—but for whom? I have no listening *volk*. For the bantering brothers here, then, endlessly joking black boys and brown boys, all sad inside if you listen close enough, but most of all the invisible one with the Korean blade who has drifted along with me from First District's yellow brick, forever laying the dark puzzle out before me like a scarred nameplate or gravestone so broad it blocks off the whole field of vision.

Mu ch___n

Answer this, s/he pleads, *I too don know what I'm spelling out Please complete for me so I* short bars of light flicker in the cigarette smoke *free of this pain of writing what I don know that   etches itself into bones of my arm my hand*

mu ch n

•

MAYBE SINCE THEN I have passed a brother or sister on the street, that very pattern of scarring weight and need altering a bit the swing of his or her arm on one side, slowing by just the width-of-a-moment the acceleration with which a hand lifts or "warms itself around a cup of coffee"

MU CH N

I guess and gaze, present it to others
Ajŏshi, i kŏs-ul chom pwa chuseyo!
Still have not made up our mind.

(1991)

This World

Jocelyn Lieu

They told her if Sidney called out at night, not to answer. His sense of the real, which had grown thin over the years, dissolved for good after dark. He won't know who you are, Ruth said. You'll confuse him, terrify him in fact. More harm than good.

"Remember," Michael said, "no matter what he says—"

"No matter what?" Diana asked.

"Don't go."

He kissed her, so softly she didn't feel the warning. Later, as she lay trying to sleep, Diana remembered what Michael had said. It wasn't exactly remembering: she heard the words again, really heard them. They came out of nowhere, with a ghostly authority, as if the wall or lamp or air had spoken. In this way, she understood that the man she lived with had instructed her to ignore his father's pain.

They'd put her in the room next to the father's, to Sidney's. The

JOCELYN LIEU was born in New York City and currently lives in Santa Fe, New Mexico, where she works as a journalist and editor. Her poetry has appeared in *The Antioch Review* and her articles and essays in numerous other publications. Educated at Yale and at Warren Wilson College, she is completing her first book of short fiction.

old man's door was open. From where she and Michael stood whispering in the hall, Diana could easily see inside.

The walls had been painted pure white, which in the fluorescence seemed tinged blue, like new milk. There were, for some reason, two single beds. The unused mattress was covered with see-through plastic while the other, on which Sidney slept, was made up with white sheets and a thin white blanket.

Sidney was the only dark and living thing in the room. Half of his body, the bottom half, was tucked into the envelope of the bed. Without his yarmulke, the balding scalp crossed by long strands of greasy hair seemed unbearably vulnerable.

"Well, good night," Michael told her.

For a year now, living together, they'd said good night in bed. But in his parents' house they were going to sleep separately: her upstairs, here, and Michael down in the living room, on the fold-out couch.

"Don't be afraid," he said.

"Why should I be afraid?" Diana spoke softly, not wanting Sidney or, for that matter, Ruth, to hear.

"No reason." Michael smiled, and it was a smile she hadn't seen on him before: the soft, proud, covert smile of a kid caught in a lie.

"Okay," he said, "sleep tight. See you en la mañana. Kiss."

She kissed him.

He stepped into the glare of his father's room and closed the door.

Standing in the hallway, which seemed colder now as well as dark, Diana heard murmurs, not just Michael's voice but Sidney's. She bent down to where the keyhole would've been, if it had been that kind of door. Words floated through the hollow wood . . . "No, Dad, she's not" . . . and then a language she only knew scraps of, Yiddish.

Maybe Michael didn't realize she was listening, but Diana felt the exclusion like a raised fist. Her grandmother and great aunts had done that, turned to Cantonese whenever talk entered the territory of sex or some other disgrace. For as long as she could remember, she had tried, and failed, to understand.

•

The room they'd put her in was Michael's from childhood. Some-one, Ruth, had placed a small bundle of carnations in a Depression glass vase on the trunk. Red flowers, green glass; the effect was like the infrared photos taken of enemy country at night.

For the first time, Diana was alone in this house, the first time besides trips to the bathroom, a chamber that had unnerved her with its seashells of potpourri and fringed towels that looked too clean to use. The rest of the house, except for Sidney and Michael's rooms, was filled with framed photographs and glass and porcelain figurines, and the needlepoint still lifes Ruth did to kill time.

Everything seemed so breakable, and arranged. In Michael's room at least she could breathe. His old cloth college books lined the shelves. There was a scarred desk, and a tensor lamp. In dresser drawers, which she lifted slightly as she pulled, so they wouldn't squeak, Diana found knitted vests and soft denim, twenty years old. The room had already been combed of secrets. The most revealing things left were the pho-tographs, and Ruth would have put those up after he'd gone.

Only one picture of Sidney and Ruth hung on the wall. It appeared to have been taken just after they'd come to America from the relo-cation camp in Germany. Childless then, looking more like brother and sister than husband and wife, they sat together on a park bench, holding hands. Though a whole garden spread out around them, they huddled close, smiling. Shadows brushed their lips and eyes. They both had the blurred, fragile look of people recovering from surgery.

Michael's image dominated, of course. Because of the war, Ruth and Sidney had married late; like Diana, Michael was an only child. Cub Scout, Indian brave. The colors were a little off, the reds not red but darker, the way dried blood is dark. Bar mitzvah, graduation. In the pictures, Michael seemed to possess a grace he'd somehow lost. Diana couldn't tell when the change had occurred. The photos ended when he moved to San Francisco. On this wall, twenty-one was as old as he'd ever get.

Diana and Michael had lived together in his flat near the Mission for a year, but though he returned to New York every two or three months—whenever he could—this was the first time she had come with him. She'd understood. She hadn't told her family either, not until the fact had grown impossible to conceal.

It wasn't subterfuge, exactly. She was no longer a child, and besides, James and Minnie Wong were modern, which meant they didn't demand marriage or someone Chinese, or even someone younger, closer to her own age. The only one who would've had something to say was Diana's grandmother, who had died two years ago, of pneumonia, and been buried in California, not Chunglao as she had wished. Chunglao was her village, their village, though Diana had never been there. To be buried in Chunglao was the desire of her grandmother's heart. That's how she'd put it: the desire of my heart. She would never know about Michael. The glitter of relief Diana felt was quickly lost in a haze of grief and shame.

She switched off the tensor lamp. In the darkness that wasn't dark—it was a city darkness, never quite complete—she listened. Sidney's door clicked shut and Michael's footsteps, sock soft, padded down the stairs. Springs creaked as he unfolded the couch.

One wall away from her, Ruth lay in the large blue bed she'd shared with Sidney before he got sick. Sheets rustled as Ruth turned and turned.

From Sidney's room, silence.

At dinner earlier that night, Diana had tried, halfheartedly, to help set the table. She'd hoped the attempt showed that she might be good daughter-in-law material after all, but Ruth, a small woman alive with energy, had beat her to it, the knives, the spoons, the napkins daubed with ancient yellow stains.

"Nothing fancy," Ruth said, "just food of the home."

Baked chicken, boiled potatoes. A salad made with iceberg lettuce and thin, glassy slices of onion and cucumber. Wishbone dressing. Sour pickles. With a tiny silver fork, Michael stabbed a spear out of the brine for her.

While they ate in the kitchen, Sidney sat in his armchair in the living-dining room.

"Aren't you going to introduce me?" Diana had asked.

"No, not yet," Michael had said. "He knows you're here. Let's wait a while. See."

Sidney was positioned in front of the television, which was on. It had been on since they arrived, as TVs had everywhere. The day before Diana and Michael landed in New York, the Gulf War had begun.

Because they'd gotten in late—there was a delay in St. Louis—they stayed the first night at a motel near J.F.K. Cross-legged on one of the beds, with a room service tray between them, they'd watched the screen of the bolted-down set fill with green fire.

"I hate to say it, but for once Bush is right," Michael said.

"Are you kidding?"

"It had to be done."

They fought in murmurs. "You don't understand. I wouldn't expect you to understand," he said. Jets rumbled over the motel roof. Neither one had wanted to look away from the TV for an instant. It had been like watching a car accident, or someone being born.

"The world," Ruth said now. She nudged the bowl of pale salad toward Diana. "The world, it only gets worse. We have people over there, he tell you? Those few of us left, a few shreds. Cousins. Children." She looked into Diana's eyes. "I am praying they are safe."

"Well," Diana said, "let's hope it's all over soon."

She tried to slice her chicken breast without getting bread crumbs on the place mat, which was made of coiled straw. Dusk had come. The kitchen window faced the backs of brick row houses identical to the one the Kaminiskis lived in. On some terraces, Weber grills glistened like wet black mushrooms. It was winter in Brooklyn, no one to be seen. Behind other windows, TVs flickered, the war.

Ruth reached behind Diana. She touched a switch, and the room was cast under a buzzing dome of light.

"This is delicious," Diana said.

"It's just Perdue's, from the supermarket. Cheaper than the butcher. The cost of things"—Ruth waved one hand—"the cost could break you."

Under the table, Michael squeezed her knee, but his face remained a careful blank. Diana wasn't sure what his gesture meant, if it had anything to do with love or allegiances.

"Relax," he'd told her that morning. "My mother's a human being." Diana was anxious not only for the usual reasons, she was ashamed of having come from a family so lightly touched by suffering.

The Wongs had their dead and tortured too, from the Cultural Revolution, but no one talked about them. Compared with the Kaminiskis' dead, her dead were nothing.

"Butcher or not, it's delicious," she said.

Ruth smiled. "Thank you, dear."

A window in the wall opened into the dining room. Through it, full or dirty dishes could be passed. The top of the window was edged with hanging crystals, the chandelier. Under this brilliant ceiling sat Sidney, his face in profile. He was rocking back and forth. Diana believed it was the Alzheimer's until Michael, following her eyes, said, "He's praying."

Sidney rose and began his slow, trembling, shuffling walk.

"Do you need help?" Ruth shouted. Her voice was a shock that radiated through the tiny kitchen. More gently, she said, "Go see if he needs help, dear."

"You need help, Dad?" Michael blotted his mouth on his napkin and got up. A greasy half-moon of dressing soaked the crumpled cloth.

"Dad?" Michael was smiling, calmer than she'd ever seen him. Back home in San Francisco, when he talked about his father or his father's disease, his jaw tensed with anger. But here, now . . .

"You going anywhere, Dad? He's not going anywhere."

Sidney had stopped so that his face was centered in the window between rooms, as if he were a portrait of himself. He smiled at Diana, and she smiled back. He kept on smiling—not stopping, the way the unafflicted did—and she saw how handsome he still was, his green eyes greener than Michael's, his jaw still strong under the stubble and flaking skin.

"He likes you," Michael said.

"He does," said Ruth.

"Listen, he's saying something. Dad?"

They all waited. *In what has become a common sight in the night sky over Baghdad . . .* The television. Michael leaned down to turn the sound off.

In the softest voice that could still be heard, a voice like paper crumbling, Sidney said, "There is one woman, two are needed."

"What, Dad?"

"There is one woman, two are needed."

The utterance seemed to drain him. Sidney tried to turn but couldn't get his feet around. "Okay Dad, let's go." Embracing him, Michael had helped his father back to his chair.

And now, alone in Michael's room, Diana puzzled over what Sidney had meant. The simplest answer was that Ruth was one woman, the one woman in the small, tight knot of this family. Another was needed. Her, Diana? That was too easy. If Diana herself were one woman? In the darkness, she blushed. One woman, two. She rolled over, and the stiff sheets scratched at her. Still too literal, and besides it didn't make sense. Maybe he meant another kind of doubleness. In Chinese, two was lucky, two pomegranates on a golden chain. That's why her grandmother had worn the pendant, down inside her flowered dress. Two of a thing showed intent, an escape from chaos. Diana's grandmother had tapped her chest; a fingernail clicked against the hidden metal fruit. "Luck," she'd said, as if presenting a proof. "You see?"

It was poetry. "Your father was speaking in poetry," Diana had whispered to Michael, as they stood in the hallway between the doors. "Everything becomes a riddle. My grandmother was like that too, in the end."

"I don't know about poetry." Michael kissed her, tired, not paying attention. "He hallucinates, sees things. He's in another world. Remember," he told her, "no matter what he says—"

"No matter what?"

"Don't go."

Diana lay waiting for sleep. She almost got there, caught in the wind tunnel, falling fast, but at the last second she clutched the sides of the bed and opened her eyes.

Pale light from the alley filtered through the blinds. Everything in the room seemed to be made from the same gray clay. What Michael said came back to her. She heard the words, really heard them.

Cruel instructions. How necessary was this prohibition? In some essential way, Sidney had recognized her. He knew who she was.

A siren whined in the distance. Diana understood the buried text in Michael's warning, or thought she did. He was keeping her from his family. If she asked, he would say he was protecting her from unpleasantness. But protection was a bad excuse. His father's illness could show her nothing she hadn't already seen with her grandmother: the oxygen tanks and bedpans, the odors, confessions and rages. No, Michael wanted to keep her apart. She could visit his home in New York, that much was allowed. She could eat chicken and pickles, sleep in his bed, talk to his mother. She could live with him, but not forever. She didn't know when the moment of leaving would come, but it would. That was clear.

Diana opened her door. Light curved up the stairway. She took it for a sign.

But Michael was asleep in a snarl of blankets and sheets. The television was on, with the sound turned low. In the changing light he looked only half formed, not thirty-seven, not even seventeen. He didn't look like someone who would leave her, or someone she'd want to leave. She slid into the bed. Like a boy, he was wearing his undershirt and Jockey shorts.

Michael flinched; he batted at her searching hands. "What?" he muttered. "What happened?"

"It's only me."

"You surprised me."

"I know," she said, "I'm sorry."

She touched his rib cage. His heart under her palm beat fast, as if he'd been running.

"Maybe you were dreaming," she said.

"Maybe," he said. "Maybe I still am."

He pushed her fingers lower, under the elastic, to where he was hard, and she felt the pang that sometimes came when he was aroused while asleep or just on waking: evidence of a desire that had nothing to do with her.

"Now?" she said. "Are you sure?"

"Why not?" Pressing down, his hand continued to guide hers.

"We have to be quiet," he murmured.

She climbed over him, to arrange their bodies the way they liked it when they were tired, her back pressed against his stomach. But when she moved, the bed exploded in a crackling squeal of springs.

Michael snorted, trying to suppress his laughs. He bit into the T-shirt she'd worn for a nightgown; his mouth left a cool wetness between her shoulder blades.

"Come on," Diana whispered. She was laughing too, soundlessly, unable to stop. "Down here." On the Persian rug, in front of the TV. Michael lay beneath her, holding her hips. While they made love, Diana found herself, almost against her will, glancing up at the screen, at the reporter in the flak jacket who stood talking on a roof somewhere under a desert sky.

Suddenly, Michael pushed her away. The smell of semen seeped between them. Diana hadn't used her diaphragm and was grateful, she thought, that he'd managed in time. She hadn't come, but she was used to not coming. She curled over him, like an infant asleep.

"Oh you seductress," Michael said. "Jezebel, how do you always get your way with me?" He kissed her ear. "Look at all this spilled seed."

The sound of shattering glass. Startled, Diana stood up. The front of her shirt sticky, stained. A broken figurine lay on the floor. It was a woman wearing a blue dress, a shepherdess. The crook in the small, translucent hand was still intact.

"Oh my God." Diana kneeled. Gathering the shards, she arranged them on her palm. She must have bumped into the knickknack stand when she stretched out her legs. Her throat tightened, as if she'd injured something that was alive.

Upstairs, the hall light blinked on. For an instant, Michael froze. "Wonderful," he said, "a real party here." He struggled into his jeans, tossed Diana his sweater. They heard one door open, then another. "If we're lucky, she's just checking on him," he whispered. He stuffed his shorts under the pillow. By the time Ruth walked slowly down the steps, her swollen legs lifting from the part in her robe, Michael and Diana were seated on the bed, breathless, staring at the set.

At the bottom of the staircase, Ruth stood looking at them. Diana couldn't see her face, just a backlit aurora of tangled hair.

"Hi, Ma."

"I can't sleep," Ruth said.

"I couldn't either," said Diana. The need to confess swelled inside her. "I have an apology to make, I broke your blue lady."

Ruth walked unsteadily toward them.

"Yes, I thought perhaps I heard sounds."

She sank into Sidney's armchair. With a brief look of sorrow, she took in the shattered figure that Diana still held.

"Don't worry, dear," she said. "What are a few pieces of clay in this world?"

Michael got up. "Want some tea, Ma? I'll make some tea."

"That would be very nice. Just dip the bag once, maybe two times. That's enough for an old woman like me."

Kitchen cabinets creaked, and the microwave began its low roar. The two women gazed straight ahead, at the television, the top of which was covered with more photos of Michael in the stages of his life. Schoolboy, pirate, a teenager with long, neat hair. In every picture, Michael's dark, unhappy eyes.

"He's quiet, thank God," Ruth said softly, a conspirator. "Like a baby, he's sleeping."

"Good. I mean, I'm glad."

Ruth pinched the flaps of her robe together. Green light streaked the televised sky: not bombs, but tracer fire.

"He was a great mind once," Ruth said. "You wouldn't know it now. All day long, reading. If we had stayed in the village we were from"—she glanced at Diana—"the village in Poland, he would have been a scholar."

"Did you know him then?"

"Of course I knew him. Everybody knew everybody. Only later," Ruth paused, "later, at the relocation camp, when we met again . . . You would not believe the happiness of being alive. We were each so grateful to find someone from home, you might say we married for gratefulness. It is not bad, to marry for this. People marry for worse."

In the kitchen, a teaspoon clinked against glass.

"Do you ever want to go back?" Diana asked.

"Where?"

"To your village. In Poland."

Ruth laughed. "What is left there for us?" she said.

They heard steps.

"He's coming," Ruth said. "Tell me what is happening with this war, this terrible and necessary war."

"Nothing," Diana told her. "They keep replaying the same footage. A lot of talk. Nothing new I can see."

Ruth had let the weak tea cool before she drank. "You'd like some?" she'd asked Diana. "Dear, offer your sweetheart some tea."

"She doesn't want any."

"That's okay," Diana said. "I don't. Really, I don't want any."

Ruth scrutinized them both. "If it's too hot, it burns," she said.

After that, they sat quietly. In the dim light, Diana fiddled with the chunks and splinters of porcelain, trying to see how they might fit together, until Ruth said, "You're making me nervous, dear."

From time to time, Michael touched the remote, changing channels. Desert Storm was everywhere.

"Excuse me, I feel sleep coming on," Diana said.

When she kissed Michael on the cheek, he gave her a suspicious look.

"Good night," she'd whispered.

"Good night."

"Good night, Ruth."

"Sleep well, dear. For what is left of this night, sleep well."

But as Diana lay between the sheets Ruth no doubt had washed that morning, the loneliness returned. To have opened herself and still be alone . . . She touched the crumpled T-shirt, the crust on her belly, the rough hair, wetness. One hand began to work. With the other, she lifted the sheet and blankets away from her body, so no one could hear the rustling.

For her imagined text, she chose what Michael and she had just done, the danger of it, the threat of discovery. But when she finally came, the image she held was of Sidney's rocking body, and his mouth and eyes.

•

She must have fallen asleep, because the voice woke her.

Help me. Please help me.

It was Sidney.

Will no one help me?

Diana's closed eyes fluttered. An unremembered dream circled the room and left. Light filled the window, but she couldn't tell if it was dawn or the glow that never deserted this city.

Will no one help?

She lay in the warm bed, listening. English. He was speaking English, to her. He wasn't in another world, he wasn't in any world but this.

Please help.

She got up. Doors creaked as she opened them. The white room shimmered with its own bluish light. Sidney lay propped on pillows. His hair was in weedy clumps around his face, his eyes impossible to read.

He was silent. Had he really spoken?

The odor of urine and shit.

Trying not to breathe, she crouched beside him.

"It's me," she said slowly, "Diana. Diana, Michael's friend. Michael, your son."

His stare shifted from her face to the hand she'd let rest on the metal bars that kept him from falling.

"Sorry," she said, and slid her fingers off the cool steel. "Sidney," she said, "I'm here to help. Tell me how to help you."

The old man's eyes gleamed. Tears slid down the dry cheeks and gathered on his chin.

"Sidney, what is it? Tell me what it is."

"Please," he said, whispering, his voice so soft it almost failed to exist. "Please . . ."

She wanted to let him know she knew.

"One woman," she told him. "I'm one woman."

Tears covered his face. "Please," he said, "please don't hurt me."

She hadn't heard him enter, but Michael was standing behind her.

"Dad," he said, "Dad, it's okay. It's all right now, it's all right." Then more words, in Yiddish, the language he and Sidney shared.

Michael nudged one shoulder under Sidney's limp arm and lifted him. With the other hand, he braced his father's chest. Slowly, together, like lovers, they began to walk.

The hall light went on. "Go back to sleep, Ma," Michael called. "I'm taking care of him. You sleep. Somebody in this house ought to get some sleep."

Diana tugged at the reeking sheets. "Leave them," he said. "Just leave them alone. I told you. You know I told you."

The bathroom door swung open. Still weeping, Sidney disappeared with his son, and Diana knew, not by the words but by Michael's cold, sad smile, that it would be over soon.

A year later, after she had moved back to her parents' house in Berkeley, Sidney died. She and Michael hadn't spoken for months— the end had been bitter—but he called to tell her.

"I'm sorry," Diana heard herself say. "I'm so sorry."

She sat in the living room, where the phone was. In the cherry-wood cabinet that used to hold the TV was a shrine to her grandmother. It wasn't an obvious shrine, just two small bunches of dried flowers and a photograph of her grandmother in a standing frame. In the portrait, she was an old woman who wore black-rimmed glasses and stared unsmiling at the person who took the picture. Old, ordinary, beloved.

Sidney had died in his sleep, kissed by God, Michael said. He and Ruth were at that stage in mourning where they didn't bathe or change their clothes. People visited the house and brought food and prayed. He was grateful for the ritual, he said, for the surprising comfort it could bring.

She told him she was glad he could find comfort somewhere.

"Well, good-bye," he said.

"I *am* sorry."

"I know."

For the rest of the week, she had trouble sleeping. On the anniversary of the war, the news channels replayed Desert Storm. Long after her parents had gone to bed, Diana stayed up in the den, switching stations. She watched the liquid green sky and remembered how, when the conflict ended and she and Michael had turned the TV off at last, the home they'd shared had filled with a silence that was never completely broken again.

"They Like You Because You Eat Dog, So What Are You Gonna Do About It?" (8 Vignettes)

Portraits

R. Zamora Linmark

The best way to describe the Sanchez family is that they are all writers. Florante. His mother, Celia. And his grandfather, Lolo Tasio, who came from and brought forth a generation of writers.

They live a block away from me in a tiny, old house that looks abandoned on Merkle Street. It's so old, the paint stopped peeling. There are vines growing from every side of the house and torn window screens that look like petals about to fall.

But the house is always alive. There is always a light on and there is always someone clicking on a typewriter.

Florante said they left the Philippines because his Lolo Tasio can no longer stand to see his country go to waste. And had they remained there, they would end up with bullet holes all over their bodies. Like

R. ZAMORA LINMARK: "I was born in Manila, Philippines, in 1968, and immigrated to Hawaii when I was eight years old. I received my B.A. in English with high honors at the University of Hawaii at Manoa, and I'm currently working on my M.A. in English at the same institution. My poetry recently appeared in *Willow Springs,* and in the forthcoming *Anthology of Philippine Writing,* which will be published in Manila."

his father, his younger brother and sister, and his Lola Neneng, who were gunned down on their way home from the market.

Why? I asked.

Because some people did not approve of what my grandparents and parents were writing about, Florante said.

Today, he takes me to his house. His Lolo Tasio greets us by the door and Florante introduces me to him. He smiles, but it's the kind of smile that tries to hide anger or solitude. Painful almost. He walks through the corridor and enters a room. Within a few minutes, I hear him tapping on the keys.

I look around the room. There are books everywhere. Shelved against the walls. Stacked on the floor and along the corridor. Books in Spanish, English, and Tagalog. Books as thick as encyclopedias and as old as the Bible.

In the center of the room is a typewriter resting on a wooden desk. The typewriter is very old, the letters and numbers faded. On the wall facing the door are three pictures pinned like a pyramid.

I walk towards the wall. At the apex is the Crucifixion cut into the shape of the Philippines. Christ is crowned in a barbed-wire tiara and wearing a red-white-and-blue loincloth.

On the bottom left is a black-and-white portrait of a man. He is blindfolded and his lips are stapled.

To the right is a colored picture of Lolo Tasio's family. They look very happy with the globe in Luneta Park behind them. There is water spouting from the top of the huge ball, covering the continents with streams.

I step a little closer. I recognize Florante and his grandfather immediately. Florante stands in front of me and points out his mother and the other members of the family.

I look at his father, his younger brother and sister, and his Lola Neneng for a long time, concentrating on their faces—the eyes, the lines between the smiles.

At the back of my head, I hear Lolo Tasio's typing. I begin to imagine ghosts seeping from his fingers as they tell him their stories. As the typing gets louder and louder, I think of the spirits rising up, ascending higher, higher than Christ.

So What Are You Gonna Do About It?

Edgar Ramirez is a faggot. Mrs. Takemoto knows it. She's always telling him to stop putting his hair behind his ears.

"And cut your hair, Edgar," she says. "It's getting long again."

Edgar Ramirez is a faggot. Christopher and Rowell, the fifth grade bulls, know it. They're always tackling him in flag football.

"A flag for a fag," they say. "Fag flag."

Edgar Ramirez is a faggot. Nelson and Carlo, the other fifth grade bulls, know it. They're always shooting him with their slingshots or tripping him each time he walks by and sways his hips, hula-style.

"What, cannot walk without heels?" they say.

Edgar Ramirez is a faggot. Caroline, Judy, and Maggie, the "Hot to Trot" girls, know it. They're always fighting over him because he looks like a Filipino John Travolta.

"Edgar, you wanna come over my house?" they say at the same time. "We can play Chinese Jacks," Caroline says. "We can read my *Sixteen* or *Teen Beat* magazines," Judy says. "We can listen to my Peaches and Herb tape," Maggie says.

Edgar Ramirez is a faggot. His mother and father know it. They're always grounding him because he spends all of his money on life-size John Travolta or Shaun Cassidy or Scott Baio posters. And pins them up on the walls, ceilings, doors, in his father's work-out room, and next to the altar.

"Anak, go to confession," his devout mother says. His father doesn't say anything. He just grabs the gardening shears and chops his hair off until he's bald or burns the posters and shoves the cinders down Edgar's throat.

Edgar Ramirez is a faggot. His friends, Katherine, Mai-Lan, Florante, Loata, and I know it.

"Since when, Edgar?" Katherine asks.

"Ever since I saw my father naked."

Edgar Ramirez is a faggot. Everyone knows it. Even Edgar himself.

"So what are you gonna do about it?" I ask.

"Nothing," he says. "Nothing."

The Pen Is a Mirror, Lonely

A lot of my classmates think that Florante and I are stupid because we speak English with accents heavier than Mai-Lan Phan's. "You talk like you're always boiling something in your mouth," Steve Johnson always says.

Sometimes I think that the only reason why Florante is only on Level 10 in Reading and I'm only on Level 14 while the others are either on Level 17 or 18 is that Mrs. Takemoto always picks on us, especially on Florante.

"Remember, f's are not p's, and v's are not b's. 'Funny', not 'punny'. 'Valley', not 'balley'. And don't roll your r's," she keeps telling us.

It makes me angry, but I don't say anything. I just stare at the clock and pray. Before the recess bell rings, Florante brings out a book or two, and hides them in his jacket.

We go to the field away from everyone and he reads to me books from his Lolo Tasio's library. Poems and stories written or translated in Tagalog or English by Filipinos. Francisco Balagtas. Hermenegildo Flores. Jose Rizal. Andres Bonifacio. Jose Corazon de Jesus.

Most of the time, he has to explain what the poem or story is about. But sometimes, the understanding comes naturally. Like the poem with commas after each word by Jose Garcia Villa. The poem that begins with "When I was no bigger than a huge star in my self, I began to write," and ends with "And I began to die, and I began to grow."

He read it so beautifully, so hauntingly, pausing after each word as if each breath was the last, that when he finished, I told him I wanted to write.

From then on, and when I don't have to serve JPO duty, Florante and I go over to his house. His mother and Lolo Tasio teach us how to read and write poems and stories. They don't care whether I read with an accent or not. As long as I understand what I'm reading.

Today, his mother makes us write about ourselves. This is what I write. I have three friends. The paper to speak to. The pen to release me. And Florante to guide me.

This is what Florante writes. My name is Florante. I am named after a poem by Francisco Balagtas. Named after a man who died fighting for his country and a woman he loved. Florante. Florante for loneliness.

My Father Picks Up My Mother Lost In The Garden

She used to stay up the whole night and wait for him to come home. When he didn't, she secretly buried the food to the very bottom of the trash bag and poured out a shot or two of Jack Daniel's into the sink. Now, she just leaves his dinner on the table and doesn't care if it spoils or not. Sometimes, she downs the Jack Daniel's and doesn't care if we found her sleeping on the floor.

Gardo, Jing, Bino, and I used to stay up the whole night and wait for him to come home. We even had a contest to see who could stay up the longest. The winner got to see our father eat the cold dinner or drink himself to sleep. But none of us ever did.

Soon, Gardo, Jing, and Bino gave up playing the game. In the morning, Gardo and Jing stopped taking turns digging through the trash bag. And Bino stopped checking the bottle. They even stopped wondering if he came home or not.

When I can, I try to take long naps. Sometimes, I stay up the whole night, waiting for him to stumble into the house, listen to the way he chews his food, and watch him sit on the La-Z-Boy and toast a shot or two to himself.

He comes home early this morning. Everyone's asleep, except me. I'm catching my second wind. I take a deep breath and walk quietly to the door. I peep out to the living room and I see him holding a bottle of whiskey. He paces back and forth, occasionally stopping to refill his mouth. He looks at the family pictures on the wall. I take another deep breath.

He picks up the only picture frame standing on top of the cabinet. It is a black-and-white picture of my mother when she was a college student. She is in her college uniform and sitting on a stone bench in a beautiful garden. She is surrounded by flowers. Behind her is a majestic fountain spouting water. She is smiling, but her eyes look lost.

He stands there holding the picture for a long time in one hand and a bottle in the other. Just standing there and staring at my mother lost in the garden with the majestic fountain behind her. He takes another swig. I hold my breath.

The Secret

Edgar thinks it's a secret. He thinks it's a secret because Mr. Campos, the custodian, always tells him that no one else can find out. He thinks no one else can find out because by the time he walks into the janitor's room where he waits for him, everyone has already left the school. Everyone except him and Mr. Campos, who sits on the bench next to the mop stand, waiting with his shirt off and his zipper undone.

Edgar thinks it's a secret because each time Mr. Campos signals him to take off his shirt from Kress or his Toughskin pants from Sears or his rubber shoes from Thom McAn, only he answers to his silent calls. He thinks it's a secret because only he and Mr. Campos know they have only a half hour before the shirt, the pants, and the shoes must be worn again. He thinks it's a secret because he never sees Mr. Campos' son who comes to pick him up every day.

Edgar thinks it's a secret when Mr. Campos tells him to lie flat on his stomach or on his back, because only he feels the words. He thinks it's a secret no one can ever find out because it is only his lips and no one else's that Mr. Campos wets, or it is only his neck and no one else's that Mr. Campos licks then blows, or it is only his chest and no one else's that Mr. Campos kisses.

Edgar thinks it's a secret because only he can feel the greying hair brushing against his skin. His skin and no one else's.

Edgar thinks it's a secret Mr. Campos must keep for the rest of his life because Mr. Campos can never tell his wife how he taught Edgar to motion him to lie flat on his stomach or on his back while Edgar runs his tongue on his cracked lips or licks then blows his neck or kisses his hairless chest.

Edgar knows it's a secret Mr. Campos can never tell his wife because only Mr. Campos can feel the child's hair, fine as silk, brushing against him. Only he can feel the rejuvenation because only Edgar can feel the white hairs pricking his face.

Edgar thinks it's a secret when Mr. Campos buries his face between his legs because only he can feel his own heart beating louder and louder as he raises his feet higher and higher. Edgar thinks it's a secret because only he can feel his feet stiffening, his small toes curling. Edgar thinks it's a secret Mr. Campos can never tell because it is forever buried in his mouth, alive and young.

Edgar thinks it's a secret when Mr. Campos, not being able to hold it in, shoots all over him and groans loud enough for the walls to hear.

Edgar thinks it's a secret despite the loud groans. He thinks it's a secret because, though the walls hear him, the walls don't have mouths. He thinks it's a secret because the sound does not escape the room, but echoes again and again in their sighing kisses.

Edgar thinks it's a secret because, though he has to wipe himself with his own shirt from Kress, he can always soak it with soap and Clorox as soon as he gets home. He thinks it's a secret because no matter how many times he tries to scrub his body, the smell of Mr. Campos is forever buried in his skin.

Mr. Campos thinks it's still a secret between him and Edgar when Edgar tells me about it. He thinks it's a secret because, before Edgar walks into the janitor's room, he does not hear Edgar telling me to wait until the green door is shut. It's a secret Mr. Campos can never find out because he does not see me looking at him through the holes in the door. Looking at him as he waits on the bench next to the mop stand with his shirt off and his zipper down.

Mr. Campos thinks it's a secret between him and Edgar because he does not see my eyes each time he signals Edgar to take off his clothes. He thinks only Edgar answers to his silent calls. He thinks only he and Edgar know about the thirty-minute rendezvous.

Mr. Campos thinks it's a secret because he does not know that I can hear his faint voice instructing Edgar to lie flat on his stomach or on his back. He does not see my eyes opening wide when he buries his face between Edgar's legs. My eyes wider and wider as Edgar's legs rise higher and higher until his small toes curl in the air.

Mr. Campos thinks it's a secret when, not being able to hold it in, he shoots all over Edgar and groans. He thinks it's a secret despite the loud groans because, though the walls hear him, the walls don't have mouths. He does not know that, though the walls don't have mouths, the door has eyes.

Mr. Campos thinks it's a secret because he does not see me watching Edgar wipe himself with his own shirt from Kress that he soaks with soap and Clorox as soon as he gets home. He thinks it's a secret between him and Edgar because he does not see Edgar reaching his arms out and telling me to smell the secret that is forever buried in his skin. Mr. Campos thinks it's still a secret.

On Marriage

My younger brother Bino says, Gross! My older sister Jing says, Maybe one of these days! My older brother Gardo says, I'm ready! My father says, Never again! My mother says, Take it back! My father says, Tomorrow! My mother says, Now! Bino says, Stop! Gardo says, I'll be just like Dad, she'll be just like Mom! Jing says, Shut up! My mother says, Take it back! My father says, Don't bother! My mother says, Take it back! My father says, No! Gardo says, Always! Jing says, Shut up! My father says, Go to your room! My mother says, Lock your doors! Bino says, No more! Jing says, Not again! My father says, Now! Gardo says, Let's go! My mother says, Take it back! My father says, I'm going out! Jing says, I'm tired! My mother says, Don't come back! Bino says, Our Father Who Art In heaven! My father says, Never! Bino says, Thy Kingdom Come, Thy Will Be Done! My mother says, Damn you! And I say, Give Us This Day, Our Daily Bread.

Edgar Kisses Me In The Dark And I Open My Eyes

This is how it goes, Katherine says, and starts singing:

> Johnny and Sandy
> Under the tree

(and Edgar joins in)

> K-I-S-S-I-N-G
> First comes love
> Then comes marriage
> Then comes Johnny
> With a baby carriage.

Florante and I look at each other. "That sounds very familiar," we say. "It sounds like . . ." And Florante starts singing in Tagalog:

> Amy, Suzy, and Tessie

(and I join in)

Romeo, Pancho, and Jose Marie
I love cinco
Pambili ng puto
Sa mga tindera
Ng bitsu-bitsu
Ting-a-ling-a-ling
Stay-tue.

"What does it mean?" Katherine and Edgar ask.

"Is it about kissing?" Mai-Lan asks.

"No," Florante answers.

"Just kids who want some rice cake," I explain.

"Time to go to sleep," Edgar's sister Jane says.

The girls go with Jane while Florante and I follow Edgar. The room is very small, clustered with paperback books and Junior Encyclopedias. The walls are plastered with posters. John Travolta as Barbarino in "Welcome Back, Kotter" displaying his blue eyes, cleft chin, and dimples only an archeologist or a psychiatrist can fathom. Shaun Cassidy in a white jumpsuit exposing his flat chest. A long, gray scarf spangled with silver around his neck. Scott Baio, pensive, in swimming trunks at the Battle of the Network Stars. And above the study table, Lindsay Wagner feeling macho as the Bionic Woman.

The three of us lie on the bed, sandwiched. I am in the middle. Within a few minutes, Florante falls asleep. He snores so loud, he reminds me of my father sleeping when he's drunk-tired.

"Are you still up?" Edgar asks.

"Yes."

He turns to face me. We laugh as we listen to Florante invent his own arpeggios.

"He sounds just like my father," I say.

"Mine, too," he says.

He moves his face closer. "Have you ever kissed someone on the lips?" he asks.

"No," I answer.

"Shhhh," he whispers. "Close your eyes."

He starts nibbling. I want to tell him to stop, but as soon as I open my mouth, he shoves his tongue in. I feel it rolling around. As if it's searching for something. I open my eyes and in the dark, I see Edgar's face. He looks like an older boy. Someone who knows what he's looking for. I push him away. I don't know what he wants.

In the morning, Mai-Lan and I walk to B.C. Market. She starts to sing the ballad of Johnny and Sandy. She sings it again and again until she gets tired.

"It's your turn," she says.

"Johnny and Sandy / Under a tree / K-I-S-S-I-N-G / First comes loooovvv . . ." I try to continue, but it feels like someone just rammed a fist into my mouth and blocked every word.

"Why'd you stop? What's wrong?" Mai-Lan asks.

"I don't know," I say. I try again. "Johnny and Sandy / Under a tree / K-I-S-S-I-N-G / First comes love? / Then comes marriage? Then comes Johnny? With a baby carriage?"

Mai-Lan looks at me. "What's the matter? You look pale," she says.

"Mai-Lan," I say, "have you ever k-k-k-kissed someone?" I stutter.

"No," she says.

"Can I kiss you, please?" I beg.

I move towards her and kiss her lips. But all I can feel is Edgar's tongue rolling around in my mouth. Just rolling around and around and around.

They Like You Because You Eat Dog

They like you because you eat dog, goat, and pig's blood.
They like you because you grind your women the way you eat *pulutan*.
They like you because you drink, play mah-jongg, and cockfight.
They like you because you go to church every Sunday.
They like you because you kneel hard, bend over quick, and spread wide.
They like you because you worship blue passports.
They like you because you guard the exiled President's body in Temple Valley.
They like you because your daughters date Marines.
They like you because you machine-gun your own kind.
They like you because your sons smoke crack, cut class, and sport tattoos.
They like you because you wear rainbow-colored clothes, toupee, and can boogie.
They like you because you are third world hip.
They like you because you have olive-skin and yellow teeth.

They like you because you say you're Spanish or Chinese.
They like you because you have big tits and tight ass.
They like you because you're the butt of everyone's joke.
They like you because you have a cock the size of a Vicks inhaler.
They like you because your favorite fruit is banana.
They like you because you sell home-grown *otong, kalamungay,* and
   eggplants at the open market on Saturdays.
They like you because you're a potato queen.
They like you because you're one hell of a gardener.
They like you because you work three full-time jobs—scraping greasy
   floors, scouring pots and pans, and scrubbing toilet bowls.
They like you because you're a walking cholera, hepatitis, and TB.
They like you because you're too proud to collect welfare.
They like you because you are a minimum-wage.
They like you because you have maids back home.
They like you because you're a doctor there and nurse's aide here.
They like you because you say you have a college degree but they say
   it's only the equivalent of a ninth grade American Education.
They like you because you can't fill out an application form.
They like you because you roll your R's, speak broken English, and
   always say yes.
They like you because you keep it all to yourself.
They like you because you take it in, all the way down.
They like you because you ask for it, adore it.
They like you because you're a copycat, want to be just like them.
They like you because, give it a couple more years, you'll be just like
   them.
And when that time comes, will they like you more?

Pangs of Love

David Wong Louie

Each night, like most Americans, my mother watches hours of TV. She loves Lucy and Carol Burnett, then switches to cable for the Chinese channel, but always concludes the broadcast day with the local news and Johnny Carson. She doesn't understand what Johnny says, but when the studio audience laughs, she laughs too, as if invisible wires run between her and the set.

My mother has lived in this country for forty years and, through what must be a monumental act of will, has managed not to learn English. This does no one any good, though I suppose when it comes to TV her linguistic shortcomings can't be anything but a positive evolutionary adaptation; dumb to the prattle that fills the airwaves, maybe her brain will wither proportionately less than the average American's.

I am thirty-five years old, and for the past nine months have lived

DAVID WONG LOUIE is the author of *Pangs of Love.* He is presently working on a novel, *The Barbarians Are Coming,* and teaches in the English department and at the Asian American Studies Center at UCLA.

267

with my mother in a federally subsidized high-rise in the lower reaches of Chinatown. After my father died, my siblings convened a secret meeting during which they unanimously elected me our mother's new apartment mate. They moved her things from Long Island, carpeted her floors, bought prints for the walls, imported me for company, then returned to their lives. I work for a midsize corporation that manufactures synthetic flavors and fragrances. We are the soul of hundreds of household products: the tobacco taste in low-tar cigarettes, the pine forests in aerosol cans, the minty pizzazz of toothpastes. We have sprays that simulate the smell of new cars; in fact, we have honed the olfactory art to a level of sophistication that enables us to distinguish between makes and models. Our mission is to make the chemical world, an otherwise noxious, foul-tasting, polysyllabic ocean of consumer dread, a cozier place for the deserving noses and tastebuds of America.

My mother's in her pajamas, her hair in a net that seems to scar her forehead. I'm sitting up with her, putting in time. I flip through the day's paper, Johnny in the background carrying on a three-way with Ed and Doc, when my mother's laugh starts revving like a siren. I shoot her a look—fat-lipped, pellet-eyed—that says, What business do you have laughing, Mrs. Pang? My mother's a sweet, blockish woman whom people generally like. She's chatty with her friends in her loud Cantonese voice and keeps her cabinets and refrigerator jammed tight with food, turning her kitchen into a mini grocery store—she's prepared for a long famine or a state of siege. Now, feeling the stab of my glare, she holds in her laughter, hand over mouth schoolgirl-style, hiding those gold caps that liven up her smiles, eyes moist and shifty dancing.

I roll my eyes the way Johnny does and return to the paper. The world's going through its usual contortions: bigger wars, emptier stomachs, more roofless lives; so many unhappy, complicated acres. As a responsible citizen of the planet, I slip into my doom swoon, a mild but satisfying funk over the state of the world. But then she starts again. Fist on cheek blocking my view of her gold mine. Her round shoulders quivering with joy. I click my tongue to let her know she has spoiled my dark mood. She turns toward me, sees the sour expression hanging on my face like dough, points at the screen where Johnny's in a turban the size of a prize pumpkin, then waves me off, swatting at flies. Ed's "ho-ho-ho" erupts from the box, the siren in her throat winds up, and all I see is the dark cave of her mouth.

What I need is a spray that smells of mankind's worst fears, something on the order of canned Hiroshima, a mist of organic putrefaction, that I'll spritz whenever the audience laughs. That'll teach her.

I stumble over my own meanness. Some son I am. What does she know about such things anyway? It's fair to say she's as innocent as a child. Her mind isn't cluttered with worries that extend beyond food and family. When she talks about the Japanese raids on her village back home, for instance, it's as a personal matter; the larger geopolitical landscape escapes her. She blinks her weary eyes. She's fighting sleep, hanging on to Johnny for one more guest before turning in. Suddenly, I have the urge to wrap my arms around her solid bulk and protect her, only she'd think I'm crazy, as I would if she did the same to me. "Go to bed," I say. "I'm not tired yet," she says. I cup my hands over my face, my fingers stinking of toilet-tissue lilacs and roses, and think things that should never enter a son's mind: a bomb explodes over the Empire State, forty blocks due north on a straight line from where we are seated, and glass shatters, and she's thrown back, the net on her hair, her pajamas, her beaded slippers on fire, and she hasn't a clue how such a thing can happen in this world. And I imagine I'll never see her again.

I fetch the newspaper, go to the couch where my mother's seated, and splash-land down beside her. I'm all set to translate the headlines, to wake her up to the world, when I stop, my tongue suddenly lead. I don't have the words for this task. Once I went to school, my Chinese vocabulary stopped growing; in conversation with my mother I'm a linguistic dwarf. When I talk Chinese, I'm at best a precocious five-year-old, and what five-year-old chats about the military budget? Still, I'm determined and gather my courage. "What's that?" I ask, pointing at the dim photo on the front page. An Afghan guerrilla, eyes to sky, on the lookout for planes, crouches near the twisted body of a government soldier; in the desolate background there's a tank, busted up in pieces. My mother pulls on the glasses she bought at the drugstore and takes a closer look. "A monkey?" she says. I finger the body. She gives up. "That's a dead person," I say, pulling the paper away. "People are dying everywhere."

"You think I don't know. Your father just died." Her voice is quivering, but combative.

I realize I'm on shaky ground. "This man's killed by another man," I say. I'm supposed to talk about freedom, about self-determination, but with my vocabulary that's a task equal to digging a grave without a shovel. "People are killing people and all you worry about is your next bowl of rice."

"You don't need to eat?" she snaps. "Fine, don't eat. It costs money to put food on the table."

She keeps talking this way, but I tune her out, giving my all to Johnny. That guy from the San Diego Zoo's on, and with him is the fleshy pink offspring of an endangered species of wild boar. It knocks over Johnny's coffee, and Johnny jumps. The audience roars; I laugh too, but it's forced, a forgery; my mother's still sore and just sits there, holding herself in like a bronze Buddha.

While I am at work the next day, she calls me. She wants to know whether I've rented a car yet. My youngest brother owns a house on the Island, and we're invited out for the weekend. My mother and I have gone over our plans many times already, so when she starts in now I lose patience in a wink. But I catch myself—with my mother repetition is a necessity, as it is when teaching a child to speak. The rental car is my idea. She says we'll save money by taking the train. But she keeps forgetting there's three of us traveling—me, my mother, and my friend Deborah. Once we agree to go in a rental car, she then tells me I should get a small model in order, again, to save money. "I'll ask for one with three wheels," I say. And she says anything's fine, but cheaper is better.

Later the same day, my boss, Kyoto, comes to my office with a problem. Every time we meet he sizes me up, eyes crawling across my body, and lots of sidelong glances. *Who is this guy?* It's the same going-over I get when I enter a sushi joint, when the chefs with their long knives and blood-red headbands stop work and take my measure, colonizers amused by the native's hunger for their superior culture. Kyoto says a client in the personal-hygiene business wants a "new and improved" scent for its men's deodorant.

"They want to change Musk 838/Lot No. i9144375941-3e?"

He bows his head, chin to chest. "You take care for Kyoto, okay?" Kyoto says.

I nod, slow and low, as if in mourning. He nods his head. I nod again.

Musk 838/Lot No. i9144375941-3e. Palm trees and surf, hibachied hotdogs topped with mustard, relish, and a tincture of Musk 838/Lot No. i9144375941-3e. Amanda Miller. Mandy Millstein. She was my love, and I followed her to Los Angeles. Within a year, about the time Sony purchased Columbia Pictures, she fell for someone named Ito, and broke off our engagement. When that happened, my siblings rushed in to fill the void Mandy's leaving left in my life, and decided I should be my newly widowed mother's apartment mate. My mother had grown accustomed to Mandy. She spoke Chinese, a stunning Mandarin that she learned at Vassar, and while that wasn't my mother's dialect Mandy picked up enough Cantonese to hold an adult conversation, and what she couldn't bridge verbally she wrote in notes. They conspired together to celebrate Chinese festivals and holidays, making coconut-filled sweet-potato dumplings, lotus-seed cookies, daikon and green onion soup, tiny bowls óf monk's food for New Year's Day. Beyond all that, Mandy had a ladylike manner of dressing that appealed to my mother's own vanity, and to her notions of what an American ("If you're going to marry a non-Chinese, she might as well look the part") should be: skirt, nylons, high-heel shoes.

Kyoto's request saddens me. Musk 838/Lot No. i9144375941-3e, a synthetic hybrid of natural deer and mink musks, spiced with a twist of mint, was, and always will be, our special scent. Taken internally, it had an aphrodisiacal effect on Mandy. One night, as was my custom, I had brought samples of our latest flavors and fragrances home from the lab. As usual, Mandy eagerly sniffed the tiny corked vials; when she tried the musk, she said it smelled dirty. I told her that to fully appreciate its essence it needed to come in contact with the heat of one's skin. She, of course, refused to experiment with her own flesh, so I volunteered my hand; as she poured, I warned her that this was a concentrate, each drop equal in potency to the glandular secretions of a herd of buck deer. Clearly my warnings unsettled her, because the next thing I know Mandy had dumped the whole works onto my palm. Later that evening, as planned, I made pizza, working the dough with my well-scrubbed hands, but Ivory soap, as it turned out, was no match for the oily compounds in Musk 838/Lot No. i9144375941-3e. The baking pie filled the apartment with a scent reminiscent of horses. But the pizza itself was a sensation, every bite bearing a snootful of joy: tomato sauce that seemed to have fangs, cheese as virile as steak, onions so pungent they ripped our eyes from our heads. "It tastes alive," Mandy said.

"Wild," I said.

"It's the basil," she said.

Her eyes caught mine. I shook my head. "Not basil," I said, "not oregano."

She creased her second slice and dipped her fingertip in the reservoir of orange grease that pooled in the resulting valley. She touched her glistening orange finger to the gap between my eyebrows, then let it slide south down the bridge of my nose, stopping at the fleshy tip of my northernmost lip. At that moment I realized we'd been eating Musk 838/Lot No. i9144375941-3e. If it had any toxic properties, it hardly mattered then. Mandy started giggling, as if she were high on grass, and I laughed to keep her company. She drew circles on my cheeks with the orange musk-laced oils. A regular pizza face. She cackled in the manner of chimps, and when I returned the favor and greased her with gleaming polka dots, I got the joke: no doubt I looked as dopey as she did then.

After that we spiked our food and beverages with Musk 838/Lot No. i9144375941-3e whenever Mandy was feeling amorous but needed a jump start.

I wonder how she has managed since she left. When she needs that little extra, does she do the same trick with Ito? Has he noticed that his California rolls smell funny—not fishy, but gamy like a herd of deer? If Mandy wants to recapture that old magic she had with me, she'll have to act quickly. Kyoto says it's time for a change. The manly scent of musk is no longer manly enough.

It's a sad day for love, Mandy, everywhere.

This is a fancy car," my mother says in Chinese as we stop-and-go up Third Avenue. "It must've cost you a bundle. Tell me, *how mucha cents*," she says conspiratorially. I look at her and say nothing.

"Isn't this nice of Bagel," my mother says a few minutes later. My youngest brother, the landowner in Bridgehampton, has always been called "Bagel" in the family. His real name is Billy, and God help him who drops "Bagel" in front of Bagel's friends. My mother's the lone exception. When she says Bagel, he knows his friends simply think that's her immigrant tongue mangling "Billy." "Out of you four brothers and sisters," she adds, "only Bagel asks me to visit."

"What are you saying? How can I invite you over when I live with you?"

"That's right. You're a good son."

"I didn't say I was a good son, but didn't I bring you out to California?"

"*Ah-mahn-da* invited me."

"I told *Amanda* to invite you while she was talking to you on the phone."

"That's right, that's right. You're a good son," she says. "Good son who doesn't know how to talk to his own mother. His American girl speaks better Chinese."

"*Forget it*," I say, waving her off.

"That's right. Always '*fo-gellit, fo-gellit.*' *Ah-mahn-da* never uses such words."

I swing across Twenty-third heading for Park. "Look at so many Puerto Ricans," she says. "Just like in California."

My brain stops, wrapped around a telephone pole that is my mother. I tell myself, *Try.* Explain the difference to your mother, who knows next to nothing: in Los Angeles what she thinks are Puerto Ricans are Mexicans and Chicanos. But I don't even know the words for Mexico, so how do I begin? In Chinese I'm as geography-poor as my mother, who knows only the streets and fields she's walked. Maybe I should use my hands. This is California, Amanda and I lived here, and over here—by my right hand—is another country Americans call Mexico. But that requires the patience of a special-ed teacher. In her mental maps, California is a few hours' drive from New York. That's what I'm up against.

Deborah is a bean pole. As a joke, my mother calls her "Mah-ti," water chestnut, the squat, bulbous tuber that tapers to a point like a mini dunce cap. She has hips that flare like the fins of an old Cadillac, but no rump to speak of. She wears glasses with a rhinestone frame —she's had the same ones since the eighth grade; this is not a stab at style here—and photosensitive lenses that have the annoying quality of never being dark enough or clear enough; she's always in a haze. On the rare occasions she's visited me at my mother's, she's come dressed in a most unladylike fashion: penny loafers or running shoes, chinos, and shirts bought in a boys' department. Today is no exception. I stop the rental car, a big Chevy four-door, at Park and Thirty-third. She grabs the front-passenger-side handle and stands there expecting my mother to climb into the back seat like a dog. I hit the power window switches. "You can sit in front when we stop to pee," I say.

Deborah slams the door behind her. She leans forward in her seat. "How are you, Mrs. Pang?" I've heard her speak more warmly to the bald mice she tends at Sloan-Kettering. That's where we met. At the lab we had had a small-scale scare, a baby version of the Red Dye No. 3 controversy a few years back, that forced Kyoto to send me, his right-hand slave, across town to have the stuff tested in Deborah's mice.

"Goot," my mother says. "How you?"

Deborah doesn't answer. Won't waste her breath on someone who can't take the conversation the next step. Mrs. Pang, the linguistic dead-end street. Barbarian, I think. But a savage in bed she is, even without Musk 838/Lot No. i9144375941-3e. Early on, my mother caught us in the sack—her sack, in fact—bony Deborah, with breasts like thimbles, on all fours. At that moment, as my mother's eyes burned holes through our nakedness, I meant to say, "What are you looking at?" full of indignation, but it came out a meek, "What do you see?" Fine, Deborah, I think, trash my mother; you're not a keeper anyway, as the fishermen say. She's the rebound among rebounds; only somehow she's stuck. If I had the words I'd straighten my mother out, allay her fears. What is she so fond of saying? "Are you planning to marry Mah-ti?" To which I tell her, emphatically, no. "So why," she says back, "you always hugging that scrawny thing?"

The trouble between Deborah and my mother runs deeper than the fact that my mother's seen the glare of Deborah's glassy bare rump. There are things I can do to soften their feelings toward each other. I might buy Deborah a pair of high-heel shoes, or register her at Hunter for Cantonese classes, or rent videos of the Frugal Gourmet cooking Chinese; I might ask my mother to stop calling Deborah Mah-ti and teach her, with patient repetition, the difficult syllables of Deborah's given name. But Deborah wants me to move out of my mother's place, says I'm a mama's boy, calls me that even as we make love; and my mother's still sad about the loss of Mandy, her surrogate Chinese daughter-in-law. My mother is subtle about this: "Mah-ti has no smell," she says, "like paper." That is to say, she misses Mandy, who made a point of showering herself with the perfumes I brought home from the lab whenever she visited my mother. There's no clean dealing with either of them.

When we pass the gas tanks along the Expressway, my mother tells me this is the very route Bagel always takes to his house. She says this with a measure of pride; I can tell what's going on in her head: I'm driving the same road my brother has driven, and to my mother's way of thinking that's not only a remarkable coincidence but a confirmation of the common thread between us, our genes, our good blood—ah, her boys, her talented womb! So why bother telling her the Expressway is the only reasonable route out to Bagel's?

Her last time out, she says, she drove with Bagel and his friend "Ah-Jay-mee" in the latter's two-seater, with Bagel folded into the rear storage area, best suited for umbrellas and tennis rackets. Then she wistfully adds that Bagel's former apartment mate Dennis had a car that had an entire backseat, but that luxury is "washed up" since he moved out.

After a while Deborah taps me on the shoulder. "What's she saying? She's talking about me, right? I heard her say my name."

"She said Dennis."

"*Dennis-ah cah bik*," my mother tells Deborah, spreading her hand to show size.

"Tell her this is a 'bik' pain in the you-know-what," Deborah says in a huff. "Tell her I'm tired of your secrecy, of being gossiped about in front of my face."

I say, "Slow down, okay? We're discussing my brother."

"What's Mah-ti saying?" my mother asks.

"She's saying her parents have a big car. She wants to take you on a drive someday."

My mother turns to Deborah and says, "*Goot!*"

There's not much traffic eastbound on a Saturday, not at this hour. Deborah's listening to her Walkman; I take the tinny *scrape scrape scrape* of the headphone's overflow as a token of peace. My mother stares out the windshield. Her eyes look glazed, uncomprehending. She seems out of place in a car, near machines, a woman from another culture, of another time, at ease with needle and thread, around pigs and horses. When I think of my mother's seventy-five-year-old body hurtling forward at eighty miles an hour, I think of our country's first astronaut, a monkey strapped into the Mercury capsule, all wires and restraints and electricity, shot screaming into outer space.

With Deborah occupied, I figure it's safe to talk. A chance to humanize the speed, the way pharmaceutical companies sweeten their chemicals with Cherry 12/Lot No. x362-4d so a new mother will eye-dropper the stuff into her baby's mouth.

We speak at the same time.

"Ah-Vee-ah," she says my Chinese name in a whisper, "why is it that *Ba-ko* has no girlfriends? You have too many. You should marry. Look at Ah-yo. See how content he is?"

Poor Ray! If she only knew half of his troubles.

"Why is *Ba-ko* so stubborn?" she asks. "I tell you something, when I offer to take him to Hong Kong to find a bride, you know what he says? He says he's already married to his cat. Ah-Vee-ah," she says, touching my hand, "he upsets me so, I wouldn't even mind if he dated your Mah-ti."

I laugh a little; she shows her gold mischievously. "Tell me," she says (we're confidants now), "what do you make of your youngest brother?"

I shrug my shoulders. "*I don't know*," I say, turning palms up. "Ask him."

"I'm talking to you now."

"Talk to Bagel."

"*Fo-gellit!*" she says.

At some time or other, my mother's offered to take all the boys on bride safaris in Hong Kong. Ray's the only one to take her up on it, and came back to the States with a Nikon and telephoto lenses and horror stories about pigeon restaurants. He's married to a Catholic girl named Polly, who insisted, probably to get back at her parents for some past sins, on taking his name—Polly Pang. Even Ray tried to dissuade her. Following my example, Bagel has turned my mother down every time. Once after a family dinner, I overheard my mother working on Bagel. She said, "I want to see Hong Kong again before I die. I first went there in 1939 because of the Japanese. How proud I'd be returning to old friends with such a fine young son! 'An overseas bandit,' they call you. They line the prettiest girls up for you. Whatever you like. You pick. Take her out. If you don't like her, you try another. *Too muchee Chinee girl.*"

My brother said, "I'm too busy for a wife."

"She cook for you."

"I won't be able to talk to her."

"They're all very modern. They're learning English. If you take a young one, you can teach her yourself."

"I'm already married to my cat."

"Such crazy talk," she said. "What kind of life is that, hugging a cat all the time. She give you babies?"

"*Forget it*," he said. "Too much trouble."

"You're killing me," she said. "Soon I'll be lying next to your father. You crazy juk-sing, you do as I say. Before it's too late, marry a Chinese girl who will remember my grave and come with food and spirit money. Left up to you, I'll starve when I'm dead."

Bagel's house is white. Even the oak floors have been bleached white. A stranger in a white turtleneck and white pleated trousers opens the door. He's very blond, with dazzling teeth and a jawline that's an archeologist's dream. "Well, look who's here," he says, "the brother, et al." We shake hands, and he says his name's Nino. Nino leads us to the sun-washed living room and introduces us to Mack, who's sprawled over a couch with the *Times*. My mother whispers that she'd warned my brother against buying a white couch because it wouldn't "withstand the dirt," but she's surprised at how clean it looks. Mack's dressed like Deborah, and this depresses me. "Billy," Nino says in a loud singsong, "big bro and Mommy's here."

Jamie of the two-seater comes into the living room. He hugs my mother, shakes my hand, and nods at Deborah. He's in a white terry-cloth robe and Italian loafers, and offers us coffee. Down the hallway someone starts to run a shower.

While Jamie grinds coffee beans in the kitchen, Nino says, "I had the worst night's sleep." He's stretched out on the other couch, his hand cupped over his eyes. "What a shock to the system, it was so damn quiet. How do the chipmunks stand it?" Then my brother makes his entrance decked out in hound's-tooth slacks, tight turquoise tennis shirt, and black-and-white saddle shoes. "God, Billy," Nino says, "you always look so pulled together."

Hugs and kisses all the way around. Bagel's got bulk. He pumps iron. I feel as if I'm holding a steer.

"Ah-Ba-ko," my mother says, once we have resettled in our seats, "come and see." She leans forward in her easy chair, a white plastic shopping bag of goodies from Chinatown at her feet. "I told her not to," I say as she unloads bundles of raw greens and paper boats of dumplings onto the armrests. When she magically lifts the roast duck from the bag, soy sauce drips from the take-out container and lands on the chair, spotting the off-white fabric. Bagel has a fit: "I invite you to dinner and you bring dinner."

"So what else is new?" I hear Deborah say.

Within seconds, Nino, Mack, Jamie, and Bagel converge on the stains with sponges. Palmolive dishwashing detergent, paper towels, and a pot of water. An eight-armed upholstery patrol.

Soon after, we're having Jamie's coffee and nibbling on my mother's dumplings, which Bagel has arranged beautifully on a Chinese-looking platter, as much a conciliatory gesture as it is his way of doing things.

"Bette Davis was buried yesterday," Mack says, from behind the paper.

"Really?" says Nino. "God, now there's a lady. Hollywood heaven, open your gates. May she rest . . . in . . . peace."

"What eyes she had," says Jamie, "like two full moons."

"Old bug eyes," Deborah says.

Nino makes a hissing sound. We all look at Deborah. "Oh, hell," Nino finally says, "what does she know?"

"How old was she?" my brother asks before Deborah can answer Nino back.

"Who knows? I saw her on Johnny Carson and she looked like hell."

"*Johnny Cahson?* He said *Johnny Cahson*, right?" My mother giggles, thrilled she understood a bit of our conversation.

Bagel rolls his eyes at me like Johnny. I shrug my shoulders as if to say, I didn't invite her to the party.

"I wanted so badly for Bette to be beautiful, but she looked like leftovers that even the cat won't touch. I swear I cried, she was such a mess."

"He did," says Mack. "Poor Nino, it was tragic. He cried the biggest tears ever. But you have to admit, she still had those fabulous eyes."

"Sure, eyes. The rest of her had been run over by Hurricane Hugo."

"I saw that show," Jamie says. "Her mind was still there. She was very sharp."

"Oh sure," says Nino, "so's broken glass."

Deborah laughs; then my mother laughs. "What is she laughing about?" my mother asks through her own laughter. I shake my head to quiet her down.

Bagel holds up a gray-skinned dumpling to the ceiling. A toast: he says, "*What Ever Happened to Baby Jane?*"

"*Jezebel*," says Jamie.

"*All About Eve.*"

"*Kid Galahad*," I say.

"Oooo, that has Edward G. Robinson in it," Nino says.

Bagel's cat, Judy, and her husband, Vavoom, enter the living room, led by their noses. My mother surreptitiously plunks a shrimp dumpling on each armrest. She sees I see her doing this, and I scowl at her and she scowls back, then covers her gold mine with her hand as she breaks into a smile. She's surrounded by cats. "Look! What an adorable picture!" says Nino. "Judy, Vavoom, and Mrs. Pang, the goddess of treats." Then he adds, "Truthfully, I wouldn't give away any of these delicacies to cats; I wouldn't give any to Bette, even if she begged from her deathbed. Mrs. Pang, you've made lifelong friends." My mother, hearing her name, looks up from the cats, but the dim heat of her eyes tells everyone she's understood little else. "Silly me," Nino says, "did I say something?"

Bagel's a commercial artist, Nino's a jewelry designer, Mack's a book editor, Jamie's a city attorney. During a lull in the conversation, which we fill by watching the cats walk across my mother's lap from one armrest to the other, Jamie asks what's new at my job. I consider the Kyoto–Musk 838/Lot No. i9144375941-3e affair, but realize if I mention Mandy's name my mother will start in on me. So, instead, I improvise: "The rumor going around the lab," I begin, "says the chemists are developing a spray for the homeless, a time-release formula that'll simulate, in succession, the smell of a living room in a Scarsdale Tudor, a regular coffee (cream and one sugar), a roast-beef dinner, and fresh sheets washed in Tide."

"How ingenious!" Nino says. "The nose is such an amazing organ."

"When someone asks you for change," says Mack, "you give him a squirt of the comforts of home."

"Picture this, a panhandler in a subway car: 'Spare spray, spare spray?' "

"This is sick," says Deborah.

"I'm just giving you the latest gossip," I say. "The other rumor is that the city plans to distribute the stuff to the homeless."

"Cheaper than shelters, I suppose," Mack says.

"This is news to me," says Jamie, the city attorney. "But I wouldn't put it past the mayor's office. Remember those prints of potted flowers the city put in the windows of abandoned buildings up in Harlem?"

He pours himself a cup of coffee. "I'm working on a homeless case right now," he says. "This couple, the Montezumas, show up at Bellevue one day. They're carrying one of those Express Mail envelopes and inside there's a baby, hot and sticky from being born, the cord still on. She's purple, in real trouble. The doctors hook her up to machines, but in a few days she dies. Only she doesn't look dead. The machines pump air into her lungs, and somehow her heart keeps beating."

"Then she's alive," I say.

"No, she *looks* alive, but that's what Montezuma claims. Her chest goes up and down. But her brain doesn't register a single blip on the screen. Specialists are called in, and they tell Montezuma the same story. But Montezuma says God is testing us all, and he won't let the hospital pull the plug. Meanwhile the city is footing the bill. More specialists are consulted; Montezuma still refuses to sign the forms, so finally the city steps in and turns off the juice. The next thing you know, half the attorneys in town are fighting for the chance to sue the city, and I have lots of work."

Bagel, Jamie, and I spend the afternoon playing tennis while my mother watches us from the car. The others take a drive around the "countryside."

We eat dinner late. Jamie barbecues chicken. My mother chops her duck into rectangular chunks. We drink three bottles of chardonnay. Afterward, we're in the kitchen, slicing pies, making coffee, putting away leftovers, washing dishes.

I hear my mother calling for Bagel. We find each other in the busy kitchen, and he asks me to see what she wants.

She's in the master bedroom standing in front of the TV set. It's turned on; the screen's filled with pink and blue snow.

"What are you doing?" I say. "This is Saturday. There's no Johnny Carson."

"You think I don't know," she says. "Saturday night has to have wrestling."

I flip through the stations with the remote control. For as long as I can remember, my mother has been a wrestling fan. It's good pitted against evil; the clean-shaven, self-effacing, play-by-the-rules good guy versus the strutting, loudmouthed, eye-gouger. No language skills required here. A dialogue of dropkicks, forearm smashes, and body slams. It's a big fake but my mother believes. And for a long time, as a kid, our family gathered in front of the set Saturday nights, drinking sodas and cracking red pistachio nuts, true believers all.

In one of my strongest memories, a man from ringside wearing a pea coat and knit cap, with a duffel bag slung over his shoulder, leapt into the ring where the champ, a vicious long-haired blond, was taking a post-victory strut on his victim's chest. The fans in the arena, my mother beside me, were voicing their indignation when this mystery man, who looked as if he had walked in off the streets, caught the champ unawares, lifted him onto his shoulder, and applied a back-breaker, soon recognized as his signature hold. What joy, what gratitude, what relief we all felt! Justice restored! Later in the program, the ringside announcer interviewed our hero. He was an Italian sailor, he said, in heavily accented English, a recent immigrant to U.S. shores.

It was myth in action. The American Dream in all its muscle-bound splendor played out before our faithful eyes.

My mother and I sit at the edge of the king-size bed. On the screen, a match is about to begin between a doe-faced boy named Bubby Arnold and the Samurai Warrior. The All-American Boy meets the Yellow Peril. The outcome is obvious to everyone except my mother. She yells encouragement to Bubby, "Kill him, kill the little Jap boy!" as he bounds across the ring, all grit and determination, but promptly collapses to the mat when he runs into the Samurai Warrior's lethal, upraised foot. I shake my head. By then my thoughts are full of Kyoto and Mandy's Ito. My Musk 838/Lot No. i9144375941-3e, testament to our love, and my tenuous hold on Mandy are crumbling, going the way of Bubby Arnold under the Samurai Warrior's assault. I ache for Bubby, the poor schnook. I can't bear to watch. But my mother hasn't given up. She screams for her man to step on his opponent's bare toes, to yank on his goatee. But that isn't in the script. He isn't paid to be resourceful, no Yankee ingenuity here. No one, not my mother and her frantic heart, can change the illusion.

At the commercial break my mother says, "The Japanese are so cruel. He almost killed that poor boy." She goes on that way, recounting the mugging, and I tell her not to take it so seriously. "It's all a fake," I say. "He's not really hurt."

"I have eyes," she says. "I know what I just saw."

I'm surprised by the sudden heat in her voice, by the wound beneath the words. The fights matter: in them, she believes her heart's desire, her words of encouragement have currency. What *she* wants counts. But the truth is she doesn't believe what she has seen. The good guy should win. Somewhere in that mind of hers she carries hope for the impossible. Bubby Arnold triumphant, Mandy back in our lives again. I look at her, a woman against the odds. What a life of disappointment!

I won't let her down as Bubby Arnold has. She needs to hear the truth: there is no Santa; the Communists aren't leaving China. Her beloved Amanda is gone for good.

"I have to tell you something." I take a deep breath and say, "Amanda," and as anticipated, she's startled, expectant, hanging on my next word.

I regret I ever started. That hope is flickering in her irises, and it's poison to my enterprise. But I have no recourse but to get on with it; as my mother likes to say at such a juncture, "You wet your hair, you might as well cut it."

I know what I want to say in English. My mind's stuffed full with the words. I pull one sentence at a time from the elegant little speech I've devised over the months for just this occasion, and try to piece together a word-for-word translation into Chinese. Yielding nonsense. I abandon this approach and opt for the shorter path, the one of reduction, simplicity, lowest common denominator. "*Ah-mahn-da*, what?

Talk if you have talk." There's music in her voice I haven't heard in years.

"I like *Amanda*," I say.

My mother nods. On the TV, wrestlers being interviewed snarl into the camera and holler threats that seem directed not so much at future opponents as at the viewers themselves.

"She doesn't like me," I say.

"Crazy boy. Like? What is this 'like'? I lived all those years with your father—who worried about who liked which one? Tomorrow, you call her back here."

Samurai Warrior's grinning face fills the screen. In the background his manager carries on about the mysteries of the Orient, tea ceremonies, karate, brown rice, and his client's Banzai Death Grip.

"Look it, look it. He's so brutal, that one is," my mother says. She touches my cheek, her hand warm but leathery. I can't remember this happening before. "You say you like her, so call her back."

"What's wrong with your ears? I said she doesn't like me. She likes him." I point at the TV.

"Crazy boy. What are you saying?" She dismisses me, her fingers pushing off my cheek, as if they have springs.

"*Amanda* likes a Japanese."

"That one?" she says, meaning the wrestler.

I pound my fists against my thighs. "No, not him." I stand up and pace the carpet between my mother and the TV set. "*Amanda*," I begin, "*Amanda* . . ." And each time I say her name and hesitate, my mother sucks in breath and inflates with new hope. I stop pacing. She looks up at me from her seat at the edge of the bed. I touch her cheeks with both hands. I don't know where the gesture comes from, movies or TV, but it has nothing to do with what went on in our household. I am on strange ground. In my palms her face is a glass bowl, open and cool. "*Amanda* likes you. She doesn't like me. She likes a Japanese boy in *California*. I can call her, but she's not coming back."

My mother pulls away, not just from my hands, but receding, a filament inside her dimming. "*Ah-mahn-da* makes a delicious dumpling," she says in a small, distant voice. "She rolls the skins so delicately."

During the next match she is uncharacteristically subdued. The fight has left her. On the screen two masked wrestlers beat up Bubby Arnold clones. Nothing issues from her, no encouragement, no outrage, no hope. I've robbed my mother of her pleasure, of her flimsy faith in Americans, in America, and in me. And I don't have the words for *I am sorry*, or fine sentences that would resurrect her faith and put things back in order. I'm the pebble in her shoe, the stone in her kidney. Now I see that she's Montezuma from Jamie's story: she would hold on to the slimmest hope, while I, as I have just done, would rush in and pull the plug on her.

At the next commercial time-out she turns to me and says, "Ah-Vee-ah, all the men in this house have good jobs, they have money, why don't they have women? Why is your brother that way? What does he tell you? I don't understand." She speaks somberly, with difficulty, as she had when she described the raids.

Her eyes, I see, are filled with tears. I know that she cries easily and often since my father's death. I've heard her in her room late at night.

I put my hand on her back, as round as a turtle's, but hot and meaty. "I don't know," I tell her, and for the first time I am stunned by my deception of her. "I don't know why there's no women here."

Bagel comes to the bedroom announcing coffee and dessert. He turns off the set. I can read his mind. He doesn't want his friends to know he dropped from the womb of one who loves something as low as wrestling. "Come eat *pie*," he says.

"*Pie*. Who made them?" she asks.

"I did, who else? I stayed up last night baking pies for you. Come on."

"Yours I won't eat," she says. "I want to taste your girlfriend's baking."

"You crazy? I don't have a girlfriend," he says. "She's driving me crazy!" he exclaims, then leaves the bedroom, and we follow.

"*Ca-lay-zee*. Who's *ca-lay-zee*? You hammerhead. Hug your dead cat the rest of your life. How fragrant is that?"

"*Forget it*, Ma," I say. I touch her shoulder, but she flicks me off.

"Ah-Ma," she says. "How can I be your mother if nobody listens to what I say?"

At the table we are confronted with big wedges of apple pie. My mother's still upset. She stares at the pie as if it were a form of torture.

"Where've you two been?" Deborah asks.

"In the bedroom, watching wrestling."

"God, how retro," she says. "What's happening to you?"

"Bagel," I say, stopping his hand as he's about to spoon sugar into my mother's coffee.

"Bagels?" Jamie says. "You're hungry for bagels? We're having bagels for breakfast."

I say nothing. I pull from my pocket gold-foil packets the size and shape of condoms. Inside each is a tablet developed at the lab. You dissolve it in your mouth, and it will disguise the sourness of whatever you drink or eat. I pass them to everyone at the table.

They won't know what has happened. They will laugh, delighted by the tricks of their tongues. But soon the old bitterness in our mouths will be forgotten, and from this moment on, our words will come out sweet.

Fourscore and Seven
Years Ago

Sixt grade, we had to give da news every morning aftah da pledge allegence and My Country Tis of Dee. "Current events time," Mrs. Ching tell, and she only call on maybe five kids fo get extra points, so first, you gotta raise your hand up and hope she call on you. You should always try be ready wit someting fo say cause sometimes nobody raise up their hands cause nobody went listen to da news on da radio or read da newspaypah last night so if you raise your hand, guarantee she call you. Bungy Lau was always waving his hand almost everyday fo give news. And if only get one chance fo tell da news left, Bungy give you da stink eye and raise his hand mo high and wave um and almost stand up awready fo make Mrs. Ching see him. Us guys and most times da girls too, dey jes put their hands down cause we no like Bungy get mad at us. Mrs. Ching try look around da room for

DARRELL LUM was born and raised in Honolulu. His interest in pidgin writing has taken both prose and dramatic forms. His most recent collections of short stories and plays are *Sun* and *Pass On, No Pass Back!*, which was the winner of the 1992 Association for Asian American Studies Outstanding Book Award. He is one of the editors of *Bamboo Ridge, The Hawaii Writers' Quarterly*.

see if get anybody else she can call besides Bungy but by den we all stay looking down at our desk so she gotta call Bungy cause he da only one left, yeah? And Bungy he stand up, he big you know, and he stay cracking his knuckles and he no mo one paper or anyting and we know dat he going to give da wrestling results from da night before.

"Las night at da Civic Auditorium, fo da Nort American Heavyweight Belt, Nicky Bockwinkle pinned Curtis 'da Bull' Iaukea in two outa tree falls and retained da Nort American Belt. In tag team ackshen 'Mister Fooge,' Fuji Fujiwara and da Masked Executionah was disqualified in a minute and thirty seconds of da first round fo using brass knuckles dat da Executionah went hide in his tights."

"Da cheatah!" Jon go tell and everybody went laugh at him. Mrs. Ching shush da class.

"Da duo of Giant Baba and da Southern Gennelman, Rippah Collins retained their tag team title."

Once I thot dat I would try dat too and I went listen to da radio, KGU Sports, da night before fo get da winners and I wrote um down because no fair if Bungy hog all da points just by giving the wrestling results. Dat wasn't news, was all fake. My fahdah said wrestling was like roller derby, all fake.

Anyway, da time I was going give da wrestling results, Bungy was looking at me cracking each knuckle in his fingers first one hand den da uddah and I went look down at my paypah wit da winnahs and da times and I thot maybe I better give da news about how da Russian Yuri Gagarin went around in space instead. After I was finished, Bungy raised his hand and said dat da Indian guy, Chief Billy White Wolf went fight Beauregarde, da guy dat always stay combing his hair and he took Beauregarde in two minutes of the third round with a half Nelson. Exact what I had on my paypah! I saw Mrs. Ching marking down our points in her book.

One time, Mrs. Ching went ask me if I like get extra points. She said she would gimme extra points if I get all dressed up like Abraham Lincoln and say da Gettysburg Address to da fift graders. I nevah like but she said I had to go cause I was da best at saying um las year. I still nevah like cause look stoopid when dey pin da black construction paper bow tie and make you wear da tall construction paper hat but she said it was one privilege fo say da speech and dat she would help me memarize um again. Ass cause when I was in da fift grade everybody had to learn da ting and had one contest in da whole fift grade and I went win cause everybody else did junk on purpose so dat dey nevah have to get up in front of da whole school, dressed up like Abe Lincoln. Shoot. I nevah know. I nevah know dat da winner had to go back da next year and say um again to da fift graders either.

Everyting was diffrent. In da sevent grade, you change classes l'dat and had all dese rules and j'like da bell stay ringing all da time. Had da warning bell before school start, had da real bell, and had da tardy bell. And da bells between classes and da tardy to class bell and da first lunch bell and da second lunch bell. And you had to tuck in your shirttails and wear shoes.

Bungy was Benjamen now. I knew cause his muddah and my muddah went make us go Chinese school summer time and we had to be in da first grade class wit all da small kids even if we was in da sixt grade going be sevent. Anyway, whenevah da teacha call Bung Mun, he tell, "My name Benjamen!" So da teacha try say "Benjamen" only ting come out "Bung-a-mun" and Bungy gotta tell again, "Benjamen!" Ass how I knew his name was Benjamen now. But most guys still yet called him "Bungy" even if he nevah answer.

And Charlene Chu had braces so she nevah smile anymore, not dat she used to smile at us anyways. Bungy, I mean Benjamen, would yell at her, "Hey, metal mout, you can staple my math papers wit your teet?" And all of a sudden, she had tits. Sixt grade nutting. Sevent grade, braces and bra.

Benjamen would always wear slippahs still yet even if he was supposed to wear shoes. He tell he get sore feet but his feet always stay bus up cause he like to go barefoot. His feet so ugly and dirty and stink, da nurse no like even look at dem, she jes give him da slippah pass. And if you had to go batroom during classtime you had to get one batroom pass. And had library pass and cafeteria pass and if you work cafeteria you had to wear da paper cap or if you get long hair da ladies make you wear da girls hairnet and you had to wear covered shoes. Even had dis yellow line painted on da stairs and down da middle of da hallway all ovah da school and you had to go up only on da right side and go down on da uddah side. Dey could nab you and make you stand hall for doing stuff like going down the up side of the stairs. Crazy yeah?

If you gotta stand hall you gotta go da vice-principal's office before school, recess, lunch time, and after school fo so many minutes and stand in da main hallway of the school facing the wall. Ass where everybody walk pass so dey can razz you anymuch dey like cause you no can talk when you standing hall. I tink Mr. Hansen went make up da rules. He was dis tall, skinny haole guy, mean-looking buggah. But he nevah do da dirty work. If you got reported to the office, you had to see da vice-principal, Mr. Higuchi. He was one short, fat guy you had to go see if you was tardy or went fight and somebody said he da one who paddle you. Bungy said watch out if you gotta go his office and he close da door. Anyway, when Higuchi tell you you gotta stand hall, he take you to your spot and he take his pencil and he make one dot on da wall and he tell, "Dis is your spot. Don't take your eyes off it." You no can talk or look around cause every now and den he come out of his office and walk up and down da hallway real soft fo check if you still dere and you not fooling around.

So in da sevent grade, I wised-up. Had me and Jon and Bungy left in da classroom spelling bee. Da winner had to represent da class in da school spelling bee and no ways we was going make "A" in front da whole school.

"Tenement," Miss Hashimoto said.

"T-E-N-A-M-E-N-T," I went spell um.

"T-E-N-T-E-M-E-N-T," Bungy went spell um.

"T-A-N-E-M-E-N-T," Jon said.

"This is easy, you guys," Hashimoto went tell.

"Nah, S-L-U-M!" Bungy went tell.

"Okay, nobody got um. Next word, syncopate."

"S-I-N-K-O-P-A-T-E," I went tell real fast. I was trying fo spell um as wrong as I could cause I nevah like spell um right by accident. Miss Hashimoto went sigh real loud.

"Definition please," Bungy went jump right in. He throw da ack him.

"To shorten or produce by syncope."

"S-Y-N-C-O-P-A-T-E . . ."

"Yes!" Miss Hashimoto said. She sounded relieved.

"E!" Bungy went yell. He knew he went spell um correct. He went spell um again, "S-Y-N-C-O-P-A-T-E-E."

Jon was laughing and I was telling, "No fair! He had two chances. Da first one was good! Was correct." Hashimoto looked pissed, she caught on. "If you boys don't shape up and start being serious I'm just going to dock your grade and send all three of you to the finals."

It ended up being me. I tink da uddah two guys was still yet missing on purpose but everytime came to me, Hashimoto went gimme me da eye and made her mout kinda mean and I could feel my heart loud in my throat and she everytime had to say, "Louder, please. Repeat the spelling." And I would spell um different jes in case I spelled um correct da first time and she would say, "Correct!" even when I tink I went spell um wrong. So I was da one.

When I was up on stage, da principal, Mr. Hansen was pronouncing da words and he went gimme "forefathers" in da first round. I went spell um "F-O-R-F-A-T-H-E-R-S" and I knew I had um wrong by da way Miss Hashimoto went look at me when I went look out at the seats and saw my homeroom class. I knew she was tinking I did um on purpose but actually I was figuring on staying in fo a coupla rounds fo make um look good before I went out. When I got back to my seat on stage I went look at her and I tink she was crying. She had one Kleenex in her hand and she was wiping her eyes. I felt *bad*, man. Wasn't my fault. I was really trying dat time. I went aftah school fo tell her sorry I went get out on da first round and she started crying again. I wanted to cry too cause I nevah mean to make da teacha cry. I hate Hashimoto fo making me go up dere in da first place. Bungy and Jon was smartah den me. My ears was hot, j'like dey was laughing at me.

Mostly da teachas was all dese old futs. But we heard dat had one cute new speech teacha, Mrs. Sherwin and dat she was one hot-cha-cha. Gordon Morikawa said da eight graders said she was good-looking. He said dat how many times Jimmy Uyehara went catch da bone while he was giving one speech cause when you give one speech you gotta go to da front and she go to da back and sometimes when she cross her legs can see her panties. "Naht," I couldn't believe dat. Besides I said, "She must be *old* if she married, she *Mrs.* Sherwin, yeah?"

Anyways we all wanted to see what she was going be like cause anyting was bettah den having chorus wit Miss Teruya who was one young old fut, and mean. She whack you wit her stick if she tink you not singing loud enough and if you no memarize da words, she make you stand next to da piano and sing solo. One time we went spend one whole class period practicing standing up and sitting down when she give da signal cause she no like when everybody stand up or go down crooked.

Da first day of da second semester we switched from chorus to speech and we went to her room and everybody was quiet cause was j'like da first day of school again. Bungy kept poking me in my back wit one book. "She cute," he whispered to me, "I heard she cute!" even though we nevah even see her yet. Some of da girls went turn around and give him stink eye and tell him, "Shhhh!" He jes went stretch out his legs and tell loud, "You tink Charlene Chu wear falsies?" I donno if he knew she was walking in da door but everybody went laugh when Charlene came through da door. Jon guys was trying fo be quiet but dey was all trying fo grab da small paperback dat Benjamen was reading behind his social studies book, *Lady Chatterley's Lover.* Jon said dat was one hot book and only da guys in their club could read um. Jon sat in front of me, and Benjamen sat behind me, so I had to pass da book back and fort between dose two guys. Nevah look like one hot book. I went look inside and nevah see no hot parts.

"Dat's because you donno which page fo read," Jon told me afterwards, "Benjamen get um all written down in his Pee Chee folder." Dey was passing da book back and fort reading da good parts all da way in social studies and now in speech. I wanted to read um too but if you stop and read um, Benjamen start kicking your chair until you pass um on. Dey was still yet passing um around when Mrs. Sherwin walked into da room and threw her cigarette case on the desk.

"Okay class, let's begin." She looked like one nint grader or little older maybe and she was wearing one short dress and everytime her bra strap was falling out and she tuck um in.

"Whoa, she smoke," Bungy was telling Jon, "She smoke!"

"See, I told you she cute," he said in my ear and put da hot book on my desk. I was supposed to pass um on to Jon but even though I was poking Jon wit da book, he nevah turn around and take um cause Sherwin went start class and he nevah like her see. I went put um undah my folder but I started fo get nervous about what if I get nabbed for having one hot book. Probably gotta stand hall for da rest of da year.

We went watch her reaching up to write her name high at da top of da board "Mrs. Sherry Sherwin—Beginning Speech" in one loose, half-printing, half-script style. She was skinny and we was watching her ass and her arm and she even write sexy and all da boys started to adjust their pants in their seats. Even her name was sexy . . . Sherry . . . Sher-wen. She turned around and we watched her lick her lips with da tip of her tongue. Da girls was looking at her and den turning around and looking at da boys. Dey probably was jes jealous.

Da rest of da time was regular. Pass out books, write your name on da card and hand um in and she gave us work on da first day, man. Was boring da beginning part so I started to read da hot book. Dis time Benjamen wasn't kicking my chair and Jon went forget about getting um, so I went read um. Mostly was about dis creepy gardener guy and he was trying fo get dis young girl. He was peeking in her window or someting and was checking out her tits and he was reaching for his dick, da book call um his "member" and somebody went kick my chair real hard and I went drop da book and quick Benjamen went kick um undah my chair. "Stoopid!" he went hiss at me. Sherwin went look up at us.

Turn out, Sherwin was the sevent-grade adviser and when came time fo the first canteen, she told the boys that we had to learn the etiquette of asking a young lady to dance. She made us practice.

"Make sure all the girls get to dance," she said. "If any of my boys notice wallflowers, I expect you to say . . ." She looked around da room and went call on me, "Daniel?"

"May I have dis dance," I mumbled.

"And ladies, how should you reply? Charlene?" Sherwin said.

"Why I'd *love* to, Daniel," Charlene said, all sassy. All da guys laughed.

"Whoa, Dan-yo! Maybe she going make you dance wit Charlene!"

"Maybe Charlene going ask you fo dance!"

Charlene straightened up and tucked her blouse tightly into her skirt. She looked at me disgusted. I wonder if dey was falsies?

"Whas one wall-fla-wah?" Jon asked.

"Stoopid," Benjamen said, "da ugly ones!"

Jon raised his hand. "Geez," Benjamen said, "he going ask someting stoopid," and he put his head down.

"Yes, Jon."

"So what if we no like dance wit da wall-fla-wahs?"

"Then you have to dance with me," Mrs. Sherwin said. "Would you like to dance with me, Jon?"

"Oh, no! Ah, I mean yes. Ah, I mean it would be an honor m'am."

"Don't gimme that bull," Mrs. Sherwin said laughing. "I just want to see you out on the floor, dear. Kicking up those heels."

I wouldn't mind dancing wit her. I was looking at my shoes. If I had Beatle boots, maybe she would dance wit me. Evans said that if you had real shiny shoes you could look up the girls' dresses. No wondah he was always rubbing the top of his shoes on the back of his pants legs. He had Beatle boots with taps and stomped on anybody with new shoes. Scuffed um up and said, "Baptize!" Like how he baptized everybody after they came back to school with a fresh haircut. Everytime he sweep his hand around my ears and tell, "Ay, whitewalls!" Evans had sideburns and a sheik cut, a razor trimmed cut around his ears that made his head look like a black helmet, hard and glistening with pomade, swept into a ducktail in the back.

"And boys," Mrs. Sherwin was saying, "if I catch you combing your hair in the dance, I'm going to confiscate your comb. Get a nice haircut before the dance and comb your hair in the bathroom." Once, I got nabbed with my comb, da long skinny kine, sticking out of my pocket and Sherwin took um cause she no even like *see* one comb. She told me I had to come back after school if I wanted um back. So I went after school fo get um back and when she went open her drawer, had uku-billion combs, all hairy and greasy and probably had real ukus on top.

"Which one is yours?" she told me.

"Uh, ass okay, I foget which one was mine," I said even though I could see mine, right dere, on top.

"You don't need to comb your hair anyway," and she went rough up my hair and I could feel her hand go down the bristly back of my neck, almost like how Benjamen baptize you.

"Eh, no make," I said. Felt good though. Could smell her perfume. Spicy. I felt hot. I wish I had one sheik cut. But I couldn't cause nutting was growing in front my ears. I no like when da barber jes buzz um off. I like get one sheik cut but I no mo nuff hair over dere to shave. Costs fifty cents more, too. Even my father no get one sheik cut. He get the 85 cent special at Roosevelt Barbershop, one time around da ears wit da machine and scissors cut on top. Pau fast.

Every time my fahdah go cut hair, I gotta go too. Even if I no like. Geez, I hope nobody see me cutting hair. Da barbah guy, Fortunato still take out da booster seat, one old worn out board dat he put across da arms of da chair and I gotta sit on um cause da stuff fo crank up da seat stay broken.

Da only good ting was da barbah shop was next to da theater dat showed hot movies. Hard fo look at da pictures when you stay wit your fahdah but you can look side-eye at da Now Playing and Coming Attractions posters: "Alexandra the Great 48 in Buxom Babes!" and "Physical Education!" Couple times I went put da *National Enquirer* inside one of the old magazines, *Soldier of Fortune* or *Guns and Ammo* or *Field & Stream,* and read the main story, "My Bosom Made Me a Nympho at Twelve." I read um so many times I almost memarized um. Had this picture of one kinda old lady bending over and could see down her dress but I knew that couldn't be one picture of da girl cause she nevah look like she was twelve and no ways you could have tits that big. Maybe trick photography. Sometimes when my fahdah stay in da chair and I stay waiting my turn, Fortunato stop cutting and quick I look up fo see if he nab me but he only stay listening to da D.J. on da radio talking Filipino. Fast, excited. He jes suck his teeth and make one "tssk" sound and cut again. And I would look at da picture again and try to imagine dat it was Mrs. Sherwin but I only could see Charlene's face in dat picture, bending ovah. Smiling at me, her braces shiny, glistening. Whoa, da spooky.

Resistance

Laureen Mar

The first time Grant Kiyoshi Ito saw his old man clearly was the morning he found him in the garage trying to hang himself with an aluminum step ladder and a nylon rope.

He'd flipped open the garage door. Disgust and panic rose, as thick and heavy as vomit. "God, Dad!" he exploded, and stared, dumbfounded. Then he ran, bumping into the ladder, sending it skittering and hearing its thin screech as he grabbed for his father's ankles.

"Mom!" he shouted. He tried to push his father high enough to put a slack in the cord. His father's pants sagged in his face, making it hard to breathe. "Mom!" He was too heavy. "Don't bend your knees!" he yelled, furious at the indignity of having to burrow his head in the soft flesh of his father's thighs. He couldn't see what was happening, he couldn't see anything except his father's fingers, short and calloused, waving above his eyes.

LAUREEN MAR is a native of Seattle; she has taught writing and literature at Washington State University and, more recently, at Pacific Lutheran University in Tacoma. Widely anthologized, her poetry earned her a public art commission for Seattle's innovative downtown transit project. Excerpted here, *Resistance* is her novel-in-progress.

His mother stood in the driveway, her purse clutched under her arm. "*Chikusho,*" she swore at the sight of her son staggering under the bewildering weight of her husband, and turned on her heels. She returned with a kitchen knife, sharply yanked the ladder into place, and on the high heels of her ivory dress shoes, cut him down.

Junichi Abiko Ito fell, crumpling to the concrete floor like a sack of potatoes. Grant backed away, watching from where he sat scrunched against the wall. His father groaned, turning his face away from his wife and coughing. Grant studied him dispassionately.

You would think that a man going to hang himself would look different somehow, either at his worst, frantic and bedeviled, or maybe at his best, supremely composed at the thought of finality. It was true, Grant conceded, that as frugal a man as his father was, he'd bought a brand new rope to hang himself, bright yellow, as if it were a new necktie he wanted to show off. Later Grant would let his sneakers toe the coils of hemp discarded on the concrete floor, the damp and dirty serpentines suddenly flaccid and obscene. This was the rope the old man used to tack down the flapping blue plastic tarps over his truckloads of manure, dead branches, grass clippings, and weeds. This was the rope that would have suited the job, but even his father had illusions of grandeur. Too little, too late, no kidding. Since when had his father tried anything new, taken any kind of risk—only now, when it couldn't possibly matter. One lousy, loud yellow cord that only someone as plastic as Mickey Mouse could successfully hang himself on.

No, the old man had tinkered with this just the way he tinkered with the lawn mower, banging his wrench against the motor to take out a distracting sputter—something he might as well do now since he had a few extra minutes. Just before he'd slipped his head into the noose he had bent down, still perched on the ladder, to take off his heavy work shoes, placing them neatly on the second rung. And even with the loop around his neck, his father appeared normal, simply as if he were taking a break standing up on the top of a ladder, then swinging gingerly away for fun, and suspended, looking as helplessly disheveled as usual: his gray work pants stained with grass and oil, his sleeves rolled bunchily to his elbows, a cowlick twirling up incongruously from his otherwise matted and streaked hair, his expression one of perpetual puzzlement and surprise, of a timid man still eager to please. To commit suicide was probably his idea of doing just that, Grant figured, and wondered if then he'd consider him a failure.

Instead he'd ended up, finally, looking pathetically out of place, as anyone would hanging from the rafters, even in the garage Grant usually avoided precisely because it seemed so much the sum of his father's life: the two lawn mowers (one permanently dismantled, its parts scattered on the floor), the hedge clipper, pole pruner, canvas drop cloths, bamboo rakes, grass shears, fork, dirt-clodded spades—tools his dad had bought as a young man trying to support a family temporarily with odd jobs and yardwork, tools that mockingly had lived up to their red-label guarantee to serve a gardener for a lifetime.

From the back wall of the garage, Grant could see everything, framed just so—as if he were watching a whole stilted and ridiculous world on his own private, miniature screen. His dad scuttling across the pavement against the wincing light. Now he watched his mother drive off in their car, his father slumped beside her. He'd stay and wait for his sisters to come home from swimming so he could tell them the lie that Mom and Dad had gone shopping at the mall. At least it was a plausible enough lie: shopping in the huge department stores made their dad dizzy, bringing him practically to a state of hyperventilation, and they'd expect to see him come home sucking his own breath back out of a brown paper sack.

The sun, with that edgy brightness peculiar to the Northwest, seemed to flinch off the white siding of their suburban tract house. On his way to the back door, Grant stopped abruptly in front of the tomato vines his father, all summer, had nursed. Their pungent leaves bristled under his fingers. He tore out the cages. Then he wrenched out the plants, flinging them behind him, leaving a trail of ripe, red Sunny Boys splattered on the concrete.

•

Grant shut the car door gently, took off his tie, and slouched low in the bucket seat of his Datsun B210. He closed his eyes. What a waste of a day. What a waste of a suit and tie. The week before, he'd signed off from Occidental Park in Pioneer Square where hundreds of homeless people from Seattle and Portland had congregated in an organized protest, overnight building a city out of sleeping bags and blankets, boxes and shopping carts in a clip that made national news. Today he'd covered a dog parade in West Seattle and the mayor singing a song about buses. After eight years of the sporadic Sunday afternoon relief, he could finally understand why a news reporter would want to become a weatherman. It was safe: the same dull rounds of rain, sun, clouds, snow, fog, an occasional blitz of hail or random earthquakes. You might get the weather wrong but at least no English-speaking, French-groomed standard poodles who barked "HARROW, HARROW" into your mike.

He put the car in reverse, shifted into first, and headed for the freeway. When he'd been at UCLA, he used to love the sprawl of traffic, the on-ramps, the off-ramps, the streets and grids so layered with metal that every day was a literal rite of passage, all the drivers nonchalantly speeding and weaving through the complicated and fragile web of their own lives. But in Seattle it was important to be polite, to act like all the other drivers who acted as if they weren't quite in their cars. So daily he drove home without his heart in it, the overpasses, the concrete walls, coming and going at the safely proscribed speed. He had time to imagine again the stark, gray titles for the documentary reports he wanted to make, ribbons and ribbons of videotape tracking the broken yellow lines of lives lost, fractured, mashed and bashed, to find the guy who walked away from it virtually unscratched, all his dignity intact. "Dogs, cats, and cockatoos were given to friends or shelters, leaving their young owners bereft"—who cared what happened to the pets? He wanted to uncover the story of the resisters, the ones who protested being impounded, moved into the doghouse of concentration camps.

The problem was that his managing editor, Gala, wouldn't buy it. Like characters in an opera, he wheedled and she flattered and it ended in death. To give him the go-ahead for a major assignment that would involve so much time and research just wasn't possible, she said. "We'd really love to have that story, Grant, but we need you for the day-to-day stuff." She'd sought to console him with a verbal shrimp puff, adding brightly, "You're so good at covering disasters."

"But Gala, it *is* a disaster, it's a disaster!" he cried. "If we don't report this, we're participating in a distortion of history. A couple hundred guys tossed into prison for resisting the draft, their protests, the fact of their existence even, squelched by community leaders who instead left us this legacy of the myth of the model minority. A violation of the First Amendment, the curtailment of Freedom of Speech! A Denver journalist denounced and tried for sedition. Let's use that angle," he argued.

"Grant," she answered, "we'll get two minutes of airtime on the day President Reagan picks up his ballpoint pen and signs the redress bill."

He knew the script. "Right. We zoom to the pen while President Reagan signs this unprecedented bill making an apology and a billion dollars in payments to 120,000 Japanese Americans who proved their loyalty, obeyed the law, went to camp, volunteered for the 442nd, the most highly decorated unit in World War II. Yadda yadda yadda. Okay, we died. We coped. And forty-eight years later, a check arrives in the mail. My father, when he gets his payment, will go out and buy a new truck. A happy ending to a sad story."

It was an important story—and yeah, he wanted the ten-second live interviews, a random pick of Seattleites who would applaud, grumble, remain oblivious, or be moved to weep. But he wanted more: a week-long series of special reports, two minutes a night, investigating the inside story, the missing chapter of Japanese American history, without which the war would never end.

No go. Gala shook her head apologetically.

He checked the rear view mirror. The amber arrow clicked quietly on the panel, flashing the message to the stream of traffic behind him that he was getting off here. He cut onto the down ramp leading to Dearborn, circling back to Jackson and passing through what used to be Japantown, now a land of concrete block mini-malls packed with Vietnamese grocery, video, and jewelry stores, noodle houses and bakeries, hair salons, and dentists.

There were vestiges of the old Japanese American community, unobtrusively part of the streetscape. Tashiro's Tools, which had started out as a hardware store on Prefontaine and moved uneasily from storefront to storefront, finally had seemed to settle down on Jackson, a block east of Rainier, its stock reduced to pruning saws and knives. On Rainier was Linc's Tackle, notable not only for its fishing tips but the fact that all four of the family's sons had been named after U.S. presidents; around the corner, Nikko, the queen bee of Japanese restaurants, modestly housed in a cedar woodframe on King; the Nisei Vets Hall on Weller; the Japanese Buddhist Church with Surefit Seatcovers parked behind its rear lot; and Tak's Body & Fender, whose mechanics ministered to the rumblings of his little car, named on the license plate "HUF"—Marianne's nickname sometimes for the car, sometimes for the driver. He shot up the hill toward Lake Washington and turned south, pulling up a few minutes later in front of her small house.

The problem was—when it wasn't Gala, who earnestly believed in her role as monitor of the day's histrionics—Marianne. Marianne Lu Tong, his lover and erstwhile psychoanalyst. When after their first few dates, she'd invited him to lie down on her living room couch, he'd done so with alacrity, imagining her lying down on top of him lying down on the couch. He'd sat up when he realized she wanted to talk about his mother.

He climbed the steps to her house. Their relationship had become so routine that he always felt the wild impulse to fling open the front door and greet her expansively with, "Hi, honey, I'm home!" or "What's for dinner, dear?" But since he didn't own a set of her keys, he knocked. So much for "The Donna Reed Show" and "Leave It to Beaver." He knocked, and then he banged on the door. Like Fred Flintstone.

Marianne came to the door looking like Wilma, her long hair swept up in a knobby ponytail. Her hairdo needed a bone. As it was, she stood there brushing leaves and twigs off her head, off the thin, nubby sweats she wore—made out of the same material as her dish rags, he'd noticed—with a look of seriousness and distraction. It wasn't the way she'd looked when he'd fallen in love with her. Why did this always happen to him? Why did the women he loved always have to change as deviously and freakishly as—well, as the weather, he grumbled to himself. An unexpected cold front, a flash flood, a tornado that came in from nowhere and tore the roof off of Dorothy's house.

"Gardening, huh?" He took off his jacket and sat down on the couch. He wanted to unlace his shoes but it seemed like too much trouble.

"Hard day?" She flopped down next to him. The leaves crinkled between them when she leaned into his lap. "Let's go out to dinner tonight." She sighed and drew her legs up on the couch, smelling like lemons and roses and something green—he didn't know. Chives?

"Can't."

"Why not?"

"Because my mother's coming in tonight. You didn't forget, did you?"

His mother had called from Los Angeles at six A.M. to remind him she was arriving that evening. "In case you forgot," she suggested gently. "Mom, how could I forget?" he'd asked jovially, and rushed to clean his house in the hour and a half left before he had to leave for the station, mentally shuddering at the thought of his mother painstakingly filing his letters and papers alphabetically. She would throw away with restrained distaste all the grimy news articles he had collected for the past year and leave him with a stack of neatly clipped coupons for orange juice, cereal, frozen peas, and boneless chicken.

He listened to the leaves crack and rustle, the itty bits shuffling scratchily between the cushions on the couch as Marianne shifted away from him.

She knew it was cruel and she didn't care. Marianne had been spoiled by a perverse kind of fortune, having had two previous boyfriends whose mothers were long and tragically departed, and as for the others (in her words), they had hardly had last names, permanent residences, jobs, scruples or morals, let alone mothers they'd want her to meet—something she'd reported more happily than regretfully, which Grant found unsettling. As miraculously as cream turns to butter, or milk turns to sour cream, she had lived to thirty-six without having had to meet a lover's mother since she was nineteen. So when she looked at him and asked with offhanded dismay, "Do I *have* to meet your mother? *Why?*"—they were, in their own way, he recognized, honest, albeit callous, questions.

He struggled not to look pained. "She's a very nice lady," he answered evenly, uncomfortably aware he'd made his mother sound like an Avon Lady or someone who arranged flowers for her church bazaar. Which come to think of it, she did once a year for the Bon Odori festival.

"Because she's my mother, for God's sake!" he wanted to shout. But then Marianne, that unrepentant heathen, would sweetly egg him with, "Christian reference."

He'd been an actor. He could do it. Modulate his voice, adjust his posture, temper his expression—fluctuating from impassivity to open relaxation to rage—which seemed to entertain her.

"Looking in your face is like looking in a funny mirror," she mused.

"Because," he said, with a reasonable smile, "because," he said, putting his arm around her waist, "I'd like you to meet her."

"Oh," she said.

And they both sat in silence, Grant remembering now with acute clarity how she'd rejoiced at having managed to avoid meeting a cousin's husband whom she'd *heard* was unbearably lugubrious or salacious or something through five years of family occasions, remembering how absolutely gleeful she'd been about having solved for once and for all the dilemma of what to do in the dire event of chain letters, copying out in false, tormented longhand the names and addresses of people she was mad at and thus neatly disposing of the twin onuses of obligation and revenge, to say nothing of hostility.

She could be irritatingly, and most annoyingly, unpredictably superstitious, despite the fact that she was trained to deal with the irrational. To the set of Chinese superstitions she claimed came from her mother, she added things willy-nilly, items about etiquette even, when she was really driven to making a point.

At the top of the list were the rules against bad luck—cleaning the house on New Year's Day, for example, not a problem since she never cleaned house. She couldn't eat bananas on her birthday, and neither could he; she shouldn't wash her hair on holidays, and neither should he. Though he still didn't understand why. The one positive superstition was that killing spiders got rid of guilt. Each spider dead by her hand not only eliminated one guilt but incidentally alerted Grant to her state of anxiety. She killed spiders with a real vengeance. Though he suspected the truth was that her parents had just gotten tired of her screams every time she'd found a spider in her bedroom and this handy superstition was simply a bribe toward self-reliance. Whenever he wanted to distract her, he resorted to the same tactic, calmly noting "spider," and pointing to the hallway, which usually was enough to forestall an argument.

"Spider," he said, pointing to the hall.

There was no way on earth she wanted to meet the woman who was responsible for the existence, the identity, the habits, the customs, the manners, of the man with whom she slept. How could she phrase this politely?

He had pried his shoes off and was sitting back with his eyes shut, his white shirt collapsing in a balloon of wrinkles. He looked exhausted, but he often seemed to be. And involuntarily, she began to take inventory.

She wished he'd cut his hair short instead of wearing it so that it rose in a wavy crest off his face, giving him an air of pomposity. His hands were small, although not refined; his fingers were squat. He was short-legged, too, and when she viewed him, naked, she couldn't help thinking he looked like her version of a Japanese farmer. She liked men who were lean and elegant and eight years younger. He was medium height, durable, his muscles and flesh compact. But completely utilitarian, although she knew he was attractive to other women.

She wished she could see the beauty in his face. She knew it was there and that she was blinded by cultural bias. His face was harsh, tough, scarred. But also sometimes too gentle for her to stand, his eyes—when he wasn't trying to make them flash darkly and spark in vehemence and anger, passion and outrage—shining and limpid as lagoons.

She just wished he didn't slurp his tea, his coffee, cocoa, soup. It was cultural, it was cultural, she knew, good manners, a sign of appreciation, and a great way to blow off the small gusts of steam rising from a hot cup. But she'd never gotten used to seeing his lip protrude like a snail clamping down over the lip of the cup. She was noise sensitive. But she liked his voice, deep, full, reassuring, and his readiness to laugh—when he could.

Three years short of forty, Grant was at the beginning of a long and terrible mid-life crisis, she thought. Some people wanted to chase after the memory—that favorite lover—of their youth, whole years in which they'd been more handsome, more hip, more limber, more sassy, and better dressed. The saddest, most shimmering spectres belonged to those modest adults whose days and nights in high school had been the apex of experience, the high point of their lives, obscured even then behind brilliant, huge pillows of pom-poms.

For the more broadly ambitious, failure was not having not taken risks or not having not had larks and adventures or not having not married or not having not had children or not having not made a building full of money, but simply not having stayed young enough to keep their entire lives before them, full of the promise of time in which to do all these things later—or postpone having to face not doing things.

But Grant was different. He wanted both a memory and a youth he'd never even had, a history, a time, a place all happening in the decade before he'd been born. He pursued the past with so much vigor, she thought, it was as if he felt he'd been left out of history, not just uninvited to the high school prom. That the subject of his obsession should be Japanese American history specific to World War II she felt in her guts was symptomatic of emotional immaturity.

And somehow, somehow, she associated this with his mom. Marianne freely blamed mothers and ex-wives for not properly socializing the men with whom she'd ended up. Unable to articulate their feelings, to be forthright, and to have a good fight. Completely incapable of remembering to flip down the toilet seat, the reason she gave Grant for not wanting to have children. "They'd get up in the middle of the night to take a pee"—she was thinking of daughters—"sit down, and fall in." With this, like the latent pragmatist she was, she'd tidily flushed away the possibility of their becoming parents. Then, too, he'd looked at her aghast and speechless.

He had told her so little about his mother, even when at the beginning of their relationship she'd tried to encourage him to open up, and frankly, what he had told her had made her recoil.

"She used to pamper me," he said fondly. When the years of adolescence threatened to crush him with their amorphous, doughy weight, his mother had hovered over him like the silver lining in a cloud, beseeching him to rest on the couch in the subdued light of their living room. In anguish, he had languished as best he could, letting her fuss quietly, placing cold, wet towels over his burning face, erupting with all the sudden violence of unspeakable urges.

She had always been solicitous of his health, he said, and remembered that at four years old he had been enamoured of the weekend golf-show programs on their black-and-white TV, watching the guys in sweaters and checkered trousers swing a club—and away the ball would go, while his mother molded vinegar-doused rice into identically pocked balls she'd putt across his plate, making him believe for a brief moment of his life that the sport of golf flew because inside every golf ball was tucked a bunched heart of seaweed, cucumber, or pickle, something to make all men strong.

Other than those slight and slightly horrifying reminiscences, he had never spoken of his mother except to describe her as a nice lady, a refined person who loved music and perfume. Though he couldn't name the type of music—popular Japanese songs? He couldn't identify the perfume.

He didn't know her favorite color. Last Christmas he had stood at a total loss in front of a glass case practically floating with silk scarves. "What colors does she like to wear?" Marianne asked. He fidgeted, fingering the cream-colored scarves ticking with clocks and chains, the filmy scarves leaping off the counter in melon and chartreuse, the overblown roses and chrysanthemums of the darker weaves and hues. And she had known what he would answer, that all he could think of was blue, beige, and maroon—the standard colors Asians were supposed to wear unless they wanted to risk looking olive, pallid, or worst of all, jaundiced. "Blue, beige," he answered, clearing his throat and trying to sound authoritative. They watched as the sales clerk efficiently wrapped in tissue a large square silk-chiffon scarf with indigo blue on one side and dark beige on the other.

She knew she was cruel but it was her job. Somehow she had ended up as a kind of pop psychologist columnist for *The Seattle Subterfuge*, or the *Fog*, as some called the alternative newsmagazine. The constant pressure to be trenchant without ever actually becoming sarcastic, frankly, was beginning to wear her down. But it was her job to remind readers that she had absolutely no sympathy for them: you marry the man, you marry his family, she wrote like everyone else. Her readers were troubled people, always asking for advice.

But in her own case, she rationalized now, it was hard to remember that Grant even had a family. He had always acted like an only child, an outsider to the proper world of mothers and fathers, sisters and brothers, grandparents, aunts, uncles, cousins. She wondered if this man—who owned a house, car, dishwasher, VCR, TV, CD, and the complete recordings of the Beach Boys—even had a single photograph of his mother. And going to wake him so that he wouldn't miss greeting his mother at the gate, Marianne concluded that she had simply absorbed Grant's own reluctance to acknowledge his family. Which, ultimately, seemed too cruel to reveal to him.

She could try, for a change, to phrase things politely.

Or she could lie.

Jean Kitayama, then Jean Ito, now Jean Miyahara, but always his mom, insisted on stopping at the supermarket on the way back from the airport. His kitchen would look like a bomb shelter before she left town.

"Why don't you come with me to meet Shikibu Daishi, Grant," she said, packing away the groceries. "I think you could learn some interesting things."

He was sure he would, judging from the booklets she had taken to sending him in the last few months. Why she thought he would be interested in joining a radical Buddhist sect was what he didn't understand.

He had never thought of his mother as being religious. He'd never had any reason to believe she was. Certainly his father didn't care about religion. Neither did George. But it was on the day she'd coaxed Grant to take her to the Bon Odori that she'd met George, in town visiting his deceased wife's sister, nieces and nephews. Really very fitting, given that the Bon Odori was a festival of the dead. Not as grim as it might sound to people accustomed to wailing dirges or the quiet pasty faces of Protestants in mourning. It was just a friendly way of remembering the dead, maybe the past. In Japan, the most traditional observers would float little lantern boats down the river, sending light to the departed. He would describe it as charming. Sweet.

In Seattle, the community celebrated with a street festival in front of the Japanese Buddhist Church. Every July, late in the month, late in the day, the women would come out dressed in lavish kimonos, bright orange and deep purple, the colors of sunset, and the men in their yukatas or hapi coats. Children would emerge from the arms of their parents and all begin to dance in the strong, measured rhythm of Japanese folk songs, the music of farmers and workers. It always amused him and slightly amazed him to see his mother dance the tanko-bushi, a coal miner's dance: digging happily twice to the right with a thrust of her hands and foot, twice to the left, her body dipping as she jauntily flung her imagined load over her shoulder.

Under the dim, bobbing glow of paper lanterns, the smoke drifting overhead from the teriyaki grill, the taiko drums striking their imperative beat with some kind of plucked stringed instrument behind it, and the shrill voice of a female singer shrieking with distortion over the loudspeakers, his mother had fallen in love. Everyone moving in a circle, repeating the same movements, celebrating the motions of ordinary life, while hands clap-clap, fans fold and unfold, and kachi-kachi, the wooden sticks, strike heart against heart.

Well, maybe not on first sight. His mother was a woman of decorum.

But where religion was concerned, he'd have to call her fickle. Since then, she'd moved with characteristic grace and great fluidity from Buddhism to Christianity and back and forth. As far as he could tell, religion, for his mother, was like playing bingo, daubing her cards of numbers with measured enthusiasm and good-natured hope with no real disappointment at losing. Or perhaps a civilized game of bridge in which invariably she played the hand of dummy. Or she went seeking strangely specific answers to the trivial, as if religion were a giant ouija board. She was too practical-minded to commit herself to any serious religious beliefs. And so it puzzled him that now she'd flown all the way up to Seattle to meet a radical sect leader from Japan.

He was, Grant gathered, the leader of a comparatively new sect, one of the many splinter groups and fanatical movements that sprang out of the devastation of World War II. Each had their following, each follower had their need to explain and grapple with their loss. But his mother?

She was impressed that the founder of the sect was an old woman who had survived the A-bomb. Rather than having given her shame, the ordeal had given her power. She fancied herself the third coming: first there was Buddha, then there was Jesus Christ, then there was her. She had linked her rise to the devastation of the war. And just as the war was indisputable, so was she.

And so, apparently, was her son, this Shikibu Daishi, who had ascended to the leadership upon her death.

Grant's mother pressed him to meet Shikibu Daishi, for her sake.

He hoped she wasn't serious.

But she was.

And so the next morning he found himself driving her to the Sheraton Hotel to meet Shikibu Daishi, shake his hand, excuse himself, and leave.

He was pleasantly surprised. For some reason, he'd pictured him as the guy on the lid of a Prince Albert can, a stiff figure in epaulets and brass buttons. In fact, although Shikibu Daishi was rather regal, he wore a dark blue business suit. His hair was slicked back, he had fine, clean-cut features, and he had good skin, Grant noticed.

Buddhism: he remembered his world religion class in college and their discussion of the popularity of Shingon in Heian Japan. Whether followers actually felt pious was a matter of speculation. There seemed to have been a fine line between the devout and the devoted, between true acceptance and appearances, given that its priests were expected to be handsome. That way, audiences could be expected to keep their attention focused. It was some form of purification.

"It's such a shame," said his mother, "about that editor of yours." She shook her head. "Asking you to rewrite your article at the last minute like that! Some people are far too particular, I think."

Grant looked sternly at Marianne, who was prodding the curly shrimp on her plate rather unkindly, he felt, with her fork.

His mother went on. "But I'm glad you could join us for lunch today."

Grant watched her smile at Marianne, his mother's face brightening with what seemed genuine pleasure. Though just the night before she had, as delicately as possible, expressed her concern that Chinese girls were not, well, you know, quite the same. "They always seem so . . . *busy*, you know. That other girlfriend of yours," she'd said, furrowing her brows faintly as if she didn't recall this exact detail, "she was Chinese, too, wasn't she? She always seemed in such a hurry." And he knew what she was thinking: that like that other girlfriend, Marianne probably prepared instant top ramen for dinner, complete with green onions, fish balls, and hard-boiled eggs. "That's not Japanese food," she'd murmured reprovingly at the time. Women and food, the two strongholds of his mother's sense of Japanese American culture.

Nonetheless, lunch had gone well, even if full of the usual inane remarks—lulling him into a sense of false security. He choked on his asparagus when he heard Marianne pause to observe, "What a *beautiful* scarf you're wearing, Mrs. Miyahara."

The blue and beige quite became her, he thought indignantly.

She had no integrity. He waited grimly for her next remark. Whenever Marianne most disliked talking with a person was when she became the most incredibly ingenuous and enthusiastic. Her friendliness and generosity, her animation, billowed in direct proportion to her true feelings of boredom and disinterest. It was only a matter of time now before she'd ask his mother for a recipe: sukiyaki, teriyaki, or for a batter that would make tempura fluff up like snowflakes and lace. It was really his father's recipe, he remembered.

And then he remembered that he wanted to ask his mother about Toshio Shimomura, who used to live in the north end, whose house they might have driven by when depositing one of her new Buddhist collaborators.

"He was a no-no boy, wasn't he, Mom?" he asked.

She chilled him with her look. God, he'd forgotten how scary she could be!

"How would I know that, Grant? You know, I haven't lived in Seattle for almost twenty years," she said, turning to Marianne. "Grant's always asking me questions about the past, and do you know what? I can't remember."

"He's a reporter," Marianne said. Grant felt a warm pulse of gratitude until she added thoughtlessly, "it's in the tradition of TV to make news out of nothing and to make nothing of news."

"Hmm." His mother seemed to consider that without criticism. "You know, she's right. You always have had such a fine imagination, ever since you were a little boy, Grant. I'm glad you found a way to use that to make a living. George and I are very proud of you these days."

He hoped she wasn't going to revive a mincing discussion of his short-lived stage career during which she'd once come to see him play Hamlet. "To be or not to be," he had muttered so quickly and in such a low tone that someone from the audience had shouted out, "WHAT?" Afterwards in the lobby Grant had overheard some malcontent remark that you couldn't cast an Asian in a role that required an actor to emote, especially a role in which enunciation mattered so terribly much. His mother had pretended enjoyment, but when he'd quit acting, she'd sent him a check for $5,000 in case he wanted to go back to school.

His mother was a master—or mistress—of the succinct. Especially when dealing with disagreeable possibilities.

He tried again. "This is for TV, Mom," he cajoled.

"Oh, who knows where he is by now," she said. "You don't need to know him, Grant. Leave the past alone. I don't think he cares to socialize with us, anyway." And she pressed the napkin to her lips, dismissing his plea as casually as she did the dirty linen. "It was so long ago. Time flies. Well, so should I," she said, glancing quickly at her watch. "George will be worried if I miss the plane."

Grant sat still, silently twisting his lips. Marianne shrugged sympathetically, but he couldn't tell whether it was meant for him or his mother.

Suddenly, he pictured a diabolical alliance between his mother and Marianne. They would send him off to a school for assimilation, aaaagghhh! The JACL! he thought. The Japanese American Citizens League! Those naive do-gooders who'd sold them out, making them all look like happy campers!

He hoped the natural tension between a mother and her son's unnatural girlfriend would be strong enough to protect him. With any ill luck, they might soon realize that they were leery of the same thing, and it wasn't each other, but a ballroom full of feisty old men. He thought of the Winter Olympic luge runners whose sunny-faced girlfriends, interviewed on TV, had flagrantly exhibited their jealousy of the sleds which the male athletes so lovingly waxed and sharpened and slept with in their bedrooms. They'd been hostile! And he knew, bang! what it was like to barrel eighty miles per hour down an icy tunnel.

He could only be grateful for Marianne's perspicacity in avoiding his mom. Three days, and that conniver had almost gotten away clean. Now he insisted that Marianne need not accompany them to the airport. "Gosh, no, you're far too busy," he said, patting her arm awkwardly as if it were a small dog, a puppy he secretly wished would frolic far away.

At the security checkpoint, he watched his mother pause in the frame of the metal detector, almost as if she were waiting for the bells to jangle, the siren to scream. Her kidskin handbag rolled silently on the belt under the flapping streamers of the X-ray box. No beeps, no buzzers, no alarms. If the security personnel, so blandly watchful, only knew the secrets she kept in her head, as sharp as shrapnel, the propaganda she disseminated so smoothly, a skyful of white leaflets showering over the land mass of his life. He thought with a comic shiver: mothers. And then, less easily: wives.

•

"Did she see your father when she was in town?" Marianne's voice drifted out of the dark.

The question surprised him. "No, she didn't even mention him. Why should she?"

"I don't know. You've never told me why they got divorced—or married, even, for that matter, in the first place. Why did they?"

It was a stupid question—obviously, they didn't get along.

Because his father was a push-over, he thought, the videotape of the camps going at half-speed through his head, the ragged fences almost all that was left. "Their lives were too confined," he said.

He shifted onto his back, realizing with sudden discomfort that what his mother probably had wanted was to marry someone like him, an educated professional, someone who traveled and wore suits and occasionally went out to dinner and concerts.

He added, wonderingly, "You know, it's really ironic that two years after she divorced my father, she married another Japanese American gardener."

"What's wrong with being a gardener?" Marianne asked.

He sighed, and turned on his side, cupping his chin in the slope of her shoulder. Marianne, in whom he loved to burrow, ferreting out a fresh discovery of himself every time, was so completely contrary even on the most unconscious level. The first time she'd visited his house, he'd offered her a cup of hot coffee and she had automatically, absently replied, "No, thanks, I drink it cold." After three years, he still hadn't adjusted. He knew he shouldn't take it personally but it still was like shaking hands with someone who palmed an electric buzzer sending small, unpleasant shocks up his spine. Even her most undeliberate gestures, even in her sleep—when she tossed restlessly, scattering her hair across the pillow, sketching her hands across his back, her knees poking into his thighs, nudging him to the top of his sleep with her occasional cries—he suspected were planned, everything calculated to send him a coded message he'd be damned if he could understand. She tossed around then, turned towards him, and sighed.

"Nothing," he answered.

excerpt from *Thousand Pieces of Gold*

Ruthanne Lum McCunn

Like the hold of the ship, the San Francisco customs shed was dimly lit, but at least the lanterns did not pitch and sway; and the air, though stale and stinking from the press of unwashed bodies, did not reek of vomit or human waste. If anything, the din from hundreds of voices, mostly male, had grown louder. But there was life and excitement in the shouting, joyful expectation in the rush for luggage, relatives, and friends.

Lalu, waiting for her turn to come before the customs officer, caught the contagion of nervous excitement, and she felt the same thrill, bright and sharp as lightning, that had shot through her when the Madam had told her she was going to America, the Gold Mountains at the other end of the Great Ocean of Peace.

RUTHANNE LUM MCCUNN is a Eurasian born in San Francisco's Chinatown who grew up in Hong Kong and was educated first in Chinese and then in English schools. Her biographical novel, *Thousand Pieces of Gold*, was made into a film and aired by PBS's *American Playhouse* in 1992. Her other books include *Sole Survivor* and an award-winning children's book, *Pie-Biter*. She lives in San Francisco and is currently working on another novel.

"I have never been there, but Li Ma, the woman for whom I bought you, says there is gold everywhere. On the streets, in the hills, mountains, rivers, and valleys. Gold just waiting to be picked up . . ."

"Gold that will make me rich. So rich, no one, not even Old Man Yang, will dare speak against me if I go home," Lalu had whispered, ignoring the rest of the Madam's words.

Hugging herself inwardly, she had pictured her parents' and brothers' faces when she gave her father the gold that would make him the richest man in the village. The pride they would have in her, their qianjin. And she had held fast to this picture, as to a talisman. First, when the Madam had turned her over to Li Ma, the crotchety, foul-mouthed woman who would take her to the Gold Mountains. Then, during the long voyage, when only the men's talk of gold had kept alive her dream of going home. And now, as she folded and refolded the forged papers Li Ma had given her. For the demons who ruled the Gold Mountains wished to keep their gold for themselves, and in order to gain the right to land, Lalu must successfully pretend to be the wife of a San Francisco merchant.

Over and over, during the long weeks crammed in the hold of the ship, Li Ma had forced Lalu and the other five women and girls in her charge to rehearse the stories that matched their papers, sternly warning, "Pass the examination by customs, and you will soon return to China a rich woman, the envy of all in your village. Fail, and you will find yourself in a demon jail, tortured as only the demons know how."

Could the torture be worse than the journey she had just endured? Lalu thought of the sweltering, airless heat and thirst that had strangled the words in her throat, making her stumble when she recited for Li Ma, earning her cruel pinchings and monotonous harangues. The aching loneliness that came from homesickness and Li Ma's refusal to permit the girls to talk among themselves. The bruising falls and the tearing at her innards each time the ship rocked, tossing her off the narrow shelf that served as bed, knocking her against the hard wood sides of the hull. The long, black periods of waiting for the hatch to bang open as it did twice each day, bringing a shaft of sunlight, gusts of life-giving salt air, the smell of the sea. The struggle to chew the hard, sour bread and swallow the slop lowered down as though they were pigs in a pen.

Lalu tossed her head, straightened her jacket, and smoothed her hair. That was all over. Behind her. No more than a bad dream. She was in America, the Gold Mountains. And soon, just as soon as she gathered enough gold, she would go home.

"Next."

Lalu felt herself shoved in front of the customs officer. She had never been close to a white man before and she stared amazed at the one that towered above her. His skin was chalk white, like the face of an actor painted to play a villain, only it was not smooth but covered with wiry golden hair, and when his mouth opened and closed, there were no words to make an audience shake with anger or fear, only a senseless roaring. Beside him, a Chinese man spoke.

"Your papers. Give him your papers," Li Ma hissed.

"My papers?" Lalu said in her native Northern dialect. "I've . . ."

She stopped, horrified. How could she have been so stupid? True, Southern speech was still strange to her, but during the long voyage, Li Ma had taught her the dialect, for the majority of Chinese immigrants on board came from the Southern province of Guongdong, and her papers claimed her as such. Now she had betrayed herself, proven her papers false. There would be no gold on the streets for her and no homecoming, only jail and torture.

Li Ma snatched the papers from Lalu. "Don't mind the girl's foolish rambling. You'll see everything's in order. Here's the certificate of departure and the slip with her husband's address here in the Great City."

Gold flashed as she passed the papers up to the Chinese man beside the demon officer. "A respected tradesman he is. Could have his pick of beauties. Why he wants this simpleton back is anyone's guess. Should have let her stay on in China when she went back to nurse his old mother. But you know how men are. So long as the woman satisfies that muscle below their belt, they don't care about anything else."

The Chinese man laughed. He passed the papers to the customs officer. Again gold flashed. They talked between them in the foreign tongue, their eyes stripping Lalu, making her feel unclean. Finally, the demon officer stamped the papers. Smirking, he thrust them down at Lalu. Her face burning with embarrassment, she hugged the precious papers against her chest and followed Li Ma past the wooden barricade. She was safe.

"Look," Li Ma barked, pointing to the huddle of waiting women and girls. "Some of them are only ten, eleven years old. Children. Yet they showed more intelligence and good sense than you. Now you mark my words. That's the first and the last time I put out good gold to save your neck, so watch yourself, do you hear?" Cuffing Lalu's ears for emphasis, she herded her charges together and out onto the wharf.

Lalu, weak from lack of nourishing food and exercise, felt as if the boat were still pitching and rolling beneath her feet. But she walked briskly, not wanting to provoke another storm of abuse from Li Ma who was speeding past heaps of crated produce, sacks of flour and beans, and stacks of barrels. Above her, she heard the screech of seagulls, and beyond the wharf, the clip-clop of horses' hooves, the creak and rattle of wagons, voices deep and shrill. But she could see no further than Li Ma's back, for the same thick fog which had shrouded the Gold Mountains when they disembarked enveloped them, its cold dampness penetrating, leaving the salty taste of tears. Lalu swallowed her disappointment. She would see the mountains soon enough. Meanwhile, she would look for the nuggets the men said lay in the street.

Beneath the sickly glow of street lamps, she saw horse droppings, rats feasting on piles of garbage, rags, broken bottles. Metal glittered. A discarded can or gold? Stooping to grab it, Lalu did not see the rock until it stung her cheek. Startled, she looked up just as a mud ball splashed against Li Ma's back.

Li Ma whirled around. "You dead girl," she screamed at Lalu. "How dare you!"

She broke off as high-pitched squeals and cries burst from the girls around her. Through the heavy mist, Lalu made out white shadows, demon boys, hurling stones and mud, yelling, words she did not understand but she could feel.

"You dead ghosts," Li Ma cried, shaking her fist at them.

Giggling, the boys concentrated their missiles on the short square woman. Without thinking, Lalu picked up the stones that landed nearest her, flinging them back at the boys as fast as they could throw them. Years of playing with her brothers had made her aim excellent and the boys soon fled.

Li Ma fell on Lalu. "Stop that you dead foolish girl or you'll have the authorities after us."

"But they started it."

"Are you so dim-witted that you don't know you're in a demon land? The laws are made by demons to protect demons, not us. Let's just hope we can get to Chinatown before they come back with officers or we'll find ourselves rotting in a demon jail."

Shouting, pushing, and shoving, she hurried them up steep cobbled streets with foul smelling gutters, past wagons pulled by huge draft horses and unwashed demon men loafing on upturned barrels until they reached narrow streets crowded with Chinese men. Chinatown. Even then, she did not permit the women and girls to rest. But the warm familiar smells and sounds soothed Lalu's confusion, and she barely felt Li Ma's parting cuff as she herded them down a flight of stairs into a large basement room with more young women and girls like herself.

"Those with contracts come over to this side, those without go stand on the platform," an old woman in black lacquer pants and jacket directed.

Lalu held out her papers. The old woman took them. She pushed Lalu in the direction of the women without contracts.

"No, I belong over there," Lalu said, trying to take back the papers.

The old woman snorted. "What a bumpkin you are! Those papers were just to get you into the country. They have to be used again."

"But Li Ma said . . ."

"Don't argue girl, you're one of the lucky ones," the old woman said. She pointed to the group of women with contracts. "Their fates have been decided, it's prostitution for them, but if you play your cards right, you may still get the bridal chair."

A shocked murmur rippled through the group of women. One of them took a paper from an inner pocket. "I have a marriage contract," she said. "Not what you suggest."

"And I! And I!" the women around her echoed.

The old woman took the contract from the young woman. The paper crackled as she spread it open. "Read it!" she ordered.

The young woman's lips quivered. "I can't."

The old woman jangled the ring of keys at her waist. "Does anyone here read?"

The women looked hopefully at each other. Some shook their heads. Others were simply silent. None could read.

"Then I'll tell you what your contracts say." Without looking at any of the papers, the old woman continued, "For the sum of your passage money, you have promised the use of your bodies for prostitution."

"But the marriage broker gave my parents the passage money," the young woman persisted.

"You fool, that was a procurer, not a marriage broker!" She pointed to the thumb print at the bottom of the paper. "Is that your mark?"

Sobbing quietly, the young woman nodded.

"Well then, there's nothing more to be said, is there?"

"Yes there is," a girl said boldly. "I put my mark on one of those contracts, and I knew what it was for." Her face reddened. "I had to," she added.

"So?" the old woman, hands on hips, prompted.

"The contract specifies the number of years, five in my case, so take heart sisters, our shame will not last forever."

"What about your sick days?"

"What do you mean?" the girl asked.

"The contract states your monthly sick days will be counted against your time: two weeks for one sick day, another month for each additional sick day."

"But that means I'll never be free!"

"Exactly."

Like a stone dropped in a pond, the word started wave after wave of talk and tears.

"Keep crying like that," the old woman shouted, "and by the time your owners come to get you, your eyes will be swollen like toads."

"What difference does it make?" a voice challenged.

"Depending on your looks, you can be placed in an elegant house and dressed in silks and jewels or in a bagnio."

"Bagnio?"

"On your way here you must have seen the doors with the barred windows facing the alleys, but perhaps you did not hear the chickens inside, tapping and scratching the screens, trying to attract a man without bringing a cop. Cry, make yourself ugly, and you'll be one of those chickens, charging twenty-five cents for a look, fifty cents for a feel, and seventy-five cents for action."

Slowly the sobs became muted sniffles and whimpers as stronger women hushed the weaker. The old woman turned to Lalu's group. "Now get up on that platform like I told you."

Silently Lalu and the other women and girls obeyed. When they were all on the platform, the old woman began to speak.

"This is where you'll stand tomorrow when the men come. There'll be merchants, miners, well-to-do peddlers, brothel owners, and those who just want to look. They'll examine you for soundness and beauty. Do yourself up right, smile sweetly, and the bids will come in thick and fast from those looking for wives as well as those looking to fill a house.

"When the price is agreed on, the buyer will place the money in your hands. That will make the sale binding, but you will turn the money over to me. Do you understand?"

The women and girls nodded. A few murmured defeat.

The old woman pointed to some buckets against the wall. "There's soap and water. Wash thoroughly. You will be stripped for auction."

"Stripped?"

"Women in the Gold Mountains are scarcer than hen's teeth and even a plain or ugly girl has value. But when a man has to pay several thousand dollars for a woman, he likes to see exactly what he is buying," the old woman said.

She grabbed a tight-lipped, thin, dark girl from the back of the group. The girl stared defiant as the old woman ripped off her jacket and pointed out scars from a deep hatchet wound, puckered flesh the shape of a hot iron. "Look carefully and be warned against any thought of disobedience or escape." She threw the girl's jacket onto the floor. "It will be the bagnio for you. If you're lucky."

She pulled the women closest to her down from the platform and herded them toward the buckets of water. "Now get going, we've wasted time enough."

All around her, Lalu could hear the sounds of women and girls preparing themselves for auction, but she made no move to join them. It had taken all her concentration to make out the words that had been spoken in the strange Southern dialect, and she was only just beginning to feel their impact.

She had been duped, she realized. By the soft-voiced, gentle Madam, a cormorant who had nothing to give except to its master. By Li Ma, the foulmouthed procuress charged with Lalu's delivery to the auction room. By the talk of freemen whose dreams could never be hers. For the Gold Mountains they had described was not the America she would know. This: the dingy basement room, the blank faces of women and girls stripped of hope, the splintered boards beneath her feet, the auction block. This was her America.

Through a haze as chilling as the fog that had surrounded her at the wharf, Lalu became aware of warm breath, an anxious nudging. It was the thin, dark girl the old woman had exposed as warning.

"Didn't you hear what the old woman said? You're one of the lucky ones."

"The Madam in Shanghai said that too."

"But it's true. There are women far worse off than you. Like those smuggled into the Gold Mountains hidden in padded crates labeled dishware or inside coal bunkers. Many of them don't survive the journey or arrive so bruised and broken they cannot be sold." The girl leaned closer and lowered her voice still further. "Those women are taken straight to the same 'hospitals' as slave girls who have ceased to be attractive or who have become diseased. There, alone in tiny, windowless cells, they're laid on wooden shelves to wait for death from starvation or their own hand." She brightened. "But you made the journey with papers and a woman to look out for you. You're thin, but beautiful and sound."

"What does that change except my price?"

The girl took Lalu's hands in hers, holding them tight, quieting their trembling. "You must learn as I have to let your mind take flight. Then you won't feel, and if you don't feel, nothing anyone does can hurt you."

Razia Begum in London

Ruxana Meer

If it didn't stop raining soon, we'd be drowned.

If the drops didn't evaporate, steaming up to open our pores like an expensive facial treatment, we'd have to learn to tread water.

If the gutters kept sailing trash down our street and the waves kept hitting the sidewalk, sometimes up to our knees, splashing us when speeding cars passed, when we got home we'd be in trouble for getting so wet.

If it didn't stop raining soon, umbrella business would go out of business 'cause everyone would know the real value of such a protective device and those who were coming in would pass theirs on to those going out.

We need it the radio and the bus driver kept saying but if it didn't stop soon, I was going to explode, hearing music outdoors and needing to dance. I would have to wait until I was inside since we need the

RUXANA MEER: "I am a Pakistani American, raised Muslima, now published in a book with new pride for my family's memories and realities. Not only staying warm and fed, I teach in Oakland, Califas, learning children worth sweet knowing. I will read them this book, but they like pictures."

rain. Under the covers I can hear it's still raining and I don't even try to get up.

Razia grandma reminds us *Don't you know better than to go out when it's pouring like this? Here,* she wraps her shawl around me. *good. choke and be dry.* If it didn't stop raining soon, the weeds would take over 'cause grandma's garden will overflow unclipped. If it didn't stop raining, I'd go insane waiting inside, to walk around, over, and above the surfaces outside where if it didn't stop raining soon, some people would drown.

It has been raining every single day since we got here and it hasn't stopped once. There are new leaks every day which spring from corners of the disintegrating brick and sometimes it's just the unsure plumbing in grandma's house that makes it rain. In her vision of modern life, it doesn't matter that these mechanics of technology don't work. As long as there is no powerful hex, she remains in spiritual control of her house, and of us, at least during the summer vacation when it never stopped raining.

From the third floor, top of the stairs spiral, I could see her standing at the bottom, talking to us and holding up her cotton shalwar, the wooden spoon directing her words at her side.

Grandma step out of the water please   you're the one getting sick. I could lie here and just watch the top her covered head, patiently waiting, her hand on the post at the bottom. I stare at the wall and find out where and what the ants go marching in between.

I can wait at the bottom for these children

Grandma why are you standing still? now moss had begun to swell, the carpet matching greens and climbing vines, tropical, uncharted and not like the pretty tidepools we saw on our class field trip. Too slippery for Grandma's wood bottom sandals. She might drown if she didn't use her spoon to paddle with.

My dreaming, sleepwalking brother had assembled a small fortress of furniture on top of the bed to prevent being found by Grandma because he didn't want to wake up and go downstairs like they do in Pakistan, maybe, before dawn, before time and light is what the clock counts and before dawn is what seeing your breath is.

I heard Kaiser, my half-asleep brother asking me *Where are you going don't leave me*

I tell him that *I'm hungry. get up. I want to eat something.* I call Grandma up again *come stay on the bed with us get out of the water there's flood.*

Kaiser stubbornly refuses to move or let me go *if you're leaving please take me with you*

What are you scared of? There's nowhere to go and we are already here I'm going downstairs

I have my head in between the bannisters, but I turn around and can see into the room where we sleep. Kaiser's face is pained but no sound comes out. The anger does not stop in his sleep because in the cycle of sleep certain conditions must continue as in waking. He is wanting to go back to California where I tell him it is raining too but at least all our friends are there. At least we know something about those people unlike foreign grandma who we are trying to get to.

Where we grew up the people shake their heads one way or another depending on who's their president, to divide up the small pie, the world's brown population, slicing the land, the resources, and the heads off mountains filled with red rock. My brother and I imagine that we could dig in our sandbox until we got to the other side of the globe, where everyone would stare at us as we climbed out of the earth patch in the middle of the market and someone would call the police. We had big dreams about the old country and when we get on the plane at the end of vacation my brother tells me his dreams kept him up at night and asleep in the morning and that's why he could never get up.

In my brother's dream, he has just gotten to sleep to find himself running down the city blocks of London in the rain and having his feet freezing through his shoes. In the run for his life, his asthma inhaler and all his change falls out of his pockets and he goes into a sandwich shop where the counters are tall enough to hide behind them. He puts two pastrami sandwiches in his jacket, which he didn't know he was still wearing. He feels invisible except to the woman having a cigarette and trying to talk to him about mayonnaise and her diet. He remembers he has to be home to eat at Grandma's and gives the sandwiches to the woman because she is really hungry. Grandma's voice and his voice are at opposite ends of the house and they are waiting to meet in the morning, hardly light 'cause the sun hasn't risen yet. She can't hear him and he knows she is down there waiting but doesn't know how long she can wait. I am watching his eyelids flicker.

I always lie on the floor, resting my stomach. I'm still trying to wake Kaiser though, as I get louder and louder, the harder he ignores me. And then periodically Grandma in a burst of surprising English, asking the same question: *Come downstairs and learn something about yourself.*

I relay the message with urgency, *soon we'll be there aye wake up and come downstairs* but my brother crawls deeper into his sheets over the mass of chairs. *Come down before you get in more trouble.*

From the bed and chair maze, his voice in the hunchback tractor wailed *Why am I in trouble?*

Because you can't wake up and everyone knows it's because you don't want to have to read Quran I'm going downstairs so are you coming or not?

Wait don't leave without me, rux.

Grandma is still asking the same question in a different way. She has never spoken English so we believe that we aren't sure she's talking to us or getting mad. She says to Ma that we are absent and mythical sort of descendants and it does no good to try to change us radically now. Our tongues are lazy and we cannot speak in the same meanings with which we are spoken to by our elders. We have not been taught in the mind and mouth properly, everyone agrees our resulting behavior is not completely our own fault.

We are raised with four place settings, three televisions and only one fireplace. At Grandma's house, even the bathroom has a fire place, plus there is one outhouse. The smells of turmeric, incense, and babies get in your hair, your clothes and your sleep when you stay there. We miss California because the smells there are not so damp. We can leave doors and windows open, the climate is mild and the seasons blur into each other.

Grandma is not looking up, reading the Quran and extra prayers in order that we be safe, jet elevated for twelve hours, suctioned in the sky and on our way home. Excited by the peanuts and the steward-esses' colorful manners, my brother and I make siren noises in the baggage check line and distract the security. We behave as world trav-elers with no manners *as if we just got off the boat.* But we are not scared, not clutching our packages, because we know our contents have insurance.

I want to take Grandma with us but that is wishful. She lives in a strangers' country anyway and so why not? In the time which Razia did travel to meet us, she was lost in the San Francisco airport, in the homelessness of the eyes of Indian and Chinese women, in the money exchange, portraitures of men, paying each other off. She discovered the New World too, and she says before America, men thought it was in our homeland, India, now Pakistan. India is hard to get near in America, which calls the Indios, people of god, Indians. My brother and I return from vacation a little clearer on the concept of those who came before us.

In the airport, Ma was holding me and I was at least her weight and holding on tighter. I stopped running around and hold my Ma's heart from falling into her lap. *What's wrong* is what I ask because *going home* is all I know. This is when she starts to cry and I tell Kaiser it's his fault because he's losing to the same video game for the fifth time and *we need our change.*

Ma tried to pass on whatever Razia said about us while she could still remember. Repeating them in that absence, in the vacuum of a plane made the pilot's head spin and caused the unexpected turbulence.

My brother, abandoned in my thoughts, missed the games we had strategized to disrupt the sleeping passengers on the long ride. He wonders what happened on that trip. To him, I never came back, didn't come back the same. I have never heard the shaking of Ma's voice like when she told me the strength of Grandma's words.

Ma apologized to Grandma for the unruly fashion of her daughter and hoped I would be grown next time we came to visit. Grandma raising nine children and ten grandchildren said it this way, *I know that the young ladies today must still be faced with fierce hostility from some who believe girls are not good for fighting for themselves, or they are no good once they begin fighting. But I think they may be more willing to persist in who they are and defend their true character, and be able to speak to one another about these times to hopefully grow very strong and energetic.*

I need to ask Grandma sometime *where does this energy come from.* Since we came back to these states, all I have are the holes where answers are needed. She would try to tell us what she could when we visited, but we don't wake up that early in the morning. When I think of her, I can't say I know all that she has taught me. The presence of her life in mine is so unmeasured. I can see only the absence so much, then I start to realize the imported way in which I act and talk and sense and the way I am hungry, so American.

The Chauvinist

Toshio Mori

Kettle whistles. Three pans of corn boil. Tall glasses tinkle with the touch of human hands. Plates rattle and scratch one another. An ancient refrigerator rumbles every once in a while. A clock on the wall ticks time, and he whistles a tune that was once the rage a few months ago. Voices in the living room murmur like a chorus in a classical work. An electric mixer whirls. Result: mayonnaise for tuna salad. Cheese crackers crackle coming out of a two-pound carton. Knives, forks, and spoons contact the forks, spoons, and knives; and the melody of the kitchen ensues.

He's a man on Ninth Street with a great calling. A calling that may some day replace priests and theology. A calling demanding dignity,

TOSHIO MORI was born in Oakland, California, in 1910 and died in 1980. Perhaps the most prominent voice chronicling the Japanese American experience, his books include *Yokohama, California*; *The Chauvinist and Other Stories*; and his first novel, *Woman from Hiroshima*. Russell Leong has written: "With wit and compassion, Toshio Mori has illuminated for us the callings and visions of gardeners, housewives, artists, students, and shopkeepers. . . . Mori's work gives meaning to the daily aspirations, struggles, and joys of ordinary people."

humbleness, humor, and the limits of human traits. The sadness of this particular man's role is that it must be kept a secret. He couldn't go out in the street and shout with all the might of his lungs just what he's doing as a contribution toward the harmony of human beings. He isn't looking for immortality; so he denounces personal immortality. He is looking for immortality of the man living today who is to die tomorrow. Call it as he does: Everyday immortality.

Takanoshin Sakoda has been at it for a long time. In his quiet solemn way he's been searching among his friends and people the solution to his school of thoughts. He isn't extraordinary. He isn't brilliant, and inside his head there isn't a bag full of philosophical ideas or tricks. There isn't a particle of outstanding skill in him which may be the undoing of his calling. There is just one thing which sets him apart from the rest of men and that's the story hereon.

People look and size him up: When he talks he is like a swirling river seeking an ocean outlet. He won't hear other people's words. He just goes on talking. He forgets the people, the background, and even himself to the point of nothingness in a subject of temporary importance.

Friends look at him from another angle: Lucky guy. Stone deaf. Doesn't have to plug cotton in his ears when to bed he goes with little wifey. Doesn't need to pick up little issues of a family circle. The innocent among the snoopy gossipers and savages of dirty insults. The babe in the gusty screechy roar of modern mads—the genius of the community due to an accidental lack of a sense.

The family in one voice (wife, daughter, and son): The blessed wit. One-half of a battleless ground. The desert of mind, culture, age, and ambition. The portrait of a man in a thousand years: a "houseband" —the meek follower of a new sufferance for power (now) and beauty (in future). The seed of a new vogue: the specialist specializing with a lack of one human sense or more. Examples of possibilities: the blind artist painting on the accepted presence of a canvas; the deaf musician composing a fresh score—new tones, new scales, new instruments; the tongueless chef concocting a new dish fit for a connoisseur; the mouthless moralist discovering in silence the language of expression; the average man on earth smelling the presence of man on Mars.

Today is the day. Takanoshin is sitting in the kitchen having finished his duties early. Everything's cooked; everything's on the table ready to be guzzled by the ladies. The women arrive. It's seven in the evening, and his wife hasn't returned. Business must've been good. Good business on Monday. Monday is Community Women's Club night.

Mrs. Tamada is looking at him and addressing Mrs. Abe. "Sometimes I believe he can hear us," she is saying. "Sometimes I see an intelligent look on his face as if he knows everything that's going on."

"Nonsense!" Mrs. Abe replies. "Look at him! Unless he's a good actor, and I know he isn't, he couldn't stare at us so long with that empty blandness of his without being genuine."

Mrs. Tamada is dubious of her companion's words. "Sometimes I feel he's laughing at us."

"Here, here! What's all this debating about?" Mrs. Tariki cuts in.

Mrs. Tamada and Mrs. Abe turn their backs on Takanoshin. "We're talking about Takanoshin. Tamada-san says he's very intelligent and can see through us," Mrs. Abe says.

"I did not!" Mrs. Tamada says.

Mrs. Tariki laughs. It's time to put everyone in place. It's about time someone definitely define the activity of Takanoshin. "Picture him sitting there night after night waiting for his wife and worrying about supper getting cold," she says. "Picture him with an apron housecleaning twice a week while his wife and daughter run the grocery store."

"He's lazy, weak, and boneless," Mrs. Abe says.

"He should be ashamed of himself staying home by the warm stove while his wife is working at the store," adds Mrs. Tamada.

The fourth woman enters the conversation. "The weasel. The tramp. The mind of a monkey," Mrs. Miyakawa says. "Good for nothing."

The four women turn and look in Takanoshin's direction.

He is nonchalantly sitting in the corner, the way immobile and wise people do. He meets their glances with a smile, the way the tolerant sages of history should have done. He is all smiles because he could not have heard the conversation. He is deaf. His ears are out of order.

He looks at the ceiling and smiles. Everything is out of order. The arrangement of his life for instance is out of order. The women are out of order; his family is out of order. The system of civilization is out of order. Ditto the people and the world.

Out of his isolation in the kitchen (cooking three meals a day is his relation to the labor problem today) he has discovered one of the biggest scoops of scientific nature. It took him eighty days and nights to see the light that one of the biggest things out of order on earth is the facts misarranged. The facts of life are; the past thus, the future thus. Proven with dignity and pomp; prophesized with sanity and bearing it is to laugh. Tonight two stars have fallen. I saw two of them fall while I was outdoors for a bit of night air. That's the fact of life for today and another day. It was time that one man on Eighth Street in the year 1939 come to grief. It was once simple to prove the fact of an event. The world in general is concerned over me because I am deaf. Even at this moment when I am sitting here peacefully and listening to the conversation as sanely and conscious as the women themselves, I am proof of the deaf living.

I the man who remains silent to the little voices about me. I did not declare myself to be anything. I am one of the living proofs of a fact purported to life. One day I simply sat down, and the family began to screech at me. It took them ten minutes to come to my side and look at each other's faces. "He can't hear," my son hoarsely whispers. "He's gone deaf!" my daughter screams. My wife pales and begins to sway and the children rush her to the sofa. Commotion arose. People came in and out. Doctors looked over me. I became the attraction of the community.

Although the news of myself being deaf became old and died, I myself knew no better than to become the beginning of a new refreshment of life. I endorse myself, my life, to the young mind—not for mischief and trouble making. I address to the suppressed, the futile, the jobless, the woman's husband, the lonely hearts. I also address the romanticist—here is something in your line. I am deaf. This is untruth but I'm not lying. A liar is a cheat who harms others. I am like a beggar who must become blind to make a living. The only difference is that I have become deaf to survive the living. The world is waiting for a new philosophy. This is the age for science and invention. People deride the experimenters' failures but we need the experimenters and the failures. We need them just as we need the untruths. Truth without untruth, it's false. By representing the truth in untruth and untruth in truth I may become someone I want to be.

Mrs. Sakoda returns home. The women stand. The meeting begins right away. Tonight is the flower arrangement night. Refreshments are served. Mrs. Sakoda is speaking, "My, he's ruined the punch again!"

"Mama! Will you taste the salad! It's salty!" the daughter calls from the next room.

The women look at Takanoshin sitting in the adjoining room and laugh. They laugh heartily and the words are heard through the house.

"I'm sorry, girls," Mrs. Sakoda is speaking again. "The evening's spoiled again. I've told him over and over and he comes right back and does the same thing again."

Pretty soon their men will be coming around to take them home. They will park their cars at the front and blow their horns. The women run out to the door and call them in. The coffee is served. The conversation is now general. The men talk of business and fishing and club activities. The art of flower arrangement is over. With the entry of each man, the men perk up and smile. The weather is fine these days. Business is good. How's yours? My car goes sixteen miles on a gallon. I caught a fifteen pounder. A striped bass near Antioch. My luck's been bad. A cop pinched me in the city. Yeah, a fine. My house needs painting. Business is so bad I put it off every year. Why don't you run up to my brother's place in San Jose? He'll be glad to see you after all these years. Why don't you? Thanks. I don't know. Oh, go ahead.

Do these men talk this way away from here? Do they in their privacy speak in such a milky language? I wonder if their thoughts run parallel to the mere words of their lips. I wonder if they are dead so soon. They talk in the same tone, same gestures, same subject, same hobbies, same duties and obligations, same destiny. Why doesn't someone talk about death (slow death) some night? The death in the flower arrangement. The death in the flower. The death in our life. The death of a birth. Some people wouldn't glibly talk; it would take their minds off talk. And the silence would be refreshing and strange. Imagine the silence at the women's club meeting. The silence in a deaf man's house. The silence wouldn't be eternal; make no mistake about that. It wouldn't be what we would like to have but ah, what is eternal? And at this moment the records of Beethoven, Sibelius, Ravel, Gershwin stop. The great poems end, Shakespeare included. The books of Tolstoy, Joyce, Whitman, Emerson, Tagore; and what have you left?

I would sit for an answer by the shore and watch the waves come in. I would lie on the hills and watch the sun for awhile. The clouds a good deal longer. I would go to the river side and watch the boats sail the waters; the trains dash by; the airliners roar overhead.

It isn't there, an early observer tells the younger generation. It isn't there. Look somewhere else. At last the young generation claim. It isn't here. It isn't nature. It isn't man's civilization or man's heredity or his environment. It isn't man's possessions or capabilities, the younger generation point. It's his possibilities that count. It's a shame to see the simplicity of each generation. This is so, that is so, all is so. The man's thoughts are the seeds of the future. The last region of man is sleep, next to nothingness. The sleep of man awake. The sleep of man sleeping. The sleep of man dreaming. The sleep of man dead. The sleep of man in birth.

The night is over. The women leave. The men follow. Goodbye, Abe-*san*. Goodnight, Tamada-*san*. Goodnight, Miyakawa, Yamamoto, Hama, Suzuki. See you next Monday. Tea ceremony next time. Oh, let's drag Karita-*san* next time. Smiles. More smiles. Handshakes. Hand waves. Brave smiles. Sad faces at departure.

The night is over for them. The night is dead. And sleep is a period between sunset and sunrise. The saddest of faces is the man or woman too lonely to be alone. The loneliest hour is the time before sleep and the awakening of conscious motor after sleep.

A man's loneliness is an offshoot of the women's club meeting every Monday night. The crowd which the theaters draw isn't due to the attraction of the picture or the stars, but the vacuum emptiness in each individual's search for the solace. A song like "Donkey's Serenade" takes hold of the audience. It is trivial and full of death, but we are impressed temporarily. Everything we touch is full of death and triviality.

And when we sense something like a poem or a symphony or a painting that would not die we are surprised. It makes us forget temporarily by reaching out for something permanent and enduring. And often when we return to ourselves our life is like the song "Donkey Serenade" (full of death and short life)—the actuality of our faces, our houses, our cars, our relatives, our bank accounts.

"Papa-*san!* Papa-*san!*"

Across the hall the daughter calls loudly. It is time for bed. Mama-*san* is upstairs in bed. The kitchen light is off; so is the dining room. The clock is a tattler. The time of man is just beginning; the theme a helplessness; action the seeds of tomorrow.

I want to talk to someone. I want to talk and listen and answer. I want to sing in a chorus in tune with the rest of the crowd. I too want to join and laugh and joke. I want sometimes to tell all the people what I know and how little I know.

I cannot flee the people's world. I am more like an inarticulate person than anyone else; the indignation for want of expression to be ignited in some little source: insignificant, impotent, a dud.

Did you note one day the sun was thus and later returned to gaze again and it was thus, but you know all was changed, the sun, the earth, yourself, the nations, the oceans.

One minute you were always light-hearted and wise-cracking. You had the sense of hearing and your friends acknowledging it. You laughed your way out of difficulties, making a lark of life. You heard laughter and you laughed. Friends came around and slapped your back. Words came easy. Gestures came abruptly in childish natural movements. And in turn of a minute you had dignity you never knew you possessed. You never lost your sense of hearing, but a day of a joke on your wife and family and friends turned the spring.

You were you yesterday. You are you today. You sit in a hole you made yourself. You sit and grin privately. You put one over. It is fun to separate for awhile from your family and friends, and descend or ascend in a different role. It's all right if you are a movie actor, dropping one role and taking up another. Unless you're an actor such a holiday is difficult on earth. You must drop one role or the other. This is the saddest thing on earth because we are all actors in our poor-lit stages, unsung, unheralded, pitied for the sake of our characters and not for our roles. One minute we are a dreamer, another minute a comic, another time a banker, a poet, a statesman, a gambler, a philanthropist, a drunk, a reverend, a murderer. All this is possible to attain in a single day. We turn and twist at a moment's mood, and the force of our surroundings is mirrored in the roles.

Did you ever have a time when you'd sit in a dark room and know every man in the world? Did you remember the time you'd have such a feeling? Was it when you were happy in a revelry or when you were alone and realized your friends had stayed away very long and you did not go out and seek them?

I sat in the kitchen and watched the women come and go. I sat in the living room among my men friends and watched them. There's really nothing to report and everything to understand. Often friendship is a fog and often you will know total strangers more intimately. I found this out in the park where I go almost daily. A warm afternoon in the park among total strangers is a lift. You talk and you are free.

I sat among my people in the living room without talk; and as I sat there without laughter, just smiling, I knew they were assembled there without laughter. I remember the way they sat around and talked. I knew they were laughing at times and were without real laughter and were feverishly together for a real one.

It was on a sunny morning three hours before noon when I had walked for seven blocks and had come to a park. It was a park I had never seen before. It was the beginning of a fresh idea and the resurrection of myself; the park life of this particular park and the parks of other American cities and Berlin, London, Tokyo, Moscow, Paris, Rome were no different; and the park life and the living room life and the dark room life were all the same dough; and laughter or no laughter was the same; and death or deathless was alike; and a joke or a tragedy was out of the same stem; and the man the same.

I sat and talked with a man who came from the Oklahoma fields. I saw him but once. He never mentioned that he was of the dust bowl clan but it was printed all over him. A man who came from Indiana talked one day for hours. He said he once worked in a nursery where he hauled the soil in a wheelbarrow. A grocer sat beside me and talked of the business conditions. A young idealist rabidly sought me for a follower. One day there was a retired capitalist sitting and talking a few seats from me, and he looked the same as anyone else. I completely lost time that day and overlooked lunch and was late cooking supper. My wife gave me hell.

Turn the disk of the earth: a bed is soaring. The clouds roar. The rivers dry. The skies drop. The sun melts. The man is bigger than the earth. Why? A dream is a better production than Warner Brothers pictures. A dream is the reality in hope; and reality the nightmare of a dream reversed. Destruction and education hand in hand. Red Cross and butchery on the same fields. Death and birth in Ward E. Asylum and earth together: fences. Barefoot and shoes, and nudism and morality. One man and one woman. One man and two women. One woman and two men. One man and many women. One woman and many men. The impatience of man. The patience of man. He sleeps. He wakes. The sleep of a man and the disk of earth continues.

Through the cracks of a cream shade the light pours in the room. The birds sing and the milk trucks rumble by. The sun is up and the room is cold. Jetliners fly; the trains whistle; the shouts of the neighbors recall the earth; the consciousness of mind awakens the presence of being.

It is morning and man is no different; the philosophy of man no different; his responsibilities are no different, his roles unchanged, and his fantasies descending. The man in bed blinks his eyes, and the rivers roll, gas and electric is on, the clock ticks, the clothes are pressed, the shoes need mending, the breakfast to make for four, the furniture to be dusted, and a park stroll scheduled.

Darkness is over, the black is grey, prison grey, and a brighter hue is present at last. And a man accepts his affliction: senseless vacuum with the waves of the earth in motion. Motionless, his nerves unflinching, he attempts communication. (Wife! Son! Daughter! Wake up . . . new morning!) End of a man of no senses: Now not only deaf but visionless, dumb, feelingless, colorless, numb . . . only a sixth sense serenity. Smile, rejoice: I was once here. Soon not a trace of my presence would remain. But who cares? (I care, says the government. I care, says the church. I do, say the friends.) I second the motion . . . while I am still alive. While I am alive, I shall smile and laugh, and in spirit grab the grits of life, scraping for crumbs while cooking up the great feast of life.

A Father

from *Darkness*

Bharati Mukherjee

One Wednesday morning in mid-May Mr. Bhowmick woke up as he usually did at 5:43 A.M., checked his Rolex against the alarm clock's digital readout, punched down the alarm (set for 5:45), then nudged his wife awake. She worked as a claims investigator for an insurance company that had an office in a nearby shopping mall. She didn't really have to leave the house until 8:30, but she liked to get up early and cook him a big breakfast. Mr. Bhowmick had to drive a long way to work. He was a naturally dutiful, cautious man, and he set the alarm clock early enough to accommodate a margin for accidents.

While his wife, in a pink nylon negligee she had paid for with her own MasterCard card, made him a new version of French toast from a clipping ("Eggs-cellent Recipes!") Scotchtaped to the inside of a

BHARATI MUKHERJEE: Born in Calcutta, she attended college in India and graduate school in the United States. She is the acclaimed author of *The Middleman and Other Stories* (winner, National Book Critics' Circle Award), *Darkness*, and the novels *Wife*, *The Tiger's Daughter*, and *Jasmine*. Her nonfiction books are *Days and Nights in Calcutta* and *The Sorrow and the Terror*. She currently holds a distinguished professorship at the University of California, Berkeley.

kitchen cupboard, Mr. Bhowmick brushed his teeth. He brushed, he gurgled with the loud, hawking noises that he and his brother had been taught as children to make in order to flush clean not merely teeth but also tongue and palate.

After that he showered, then, back in the bedroom again, he recited prayers in Sanskrit to Kali, the patron goddess of his family, the goddess of wrath and vengeance. In the pokey flat of his childhood in Ranchi, Bihar, his mother had given over a whole bedroom to her collection of gods and goddesses. Mr. Bhowmick couldn't be that extravagant in Detroit. His daughter, twenty-six and an electrical engineer, slept in the other of the two bedrooms in his apartment. But he had done his best. He had taken Woodworking I and II at a nearby recreation center and built a grotto for the goddess. Kali-Mata was eight inches tall, made of metal and painted a glistening black so that the metal glowed like the oiled, black skin of a peasant woman. And though Kali-Mata was totally nude except for a tiny gilt crown and a garland strung together from sinners' chopped off heads, she looked warm, cozy, *pleased*, in her makeshift wooden shrine in Detroit. Mr. Bhowmick had gathered quite a crowd of admiring, fellow woodworkers in those final weeks of decoration.

"Hurry it up with the prayers," his wife shouted from the kitchen. She was an agnostic, a believer in ambition, not grace. She frequently complained that his prayers had gotten so long that soon he wouldn't have time to go to work, play duplicate bridge with the Ghosals, or play the tabla in the Bengali Association's one Sunday per month musical soirees. Lately she'd begun to drain him in a wholly new way. He wasn't praying, she nagged; he was shutting her out of his life. There'd be no place in the house until she hid Kali-Mata in a suitcase.

She nagged, and he threatened to beat her with his shoe as his father had threatened his mother: it was the thrust and volley of marriage. There was no question of actually taking off a shoe and applying it to his wife's body. She was bigger than he was. And, secretly, he admired her for having the nerve, the agnosticism, which as a college boy in backward Bihar he too had claimed.

"I have time," he shot at her. He was still wrapped in a damp terry towel.

"You have time for everything but domestic life."

It was the fault of the shopping mall that his wife had started to buy pop psychology paperbacks. These paperbacks preached that for couples who could sit down and talk about their "relationship," life would be sweet again. His engineer daughter was on his wife's side. She accused him of holding things in.

"Face it, Dad," she said. "You have an affect deficit."

But surely everyone had feelings they didn't want to talk about or talk over. He definitely did not want to blurt out anything about the sick-in-the-guts sensations that came over him most mornings and that he couldn't bubble down with Alka-Seltzer or smother with Gas-X. The women in his family were smarter than him. They were cheerful, outgoing, more American somehow.

How could he tell these bright, mocking women that, in the 5:43 A.M. darkness, he sensed invisible presences: gods and snakes frolicked in the master bedroom, little white sparks of cosmic static crackled up the legs of his pajamas. Something was out there in the dark, something that could invent accidents and coincidences to remind mortals that even in Detroit they were no more than mortal. His wife would label this paranoia and dismiss it. Paranoia, premonition: whatever it was, it had begun to undermine his composure.

Take this morning, Mr. Bhowmick had woken up from a pleasant dream about a man taking a Club Med vacation, and the postdream satisfaction had lasted through the shower, but when he'd come back to the shrine in the bedroom, he'd noticed all at once how scarlet and saucy was the tongue that Kali-Mata stuck out at the world. Surely he had not lavished such alarming detail, such admonitory colors on that flap of flesh.

Watch out, ambulatory sinners. Be careful out there, the goddess warned him, and not with the affection of Sergeant Esterhaus, either.

"French toast must be eaten hot-hot," his wife nagged. "Otherwise they'll taste like rubber."

Mr. Bhowmick laid the trousers of a two-trouser suit he had bought on sale that winter against his favorite tweed jacket. The navy stripes in the trousers and the small, navy tweed flecks in the jacket looked quite good together. So what if the Chief Engineer had already started wearing summer cottons?

"I am coming, I am coming," he shouted back. "You want me to eat hot-hot, you start the frying only when I am sitting down. You didn't learn anything from Mother in Ranchi?"

"Mother cooked French toast from fancy recipes? I mean French Sandwich Toast with complicated filling?"

He came into the room to give her his testiest look. "You don't know the meaning of complicated cookery. And mother had to get the coal fire of the *chula* going first."

His daughter was already at the table. "Why don't you break down and buy her a microwave oven? That's what I mean about sitting down and talking things out." She had finished her orange juice. She took a plastic measure of Slim-Fast out of its can and poured the powder into a glass of skim milk. "It's ridiculous."

Babli was not the child he would have chosen as his only heir. She was brighter certainly than the sons and daughters of the other Bengalis he knew in Detroit, and she had been the only female student in most of her classes at Georgia Tech, but as she sat there in her beige linen business suit, her thick chin dropping into a polka-dotted cravat, he regretted again that she was not the child of his dreams. Babli would be able to help him out moneywise if something happened to him, something so bad that even his pension plans and his insurance policies and his money market schemes wouldn't be enough. But Babli could never comfort him. She wasn't womanly or tender the way that unmarried girls had been in the wistful days of his adolescence. She could sing Hindi film songs, mimicking exactly the high, artificial voice of Lata Mungeshkar, and she had taken two years of dance lessons at Sona Devi's Dance Academy in Southfield, but these accomplishments didn't add up to real femininity. Not the kind that had given him palpitations in Ranchi.

Mr. Bhowmick did his best with his wife's French toast. In spite of its filling of marshmallows, apricot jam and maple syrup, it tasted rubbery. He drank two cups of Darjeeling tea, said, "Well, I'm off," and took off.

All might have gone well if Mr. Bhowmick hadn't fussed longer than usual about putting his briefcase and his trenchcoat in the backseat. He got in behind the wheel of his Oldsmobile, fixed his seatbelt and was just about to turn the key in the ignition when his neighbor, Al Stazniak, who was starting up his Buick Skylark, sneezed. A sneeze at the start of a journey brings bad luck. Al Stazniak's sneeze was fierce, made up of five short bursts, too loud to be ignored.

Be careful out there! Mr. Bhowmick could see the goddess's scarlet little tongue tip wagging at him.

He was a modern man, an intelligent man. Otherwise he couldn't have had the options in life that he did have. He couldn't have given up a good job with perks in Bombay and found a better job with General Motors in Detroit. But Mr. Bhowmick was also a prudent enough man to know that some abiding truth lies bunkered within each wanton Hindu superstition. A sneeze was more than a sneeze. The heedless are carried off in ambulances. He had choices to make. He could ignore the sneeze, and so challenge the world unseen by men. Perhaps Al Stazniak had hayfever. For a sneeze to be a potent omen, surely it had to be unprovoked and terrifying, a thunderclap cleaving the summer skies. Or he could admit the smallness of mortals, undo the fate of the universe by starting over, and go back inside the apartment, sit for a second on the sofa, then re-start his trip.

Al Stazniak rolled down his window. "Everything okay?"

Mr. Bhowmick nodded shyly. They weren't really friends in the way neighbors can sometimes be. They talked as they parked or pulled out of their adjacent parking stalls. For all Mr. Bhowmick knew, Al Stazniak had no legs. He had never seen the man out of his Skylark.

He let the Buick back out first. Everything was okay, yes, please. All the same he undid his seatbelt. Compromise, adaptability, call it what you will. A dozen times a day he made these small trade-offs between new-world reasonableness and old-world beliefs.

While he was sitting in his parked car, his wife's ride came by. For fifty dollars a month, she was picked up and dropped off by a hard up, newly divorced woman who worked at a florist's shop in the same mall.

His wife came out the front door in brown K-Mart pants and a burgundy windbreaker. She waved to him, then slipped into the passenger seat of the florist's rusty Japanese car.

He was a metallurgist. He knew about rust and ways of preventing it, secret ways, thus far unknown to the Japanese.

Babli's fiery red Mitsubishi was still in the lot. She wouldn't leave for work for another eight minutes. He didn't want her to know he'd been undone by a sneeze. Babli wasn't tolerant of superstitions. She played New Wave music in her tapedeck. If asked about Hinduism, all she'd ever said to her American friends was that "it's neat." Mr. Bhowmick had heard her on the phone years before. The cosmos balanced on the head of a snake was like a beach ball balanced on the snout of a circus seal. "This Hindu myth stuff," he'd heard her say, "is like a series of super graphics."

He'd forgiven her. He could probably forgive her anything. It was her way of surviving high school in a city that was both native to her, and alien.

There was no question of going back where he'd come from. He hated Ranchi. Ranchi was no place for dreamers. All through his teenage years, Mr. Bhowmick had dreamed of success abroad. What form that success would take he had left vague. Success had meant to him escape from the constant plotting and bitterness that wore out India's middle class.

Babli should have come out of the apartment and driven off to work by now. Mr. Bhowmick decided to take a risk, to dash inside and pretend he'd left his briefcase on the coffee table.

When he entered the living room, he noticed Babli's spring coat and large vinyl pocketbook on the sofa. She was probably sorting through the junk jewelry on her dresser to give her business suit a lift. She read hints about dressing in women's magazines and applied them to her person with seriousness. If his luck held, he could sit on the sofa, say a quick prayer and get back to the car without her catching on.

It surprised him that she didn't shout out from her bedroom, "Who's there?" What if he had been a rapist?

Then he heard Babli in the bathroom. He heard unladylike squawking noises. She was throwing up. A squawk, a spitting, then the horrible gurgle of a waterfall.

A revelation came to Mr. Bhowmick. A woman vomiting in the privacy of the bathroom could mean many things. She was coming down with the flu. She was nervous about a meeting. But Mr. Bhowmick knew at once that his daughter, his untender, unloving daughter whom he couldn't love and hadn't tried to love, was not, in the larger world of Detroit, unloved. Sinners are everywhere, even in the bosom of an upright, unambitious family like the Bhowmicks. It was the goddess sticking out her tongue at him.

The father sat heavily on the sofa, shrinking from contact with her coat and pocketbook. His brisk, bright engineer daughter was pregnant. Someone had taken time to make love to her. Someone had thought her tender, feminine. Someone even now was perhaps mooning over her. The idea excited him. It was so grotesque and wondrous. At twenty-six Babli had found the man of her dreams; whereas at twenty-six Mr. Bhowmick had given up on truth, beauty, and poetry and exchanged them for two years at Carnegie Tech.

Mr. Bhowmick's tweed-jacketed body sagged against the sofa cushions. Babli would abort, of course. He knew his Babli. It was the only possible option if she didn't want to bring shame to the Bhowmick family. All the same, he could see a chubby baby boy on the rug, crawling to his granddaddy. Shame like that was easier to hide in Ranchi. There was always a barren womb sanctified by marriage that could claim sudden fructifying by the goddess Parvati. Babli would do what she wanted. She was headstrong and independent and he was afraid of her.

Babli staggered out of the bathroom. Damp stains ruined her linen suit. It was the first time he had seen his daughter look ridiculous, quite unprofessional. She didn't come into the living room to investigate the noises he'd made. He glimpsed her shoeless stockinged feet flip-flop on collapsed arches down the hall to her bedroom.

"Are you all right?" Mr. Bhowmick asked, standing in the hall. "Do you need Sinutab?"

She wheeled around. "What're you doing here?"

He was the one who should be angry. "I'm feeling poorly too," he said. "I'm taking the day off."

"I feel fine," Babli said.

Within fifteen minutes Babli had changed her clothes and left. Mr. Bhowmick had the apartment to himself all day. All day for praising or cursing the life that had brought him along with its other surprises an illegitimate grandchild.

It was his wife that he blamed. Coming to America to live had been his wife's idea. After the wedding, the young Bhowmicks had spent two years in Pittsburgh on his student visa, then gone back home to Ranchi for nine years. Nine crushing years. Then the job in Bombay had come through. All during those nine years his wife had screamed and wept. She was a woman of wild, progressive ideas—she'd called them her "American" ideas—and she'd been martyred by her neighbors for them. American *memsahib. Markin mem, Markin mem.* In bazaars the beggar boys had trailed her and hooted. She'd done provocative things. She'd hired a *chamar* woman who by caste rules was forbidden to cook for higher caste families, especially for widowed mothers of decent men. This had caused a blowup in the neighborhood. She'd made other, lesser errors. While other wives shopped and cooked every day, his wife had cooked the whole week's menu on weekends.

"What's the point of having a refrigerator, then?" She'd been scornful of the Ranchi women.

His mother, an old-fashioned widow, had accused her of trying to kill her by poisoning. "You are in such a hurry? You want to get rid of me quick-quick so you can go back to the States?"

Family life had been turbulent.

He had kept aloof, inwardly siding with his mother. He did not love his wife now, and he had not loved her then. In any case, he had not defended her. He felt some affection, and he felt guilty for having shunned her during those unhappy years. But he had thought of it then as revenge. He had wanted to marry a beautiful woman. Not being a young man of means, only a young man with prospects, he had had no right to yearn for pure beauty. He cursed his fate and after a while, settled for a barrister's daughter, a plain girl with a wide, flat plank of a body and myopic eyes. The barrister had sweetened the deal by throwing in an all-expenses-paid two years' study at Carnegie Tech to which Mr. Bhowmick had been admitted. Those two years had changed his wife from pliant girl to ambitious woman. She wanted America, nothing less.

It was his wife who had forced him to apply for permanent resident status in the U.S. even though he had a good job in Ranchi as a government engineer. The putting together of documents for the immigrant visa had been a long and humbling process. He had had to explain to a chilly clerk in the Embassy that, like most Indians of his generation, he had no birth certificate. He had to swear out affidavits, suffer through police checks, bribe orderlies whose job it was to move his dossier from desk to desk. The decision, the clerk had advised him, would take months, maybe years. He hadn't dared hope that merit might be rewarded. Merit could collapse under bad luck. It was for grace that he prayed.

While the immigration papers were being processed, he had found the job in Bombay. So he'd moved his mother in with his younger brother's family, and left his hometown for good. Life in Bombay had been lighthearted, almost fulfilling. His wife had thrown herself into charity work with the same energy that had offended the Ranchi women. He was happy to be in a big city at last. Bombay was the Rio de Janeiro of the East; he'd read that in a travel brochure. He drove out to Nariman Point at least once a week to admire the necklace of municipal lights, toss coconut shells into the dark ocean, drink beer at the Oberoi-Sheraton where overseas Indian girls in designer jeans beckoned him in sly ways. His nights were full. He played duplicate bridge, went to the movies, took his wife to Bingo nights at his club. In Detroit he was a lonelier man.

Then the green card had come through. For him, for his wife, and for the daughter who had been born to them in Bombay. He sold what he could sell, and put in his brother's informal trust what he couldn't to save on taxes. Then he had left for America, and one more start.

All through the week, Mr. Bhowmick watched his daughter. He kept furtive notes on how many times she rushed to the bathroom and made hawking, wrenching noises, how many times she stayed late at the office, calling her mother to say she'd be taking in a movie and pizza afterwards with friends.

He had to tell her that he knew. And he probably didn't have much time. She shouldn't be on Slim-Fast in her condition. He had to talk things over with her. But what would he say to her? What position could he take? He had to choose between public shame for the family, and murder.

For three more weeks he watched her and kept his silence. Babli wore shifts to the office instead of business suits, and he liked her better in those garments. Perhaps she was dressing for her young man, not from necessity. Her skin was pale and blotchy by turn. At breakfast her fingers looked stiff, and she had trouble with silverware.

Two Saturdays running, he lost badly at duplicate bridge. His wife scolded him. He had made silly mistakes. When was Babli meeting this man? Where? He must be American; Mr. Bhowmick prayed only that he was white. He pictured his grandson crawling to him, and the grandson was always fat and brown and buttery-skinned, like the infant Krishna. An American son-in-law was a terrifying notion. Why was she not mentioning men, at least, preparing the way for the major announcement? He listened sharply for men's names, rehearsed little lines like, "Hello, Bob, I'm Babli's old man," with a cracked little laugh. Bob, Jack, Jimmy, Tom. But no names surfaced. When she went out for pizza and a movie it was with the familiar set of Indian girls and their strange, unpopular, American friends, all without men. Mr. Bhowmick tried to be reasonable. Maybe she had already gotten married and was keeping it secret. "Well, Bob, you and Babli sure had Mrs. Bhowmick and me going there, heh-heh," he mumbled one night with the Sahas and Ghosals, over cards. "Pardon?" asked Pronob Saha. Mr. Bhowmick dropped two tricks, and his wife glared. "Such stupid blunders," she fumed on the drive back. A new truth was dawning; there would be no marriage for Babli. Her young man probably was not so young and not so available. He must be already married. She must have yielded to passion or been raped in the office. His wife seemed to have noticed nothing. Was he a murderer, or a conspirator? He kept his secret from his wife; his daughter kept her decision to herself.

Nights, Mr. Bhowmick pretended to sleep, but as soon as his wife began her snoring—not real snores so much as loud, gaspy gulpings for breath—he turned on his side and prayed to Kali-Mata.

In July, when Babli's belly had begun to push up against the waist-less dresses she'd bought herself, Mr. Bhowmick came out of the shower one weekday morning and found the two women screaming at each other. His wife had a rolling pin in one hand. His daughter held up a *National Geographic* as a shield for her head. The crazy look that had been in his wife's eyes when she'd shooed away beggar kids was in her eyes again.

"Stop it!" His own boldness overwhelmed him. "Shut up! Babli's pregnant, so what? It's your fault, you made us come to the States."

Girls like Babli were caught between rules, that's the point he wished to make. They were too smart, too impulsive for a backward place like Ranchi, but not tough nor smart enough for sex-crazy places like Detroit.

"My fault?" his wife cried. "I told her to do hanky-panky with boys? I told her to shame us like this?"

She got in one blow with the rolling pin. The second glanced off Babli's shoulder and fell on his arm which he had stuck out for his grandson's sake.

"I'm calling the police," Babli shouted. She was out of the rolling pin's range. "This is brutality. You can't do this to me."

"Shut up! Shut your mouth, foolish woman." He wrenched the weapon from his wife's fist. He made a show of taking off his shoe to beat his wife on the face.

"What do you know? You don't know anything." She let herself down slowly on a dining chair. Her hair, curled overnight, stood in wild whorls around her head. "Nothing."

"And you do!" He laughed. He remembered her tormentors, and laughed again. He had begun to enjoy himself. Now *he* was the one with the crazy, progressive ideas.

"Your daughter is pregnant, yes," she said, "any fool knows that. But ask her the name of the father. Go, ask."

He stared at his daughter who gazed straight ahead, eyes burning with hate, jaw clenched with fury.

"Babli?"

"Who needs a man?" she hissed. "The father of my baby is a bottle and a syringe. Men louse up your lives. I just want a baby. Oh, don't worry—he's a certified fit donor. No diseases, college graduate, above average, and he made the easiest twenty-five dollars of his life—"

"Like animals," his wife said. For the first time he heard horror in her voice. His daughter grinned at him. He saw her tongue, thick and red, squirming behind her row of perfect teeth.

"Yes, yes, yes," she screamed, "like livestock. Just like animals. You should be happy—that's what marriage is all about, isn't it? Matching bloodlines, matching horoscopes, matching castes, matching, matching, matching . . ." and it was difficult to know if she was laughing or singing, or mocking and like a madwoman.

Mr. Bhowmick lifted the rolling pin high above his head and brought it down hard on the dome of Babli's stomach. In the end, it was his wife who called the police.

Fictive Fragments of a Father and Son

from *Turning Japanese*

David Mura

Someone must have been telling lies about Joseph K., for without having done anything wrong he was arrested one fine morning.

—Franz Kafka, *The Trial*

Henry went to the control station to register his family. He came home with twenty tags, all number 10701, tags to be attached to each piece of baggage, and one to hang from our coat lapels. From then on we were known as family #10701.

—Monica Sone, *A Nisei Daughter*

When I was in college, I once asked my father what it was like in the camps.

"Well, before the war, when I got home from school, I had to work in my father's nursery," he said. "In the camps, after school, I could just go out and play baseball."

It's amazing to me how many years I accepted this precis. Or my father's homily, "If you look for prejudice, you'll find it." Or his insistence that his Horatio Alger rise to upper middle class in the years after the war had been without incidents or insults, without discrimi-

---

DAVID MURA is a Sansei, a third-generation Japanese American. He is the author of the award-winning *Turning Japanese: Memoirs of a Sansei*. His other books include poetry —*After We Lost Our Way*—and the essay *A Male Grief: Notes on Pornography & Addiction*. His essays on race and multiculturalism have appeared in *The Graywolf Annual V: Multicultural Literacy*, *Mother Jones*, and *The New York Times*. He lives in Minnesota and is at work on an autobiographical book on Asian Americans and race.

nation. All he had to do was work his ass off. (A lesson I never quite seemed to learn.)

And then, after I visited Hiroshima last year, during a year long visit to Japan, I started to think of where my father was on the day the war ended. And something changed. There was this story there that hadn't been told. Or many stories. Stories my father would call fictions. Completely untrue.

By the last year of the war, my father had been released from the internment camp in Jerome, Arkansas, for more than a year and was going to Western Michigan University in Kalamazoo, living with the family of a professor.

Probably my father is both pleased and anxious about this precarious new freedom. Perhaps he has looked through the pages of *Life* or *Time*, has seen the cartoons depicting the Japanese: they are lice, vermin, tiny thoraxes with huge heads attached, a buck tooth smile and squinty eyes behind thick glasses; they are small, slant-eyed rats squirming under a huge boot of a GI giant smashing down with unfathomable power. Perhaps he has seen the way some of his classmates look at him, casting glances sideways in history or English, as he passes in the halls. Perhaps they whisper loud enough for him to hear. Perhaps not. (Is he imagining this? Or am I?) I know he does not date in college. There are no other *Nisei*, none of his kind. Does he admit to himself his desire for the white girls in his classes? Or is the sexual conflict inside him too dangerous to acknowledge?

It is the year the war has ended, the summer between his freshman and sophomore year. August, a few days after Hiroshima and Nagasaki. A holiday has been declared, men sweep women up in their arms in the middle of streets and kiss them, and the women, abandoned for a moment, respond; firecrackers, streamers, confetti, all the trappings of a carnival, whirl through intersections and squares throughout the country. People sport the smiles and laughter of peace, as if the muscles, clenched like a fist for so long, have moved on to another task, all brightness, promise and plenty.

On August 11, 1945, my father is sitting on the steps of a house in

Kalamazoo, Michigan. He hears the swooping sirens of the firetrucks from the center of town, the high school band blaring "Stars and Stripes Forever," the tooting of horns, loudspeakers filling with speeches. He sees in his mind the street filled with banners and flags, the men with faces bright and beet-red from joy and drink, the women yanking their children at the wrist, dabbing their eyes with handkerchiefs. A squirrel comes chittering across the lawn, rears up on its haunches, begging as usual for a handout. My father picks up a stone from the dirt, pulls back his arm, and then drops the stone to his feet. A voice rises inside him, insistent and restless, a twitch in his muscles, an urge to move, go somewhere, do something. "It won't always be like this," he remembers his teacher in the camps saying. "After the war you will be free again and back in American society. But for your own sakes try and be not one, but two hundred percent American. . . ."

I am American he says to himself. I am glad we won. The light through the leaves is bright, blinding. The heat immense, oppressive. The sounds all over town joyous. He repeats his mantra over and over. He learns to believe it.

My father never slept with a white woman, never, I think, slept with anyone but my mother. Still, I know he must have thought of crossing that line, must have been aware it was there to cross.

One fall afternoon in eighth grade, I am home from school with a slight fever. My mother is out shopping. For some reason, I start rummaging in their closet, pushing back the pumps and flats, all lined in a row on the rack, unzipping the garment bags. (What am I looking for? Years later, my therapist will tell me that news travels quickly and silently in families; no one has to speak of it.) From beneath a stack of folded sweaters, I pull a *Playboy* magazine. I start moving through the pages, the ads for albums and liquor, cartoons, the interview with Albert Schweitzer, with photos of the great man in pith helmet and bow tie, his famous walrus mustache. And then the foldout undoes itself, flowing before me with its glossy shine.

I've seen a *Playboy* someone brought into the locker room at school. But now I'm alone, in my parents' bedroom. I worry about when my mother is coming back, I forget she is gone. I'm entranced by the woman's breasts, the aureoles seem large as my fists. She is blonde, eighteen, a UCLA coed. She leans against a screen, half her body exposed to the camera.

And so, like many other American boys, I discover my sexuality in the presence of a picture. And, like many other American boys, I do not think of the color of the woman's skin. Of course, if she were black or brown or yellow . . . but she is white, her beauty self-evident. I sense somehow that she must be more beautiful than Asian women, more prestigious. But the forbidden quality of sex overpowers any thought of race. I do not wonder why my father looks at these pictures, these women who are not my mother. The sensations of pleasure, of momentary possession and shame, flood over me quickly, easily, sliding through my body.

A few minutes later, I pick up the magazine, slip it back in the garment bag beneath the sweaters.

In one of my poems, there's a line about my father, "he worked too hard to be white, he beat his son." Of course, it's more complicated than that.

I know that his father, my grandfather, would chase my father around the yard in L.A., brandishing a two by four. Whenever my father referred to this, his manner was surprisingly casual. The beatings were no different from the long distances he had to walk to school or the work he performed in his father's nursery. They were simply proof that my father's childhood was harsher than mine.

Sometimes I try to picture my father running from my grandfather, as he holds his weapon aloft. At a certain moment, the board comes down on flesh, whacks the sweaty, t-shirted back of the young boy, knocking him forward, a flat, dull driving pain, the wind rushing from his lungs, a dizziness of fear, panic, and perhaps relief erupting from his stumbling body. The next blow is harder, more solid; the thought rises in my father that he cannot go on, this can't be happening, each blow softened only by the fact that there is one less to go, it will somehow end.

But when I try to imagine my father, squirming in his father's grip, in all likelihood, it is not my father I am seeing, but myself, as my father hovers over me in my room, having read the note from my teacher or having heard from my mother. I've been bad, have talked too much. He grabs my toy whip from the floor, the one modelled after Zorro's. The whip comes down; I do not go limp. I scramble about. The room is small, he catches me and hauls me on his lap. I'm held in this vise. I can't move, can't bear knowing this will happen again and again.

Somehow, behind these acts of fathers and sons lies the backdrop of race and relocation.

As the war went on, the internees at the Jerome, Arkansas relocation center were given weekend passes. They could travel to Little Rock to eat at a restaurant or watch a movie. My grandfather or grandmother did not go on these trips, only their children. The children spoke English, were enamored of Hollywood's stars.

It is summer, 1942. On a dust dry country road, my father waits for the bus with other young *Nisei*. Behind them, like a bad dream, the fences of barbed wire, the rifle towers, the gates, the barracks filled with mothers, fathers, and bawling babies, with aging bachelors, with newlyweds. Down the ridge they can see the shacks of sharecroppers, more ramshackle than any of the barracks, with gaps in the walls and their boards weatherbeaten and cracked. Rougher, looser than his older brother Ken—less Japanese—my father and his friends jostle and joke, talk about the baseball game yesterday, about Carol Hiyama or Judy Endo. These boys frighten some of the *Issei* in camp. They play cards behind the barracks, smoke cigarettes, curse in English.

When the bus comes, it is nearly empty. They take their seats in the front, behind an old white woman with a pillbox hat, her purse planted in her lap. Behind them, the anonymous faces of a few Negroes, a couple men in overalls, a mother and her child with pigtails. There's never a question for my father of sitting in the back.

It is the same at the lunch counter where they order hamburgers and malts. Perhaps they notice the stares of the whites around them, but most likely they are too engrossed in their own conversation, in teasing Tosh about his crush on Carol, to notice where the negroes are sitting. Later, these boys will sit below the balcony, below the section for negroes. The faces of Cary Grant and Katharine Hepburn flow off the screen, borne on light, enlarged by glamour and celluloid, becoming part of my father's dreams.

Two years later, he's in college, away from the camps, entering the Episcopalian church with Professor Bigelow and his family. It is a sunny fall morning, the leaves, splashes of red and yellow and orange, swirling down to the street, crackling on the walk. The church is white, spired, clean in the sunlight. My father has no suit. He's wearing a white shirt, a tie. It is his first time inside this church.

Had my grandfather been a fervent Buddhist, things might have turned out differently. But my grandfather was too much a man of this world. Sharing with most Japanese a passive attitude towards religions, he had grown away from Buddha and the Shinto gods during this time in America. My father is an empty vessel, waiting to be filled.

As he ambles along with the Bigelows, he's a little stiff, a bit nervous, not knowing what to do. Inside, he's greeted by streams of light from great stained glass windows: Christ in the garden of Gethsemane, kneeling in prayer with the cross of his destruction in the distance, the disciples gathered around him, questioning, listening; the fish and bread of life laid out in jagged triangles; the haggard bearded man stretched out on the cross, eyes closed, giving up the ghost. What strikes my father more, the beautiful colors or this progression towards suffering? The light or the dark?

He sees notices in front of the benches, a little platform that swings down, cushioned green leather. Just as the children enter the pew, they suddenly kneel down, facing straight ahead towards the altar; Mrs. Bigelow and the professor do the same. My father wonders what he should do. Self-conscious, he does the best he can with a half-way gesture, the way seventh-graders in our parish years later used to bow. The professor smiles and tries to reassure him, but my father, watching the altar boy light the candles on the altar, hearing the organ and the voices of the choir, is again wondering what to do. As the service continues and the members in the pews rise up to speak in unison, kneel, rise, kneel, over and over at exactly the right time, my father is disoriented. He feels a slight ache in his back, is thankful at least for the cushioned platform.

"This is the body and blood which is shed for you and the New Testament. Take this and drink. Do this often in rememberance of me."

Thank God, he thinks, I understand the words. And in all of this there is a music that takes over my father, something beyond sense, beyond God or Christ. What attracts him is a sense of belonging, of crossing some line, a way out of the Buddhist temples and streets of L.A., something he first felt in the radios and comic books, the very language that poured from his mouth, in the games of mumblety-peg, marbles and baseball, in the pledge he recited in school each morning. Something that wasn't foreign, that did not keep him out.

He will convert, he will take up the cross, he will bring us to Church all through my childhood, up until the time we move from our middle class home in Morton Grove to our upper class one in Northbrook, a time when he is finally a vice-president, when religion is no longer needed. By then I will be estranged from the Church, an atheist, wondering what brought him to think a white man must be God.

Growing up, I had the usual complaints of most Asian kids about their hard driving parents. There were never enough excellents, enough hundreds on tests, there were always errors I'd made on the field, tackles I missed. When I was seven, my father took me to the sidewalk on Lake Shore drive and pushed me off on my bike, screamed "pedal, pedal," and quickly became disgusted when I fell, yelling I didn't listen to him. Ten years later when I learned to drive, it was the same; sitting beside me in our Buick, he slammed on some imaginary brake in front of him and shook my arm. A terrible teacher, he always ended up screaming and shouting, muttering about my lack of concentration, my refusal to perform.

Perhaps the problem was how I took all this. I believed whatever it was that reddened his face, that clenched it so tight, that coiled his fist into a tight ball, must have come from me. I must have created this force, it was what I deserved. I was simply unable to brush it off.

Years later, I wonder, where did my father's rage come from?

I see my father now as a successful executive, writing speeches for other executives, writing videos, public relations campaigns, giving speeches at conventions and meetings, splicing bits of information with familiar corn-pone jokes. I see him at evening striding down the fairway in back of his house, shading his eyes as his drive soars into the sun, the tiny white ball disappearing in the last blaze of orange light, the first crickets of evening, gnats scribbling their mad circles around his head. His body looks ten years younger, hardened by weights, by Nautilus, though it has begun to stoop, just a touch, to descend towards earth. He is sixty, he is content, the fairway stretches out before him, he wants no other life than this. He has no problems with identity, with the past or race. He has been freed from history.

And I am still his son.

In the light of Kafka, the story of the camps becomes a parable, a parable whose meaning I must somehow solve.

One day, K. steps out of his door to find a notice: he must report to the authorities. Who are the authorities? He does not know, only that he must report to them. When he reports to them, they give him a number, tell him to come back tomorrow. When he comes back the next day, he is taken by bus to a train and then by train to a place with others who have been given numbers and notices. He realizes he has been imprisoned. He is no longer singular, no longer private. The communal beds, shower stalls and toilets only confirm this, as do the barbed wire and rifle towers with guards. What is his crime? He is K. That is his crime.

My father's name was originally Katsuji Uyemura. Then Tom Katsuji Uyeumura. Then Tom Katsuji Mura. Then Tom K. Mura.

What is the job of the son of K.? To forgive his crime? To try him again?

A Red Sweater

Fae Myenne Ng

I chose red for my sister. Fierce, dark red. Made in Hong Kong. Hand Wash Only because it's got that skin of fuzz. She'll look happy. That's good. Everything's perfect, for a minute. That seems enough.

Red. For Good Luck. Of course. This fire-red sweater is swollen with good cheer. Wear it, I will tell her. You'll look lucky.

We're a family of three girls. By Chinese standards, that's not lucky. "Too bad," outsiders whisper, ". . . nothing but daughters. A failed family."

First, Middle, and End girl. Our order of birth marked us. That came to tell more than our given names.

FAE MYENNE NG made a stunning debut with her novel *Bone*. Born in San Francisco and raised in Chinatown, she attended the University of California, Berkeley, and Columbia University. Her award-winning stories have appeared in *Harper's* magazine, *The American Voice*, the *Pushcart Prize Anthology*, the *City Lights Review*, *Home to Stay: Asian American Women's Fiction*, and other publications.

My eldest sister, Lisa, lives at home. She quit San Francisco State, one semester short of a psychology degree. One day she said, "Forget about it, I'm tired." She's working full time at Pacific Telephone now. Nine hundred a month with benefits. Mah and Deh think it's a great deal. They tell everybody, "Yes, our Number One makes good pay, but that's not even counting the discount. If we call Hong Kong, China even, there's forty percent off!" As if anyone in their part of China had a telephone.

Number Two, the in-between, jumped off the 'M' floor three years ago. Not true! What happened? Why? Too sad! All we say about that is, "It was her choice."

We sent Mah to Hong Kong. When she left Hong Kong thirty years ago, she was the envy of all: "Lucky girl! You'll never have to work." To marry a sojourner was to have a future. Thirty years in the land of gold and good fortune, and then she returned to tell the story: three daughters, one dead, one unmarried, another who-cares-where, the thirty years in sweatshops, and the prince of the Golden Mountain turned into a toad. I'm glad I didn't have to go with her. I felt her shame and regret. To return, seeking solace and comfort, instead of offering banquets and stories of the good life.

I'm the youngest. I started flying with Pan Am the year Mah returned to Hong Kong, so I got her a good discount. She thought I was good for something then. But when she returned, I was pregnant.

"Get an abortion," she said. "Drop the baby," she screamed.

"No."

"Then get married."

"No. I don't want to."

I was going to get an abortion all along. I just didn't like the way they talked about the whole thing. They made me feel like dirt, that I was a disgrace. Now I can see how I used it as an opportunity. Sometimes I wonder if there wasn't another way. Everything about those years was so steamy and angry. There didn't seem to be any answers.

"I have no eyes for you," Mah said.

"Don't call us," Deh said.

They wouldn't talk to me. They ranted idioms to each other for days. The apartment was filled with images and curses I couldn't perceive. I got the general idea: I was a rotten, no-good, dead thing. I would die in a gutter without rice in my belly. My spirit—if I had one—wouldn't be fed. I wouldn't see good days in this life or the next.

My parents always had a special way of saying things.

Now I'm based in Honolulu. When our middle sister jumped, she kind of closed the world. The family just sort of fell apart. I left. Now, I try to make up for it, but the folks still won't see me, but I try to keep in touch with them through Lisa. Flying cuts up your life, hits hardest during the holidays. I'm always sensitive then. I feel like I'm missing something, that people are doing something really important while I'm up in the sky, flying through time zones.

So I like to see Lisa around the beginning of the year. January, New Year's, and February, New Year's again, double luckiness with our birthdays in between. With so much going on, there's always something to talk about.

"You pick the place this year," I tell her.

"Around here?"

"No," I say. 'Around here' means the food is good and the living hard. You eat a steaming rice plate, and then you feel like rushing home to sew garments or assemble radio parts or something. We eat together only once a year, so I feel we should splurge. Besides, at the Chinatown places, you have nothing to talk about except the bare issues. In American restaurants, the atmosphere helps you along. I want nice light and a view and handsome waiters.

"Let's go somewhere with a view," I say.

We decide to go to FOLLOWING SEA, a new place on the Pier 39 track. We're early, the restaurant isn't crowded. It's been clear all day, so I think the sunset will be nice. I ask for a window table. I turn to talk to my sister, but she's already talking to a waiter. He's got that dark island tone that she likes. He's looking her up and down. My sister does not blink at it. She holds his look and orders two Johnny Walkers. I pick up a fork, turn it around in my hand. I seldom use chopsticks now. At home, I eat my rice in a plate, with a fork. The only chopsticks I own, I wear in my hair. For a moment, I feel strange sitting here at this unfamiliar table. I don't know this tablecloth, this linen, these candles. Everything seems foreign. It feels like we should be different people. But each time I look up, she's the same. I know this person. She's my sister. We sat together with chopsticks, mismatched bowls, braids, and braces, across the formica tabletop.

"I like three pronged forks," I say, pressing my thumb against the sharp points.

My sister rolls her eyes. She lights a cigarette.

I ask for one.

I finally say, "So, what's new?"

"Not much." Her voice is sullen. She doesn't look at me. Once a year, I come in, asking questions. She's got the answers, but she hates them. For me, I think she's got the peace of heart, knowing that she's done her share for Mah and Deh. She thinks I have the peace, not caring. Her life is full of questions, too, but I have no answers.

I look around the restaurant. The sunset is not spectacular and we don't comment on it. The waiters are lighting candles. Ours is bringing the drinks. He stops very close to my sister, seems to breathe her in. She raises her face toward him. "Ready?" he asks. My sister orders for us. The waiter struts off.

"Tight ass," I say.

"The best," she says.

My scotch tastes good. It reminds me of Deh. Johnny Walker or Seagrams 7, that's what they served at Chinese banquets. Nine courses and a bottle. No ice. We learned to drink it Chinese style, in teacups. Deh drank from his rice bowl, sipping it like hot soup. By the end of the meal, he took it like cool tea, in bold mouthfuls. We sat watching, our teacups of scotch in our laps, his three giggly girls.

Relaxed, I'm thinking there's a connection. Johnny Walker then and Johnny Walker now. I ask for another cigarette and this one I enjoy. Now my Johnny Walker pops with ice. I twirl the glass to make the ice tinkle.

We clink glasses. Three times for good luck. She giggles. I feel better.

"Nice sweater," I say.

"Michael Owyang," she says. She laughs. The light from the candle makes her eyes shimmer. She's got Mah's eyes. Eyes that make you want to talk. Lisa is reed-thin and tall. She's got a body that clothes look good on. My sister slips something on and it wraps her like skin. Fabric has pulse on her.

"Happy birthday, soon," I say.

"Thanks, and to yours too, just as soon."

"Here's to Johnny Walker in shark's fin soup," I say.

"And squab dinners."

"I LOVE LUCY," I say.

We laugh. It makes us feel like children again. We remember how to be sisters.

I raise my glass. "To I LOVE LUCY, squab dinners, and brown bags."

"To bones," she says.

"Bones," I repeat. This is a funny that gets sad, and knowing it, I keep laughing. I am surprised how much memory there is in one word. Pigeons. Only recently did I learn they're called squab. Our word for them was pigeon—on a plate or flying over Portsmouth Square. A good meal at 40 cents a bird. In line by dawn, we waited at the butcher's listening for the slow, churning motor of the trucks. We watched the live fish flushing out of the tanks into the garbage pails. We smelled the honey-brushed cha sui bows baking. When the white laundry truck turned onto Wentworth, there was a puffing trail of feathers following it. A stench filled the alley. The crowd squeezed in around the truck. Old ladies reached into the crates, squeezing and tugging for the plumpest pigeons.

My sister and I picked the white ones, those with the most expressive eyes. Dove birds, we called them. We fed them leftover rice in water, and as long as they stayed plump, they were our pets, our baby dove birds. And then one day we'd come home from school and find them cooked. They were a special, nutritious treat. Mah let us fill our bowls high with little pigeon parts: legs, breasts, and wings, and take them out to the front room to watch I LOVE LUCY. We took brown bags for the bones. We balanced our bowls on our laps and laughed at Lucy. We leaned forward, our chopsticks crossed in mid-air, and called out, "Mah! Mah! Come watch! Watch Lucy cry!"

But she always sat alone in the kitchen sucking out the sweetness of the lesser parts: necks, backs, and the head. "Bones are sweeter than you know," she always said. She came out to check the bags. "Clean bones," she said, shaking the bags. "No waste," she said.

Our dinners come with a warning. "Plate's hot. Don't touch." My sister orders a carafe of house white. "Enjoy," he says, smiling at my sister. She doesn't look up.

I can't remember how to say scallops in Chinese. I ask my sister, she doesn't know either. The food isn't great. Or maybe we just don't have the taste buds in us to go crazy over it. Sometimes I get very hungry for Chinese flavors: black beans, garlic and ginger, shrimp paste and sesame oil. These are tastes we grew up with, still dream about. Crave. Run around town after. Duck liver sausage, beancurd, jook, salted fish, and fried dace with black beans. Western flavors don't stand out, the surroundings do. Three pronged forks. Pink tablecloths. Fresh flowers. Cute waiters. An odd difference.

"Maybe we should have gone to Sun Hung Heung. At least the vegetables are real," I say.

"Hung toh-vee-foo-won-tun!" she says.

"Yeah, yum!" I say.

I remember Deh teaching us how to pick bok choy, his favorite vegetable. "Stick your fingernail into the stem. Juicy and firm, good. Limp and tough, no good." The three of us followed Deh, punching our thumbnails into every stem of bok choy we saw.

"Deh still eating bok choy?"

"Breakfast, lunch and dinner." My sister throws her head back, and laughs. It is Deh's motion. She recites in a mimic tone. "Your Deh, all he needs is a good hot bowl of rice and a plate full of greens. A good monk."

There was always bok choy. Even though it was nonstop for Mah —rushing to the sweatshop in the morning, out to shop on break, and then home to cook by evening—she did this for him. A plate of bok choy, steaming with the taste of ginger and garlic. He said she made good rice. Timed full-fire until the first boil, medium until the grains formed a crust along the sides of the pot, and then low-flamed to let the rice steam. Firm, that's how Deh liked his rice.

The waiter brings the wine, asks if everything is alright.

"Everything," my sister says.

There's something else about this meeting. I can hear it in the edge of her voice. She doesn't say anything and I don't ask. Her lips make a contorting line; her face looks sour. She lets out a breath. It sounds like she's been holding it in too long.

"Another fight. The bank line," she says. "He waited four times in the bank line. Mah ran around outside shopping. He was doing her a favor. She was doing him a favor. Mah wouldn't stop yelling. 'Get out and go die! Useless Thing! Stinking Corpse!' "

I know he answered. His voice must have had that fortune teller's tone to it. You listened because you knew it was a warning.

He always threatened to disappear, jump off the Golden Gate. His thousand-year-old threat. I've heard it all before. "I will go. Even when dead, I won't be far enough away. Curse the good will that blinded me into taking you as wife!"

I give Lisa some of my scallops. "Eat," I tell her.

She keeps talking. "Of course, you know how Mah thinks, that nobody should complain because she's been the one working all these years."

I nod. I start eating, hoping she'll follow.

One bite and she's talking again. "You know what shopping with Mah is like, either you stand outside with the bags like a servant, or inside like a marker, holding a place in line. You know how she gets into being frugal—saving time because it's the one free thing in her life. Well, they're at the bank and she had him hold her place in line while she runs up and down Stockton doing her quick shopping maneuvers. So he's in line, and it's his turn, but she's not back. So he has to start all over at the back again. Then it's his turn but she's still not back. When she finally comes in, she's got bags in both hands, and he's going through the line for the fourth time. Of course she doesn't say sorry or anything."

I interrupt. "How do you know all this?" I tell myself not to come back next year. I tell myself to apply for another transfer, to the East Coast.

"She told me. Word for word." Lisa spears the scallop, puts it in her mouth. I know it's cold by now. "Word for word," she repeats. She cuts a piece of chicken. "Try," she says.

I think about how we're sisters. We eat slowly, chewing carefully, like old people. A way to make things last, to fool the stomach.

Mah and Deh both worked too hard; it's as if their marriage was a marriage of toil—of toiling together. The idea is that the next generation can marry for love.

In the old country, matches were made, strangers were wedded, and that was fate. Those days, sojourners like Deh were considered princes. To become the wife to such a man was to be saved from the war-torn villages.

Saved to work. After dinner, with the rice still in between her teeth, Mah sat down at her Singer. When we pulled out the wall-bed, she was still there, sewing. The street noises stopped long before she did. The hot lamp made all the stitches blur together. And in the mornings, long before any of us awoke, she was already there, sewing again.

His work was hard, too. He ran a laundry on Polk Street. He sailed with the American President Lines. Things started to look up when he owned the take-out place in Vallejo, and then his partner ran off. So he went to Alaska and worked the canneries.

She was good to him too. We remember. How else would we have known him all those years he worked in Guam, in the Fiji Islands, in Alaska? Mah always gave him majestic welcomes home. It was her excitement that made us remember him.

I look around. The restaurant is full. The waiters move quickly.

I know Deh. His words are ugly. I've heard him. I've listened. And I've always wished for the street noises, as if in the traffic of sound, I believe I can escape. I know the hard color of his eyes and the tightness in his jaw. I can almost hear his teeth grind. I know this. Years of it.

Their lives weren't easy. So is their discontent without reason?

What about the first one? You didn't even think to come to the hospital. The first one, I say! Son or daughter, dead or alive, you didn't even come!

What about living or dying? Which did you want for me that time you pushed me back to work before my back brace was off?

Money! Money!! Money to eat with, to buy clothes with, to pass this life with!

Don't start that again! Everything I make at that dead place I hand . . .

How come . . .
What about . . .
So . . .

It was obvious. The stories themselves meant little. It was how hot and furious they could become.

Is there no end to it? What makes their ugliness so alive, so thick and impossible to let go of?

"I don't want to think about it anymore." The way she says it surprises me. This time I listen. I imagine what it would be like to take her place. It will be my turn one day.

"Ron," she says, wiggling her fingers above the candle. "A fun thing."

The opal flickers above the flame. I tell her that I want to get her something special for her birthday, ". . . next trip I get abroad." She looks up at me, smiles.

For a minute, my sister seems happy. But she won't be able to hold onto it. She grabs at things out of despair, out of fear. Gifts grow old for her. Emotions never ripen, they sour. Everything slips away from her. Nothing sustains her. Her beauty has made her fragile.

We should have eaten in Chinatown. We could have gone for coffee in North Beach, then for jook at Sam Wo's.

"No work, it's been like that for months, just odd jobs," she says.

I'm thinking, it's not like I haven't done my share. I was a kid once, I did things because I felt I should. I helped fill out forms at the Chinatown employment agencies. I went with him to the Seaman's Union. I waited too, listening and hoping for those calls: "Busboy! Presser! Prep Man!" His bags were packed, he was always ready to go. "On standby," he said.

Every week. All the same. Quitting and looking to start all over again. In the end, it was like never having gone anywhere. It was like the bank line, waiting for nothing.

How many times did my sister and I have to hold them apart? The flat ting! sound as the blade slapped onto the linoleum floors, the wooden handle of the knife slamming into the corner. Was it she or I who screamed, repeating all their ugliest words? Who shook them? Who made them stop?

The waiter comes to take the plates. He stands by my sister for a moment. I raise my glass to the waiter.

"You two Chinese?" he asks.

"No," I say, finishing off my wine. I roll my eyes. I wish I had another Johnny Walker. Suddenly I don't care.

"We're two sisters," I say. I laugh. I ask for the check, leave a good tip. I see him slip my sister a box of matches.

Outside, the air is cool and brisk. My sister links her arm into mine. We walk up Bay onto Chestnut. We pass Galileo High School and then turn down Van Ness to head toward the pier. The bay is black. The foghorns sound far away. We walk the whole length of the pier without talking.

The water is white where it slaps against the wooden stakes. For a long time Lisa's wanted out. She can stay at that point of endurance forever. Desire that becomes old feels too good, it's seductive. I know how hard it is to go.

The heart never travels. You have to be heartless. My sister holds that heart, too close and for too long. This is her weakness, and I like to think, used to be mine. Lisa endures too much.

We're lucky, not like the bondmaids growing up in service, or the new-born daughters whose mouths were stuffed with ashes. Courtesans with the three-inch foot, beardless, soft-shouldered eunuchs, and the frightened child-brides, they're all stories to us. We're the lucky generation. Our parents forced themselves to live through the humiliation in this country so that we could have it better. We know so little of the old country. We repeat the names of Grandmothers and Uncles, but they will always be strangers to us. Family exists only because somebody has a story, and knowing the story connects us to a history. To us, the deformed man is oddly compelling, the forgotten man is a good story. A beautiful woman suffers.

I want her beauty to buy her out.

The sweater cost two weeks' pay. Like the 40-cent birds that are now a delicacy, this is a special treat. The money doesn't mean anything. It is, if anything, time. Time is what I would like to give her.

A red sweater. 100%. The skin of fuzz will be a fierce rouge on her naked breasts.

Red. Lucky. Wear it. Find that man. The new one. Wrap yourself around him. Feel the pulsing between you. Fuck him and think about it. 100% angora. Hand Wash Only. Worn Once.

Chang

The first time I ever heard my father speak Chinese was at Coney Island. I don't remember how old I was then, but I must have been very young. It was in the early days, when we still went on family outings. We were walking along the boardwalk when we ran into the four Chinese men. My mother told the story often, as if she thought we'd forgotten. "You kids didn't know them and neither did I. They were friends of your father's, from Chinatown. You'd never heard Chinese before. You didn't know what was up. You stood there with your mouths hanging open—I had to laugh. 'Why are they singing? Why is Daddy singing?' "

I remember a little more about that day. One of the men gave each of my sisters and me a dollar bill. I cashed mine into dimes and set out to win a goldfish. A dime bought you three chances to toss a ping-pong ball into one of many small fishbowls, each holding a quivering

---

SIGRID NUNEZ: "I was born in New York City and educated at Barnard College and Columbia University. My short fiction has appeared in *The Threepenny Review, Iowa Review, Salmagundi*, and other journals. I have been the recipient of two Pushcart awards and a 1990 G.E. Foundation Award for Younger Writers."

tangerine-colored fish. Overexcited, I threw recklessly, again and again. When all the dimes were gone I ran back to the grown-ups in tears. The man who had given me the dollar tried to give me another, but my parents wouldn't allow it. He pressed the bag of peanuts he had been eating into my hands and said I could have them all.

I never saw any of those men again or heard anything about them. They were the only friends of my father's that I would ever meet. I would hear him speak Chinese again, but very seldom. In Chinese restaurants, occasionally on the telephone, once or twice in his sleep, and in the hospital when he was dying.

So it was true, then. He really was Chinese. Up until that day I had not quite believed it.

My mother always said that he had sailed to America on a boat. He took a slow boat from China, was what she used to say, laughing. I wasn't sure whether she was serious, and if she was, why coming from China was such a funny thing.

A slow boat from China. In time I learned that he was born not in China but in Panama. No wonder I only half believed he was Chinese. He was only half Chinese.

The facts I know about his life are incredibly, unbearably few. Although we shared the same house for eighteen years, we had little else in common. We had no culture in common. It is only a slight exaggeration to say that we had no language in common. By the time I was born my father had lived almost thirty years in America, but to hear him speak you would not have believed this. About his failure to master English there always seemed to me something willful. Except for her accent—as thick as but so different from his—my mother had no such trouble.

"He never would talk about himself much, you know. That was his way. He never really had much to say, in general. Silence was golden. It was a cultural thing, I think." (My mother.)

By the time I was old enough to understand this, my father had pretty much stopped talking.

Taciturnity: they say that is an Oriental trait. But I don't believe my father was always the silent, withdrawn man I knew. Think of that day at Coney Island, when he was talking a Chinese blue streak.

Almost everything I know about him came from my mother, and there was much she herself never knew, much she had forgotten or was unsure of, and much that she would never tell.

I am six, seven, eight years old, a schoolgirl with deplorable posture and constantly cracked lips, chafing in the dollish old-world clothes handmade by my mother; a bossy, fretful, sly, cowardly child given to fits of temper and weeping. In school, or in the playground, or perhaps watching television, I hear something about the Chinese—something odd, improbable. I will ask my father. He will know whether it is true, say, that the Chinese eat with sticks.

He shrugs. He pretends not to understand. Or he scowls and says, "Chinese just like everybody else."

("He thought you were making fun of him. He always thought everyone was making fun of him. He had a chip on his shoulder. The way he acted, you'd've thought he was colored!")

Actually, he said "evvybody."

Is it true the Chinese write backwards?

Chinese just like evvybody else.

Is it true they eat dog?

Chinese just like evvybody else.

Are they really all Communists?

Chinese just like evvybody else.

What is Chinese water torture? What is footbinding? What is a mandarin?

Chinese just like evvybody else.

He was not like everybody else.

The unbearably few facts are these. He was born in Colón, Panama, in 1911. His father came from Shanghai. From what I have been able to gather, Grandfather Chang was a merchant engaged in the trade of tobacco and tea. This business, which he ran with one of his brothers, kept him travelling often between Shanghai and Colón. He had two wives, one in each city, and, as if out of a passion for symmetry, two sons by each wife. Soon after my father, Carlos, was born, his father took him to Shanghai, to be raised by the Chinese wife. Ten years later my father was sent back to Colón. I never understood the reason for this. The way the story was told to me, I got the impression that my father was being sent away from some danger. This was, of course, a time of upheaval in China, the decade following the birth of the Republic, the era of the warlords. If the date is correct, my father would have left Shanghai the year the Chinese Communist Party was founded there. It remains uncertain, though, whether political events had anything at all to do with his leaving China.

One year after my father returned to Colón his mother was dead. I remember hearing as a child that she had died of a stroke. Years later this would seem to me odd, when I figured out that she would have been only twenty-six. Odder still, to think of that reunion between the long-parted mother and son; there's a good chance they did not speak the same language. The other half-Panamanian son, Alfonso, was either sent back with my father or had never left Colón. After their mother's death the two boys came into the care of their father's brother and business partner, Uncle Mee, who apparently lived in Colón and had a large family of his own.

Grandfather Chang, his Chinese wife, and their two sons remained in Shanghai. All were said to have been killed by the Japanese. That must have been during the Sino-Japanese War. My father would have been between his late twenties and early thirties by then, but whether he ever saw any of his Shanghai relations again before they died, I don't know.

At twelve or thirteen my father sailed to America with Uncle Mee. I believe it was just the two of them who came, leaving the rest of the family in Colón. Sometime in the next year or so my father was enrolled in a public school in Brooklyn. I remember coming across a notebook that had belonged to him in those days and being jolted by the name written on the cover: Charles Cipriano Chang. That was neither my father's first nor his last name, as far as I knew, and I'd never heard of the middle name. (Hard to believe that my father spent his boyhood in Shanghai being called Carlos, a name he could not even pronounce with the proper Spanish accent. So he must have had a Chinese name as well. And although our family never knew this name, perhaps among Chinese people he used it.)

Twenty years passed. All I know about this part of my father's life is that it was lived illegally in New York, mostly in Chinatown, where he worked in various restaurants. Then came the Second World War and he was drafted. It was while he was in the Army that he finally became an American citizen. He was no longer calling himself Charles but Carlos again, and now, upon becoming a citizen, he dropped his father's family name and took his mother's. Why a man who thought of himself as Chinese, who had always lived among Chinese, who spoke little Spanish and who had barely known his mother would have made such a decision in the middle of his life is one of many mysteries surrounding my father. My mother had an explanation: "You see, Alfonso was a Panamanian citizen, and *he* had taken his mother's name" (which would, of course, be in keeping with Spanish cultural tradition). "He was the only member of his family your father had left—the others were all dead. Your father wanted to have the same last name as his brother. Also, he thought he'd get along better in this country with a Spanish name." This makes no sense to me. He'd been a Chinatown Chang for twenty years—and now all of a sudden he wanted to pass for Hispanic?

In another version of this story, the idea of getting rid of the Chinese name was attributed to the citizenship official handling my father's papers. This is plausible, given that immigration restrictions for Chinese were still in effect at that time. But I have not ruled out the possibility that the change of names was the result of a misunderstanding between my father and this official. My father was an easily fuddled man, especially when dealing with authority, and he always had trouble understanding and making himself understood in English. And I can imagine him not only befuddled enough to make such a mistake but also too timid afterwards to try to fix it.

Whatever really happened I'm sure I'll never know. I do know that having a Spanish name brought much confusion into my father's life and have always wondered in what way my own life might have been different had he kept the name Chang.

From this point on the story becomes somewhat clearer.

With the Hundredth Infantry Division my father goes to war, fights in France and Germany and, after V-E Day, is stationed in the small southern German town where he will meet my mother. He is thirty-four and she not quite eighteen. She is soon pregnant.

Here is rich food for speculation: How did they communicate? She had had a little English in school. He learned a bit of German. They must have misunderstood far more than they understood of each other. Perhaps this helps to explain why my eldest sister was already two and my other sister on the way before my parents got married. (My sisters and I did not learn about this until we were in our twenties.)

By the time I was three they would already have had two long separations.

"I should have married Rudolf!" (My mother.)

1948. My father returns to the States with his wife and first daughter. Now everything is drastically changed. A different America this: the America of the citizen, the legal worker, the family man. No more drinking and gambling till all hours in Chinatown. No more drifting from job to job, living hand to mouth, sleeping on the floor of a friend's room or on a shelf in the restaurant kitchen. There are new, undreamed-of expenses: household money, layettes, taxes, insurance, a special bank account for the children's education. He does the best he can. He rents an apartment in the Fort Greene housing project, a short walk from the Cantonese restaurant on Fulton Street where he works as a waiter. Some nights after closing, after all the tables have been cleared and the dishes done, he stays for the gambling. He weaves home to a wide-awake wife who sniffs the whiskey on his breath and doesn't care whether he has lost or won. So little money —to gamble with any of it is a sin. Her English is getting better ("no thanks to him!"), but for what she has to say she needs little vocabulary. She is miserable. She hates America. She dreams incessantly about going home. There is something peculiar about the three-year-old: she rarely smiles; she claws at the pages of magazines, like a cat. The one-year-old is prone to colic. To her horror my mother learns that she is pregnant again. She attempts an abortion, which fails. I am born. About that attempt, was my father consulted? Most likely not. Had he been I think I know what he would have said. He would have said: No, this time it will be a boy. Like most men, he would have wanted a son. (All girls—a house full of females—a Chinese man's nightmare!) Perhaps with a son he would have been more open. Perhaps a son he would have taught Chinese.

He gets another job, as a dishwasher in the kitchen of a large public health service hospital. He will work there until he retires, eventually being promoted to kitchen supervisor.

He moves his family to another housing project, outside the city, newly built, cleaner, safer.

He works all the time. On weekends, when he is off from the hospital, he waits on table in one or another Chinese restaurant. He works most holidays and takes no vacations. On his rare day off he outrages my mother by going to the racetrack. But he is not self-indulgent. A little gambling, a quart of Budweiser with his supper—eaten alone, an hour or so after the rest of us (he always worked late)—now and then a glass of Scotch, cigarettes—these were his only pleasures. While the children are still small there are occasional outings. To Coney Island, Chinatown, the zoo. On Sundays sometimes he takes us to the children's matinee, and once a year to Radio City, for the Christmas or Easter show. But he and my mother never go out alone together, just the two of them—never.

Her English keeps getting better, making his seem worse and worse.

He is hardly home, yet my memory is of constant fighting.

Not much vocabulary needed to wound.

"Stupid woman. Crazy lady. Talk, talk, talk, talk—never say nothing!"

"I should have married Rudolf!"

Once, she spat in his face. Another time, she picked up a bread knife and he had to struggle to get it away from her.

They slept in separate beds.

Every few months she announced to the children that it was

over: we were going "home." (And she did go back with us to Germany once, when I was two. We stayed six months. About this episode she was always vague. In years to come, whenever we asked her why we did not stay in Germany, she would say, "You children wanted your father." But I think that is untrue. More likely she realized that there was no life for her back there. She had never got on well with her family. By this time I believe Rudolf had married another.)

Even working the two jobs, my father did not make much money. He would never make enough to buy a house. Yet it seemed the burden of being poor weighed heavier on my mother. Being poor meant you could never relax, meant eternal attention to appearances. Just because you had no money didn't mean you were squalid. Come into the house: see how clean and tidy everything is. Look at the children: spotless. And people did comment to my mother—on the shininess of her floors and how she kept her children—and she was gratified by this. Still, being poor was exhausting.

One day a woman waist-deep in children knocked at the door. When my mother answered, the woman apologized. "I thought—from the name on the mailbox I thought you were Spanish, too. My kids needed to use the toilet." My mother could not hide her displeasure. She was proud of being German, and in those postwar years she was also bitterly defensive. When people called us names—spicks and chinks—she said, "You see how it is in this country. For all they say how bad we Germans are, no one ever calls you names for being German."

She had no patience with my father's quirks. The involuntary twitching of a muscle meant that someone had given him the evil eye. Drinking a glass of boiled water while it was still hot cured the flu. He saved back issues of *Reader's Digest* and silver dollars from certain years, believing that one day they'd be worth lots of money. What sort of backward creature had she married? His English drove her mad. Whenever he didn't catch something that was said to him (and this happened all the time), instead of saying "what?" he said "who?" "Who? Who?" she screeched back at him. "What are you, an owl?"

Constant bickering and fighting.

We children dreamed of growing up, going to college, getting married, getting away.

And what about Alfonso and Uncle Mee? What happened to them?

"I never met either of them, but we heard from Mee all the time those first years—it was awful. By then he was back in Panama. He was a terrible gambler, and so were his sons. They had debts up to here—and who should they turn to but your father. Uncle What-About-Mee, I called him. 'Think of all I've done for you. You owe me.'" (And though she had never heard it she mimicked his voice.) "Well, your father had managed to save a couple of thousand dollars and he sent it all to Mee. I could have died. I never forgave him. I was pregnant then, and I had one maternity dress—one. Mee no sooner got that money than he wrote back for more. I told your father if he sent him another dime I was leaving."

Somehow the quarrel extended to include Alfonso, who seems to have sided with Mee. My father broke with them both. Several years after we left Brooklyn, an ad appeared in the Chinatown newspaper. Alfonso and Mee were trying to track my father down. He never answered the ad, my father said. He never spoke to either man again. (Perhaps he lied. Perhaps he was always in touch with them, secretly. I believe much of his life was a secret from us.)

I have never seen a photograph of my father that was taken before he was in the Army. I have no idea what he looked like as a child or as a young man. I have never seen any photographs of his parents or his brothers, or of Uncle Mee or of any other relations, or of the houses he lived in in Colón and Shanghai. If my father had any possessions that had belonged to his parents, any family keepsakes or mementoes of his youth, I never saw them. About his youth he had nothing to tell. A single anecdote he shared with me. In Shanghai he had a dog. When my father sailed to Panama, the dog was brought along to the dock to see him off. My father boarded the boat and the dog began howling. He never forgot that: the boat pulling away from the dock and the dog howling. "Dog no fool. He know I never be back."

In our house there were no Chinese things. No objects made of bamboo or jade. No lacquer boxes. No painted scrolls or fans. No calligraphy. No embroidered silks. No Buddhas. No chopsticks among the silverware, no rice bowls or tea sets. No Chinese tea, no ginseng or soy sauce in the cupboards. My father was the only Chinese thing, sitting like a Buddha himself among the Hummels and cuckoo clocks and pictures of alpine landscapes. My mother thought of the house as hers, spoke of *her* curtains, *her* floors (often in warning: "Don't scuff up my floors!"). The daughters were hers, too. To each of them she gave a Teutonic name, impossible for him to pronounce. ("*What* does your father call you?" That question—an agony to me—rang through my childhood.) It was part of her abiding nostalgia that she wanted to raise the children as Germans. She sewed dirndls for them and even for their dolls. She braided their hair, then wound the braids tightly around their ears, like hair earmuffs, in the German style. They would open their presents on Christmas Eve rather than Christmas morning. They would not celebrate Thanksgiving. Of course they would not celebrate any Chinese holidays. No dragon and firecrackers on Chinese New Year's. For Christmas there was red cabbage and sauerbraten. Imagine my father saying sauerbraten.

Now and then he brought home food from Chinatown: fiery red sausage with specks of fat like teeth embedded in it, dried fish, buns filled with bean paste which he cracked us up by calling Chinese peenus butter. My mother would not touch any of it. ("God knows what it really is.") We kids clamored for a taste and when we didn't like it my father got angry. ("You know how he was with that chip on his shoulder. He took it personally. He was insulted.") Whenever we ate at one of the restaurants where he worked, he was always careful to order for us the same Americanized dishes served to most of the white customers.

•

An early memory: I am four, five, six years old, in a silly mood, mugging in my mother's bureau mirror. My father is in the room with me but I forget he is there. I place my forefingers at the corners of my eyes and pull the lids taut. Then I catch him watching me. His is a look of pure hate.

"He thought you were making fun."

A later memory: "Panama is an isthmus." Grade-school geography. My father looks up from his paper, alert, suspicious. "Merry Isthmus!" "Isthmus be the place!" My sisters and I shriek with laughter. My father shakes his head. "Not nice, making fun of place where people born."

"*Ach*, he had no sense of humor—he never did. You couldn't joke with him. He never got the point of a joke."

It is true that I hardly ever heard him laugh. (Unlike my mother, who, despite her chronic unhappiness, seemed always to be laughing —at him, at us, at the neighbors. A great tease she was, sly, malicious, often witty.)

Chinese inscrutability. Chinese sufferance. Chinese reserve. Yes, I recognize my father in the clichés. But what about his Panamanian side? What are Latins said to be? Hot-blooded, mercurial, soulful, macho, convivial, romantic. No, he was none of these.

"He always wanted to go back, he always missed China."

But he was only ten years old when he left.

"Yes, but that's what counts—where you spent those first years, and your first language. That's who you are."

I had a children's book about Sun Yat Sen, The Man Who Changed China. There were drawings of Sun as a boy. I tried to picture my father like that, a Chinese boy who wore pajamas outdoors and a coolie hat and a pigtail down his back. (Though of course in those days after Sun's Revolution he isn't likely to have worn a pigtail.) I pictured my father against those landscapes of peaks and pagodas, with a dog like Old Yeller at his heels. What was it like, this boyhood in Shanghai? How did the Chinese wife treat the second wife's son? (My father and Alfonso would not have had the same status as the official wife's sons, I don't think.) How did the Chinese brothers treat him? When he went to school—did he go to school?—was he accepted by the other children as one of them? Is there a Chinese word for half-breed, and was he called that name as we would be? Surely many times in his life he must have wished he were all Chinese. My mother wished that her children were all German. I wanted to be an all-American girl with a name like Sue Brown.

He always wanted to go back.

In our house there were not many books. My mother's romances and historical novels, books about Germany (mostly about the Nazi era), a volume of Shakespeare, tales from Andersen and Grimm, the *Nibelungenlied*, Edith Hamilton's *Mythology*, poems of Goethe and Schiller, *Struwwelpeter*, the drawings of Wilhelm Busch. It was my mother who gave me that book about Sun Yat Sen and, when I was a little older, one of her own favorites, *The Good Earth*, a children's story for adults. Pearl Buck was a missionary who lived in China for many years. (Missionaries supposedly converted the Changs to Christianity. From what? Buddhism? Taoism? My father's mother was almost certainly Roman Catholic. He himself belonged to no church.) Pearl Buck wrote eighty-five books, founded a shelter for Asian-American children, and won the Nobel Prize.

The Good Earth. China a land of famine and plagues—endless childbirth among them. The births of daughters seen as evil omens. "It is only a slave this time—not worth mentioning." Little girls sold as a matter of course. Growing up to be concubines with names like Lotus and Cuckoo and Pear Blossom. Women with feet like little deer hooves. Abject wives, shuffling six paces behind their husbands. All this filled me with anxiety. In our house the man was the meek and browbeat one.

I never saw my father read, except for the newspaper. He did not read the *Reader's Digest*s that he saved. He would not have been able to read *The Good Earth*. I am sure he could not write with fluency in any tongue. The older I grew the more I thought of him as illiterate.

Hard for me to accept the fact that he did not read books. Say I grew up to be a writer. He would not read what I wrote.

He had his own separate closet, in the front hall. Every night when he came home from work he undressed as soon as he walked in, out there in the hall. He took off his suit and put on his bathrobe. He always wore a suit to work, but at the hospital he changed into whites and at the restaurant into dark pants, white jacket, and black bow tie. In the few photographs of him that exist he is often wearing a uniform—his soldier's or hospital-worker's or waiter's.

Though not at all vain, he was particular about his appearance. He bought his suits in a men's fine clothing store on Fifth Avenue, and he took meticulous care of them. He had a horror of cheap cloth and imitation leather, and an equal horror of slovenliness. His closet was the picture of order. On the top shelf, where he kept his hats, was a large assortment—a lifetime's supply, it seemed to me—of chewing gum, cough drops, and mints. On that shelf he kept also his cigarettes and cigars. The closet smelled much as he did—of tobacco and spearmint and the rosewater-glycerin cream he used on his dry skin. A not unpleasant smell.

He was small. At fourteen I was already as tall as he, and eventually I would outweigh him. A trim sprig of a man—dainty but not puny, fastidious but not effeminate. I used to marvel at the cleanliness of his nails, and at his good teeth, which never needed any fillings. By the time I was born he had lost most of his top hair, which made his domed forehead look even larger, his moon-face rounder. It may have been the copper-red cast of his skin that led some people to take him for an American Indian—people who'd never seen one, probably.

He could be cruel. I once saw him blow pepper in the cat's face. He loathed that cat, a surly, untrainable tom found in the street. But he was very fond of another creature we took in, an orphaned nestling sparrow. Against expectations, the bird survived and learned how to fly. But, afraid that it would not be able to fend for itself outdoors, we decided to keep it. My father sometimes sat by its cage, watching the bird and cooing at it in Chinese. My mother was amused. "You see: he has more to say to that bird than to us!" The emperor and his nightingale, she called them. "The Chinese have always loved their birds." (What none of us knew: at that very moment in China keeping pet birds had been prohibited as a bourgeois affectation, and sparrows were being exterminated as pests.)

It was true that my father had less and less to say to us. He was drifting further and further out of our lives. These were my teenage years. I did not see clearly what was happening then, and for long afterwards, whenever I tried to look back, a panic would come over me, so that I couldn't see at all.

At sixteen, I had stopped thinking about becoming a writer. I wanted to dance. Every day after school I went into the city for class. I would be home by 8:30, about the same time as my father, and so for this period he and I would eat dinner together. And much later, looking back, I realized that that was when I had—and lost—my chance. Alone with my father every night like that, I could have got to know him. I could have asked him all those questions that I now have to live without answers to. Of course he would have resisted talking about himself. But with patience I might have drawn him out.

Or maybe not. As I recall, the person sitting across the kitchen table from me was like a figure in a glass case. That was not the face of someone thinking, feeling, or even daydreaming. It was the clay face, still waiting to receive the breath of life.

If it ever occurred to me that my father was getting old, that he was exhausted, that his health was failing, I don't remember it.

He was still working seven days a week. Sometimes he missed having dinner with me, because the dishwasher broke and he had to stay late at the hospital. For a time, on Saturdays, he worked double shifts at the restaurant and did not come home till we were all asleep.

After dinner, he stayed at the kitchen table, smoking and finishing his beer. Then he went to bed. He never joined the rest of us in the living room in front of the television. He sat alone at the table, staring at the wall. He hardly noticed if someone came into the kitchen for something. His inobservance was the family's biggest joke. My mother would give herself or one of us a new hairdo and say, "Now watch: your father won't even notice," and she was right.

My sisters and I bemoaned his stubborn avoidance of the living room. Once a year he yielded and joined us around the Christmas tree, but only very reluctantly; we had to beg him.

I knew vaguely that he continued to have some sort of social life outside the house, a life centered in Chinatown.

He still played the horses.

By this time family outings had ceased. We never did anything together as a family. But every Sunday my father came home with ice cream for everyone.

He and my mother fought less and less—seldom now in the old vicious way—but this did not mean there was peace. Never any word or gesture of affection between them, not even, "for the sake of the children," pretense of affection.

(Television: the prime-time family shows. During the inevitable scenes when family love and loyalty were affirmed, the discomfort in the living room was palpable. I think we were all ashamed of how far below the ideal our family fell.)

Working and saving to send his children to college, he took no interest in their school life. He did, however, reward good report cards with cash. He did not attend school events to which parents were invited; he always had to work.

He never saw me dance.

He intrigued my friends, who angered me by regarding him as if he were a figure in a glass case. Doesn't he ever come out of the kitchen? Doesn't he ever talk? I was angry at him, too, for what he seemed to me to be doing: *willing* himself into stereotype: inscrutable, self-effacing, funny little chinaman.

And why couldn't he learn to speak English?

He developed the tight wheezing cough that would never leave him. The doctor blamed cigarettes, so my father tried sticking to cigars. The cough was particularly bad at night. It kept my mother up, and so she started sleeping on the living-room couch.

I was the only one who went to college, and I got a scholarship. My father gave the money he had saved to my mother, who bought a brand-new Mercedes, the family's first car.

He was not like everybody else. In fact, he was not like anyone I had ever met. But I thought of my father when I first encountered the "little man" of Russian literature. I thought of him a lot when I read the stories of Chekhov and Gogol. Reading "Grief," I remembered my father and the sparrow, and a new possibility presented itself: my father not as one who would not speak but as one to whom no one would listen.

And he was like a character in a story also in the sense that he needed to be invented.

The silver dollars saved in a cigar box. The *Reader's Digests* going back to before I was born. The uniforms. The tobacco-mint-rosewater smell. I cannot invent a father out of these.

I waited too long. By the time I started gathering material for his story, whatever there had been in the way of private documents or papers (and there must have been some) had disappeared. (It was never clear whether my father himself destroyed them or whether my mother later lost or got rid of them, between moves, or in one of her zealous spring cleanings.)

The Sunday-night ice cream. The Budweiser bottle sweating on the kitchen table. The five-, ten-, or twenty-dollar bill he pulled from his wallet after squinting at your report card. "Who? Who?"

We must have seemed as alien to him as he seemed to us. To him we must always have been "others." Females. Demons. No different from other demons, who could not tell one Asian from another, who thought Chinese food meant chop suey and Chinese customs matter for joking. I would have to live a lot longer and he would have to die before the full horror of this would sink in. And then it would sink in deeply, agonizingly, like an arrow that has found its mark.

●

Dusk in the city. Dozens of Chinese men bicycle through the streets, bearing cartons of fried dumplings, Ten Ingredients Lo Mein, and sweet-and-sour pork. I am on my way to the drugstore when one of them hails me. "Miss! Wait, Miss!" Not a man, I see, but a boy, eighteen at most, with a lovely, oval, fresh-skinned face. "You—you Chinese!" It is not the first time in my life this has happened. As shortly as possible I explain. The boy turns out to have arrived just weeks ago, from Hong Kong. His English is incomprehensible. He is flustered when he finds I cannot speak Chinese. He says, "Can I. Your father. Now." It takes me a moment to figure this out. Alas, he is asking to meet my father. Unable to bring myself to tell him my father is dead, I say that he does not live in the city. The boy persists. "But sometime come see. And then I now?" His imploring manner puzzles me. Is it that he wants to meet Chinese people? Doesn't he work in a Chinese restaurant? Doesn't he know about Chinatown? I feel a surge of anxiety. He is so earnest and intent. I am missing something. In another minute I have promised that when my father comes to town he will go to the restaurant where the boy works and seek him out. The boy rides off looking pleased, and I continue on to the store. I am picking out toothpaste when he appears at my side. He hands me a folded piece of paper. Two telephone numbers and a message in Chinese characters. "For father."

He was sixty when he retired from the hospital, but his working days were not done. He took a part-time job as a messenger for a bank. That Christmas when I came home from school I found him in bad shape. His smoker's cough was much worse, and he had pains in his legs and in his back, recently diagnosed as arthritis.

But it was not smoker's cough, and it was not arthritis.

A month later, he left work early one day because he was in such pain. He made it to the train station, but when he tried to board the train he could not get up the steps. Two conductors had to carry him aboard. At home he went straight to bed and in the middle of the night he woke up coughing as usual, and this time there was blood.

His decline was so swift that by the time I arrived at the hospital he barely knew me. Over the next week we were able to chart the backward journey on which he was embarked by his occasional mur-murings. ("I got to get back to the base—they'll think I'm AWOL!") Though I was not there to hear it, I am told that he cursed my mother and accused her of never having cared about him. By the end of the week, when he spoke it was only in Chinese.

One morning a priest arrived. No one had sent for him. He had doubtless assumed from the name that this patient was Hispanic and Catholic, and had taken it upon himself to administer extreme unc-tion. None of us had the will to stop him, and so we were witness to a final mystery: my father, who as far as we knew had no religion, feebly crossing himself.

The fragments of Chinese stopped. There was only panting then, broken by sharp gasps such as one makes when reminded of some important thing one has forgotten. To the end his hands were restless. He kept repeating the same gesture: cupping his hands together and drawing them to his chest, as though gathering something to him.

Now let others speak.

"After the war was a terrible time. We were all scared to death, we didn't know what was going to happen to us. Some of those soldiers were really enjoying it, they wanted nothing better than to see us grovel. The victors! Oh, they were scum, a lot of them. Worse than the Nazis ever were. But Carlos felt sorry for us. He tried to help. And not just our family but the neighbors, too. He gave us money. His wallet was always out. And he was always bringing stuff from the base, like coffee and chocolate—things you could never get. And even after he went back to the States he sent packages. Not just to us but to all the people he got to know here. Frau Meyer. The Schweitzers. They still talk about that." (My grandmother.)

"We know the cancer started in the right lung but by the time we saw him it had spread. It was in both lungs, it was in his liver and in his bones. He was a very sick man and he'd been sick for a long time. I'd say that tumor in the right lung had been growing for at least five years." (The doctor.)

"He drank a lot in those days, and your mother didn't like that. But he was funny. He loved that singer—the cowboy—what was his name? I forget. Anyway, he put on the music and he sang along. Your mother would cover her ears." (My grandmother.)

"I didn't like the way he looked. He wouldn't say anything but I knew he was hurting. I said to myself, this isn't arthritis—no way. I wanted him to see my own doctor but he wouldn't. I was just about to order him to." (My father's boss at the bank.)

"He hated cats, and the cat knew it and she was always jumping in his lap. Every time he sat down the cat jumped in his lap and we laughed. But you could tell it really bothered him. He said cats were bad luck. When the cat jumped in your lap it was a bad omen." (My mother's younger brother, Karl.)

"He couldn't dance at all—or he wouldn't—but he clapped and sang along to the records. He liked to drink and he liked gambling. Your mother was real worried about that." (Frau Meyer.)

"Before the occupation no one in this town had ever seen an Oriental or a Negro." (My grandmother.)

"He never ate much, he didn't want you to cook for him, but he liked German beer. He brought cigarettes for everyone. We gave him schnapps. He played us the cowboy songs." (Frau Schweitzer.)

"Ain't you people dying to know what he's saying?" (The patient in the bed next to my father's.)

"When he wasn't drinking he was very shy. He just sat there next to your mother without speaking. He sat there staring and staring at her." (Frau Meyer.)

"He liked blonds. He loved that blond hair." (Karl.)

"There was absolutely nothing we could do for him. The amazing thing is that he was working right up till the day he came into the hospital. I don't know how he did that." (The doctor.)

"The singing was a way of talking to us, because he didn't know German at all." (My grandmother.)

"Yes, of course I remember. It was Hank Williams. He played those records over and over. Hillbilly music. I thought I'd go mad." (My mother.)

Here are the names of some Hank Williams songs: Honky Tonkin'. Ramblin' Man. Hey, Good Lookin'. Lovesick Blues. Why Don't You

Love Me Like You Used To Do. Your Cheatin' Heart. (I heard that)
Lonesome Whistle. Why Don't You Mind Your Own Business. I'm So
Lonesome I Could Cry. The Blues Come Around. Cold, Cold Heart.
I'll Never Get Out of This World Alive. I Can't Help It If I'm Still in
Love with You.

excerpts from *The Stranded in the World*, a novel-in-progress

Han Ong

Portions of the city which appear harmless enough during the daytime—rows of blocks occupied by houses and storefronts indistinguishable from one another, each mimicking the other's blandness, the other's innocuousness, as if all that was needed to make a neighborhood a neighborhood was visual unity; as if in observance of some misguided notion that equated banality with normality (but it could be true, too, for looking at these houses, which appear spread out like immaculate ink dots in a row, hypnotic in their sameness, their blandness, one is lulled into a warm feeling of familiarity, safeness: home is nothing more than a symmetrical alignment of furniture, you can count on everything to be as you left it, where you left it, it will

HAN ONG is a playwright/performer whose plays and texts include: "The L.A. Plays: In a Lonely Country & A Short List of Alternate Places," "Reasons to Live. Reason to Live. Half. No Reason," "Symposium in Manila," and "Corner Store Geography." They have been presented nationally and internationally in such places as the New York Shakespeare Festival's Public Theater, the Mark Taper Forum, American Repertory Theatre and the Almeida in London, England. Born and raised in Manila, Philippines, of Chinese parents, Han Ong came to the United States in 1984 and now lives in Los Angeles.

all be there, in its obedient, visually repetitive stillness)—these harmless-appearing portions of the city become at night transformed into something else entirely. A subversion.

Cars driven by men begin patrolling as early as six, as soon as the light goes out. The objects of their furtive search pock the streets outlined in neon: Young boys, each staking claim to a corner, a little cut of pavement, parade in a variety of poses, some with a calculated lewdness to help draw attention to themselves, others seeming as if slung back from a great weariness, knowing that a kind of appeal lies in this masquerade of being beyond it all. Their eyes move constantly, little dancers flashing their semaphore inquiries from car to car, seeing if some interest's been sparked in the drivers, that silent, mutual contract based on the look of the eyes.

Windows roll down soon afterwards, car doors open, an invitation flung out to the desired party to hop into the darkness of the car, to take a chance with that darkness whose character is determined by its owner, an extension of his character, motives.

Night after night, this procession of cars, with no shortage of places in which to conduct business—alleys, backstreets, abandoned lots, poorly lit corners, schoolgrounds—the entire section seems as if intended for just this purpose, all that was needed was some darkness, night, with its guarantee of blindness.

To say then that this place becomes "transformed" would be excessive. Even in its daytime blandness this aspect—a potential for a cruising ground—exists. All that was needed was someone perceptive enough to see this, and then after that, for him to draw others, and for those others to draw yet more, until the math grew to one capable of sustaining for days, months, years, legendary time able to perpetuate past police censure and neighborhood vigilance. To use the word "transformed" would be tantamount to saying that these boys are "transformed" into prostitutes. Even before prostitution, there already resides in them the vulgarity, the attraction to the same sex, or the monetary lust that are the key characteristics of male prostitutes. To use "transformed" is to believe in victims, victimizers, that good and evil exist independent of each other, it's to believe in childhood, to portray—as American movies often do—the royal stupidity of children as something on the order of the divine.

It's the heart of the night: a center filled with cars slowly bobbing up and down as if afloat on a sea, an automobile parade. Cruising. Motored by hunger, panic, guilt. Drawn in ink, a field of black so dark it rivals nothingness.

Male prostitution, unlike a lot of female prostitution, makes do without the tyrannies of a pimp. Young boys become prostitutes on their own initiative, not, as cliche would have it, through the amoral coaxing of a recruiter, a seducer. It is the essence of private enterprise, the self-started business, American to the bone. What draws them to the practice is the obscenity, the attractive amorality of it all. And its seeming ease, money for nothing, for just lying back and allowing a stranger to touch that body, to have its way with all that that inert stretch of skin suggests, the pleasure and the violence. To the monumental laziness of youth, this idea of money for nothing is supremely attractive. What attracts them, too, though saying this right now makes me cringe because the equation seems too pat, too convenient, what attracts them, too, is being made to feel wanted, recognizing that they possess qualities to which value is attached, quantifiable, tactile, like dough to knead between cold fingers, warm, a warming thought is the ownership of such traits, money in the bank. Goods off a shelf. Valuables.

Same with me.

He hit me, drew blood.

But at least I have the solace of six thousand dollars, a sturdy figure: all of it from him, given to me during the course of our affair and which I've saved up.

Same with me.

Two weeks after the evaporation of that six thousand dollars in a fairytale poof of smoke I'm in it—prostitution—and then awakened— somehow, though I don't know how—I leave. I walk to the light, respectable again, having no memory of wrongdoing, no shame. I go into a corporate office several floors below the ground in a white shirt and pants; no variance from that daily monotony of white—it's my color now, I will gladly wear the uniform of anyone who will have me. It's the mail room I'm in, letters pour in but none are meant for me except in the cursory sense of being a middleman, sieve-fingers of a go-between. I lick, I stamp, paste, knead, push in, seal, tie, everything having to do with containment. Words are being hurled from myriad corners, the envelopes are full of intimations of a life I will never know, one in which forward motion is possible, containing the undying buzz of activity, lunch dates and such. I gather documents and fold them into envelopes for mailing, make them as flat and wide as possible, parcels replicating the character—physical and otherwise—of the city. I'm happy. I lick, I stamp, paste, knead, push in, seal. Containment. Mainly that's it. I'm contained. And contain everything else around me in turn. Keep. Push. Seal. Keep.

We've gone out. An "evening on the town." We're in his car. He doesn't speak. I've moved from a house of noise, I'm thinking, from that place where one can't hope for escape, from there to him, the silent man.

We disembark. He hands the keys to someone costumed in red. We go in. He takes my elbows. We're shuttled past a glass door—a Hello for him from a doorman—into an elevator. Seventh floor, he tells the man. We go up.

When the door opens music floats in. We go out. There's a stretch of red carpet ahead of us which it's obvious someone takes great pains to keep immaculate. Everything is red and gold. Chairs and tables set up by windows looking down onto the city are lacquered in those colors as if in appeal to the tasteless in each of us. We're seated. He smiles, nods to the waiter who, in turn, smiles back. Piano key white. He asks me what I want. I look at the menu. The prices are higher than anything I'd pay for. Or that my family would. He asks again. I tell him. All right. He motions for the waiter, who arrives prompt and eager to please, lips to my lover's heel. He gives out our orders, the waiter takes them down, a scrawl on a pad, blue ball point hieroglyphics. He leaves, thanks us.

Someone notices my lover, a familiar, and he comes over to shake hands. I'm introduced. My lover says something, modifier which I don't hear. Friend. I think that's what's used. Friend. The familiar is introduced as an acquaintance. Business acquaintance. He asks to join us. My lover looks to me. Sure, I look back. Sure, my lover says. The man motions to the waiter, asks for a third chair, which is brought to him quick, and asks that his order be brought to our table instead. He sits.

The two of them launch into a conversation in which sums and numerical figures are toted up as if a competitive tally session. My lover looks, asking me to join in, asking what I'd like to talk about, and I shrug, saying, Whatever you have in mind. Stories about me are brought up for this business acquaintance's benefit. Setting me in context. A high-schooler. That's how I'm set.

Oh are you? this person asks.

Yes Yes. What more is there to say? The man looks, though not much older than my lover, to be of an entirely different generation. A face to freeze liberalness cold. I presume nowhere down the conversational road will there be any divulging of my truer *context*. Ha-ha. For him "friend" would do. That, and "high-schooler."

He asks me a series of inane questions, knowing my age, from which he interpolates an intellectual level. It's all I could do to keep from spitting at him, but when I look at my lover, he doesn't seem to be aware of any wrongdoing on his acquaintance's part. I stiffen my smile in place and keep nodding, which seems like the thing to do.

He leaves to get up long after he should have, bows his apologies, and walks away.

My lover continues talking as if nothing's transpired. I ask him who this acquaintance is, what connection to him. Backer, he says. Wealthy person. All right, I nod.

We leave. Everyone looks droopy, rubber faces further distended by being lowered onto plates, framed by wrists busily tossing in the air like toy attachments, loose-hinged and creaky. Forks scrape their steely cough onto plates and glasses crackle, dropped from limp palm to table. No one looks up. In an instant we're gone, down the steel elevator whose door, too—I'm noticing this for the first time—is gold, and out through glass doors, into our car, away from this building dropped into the middle of this hill, this hideaway inaccessible to all but this group, moneyed class who are all lips, all kiss and chew, eyeless. Back home.

Many more of this in succeeding nights. Many such places. Access there. And many other familiars, introductions, dead-end conversation, nods, a lot of nodding. An arena he functions well in. He's beautiful like that, lying, not saying much, dodging. He's beautiful dodging. Always a confession threatening to enter from the sides of the mouth, but nothing comes of it. Always back to civility, things beautiful. That American mouth, enviable dentistry, white. Marble keys circled by red red lips. I want to kiss him most when he lies, when he curses, all things vile made sweet by that thing, that animal in its hole, darting in and out.

Sometimes, though, I'll catch him in the middle of a passage, as he narrates something, there'll be a slowing down, a creak in the otherwise smooth fabrication, a sudden braking to reveal having stumbled onto a backwoods forest, stranded. He'll be revealed to be less than varnished. Incomplete. And I'll know. That's the truth of him. Silent. Slow. A slow man. All this despite his well-rehearsed routines, oil on ice theatrics. A kin to me. We're singular, he and I. Only with each other do we become plural. We have a loneliness in common, his of course burnished by age, made more inaccessible, and in this distance, more royal, elegant, but we have at our core the same loneliness really: the look on his face as he stares out the window in the middle of a passage—cold, distant—is my look, too, sometimes. Our conversations are filled with brief silences during which the loneliness appears. Like me he doesn't speak of a family. No thing which precedes him, without source. Mr. Mystery Man. He's estranged. Ran away at an early age, teens, and was never heard from again. A successful businessman, money as a wall between how he saw himself then, annexed to that family who would have little of him, and how he is now, remade. A buffer. It's a story I attribute to him of course, aspects of my own modified to fit that image of him I have in my head. Undisturbed. Then one day he brings home a brother. Younger brother. They look like twins. Suddenly I'm excluded. That field from which I can only stand at the periphery, looking in. They go places, laugh, always that laugh, conspiratorial. We go out, a threesome, but it's clearly me who's out of place. Always nothing from him about brothers, a brother, parents, and then all of a sudden, this dropping in. He's concerned about his brother. Any day he might just drop out. Fall by the wayside. A handsome boy, and privileged too, from a privileged family. Spoiled. All things open to him, choices to which money and beauty gives you access, without which it would be easier to continue along established lines, sturdy, a sturdy growth, respectable. His brother doesn't have the requisite strength to resist the easy choice, those temptations proffered in color, packaged. Wasted, that's the easiest thing to imagine him as. A lazy youth. He asks me to go talk to him, we're almost the same age, he younger by a year or two. And although I have nothing to say, nothing remotely resembling empathy or understanding, I go to him. I say Hi, ask him what's going on. He brightens up. He says he's wanted to talk to me for some time. Says he approves of his brother and me. Approves. That's the word he uses. It makes me picture him as old suddenly, emissaried from his parents. He goes on and on. Says he thinks I'm great. Admirable. Suddenly all these words which make me think his brother's concern foolish. A smart kid. After all his brother's worrying, he's proven himself otherwise. But then there's that cheeriness too at sixteen which I can remember in myself, that cheeriness which through the course of time curdles, a dramatic turnaround, from smile to smirk to deadpan, nothing all of a sudden. Joyless. It's never good to start out cheery. Unable to ask him what his brother wants to know—what's been happening, is he taking drugs, any sexual hint—I nod on. The day he goes we have breakfast together, the three of us. We sit out in the sun, faces bleached under that light, unrecognizable. My lover's brother looks sad, he's sad to go, he says this and my lover looks away. If given his choice, his brother would want to live with us indefinitely, that's what he told me once. It's been nice being here, his brother finally says, his head awkward from the weight of the admission. My lover doesn't say anything, just smiles.

The next day we're back to routine, he and I apart from the rest of the world, a return to my original version of him, familyless. Months after that news arrives, though from whom I don't discern, that his brother has died. Strangled. Mysterious circumstances. That's what he first tells me, those words. A sketchy thing, he keeps saying. And then when enough time has elapsed, he sits me down, and says, This is what happened. Someone took him in. He ran away from home, some-one took him in, whether they were lovers I don't know but this per-son, this man took him in. And the next day he ran away from him as well. First from my family, whose confines I can understand wanting to escape. But this man. Admittedly nothing is known about him ex-cept the superficials, a businessman, well-respected, wealthy, able to support my brother the way he's accustomed to with my family, and supposedly in love with him too. All things in place. And yet my brother had to run.

What follows, he says, is not so clear. Whose hands he fell into. This would happen, we always knew this would happen, a matter of time before it did, and now that it has, ended finally, confirmed for us all our worst fears, now that that's done, it's almost a relief, except for the mystery, whose hands on his neck, only in that area do we feel as if life has betrayed us. Everything else in order but that.

This is where, months later, he would turn things against me. He'd come up to me, right to my face, a push, then say things like, You're who's responsible. I shouldn't have let you talk to him. Not my brother. Before you there was only him and his laziness. After you spoke to him a change came in and took over. I could tell, all at once someone in my brother's place who looked like my brother but wasn't him, was in fact no one else but you. A replica. You taught him to whore. That's what you did. That's what happened to him. A stupid boy inspired to whoring by example from you, what match is that for a crazed john? What match? That's what happened, oh yes you can be sure, death at the hands of a wayward man, an itinerant with a feel for young boys' necks, the promise of a bill on a rainy night, a warm ride, and then straight to hell, the body disposed of in a ditch at a park, all around him grass—here he breaks down—all around my poor young brother grass and nothing else, no other witness. That's what he'd say, hands to my shoulders shaking me in paroxysms of comic hatred that would end in a slap, slaps. He'd push me to a wall and hit my head there. Blood of course, always that predictable punctuation mark, after which profuse apologies would spill. I let him do as he pleased because I knew I was indebted to him, his rescue of me from my family, whose monstrosity was even more unbearable than this, than physical violence at the hands of a man I knew, really, only for a brief length before I'd agreed to commit myself to our arrangement.

So this is what he did to me. Slaps. A slap. A myriad things would begin these episodes. Sometimes the reason was arcane, sometimes no reason. Mostly I deserved them. That was how I saw it. But before then, several months before, just at the first relay of the news of his brother's death, my lover held me very close to him, listened to my breathing at night, made sure I hadn't stopped breathing, that I too hadn't deserted him. He kept his fingers to my chest when we were in bed to monitor my skin, its proximity to him, to this life and not to the other, that life which supposedly awaits at the other side where he's said he's seen his brother in dreams, a dream, his brother surrounded by white white light he said, as if the carpet of grass that was his last resting place before the false comfort of the coffin had transfigured itself into blades of light. He began with concern, locking my chest in the grove of his arms nightly, and ended more or less in the same position, but the grove had thickened overnight, branches transformed into bars of prison. Hitting. A continual slamming of body to wall until the very end of our relationship, that tennis game.

On some nights, specially after those times when little things I'd catch on television would call to mind my family, I'd think of my lover's brother. Fleeing from thoughts of my family, my mind would settle on him instead. And also, but lightly, on my brother, who'd be my lover's brother's age in a few years. I'd see my brother through the veil, the superimposed image of that other, the murder victim discarded by the side of the road one rainy night. And—though for what reason I don't know—I'd see my brother heading down the very same road, him in a few years a cursory item in the daily papers, not even a column, just a bare mention, body to serve as a validation of all my mother's worst fears of this country. Two sons gone, eaten up. I'd see my brother in a glass coffin. Typical of that family: body trussed up and encased in glass for public display. Visual aid for my mother as she declaims about the dead-endedness of American morality. There are certain images so true as you dream of them that they are virtually assured occurrence in real life. This is one of them, my brother's death. My brother's death at the hands of some night butcher only to wind up as fodder for my mother's sermons. Or maybe it's myself I see murdered, not my brother at all but me. On those evenings out on the streets, in full view of passing cars, the driver of each of which could be the same one who disposed of my lover's brother. Myself in danger all those nights. Thumb hitched to attract traffic, thumb hiked up as indifference to death to morality.

Sugar & Salt

Ninotchka Rosca

So much wisdom had come to her through the years that the bird of her soul couldn't break the shell of her mortality. Tandang Sora had to have help in her dying. With 200 pounds on a frame barely topping five feet, with perfect vision, keen hearing, and a third growth of teeth, she knew she could live to twice her age and girth with ease—which only made sharper and more poignant the just recriminations of the spirits of those whose funeral cortege she had attended. Accordingly, after the November Feast of the Dead, when memory had had its fill of indulgence, Tandang Sora composed a message summoning her descendants to her nipa-and-bamboo house which clung like tree fungus to the mountainside. The message she entrusted to three couriers: the sun peeping into and at everything, the wind which went everywhere, and the postman who rode his bicycle through the upland routes twice a week.

NINOTCHKA ROSCA was born in the Philippines but lived in exile in the United States during the Marcos years. She has published five books, among them the novels *State of War* and *Twice Blessed*.

One lunar cycle later, her daughters, sons-in-law, grandchildren and great- and twice-great-grandchildren began arriving in threes and fives. They found their proper spot in the house, according to their disposition: the men near doors and windows, as far as possible from the wicker chair which served as Tandang Sora's bed as well, for she hardly slept now, spending the nights instead telling the beads of her years; the women in a semicircle about her, claiming their place by a touch of the fingertips before scattering through the house to clean, cook, and make sure there was enough beer in the icebox for warm evenings.

Tandang Sora waited patiently, knowing that unlike men who were trees, women were the wind and had to check everything before settling down. Finally, her eldest daughter, herself exhibiting formidable wisdom, voiced the need for silence, right after dinner, saying that Tandang Sora had to slough off knowledge. At which, the eldest great-granddaughter, who was in her third year of college, brightened considerably and in the language of her group of church volunteers, exclaimed that nana meant to share.

Tandang Sora hooted. She wanted no part of it, not even a tenth, she said; it was all for giving away. Great-granddaughter blushed. Tandang Sora closed her eyes, the better to select among her visions, and gave:

THE FIRST GIFT

As soon as they had seen to their living quarters, the strangers from the edge of the world decided that their next duty lay in the building of two structures: a church in the volcano's shadow and a watchtower on a crag overlooking the seashore. As they explained to the natives, whom they called *indios*, after another people whom the natives in turn called *bumbai*, the church would be for the care of men's souls and the watchtower for the care of their bodies. From the first would come warnings against sin and from the second, warnings against pirate raiders who came from islands peregrinating through the seas. Surely, said the strangers, the *indios* would not object to donating labor for a year or two since their well-being would be doubly guaranteed.

No, not at all, except that . . . And here, the natives tried to explain to the fair-skinned strangers who rapidly lost their temper and began to bluster in the name of the King, the Pope and the whiplash. It was useless. The idea that the construction of a house, even of a house of God, involved not only binding space but binding time as well was too rudimentary, too inelegant, to find expression in the complex language of the foreigners. The natives gave up, finding it impossible to convey to the foreigners how it was necessary not only to define the length and width and height of a structure but also to locate its proper niche in the honeycomb of time, there to be fixed where the currents of its past and future met. Instead, they set to work, mumbling among themselves at the strangers' foolishness, while quarrying adobe blocks and felling trees.

Directly after the Chinese artisans had given the walls and pillars a final stroke with their chisels, and when all the saints had donned their glittering finery, the volcano belched and shifted its feet under the earth. The church stones lost their grip upon each other and fell to the ground.

The watchtower, a project less grand than the church, fared better. Because the natives here were laxly watched, the men were able to query the women who passed by on their way to the river. The women, faces hidden by the beaked shadow of woven reed hats, touched the earth with the tips of their forefingers, and told the men to mix eggshell and albumin with the mortar, in this order and descending amount: the shell and white of turtle eggs, of flamingo eggs, of quail eggs, and lastly, of swallow eggs. When the men thanked them, the women glanced away with half-hooded eyes and said it was nothing; everyone knew nothing held the elements of time better than an egg.

THE SECOND GIFT

Though in due time, the strangers lost their newness and became the visitors, they were not happy. Because the 300 of them were males, they needed to acquire wives. From the sea chests in their ships' holds, they brought out mirrors, curved to fit the hand's palm. In the custom of the islands, they offered these as bride price but erred in making the offer to the fathers of the women they wanted. They were refused with much laughter. That men could presume to accept gifts for women was so preposterous the fathers thought it was an elaborate foreign joke.

A dozen visitors lost patience and forced the women they had chosen to their beds. Here, with their bodies and in the custom of their own homelands, they imprinted upon the women the spoor of ownership. The women however shook their hair free of their necks' sweat, retied their skirts of woven cloth about their hips and ran away to the mountains. They returned a few days later, freshly washed, and walked among their folks with clear eyes and brows. They called out a sharp clear warning, however, a trill of birdsong, to other women whenever a visitor approached.

A male *indio*, taking pity on the visitors, explained that while men's souls fled to littoral havens, women's souls found refuge in mountaintops—temporarily when the woman was surprised or frightened, or permanently, in death. Once a year, when the sky wore the sun for its left eye and the moon for its right, the souls of the dead would gather in a plateau for feasting and storytelling.

When the strangers assaulted the women, their souls quickly departed their bodies. The men were thus left with insignificant matter and what was done to that could not affect the women's fate.

That made no sense to the exasperated visitors. Because it was a chance to show off his wisdom, the *indio* betrayed his sisters. "Show the mirror," he instructed his wretched audience, "each of you, to the woman of your choice."

It was captain who took his advice, sidling up to a woman of fifteen summers washing clay pots and porcelain bowls in the silver river. Her untattooed skin showed her youth and her singleness. Easing his right arm about her carefully, while she was barely aware of his presence, he raised his cupped hand to her face so that her eyes fell on the mirror. She looked. And accepted.

Thereafter, during thunderstorms, women had to hide small mirrors and cover large ones with black cloth, for fear that the *lintik*, strongest, swiftest and most lethal of lightning bolts, would leap for the bright surface which had trapped the souls of its mountaintop playmates in the game of churning the weather.

The visitors' ships crisscrossed the world's waters and returned with finery for the wives: petticoats of six to twelve tiers, dresses tight at the top and loose below, tall combs encrusted with bits of mica and colored stones, embroidered and fringed shawls, and shoes which would only walk the smoothened town roads. To accommodate the ample circle of the wives' skirts—which hid the pain of their steps in the tight shoes—roadways had to be widened. The houses followed since rooms and doorways had to expand; unlike their sisters in the unsewn cloth skirts, sleeveless boleros and gold bracelets and anklets, the wives could no longer flit and dart about like dragonflies. They had to have two feet of space to their left, to their right and before and behind them.

The town's skin thus shifted constantly, caught as it was in the paradox of growing larger and smaller at the same time. The visitors, however, were satisfied. They found a new name for themselves and taught it to the natives: *autoridad.*

THE FOURTH GIFT

Misfortune being a cloak that fitted the size of its recipients, the town's bad luck started with a very small discovery. The first woman to accept a mirror now learned that her husband had gaps in his jaw where some of his teeth had pulled out their roots and run away. She noticed this only when her husband guffawed, so awed had she been by the metal guards of his helmet and the tangled hair of his beard. She told her neighbor who proceeded to tickle her husband, promptly making the same discovery.

Two of the wives, being more venturesome, shed their petticoats, shawls, shoes and combs, and tying their old handwoven cloth about their hips, hied off to the mountainside healing hut. They brought back little blue porcelain jars where, in the days before they became wives, they had kept their medicine: salt gathered where hot springs met seawater, crystalized moonmilk from nightrocks, mashed red roots, all mixed with such elements as were seen daily but unperceived, like a tree's height, the curve of a wave, the heat of sunray.

The two told their husbands that the unguent, packed in the spaces where the old teeth had been, would turn the gums soft and coax toothbuds to form. No one in the islands, they told their husbands, was missing a tooth, the women being too wise to let that happen.

During their absence though, the missing teeth had become common knowledge in the town and the visitors awoke one morning to an ululating laughter moiling like thin smoke between and among the houses. What manner of men, the natives asked, their eyebrows flapping like birdwings, would cause their teeth to jump ship as it were? They laughed. Along the shore, by the river, over the granite pestle for husking rice, in the parlors and the kitchens, and even the littlest child perched next to a kingfisher in the tree chuckled, his amusement spewing around bites of ripe guava.

The knowledge of the blue porcelain jars was lost then, for the visitors heard not laughter but humiliation. It was unconscionable, they said, that women—who should never touch strange flesh—should be healers. The wives protested in vain that even their husbands were strangers until the marriage was many seasons old. Silence, *autoridad* roared at the women and gathered many young men to board their ships for lands at the world's edge where they would receive proper training in healing.

Because the women thereafter said not a word, the clouds, the rain, the reeds and even the typhoon all lost their female voice.

THE FIFTH GIFT

The harvest of salt, of which there were nine times seven varieties, was women's work. Only their fingertips, which were as knowing as a cat's tongue, could coax the white crystals from warm and moist places. With the exception of sea salt which was taken home directly, the salt was then stored in clay jars, each to its kind: that which came from caves, that which came from insect dwellings, that which were scraped off rocks, that which lined lichen beds and tree fungi, that which oozed out of plants and hardened in the air. Mixed, sung over, fermented and aged, packed in porcelain jars obtained from Chinese traders, these kinds of salt were used for medicine.

The wisdom of the nine times seven varieties of salt frightened *autoridad.* They forbade the harvest of crystals, forbade the possession of blue porcelain jars, forbade the women from going out with the moon. When the native males protested, asking what would be used to tickle the tongue and awaken the body, the visitors showed them a powder so much whiter, so much more precise. This, they said, was sugar.

THE SIXTH GIFT

The rain no longer tidied up after itself. Instead of playing at plaiting themselves, clouds climbed on each other, piled up and grew dark and glowering at the horizon. Reeds clung so ferociously to the river that water was forced to heave up and sprawl upon the land. The typhoon walked in, looking neither left nor right, and laid its heavy feet upon houses and trees, and departed without a backward glance.

The settlements were abandoned because the making of sugar required such effort men and women had to pretend to be water buffaloes, living in herds and working ceaselessly day and night. *Autoridad* had long, rectangular structures without windows built for the natives who then created flat fields as far as the eye could span which became the cradle for sugar cane. Close by, a refinery spewed a drunken black roil of smoke into an orange sky.

After a while, *indio* sweat acquired the consistency of syrup and even the flesh of the river fish had the taste of taffy.

THE SEVENTH GIFT

Though the games were forgotten, still one survived, played by girls between the ages of nine and twelve. Each hollowed out nine small nests the size of a child's fist in the earth and placed seven shells each in eight of the hollows. Pairing off, they would then pass the shells among the holes rapidly, singing a tune without words under their breath, filling and emptying the nests. The first to hit an empty nest would then rise to her feet, turn once, turn twice, feel the air currents with crane steps and then swirl four feet above the ground, looping about trees, between houses, circumnavigating the town well, before settling back to the sparkling laughter of her playmates.

THE EIGHTH GIFT

Overnight, it seemed, land sprouted in the far horizon and the natives took to crisscrossing the oceans. Some women followed their men. But they never found the males' routes and were scattered to the earth's five corners. Here, to ease their longing, they built homes which, being outside of time, creaked and groaned at daybreak and dusk, the sound touching the exiled women with fingertips as cold as the lips of blue porcelain jars.

THE FINAL GIFT

The new natives died young but the old ones lived long, wisdom thickening the chain that bound them to the earth. It took many nights to unplait that chain, for care had to be taken that knowledge was divided and distributed among the living fairly, to each according to his or her need. On the last daybreak when light lined the night reminding everyone that even the darkest flower was rimmed with paleness, something lithe and shining hopped with crane legs from Tandang Sora's death-chair. It turned once, turned twice, turned thrice, before gliding out the window toward the mountaintop. In its flight, it conveyed the last gift—the knowledge that wisdom was of the soil and had to be left behind, and that the soul could only soar in innocence. This gift was given in such a manner that even the littlest twice-great-granddaughter understood.

Walk-In Closet

Kerri Sakamoto

Walking down the street people glance at me then wince. They can't quite put their finger on it, wouldn't even want to, especially women. They don't want to touch me, afraid it might rub off on them. For one thing, I have a bad complexion. I used to have acne, I still get pimples here and there. In high school they called me craterface. There are small purplish dents left, just the size I can rest my fingertips in. My mother says I've made the scars even bigger. After work sometimes in front of the mirror, I splay out my fingers over each of the dents and peek out to see how I'd look without them.

My features are a bit lopsided, as if the two hemispheres didn't quite mesh. My skin's darkened from the scarring, and it's always slick with oil. When I arrive home, my mother soaks a large cotton ball with rubbing alcohol and drags it down my face in rows, she'd like to strip

KERRI SAKAMOTO: "I am originally from Toronto, and now live in New York City. . . . My short fiction has appeared in Canada and the U.S. I served as co-writer and associate producer for *Little Baka Girl*, a short film by Helen Lee. . . . I am currently collaborating on an experimental narrative screenplay with video artist Rea Tajiri and writing a novel whose working title is *Anywhere but Japan*. . . ."

the skin right off. She drops the grey-brown wad into her powder-white palm and shakes her head at me. Tsk, she says, as if I did this to my face on purpose. It's the dust falling from the library shelves, I tell her. She tries to say 'tsk' the way mothers do, the way she imagines nannies to wealthy WASP families do, with a wagging finger. But I know it's a catch in her throat she'll never be able to swallow, it snagged the minute they handed me to her, this balled-up bundle, in the hospital.

My mother is exquisite. Someone once said she's the epitome of Japanese beauty and it's true. Her face is a slender oval, all smooth lines running into one another precisely where they should. Each feature in repose is a blossom yet to unfold. She's one of the women in Utamaro's woodblock prints, facing their vanity mirrors, their bosoms puffy under the folds of their kimonos. My infant ear settled into that pillow of flesh. Let's go nen ne, she'd blow, low like bubbles, go nen ne. Sleepy bye. I only heard Japanese words in the dark, in floating whispers. By day I was taunted by other boys in the schoolyard, by night, close to her breast, I was safe, like Momotaro, the boy inside the peach. Nowadays, alone in my bed, I feel nothing, I wake up shunned by my double in the mirror.

I felt the rise and fall of my mother's breast under my head like the ocean's breath in a seashell. For years I didn't know what I was feeling was the pump of oxygen into her lungs and the flood of blood into her heart. I don't know what I'd do if it ever stopped.

The glare of morning light is unbearable. We keep the drapes drawn in the livingroom of our suburban apartment, which faces north, and the lamps down low. Our eyes are sensitive to direct light. My mother buys the blue-tinted bulbs, she says the regular ones make her look unnaturally yellow, even damage her skin with their rays.

I can't imagine why a man would leave her—I never would—but my father, who is this little white speck in my head, did, some 25 years ago. She keeps the only photo of him and her together in the drawer by her bed. Sleep tight, don't let the bedbugs bite, she cheerily calls each night from her room as I turn out my light. (It's a saying she must have learned long ago from him, or maybe it's from Mrs. Lawrence, our jowly neighbour who spills her street gossip to my silent nodding mother.) Then I hear the squeak and pull of the drawer, right on schedule, slowing in its tracks as she takes out the photograph. Years ago, shuffling to the bathroom, I glimpsed her through her cracked-open doorway, and every night, hearing that sound, I say goodnight to that vision. She's sitting up tucked into the right side of her queen-size bed in her white linen gown, creaseless pillow propped behind her, the picture in her lap. She's leaning over the picture and her hair, which she always wears tied back during the day, is a black cape around her shoulders. She stares right into his face, but he's looking elsewhere, he's looking at her 30 years ago.

I know this because I studied the picture when she wasn't home. I went into her room one day when I came home early from school feverish with flu. She was working at the job she still has, selling lingerie in a large department store. I was six or seven then, and I found it there, face down beside her white powder make-up, red lipstick and hairbrush.

He's one of them, I thought, a fluey sweat beading on my face. White. One of the billions of people in the world that I line up on one side of the giant room inside my head, while my mother and I stand on the other, alone. I saw myself in my mother's mirror, clutching the picture frame.

I felt sick, seeing the hard circle of his face, the two holes of his eyes fixed on my mother turned demurely from the camera in a pink dress, it was her favourite color even back then, her hair stiffened into squarish curlicues. I slumped down. I wanted to vomit, but nothing. I coughed up spit and froth into my hand, I was empty and clean. On my mother's velvet stool I twisted. No no no, I cried soundlessly. My reflection was a double-headed blur. I grabbed for the lipstick tube inside the drawer. I wanted to blot out that white speck. I rotated the bottom, red climbed out, rich, solid and round, and instead I pressed it to my lips. It must have been soft, melted from the summer air, because it broke against my mouth, smeared down my chin. I looked at the red line and where it broke off, half-swallowed into the part of my lips.

By the time my mother arrived home, I'd cleaned myself up, replaced the photograph, and molded the jagged end of her lipstick to a rounded tip the best I could. I was calm with her when she cupped her palm over my forehead to gauge my fever. Poor thing, she uttered (another phrase she'd learned somewhere), smoothing my hair then the embroidered doily on the arm of our shabby couch. When she tucked me in, her shadow arched overhead, catlike, and she whispered, Kawaii-so, Nobu-chan. Go nen ne. I saw the words wisp by, but this time, I had to grab them, hold them to the light. I darted my hand out to the lamp beside my bed, nearly knocked it over. I shone it right in my mother's eyes. She gasped, her hands flew up to block me. Before she flicked off the lamp, I saw her face: It was lumpy, as I'd never seen it before, her mouth lolling behind a quick flutter of white powder. Baka, Nobuo-san, bad, she finally spit out, slamming the door behind her.

I feel desolate when my mother and I argue, which nowadays is rare. I make up with her right away, even if she's in the wrong. I can't be left alone in that room inside my head, I can't face those throngs of people on the one side, with her nowhere in sight.

Often at work, I catch my fingers climbing over my face into the holes and I stop, look around to make sure no one's seen me. The people I work with have gotten used to me. I know they take my face for granted now, it's mere surface. Looks don't count in the public library business. The men in the offices upstairs didn't consider my face an impediment, they didn't read anything extreme like divine retribution into it, or an evil nature; they hired me.

Then again, they're not the ones who have to see me every day. My co-workers stared as everyone does. First they flinch, but they keep looking, they can't help themselves. During the first few days, I felt them peeking out of the backroom as I sat at the front desk. Their eyes roamed over me as if at a road accident or a zoo.

How dare they, I think. They're misfits too. I feel sorry for every one of them. Nobody is lily-white, they're Indian, Pakistani, Puerto Rican, Jamaican, Chinese, all beneficiaries of affirmative action, no doubt. I'm the only one without an accent. I've begun to catalogue the nervous tics they each have, subtle, yet more pronounced when they're at the front desk, dealing with the public. Some have a general body twitch, some blink like a vertical hold out of whack, some sweat excessively. From others, there's a slow seeping of unpleasant odours and a spreading stain at their armpits. The young Chinese man shuffles his feet behind the desk, up top, he's all calm. Their energy goes into keeping those tics under control.

But I know how they feel, standing before a growing line of teen-agers from nearby Rosedale. They're girls whose complexions are kept creamy and their hair glossy chestnut with Swiss cosmetics from their mothers' salons. Boys with thick hedges of hair starting at the right place above their foreheads, faces fresh with early fuzz. They've never had to wait for anything, they get impatient in line. Their eyes are translucent colors—blue, green, hazel— and they fix them hard on whoever's at the desk, demanding attention, though others are ahead. The trick is not to look up. I've thought of telling them this, the Chinese man, Lei, or the Indian girl, who look especially nervous. But I see they've already learned not to offer too much. I know when I'm too eager, I hear my voice come out edgy and strange.

In the end, I don't say anything. I keep to myself. I never address co-workers by their first names.

The other day, the Pakistani man smiled, leaned over my desk and placed his finger on the photo pinned to my bulletin board. He blinked. Hey Norman (that's what they call me here, it's easier than Nobuo), your girlfriend is it? He wriggled his finger along its length. I kept busy with my work as his warm breath snaked down my neck. I wonder if it's true, he mused, catching my eye when I turned sharply. He gave a knowing, unblinking glance. I wouldn't know because I've never . . . Is it true about these Oriental women? That there's something different, some special . . . ?

I swatted his hand. (The clap of my palm on his wrist was heard by others, who looked over in alarm.) It's my mother, I said, flatly. He stepped back. I'm sorry, he stuttered, looking sheepish. I resumed my work. It's not that I minded him touching the photograph. It's only a picture. But I let him believe I was offended. From the corner of my eye, I watched him slink off toward the book shelves.

I've often wondered which might be the greater surprise to him: how my mother's youthful looks belie her age, or how little I resemble my mother.

Later that day, the Indian girl approached me. I saw what Anwar did, she said, inclining her head toward my mother's photo. I heard what he said. Her large eyes looked directly into mine. They were the same colour as my mother's. The dark toffee tone of her skin distracted me from seeing that. You were right to slap him, she said firmly. I took a closer look. Her features were perfectly formed, all fine and dainty, more pointed than my mother's, yet still quite lovely. Your mother is very beautiful, she added, as if reading my thoughts.

I merely nodded, because I didn't know what else to say. My face felt hot and flushed. All I could think of was how much worse my skin must have looked, red and up close. I've avoided her since then, so I won't get flustered.

Except the other day, walking past the ladies' washroom, the door swung open and her reflection flashed at me from the mirror inside. She was holding a tube of the plum lipstick she always wears (I've never seen her without it), raising it to her lips. The door slammed shut. I stood there for several seconds before the closed door until someone, a young boy brushed past and looked at me oddly.

I hurried back to my desk, afraid of someone else spotting me.

I've always kept myself groomed impeccably, it's my mother's influence. I do the best with what I have. I shave every morning (though I hardly need to), I shower twice a day. I use my mother's facial scrubbing grains once a week. I've never had body odor, that's one saving grace, and I don't need glasses, but I wonder if eyeglasses might be flattering. We buy fine wool pants for me, navy, grey or dark brown, custom-fitted. We pick them out together, my mother knows how self-conscious I am with salespeople.

She buys me fine combed all-cotton dress shirts. She sends them out to be bleached blue-white and starched. When I'm checking out books at the library, I can observe the clean stiff cuffs of my shirt grazing my wrists as my hands deftly slip cards in back pockets. In the moment before I look up, place a leatherbound tome into the pinkish hands of a Rosedale youth, I imagine this crisp white Swiss cotton shirt is all anyone sees of me.

Dressing well has been my mother's guiding principle through life. She learned to sew from her mother who made her own kimonos here to avoid relying on mail-order or relatives back home. As a teenager, my mother copied the latest chic styles from Vogue magazines. Remembering the first Western-style dress she concocted, she giggles convulsively (masking her face with her hands knowing she looks less attractive this way). She hadn't yet mastered the form-fitting lines absent from straight-seamed kimonos, and the dress, she says, resembled a squat cardboard box.

I built the large walk-in closet which takes up most of my mother's bedroom. I took a lot of care erecting it with my mother helping a bit, steadying beams while I hammered away. I installed a continuous dowel along each side of the closet so that her clothes form a looping pastel rainbow. This wasn't her own idea. My mother copied it from the closet of a Rosedale matron whom she worked for as a live-in domestic when she first arrived in the city from the west coast. Each morning, she reversed inside-out sleeves, smoothed creases and hung up the clothes flung about in indecision the evening before. My mother had to find the correct place for each article so the colors progressed smoothly from one shade to another.

She lived for about four months on the top floor of the house inside another walk-in compartment within the woman's former bedroom. Now my mother flings her arms out to embrace her own rainbow of apparel, runs one graceful hand along it as she does a tour of the closet.

Those people were good to me, she says, remembering. When I didn't know anything, wearing those shabby rags, they let me into their home. She forgets other things she's told me, how she trudged up the winding fire escape (treacherous in winter) to the top floor, passing on the second floor, the window of the livingroom where the matron, her husband, and their son, daughter and nanny sat.

Inspired by that daily glimpse, my mother redecorated our apartment ten years ago. She thought how a glance into our apartment (perhaps from the building across the street) might give rise to the same feeling she felt on her climb up or down, thirty years ago. She boxed up every Japanese trinket, calendar, vase we had in the place, they didn't match the brocade drapes. She even traded the silk wallhanging to Mrs. Lawrence for a knuckle-sized Royal Doulton porcelain flower basket. The French provincial dining set and framed mirror we purchased at discount from the department store. She swears it's identical to the set she dusted.

Glancing at the line of faces before the library's front desk, I wonder which one comes from that mansion with the two walk-in wardrobes and winding fire escape.

My mother learned a lot from this woman who would brush past her in the expansive hallway. When you walk by, my mother says, leave only this. She demonstrates her glide which after ten years, she's perfected. Her one arm undulates behind her, the pink scarf around her neck trailing. She stands to the left of the space she's come and gone from, extends her delicate neck and sniffs. Traces, she declares, composing her features to their best advantage. Leave only traces, she repeats. She does this every so often: dresses up, pats Givenchy behind her ears. Then, before she leaves for the department store, she changes back into everyday wear then inspects herself before the mirror. Then she pivots to face me with a look that asks for approval and knows it will be given.

Whenever I've reached out to blend the seam of make-up and powder between her chin and her neck, she pulls away, leaving my outstretched hand dangling cold and awkward. She ignores it, turning to the mirror, dips the tip of her finger in her mouth and dabs at the telltale line. When she's finished, I can almost see dainty paw prints all along her neck.

I wonder if I'm enough for her. I know she still thinks of him, though it's only a photograph she fondles, not a man.

At the end of the day, when she's running the cotton ball down my face, she's sometimes looking off, not watching what she's doing. She's stung my eye a few times with the astringent. Today, she's doing just that: not looking at me, she could be stripping bark from a tree.

Ah-hem, I clear my throat. She focuses and smiles. Tsk, tsk, she says with two skips of the tongue.

I met a man today, she says finally, her voice lighter than usual for the end of the day. She plops the cotton ball into the toilet bowl. You shouldn't do that, I scold, nervously diverting the subject to where it belongs. Those things clog up the pipes, I add.

I don't know why she tells me this. She knows how it upsets me, even though nothing's ever happened. Not even a visitor, only odd nights out in mixed groups to the theatre or cinema. But no nightcaps, no escort to the door. I couldn't fall asleep until she arrived, clicking her heels across the kitchen floor, to let me know. To let me sleep.

Ben, his name is, she's saying.

You met him at work? I ask, without looking up. I suppress a snort, it might come spurting out and never stop.

Yes, she replies, slowly drawing it out. I notice her one hand caressing the other. She's talked about men before, but her voice sounds different this time. He was buying slippers for his sister, she says.

I think of my mother unsnapping those pocket-sized, see-through plastic pouches, bending and unbending curled-up slipper soles for this stranger. There are only two reasons why a man would be shopping in a lingerie department.

Ben, she says, is Jewish. Asian men don't interest my mother. I've seen her dismiss their attentive stares with a haughty turn of her lovely head. Not enough hair on the chest, I overheard her telling Mrs. Lawrence on the front stoop, one of the few times she did the talking. Not manly enough, she declared. I remember opening my shirt in front of the mirror to count the hairs growing there (there still aren't any).

Ben, she sighs. One meeting and already he's inside our home, his name passed between her lips, between us. I begin filling in the empty oval of his face, maliciously: First, a long, large nose, then a thin frugal mouth curving around its overhanging tip. I add a full beard (which I'll never be able to grow). I look at my mother, staring off: her nose is so fine, not sprawling and round like so many Asian noses, not like mine. Her skin is soft and hairless, poreless really, her arms are hairless too. She's never shaved her legs in her life, I know. For a Japanese woman, it's unheard of.

I took my coffee break with him, she goes on. He lived in Tokyo for a year, so he knows some Japanese. He's a businessman. Very successful. She giggles. Konichi-wa he said. He could tell I was Japanese right away. Not Chinese, not Korean. Not one of those boat people. Nihonjin.

There's a difference, you know, she says, meaningfully.

Ben says Japanese women are the most beautiful in the world, do you think it's true? She dips her gaze on me briefly, not expecting an answer. She's blushing under her powder, her hands are curled over her mouth as her laughter thins into a barely audible tweeking, like fingernails over a blackboard.

She isn't home yet. It's after midnight, quiet outside. The street lamps have gone out. I've tried to keep calm, followed the swirling pattern of the plaster ceiling again and again. I've told myself: Soon. As soon as I find my way out of this maze of swirls to the outer rim, she'll be home. Soon you'll hear her come in the door. But I can't find my way out, I'm too nervous to concentrate, I keep getting trapped in the centre swirl. Finally I can't stand it. I flip over, curl up, plunge my face into the pillow, pushing out and sucking in to breathe. Soon she'll be home, soon, soon, soon, I repeat, trying to calm the pulsing of my body. Go nen ne, I hear drift through my head, but I can't. I quiver with each creak in the hallway, skitter of the door in its frame. Then, suddenly, the lock clunks loudly, I stop breathing. I wait: for the door to be held open a second too long, for an extra voice, or a shush blown over a finger. But nothing. Just the click of her heels up to the mirror to make sure she looked the way she'd wanted to right to the end.

I inhale slowly and carefully, I straighten and rotate in my bed, smooth the bedsheets and my pyjamas. Lying face up, I close my eyes. I hear her footsteps pass my room then the crank of the water pipes in her bathroom. She's brushing her teeth now, swishing the water from cheek to cheek.

Her light clicks out. I wait again but there's no squeak of the dresser drawer. No nightie night, sleep tight, though she must know I'm still awake.

The next morning she sleeps in. I don't wake her, I don't know what to do, she's never done this before. I leave for work. I sit down to her picture facing me, as always, from the bulletin board. I take out a pushpin holding up a flyer that drops to my desk. I press it into the photograph, leaning my entire weight forward to puncture it. I hear the squish of cheap leather shoes behind me and a slow tsk tsk, turn to see the back of Anwar walking away. My mother's eyes stare at me above the red cone tacked over her mouth.

You need to get out more, she's telling me, stroking my hand. Make some friends. I don't say a word.

Look, she says. She's holding up a square white box with slits across one side and a series of buttons across the other. She takes it out of its plastic wrapper and plugs it in. A red dot pulses. It's an answering machine, she declares. In case Mrs. Lawrence or work or Ben has to call and I'm not home.

I don't know why we need this machine when we hardly get any phone calls.

It's not for Ben, I say. It's not, because the only time you're out is when you're with him.

She ignores this comment. When the red dot flashes it means there's messages, she explains.

She presses one of the buttons with her slender finger. It's her voice saying: Ayame and Norman aren't home just now. Please leave a message after the tone.

Why is she using her Japanese name now, after all these years? Why bother with my name? The voice is hollow, comes from far away, from a person who is too busy for me. It's not the voice that says, sleep tight, or calls me Nobu-chan.

I hate them, they smell, they're dirty, they push push push to get the seats, she says. Especially the old ones. My mother's returned from Chinatown, and a ride on the downtown bus. She's bought two full bags of groceries from the Japanese food store to cook Ben a meal here. It'll be our first meeting.

They wear their little soiled uniforms and no socks, she rants. They drop their fat cabbages on my feet, on my good shoes. She bends down to dust them off. Her face is twisted with distaste she's not bothering to conceal.

I'm exhausted and I haven't even begun, she groans. Everything has to be perfect. Help me, Nobu.

She rests her arm on my shoulder and leans her head down. I'm smelling her fragrance close, smelling it from her skin, instead of from a space she's left behind. I feel my hand trembling, I want to stay like this forever, it's been so long since she's let me this close. Abruptly she pulls away.

She takes out a *Time-Life Japanese Cookbook* from the last of the shopping bags she's brought in. Better not let Ben see this. She winks. He's used to Tokyo food, but all I know is country style, she laments. She unrolls a complimentary calendar and hangs it by the kitchen table, a lone bit of Japanese decor. A bright-eyed girl in a multi-coloured kimono, Miss October, now stands over us, a fan demurely held under her chin. My mother imitates the girl by holding a folded paper bag. I was that beautiful once, she sighs.

Ordinarily, I'd say, but mother, you still are. But I don't.

She doesn't notice. She's pulling out the saucepans, the cutting board, rummaging through the cutlery drawer for spare chopsticks. She's flipping anxiously through the cookbook.

All at once I take a deep breath and say it: Why does he have to come? She hasn't heard.

I say it again, a little stronger. Why does HE have to come? Still she keeps on. I touch my lips and know they haven't moved. They're dry and sealed shut.

I flee to my room, try reading, but can't concentrate. It's only a dinner, I tell myself. Only a date. But I can't fool myself. Pots clang in the kitchen, cupboards bang. It upsets the beating of my heart.

I shut my door tight, turn out the lights and put on the stereo. Is she punishing me? For not paying enough attention? For not being enough? For looking like this?

I need to hear some music, soothing, to calm me. I know what it is. My hands are shaking, I can barely fit the cassette into the player. Then I get it, it starts up, filtering through the last bit of afternoon light. Tiny voices fill my ears: Mo-mo-ta-ro, I sing with them, shaky and off-key. I try to remember little Momotaro jumping out of the peach, Momotaro going nen ne after a long day of playing, the story she used to tell me. She doesn't know I kept this when she threw everything else away.

I try stretching out on the bed, folding my arms under my head.

But my feet start fidgeting, then my fingers grope from under my head and start scaling either side of my face to pick at my scars. I want to curl up and flip over, push my face into the pillow, push that deep gouge in my belly against the mattress. But I can't. She'll hate that.

I bound off the bed. I feel my collars and cuffs droopy and grey. She'll hate me like this. She'll want me to change. I throw open my cupboards. I grab at my just laundered shirts still in their wrapping. My fingers are spidery, clumsy and get in the way. I'm tearing at the paper, then use my teeth. I'd like to rip them, rip the stiff white cuffs I've watched skirt my wrists so gracefully. I taste soap and bleach and salt, biting until my teeth hurt.

Then I fall back onto the bed, try to catch my breath. The song finishes. I lie there, breathing deeply for several minutes as the tape swishes round. I feel a thread between my front teeth.

I get up and head back to the kitchen.

The lights are up, brighter than they've ever been. I shield my eyes. I couldn't see, she mutters as she removes her apron. Behind her on the dining table, there's an array of food, sitting primly in bowls and plates of various shapes and sizes. In the light, the brightly coloured centres of rolled rice glisten.

Do you think he'll like it? she asks.

The cooking has steamed half the powder from her face. A few strands of hair have fallen down, exposing grey roots here and there. When did she begin dyeing it? Her skin looks like patchwork, all yellow and white. Her face looks strangely lopsided, like a cat with different colored eyes.

She looks different, yet familiar.

What? she says watching me look, her hands flitting from her hair to her face to her skirt. Set the table, she orders, throwing down the apron. And change your clothes, your trousers are creased and your collar's drooping. She's halfway down the hallway toward her bedroom as she says this.

I follow after her quietly, see her disappear around the corner into her bedroom. I pause at the threshold, I'm not allowed in her room ordinarily. I look around. Nothing has changed since the last time I was in here. The bed is in the same place, the dresser with the white linen runner is still beside it. I smell Givenchy.

The door to the closet is partly open. I hear the raking of hangers along the dowel. She's deciding what to wear.

I slip up and close the door behind me, shutting us in darkness. I hear her gasp. I grope for the string attached to the lightbulb in the middle of the closet.

The light is harsh. The clothes hang in a jumble of colours. She hasn't kept them in order.

My mother looks aghast, then angry. Nobu, she says, scolding, What are you doing?

Sit down, I say. She looks at my finger pointed at a chair.

He'll be here in half an hour, she says. She twists her watch on her wrist, stamps her tiny foot. She walks up to me as I stand barring the door. Let me through, she demands.

I raise my arm in front of me, lean forward so my hand rests squarely above her breast. Then gently but firmly, I push back, sinking my hand into the soft flesh rising between my fingers.

Her eyes widen, she looks down at my hand. She tries to swat it but misses.

You're just fine, I say. I take my hand from her breast then move to grip her upper arm. It takes a long time to do that, as if I'm alone until I feel the flesh under my fingers again. My shirt cuffs are filthy and ragged, I notice. I slip my arms around her and guide her to a chair that's beside the mirror I hung in the corner. She feels old in my arms. Then I yank a dress from its hanger and toss it over the light to soften it.

Not my good pink silk, she groans.

In the rosy light she looks more like herself, but tired. She reaches out to touch my cheeks with the back of her hand. I flinch, expecting a slap.

Nobu-chan? She hasn't called me chan in years.

I have to fix myself up, she says. I have to get ready.

You look fine, I answer.

He won't like me, she says.

Then we won't let him in, I say.

Suddenly she springs toward the mirror, presses her face close, licks her finger to smooth what's left of her make-up over her face. She rakes at her hair, wets her palms to smooth the front strands to cover the grey, but strips keep flopping down in her face. I see her scanning the floor for her hairclip.

She turns to me with a helpless look. Nobu. Baka, she says. Stupid boy. Let me out. She's trying to scare me—me, the little boy who shone that light in her eyes. But her voice is a whisper, she's tired.

She falls into the chair. Then tears flow down her cheeks, flow and flow, they fall into her lap and pool there. I've never seen my mother cry.

The buzzer sounds, startling us both though it's muffled by two sets of walls. It freezes my heart for seconds on end. Down in the lobby, his finger's on the button. It starts and stops, starts and stops. My body is racked by the sound, like it's drilling into me.

My mother gets up, sits down, gets up, sits down. She shakes her fists at me. She twists her face. Finally the buzzing stops. I keep waiting for it to start again, but it doesn't. I walk over to where she sits, rest my hand on the back of the chair and look in the mirror at the two of us.

The last of her make-up has caked off. She looks terrible. I don't tell her this.

The telephone rings. Three rings then a heavy click. The answering machine hums. Ayame and Norman aren't home just now, the voice squeaks out in the kitchen, then there's a long beep. At the end of it, a low rumbling travels from the kitchen down the hall and into the closet. My mother's sitting up in the chair, alert, her ear cocked.

Immigration Blues

from *The Man Who (Thought He) Looked like Robert Taylor*

Bienvenido Santos

—*I'm only trying to help you. We should help each other in this country.*
—*Look who's talking. You the guy who run away when you see an old Pinoy approach you. You tell me that yourself. You can't deny.*
—*That's different. Most of these o.t.'s are bums.*
—*Ina couple more years, you'd be one of 'em.*
—*Not me. I save. I make no monkey business. When I retire I'll have everything I need.*
—*Except friends.*
—*Who need friends. Besides, I got friends.*

BIENVENIDO SANTOS wrote his first book, *You Lovely People,* in 1955. One of the most important, beloved, and widely read writers in the Philippines, he has written five short-story collections, including *Brother, My Brother* and *The Scent of Apples*; two books of poetry, *The Wounded Stag* and *Distances in Time*; and five novels, including *The Praying Man, The Man Who (Thought He) Looked like Robert Taylor,* and *What the Hell for You Left Your Heart in San Francisco.* Now retired, he has taught at Ohio State University, the Aspen Creative Writing Workshop, and Wichita State University. He commutes between homes in Greeley, Colorado, and Sagpon, Albay, Philippines.

—*That's what you think. You're gonna lose one now. These guys you're scare are our countrymen.*

—*Who told you I'm scare? I just avoid 'em, that's all. Some of 'em give me bad time, like I'm a sucker.*

—*You look like one, that's why. But don't you see, these old guys are lonely.*

—*Lonely, my balls! After the soft talk come the soft touch, the cry story.*

—*How I pity you. . . . Because you should've experience the other vice versa. Like I have. They take you to their homes, feed you till you burp. Especially those Pinoys who don't have no contact with other Pinoys. They show you off to their American wife like lost brother. Like they never get a chance to speak the dialect for years and they just keep talking, never mind the wife who don't understand. And when it's time for you to leave, you know you aren't going to see each other no more. Their eyes shine like they're crying. . . .*

—*I seen tearful fellow myself, but I think he got sore eyes. He should've been ina hospital.*

—*Have you been to their homes? The walls, they're cover with Philippine things. They're always shoving albums to you. Some of 'em even got the map of Philippines embroidered somewheres. But what's the use, my smart aleck* paisano, *you won't recognize loneliness even it's serve to you on a bamboo tray. . . .*

Through the window curtain, Alipio saw two women, one seemed twice as large as the other. In their summer dresses, they looked like the country girls he knew back home in the Ilocos, who went around peddling rice cakes. The slim one could have passed for Seniang's sister as he remembered her in the pictures his wife kept. Before Seniang's death, they had arranged for her coming to San Francisco, filing all the required petition papers to facilitate the approval of her visa. She was always "almost ready, all the papers have been signed," but she never showed up. His wife had been ailing and when she died, he thought that, at least, it would hasten her sister's coming. The wire he had sent informing her of Seniang's death was not returned nor acknowledged.

The knocking on the door was gentle. A little hard of hearing, Alipio was not sure it was distinctly a knocking on wood that sounded different from the little noises that sometimes hummed in his ears in the daytime. It was not yet noon, but it must be warm outside in all that sunshine otherwise those two women would be wearing warm clothes. There were summer days in San Francisco that were cold like winter in the mid-West.

He limped painfully towards the door. Until last month, he wore crutches. The entire year before that, he was bed-ridden, but he had to force himself to walk about in the house after coming from the hospital. After Seniang's death, everything had gone to pieces. It was one bust after another, he complained to the few friends who came to visit him.

"Seniang was my good luck. When God decided to take her, I had nothing but bad luck," he said.

Not long after Seniang's death, he was in a car accident. For about a year, he was in the hospital. The doctors were not sure he was going to walk again. He told them it was God's wish. As it was he was thankful he was still alive. It was a horrible accident.

The case dragged on in court. His lawyer didn't seem too good about accidents like his. He was an expert immigration lawyer, but he was a friend. As it turned out, Alipio lost the full privileges coming to him in another two years if he had not been hospitalized and had continued working until his retirement.

However, he was well provided. He didn't spend a cent of his own money for doctor and medicine and hospitalization bills. Now there was the prospect of a few thousand dollars coming as compensation. After deducting his lawyer's fees it would still be something to live on. There was social security, partial retirement pension. It was not bad. He could walk a little now although he still limped and had to move about with care.

When he opened the door, the fat woman said, "Mr. Palma? Alipio Palma?"

"Yes," he said. "Come in, come on in." He had not talked to anyone the entire week. His telephone had not rung all that time. The little noises in his ears had somehow kept him company. Radio and television sounds lulled him to sleep.

The thin one was completely out of sight as she stood behind the big one who was doing the talking. "I'm sorry, I should have phoned you first, but we were in a hurry."

"The house a mess," Alipio said truthfully. He remembered seeing two women on the porch. There was another one, who looked like Seniang's sister. Had he been imagining things? Then the thin one materialized, close behind the other, who walked in with the assurance of a social worker, about to do him a favor.

"Sit down," Alipio said, passing his hand over his face, a mannerism which Seniang hated. Like you have a hangover, she chided him, and you can't see straight.

There was a TV set in the small living room crowded with an assortment of chairs and tables. There was an aquarium on the mantelpiece of a fake fireplace. A lighted bulb inside the tank showed many colored fish swimming about in a haze of fish food. Some of it lay scattered on the edge of the mantelpiece. The carpet beneath it was sodden and dirty. The little fish swimming about in the lighted water seemed to be the only sign of life in the room where everything was old, including, no doubt, the magazines and tabloids scattered just about everywhere.

Alipio led the two women through the dining room, past a huge rectangular table in the center. It was bare except for a vase of plastic flowers as centerpiece.

"Sorry to bother you like this," the fat one said as she plunked herself down on the nearest chair, which sagged to the floor under her weight. The thin one chose the near end of the sofa that faced the TV set.

"I was just preparing my lunch. I know it's quite early, but I had nothing else to do," Alipio said, pushing down with both hands the seat of the cushioned chair near a movable partition, which separated the living room from the dining room. "I'm not too well yet," he added as he finally made it.

"I hope we're not really bothering you," the fat one said. The other had not said a word. She looked pale and sick. Maybe she was hungry or cold.

"How is it outside?" Alipio asked. "I have not been out all day." Whenever he felt like it, he dragged a chair to the porch and sat there, watching the construction going on across the street and smiling at the people passing by. He stayed on until it felt chilly.

"It's fine. It's fine outside. Just like Baguio."

"You know Baguio? I was born near there."

"We're sisters," the fat one said.

Alipio was thinking, won't the other one speak at all?

"I'm Mrs. Antonieta Zafra, the wife of Carlito. I believe you know him. He says you're friends. In Salinas back in the thirties. He used to be a cook at the Marina."

"Carlito, yes, yes, Carlito Zafra. We bummed together. We come from Ilocos. Where you from?"

"Aklan. My sister and I speak Cebuano."

"She speak? You don't speak Iloco."

"Not much. Carlito and I talk in English. Except when he's real mad, like when his cock don't fight or when he lose, then he speaks Iloco. Cuss words. I've learned them. Some."

"Yes. Carlito. He love cockfighting. How's he?"

"Retired like you. We're now in Fresno. On a farm. He raises chickens and hogs. I do some sewing in town whenever I can. My sister here is Monica. She's older than me. Never been married."

Monica smiled at the old man, her face in anguish, as if near to tears.

"Carlito. He got some fighting cocks, I bet."

"Not any more. But he talks a lot about cockfighting. But nobody, not even the Pinoys and the Latin Americanos around are interested in it." Mrs. Zafra appeared pleased at the state of things on the home front.

"I remember. He once promoted a cockfight. Everything was ready, but the roosters wouldn't fight. Poor Carlito, he did everything to make 'em fight like having them peck at each other's necks, and so forth. They were so tame. Only thing they didn't do was embrace." Alipio laughed showing a set of perfectly white and even teeth, obviously dentures.

"He hasn't told me about that; I'll remind him."

"Do that. Where's he? Why isn't he with you?"

"We didn't know we'd find you here. While visiting some friends this morning, we learned you live here." Mrs. Zafra was beaming on him.

"I've always lived here, but I got few friends now. So you're Mrs. Carlito. I thought he's dead already. I never hear from him. We're old now. We're old already when we got our citizenship papers right after Japanese surrender. So you and him. Good for Carlito."

"I heard about your accident."

"After Seniang died. She was not yet sixty, but she had this heart trouble. I took care of her." Alipio seemed to have forgotten his visitors. He sat there staring at the fish in the aquarium, his ears perked as though waiting for some sound, like the breaking of the surf not far away, or the TV set suddenly turned on.

The sisters looked at each other. Monica was fidgeting, her eyes seemed to say, let's go, let's get out of here.

"Did you hear that?" the old man said.

Monica turned to her sister, her eyes wild with fright. Mrs. Zafra leaned forward, leaning with one hand on the sofa where Alipio sat, and asked gently, "Hear what?"

"The waves. They're just outside, you know. The breakers have a nice sound like at home in the Philippines. We lived near the sea. Across that water is the Philippines, I always tell Seniang, we're not far from home."

"But you're alone. It's not good to be alone," Mrs. Zafra said.

"At night I hear better. I can see the Pacific Ocean from my bedroom. It sends me to sleep. I sleep soundly like I got no debts. I can sleep all day, too, but that's bad. So I walk. I walk much before. I go out there. I let the breakers touch me. It's nice the touch. Seniang always scold me, she says I'll be catching cold, but I don't catch cold, she catch the cold all the time."

"You must miss her," Mrs. Zafra said. Monica was staring at the hands on her lap while her sister talked. Her skin was transparent and the veins showed on the back of her hands like trapped eels.

"I take care of Seniang. I work all day and leave her here alone. When I come, she's smiling. She's wearing my jacket and my slippers. Like an Igorot. You look funny, I says, why do you wear my things?

She chuckles, you keep me warm all day, she says. We have no baby. If we have a baby . . ."

"I think you and Carlito have the same fate. We have no baby also."

"God dictates," Alipio said, making an effort to stand. Monica, in a miraculous surge of power, rushed to him and helped him up. She seemed astonished and embarrassed at what she had done.

"Thank you," said Alipio. "I have crutches, but I don't want no crutches. They tickle me." He watched Monica go back to her seat.

"It must be pretty hard alone," Mrs. Zafra said.

"God helps," Alipio said, walking towards the kitchen as if expecting to find the Almighty there.

Mrs. Zafra followed him. "What are you preparing?" she asked.

"Let's have lunch," he said. "I'm hungry. Aren't you?"

"We'll help you," Mrs. Zafra said, turning back to where Monica sat staring at her hands again and listening perhaps for the sound of the sea. She did not notice nor hear her sister when she called, "Monica!"

The second time, she heard her. Monica stood up and went to the kitchen.

"There's nothing to prepare," Alipio was saying, as he opened the refrigerator. "What you want to eat? Me, I don't eat bread, so I got no bread. I eat rice. I was just opening a can of sardines when you come. I like sardines with lots of tomato sauce and hot rice."

"Don't you cook the sardines?" Mrs. Zafra asked. "Monica will cook it for you if you want."

"No! If you cook sardines, it taste bad. Better uncooked. Besides, on top of the hot rice, it gets cooked. You chop onions. Raw not cooked. You like it?"

"Monica loves raw onions, don't you, Sis?"

"Yes," Monica said in a voice so low Alipio couldn't have heard her.

"Your sister, is she well?" Alipio asked, glancing towards Monica.

Mrs. Zafra gave her sister an angry look.

"I'm okay," Monica said, a bit louder this time.

"She's not sick," Mrs. Zafra said, "but she's shy. Her own shadow frightens her. I tell you, this sister of mine, she got problems."

"Oh?" Alipio exclaimed. He had been listening quite attentively.

"I eat onions," Monica said. "Sardines, too, I like."

Her sister smiled. "What do you say, I run out for some groceries," she said, going back to the living room to get her bag.

"Thanks. But no need for you to do that. I got lots of food, canned food. Only thing I haven't got is bread," Alipio said.

"I eat rice, too," Monica said.

Alipio had reached up to open the cabinet. It was stacked full of canned food: corned beef, pork and beans, vienna sausage, tuna, crab meat, shrimp, chow mein, imitation noodles, and, of course, sardines, in green and yellow labels.

"The yellow ones with mustard sauce, not tomato," he explained.

"All I need is a cup of coffee," Mrs. Zafra said, throwing her handbag back on the chair in the living room.

Alipio opened two drawers near the refrigerator. "Look," he said as Mrs. Zafra came running back to the kitchen. "I got more food to last me . . . a long time."

The sisters gaped at the bags of rice, macaroni, spaghetti sticks, sugar, dried shrimps wrapped in cellophane, bottles of soy sauce and fish sauce, vinegar, ketchup, instant coffee, and more cans of sardines.

The sight of all that foodstuff seemed to have enlivened the old man. After all, it was his main sustenance, source of energy and health. "Now look here," he said, turning briskly now to the refrigerator, which he opened. With a jerk he pulled open a large freezer, crammed full of meats. "Mostly lamb chops," he said, adding, "I like lamb chops."

"Carlito, he hates lamb chops," Mrs. Zafra said.

"I like lamb chops," Monica said, still wild-eyed, but now with a bit of color tinting her cheeks. "Why do you have so much?" she asked.

Alipio looked at her before answering. He thought she looked younger than her married sister. "You see," he said, "I read the papers for bargain sales. I can still drive the car when I feel all right. It's only now my leg's bothering me. So. I buy all I can. Save me many trips."

Later they sat around the enormous table in the dining room. Monica shared half a plate of the boiled rice topped with a sardine with Alipio. He showed her how to place the sardine on top, pressing it a little and pouring spoonfuls of the tomato sauce over it.

Mrs. Zafra had coffee and settled for a small can of vienna sausage and a little rice. She sipped her coffee meditatively.

"This is good coffee," she said. "I remember how we used to hoard Hills Bros. coffee at . . . at the college. The sisters were quite selfish about it."

"Antonieta was a nun, a sister of mercy," Monica said.

"What?" Alipio exclaimed, pointing a finger at her for no apparent reason, an involuntary gesture of surprise.

"Yes, I was," Mrs. Zafra admitted. "When I married, I had been out of the order for more than a year, yes, in California, at St. Mary's."

"You didn't . . ." Alipio began.

"Of course not," she interrupted him. "If you mean did I leave the order to marry Carlito. Oh, no. He was already an old man."

"I see. We used to joke him because he didn't like the girls too much. He prefer the cocks." The memory delighted him so much, he reared his head up as he laughed, covering his mouth hastily, but too late. Some of the tomato-soaked grains of rice had already spilled out on his plate and the table in front of him.

Monica looked pleased as she gathered carefully some of the grains on the table.

"He hasn't changed," Mrs. Zafra said vaguely. "It was me who wanted to marry him."

"You? After being a nun, you wanted to marry . . . Carlito? But why Carlito?" Alipio seemed to have forgotten for the moment that he was still eating. The steam from the rice passed across his face, touching it. He was staring at Mrs. Zafra as he breathed in the aroma without savoring it.

"It's a long story," Mrs. Zafra said. She stabbed a chunky sausage and brought it to her mouth. She looked pensive as she chewed on it.

"When did this happen?"

"Five, six years ago. Six years ago, almost."

"That long?"

"She had to marry him," Monica said blandly.

"What?" Alipio said, visibly disturbed. There was the sound of dentures grating in his mouth. He passed a hand over his face. "Carlito done that to you?"

The coffee spilled a little as Mrs. Zafra put the cup down. "Why, no," she said. "What are you thinking of?"

Before he could answer, Monica spoke in the same tone of voice, low, unexcited, saying, "He thinks Carlito got you pregnant, that's what."

"Carlito?" She turned to Monica in disbelief. "Why, Alipio knows Carlito," she said.

Monica shrugged her shoulders. "Why don't you tell him why," she said.

"It's a long story, but I'll make it short," she began. She took a sip from her cup and continued, "After leaving the order, I couldn't find a job. I was interested in social work, but I didn't know anybody who could help me."

As she paused, Alipio said, "What the heck does Carlito know about social work?"

"Let me continue," Mrs. Zafra said.

She still had a little money, from home, and she was not too worried about being jobless. But there was the question of her status as an alien. Once out of the order, she was no longer entitled to stay in the country, let alone get employment. The immigration office began to hound her, as it did other Filipinos in the same predicament. They were a pitiful lot. Some hid in the apartments of friends like criminals running away from the law. Of course, they were law breakers. Those who had transportation money returned home, which they hated to do. At home they would be forced to invent lies as to why they had come back so soon. They were defeated souls, insecure, and no longer fit for anything. They had to learn how to live with the stigma of failure in a foreign land all their lives. Some lost their minds and had to be committed to insane asylums. Others became neurotic, antisocial, depressed in mind and spirit. Or parasites. Some must have turned to crime. Or just folded up, in a manner of speaking. It was a nightmare. She didn't want to go back to the Philippines. Just when she seemed to have reached the breaking point, she recalled incidents in which women in her situation married American citizens and, automatically, became entitled to permanent residency with an option to become U.S. citizens after five years. At first, she thought the idea was hideous, unspeakable. Other foreign women in a similar situation could do it perhaps, but not Philippine girls. But what was so special about Philippine girls? Nothing really, but their upbringing was such that to place themselves in a situation where they had to tell a man that they wanted to marry him for convenience was degrading, an unbearable shame. A form of self-destruction. Mortal sin! Better repatriation. A thousand times.

When an immigration officer finally caught up with her, he proved to be very understanding and quite a gentleman. He was young, maybe of Italian descent, and looked like a star salesman for a well-known company in the islands that dealt in farm equipment. Yet he was firm.

"I'm giving you one week," he said. "You have already overstayed by several months. If, in one week's time, you haven't yet left, I shall have to send you to jail, prior to deportation proceedings."

She cried, oh, how she cried. She wished she had not left the order, no, not really. She had no regrets about leaving up to this point. Life in the convent had turned sour on her. She despised the sisters and the system, which she found tyrannical, inhuman. In her own way, she had a long series of talks with God and God had approved of the step she had taken. She was not going back to the order. Even if she did, she would not be taken back. To jail then?

But why not marry an American citizen? In one week's time? How? Accost the first likely man and say, "You look like an American citizen. If you are, will you marry me? I want to remain in this country."

All week she talked to God. It was the same God she had worshipped and feared all her life. Now they were palsy walsy, on the best of terms. As she brooded over her misfortune, He brooded with her, sympathized with her, and finally advised her to go look for an elderly Filipino, who was an American citizen, and tell him the truth of the matter. Tell him that if he wished, it could be a marriage in name only. If he wished . . . Otherwise . . . Meanwhile He would look the other way.

How she found Carlito Zafra was another story, a much longer story, more confused. It was like a miracle. Her friend God could not have sent her to a better instrument to satisfy her need. That was not expressed well, but amounted to that, a need. Carlito was an instrument necessary for her good. And, as it turned out, a not too unwilling instrument.

"We were married the day before the week was over," Mrs. Zafra said. "And I've been in this country ever since. And no regrets."

They lived well and simply, a country life. True, they were childless, but both of them were helping relatives in the Philippines, sending them money, goods.

"Lately, however, some of the goods we've been sending do not arrive intact. Do you know, some of the good quality material we send never reach my relatives. It's frustrating."

"We got lots of thieves between here and there," Alipio said, but his mind seemed to be on something else.

"And I was able to send for Monica. From the snapshots she sent us, she seemed to be getting thinner and thinner, teaching in the barrio, and she wanted so much to come here."

"Seniang was like you also. I thank God for her," Alipio told Mrs. Zafra in such a low voice he could hardly be heard.

The sisters pretended they didn't know, but they knew. They knew practically everything about him. Alipio seemed pensive and eager to talk so they listened attentively.

"She went to where I was staying and said, without any hesitation, marry me and I'll take care of you. She was thin then and I thought what she said was funny, the others had been matching us, you know, but I was not really interested. I believe marriage means children. And if you cannot produce children, why get married? Besides, I had ugly experiences, bad moments. When I first arrived in the States, here in Frisco, I was young and there were lots of blondies hanging around on Kearny Street. It was easy. But I wanted a family and they didn't. None of 'em. So what the heck, I said."

Alipio realized that Seniang was not joking. She had to get married to an American citizen otherwise she would be deported. At that time, Alipio was beginning to feel the disadvantages of living alone. There was too much time on his hands. How he hated himself for some of the things he did. He believed that if he were married, he would be more sensible with his time and his money. He would be happier and live longer. So when Seniang showed that she was serious, he agreed to marry her. But it was not to be in name only. He wanted a woman. He liked her so much he would have proposed himself had he suspected he had a chance. She was hard working, decent, and, in those days, rather slim.

"Like Monica," he said.

"Oh, I'm thin," Monica protested, blushing deeply. "I'm all bones."

"Monica is my only sister. We have no brother," Mrs. Zafra said, adding more items in her sister's vita.

"Look!" Monica said, "I finished everything on my plate. I haven't tasted sardines for a long time now. They taste so good, the way you eat them. I'm afraid I've eaten up your lunch. This is my first full meal. And I thought I've lost my appetite already."

Her words came out in a rush. It seemed she didn't want to stop and paused only because she didn't know what else to say. But she moved about, gaily and at ease, perfectly at home. Alipio watched her with a bemused look in his face as she gathered the dishes and brought them to the kitchen sink. When Alipio heard the water running, he stood up, without much effort this time, and walked to her, saying, "Don't bother. I got all the time to do that. You got to leave me something to do. Come, perhaps your sister wants another cup of coffee."

Mrs. Zafra had not moved from her seat. She was watching the two argue about the dishes. When she heard Alipio mention coffee, she said, "No, no more, thanks. I've drunk enough to keep me awake all week."

The two returned to the table after a while.

"Well, I'm going to wash them myself, later," Monica said as she took her seat.

"You're an excellent host, Alipio," Mrs. Zafra commended him, her tone sounding like a reading from a citation on a certificate of merit or something. "And to two complete strangers at that. You're a good man," she continued, the citation-sounding tone still in her voice.

"But you're not strangers. Carlito is my friend. We were young together in the States. And that's something, you know. There are lots like us here. Old timers, o.t.'s, they call us. Permanent residents. U.S. citizens. We all gonna be buried here." He appeared to be thinking deeply as he added, "But what's wrong about that?"

The sisters ignored the question. The old man was talking to himself.

"What is wrong is to be dishonest. Earn a living with both hands, not afraid any kind of work. No other way. Everything for convenience, why not? That's frankly honest. No pretend. Love comes in the afterwards. When it comes. If it comes."

Mrs. Zafra chuckled, saying, "Ah, you're a romantic, Alipio. I must ask Carlito about you. You seem to know so much about him. I bet you were quite a . . ." she paused because what she wanted to say was "rooster," but she did not want to give the impression of over familiarity.

But Alipio interrupted her, saying, "Ask him, he will say, yes, I'm a romantic." His voice had a vibrance that was a surprise and a revelation to the visitors. He gestured as he talked, puckering his mouth every now and then, obviously to keep his dentures from slipping out. "What do you think? We were young, why not? We wowed 'em with our gallantry, with our cooking. Boy, those dames never seen anything like us. Also, we were fools, most of us, anyway. Fools on fire!"

Mrs. Zafra clapped her hands. Monica was smiling.

"Ah, but that fire is gone. Only the fool's left now," Alipio said, weakly. His voice was low and he looked tired as he passed both hands across his face. Then he lifted his head. The listening look came back to his face. Now his voice shook as he spoke again.

"Many times I wonder where are the others. Where are you? Speak to me. And I think they're wondering the same, asking the same, so I say, I'm here, your friend Alipio Palma, my leg is broken, the wife she's dead, but I'm okay. Are you okay also? The dead they can hear even they don't answer. The alive don't answer. But I know. I feel. Some okay, some not. They old now, all of us, who were very young. All over the United States. All over the world . . ."

Abruptly, he turned to Mrs. Zafra, saying, "So. You and Carlito. But Carlito he never had fire."

"You can say that again," Mrs. Zafra laughed. "It would have burned him. Can't stand it. Not Carlito. But he's a good man, I can tell you that."

"No question. Da best," Alipio conceded.

Monica had been silent, but her eyes followed every move Alipio made, straying no farther than the reach of his arms as he gestured to help make clear the intensity of his feeling.

"I'm sure you still got some of that fire," Mrs. Zafra said.

Monica gasped, but recovered quickly. Again a rush of words came from her lips as if they had been there all the time and now her sister had said something that touched off the torrent of words. Her eyes shone as in a fever as she talked.

"I don't know Carlito very well. I've not been with them long, but from what you say, from the way you talk, from what I see, the two of you are different . . ."

"Oh, maybe not," Alipio said, trying to protest, but Monica went on.

"You have strength, Mr. Palma. Strength of character. Strength in your belief in God. I admire that in a man, in a human being. Look at you. Alone. This huge table. Don't you find it too big sometimes?" Monica paused, her eyes fixed on Alipio.

"I don't eat here. I eat in the kitchen," Alipio said.

Mrs. Zafra was going to say something, but she held back. Monica was talking again.

"But it must be hard, that you cannot deny. Living from day to day. Alone. On what? Memories? Cabinets and a refrigerator full of food? I repeat, I admire you, sir. You've found your place. You're home safe. And at peace." She paused again, this time to sweep back the strand of hair that had fallen on her brow.

Alipio had a drugged look. He seemed to have lost the drift of her speech. What was she talking about? Groceries? Baseball? He was going to say, you like baseball also? You like tuna? I have all kinds of fish. Get them at bargain price from Safeway. But, obviously, it was not the proper thing to say.

"Well, I guess, one gets used to anything. Even loneliness," Monica said in a listless, dispirited tone, all the fever in her voice suddenly gone.

"God dictates," Alipio said, feeling he had found his way again and he was now on the right track. What a girl. If she had only a little more flesh. And color.

Monica leaned back on her chair, exhausted. Mrs. Zafra was staring at her in disbelief, in grievous disappointment. What happened, you were going great, what suddenly hit you that you had to stop, give up, defeated, her eyes were asking and Monica shook her head in a gesture that quite clearly said, no, I can't do it, I can't anymore, I give up.

Their eyes kept on talking a deaf-mute dialogue. Mrs. Zafra: Just when everything was going fine, you quit. We've reached this far and you quit. I could have done it my way, directly, honestly. Not that what you were doing was dishonest, you were great, and now look at that dumb expression in your eyes. Monica: I can't. I can't anymore. It's too much.

"How long have you been in the States?" Alipio asked Monica.

"For almost a year now!" Mrs. Zafra screamed and Alipio was visibly shaken, but she didn't care. This was the right moment. She would take it from here whether Monica liked it or not. She was going to do it her way. "How long exactly, let's see. Moni, when did you get your last extension?"

"Extension?" Alipio repeated the word. It had such a familiar ring like "visa" or "social security," it broke into his consciousness like a touch from Seniang's fingers. It was almost intimate. "You mean . . ."

"That's right. She's here as a temporary visitor. As a matter of fact, she came on a tourist visa. Carlito and I sponsored her coming, filed all the papers, and all she had to do was wait another year in the Philippines, but she couldn't wait. She came here as a tourist. Now she's in trouble."

"What trouble?" Alipio asked.

"She has to go back. To the Philippines. She can't stay here any longer."

"I have only two days left," Monica said, her head in her hands. "And I don't want to go back."

Alipio glanced at the wall clock. It was past three. They had been talking for hours. It was visas right from the start. Marriages. The long years and the o.t.'s. Now it was visas again. Were his ears playing a game? They might well, as they sometimes did, but his eyes surely were not. He could see this woman very plainly, sobbing on the table. She was in great trouble. Visas. Oh, oh! Now he knew what it was all about. His gleaming dentures showed a half smile. He turned to Mrs. Zafra.

"Did you come here . . ." he began, but Mrs. Zafra quickly interrupted him.

"Yes, Alipio. Forgive us. As soon as we arrived, I wanted to tell you without much talk, 'I'll tell you why we're here. I have heard about you. Not only from Carlito, but from other Filipinos who know you, how you're living here in San Francisco alone, a widower, and we heard of the accident, your stay in the hospital, when you came back, everything. Here's my sister, a teacher in the Philippines, never married, worried to death because she's being deported unless something turned up like she could marry a U.S. citizen, like I did, like your first wife Seniang, like many others have done, are doing in this exact moment, who knows? Now look at her, she's good, religious, any arrangement you wish, she'd accept it.' But I didn't have a chance. You welcomed us like old friends, relatives. Later, every time I began to say something, she interrupted me. I was afraid she had changed her mind and then she began to talk, then stopped without finishing what she really wanted to say, why we came to see you, and so forth."

"No, no!" Monica cried, raising her head, her eyes red from weeping, her face wet with tears. "You're such a good man. We couldn't do this to you. We're wrong. We started wrong. We should've been more honest, but I was ashamed, I was afraid! Let's go! Let's go!"

"Where you going?" Alipio asked.

"Anywhere," Monica answered. "Forgive us. Forgive me, Mister. Alipio."

"What's to forgive? Don't go. We have dinner. But first, *merienda*. I take *merienda*. You do also, don't you?"

The sisters exchanged glances, their eyes chattering away.

Alipio was chuckling. He wanted to say, talk of lightning striking same fellow twice, but thought better of it. A bad thing to say. Seniang was not lightning. At times only. Mostly his fault. And this girl Moni? Nice name also. How can she be lightning?

Mrs. Zafra picked up her purse and before anyone could stop her, she was opening the door. "Where's the nearest grocery store around here?" she asked, but like Pilate, she didn't wait for an answer.

"Come back, come here back, we got lotsa food," Alipio called after her, but he might just as well have been calling to the Pacific Ocean.

Mrs. Zafra took her time although the grocery store was only a few blocks away. When she returned, her arms were full of groceries in paper bags. The two met her on the porch.

"*Kumusta*," she asked, speaking for the first time in the dialect as Monica relieved her of her load. The one word question meant much more than "how are you" or "how has it been?"

Alipio replied, as always, in English. "God dictates," he said, his dentures sounding faintly as he smacked his lips, but he was not looking at the foodstuff in the paper bags Monica was carrying. His eyes were on her legs, in the direction she was taking. She knew where the kitchen was, of course. He just wanted to be sure she wouldn't lose her way. Sometimes he went to the bedroom by mistake. Lotsa things happen to men of his age.

Faith

John J. Song

I.

It's winter and the trees have raised their bare arms to the cold. The cloudless, navy-colored sky swells in stunned silence. Someone has punched the full moon to bruises, its thin blue light trims the shadows to slivers. In a warm room overlooking West Park Boulevard, Keith takes a draw off his cigarette, watching the smoke curl toward the window, toward the swollen moon, as if drawn there by the mystery of open space. His girlfriend Claudia sleeps next to him, her head wrapped in the thick ribbons of a dream, lips mouthing silent and mysterious vowels. He should be there too, at the door of a dream, poised and ready to enter. But the sudden explosive pop of bottles breaking in the distance calls him back and he thinks again of his mother. Four years since he spoke with her. Now this. She sounded so old over the phone. He wondered, listening to her speak, about who

JOHN J. SONG, born in 1968 and originally from South Korea, was raised in southern California and educated at the University of California, Berkeley. A poet and fiction writer, he is "most interested in the continuing evolution of Asian American identity —the clashes/hybrids between and within cultures and ethnicities, generations, and sensibilities." This is his first fiction publication.

she was and who she had become; the years of quiet acquiescence to his father's intractable authority; the quiet, measured cadence of her voice sounding somewhat like wisdom but not wisdom. Her voice tempered by the expectation of no apologies. She told him tonight, almost apologetically, that her once aristocratic face was losing value; creasing, she said with an inspired and regretful laugh, like paper money. She wove Korean words into her speech and called him by his Korean name, Ki Young. He recalled, in that moment, the simple pleasure of his mother's smooth, familiar voice, the intimacy of his name spoken with his mother's fluid inflections; he recalled her storyteller's voice, the way it would unfold drama and humor, exposing always some moral at the center. "Your father has passed away," she told him. In Korean: *Your father has gone to return to where he came from.* Her voice was flat.

Keith pulls back the covers and climbs back into bed. Reaching for the familiar scar on Claudia's right hip, just below the elastic of her underpants, he pushes the elastic down an inch and fingers the jagged line, trying to fuse the smooth angles of once-broken skin into memory. This is the world as it turns blue: blue like the inside of a saxophone, or the bottom of a vase; blue like a slow, drowning river, or the scribbled lines of one's own veins, ordered even in the appearance of disorder. Blue like memory, like faith. He lifts the folds of her long hair and kisses the back of her neck, her beauty spot. He searches for what he loves, the subtle and distinctive female odor of her body, the alkaline bitterness of her hair. The way she burrows her body into his, her rear cased into the hollow of his body, her body producing such heat even as it sleeps. He ignores the tingling in his arm as it numbs beneath Claudia's sleeping hair, drawn instead to the even rhythm of her chest doing its tireless business of breathing, her heart pulsing and pulsing.

II.

His mother wept quietly on the phone, happy to hear Keith's voice. She told him that it had been too long since she had last seen him, that her life had become mournful, nothing but gardening and reading books and going to church. "Life has proven to be sorrowful," she said. It has always been that way, Keith thought, in the silence that followed; his mother's basic understanding of life began with the acceptance of some kind of loss. Not loss as sorrow so much as surrender. Korean people, his mother used to say, have always undergone *ghoseng*—struggle, hardship. Koreans have had to keep a very wise sense of resignation in order to survive. After all, she would say, how else to know the true depth of good fortune but by testing first the depth of struggle? So Keith's mother believed that one must barter for things, constantly surrender one thing for the other. Keith has always hated this about his mother the most.

Eyes closed and moving towards sleep, Keith dreams again about his mother and father: The day he leaves to join Claudia at her new job in Sacramento. He has stopped by his parents' house to say goodbye. He sees it unfold as if watching from a neighbor's window. But Keith is also acting in it, and he sees himself with the disembodied and clairvoyant vision of the dreamer: *It's overcast and father is wearing a blue parka and slippers; a cigaret dangles from his mouth. Mother wears her red wool melton coat and pink sweatpants. I tell them that Sacramento is a temporary situation—something to see if Claudia and I can make it. But we all seem to understand; we recognize the thickness of the moment, even as we refuse to name it. Mother senses the truth deepest, even more, perhaps than me: This will be the last time. When she kisses me goodbye, she weeps, pats my hands over and over again, praising them. She says that I have beautiful hands, that she knew it would be that way, that between me and Ji Min, I was the one who had learned how to pray, the hyoja—filial son—who had learned what a rosary was and how to hold it; she says that between the thin, zippered fingers of my praying hands, God has passed a thousand blessings.*

Sleep exposes this memory with the clarity of the frozen image, like a slide held up to the sunlight. Keith sees in his mother's face the premonition of aging and loneliness. Whose he can't say. Keith's father will miss him. They hug awkwardly and shake hands. Mr. Lee tells Keith to call when he gets to Sacramento. "Don't forget to call Mr. Kim," his father says, one last time, "he can get you a job at his company." Keith nods his head and settles into his car. As he drives away, the two figures of his mother and father stand framed in the rear view mirror, his father with his arm around his mother. He wants at that moment to stop and take his mother with him. But he waves his arm instead and honks as he takes the slow curve of the street like he has a hundred times before, but then he disappears from view for the last time.

Keith's mother lives by faith. *Rely on God.* It's easy to have faith when things are going well; it's when God steps away that faith is tested. Over her cheap cordless telephone, his mother told him that she still believes in heaven, still believes that when the family has all passed, they will meet again in a white room where there will be chairs with their names on them—his, Ji Min's, father's, and her's. There, the rough splinters of their lives will heal themselves into a perfect and holy thing, the reunion gleaming with the sanctity of God's fulfilled promises. It will happen, she says.

Keith had learned early, it was true, what a rosary was and how to hold it. It was his sister, his elder by eighteen minutes, that had shown him how to hold the beads between forefinger and thumb. Let the small wooden crucifix of the rosary hang elegantly from the hands. Rock slightly when saying the Our Father and the Hail Mary. They had both learned, from the nuns at St. Martha's Catholic School, the Seven Sacraments, the Fourteen Stations of the Cross, and Keith kneeled, crying, on a flat tray of uncooked rice in the corner of the classroom, until he learned the Apostles' Creed the way it was meant to be said, with pious faith and conviction; they learned that bread and wine could become flesh and blood, that Ash Wednesday meant a cross fingered on their forehead by Father Killian, Immaculate Conception meant no school, and free-dress days meant any shirt with a collar, except red shirts, because red was the color of the devil.

Keith learned, for the first time, how to speak his name in public, *Ki Young*, before it was changed to Keith. It was in second grade, the first day at St. Martha's. Keith was sent to Sister Nieves' class. Ji Min was not there, placed instead with Sister Josephina, the better to make new friends. It was religion hour and everyone stared. He could remember how small he felt in his new black corduroys, his starched white shirt. Sister Nieves smiled and took his hand, and sat him in the rear of the class near the windows. Speaking an english that did not sound like real english, but like the kind the Mexicans who lived next door spoke, more musical and full of words he did not know, Sister Nieves told him to stand up and say his name to the class. She said, "This is Ki Young Lee," and it was strange because he had never heard it pronounced that way, formally, out loud in a public space, with everybody watching and waiting for him to follow. He was frightened, made mute by the strangeness of his own name, pronounced hard and garbled, not at all like how mother said it, or father, or Ji Min. Sister Nieves wrote his name on the board, *Ki Young* ahead of *Lee*, instead of how he said it at home, *Lee Ki Young*. Everyone waited for him to say his name. He heard laughter then. He tried hard to sound his name the way that father had taught him, trying to keep in mind how he had told him, "Don't let the kids laugh at you." But he couldn't do it, he was not in that word that Sister Nieves spoke; the letters written on the blackboard spelled his name but did not call him. He sat down then, and his body shook but he did not cry.

III.

Every day, Mrs. Lee prays for her children, Keith and Ji Min. She prays that Keith is kind and considerate, a good provider; she prays that he has not forgotten the rosary, the awesome power of faith and the wrath of God. She prays for his health and his happiness with Claudia. She and her husband did not give their blessings to Keith's life with Claudia, not because they sleep together unmarried but because Claudia is a Chicana. To Mr. Lee, this was worse than betrayal, more than just a choice or an act of independence—it was willful destruction, an annihilation of familial history. With one act, the long line of ancestral faces would begin losing its definition, and the exquisite calligraphy of names would cease living. But Mrs. Lee knows otherwise; this is the real price of America—that to gain one thing is to lose something else. The rhythm of America is change: something new and dangerous every day. It is both a taunt and a test. Mrs. Lee knows that her life in America is a kind of test, that her situation now is a kind of test, that to lose Ji Min is a test, and that only God is permanent in a world of impermanence. So she prays for Keith's happiness now, afraid that she in some way will lose him too. Keith knows that deep down, his mother still hopes that he will one day marry a Korean woman, and she tells her close friends about him, her son, how he could match up with their daughter, or so-and-so's sister, cousin, niece.

But Mrs. Lee saves her rosaries for Ji Min. The one who came first, whose womb will never round into motherhood, shy daughter forever lost—the unhappy one who opened her arms to the waters beneath the Golden Gate and swam away like a fish. To Mrs. Lee, between absence and memory comes faith. She prays that out of faith will come God's forgiveness, that He will not forsake Ji Min, her only daughter. She prays too that God will open her own eyes, allow her to see the world so she might come to understand her daughter. So Mrs. Lee mumbles her Hail Marys in a quiet, song-like whisper in the darkened pews at the back of the church. Every Wednesday afternoon, she takes the bus to St. John the Baptist's, where they held Ji Min's memorial service, and lights votive candles, asking Mary the Mother of Jesus to allow Ji Min into that whitened room, allow her to sit in that pearled chair with her name on it, where she can face God and plead innocence.

IV.

I carry my sister's ghost around like a shadow. It's sleep that pumps blood into memory, warms it to life: that's when Ji Min appears so clearly that I can almost touch her, smell her humanness. The outlines are as recognizable as my own—my body is her body, shadows identical. Usually, it's Ji Min who calls first, as if impatient for me to reach her. She waits until sleep dissolves my body then enters stealthily, unannounced, the same way that father would enter her darkened room at the end of the hallway, or the overgrown arbor in the corner of the backyard where we would sometimes play. I do not know when she will appear, only that she will. So I prepare, make myself clean. And always, she comes. Wordless, she tells me things; we share the same stories.

When we were young, mother and father built a Japanese garden in the backyard of our small house in Walnut Hills. Together, Ji Min and I remember the backyard in great detail: the horsetail planted around the koi pond, the articulate branches of crafted pine balanced by a thin grove of bamboo, the juniper garden and African lilies anchored by broad, flat stones. On the arbor, jasmine and wisteria tumbled over the latticed trellis, and in early spring the scent of blossoms would overpower you. One could sit on the small redwood bench and forget oneself, surrender completely. It was mother's favorite space, her special project. It was this garden that made us feel like we were getting somewhere in this country, moving up in life. Tending a garden meant having time; it meant having the money to purchase plants, tools, fertilizers, pots.

Ji Min and I liked the pond best; this was the special place where we would sit and talk, sister to brother. Twin to twin. It was in these moments, I sometimes recall, that Ji Min's movements seemed most natural, most at ease with herself. The tight fist of her speech would unpack itself then, her body no longer stiff, her face calm and polished. Tonight, in my dream, we are thirteen again. It's late summer, and the sun has already set behind the hillside, smearing the sky red and orange. Ji Min sits with her feet in the pond, the koi nuzzling up to her feet, her toes. I'm sitting next to her, cross-legged, listening to her and watching the fish. She slaps at the water lightly with her feet, scattering the koi with a roiling rush. "Remember what mom said about the koi?" she asks. " 'Strive to live like the koi, slide through the tangles gracefully, swim clear of mud; be proud but simple.' " She slaps at the water with her feet again. "That's not possible, Ki Young. Sometimes you have to be mean. Mom taught us good but she didn't teach us everything."

For one of the few times between us, I do not know what to say. She tells me that something has happened to her body, that even though she's okay, something has changed her. Though I say I do, I do not understand.

"Don't say anything," she says, getting up. "Don't even tell mom."

"What are you talking about?" I ask, pressing her.

"Nothing. Nothing at all."

Through the blue hallways of memory, another dream approaches, new yet familiar. It comes to me as if from the dark corners of shared experience. It pulls heavily at the bottom of my stomach like a wide, powerful current threatening to sweep me away.

It's autumn, sister, and you're sitting on the wide front porch of the old house we used to live in when we first came to America. The house looks the same, sad and tired, and the large chestnut tree that shades the lawn has dropped its prickly husks, scattering them like sea urchins on an ocean floor. It's Halloween, and you are maybe eleven or twelve. Mother is gone and I am also not present. You and father are going to carve pumpkins for the front porch. You spread some newspaper across the kitchen table and father sets a fat, ripe pumpkin on it. He inserts a knife through the top of the pumpkin and circles out an opening. He pulls the top off by the stem. He makes you laugh by wearing the orange crown on his head, not caring about the orange threads tangling in his hair. He plunges his hands in the bright pumpkin and scoops out a fistful of orange mash and wet seeds. He smiles and takes your hands, guiding them into the pumpkin. His fingers weave and squish playfully with yours and you are both laughing. Slowly, he eases behind you and gently encloses you with his arms. With his left hand, he grips both of your slender wrists and mashes them greedily along the inside of the pumpkin, the way a pig roots in wet earth. Father makes you laugh again. With his other hand, he takes a fistful of seeds and pumpkin mash and splatters it on the table. His mouth at your ear, he whispers that the seeds are good for roasting. Then he begins to lick your earlobe, sticks his tongue into your ear. The smile on your face is anxious, tentative. You grimace and shudder as he licks the seeds and ripeness from his fingers. You feel the power of his thighs against your backside, the bent knees trapping you, and the urgency of his attention. He kisses your neck and pulls down your pants with the wet hand, slimy still, and places it on tender spots

*that he has touched only through your clothes. His fingers run their
course until they find the small opening of your sex.*

This the beginning.

Still yet, another story, this time we are eleven. Father is still at
work, staying late at the store. Ji Min and mother fight, yelling at each
other, both of them accusers, both crying. Mother locks herself in the
bathroom; I can hear the sound of water running. Ji Min is in her
room, and the door is also locked. I kneel on the floor outside, the
rough shag of the carpet against my face, as I try to peer under the
crack of the door, calling out, "Let me in, Ji Min, let me in." I cannot
get small enough to see her. I want at that moment to flatten myself
into a thin envelope, a small package with a message inside—come
out, sister, come out and speak to me. I sit outside Ji Min's room until
father wakes me and sends me back to my own room. Ji Min, you do
not wake up for breakfast. That day, I go to school alone.

V.

Keith awakes and reaches for a cigaret. It is just before dawn and
the sky is lightening in streaks of peach and yellow. He sways under
the weight of memory. The smoke from his cigaret curls like a
questionmark. He tries to forget, then tries to remember, unsure of
what is memory and what is dreams. Memories of dreams and dreams
of memories: they keep coming, scattering through his head like restless children at morning recess, this way, that way. His father has
passed away. But he had left Keith's life long ago, expelled from
Keith's life the same way that Ji Min was once expelled from the
history of their family. Her ghost was kept waiting, silent as a coffin;
his father had learned to forget or refused to remember. Last night,
his mother mentioned that it was not that his father didn't want to
remember, but that he didn't know how to remember. Keith wonders
if his mother has recited any prayers for his father, and whether his
story too, will gather dust. Keith looks at Claudia, her back turned to
him in sleep, and wonders what he will tell his mother. Will she come

to see them? He doesn't know; the Holy Spirit has yet to make a believer out of him. *God is less reliable than memory.* Turning toward the bed once again, he reaches for Claudia, pulls her close to him and holds her. He ignores the sun rising in the corner of the window and closes his eyes. Everything evaporates and all he feels is Claudia breathing, her chest rising and falling.

Alien Relative

An Outtake from The Kitchen God's Wife

Amy Tan

I was there at San Francisco Airport when Helen arrived in this country from Formosa. That was in 1956, maybe sooner than that. In any case, back then she was called Hulan, "Lake Mist." She said her mother named her that because she came into this world like the Queen of Clouds rising from the water at dawn. But I think Helen just made that up. I think probably her mother called her that because she was born already crying a lake of tears.

As I was saying, I was there at the airport with my husband and children, waiting for Hulan to come, this woman I call sister, although

AMY TAN was born in Oakland, California, in 1952. Her father immigrated to America in 1947. Her mother came to the United States in 1949, shortly before the Communists seized control of Shanghai; she was forced to leave behind three daughters from a previous marriage. Tan's first book, *The Joy Luck Club*, was a finalist for both the National Book Award and the National Book Critics' Circle Award. It has been translated into nineteen languages, including Chinese, and has been made into a film by director Wayne Wang. Her second novel, *The Kitchen God's Wife*, became a bestseller nationally and internationally shortly after publication. She is also the author of a children's book, *The Moon Lady*, and is currently at work on a third book, *The Year of No Flood*.

she is no such thing. I just said that for the Immigration officials, so I could sponsor her—also because I owed Hulan a debt I had to repay. She helped me leave my first marriage, that time I was married to a bad man. Actually, she did not really help help, only promised not to interfere. In China, that was almost like helping. As for myself, I really did help Hulan. I helped her come to this country. In America, that meant I had to interfere.

"Hey!" I called when I saw Hulan come out of the Customs swinging door, her face bouncing up and down in the crowd. And just like her name, she had mist in her eyes, crying so hard she couldn't see us. It was seven years since the last time I saw her, but she looked as if it had been twice as long, she was so old. Her hair was unstylish, same as always, only now it was hanging down just like a washerwoman's, no curly parts to frame her round face. And she wore an ugly fur coat, the skins bent all stiff to pieces, like an old dead dog dried out on the road. So of course I didn't recognize it, my mink coat, I mean, the same one I loaned her in Shanghai last time I saw her, when I was still dreaming I could buy ten just like it in my rich new American home. Oh, I was mad when I found out later that her ruined coat was mine!

But, as I was saying, that day at the airport, at the Customs door, our whole family was happy to welcome her—her husband and her children, too. I was standing on my tiptoes, holding my young daughter's hand. Actually, I squeezed Pearl's hand too hard. I didn't mean to, of course, but then, with so much waiting and excitement, and then to finally see Hulan, my old friend who knew all the troubles of my life—well, how did I know what I had done until Pearl screamed, "Let me go, Mommy, let me go!" In front of all those people, she said that. All my life, it seems, Pearl's been saying the same thing. Let me go.

Anyway, we were there, only a few faces away, and still Hulan couldn't see us. Of course she couldn't—she didn't have her glasses on. So my husband, Johnny, lifted our four-year-old son high in the air to call Hulan's attention our way. And little Samuel shouted, "Whoa, horsey! Whoa!" and waved three cowboy hats, two white, one black, two for boys, one for girl, because that's how many children

Hulan had. Finally Hulan saw us, and cried back, "Brother! Sister!" I think she called us that just in case the Immigration officials were watching.

She pushed her way through the crowd. Her husband, Henry, came next, just like a person still dream-walking, not believing he was really here. He was holding the baby, Bao-bao Roger. Then came Ming-fei Mary, so small for eight years old . . . then two suitcases . . . one box . . . no more.

Right away I noticed: Only two children, why not three? Where was their middle child, the son who was six years old?

"Feng-yi Frank, where is he?" I asked, still looking.

"Oh, he is coming," Hulan answered slowly, "only later."

Johnny and I looked behind her, thinking she meant one minute later. Then one minute later, when we were still waiting and looking, Henry finally explained it this way: "The money you sent for five tickets, later it was enough for only four."

And still we didn't understand, until Hulan began to cry in a scared way. "You already did so much. How could we ask for more?" Then Henry sat down on a suitcase and covered his face. And Ming-fei Mary started wailing. And little Bao-bao saw all this, turned his mouth down, and cried loud, too.

So that's how we found out: They left Feng-yi behind. Too polite to ask for more money! Too polite to let their middle son come to America! Oh, isn't that the Chinese way—to make all that pain seem like just a small inconvenience?

That day at the airport I can never forget. We were all standing together at last, so many happy people rushing by us. My heart hurt, filled with Hulan's troubles, my stomach ached, mixed with my own anger. I wanted to shout at Hulan, "So stupid! So stupid!" Because I was remembering how much we too had suffered. How Johnny worked overtime, one-dollar-eighty-five for an hour, stacking boxes weekends and nights. How I always bought the fatty pork, twenty cents' saving here and there. How I scolded Pearl so hard for one sock missing, until she shouted, "Leave me alone," and I left her with a big slap mark on her face instead. All those sacrifices to bring so much unhappiness to America!

Of course, we tried to send for Feng-yi right away, as soon as we had more money. But then we found out: no applications for nephews, ten-years waiting list for sons, but first you must be a citizen, no breaking the rules. So, it was seven years more before Hulan and Henry received their citizenship papers, four years more before they were brave enough to tell the authorities, "We have another son." Eleven years altogether before they finally got Feng-yi Frank back. And telling it this way, I make it sound simple.

Anyway, that was long time ago, more than twenty years gone by, all those troubles now forgotten. Today Hulan's an American. Now days she calls herself Helen. Now she thinks life is so easy, doing everything the American way. Like what she said yesterday. I was complaining about my daughter, Pearl, how she never comes to visit, how she never tells me anything over the phone, just, "Oh, Mom, we're fine, don't worry."

And Helen said, "You want her to visit you more often, it's easy. You invite her to your house. That's the American way. These days, kids don't drop in, drop out. You have to ask. Come on this date, such-and-such a time. Like an appointment, see, easy to make."

And I wanted to tell Helen: Easy? You don't remember? It's not so easy to claim back your child.

I was with her, standing in long lines at the Department of Justice. You think Hulan could speak up for herself, a mother who left her son behind? So I came along to use the American rules to push us through first one line then another, one place to get forms, one place to ask questions.

Finally we found the right line, but the woman authority acted like she was too busy stamping official documents—toong! toong!—oh yes, what she was doing was more important than us. Helen pushed forward the application, the one that said, "Petition for Alien Relative." I whispered to Helen from behind, "Talk, talk, tell her your situation."

"I came to this country," Helen began, "but forgot my son."

"Forgot?" the woman said, still stamping, not even looking up. "How can you forget a son?"

"No, no! I can never forget my son," Hulan said, leaning back, scared. "This is not what I meant." The woman authority now looked at Hulan. Hulan looked at me. And I knew what she wanted to say, all those things she told me at her kitchen table these past eleven years. So I stepped to the counter and I told the Immigration authority how this could happen, how you can lose a child, and really, this was nobody's fault.

They were sitting in a courtyard in Formosa, Henry and Hulan, when our telegram came. They took it inside their room, so the neighbors could not see, these strangers who envied you if you had even one grain of rice more. But already, people were whispering, "Overseas! They got a telegram from overseas!"

Hulan dried their hands, it was so steamy hot that day. Then carefully, so carefully, she used a small knife to cut open the envelope and read our one-page message, the words we tried to say clearly, so there would be no delay: "The Red Cross, the church sponsor, all of us are saying to come now, come through. There is an opening. The money is being wired to you."

They walked out of their room, into the courtyard. They looked at their neighbors, who were by their doors watching. Hulan had waited for the day she could do this. "Soon this room will be available," she announced, just like a victor. "We are moving to America!"

Then came the first problem. Their daughter had a TB test, and it said maybe the TB was active, maybe not. In any case, Ming-fei Mary couldn't leave. So they gave an official some of their plane ticket money to say it was not, and later it really turned out it was not. "But in those days," Helen argued with me later, "who knew which way things would go for you without paying a price?"

Now they had only enough money to buy four plane tickets. They didn't think ahead that this would happen, that's how it is when you are scared. So Henry said, "We should write to Winnie and Johnny, ask them for more money."

But Hulan said, "They will think we were careless! Besides, too much time will be wasted before they can answer us yes or no." Because they both knew: In Formosa, wait too long and you can lose your chance forever. Just that day, they had heard it on the radio: at a black-market booth, hundreds of people had pushed and shoved, shouted and fought—then fourteen people were hurt, two people crushed—over one special visa to America, which turned out to be illegal.

For two days and two nights, they argued and cried, deciding what to do. Hulan even tried to sell the mink coat, the same one I gave her before I left China. But then the pawnshop man told Hulan the coat was dirty, trying to bargain her down. So Hulan washed that mink coat with soap and water, washed it until there was nothing left to sell. After that, Henry decided what to do.

"I will stay," he said. "You and the children, you go first." He was once a military official. He knew how to be brave like that, ordering his family to a second-place victory.

But Hulan scolded him bitterly, "What good is a family in America with no father to feed them? I will stay."

Then Henry shouted, "Crazy woman! No mother to guide her children to the right opportunities? You want them to become wild Americans? We are all staying then."

That evening they felt too sick to eat. They lay wide awake on their bed, grieving silently over the opportunity they could no longer use. Then they looked at their three sleeping children, crowded on another bed in the same room, two boys, one girl, growing bigger every day. I have done the same with my own children, so I know. And seeing this, all their anger turned to grief. Because at that moment, as with every moment, neighbors were arguing: "That's my pot! Who said you can use it to cook your smelly food!" Then more people were shouting, "Your food stinks worse!" Every day they heard this, the cursing and shouting, accusing and pleading. They were listening to all this hopelessness coming from rooms filled with people who had once been so rich and powerful in different parts of China, and were now the same kind of poor in one courtyard in Formosa.

In the middle of the night, when the courtyard was finally quiet, Hulan and Henry rose from the bed and went outside. They sat on the ground, looked at the sky, but not at each other.

Hulan spoke first: "Ming-fei's health, it's always been poor."

Then Henry said, "And little Bao-bao—so helpless! Only one year old."

After that they were silent for a long time. The night was black, no stars, no moon. They heard no crickets, felt no cooling wind. Finally Hulan spoke in a trembly voice.

"Yesterday afternoon I saw Feng-yi holding a cocoon in his hand. Just like this, so softly. He was blowing his breath on it, thinking this would make the butterfly pop out and play."

"Six years old, and already so clever," said Henry.

"So patient, so playful," Hulan said, now starting to cry.

"Strong," said Henry, then more loudly, "and obedient, too."

"Our favorite," Hulan whispered in a hoarse voice, "and he knows this, too. Old enough to never forget us."

That morning, Hulan grasped her middle child to her heart and promised him, "I will never forget you, never lose you." And Feng-yi smiled, not knowing what she meant.

In the evening, they took Feng-yi to visit his grandmother. Actually, she was not the real grandmother but a bondservant who married Henry's father after the real grandmother died. In any case, the old lady was glad to take in the little boy. Although, after she put the boy to bed, she scolded Hulan and Henry: "Leaving China was bad enough. Now you're going to America, where it is even worse. What will become of us Chinese people?" They went to the airport that night, when Feng-yi was already dreaming.

On the airplane, they practiced everything about the new country in their minds. They imagined a large Immigration official greeting them with pale eyes and a sly mouth, smiling and encouraging them, "Say anything. In our country, you are free to say anything. Do you love our government?"

"Yes," they practiced saying in English. "We love America, very, very much, more than China, more than Formosa."

And then they imagined this pale-eyed man asking them more questions, trickier ones: "Then where is your other son, the one on this document? Why did you leave him behind? Is he a Communist spy?"

"Oh no, not a spy, just a little boy. He loves America, too."

"Then why didn't you bring him?"

"He was sick, too sick to come."

"I see, and the rest of you, did you bring this same sickness here?"

"Actually he is not sick, nobody is. It's just that we didn't have the money to bring him. This is the truth, only that reason, no money."

"What! You came to our country with not enough money? You came here to beg? Police! Police!"

Before they landed, the visa papers with their names had one name crossed out. I always thought that was a bad-luck thing to do, crossing Feng-yi's name out, like wishing he would be banished from the world—which, of course, is what happened four months later.

I read the letter in Hulan's kitchen. That grandmother, who was not even the real grandmother, wrote to say she was returning to China. "Fukkien food is bad for the stomach," she wrote. "I would rather die in Shanghai than live in Formosa. No more running away. We are going home, Feng-yi and I."

"Henry did this!" cried Hulan. "I insisted I should be the one to stay, Feng-yi should go. Now look what's happened!"

"I said we all should stay," Henry shouted back. "But you! You were dreaming of American cars, a car we could drive back to Formosa to fetch Feng-yi back!"

Day after day, year after year, we heard them arguing like that. I used to sit in Hulan's kitchen. So many times I had to watch the steam rise from her cook pot, the mist clouding her eyes, while she whispered to me—every birthday, every festival day, every time I brought my same-age daughter to her house—how she would never forget him.

Let me tell you, that little boy, Feng-yi, none of us could forget him. For so many years we could not see him. We could not hear him. We could not write to him. He was just a little boy, living in Red China, cut off from the world. But I remember, it was just like he was living in Hulan's kitchen all those years, shouting back, as powerful as any angry ghost.

"My sister, she only forgot to claim her son on the paper," I explained to the Immigration authority. "Now do you understand?"

The authority was not smiling. She said, "Then here's what you should do."

For her forgetfulness, Hulan and Henry had to hire an expensive immigration lawyer. The lawyer they found in the Yellow Pages was

Chinese but born in this country. Hulan didn't listen when I told her, "A Chinese name doesn't mean Chinese thinking."

Sure enough, this lawyer said—in English—that we needed proof, "a birth certificate," to show this Alien Relative on the application paper had a true relationship with his mother.

"In China," I told the lawyer carefully, "you don't need a certificate to be born. See, when a baby is born, if he is crying, this is proof he is born live. If a woman sacrifices her own breast to feed him, this is proof she is his mother. Okay?"

"What you need," the lawyer said to Hulan, "is an affidavit witnessed by a notary public, signed by witnesses who knew you in China when your son was born."

Hulan shook her head quickly and said, "All those people are dead." But what she really meant was, "All those people are scared to death." Who would be willing to sign an official document when they had their own problems to hide? Maybe they were renting a room for two, when they really had eight or ten people living inside. Maybe they told the officials they were working one job, nine-to-five, but it was really three jobs—graveyard, overtime, weekends—and who knew if all that extra work was illegal to do. In any case, why should anyone lift a hand to help only to have it chopped off?

"Chinese people always help each other out," said the lawyer.

Lucky for Hulan, I remembered Old Auntie Du, her aunt married to her father's brother from long time ago. And this old aunt, over seventy years old, knew she would die soon anyway.

"They can kick me out of this country, okay!" laughed Auntie Du. "Send me back to China, doesn't matter. Anyway, I want to be buried there."

Old Auntie Du signed the affidavit, and she told the notary public several times, "I was right there. These two eyes, these two hands—right there inspecting the cord that tied mother to son, son to mother. Write that down."

Six months later, Feng-yi Frank, the Alien Relative on the petition, arrived at the airport. We were there, at the Customs swinging door, same as in 1956, only now it was 1967. Henry brought his never-forgotten son a cowboy hat. Samuel and Pearl brought their new cousin Silly Putty and a water pistol. And Hulan, I remember, she brought her dreams. Her face had two dark spots under her eyes, two hungry hollows in her cheeks. So many nights of dreaming awake!

I saw how her eyes grew big with hope, staring at each little boy who walked through the Customs door. Her feet were ready to run toward this one—then that one—here, no, over there!

I was the first to know it was Feng-yi Frank standing in front of us. And Hulan was right, when she left her son, he was old enough never to forget. He stared right at his mother, nobody else. That's when Helen's eyes looked up, turned scared, searching for her memory.

His smooth, plump chin, the one she used to lift to her face to kiss, now it pointed down at her, rough and bony hard. His soft little hands, the ones that reached up to her, demanding to be held, now they held tight onto two boxes tied with string, and he didn't even put them down when Hulan hugged him American-style.

But his eyes—they had changed the most, she whispered to me later. Not curious, not eager, never looking back or farther ahead. He seemed to see only what was in front of him, and he showed no opinion in his eyes about any of it. That son, already seventeen years old when he arrived, never let his mother forget what she had done.

Maybe I should have felt more sorry for Hulan. But then I thought, She never told Feng-yi she was sorry. I heard what she said: how Formosa, then America, then China were the reasons for the long delay. "How could I fight three countries?" she told him at the beginning. Later, she bragged about all her hardships to bring him over: "Lawyers, money, affidavit—more complicated than you think!"

Now Feng-yi is an American, life is so easy. He tells everyone to call him Frank. He is almost forty, same as my daughter, Pearl. He lives with his mother and father. Lucky he still has a living father, not like my children. Every evening he has dinner at home, so polite, saying thank you, no thanks when his mother says, "Eat more, eat more!" At night he goes to his job as a security guard, signing people in, signing people out. And when he gets up late in the afternoon, he smokes too many cigarettes, or plays video games on his TV set, or lies underneath an old greasy car and sings to its stomach, "How much is that doggie in the window, the one with the waggle-ly tail."

An American lady from our church once asked Frank, "What was it like living in China, aren't you so glad to be here?" And Frank said, "China wasn't too bad, just boring, same old clothes, nothing to do. Oh, and they didn't let you have pets."

Helen then told that church lady how much Frank always wanted a dog. And that's what he got, a fancy poodle dog, for his twenty-fifth birthday. Puffy head, puffy tail. I tell you this, though, that dog, all those years, lived outside on a cold little porch, because Helen didn't want it to messy up her house. And I saw that dog every time I went to visit—I saw it through the sliding glass door. It was matted and dirty, so skinny, shaking and dancing in a circle every time he saw Frank come home. But Frank didn't even look at that doggie in the window. Although sometimes he still sang that same song, the one with the waggle-ly tail.

I heard Helen complain only one time, about her son, I mean. We were watching Frank, and Frank was watching cars race round and round on the TV set. He sat up, he sat back, he shook his fist and shouted, "Go, you sonabitch, go!" That's when Helen whispered to me, "Look what the Communists did to my son."

I still see Helen almost every day. But she doesn't tell me her troubles. She doesn't cry in her kitchen. She doesn't take my advice anymore. Now she thinks she's giving me advice, helping me. Like the other day. We were sitting in her kitchen, near the sliding glass door. I was watching her dog lying outside, so sad. She was telling me how I should call Pearl.

"Make her some Chinese dumplings," Helen said. "Invite her to come eat. She eats your food, she's just like your little girl again, thanking her mommy."

I pretended not to listen. What does she know? Why should I let her interfere? So instead I told her, "That poodle dog looks sick, real bad."

And she said, "Oh, that dog's okay. It's just old."

The next day that dog died. I was in Helen's kitchen a few days after it happened. I didn't say anything about the dog that was no longer there. I didn't tell Helen how I made the dumplings, how Pearl didn't come. We were just sitting and drinking tea, same as always. Then Helen started to scratch her ankles, then her legs, until she cried out, "Why are those fleas still pinching me? That dog's already dead!"

And I didn't explain to her, because I know how Helen has become. She doesn't understand, not anymore, how something can still hurt you after it's gone.

Untitled Story

from *Selected Stories*

Jose Garcia Villa

1

FATHER DID NOT UNDERSTAND MY LOVE FOR VI, so Father sent me to America to study away from her. I could not do anything and I left.

2

I was afraid of my father.

JOSE GARCIA VILLA was born in Manila, Philippines, circa 1911. A legendary poet, editor, and fiction writer, he has been a seminal influence on many poets in the Philippines and has edited several anthologies of Philippine poets under his nom de plume, "Doveglion." He has lived in America for over fifty years, and is the recipient of numerous grants and awards, including Guggenheim, Rockefeller, and Bollingen Foundation fellowships, as well as a Philippines Cultural Heritage Award and an American Academy of Arts and Letters Award. An associate editor at New Directions Books from 1949 to 1951, he has had poetry and short stories anthologized widely and studied throughout the world—from *Best American Short Stories of 1932* to the more recent *Language and Composition* and *Elements of Writing*. Published extensively in the Philippines, his works in the United States include a collection of fiction, *Footnote to Youth*, and poetry, *Have Come, Am Here* and *Selected Poems and New*.

3

On the boat I was seasick and I could not eat. I thought of home and my girl and I had troubled dreams.

4

The blue waves in the young sunlight were like azure dancing flowers but they danced ceaselessly to the tune of the sun, to look at them made me dizzy. Then I would go to my cabin and lie down and sometimes I cried.

5

We were one month at sea. When I arrived in America I was lonely.

6

I window-shopped at Market Street in San Francisco and later when I was in Los Angeles I went to Hollywood but I remained lonely.

7

I saw President Hoover's home in Palo Alto but I did not care for President Hoover.

8

In California too I saw a crippled woman selling pencils on a sidewalk. It was night and she sat on the cold concrete like an old hen but she had no brood. She looked at me with dumb faithful eyes.

9

The Negro in the Pullman hummed to himself. At night he prepared our berths and he was automatic like a machine. As I looked at him I knew I did not want to be a machine.

10

In the university where I went there were no boys yet. It was only August and school would not begin until September. The university was on a hill and there the winds blew strong. In my room at night I could hear the winds howling like helpless young puppies. The winds were little blind dogs crying for their mother.

11

Where was the mother of the winds? I lay in bed listening to the windchildren crying for their mother but I would fall asleep before their mother had returned to them.

12

During the day the little blind puppies did not whimper much. It was only at night they grew afraid of the dark and then they cried for their mother. Did their mother ever come to them? Maybe their mother had a lover and she loved this lover more than the little blind puppies.

13

I had nothing to do and I wrote home to my friends but my friends did not write to me.

14

One day a boy knocked at my room. He was young and he said he was alone and wanted to befriend me. He became dear to me.

15

The boy's name was David. He was poor and he wore slovenly clothes but his eyes were soft. He was like a young flower.

16

When David was sick I watched over him.

17

Afterwards David would not go anywhere without me.

18

Of nights David and I would walk through the streets and he would recite poetry to me.

> *"Sunset and evening star*
> *And one clear call for me . . ."*

This was the slowness of David, the slowness of the sunset, of the evening star.

19

One night David came to me and said he was returning home the next morning. He could not earn enough money on which to go to school.

I died in myself.

After David had gone I walked the streets feeling I had lost a great, great something. When I thought of him it hurt very much.

School opened in September. At my table in the dining hall we were eight. I liked Georgia, Aurora, Louise and Greg. There was another girl and her name was Reynalda but she was a little haughty.

The boys were Joe and Wiley. Joe came from David's town and when I asked him about David he said they had been like Jonathan and David in high school. Joe loved David and David, who was far away now, became a bond between Joe and me.

Sometimes Joe and I got sore at each other but when we thought of David we became friends again.

Joe wanted to become a preacher and Wiley would be a sports editor. I did not know what I wanted to be. First when I was a boy I wanted to be a movie actor but later I did not want to be a movie actor. I wanted to paint but Father objected to it because he said painters did not make much money.

26

Father was a moneymaker. When he had made it he did not want to spend it. When I needed money I went to my mother and she gave it to me because she was not a moneymaker.

27

Then I fell in love with Georgia. Georgia had golden hair and I became enamored of it. In my country all the girls were blackhaired. I asked Georgia to let me feel her hair and when I ran my fingers through it I became crazy about her.

28

Georgia and I went running around. Afterwards she wrote me love letters.

29

In one letter she called me My Lord, in another Beloved. But I called her just Georgia although sometimes I called her Georgie. When I called her Georgie I smiled because it was like a boy's name.

30

One day Georgia and I quarrelled and many nights thereafter I walked the streets muttering to myself. I did not know what I was saying. I called myself, "You . . ." but the sentence did not get finished. I would look at the sky and behold the stars and talk to myself.

31

One night I stopped talking to myself. I was no longer incoherent and the sentence on my lips that began with "You . . ." got finished.

32

The finished sentence was beauteous as a dancer in the dawn. The sentence was finished at night but it was not like the night but like the dawn.

33

Later Georgia and I made up but everything was not as it used to be. The finished sentence was beauteous like a dancer in the dawn. After a time I did not care for Georgia nor she for me.

34

I went to school but I did not like going to school.

35

I said to myself I would be through with girls and love only the girl back home. I wondered if what had happened to me had happened too or was happening to Vi. As I thought it I got angry not at myself but with Vi.

36

A girl should be constant.

37

I was angry with Vi and in my fancy I saw many pictures of her with other boys. She was dancing and smiling and she had no thoughts of me.

38

Finally I dreamt Vi had got married and I woke up crying. Then I was no longer angry with Vi but with my father who had separated us. I wrote Father an angry letter blaming him. I said I would quit studying and did not care if he cut me off.

39

I was very angry I became a poet. In fancy my anger became a gorgeous purple flower. I made love to it with my long fingers. Then when I had won it and it shone like a resplendent gem in my hands I offered it to my father.

40

My father could not understand the meaning of the gorgeous purple flower. When I gave it to him he threw it on the floor. Then I said, "My father is not a lover."

41

I picked the flower and it lived because my father refused it.

42

One morning at breakfast I told Wiley and Joe and the girls that I was quitting school and leaving for New York that afternoon. At first they would not believe me but I was quiet and pensive throughout the meal and finally they believed me. They wanted to know why I was leaving but I told them I did not know it myself.

43

At lunch they looked at me wistfully and I said, "This is our last meal together." I became very sad.

44

I shook their hands and Louise and Aurora asked me if I would write to them. When I left the table they followed me softly with their eyes until I turned at the door.

45

Joe and Wiley walked with me to my room at the dorm. They did not want to leave me and in my room I said they must go for I must pack my things. They wanted to help me but I said I was not packing many things. I made them go after we had shaken hands and promised to write each other. Joe and Wiley wanted to go to the station to see me off but I begged them not to. It would make me feel bad, I said.

46

And so I made Joe and Wiley go but when they had left my room I went to the window and looked at them long and I cried. I liked Joe and Wiley and Aurora and Louise—why was I leaving them?

47

Then I lay on the bed without moving. All the time I knew I was not truly leaving for New York yet I felt greatly hurt. In myself I was leaving and behind me I would leave Joe and Wiley and the girls. I would be lonely again as when I had first come to America.

48

I had said I was leaving for New York but it was not true. I was a liar because I had felt like telling a lie and I was angry with my Father and in my mind I wanted to do something rash like leaving college and going about starving in a big city like New York.

49

In the big city of New York, where I had never been I was hungry and without money. I lived in a little dark room and it was dark and ugly for the rent was cheap. There was only one little window in the room and it was tight to open.

50

One night I opened the little window and a piece of paper blew in. It settled on the floor and then my mind began to work about it.—I am not alone. A lover is waiting for me outside. She has written me a letter calling me to her side. . . . "I will go to you, sweetheart," I whispered tenderly.

51

Then a strong wind blew in and the paper moved.—It is a white flower trembling with love. It is God's white flower.—It made me think of my gorgeous purple flower which my father had refused and I wanted it to become God's white flower. Make my purple flower white, God, I prayed.

52

In New Mexico I had prayed before about my father, mother and sisters but in New York I prayed about a flower.

53

In New York it was colder than in New Mexico.

54

I wanted to buy a new suit and go to see a new UFA film but I had no money.

55

Because I wanted to have a new suit and to see a new German film and I had no money I walked around in the streets. I looked at the haberdashery windows and gazed at the new styles. There was a wine-colored suit with padded shoulders and if I only had money I could have it. It cost sixty-five dollars.

56

In front of the big cinema it was very bright. In San Francisco I saw the Fox Theatre and I thought it was very big but this was much bigger. It was very lavish. Rich young ladies and thin gay gentlemen poured in. They laughed goldenly.

57

Then I got tired walking and I returned to my little dark room and the dark made me want a woman.

58

It was cold in the room and I thought if I had a woman I would not feel so cold. We would share each other's warmth.

59

"Warming woman, warming woman," I sang. How beautiful the words. How beautiful the thought.

60

Then I turned on the light and in the lighted room I took a book and read. The story was about a liar. I thought of myself. I had lied to Joe and Wiley and to Aurora and Louise and to every one at the table. It had occurred to me to lie and I did and now I was living up to my lie.

61

All these adventures in New York I have been telling you about happened in my room as I lay on the bed crying because I was a liar. But I was not afraid to cry.

62

Later I dressed and pretended I was going to the station where I was leaving. After a time when I got dressed I did not want to merely pretend and I left my room to go to the station.

63

On the way I met Aurora. She walked with me to the street corner to bid me good-bye. She held my hands long and her hold was tight. Her hands were soft like flowers and thin like roots but they were strong lovers. Her hands made cruel love to my hands.

64

"Write to me," her mouth said—but her hands, "Have we not touched the touch to last us forever? the touch of music that knows no forgetting?"

65

When I had already gotten into the bus and the bus started Aurora did not move. She stood at the corner, her eyes following me. She stood there long, immobile, and I waved my hand at her but only her eyes moved. Her hands that had been lovers were quiet now. Her whole body has become a quiet lover. As the bus moved away, in the far corner she was no longer a quiet lover but a song of serenity.

66

In the bus strange thoughts came to me: I have touched her hands. Why do I not love her the way I loved Georgia? Why have I not asked to touch her hair? Maybe if I touched her hair I would love her like I was maddened by Georgia. . . . I should have touched her hair. She would have liked it. We would have become lovers.

67

As to Georgia I did not bid her good-bye and I did not care.—I touched her hair. I ran my fingers through her hair. After I finished the sentence that was beauteous as a dancer in the dawn I did not care to touch her hair.—In the bus I could not understand why and it made feel sad.

68

I got off at the station and waited for the 5:30 train. It came and then it left. I watched it till I could not see it. I wondered if I was in it.

69

Had I bidden myself good-bye?

70

Afterwards I walked through the town as if I had gone out of myself. I looked for myself vainly. I was nowhere. I was now only a shell, a house. The house of myself was empty.

71

My god had flown away and carried with him my gorgeous purple flower. Will Father laugh now?

72

Where had my god fled? Where was he taking my purple flower which my father had refused?

73

In the morning, on the campus, I met Aurora and she said I fooled her. Later everybody said I fooled them. But to Aurora, as I thought of her as she stood at the street corner, her hands making love to my hands, and of her when she was a song of serenity, I said: "Your hands have told me an unforgettable story. Your song of serenity has awakened me. Now let me feel your hair . . ."

74

My god was in her hair. My god was there with my purple flower pressed gently to his breast. I opened his hands and he yielded to me my flower. I pinned it to Aurora's hair. And as the purple petals kissed the soft dark of her hair, my flower turned silver, then white—became God's white flower. Then I was no longer angry with my father.

Lenox Hill, December 1991

Marianne Villanueva

I would have liked to say: I took the first plane to New York, but I did not. I am ashamed to say it, but I didn't at first believe my brother-in-law when he called and said she was very sick. I remember listening to his foreign, English voice, and a host of memories came over me—memories of other times, other crises and emergencies, times that left me feeling helpless and angry. And he sounded so matter-of-fact, so *English* and above it all, and when he said she had strep I thought: Now you are really pulling my leg—you say all these awful things are happening and she has STREP? I had wanted to hang up on him, but did not, and the rest of that day I busied myself with office work and did not think about my sister anymore.

MARIANNE VILLANUEVA: "I was born in Manila in 1958. I left Manila in 1979 to begin a master's program in East Asian studies at Stanford University. . . . My current job is as grant administrator for Stanford University's East Asia National Resource Center. . . . I've written for *Asiaweek* and *The Filipinas Journal* . . . and was at one time a playwright and a fellow at the University of the Philippines Summer Writing Workshop." She has published a collection of stories, *Ginseng and Other Tales from Manila*, and lives in Redwood City, California, with her husband and son.

When my sister and I first came to America, she chose to settle on the East Coast, I on the West. She was always more adventurous, more self-confident, tough. I wanted to be close to my mother's relatives, who lived in various San Francisco suburbs. Later, I came to regret my decision. My sister seemed so free there in that big city, and I was entrammeled with family disputes and family obligations. My sister married an Englishman and had three children. She lived on Park Avenue and had two maids. She was very happy.

It was a Dr. Sterling who called the house, early on the morning of my sister's third day in the hospital. He said: Come as soon as you can, there's not much time.

An aunt drove me to the airport. I asked for a seat by the window and curled up with my legs tucked under me. Strong sunlight filled the airplane cabin. It was impossible to sleep. I looked down and saw clouds; a mountain; a river snaking through brown canyons. Throughout the long flight I read passages from the book I happened to check out of the library the previous week: *The Four Winds: A Shaman's Journey into the Amazon.* It was written by two men, Erik Jendresen and Antonio Villoldo, but it was really Villoldo's story, Villoldo's journey to the Amazon. In the early section of the book, I came across a passage about an autopsy: the corpse was that of a 37-year-old woman, and as he watches a medical student put a piece of her brain on a slide Villoldo asks himself, Where is the consciousness that was Jennifer, where were her memories, the unique trace that had made her who she was?

When I arrived in New York, it was late at night. Strange men held up signs near the baggage carousels, and I was frightened and tried to get away from them, but one of them spotted me and asked me if I needed a limousine. Yes! I said, But I will not ride alone with you. I must have seemed hysterical. He looked at me carefully and then said, Wait here, I will find someone to share the ride.

After what seemed like an interminable wait, he returned with a young student: a Korean visiting friends at Columbia. The Korean talked and talked, all the way into Manhattan. I think we passed a bridge and entered a tunnel. With startling suddenness we were in the middle of canyons of buildings. The driver dropped off the Korean and we began to talk. He was a young black man, with two children, and he told me he had been waiting at the airport for hours, and he was hungry and wanted to go home and have his dinner. He didn't charge me very much. I was sorry when I got out of the limousine.

This is the part where things become difficult. I have to switch to another way of writing about events, in order to get through the rest of what happens. I can describe things more accurately if I present, briefly, scenes that stand out in my mind, as of—

Memory 1: Arrival

I am at the apartment on Park Avenue. It must be after 10 at night. All the lights in the apartment are blazing, and my sister's three children, aged 5, 4, and 1, are wide awake and my first impression upon walking in the door is of loud screams and an atmosphere of general hubbub and disorder. My brother-in-law walks up, holding the youngest upside down in his arms. It is the first time I have seen this fabled place, this place that all my sister's classmates in Manila know to visit when they are in New York. And now I note the mirrored hallway, the high-ceilinged kitchen with its capacious island, the various suites of rooms. I ask for my mother and with barely a word my brother-in-law relieves me of my bag and directs me to the hospital. I go out into a night which is much warmer than I had come to expect. All up and down Park Avenue, an amazing sight: Christmas trees are blinking bravely in the darkness. I pass lighted doorways, behind which stand doormen with surly faces. I pass women in fur coats walking their dogs. I do not feel the cold.

Memory 2: Lenox Hill

I am at the intensive care ward. There, at the end of a long row of beds, I see a swollen shape, lying with legs awkwardly spreadeagled. Long, thick, black hair is spread out on a pillow. I instinctively head towards this head of black hair, and pass beds filled with old, old people, some with their hospital gowns pushed all the way up to their stomachs, revealing bone-thin limbs. Some with their mouths twisted open, as though gasping for air. I at first do not believe this swollen body I am approaching to be my sister's, but when I come close and see my mother there, my heart fills with grief, a grief so great I want to shout over and over: WHAT HAVE THEY DONE TO YOU?

My mother looks up at me, and whatever I prepared myself to find when I arrived at the hospital, it certainly wasn't this: my mother looks at me, and her face is happy and peaceful. "Come," she says, sensing my fear, coaxing me forward. She is strength, strength itself, sitting there in the intensive care ward, while all my insides seem in danger of cracking open, and something snakes into my heart, cold.

I look into my sister's eyes: they are flaming red and twice the normal size. A thick, opaque film of fluid coats them and oozes out at the corners. Her swollen hand makes a faint movement toward the ventilator in her mouth.

This is what my sister has: three IVs, one in each arm to push drugs and fluids, an arterial line in her left arm to draw blood and for hooking up to a transducer for constant blood pressure readings; a nasogastric tube running through her nose and into her stomach, hooked up to a suction machine on the floor to drain her stomach constantly so that she won't aspirate, regurgitate into her trachea; an endotracheal tube down her throat; a ventilator because she can't breathe by herself. Whenever she moves her tongue the monitor emits a faint beep.

I grab her limp hand, knowing that now she cannot pull away, as she would have done were she not so seriously ill. I sob, because I realize this is something I had not been able to do for many years, and it has to be now, now in these circumstances. I sob, too, because my sister, who I had always remembered as a rather vain person, who when she was 16 had had a nose job and an eye job and various other things done to make her look less "Oriental," who was 34 and had three young children, was no more, and this new physical reality, this shape that allowed me to hold her hand without resistance, had taken her place.

Now there is a flurry of beeps from the ventilator. My mother bends forward and tells my sister not to talk. My mother tells her, "There will be plenty of time later." But my sister is still biting down, moving her tongue. Nurses hurry over. The beeps increase. I feel something terrible is happening, and whatever it is I feel I must be the cause. I step back from the bed while the nurses call out, "Paz, Paz, stop biting the ventilator. Stop it!" I can not bear to hear my sister addressed in such a way, as though she were a five-year-old. She is helpless, she cannot move. If she were able to, she might flail away at one of these nurses, but now she can only lie there, her tongue perhaps the only part of her capable of movement.

I want to shout: "Can't you let her speak? Can't you get the ventilator out of her mouth?" Because I can see how it hurts her: that monstrous thing, pushing her swollen tongue to the inside of her cheek, pressing on her cracked lips. But I stand there, dumb. Already there are at least two other nurses there, hurrying, hurrying, preparing to inject my sister with a sedative. I do nothing. Instead I flee from them and head for the waiting lounge, cursing my cowardice.

Memory 3: The Waiting Lounge

It is a tiny room with two lumpy, plastic-covered sofas in a sick shade of avocado green, and a window that overlooks a side street and some brownstone buildings. Against one wall is a pay phone, and newspapers scattered on a coffee table. Later I will come to know every particular of this room: the squares of graying linoleum, the exact depressions on the sofa cushions, the coffee rings on the cheap wooden tables, the television suspended by a steel arm from the wall. I will cradle the phone receiver against my ear and make numerous, teary calls to California, to my husband. My mother and I will sit on the green sofa and wait for the doctor to tell us about my sister's latest blood gas readings, minute improvements in her lung capacity. We will sit here and pace and get to know the relatives of Mrs. Beatrice Sulkin—a son, a daughter, a husband—who pace with us. We will come to know all this.

Memory 4: Filipina Nurses

Two of them come to me as I sob on the sofa and one of them hands me a box of tissues. "Calma lang," she says. Her companion says, "Don't worry. She is much better now. She was very bad this morning."

Their words comfort me but I continue to sob, though I realize it is now more for myself than for my sister—sobbing because the long trip in the airplane, the leave-taking from my son and husband this Christmas, was so very hard, and because I am exhausted. "Calma lang."

A young Filipina named Lourdes is her nurse that first night. She is pretty, with thick black hair plaited and fastened up at the back of her head. She jokes with the young interns, and keeps injecting my sister with Benadryl. Lourdes tells me that my sister keeps fighting the ventilator. She tells me that earlier they had to strap her down to the bed. I had noticed the purplish marks on her wrists and ankles and wondered where they came from. Tuesday morning, two days earlier, was when they had almost lost her. It was the night my brother-in-law had gone home to spend some time with the children.

They said she was thrashing in the bed. Perhaps it wasn't fear so much as the feeling that she was drowning, her lungs filling up with fluid. But the thrashing was using up whatever little oxygen was going to her brain. And they had to strap her down.

Since my mother arrived, Thursday morning, she has been quiet. She looks at my mother, and she knows her. My mother strokes her hair tenderly. Tenderly she fans my sister's legs and pushes up the hospital gown because my sister needs air. She needs air more than anything in the world. Look at her fingers and toes, already turning blue . . .

Memory 5: Doctors

It may be the third or fourth day, and I am already feeling how ineffectual my presence is. I am standing by my sister's bed, but I don't—can't—speak. I stand, dumb with misery, by my sister's hospital bed.

The doctors have injected her with Pavulon, a paralyzing agent. They say they had to sedate her because anxiety increases the heart rate and uses up oxygen and they are worried she might suffer brain damage. They say she can still hear. I ask them, What is it like, this hearing? They tell me, like hearing voices in your sleep. Yet I hesitate to speak to my sister in the same loud voice the nurses use: Paz, I'm going to put eyepatches on you now; Paz, I'm going to put drops in your eyes. I stand there, dumb with misery.

Memory 6: My Uncle

I am jealous of my mother's younger brother because he has managed to make my sister giggle. It is the last time we see her conscious and awake. He takes one of her swollen feet and starts to tickle it. My sister's shoulders rise and her swollen mouth parts and even with the ventilator in her mouth she does look strangely happy. I watch, dumb with misery.

Later, I try to tell her things. My voice is soft. I can think of nothing to say. Only things like, "Panggoy," using the name I much prefer to her Christian name, "I am here." Here! But what does that mean, exactly? Even my touch is light and tentative. I am unable to stroke her arms with my mother's vehemence, my brother-in-law's vigor. They seize the parts of her body as though claiming her, inciting her to struggle. But I am afraid.

Memory 7: Sunday Night

My mother and I are stretched out, one to a sofa, in the tiny waiting room. It feels as though we have just fallen asleep when someone comes in and switches on the light. My mother and I are up instantly. It is the young doctor, Dr. Rosen, wearing green scrubs. He gives us my sister's latest blood gas count. He is ecstatic. We are, too. We think now that my sister will surely live.

Memory 8: In the Kitchen

In this bright place, all white tile and chrome appliances, I sit on a high stool and tell my brother-in-law about my sister's latest blood gas reading. He is happy but trying hard not to lose control. I tease him that he should take my sister on a long cruise for their tenth anniversary, which is coming up in May. He tells me they have planned to go to Egypt.

Memory 9: Monday

I spend the whole day away from the hospital. I feel light-headed and happy. I walk down Fifth Avenue and marvel at the giant golden snowflakes strung across the street. When I finally check back at the hospital, it is late at night. My mother is at her customary place, but her head is bowed. Poor woman, I think. She must be exhausted. But when she looks up, the expression on her face frightens me and I ask, What is it, what is it? The ventilator, she says. They tried to take her off it today, but she had a setback. A terrible setback. Her body just couldn't take it.

Memory 10: Doormen

I begin to look forward to the walks in the cold, and know buildings and doormen. I know all the doormen in my sister's building. One in particular, an old man named George, is very kind. He is the one who runs after me if I happen to get into the elevator without speaking to him and asks: "How is she?" My chin pressed down into my overcoat, I invariably shake my head and say, "Not good." George lifts his hands, shrugs his shoulders. "It's in God's hands," he says.

Memory 11: Other People

I sit on a sagging chair in the foyer. It is 3, 4 in the morning. I sit and look out the window and wait for it to get light. In the room behind me, a doctor is shouting into a phone: Are you crazy? What do you think I am, stupid? Do you think I'm stupid? And she goes on and on like that, interminably.

There is someone else with a terrible cough. Choking on phlegm. It is an old man or an old woman. I want to cover my ears, to shout: Stop it! Stop it!

I am alone, waiting for my mother to come. Waiting for my brother-in-law. I am tired. Who are all these strangers yakking in the foyer?

Now and then I walk past the rows of sick old people, being careful to keep my eyes down. I see my sister lying there, her bloated shape, her eyes taped shut, no sign of life or movement. There is no one with her. The children's nanny, a Filipina who has left her two young boys with her mother so she can come to America and care for my sister's children, was supposed to have been there at 10. It is now almost 11. Not even my brother-in-law is there.

Memory 12: Tuesday

My sister has a bad night. In fact, we nearly lose her. My mother rushes to the apartment to get me. It is cold and raining. In her panic, she slips and hurts her knee. The wound has bled through her pants when she arrives at the apartment, but she immediately rushes back with me to the hospital without bothering to change. When we arrive at the hospital, I am annoyed to see that the nurse on duty, an elderly Filipina, is wandering aimlessly around with a nonchalant air, as though nothing is happening. "She is all right now, she is stable," she keeps telling my distraught mother. Stable, but only for the moment, I think bitterly.

Memory 13: Mary Ellen

I do not recognize the nurse, though thank God it is not the other one of last night, the old Filipina who seemed only to want to sit down and smoke her cigarette in the waiting room and read the newspapers scattered on the floor.

Mary Ellen looks Irish. She has red hair, calm grey eyes, a wide mouth that seems always on the verge of saying something sarcastic. To all my queries of "How is she?" she has only one answer: "The same." But I like this nurse, with her warm, stolid, squarish body, and her clean smell. I think to myself: my sister will not die as long as *she* is there.

When her shift is over, I want to tell her: come back soon. I watch her leave the ward in her going-out clothes. She and another nurse, another Filipina, are heading for the elevators, and they look different, almost coquettish, in short skirts and sheer black stockings. I wander back alone to my sister's bed.

Memory 14: Wednesday

My sister is no longer the only young woman in the intensive care ward. Everyone seems to be gathered around the latest arrival: a woman who has been placed in Bed No. 1, closest to the nurses' station. I watch them wheel her in and, in my confused state, mistake her black hair for my sister's. I go to my sister's bedside, but I cannot sit down. Someone has taken away the chair.

Beside her someone has placed a small pocketbook: *Furrow*, the collected writings of Jose Maria Escriva, the founder of Opus Dei. He is about to be beatified and Mrs. Yujuico who works in my office tells me the period just before his beatification is when prayers to him have the most potency. On the window sill my brother-in-law has propped up a picture of Georgina and William, sitting on Santa Claus' lap.

Memory 15: The Pay Phone

The pay phone in the waiting room rings annoyingly. Hello, a young woman says. Can I speak to Mrs. Greenfeld? There is no Mrs. Greenfeld here, I say. I hang up. Not five minutes later, it rings again. I know there is a Mrs. Greenfeld there, with Mr. Weinberger. What am I? An answering service? I go to call someone. A young male intern comes to the phone. No, no, he says, and hangs up. Ten minutes later, the phone rings again. Please, says the young woman. I need to speak to my mother. I know she is there: a Mrs. Greenfeld who is with Mr. Weinberger. I go back to the ward. There, next to Bed No. 2, is a thirty-ish woman in a tweed overcoat and a slouchy hat. Are you Mrs. Greenfeld? I ask. Yes, she says. Mr. Weinberger looks very pale, and his mouth is twisted in a kind of grimace. You have a phone call, I say. She comes to the phone and I can hear rapid-fire Yiddish and I know that somewhere in there is some mention about me and the number of times I have hung up on the daughter saying, There is no Mrs. Greenfeld here.

I collect my things and go back to the apartment. There is no one in the study. I lie down on the leather couch. I look out and see it has begun to snow. The phone keeps ringing: someone called Donna Lopez from Washington, D.C.; Matt Skidmore, my sister's boss at Chemical Bank; Fletcher, a friend of my brother-in-law from Merrill Lynch.

I see Georgina and William playing outside in the hallway with the chocolate egg I had given them as a Christmas present. Georgina has black hair, and William is blond. Georgina is beautiful, but William, with his blond hair and slanted eyes, looks mournful and lost.

The chocolate egg has rolled to one corner and they are fascinated with the wooden box and the synthetic straw, and Georgina says she will put a little bird in it—a bird with a broken wing. I go with her to her room and I start pretending to cook with her pots and pans. She stares at me at first, with big, round eyes, and then gradually it dawns on her what I am doing and she begins to smile. Then the nanny comes to say my mother has called for me to take her place at the hospital for a while. I am flustered and run out, forgetting about Georgina. She runs after me, screaming, but her nanny catches her and holds her firmly. I am not going anywhere, the nanny says.

Memory 16: Good-Bye

The day my father arrives from the Philippines. No one told me he was coming. I simply enter the intensive care ward early one morning, and he is there. He is wearing a fine, brown cardigan, and his hair is neatly combed. He sits back on a hospital chair, not saying anything. His eyes are dry. He looks essentially the same person as the one who sat at the breakfast table every morning when I was growing up. Yet, how strange it is to see him sitting here. This cold winter morning, with the snowflakes blowing by the half-open window.

I know I have to leave. There are too many people in the apartment, everyone getting on each other's nerves, and Mary Ellen has told me that my sister can continue in her present state for a long, long time. I go to the hospital alone and see my sister lying on the bed, inert, her eyes taped shut. I look at her cracked, swollen lips and jowls, her bluish fingers and toes, trying to fix her image in my mind. I am anxious when I see that she is alone again, no one there to massage her limbs or comb her hair. The nurses are busy with other patients and leave me alone. I stand there for a long time, simply watching. Now is the time, I think. Now is the time to tell her what she has meant to me, and how much I love her. I see her shudder, a movement I have observed before and which had distressed me until my mother said, "She is coughing." Now she coughs, and coughs some more. Her hand moves up slightly toward her stomach, but it is a half-gesture. Before the motion can be completed, the hand sinks down again, and she is still.

"I love you," I say, with all the strength I can muster, but the sound comes out small, almost inaudible. I stand there, immobilized. I want to kiss her, but dare not. I remember the doctor's words: "The next 48 hours are crucial. Any little infection could kill her." And I can feel, at the back of my throat, the scratchy beginnings of a cough. And I do not want anything to harm my sister. I do not want any harm to come to her at all.

I say good-bye to Mary Ellen, who is once again her nurse, and Mary Ellen gives me a tight little smile and her eyes remain detached, though I tell myself she is not unkind.

A few days later, when I receive word, I am at the office. I am speaking to someone and telling her how my mother has brought in a very famous faith healer from Mexico, and how this woman touched my sister's foot and said, with purest certainty, "She will recover." Then the phone rings, and it is my aunt. She says the words quietly. My head drops to the table and I realize now my aunt's words were the ones I was expecting to hear. My sobs are shattering and everyone in the office comes running and yes, I want everyone to know it, my sister is no more.

Later, there are other phone calls. From my mother, sounding far, far away, as if she has fallen into some deep well of grief and exhaustion and not even the sound of my voice will suffice to pull her out of it. She keeps repeating, "To see her in a shroud—" I think of my sister in a winding sheet, on a hospital bed. Later, there is some back and forth on whether or not she should be cremated. I think it is important for my sister's body to be brought home—important because that is the Filipino way: to have an open casket for nine days, where everyone can come and look and say their farewells. But it is my brother-in-law who objects, and his wish prevails. He does not want his children to see their mother in a casket. She is cremated in New York, and her ashes are flown home to Manila by my mother. My niece, my sister's eldest child, draws a picture—a figure ascending to clouds, and beneath it, she has her father write the words: "My mother goes up to heaven, and leaves behind her bones."

Talking to the Dead

We spoke of her in whispers as Aunty Talking to the Dead, the half-Hawaiian kahuna lady. But whenever there was a death in the village, she was the first to be sent for; the priest came second. For it was she who understood the wholeness of things—the significance of directions and colors. Prayers to appease the hungry ghosts. Elixirs for grief. Most times, she'd be out on her front porch, already waiting—her boy, Clinton, standing behind with her basket of spells —when the messenger arrived. People said she could smell a death from clear on the other side of the island, even as the dying person breathed his last. And if she fixed her eyes on you and named a day, you were already as good as six feet under.

I went to work as her apprentice when I was eighteen. That was in

SYLVIA WATANABE was born in Hawaii on the island of Maui. Her collection of stories, *Talking to the Dead*, was published in 1992. She was coeditor with Carol Bruchac of *Home to Stay: An Anthology of Asian American Women's Fiction*. Her fiction has appeared in numerous literary journals and been published in many anthologies, including *The Best of Bamboo Ridge*, edited by Eric Chock and Darrell Lum, *My Father's Daughter*, edited by Irene Zahava, and *Passages to the Dream Shore*, edited by Frank Stewart.

'48, the year Clinton graduated from mortician school on the GI bill. It was the talk for weeks—how he'd returned to open the Paradise Mortuary in the heart of the village and had brought the scientific spirit of free enterprise to the doorstep of the hereafter. I remember the advertisements for the Grand Opening, promising to modernize the funeral trade with Lifelike Artistic Techniques and Stringent Standards of Sanitation. The old woman, who had waited out the war for her son's return, stoically took his defection in stride and began looking for someone else to help out with her business.

At the time, I didn't have many prospects—more schooling didn't interest me, and my mother's attempts at marrying me off inevitably failed when I stood to shake hands with a prospective bridegroom and ended up towering a foot above him. "It would be bad enough if she just looked like a horse," I heard one of them complain, "but she's as big as one, too."

My mother dressed me in navy blue, on the theory that dark colors make things look less conspicuous. "Yuri, sit down," she'd hiss, tugging at my skirt as the decisive moment approached. I'd nod, sip my tea, smile through the introductions and small talk, till the time came for sealing the bargain with handshakes. Then, nothing on earth could keep me from getting to my feet. The go-between finally suggested that I consider taking up a trade. "After all, marriage isn't for everyone," she said. My mother said that that was a fact which remained to be proven, but meanwhile it wouldn't hurt if I took in sewing or learned to cut hair. I made up my mind to apprentice myself to Aunty Talking to the Dead.

The old woman's house was on the hill behind the village, just off the road to Chicken Fight Camp. She lived in an old plantation worker's bungalow with peeling green and white paint and a large, well-tended garden—mostly of flowering bushes and strong-smelling herbs.

"Aren't you a big one," a voice behind me said.

I started, then turned. It was the first time I had ever seen her up close.

"Hello, uh, Mrs. Dead," I stammered.

She was little, way under five feet, and wrinkled. Everything about her seemed the same color—her skin, her lips, her dress. Everything was just a slightly different shade of the same brown-gray, except her hair, which was absolutely white, and her tiny eyes, which glinted like metal. For a minute those eyes looked me up and down.

"Here," she said finally, thrusting an empty rice sack into my hands. "For collecting salt." Then she started down the road to the beach.

In the next few months we walked every inch of the hills and beaches around the village, and then some. I struggled behind, laden with strips of bark and leafy twigs, while Aunty marched three steps ahead, chanting. "This is *a'ali'i* to bring sleep—it must be dried in the shade on a hot day. This is *noni* for the heart, and *awa* for every kind of grief. This is *uhaloa* with the deep roots. If you are like that, death cannot easily take you."

"This is where you gather salt to preserve a corpse," I hear her still. "This is where you cut to insert the salt." Her words marked the places on my body, one by one.

That whole first year, not a day passed when I didn't think of quitting. I tried to figure out a way of moving back home without making it seem like I was admitting anything.

"You know what people are saying, don't you?" my mother said, lifting the lid of the bamboo steamer and setting a tray of freshly steamed meat buns on the already crowded table before me. It was one of my few visits since my apprenticeship, though I'd never been more than a couple of miles away, and she had stayed up the whole night before, cooking. She'd prepared a canned ham with yellow sweet potatoes, wing beans with pork, sweet and sour mustard cabbage, fresh raw yellowfin, pickled eggplant, and rice with red beans. I had not seen so much food since the night she tried to persuade Uncle Mongoose not to volunteer for the army. He went anyway, and on the last day of training, just before he was to be shipped to Italy, he shot himself in the head while cleaning his gun. "I always knew that boy would come to no good," was all Mama said when she heard the news.

"What do you mean you can't eat another bite?" she fussed now. "Look at you, nothing but a bag of bones."

The truth was, there didn't seem to be much of a future in my apprenticeship. In eleven and a half months I had memorized most of the minor rituals of mourning and learned to identify a couple of dozen herbs and all their medicinal uses, but I had not seen, much less gotten to practice on, a single honest-to-goodness corpse. "People live longer these days," Aunty claimed.

But I knew it was because everyone, even from villages across the bay, had begun taking their business to the Paradise Mortuary. The single event that had established Clinton's monopoly was the untimely death of old Mrs. Parmeter, the plantation owner's mother-in-law, who'd choked on a fishbone in the salmon mousse during a fundraising luncheon for Famine Relief. Clinton had been chosen to be in charge of the funeral. After that, he'd taken to wearing three-piece suits, as a symbol of his new respectability, and was nominated as a Republican candidate for the village council.

"So, what are people saying?" I asked, finally pushing my plate away.

This was the cue that Mama had been waiting for. "They're saying that That Woman has gotten herself a pet donkey, though that's not the word they're using, of course." She paused dramatically; the implication was clear.

I began remembering things about living in my mother's house. The navy-blue dresses. The humiliating weekly tea ceremony lessons at the Buddhist temple.

"Give up this foolishness," she wheedled. "Mrs. Koyama tells me the Barber Shop Lady is looking for help."

"I think I'll stay right where I am," I said.

My mother fell silent. Then she jabbed a meat bun with her serving fork and lifted it onto my plate. "Here, have another helping," she said.

A few weeks later Aunty and I were called outside the village to perform a laying-out. It was early afternoon when Sheriff Kanoi came by to tell us that the body of Mustard Hayashi, the eldest of the Hayashi boys, had just been pulled from an irrigation ditch by a team of field workers. He had apparently fallen in the night before, stone drunk, on his way home from the La Hula Rhumba Bar and Grill.

I began hurrying around, assembling Aunty's tools and potions, and checking that everything was in working order, but the old woman didn't turn a hair; she just sat calmly rocking back and forth and puffing on her skinny, long-stemmed pipe.

"Yuri, you stop that rattling around back there," she snapped, then turned to the sheriff. "My son Clinton could probably handle this. Why don't you ask him?"

Sheriff Kanoi hesitated before replying, "This looks like a tough case that's going to need some real expertise."

Aunty stopped rocking. "That's true, it was a bad death," she mused.

"Very bad," the sheriff agreed.

"The spirit is going to require some talking to," she continued. "You know, so it doesn't linger."

"And the family asked especially for you," he added.

No doubt because they didn't have any other choice, I thought. That morning, I'd run into Chinky Malloy, the assistant mortician at the Paradise, so I happened to know that Clinton was at a morticians' conference in Los Angeles and wouldn't be back for several days. But I didn't say a word.

When we arrived at the Hayashis', Mustard's body was lying on the green Formica table in the kitchen. It was the only room in the house with a door that faced north. Aunty claimed that a proper laying-out required a room with a north-facing door, so the spirit could find its way home to the land of the dead without getting lost.

Mustard's mother was leaning over his corpse, wailing, and her husband stood behind her, looking white-faced, and absently patting her on the back. The tiny kitchen was jammed with sobbing, nose-blowing mourners, and the air was thick with the smells of grief—perspiration, ladies' cologne, the previous night's cooking, and the faintest whiff of putrefying flesh. Aunty gripped me by the wrist and pushed her way to the front. The air pressed close, like someone's hot, wet breath on my face. My head reeled, and the room broke apart into dots of color. From far away I heard somebody say, "It's Aunty Talking to the Dead."

"Make room, make room," another voice called.

I looked down at Mustard, lying on the table in front of me, his eyes half open in that swollen, purple face. The smell was much stronger close up, and there were flies everywhere.

"We'll have to get rid of some of this bloat," Aunty said, thrusting a metal object into my hand.

People were leaving the room.

She went around to the other side of the table. "I'll start here," she said. "You work over there. Do just like I told you."

I nodded. This was the long-awaited moment. My moment. But it was already the beginning of the end. My knees buckled, and everything went dark.

Aunty performed the laying-out alone and never mentioned the episode again. But it was the talk of the village for weeks—how Yuri Shimabukuro, assistant to Aunty Talking to the Dead, passed out under the Hayashis' kitchen table and had to be tended by the grief-stricken mother of the dead boy.

My mother took to catching the bus to the plantation store three villages away whenever she needed to stock up on necessaries. "You're my daughter—how could I *not* be on your side?" was the way she put it, but the air buzzed with her unspoken recriminations. And whenever I went into the village, I was aware of the sly laughter behind my back, and Chinky Malloy smirking at me from behind the shutters of the Paradise Mortuary.

"She's giving the business a bad name," Clinton said, carefully removing his jacket and draping it across the back of the rickety wooden chair. He dusted the seat, looked at his hand with distaste before wiping it off on his handkerchief, then drew up the legs of his trousers, and sat.

Aunty retrieved her pipe from the smoking tray next to her rocker and filled the tiny brass bowl from a pouch of Bull Durham. "I'm glad you found time to drop by," she said. "You still going out with that skinny white girl?"

"You mean Marsha?" Clinton sounded defensive. "Sure, I see her sometimes. But I didn't come here to talk about that." He glanced over at where I was sitting on the sofa. "You think we could have some privacy?"

Aunty lit her pipe and puffed. "Yuri's my right-hand girl. Couldn't do without her."

"The Hayashis probably have their own opinion about that."

Aunty dismissed his insinuation with a wave of her hand. "There's no pleasing some people," she said. "Yuri's just young; she'll learn." She reached over and patted me on the knee, then looked him straight in the face. "Like we all did."

Clinton turned red. "Damn it, Mama," he sputtered, "this is no time to bring up the past. What counts is now, and right now your right-hand girl is turning you into a laughingstock!" His voice became soft, persuasive. "Look, you've worked hard all your life, and you deserve to retire. Now that my business is taking off, I can help you out. You know I'm only thinking about you."

"About the election to village council, you mean." I couldn't help it; the words just burst out of my mouth.

Aunty said, "You considering going into politics, son?"

"Mama, wake up!" Clinton hollered, like he'd wanted to all along. "You can talk to the dead till you're blue in the face, but *ain't no one listening*. The old ghosts have had it. You either get on the wheel of progress or you get run over."

For a long time after he left, Aunty sat in her rocking chair next to the window, rocking and smoking, without saying a word, just rocking and smoking, as the afternoon shadows spread beneath the trees and turned to night.

Then she began to sing—quietly, at first, but very sure. She sang the naming chants and the healing chants. She sang the stones, and trees, and stars back into their rightful places. Louder and louder she sang, making whole what had been broken.

Everything changed for me after Clinton's visit. I stopped going into the village and began spending all my time with Aunty Talking to the Dead. I followed her everywhere, carried her loads without complaint, memorized remedies, and mixed potions till my head spun and I went near blind. I wanted to know what *she* knew; I wanted to make what had happened at the Hayashis' go away. Not just in other people's minds. Not just because I'd become a laughingstock, like Clinton said. But because I knew that I had to redeem myself for that one thing, or my moment—the single instant of glory for which I had lived my entire life—would be snatched beyond my reach forever.

Meanwhile, there were other layings-out. The kitemaker who hanged himself. The crippled boy from Chicken Fight Camp. The Vagrant. The Blindman. The Blindman's dog.

"Do like I told you," Aunty would say before each one. Then, "Give it time," when it was done.

But it was like living the same nightmare over and over—just one look at a body and I was done for. For twenty-five years, people in the village joked about my "indisposition." Last fall, my mother's funeral was held at the Paradise Mortuary. While the service was going on, I stood outside on the cement walk for a long time, but I never made it through the door. Little by little, I'd begun to give up hope that my moment would ever arrive.

Then, a week ago, Aunty caught a chill, gathering *awa* in the rain. The chill developed into a fever, and for the first time since I'd known her, she took to her bed. I nursed her with the remedies she'd taught me—sweat baths; eucalyptus steam; tea made from *ko'oko'olau*—but the fever worsened. Her breathing became labored, and she grew weaker. My few hours of sleep were filled with bad dreams. Finally, aware of my betrayal, I walked to a house up the road and telephoned for an ambulance.

"I'm sorry, Aunty," I kept saying, as the flashing red light swept across the porch. The attendants had her on a stretcher and were carrying her out the front door.

She reached up and grasped my arm, her grip still strong. "You'll do okay, Yuri," the old woman whispered hoarsely. "Clinton used to get so scared, he messed his pants." She chuckled, then began to cough. One of the attendants put an oxygen mask over her face. "Hush," he said. "There'll be plenty of time for talking later."

On the day of Aunty's wake, the entrance to the Paradise Mortuary was blocked. Workmen had dug up the front walk and carted the old concrete tiles away. They'd left a mound of gravel on the grass, stacked some bags of concrete next to it, and covered the bags with black tarps. There was an empty wheelbarrow parked to one side of the gravel mound. The entire front lawn had been roped off and a sign had been put up that said, "Please follow the arrows around to the back. We are making improvements in Paradise. The Management."

My stomach was beginning to play tricks, and I was feeling shaky. The old panic was mingled with an uneasiness which had not left me ever since I'd decided to call the ambulance. I kept thinking that it had been useless to call it since she'd gone and died anyway. Or maybe I had waited too long. I almost turned back, but I thought of what Aunty had told me about Clinton and pressed ahead. Numbly, I followed the two women in front of me.

"So, old Aunty Talking to the Dead has finally passed on," one of them, whom I recognized as Emi McAllister, said. She was with Pearlie Woo. Both were old classmates of mine.

I was having difficulty seeing—it was getting dark, and my head was spinning so.

"How old do you suppose she was?" Pearlie asked.

"Gosh, even when we were kids it seemed like she was at least a hundred," Emi said.

Pearlie laughed. " 'The Undead,' my brother used to call her."

"When we misbehaved," Emi said, "our mother always threatened to abandon us on the hill where Aunty lived. Mama would be beating us with a wooden spoon and hollering, 'This is gonna seem like nothing then.' "

Aunty had been laid out in a room near the center of the mortuary. The heavy, wine-colored drapes had been drawn across the windows and all the wall lamps turned very low, so it was darker indoors than it had been outside. Pearlie and Emi moved off into the front row. I headed for the back.

There were about thirty of us at the viewing, mostly from the old days—those who had grown up on stories about Aunty, or who remembered her from before the Paradise Mortuary. People got up and began filing past the casket. For a moment I felt dizzy again, but I glanced over at Clinton, looking prosperous and self-assured, accepting condolences, and I got into line.

The room was air conditioned and smelled of floor disinfectant and roses. Soft music came from speakers mounted on the walls. I drew nearer and nearer to the casket. Now there were four people ahead. Now three. I looked down at my feet, and I thought I would faint.

Then Pearlie Woo shrieked, "Her eyes!" People behind me began to murmur. "What—whose eyes?" Emi demanded. Pearlie pointed to the body in the casket. Emi cried, "My God, they're open!"

My heart turned to ice.

"What?" voices behind me were asking. "What about her eyes?"

"She said they're open," someone said.

"Aunty Talking to the Dead's eyes are open," someone else said.

Now Clinton was hurrying over.

"That's because she's not dead," still another voice added.

Clinton looked into the coffin, and his face went white. He turned quickly around and waved to his assistants across the room.

"I've heard about cases like this," someone was saying. "It's because she's looking for someone."

"I've heard that too! The old woman is trying to tell us something."

I was the only one there who knew. Aunty was talking to *me*. I clasped my hands together, hard, but they wouldn't stop shaking.

People began leaving the line. Others pressed in, trying to get a better look at the body, but a couple of Clinton's assistants had stationed themselves in front of the coffin, preventing anyone from getting too close. They had shut the lid, and Chinky Malloy was directing people out of the room.

"I'd like to take this opportunity to thank you all for coming here this evening," Clinton was saying. "I hope you will join us at the reception down the hall."

While everyone was eating, I stole back into the parlor and quietly—ever so quietly—went up to the casket, lifted the lid, and looked in.

At first I thought they had switched bodies on me and exchanged Aunty for some powdered and painted old grandmother, all pink and white, in a pink dress, and clutching a white rose to her chest. But there they were. Open. Aunty's eyes staring up at me.

Then I knew. This was *it*: my moment had arrived. Aunty Talking to the Dead had come awake to bear me witness.

I walked through the deserted front rooms of the mortuary and out the front door. It was night. I got the wheelbarrow, loaded it with one of the tarps covering the bags of cement, and wheeled it back to the room where Aunty was. It squeaked terribly, and I stopped often to make sure no one had heard. From the back of the building came the clink of glassware and the buzz of voices. I had to work quickly—people would be leaving soon.

But this was the hardest part. Small as she was, it was very hard to lift her out of the coffin. She was horribly heavy, and unyielding as a bag of cement. I finally got her out and wrapped her in the tarp. I loaded her in the tray of the wheelbarrow—most of her, anyway; there was nothing I could do about her feet sticking out the front end. Then I wheeled her out of the mortuary, across the village square, and up the road, home.

Now, in the dark, the old woman is singing.

I have washed her with my own hands and worked the salt into the hollows of her body. I have dressed her in white and laid her in flowers.

Aunty, here are the beads you like to wear. Your favorite cakes. A quilt to keep away the chill. Here is *noni* for the heart and *awa* for every kind of grief.

Down the road a dog howls, and the sound of hammering echoes through the still air. "Looks like a burying tomorrow," the sleepers murmur, turning in their warm beds.

I bind the sandals to her feet and put the torch to the pyre.

The sky turns to light. The smoke climbs. Her ashes scatter, filling the wind.

And she sings, she sings, she sings.

Eye Contact

from *American Knees*

Shawn Wong

Being the only two Asians at a party, they tried to avoid each other, but failed. They touched accidentally several times. They watched each other furtively from across the room.

Aurora Crane had arrived first. They were her friends, her office mates, and it was their party. Raymond Ding was only a guest of her boss, who was the host of the office party. A visitor from out of town invited at the last minute. A friend of a friend in the city for only three days to do some business. When he arrived at the front door, she knew before he did that they were the only two Asians at a party. With dread she knew her boss would make a special point of introducing him to her and that one by one her friends, the loyal, would betray

SHAWN WONG is the author of an acclaimed first novel, *Homebase*, and is one of the coeditors of the Asian American anthologies *Aiiieeeee!* and *The Big AIIIEEEEE! The History of Chinese America and Japanese America in Literature.* He is also coeditor of *Before Columbus Foundation Fiction/Poetry Anthology: Selections from the American Book Awards, 1980–1990,* two volumes of contemporary American multicultural writings. Active in the lively Seattle arts community, he is at present an associate professor of American ethnic studies at the University of Washington and director of the Asian American Studies Program. He is at work on a new novel, *American Knees.*

her and pair her with him. They would probably be introduced several times during the evening. It made sense to them. There was no real covert activity, no setup, no surprise blind date, no surprise dinner companion seated not so coincidentally next to her. She was not at home with mother meeting not so coincidentally her mother's idea of a "nice Japanese boy." She had a boyfriend (unfortunately in another city and not Asian and a lover none of the loyal had met and to add to the further misfortune, some knew she had moved away from him to define a future without him making it very complex in her mind, but simple in the minds of the now distrustfully loyal).

Prior to the impending introductions, she wondered when they would make eye contact, when he would realize they were the only two Asians at the party. She hoped to God he wasn't an insecure Asian male who would only talk to her. She hoped to God he wouldn't see her as every Asian boy's answer to the perfect woman—half white, half Asian, just enough to bring home to Mother while maintaining the white girl fantasy. This gets somewhat complex, certainly more complex than *Love Is a Many-Splendored Thing*. Aurora Crane is Eurasian Jennifer Jones. Is the Asian boy William Holden? He'd like to think so.

When he eventually gets around to asking, "What are you?" will it be any different than any other obnoxious bore? Or would he simply be overly curious, but too polite to ask? It would be that slow realization creeping over his face, the ponderings and machinations that nestle in the eyes, the slight squint as if squinting can detect racial ancestry and blood lines. He would ask finally when she noticed he was no longer listening to her and merely watching her talk, all the while trying to decipher and calibrate the skin tone, the shape of her eyes, the color of her hair. In the past, the truly devious and ignorant would ask where she was from. A city in California was not the answer. Where are your parents from? Also from California was not the answer. Sometimes she would return the favor and ask where the interrogator's parents were from because, ha ha, nearly everyone in Washington, D.C. was from somewhere else, a standard cliche. The truly inept (which were sometimes failed devotees of the truly devious and ignorant) would blurt out the question, "What nationality are you?" American and my parents. "What are you, you know, what race?" Was ethnicity so hard a word to use? "Oh, how wonderful to be Japanese and Irish! You're so pretty." At which point some D.C. matron and patron of the arts would exclaim to her friend, "Miriam, don't you think she's pretty? That skin coloring!" Sometimes they reach out and touch her skin without asking.

"Don't you think he's pretty?" Annie, the betrayer from work, nudged Aurora. She was, of course, referring to the visitor from the Orient. "Maybe he's a Japanese businessman in town to argue against import duty and the trade deficits, but then he's kind of tall."

Aurora, without looking at him, replied, "His suit is the wrong color. Euro-trash natural shoulders olive brown, not Brooks Brothers American cut charcoal grey. Handpainted tie. West Hollywood is about as far east as this guy goes."

Asian people could tell she was part Asian, perhaps not part Japanese, but something. They would know at first eye contact. This eye contact thing between Asian men and Asian women was where the war began.

This is how it happens.

An Asian woman and an Asian man are the only two people on opposite sides of an intersection waiting to cross the street. First there's usually one momentary point of eye contact to register race. He looks to see if he knows you or your relatives. If he doesn't, the competition begins. The men always weaken first. They look at the traffic, check the lights, check the wrist watch, then walk, never making eye contact again. At the critical point when eye contact should occur between the only two people on the street caught between the boundaries of a crosswalk, the men chicken out and check the time again or run as if they were late. Just once she'd like to shock one of these boys and say, "Hey, home. What it is?" Whenever she was with her black friend Steve Dupree on the street and heard him say that to another black man, she would ask if he knew that man. The fact that he never did made her wonder why it wasn't ever possible between two Asians. Was it distrust and suspicion? Was it historical animosity? Was it because Japan invaded China and Korea? Mao versus Chiang Kai Shek? Chinatown versus Japantown? Fourth generation Chinese American versus fresh off the boat?

Since the "mysterious and exotic visitor from the east" didn't have any Polo trademarks on his clothes, Aurora ruled out Korean and decided he was Chinese. She set out to find the most typically Chinese feature about him, but couldn't find the usual landmarks: cheap haircut with greasy bangs falling down across the eyebrows, squarish gold rimmed glasses askew because there's no bridge to hold them up, polyester balls on his pants with a baggy butt, a shirt tucked in way too tight, and perhaps a slab of jade on a thick 24 kt gold chain around his neck. He had none of the above except for a gift for the host and hostess in a plastic shopping bag. *Please, please*, Aurora thought, *let it be oranges!* Oh, it would be so Chinese to bring oranges. And, of course, the plastic shopping bag—Chinese Samsonite. He was made.

She knew she was being cruel. She had to be cruel in order to steel herself for the impending introductions. Why she needed to be cruel, she wasn't sure, but she found herself now looking for and analyzing the most un-Asian features about him. Okay, the clothes were certainly Melrose Avenue, West Hollywood, all natural fiber, beautiful colors. No man dressed like that in D.C. which was a lawyer's dark grey or navy blue and red tie town. No exceptions. Maybe on Saturdays they would walk on the wild side and wear a yellow tie. She doubted if Asian American men in West Hollywood dressed like him. That gave Aurora a clue. Okay, he was tall, nearly six feet, which gave Asian men that attitude that they're tall enough to qualify to flirt with white women eye to eye and not have to resort to either dominance or the cleverness of their shorter counterparts with the Napoleon complex.

"Isn't he pretty, Ro?" Annie repeated.

"He's obviously got some Wonder Bread squeeze at home who dresses him."

"Well there's one you don't have to make over," Annie said. "We deserve once in a while to find one that's already been made over with the cute clothes, contact lenses, cute haircut, nice shoes by some other woman. Jeez, the work we put into some of these guys, then they leave us because they're so presentable and de-polyesterized."

Aurora was reloading another salvo about a Chinaman shopping on Melrose Avenue in a four wheel drive Jeep Cherokee with a golden retriever, when Annie said what she always said about Aurora's analysis of men, "Yeah, yeah, I know, we weren't born cynical."

Aurora looked away when she saw her boss leading the Chinaman by the arm to the front room where she was sitting. Instead of the impending introduction she feared, she heard her boss announce, "Everybody, this is Raymond Ding from San Francisco. This is everybody." Turning to Ding, her boss continued, "I'll let everybody introduce themselves, and the food's coming soon." That was it.

When Ding surveyed the room and nodded hello, he didn't do a double-take on Aurora, instead said hello to the group, nodded his head. Those of the loyal closest to him, began a discussion of San Francisco out of which Aurora heard snatches of conversation about fog and Italian food. Maybe he thought he was too good for her.

Aurora didn't know if she was relieved or disappointed. She was willing to give him a chance. Later, through some miscalculation on both their parts they had ended up at the food table together, each entering the dining room from different doors. She handed him a plate by the buffet. They spoke briefly about the food and exited the same separate doors. Upon re-entering the living room again by separate entrances they noticed that their seats had been taken by others. A piano bench large enough for two remained. From across the room, he made eye contact, didn't look away, and motioned for her to share the chair.

Brave Chinese boy, she thought.

"Do you play?" he asked pointing with his dinner plate to the piano. He wished those weren't his first words to her. Prop dependent, boring, and unoriginal introductory comment. Raymond suddenly felt like an interloper who sidles up to an attractive woman at a piano bar only to realize the vacant seat beside her belongs to her boyfriend only temporarily absent. Of course, he'd never do that anyway, unless the woman spoke to him first.

Her answer was a simple truth, "No." The intonation in her "no" closed doors, broke hearts, melted romantic inscriptions on sterling silver keepsake lockets with acid.

He said, "Food looks good." Prop dependent, boring, unoriginal again. Should he say something funny now like, "My how your eyes slant in this rich light. Hey, it's tough to get that *yin/yang* thing just right. How about that war bride thing?"

Aurora snaps a carrot stick in her mouth. Perhaps, Aurora thought, she should speak a little to the "Oriental" at hand just in case people were watching. "Was it Ray or Raymond?"

"Either way is fine, but go easy on the Ding jokes."

"Aurora Crane."

Raymond smiled. He was being witty and clever in his mind. He knew without asking that her parents had named her Aurora because of the aurora borealis, a child of many colors. Perhaps her girlhood friends teased her and called her "AB" for short. She was looking away from him after her introduction as if she were bracing herself for questions about her name, but Raymond posed the questions only in his mind and smiled to himself at the answers.

Back to back they entered conversations on opposing sides of the room. At first they spoke at the same time, each conversation drowning out the conversations on the opposite side of the room. The piano bench had a sensory induced demilitarized zone in which all touch and invasion should be avoided. But each time she laughed she leaned back touching, no, grazing him slightly. Each time after the first touch, the feeling lingered as if they were holding a flower petal between them without bruising it, or a potato chip, depending on how sentimental the touch. The touching worked its way into their conversations as each one of them paused in their own talk to eavesdrop on the other while feigning to pay attention to their own. Their touching became a way of flirting with each other. A simple touch from one would cause the other to stop their conversation, stutter over a word, be distracted. They would need this information later in order to gauge and measure the ground on which they would talk when the time came.

The Chinese "six breaths of nature" moved between them: wind, rain, darkness, light, *yin*, and *yang*. The perfect blend of each breath of nature settles the heart, mind, and body. Indeed, if something were to begin between Raymond and Aurora, neither one of them paid much attention to the fact that it had been raining for days, it was dark, a bright piano lamp was glaring in their eyes as they spoke and each of them now were situated antagonistically back to back rather than allowing the complementary *yin* which is dark and feminine and the *yang* which is light and masculine to find a sense of place between them. But then, that was just so much Orientalism under the rug.

He wanted to begin again. He prepared for a new beginning knowing that the conversation would eventually turn and it would include the two of them together. The piano bench's north and south would be joined together. The longer the delay, the later the party went, the more impossible to get over this Asian thing between them. Solve the dilemma, get the facts about each other's preference for lovers not of their own race. Nothing personal, you know. It's an individual thing, that love thing. We can get on with it, maybe even be friends, double date to prove how comfortable we are with voicing our racial preference to each other honestly and forthrightly. How adult of us; how politically correct.

Was she part Korean or Japanese? he wondered. Or maybe he was altogether wrong and she was native Alaskan or Indian or Latino? What a relief that would be.

He tells her in his mind, with his back turned to her, "Let's say we've just arrived here in America from a foreign country; you from Korea, Ceylon, or Mongolia, me from the Forbidden City. I say to you at the supermarket checkout line where we meet, 'Hi, how are you?' in broken English. You, having just learned about standing in the express lines, look down and say, in Korean, 'You have two too many items.' I give you my salami and oatmeal cookies because you only have four items. You buy them and leave.

"The next time I see you, you're taking English and Pre-Nursing classes at Seattle Central Community College. In the school cafeteria, I say, 'Hey, how *are* you? What's your major?' You buy green Jell-O and leave.

"The next time I see you, you're getting an MBA degree from Kansas and dating a Jayhawk, 6910" power forward, full scholarship. He's no walk-on. You're his tutor. I see you in the library. I ask, 'Would you like to read my *Wall Street Journal*?' You put down your copy of *Die Zeit* and glare at me. I say, 'I'm majoring in social work.'

"The next time I see you, you're at a dude ranch in Arizona wearing cowboy boots with your jade. I resist calling you 'slim.'

"The next time I see you, you're buying leopard print black tights at Bloomingdale's. You're wearing a black suede dress with fringe. You've changed your name from something with too many syllables to Connie. 'How about some espresso, Connie?' I ask. You look down at the women's socks in my hands and I explain, 'I buy women's socks because I have small feet.'

"The next time I see you, you're trading in your Toyota and buying a Ford Bronco 4WD equipped with monster mudder tires and a chrome brush guard. Safest car in America. *You'll never get in it with that skirt*, I think. 'What's she got under the hood?' I ask. You peel out in reverse.

"The next time I see you, you're anchoring the news on television. 'How's the weather and what's the score?' I ask."

He feels Aurora rise from the piano bench, glances up at her as she gathers some empty plates to take to the kitchen. When she returns someone else has taken her place on the piano bench. Raymond and Aurora's eyes meet. He wants her to come and sit on his lap, sit on the floor beside him with the arm casually draped across his leg, share a glass of wine. Eye contact, then it's gone.

He rises from the bench because there isn't a place for her to sit, makes the same motion he made when they first shared the bench. She shakes her head and points at him, then at the kitchen. *Follow me.*

In the kitchen they talk for nearly an hour. No one interrupts them because they're the only two Asians at the party. Private and natural. There's an occasional "oh, I'm glad you two have met." Guarding against any further cleverness, he withholds anymore prop dependent glib comments and she finds out he's actually a little shy. He doesn't squint to determine her ethnicity. She doesn't leave him guessing. Their conversation is complementary. She offers information and he fills in the blanks without asking embarrassing questions. "I'd like to study Japanese at a language school in Kyoto," she tells him. He responds by asking if her mother is *Issei* or *Nisei*. She says she's *Nisei* and that her Irish American father met her while buying strawberries from the family farm.

She finds herself not needing to explain herself or her identity. Twice she reaches out and pulls him toward her to keep him from backing into someone carrying a tray of food. When the danger passes each time, he retreats a step. Perhaps he should have read Sun Tzu's *The Art of War*.

In just this hour of talk, Raymond sees that Aurora is not the kind of woman who places stuffed animals in her car or would wear a dress with a zipper from the neckline to the hemline. She doesn't buy Tupperware.

Two days later, this is how she made him kiss her. He was leaning against a column at the top of the stairs on the portico of the Lincoln Memorial. She walked toward him saying something he couldn't hear and leaned next to him, covering his arm with her back. She nestled. He put his arm around her waist. She denies this to this day claiming her eyesight isn't that good and she simply misjudged how close she was to him, yet at the time she didn't move away. They kissed at the top of the stairs of the Lincoln Memorial, at lunch time, in full view of school children on a field trip from North Carolina. He suddenly felt too conspicuously Chinese. She held him close and he kissed her on her neck just under her left ear which was exactly the right thing to do. She didn't breathe until she whispered in his ear, "Public and demonstrative Asian love. A rare sight."

One of the little southern white children asked their teacher, "Are they making a movie?"

Three years later, in San Francisco, they were packing their separate things and parting.

Raymond watches Aurora walk across the room and sit on the floor in front of the dresser. She pulls open a drawer and begins to sort through it, placing her things in a box. Raymond remembers their first kiss at the Lincoln Memorial was followed by several weeks of absence as Raymond returned to San Francisco. In the space between them they flirted, she scolded, he reminisced about their delicate kiss, she changed the subject, he probed politely the boundaries of their intimate talk, and she questioned his motives. With each answer, Raymond discovered the power of his voice in her ear. And with each answer he moved the boundaries closer to her heart.

He tells her a week after kissing her, "I miss you."

"Because of one kiss, Ray?"

"Another kiss under the ear."

Raymond doesn't know Aurora at all, except for their talk at the party, except for a kiss that grew out of an abrupt infatuation stalled by distance. If he were there he would know what to do.

"What would you do if you were here?" Aurora offers her own answer, "Would you take me on a *date*, Ding?"

"Maybe we're past the formal date period."

"We never had a date."

"The Lincoln Memorial."

"That wasn't a date. I met you there after work and you go and kiss me."

"You wanted me to kiss you."

"*I wanted it*. Listen to you! That'll stand up in court, bud."

"You know it's true."

"Cliche number two."

"What did you do today?" Raymond wonders if she would let him wimp out and change the subject.

"I got my first photo in the newspaper."

Raymond is relieved and pushes congratulations to her much too loudly.

"Yes, Ray," Aurora sighs, "years of training, months of hauling camera equipment around and setting up lights for other photographers and just when the newspaper is short staffed I get my chance and the editor sends me out on my own to do what? Take a photo of the President? Perhaps some visiting King? Stalk a bad boy Congressman? No, none of the above, I, Aurora Crane, hit the big time, hit the pages of print with a photo of a pothole in front of the White House."

"Is your name on it? Send me one. Signed 'Love and kisses.' "

"When are you coming back?"

"Do you want me to?"

Raymond finds out later that Aurora doesn't say the word "yes" much, one simply knows when she agrees. "I wish I were there now," Raymond says while searching for some way to find some detail, some familiarity in imagining her at home, but he's never been to her apartment and has seen her in only two different dresses. He resists asking, "What are you wearing?"

"I'm in bed," Aurora says. "Say it again."

"I wish I were there." There is a silence on the line then he hears her breathing change.

"What does your room look like?" Raymond retreats.

"It's a mess."

"Let me guess. The shoes are thrown in a jumbled mess on the closet floor, there are old magazines and newspapers on the floor, an old coffee cup from this morning sits on the bed stand with a little cold coffee in the bottom, the bookshelf is too small for all your books, there are photographs unframed and thumb-tacked to the wall, none of the photographs are your own, there are sweat pants, jogging shoes, and a bra lying on the floor. You're wearing an extra large Columbia University T-shirt in bed."

Aurora is silent.

"Aurora?"

"Where are you calling from?"

"Home."

"Did you talk to my roommate? You have a sister you're not telling me about? You left out the color of my panties."

"No. And, no to the second question. I was being polite on the third. The panties on the floor have purple dots and the ones you're wearing have Mickey Mouse on them."

"You're wrong, they're both on the floor."

"I guess this means we're past the formal date period." Raymond's breathing has changed.

"I'm wet."

Without hesitation Raymond proposes a scene in a lower voice, raising the humidity over the phone. "You are seated on top of your desk when I come into the room. Your legs are crossed. I walk up to you and put my hand under your knees and uncross your legs."

"What are you doing?"

"I'm doing the same thing you're doing."

"I didn't know forty year old Asian men masturbate."

She knows he's thirty-nine, but he lets it go. "We can even use the

other hand to calculate logarithms on our Hewlett-Packard calcula-
tors." Aurora doesn't laugh. Her breathing sounds muffled as if she's
talking from underneath the covers of her bed. "The backs of your
knees are moist as I hold them down on the desk. I slide my hands up
the sides of your thighs, feeling the muscles of your thighs tighten.
I'm moving so slowly that you relax. Your legs part slightly. I can feel
your breathing on my neck. I reach around your hips, up the fabric of
your panties to the waistband."

"I have tights on."

"I reach for the waistband of your tights."

"You can't get to them from where you are."

"My fingers are feathers. You can barely feel them, but they can
lift you, they can warm you, they have a tropical humidity of their
own. Your tights melt away. Your panties are a warm breeze that
comes up suddenly then vanishes, exposing a humid scented moss.
My feathers flutter and nestle on the mound. My tongue is an orchid
petal."

"That's too pastoral, but I like the fluttering."

"I'm trying to be polite on our first seduction. More graphic, dear?"

"No."

"How about mythic and heroic?"

"Yes, try mythic."

Like the voice that narrates NFL Films, Raymond is mythic and
heroic. "The pulsating and golden aura of my manhood rises majes-
tically in the east and blocks the sun. It presses, advances, draws you
quivering toward me. It beckons you to embark on a voyage on the
surging waves of a melting earth, a field of erupting, heaving mountains pouring white hot magma down down down to the crashing
waves of the ocean pounding the burning sand of your desire. We are
reborn. We are immortal. Come with me. Come."

"Your manhood blocks the sun?"

"Yes, child."

"How big is this golden aura of manhood?"

"How big do you want it to be?"

"Big as a cucumber."

"How about a pickle?"

"I'm hanging up."

Long distance phone sex and making love with Aurora in person are the same seduction to her. A good lover must be articulate first and skillful and attentive second. Aurora's bedtime stories. Raymond has to flirt, and be romantic, and be seductive, and undress her, and make love to her in complete sentences and full paragraphs. She wants to be the center of his fantasy while they're making love. Each time the details must be different; different clothing, different order in which the clothing comes off, different circumstances, different places. They are characters in a story that has a beginning and a middle.

She pins Raymond to the wall and pulls his shirt out of his pants, presses her face to his chest and tries to smell him through the fabric of his shirt. She unbuckles his pants, lets them slide to the floor around his ankles, and blocks his attempts to kick his shoes off and free his pants by placing her knee between his legs. She wants him to be slightly hobbled and awkward.

She whispers in his ear and pressures him, "What do you want to do to me?" She wants him to think and be coordinated and be skillful at the same time. She turns her back to him and leans against Raymond, pinning him between her and the wall. She reaches behind her and tucks her fingers in the waistband of his underwear and pushes them down. He lifts her skirt. She stands on his shoes so that she's taller and accepts the way he nestles his erection between her legs. She likes the feeling of him being hard against the crotch of her panties. He presses his penis against the fabric pretending to be frustrated by his inability to enter her. He covers her right hand with his own hand and places it on the buttons of her blouse. He kisses her neck and watches her unbutton her blouse. He kisses her under her ear and whispers his story. The story is told slowly so that Raymond never has to change his mind, or revise, or edit. The sex stories he tells Aurora are plotted to indulge Aurora's point of view and descriptively polite in his choice of words. It is Aurora who interrupts and poses questions. Her questions are partly her own voice and partly Raymond's. She says the words "suck" and "cunt" and "fuck" deliberately as if she were quoting Raymond, as if Raymond had said them, as if one could hear the quotes surrounding each word. Each question pursues Raymond's motives and each question can only be answered with "yes." She likes to hear him say "yes." Sometimes he stops in mid-sentence as he searches for ways of speaking with his hands. Aurora unbuttons, un-hooks, unsnaps, unzips.

It's very hot. Very humid. We couldn't sleep the night before. In our exhaustion the following afternoon we've fallen asleep fully clothed on our bed in a hotel room with enormous windows and billowing white curtains.

We're bathed by the filtered sunlight of the opaque curtains. We're only one floor above a noisy street. Each time the breeze separates the curtains, there's a view across the street of other build-ings, of windows mirroring the reflection of our hotel.

Are we in a foreign country? I'm not sure. The noise from the street stirs you from your deep sleep.

My hand rests inside your loose blouse cupping your breast. Before opening your eyes you can feel my thumb brush lightly against your nipple each time your breathing rises and falls. You push my hand away and the sweat pooled there is cooled by the breeze pushing through the curtains.

Was it a tire screech or a bottle shattering against the pavement that woke you? You unbutton your blouse, but you're too tired to sit up and shed it from your damp back. Your skirt is twisted and gathered and folded in the sheets. Some of the fabric of the skirt is matted against your thighs where you've been sweating. It irri-tates your skin. You push your skirt off. You're not wearing un-derwear and worry about the curtains parting.

You're beginning to remember your dream. You're angry with me. Something you dreamt made you angry. I was with two women and we were laughing at you and how you discovered my infidelity. You're angry now for being naked and vulnerable while I'm fully clothed and disloyal. Your heartbeat is pushed by your anger. An-other bottle shatters on the street. You weren't dreaming, you say.

Your fear wakes me. You turn on your side and look into my brown eyes before I'm fully awake to see where I've been, to con-

firm my infidelity. Instead of seeing guilt and fear, you see a sleepy insouciance. Your anger changes to irritation at having been woken by your rapid heartbeat. By the time your hand reaches across and feels my slow heartbeat, you are convinced of my innocence.

"A little boy, a woman's fear," you whisper. I can't hear you over the noise from the street. Other people are talking. We are in a foreign country.

I lift your hand from my chest and place your palm against my forehead. "It's hot." You feel my cheeks with the cool backside of your hand. When I lick my dry lips you rest a fingertip on the tip of my tongue. I expect to taste the salt of my own sweat, instead I taste you. You push your finger down against my tongue. I take your hand from my mouth and place it back down there, our fingers intertwine, you push my finger inside you, pull my hand from you, brush the wetness against your clit. My finger is cradled by yours. You teach me each delicate stroke. "The curtains," you say, "people can see us." My tongue circles your nipple. "We are in a foreign country," I whisper.

After Raymond and Aurora make love, she lays her head against his chest, listens to his rapid heartbeat, his deep breathing, and she feels his body heat. Aurora is always amused by his exhaustion which she once thought was an exaggerated performance as if he were trying to please her. Aurora thought that men could not be so consumed by their orgasm, that in reality they are only consumed by the satisfaction of having completed a task that required coordination, timing, and unselfishness. *How was I?*

She thinks that his heart beats more rapidly than that of anyone she knows, like a small animal nearly frightened to death. When they first made love and she questioned his state of exhaustion, he would only say, "I'm old." Raymond is not a man of routine habits like some who eat the same breakfast morning after morning, but he is a man of routine habits after making love. He places his right hand over his forehead then drags it down over his eyes as if he's thinking about something he can't believe. He doesn't move his hand from his eyes until his breathing slows as if reality sinks in. "I'm a dream that comes true," Aurora teases.

In remembering their parting, Raymond wasn't sure he and Aurora had this conversation all in one sitting, but it survives in his mind as one.

"Let's have an argument," Aurora says.

Raymond agrees.

"You're a man, I hate men."

"Yes, I agree, I am one."

"Men are scum."

"Yes."

"I have no life."

"You have me."

Raymond says something that he's said before only this time Aurora is listening. "The disagreement between us is not the difference between men and women, but between sons and daughters."

"What's the difference?" Aurora is beginning to look upset at Raymond in that familiar way, for the way she thinks he changes subjects in order to deflect an argument. She's upset at herself for asking another question; falling into a trap.

"What did your mother want to be?" *There's no trap*, Raymond wants to tell her.

"She was my mother."

"No, what did she want to be? An artist, a ballet dancer? Did she ever want to be Myrna Loy?"

"What are you talking about? I don't know."

"The difference between us is in the way our mothers raised us. I was raised by a mother who raised me on extravagance and perfection. When my mother arrived from China, she took photography and painting. We were a Picasso-esque 'self-portrait with baby.' Despite our disjointed image, some said I had my mother's nose. My baby pictures were social statements, natural light black and white photos heavily shaded with shadow and bleakness, symbolizing man's alienation from society. A baby seated in a desolate corner of a room framed against an immense blank wall. A baby's innocence measured against some large impersonal machine of industry. The tender smooth skin of a baby, a shard of glass, a broken gear. In between painting my mother went to the movies. In America she wanted to be Nora Charles in *The Thin Man*. She bought me a wire hair terrier like Asta. Maybe she didn't want to be Nora Charles, but I know she wanted her life to be like Nick and Nora Charles' life—rich, affluent—but more importantly than affluence, she wanted to move through her daily life with the same ease that Nora Charles moved through the daily routine of her life. Things get done, people open doors, taxis are hailed, mysteries are solved. It was her way of being an American. My father wouldn't let her name me Nick Charles Ding."

"You know the sexiest thing about you?"

Aurora's trap. She tells Raymond men are scum, then pushes an idea toward him he can't resist. She never asks questions that are soft and open-ended like, "What are you thinking, honey?" She argues and makes love with him by asking questions, both are forms of entrapment and seduction.

"I asked, 'Do you know the sexiest thing about you?' "

"Do you remember the first time we made love."

Aurora looks up at Raymond in frustration.

"On the phone."

Her look changes to resignation.

"Why did you open yourself up like that? We hardly knew each other."

"You're complaining?"

Raymond shakes his head.

"I felt it would be fine. I told my friend Brenda about how we had phone sex. She thought you were a pervert. Don't worry, I told her the truth, how I started it, I wanted it to happen. There was something about you being my first Asian lover; there was a lot I didn't need to guard against, second guess, protect."

"I don't understand."

"You don't see it, Raymond?"

Raymond shakes his head again.

"You ever go into a Chinese restaurant or a Japanese restaurant with a date who was white or black? Well, how do you feel? You're made to feel like the outsider as you're scrutinized. Your date doesn't feel any of this friction and tension. He feels like he's part of the inside; you're going to order the good stuff, maybe talk a little lingo with the waitress for his benefit. He might even throw in a little *arigato* trying to get on your good side. There you are eating, perhaps feeling the disapproval of the waitress, the busboy, all the while you're trying to figure out if your date is one of those guys who got some kind of Asian woman thing. And that 'thing' runs the gamut from asking you to teach him how to use chopsticks, to figuring he's going to get a *shiatsu* massage, to wanting his tea leaves read, to trying to find out if my vagina is slanted. I keep my hair short just to keep the white guys with the Nancy Kwan fetish screened out immediately. I've never been with any non-Asian man who hasn't at one time or another during our relationship tripped himself up and said something racist. Their defense is that I'm half white. They don't understand it when I say I'm not white. Hearing your voice on the phone, remembering how you kissed me on the neck, I felt free to leave myself unprotected, unguarded. The worst you could do was say something sexist. I could teach you to be less sexist and lower the toilet seat and all. As I started talking with you on the phone, I realized you'd let me just be a woman, not make me be an Asian woman, which is, ironically, what Asian women say they want to be when they're with a non-Asian man. I knew you wouldn't make being an Asian woman part of the sexual fantasy, you know, 'Speak Japanese to me baby while I whack off.' That's why I wanted you." Aurora said all of this without looking at Raymond.

"You make it sound so romantic."

"You're the only boyfriend I've ever had who uses the word 'romantic.' It was romantic, Raymond. Our fantasies were on the same plane. I thought you had the will and the desire to make me happy." She pushes the drawer in and suppresses a sudden urge to change her mind and stay with Raymond. "You didn't answer my question about the sexiest thing about you."

"We had simultaneous orgasms over the phone?"

"So you say," Aurora shoots him a look of disapproval. "You didn't have to describe your orgasm over the phone."

"I was inspired."

"You're avoiding my question."

"Do you want me to guess?"

"Your patience with women. I've noticed it's how you flirt with women. You sit and listen. You actually want to be friends and maybe several years down the road, something hits them and they want to go to bed with you. Women come up and kiss you, sometimes right in front of me."

"Friendly kisses—"

"That's the way you flirt. You walk into a room, or a party, or a dinner never expecting a kiss, giving a kiss, nor do you look comfortable giving or receiving kisses. Keeping your distance is in itself a very flirtatious act." Aurora felt stupid saying this. She knew some of the women only did this because they were older than Aurora, closer to Raymond's age and only kissed him in front of her as a way of holding ground, sticking a spear into her youth and beauty. The look on Raymond's face told her he wasn't going to argue with her illogical observations. What she said was true. Aurora noticed how women would greet other men and stiffly accept their friendly kiss on the cheek, even return a peck with complete insincerity, then these same women would greet Raymond with a kiss, sometimes on the lips, sometimes while he was in the midst of talking to someone else. Aurora suspected they liked to see Raymond's surprise and watch his insecurities and even a slight inferiority complex rise to the surface. It was like having a certain power over him and the more beautiful the woman the more forward the kiss. The best evidence was Aurora had done the same with their first kiss with the exception she made him kiss her by asking him.

Raymond was going to say perhaps the women just wanted to kiss someone Chinese, but he didn't.

Aurora wants to describe him as inscrutable, in the most well-meaning version of the word, the Sam Shepard inscrutable silence attractive version of the word, but obviously can't use that word.

Aurora knows that Raymond's relationships with other women and his marriage to his ex-wife made him what he is to her. He's a man who admits he's made mistakes in relationships, then improves his behavior for the next woman. At the same time Raymond has built a wall around those relationships sealing them off from view. He doesn't know Aurora wants to know exactly what he thinks the mistakes were. He blames himself, but that's not enough for Aurora. She knows he tries to protect her and that he's cautious about the past. Too much history, too many experiences measure too much of Raymond's age against Aurora's age. What stands between them is an excuse about difference in age.

Aurora pushed her argument aside and moved it closer to the two of them. "Look at the way you make love. You want to talk and play at the same time. There's no rush. Most guys approach women like some lone dog with the rest of the pack behind them barking encouragement. They measure their advances as victories and defeats. Why am I the one saying the dirty words? Where did you learn how to flirt like that? Are you conscious of it?"

"I must have learned it from my mother."

"Flirting and seduction?"

"No, patience." Raymond laughs, "I learned it by following my mother on shopping trips to San Francisco, to I. Magnin, City of Paris, Macy's. I remember her being very proud of the way the women clerks used to compliment me on my ability to stay interested in shopping for my mother's clothes. In the old days the department stores had huge elegant dressing rooms and I'd sit there and watch my mother try on clothes. The clerks thought it was so cute the way my mother asked my opinion. I'd sit there like some midget sugardaddy and say, 'I like it. I'll buy it for you.'"

It struck Raymond that after his mother's death he learned to become a man from his father and learned his patience by re-examining his mother's life as if everything she did or they did together had symbolic meaning, as if she knew she would exist mostly in his memory.

"You see, Ro, a Chinese son's life is bound by duty and obligation to mother and father. I guess patience is practiced across several generations for Chinese. Now, I'm suddenly older than my mother was, there's nothing I need from her. My father's got his notion about having a second wife and a second life. Our lives are running parallel to each other. Somehow my life is safe, perhaps even free from filial duty."

"Sometimes I think it's easier for you, than me. You're the loner.

You're free to do whatever you want. Your mother is whatever you want her to be in your mind. Your father is content to start a new life and isn't dependent on you. Why am I struggling? Why don't I understand *my* father?" Aurora asks. "Maybe because I'm a daughter."

"If you had been born the first son rather than the first of two daughters would life have been different? Perhaps your mother's life would have been more extravagant. What are you afraid of?"

"We were arguing about us."

"We were not arguing. You said, 'Men are scum.' I agreed."

"Why do you always buy green onions when we go to the grocery store?"

"The last bunch is rotten." Raymond lets Aurora retreat.

"It's rotten because we didn't eat it."

It's an inheritance. Raymond's mother always bought green onions every trip to the market. His mother broke off and stole thumb size pieces of ginger from the Safeway. "It's not even enough to weigh," she tells him. Aurora's inheritance is that she saves things like her mother did: useful things like the Styrofoam trays the meat is packaged in, rubber bands, used wire ties, plastic soup containers from the take-out, plastic Ziploc bags. Letters. Raymond's mother never saved anything, never bought the economy size. What doesn't seem to change between them is what they inherit from their parents.

"Things have changed," Aurora says.

Raymond wants to be saved from the way things change, from fear of change. He suddenly feels like he should quit before he's fired. He wants to separate his things into separate drawers before Aurora speaks again, before she's finished sorting his things from hers. He doesn't want to get caught showing Aurora how much he's in love with her when she changes her mind.

I can be your friend. Raymond wants to tell her.

"It's ironic how your conceit involves other people in your life—the way it involves me. You're proud of your patience in my presence. You're proud of your shyness which you say is confidence. You can be weak and vain about your image in my presence. Is that possible?" Aurora prattles in a way that seems as if she's talking to herself half the time as she sits on the floor in front of another drawer examining things that are both hers and Raymond's. "I think I've fallen in love with the image of you being alone, aloof, shy. You give people close to you their freedom to grow and, yet you don't allow this relationship to end. Trust the memory more than the thing itself. I don't want to hurt you."

Raymond can't speak. Each time she says she doesn't want to hurt him, it hurts him. *Yes, I can be a friend. Yes, I can be a brother. I can help you get a job. I can fix your car. Men like me have tools.*

"Things have changed." Everything Aurora has taken out of the drawer she puts back. "We need to clean our house. There are things we need to throw away, but I can't throw anything away."

Aurora realizes the double meaning in what she's said and steels herself against Raymond's self-pity, how he wants to say that he wishes it were true. The silence is worse. Aurora is relieved when Raymond shows some strength and tries to be funny. She laughs as Raymond offers a guide to throwing things away.

"Why do you save old copies of *People* and of all things, *TV Guide*? Of what use is six month old news about shoulder pads, Calvin Klein, Paula Abdul, Soul II Soul, Arsenio Hall? If you need a halfway house and can't bear to throw the magazine away, tear out the articles you want to save, put them all in one box, save them for exactly one month, then throw them away.

"Throw away socks, T-shirts, underwear, tights, if any of the following are true: (1) none of the above have any elastic left, (2) there are holes in, pick one, toes, butt, crotch, armpit, sleeves, heel, (3) you haven't worn them in five years, (4) haven't worn them since high school, or (5) have never worn them because they're too damn ugly.

"Throw away cosmetics or medicine if: (1) you're allergic to it, (2) you haven't used it in five years, (3) it's not the same color it once was, (4) you hate the color, (5) it belongs to your sister and you stole it from her, or (6) the bottle/box/tube is empty."

"You make it sound so easy." The self-pity shifts as if it's being pushed. Then it's shared.

"Things of sentimental value are difficult to throw away. There are sacred items that can never be thrown away except in a fit of pique or despair such as letters, photographs, high school dance corsages, teddy bears, ticket stubs, college sweat shirts, diaries. The more you throw away in this category, the more you feel like your life will move forward, like forcing motion in your life will cause motion, like our theory of moving the furniture in our apartment—the law of interior space physics—which states that if you move the furniture in our home, we will create movement in our lives."

This last part Aurora recites with him and laughs again. She reaches into the same drawer and begins to sort again. "Do you remember what I said to you when I thought you might try to seduce me after we kissed at the Lincoln Memorial?"

"Yes."

"Well?"

"You said, 'You're either genuinely nice or very very smart.' "

"Why didn't we sleep together that night?"

"It took me weeks to decide on an answer."

There are things Raymond can't say to Aurora now. He wants to say, *look at the thing you're throwing away, remember the moment, the time, the person, the feeling, then throw it away, it will stay with you. There are things I can't bear to throw away like everything I have that belonged to my father and mother. Yet, everything that I've lost of theirs, the memory of that object, that thing, is burned in my memory. Somewhere in my moving years ago I lost a family album. I've memorized every photo in the album.*

"You bought me a dress. I haven't worn it in years."

"Trust the memory more than the thing itself."

Aurora is tapping a pencil on the floor and flipping it in the air. "That's my expression, you stole it from me." Aurora puts everything back in the same drawer again and pushes it back into the bureau. "I don't know who I am when I'm with you. I look at you and I think you're beautiful, but I don't see me anywhere in you. I'm not on the surface." Raymond moves to speak, but doesn't have a defense against the truth. Aurora stops him before he ends up in an awkward space between lying and insincerity. Aurora is afraid of her last statement. Even in separating from Raymond she appreciated the way he made their conversation specific to them, to who they were, and kept away from the cliches. Now she sounded whiny like a white Yuppie couple mouthing things they'd heard on television or in a college psychology class about distancing oneself, about finding one's own space, about having other needs, about dysfunctional relationships. "I'm not on the surface. You look at some men and they have an aura about them that says how much they love their wife, their girlfriend. Or they wear their obligation on the outside; it says they have to run, get home, bring the paycheck home, buy groceries, make sure there's air in the spare for their daughter's date." She tries to sound more specific, but ends up drawing a picture neither one wanted or was capable of producing between them. She sees Raymond trying to reimagine himself in each of the examples. She wants to say, *but not you.*

Aurora pushes herself along the floor further away from Raymond while at the same time stretching out her legs and resting her foot on his ankle. "Maybe it's my fault. I wanted my father to give me this too. I know my mother wanted him to publicly exhibit that he was a part of our lives; his Japanese wife, his two Eurasian daughters. But I don't think he really knew how. There were the three of us and him. He never looked like he belonged to us and we never looked like we belonged to him. My father's an old Navy man, Chief Petty Officer. He's got tattoos on his arms for chrissakes. I remember he came to visit me when I was going to Columbia and we're walking down the street on the Upper West Side. People were staring at us, my father with his midwest plaid shirt, windbreaker advertising our auto parts store, his arm around my waist. He's still got his Navy crew cut. I thought people were staring because he's so midwest, but they weren't. People were staring at me and I saw it in their eyes. I wasn't his daughter, I was a prostitute. They've seen me in the movies. Sailor and the pretty Asian girl. When I'm with you I'm safe from blame."

"Just because I'm Asian."

"That's part of it and it's what I wanted. I wanted at least our identity together to influence me, to lead me, to feel like I belonged to you."

"Feminists—"

"Not in the way that'll have every Asian feminist up in arms hearing my proclamation, pointing their fingers at me—"

"At me, the misogynist or at the very least, the domineering Asian man and you, the young impressionable girl slave."

"No one will ever accuse you of being a misogynist or domineering.

My friend Brenda once said you were a man who was taught how to be a man by a woman."

"Brenda said that? I'm suspicious of the meaning of that statement since Brenda doesn't like Asian men."

"She thinks Asian men are sexy."

"I've never seen her with one."

"She doesn't want to go out with them, she just likes their hairless chests and they certainly don't have hair on their backs and the fact they don't smell when they sweat. She sees all of you as sweet smelling mute Bruce Lees."

"How do you see me?"

"I was in love with the way we were a family. People saw us and it made sense to them."

"Except you're nearly thirteen years younger and look twenty years younger."

"That never bothered you, why? Even that woman who thought I was your daughter didn't bother you. Nor did you ever put me on display, you know, forty-two year old codger with young trophy wife."

"Every Asian woman I've ever had a date with has always looked fifteen years younger than me even when they were older than me. People think my Aunt is my sister. Besides forty—"

"I'm still in love with you."

Aurora accepts and shoulders the guilt for why she and Raymond are separating. He's hurt but rarely shows it. He tries to be strong and tries to say things that are meant to be ironic and wry as if they had just met, as if she had no knowledge of how much he loved her. He can do this because he knows she still loves him. He thinks if he can keep Aurora talking and if he pretends he's strong, she'll be able to find her belief again. He tries not to give in to everything Aurora wants. Raymond picks an argument, but he's not very good at it.

"It's the age thing."

"It's not the age thing."

"It's the voice of experience thing."

"It's not the experience thing."

"I give too much advice."

"I ask you for advice."

"I'm Chinese and you're not."

"It's not racial."

"I'm a bad lover."

"You know the answer to that."

"I think your friends are young and silly."

"Some of them are."

"I patronize."

"You never patronize."

"I'm perfect."

"It's my fault, not yours."

"It's not your fault."

"I think I'm frightened by something."

"What is it Aurora?"

They both know, but can't say. It's hard for Aurora to believe in her own safety, that she can feel protected, that she believes she wants Raymond to protect her. Protect her from what? From what happens, from what ifs? No. It's identity. A sense of self. She wants to be as strong by herself as she is with Raymond. She wants to have a "son's" sense of the world. She wants an inheritance from her father. She wants her father to pass his power and authority to her as if she were a son. Perhaps he has already, she thinks. She wants people to witness and acknowledge King Lear handing the kingdom over to the loyal daughter. *Give me the pocket watch from grandpa, turn over the business, pat me on the back when I follow you into the Navy, live your life through me, your son, and grab me another beer, will ya?* The witnesses Aurora sees only hear her saying, "Hey, sailor." She can't be part of the same inheritance. She's not white. She's part white, but it still makes her not white. Was Raymond the father that makes sense and joins two mutually agreeable identities together? He's more than just my lover, Aurora admits. It upsets her that Raymond knows he's not as strong without her. Has she had enough chances to prove herself, like Raymond has? "I'm older," Raymond has said more than once, "maybe I know there are things I simply can't do anymore, I can't prove anymore, or there are things I don't want anymore, or things I accept as is." Aurora remembers how Raymond talks about himself like a car, "As is, no warranty."

Raymond wonders if it is racial. Raymond argues with himself about race and gender, about race and identity being a flimsy excuse, a coverup, a scapegoat. He's interrogating himself and his answers sound defensive. "What is it you don't know? What is it you can't find out with me?" he wants to ask her.

Aurora wonders if it is racial. Perhaps Raymond makes too much of the race issue. Their union was never always just love and desire and friendship. Race was always present in public and in private. Sometimes she felt that he treated his ancestry as a gift to her that would make sense of who she was. She knew she didn't have to be with Raymond to simply say to herself that she was Japanese American and that she felt Japanese American even though some people found it difficult to see it in her face. Being with Raymond people assumed she was Asian and didn't have to guess. She found herself explaining less, but at the same time wanting to harbor the definition of herself that she had to defend against while growing up. Sometimes it was "the age thing" between them. Raymond knew himself better because he was older. Aurora sometimes wanted to be more adrift, more unsure, make more decisions. Raymond and Aurora fit together. There's a common bond. People can see it when they're together. She likes being in a city with a huge Asian population. She can identify with the city in the same way she can be identified with Raymond.

The first few months with Raymond was like being in a college ethnic studies class as they compared notes about being Asian in America and being biracial. Raymond spoke of the sixties and self-determination, then the seventies and used terms like "multicultural" that she had only heard in school and never between two lovers. Perhaps Raymond and Aurora were no different, neither one really knew they were Asian when they were young and each had to prove it in their own way. For Raymond the opportunity to find his identity came in the sixties. Negroes became Blacks and Raymond became "Asian American" without a hyphen. She knew all this information in a general way, yet Aurora would listen and be kind, but in reality only wanted to know how long Raymond's hair was and what he wore. Sometimes he lectured in bed about Berkeley in the sixties.

Aurora is afraid that she'll never forget the way she and Raymond make love.

"How can you be afraid of that?" Raymond asks. "Is that something you want to forget?"

Weeks later, after their separation, Aurora is sitting on the edge of the bed, her bathrobe is untied and hangs open, she is naked underneath. The phone rings. She doesn't move to answer it, instead her phone machine answers. When she hears Raymond's voice, she pulls her bathrobe close around herself. He sounds distracted, admits there is no reason he called, then says there was a reason, but he's forgotten. Then he remembers that he called to tell her his new phone number, but he doesn't tell her. He'll call again.

Face

Yoji Yamaguchi

Whores worked out of clapboard shacks in a place called China
Alley—a misnomer, as it was not really an alley but a labyrinth
of paths running behind and between a cluster of shops and saloons;
nor were there any Chinese to be found. The Chinese had quit the
town nearly a decade ago, after the Japanese, fresh off the boat and
hungry for riches, underbid their hire for all the laborers' jobs and
quickly laid claim to the entire immigrant quarter. But the name had
been coined by Americans, and none of the Issei felt inclined to quib-
ble over the name of those ramshackle huts—"floating world" or
"pleasure district" would have sounded rather high-handed, anyway—
so China Alley it remained.

One of the women who worked there, Kikue, was the subject of
much conjecture among her colleagues. She was older than most of
the others, approaching her thirties, so it was said, and not especially

YOJI YAMAGUCHI was born in New Jersey in 1963. He holds degrees from Duke University, The Johns Hopkins University, and the University of Virginia. "Face" is excerpted from a novel-in-progress.

beautiful. Yet, she attracted only the most reputable and prosperous Issei, local merchants, artisans, and farmers who were almost all of them well-mannered and well-kempt, with plenty of money in their pockets. The other women, alas, had to contend with the seamier elements—the gamblers, loan sharks, thugs, and indigents—coarse, unruly men, hardly fastidious about their appearances and even less so about such niceties as payment for services rendered. So it was a mixture of curiosity and envy that started tongues wagging.

One story had it that Kikue had been married once, until her husband caught her in bed with another man, whereupon he killed him and tried to kill her as well; she escaped, but fell into the clutches of a pimp, who promptly shipped her off to America. Another version was that her husband lost a wager to a labor contractor who had come to their town recruiting workers, and gave her away, as he hadn't enough cash.

Yet the most widely accepted version was that a pimp, posing as a wealthy merchant from San Francisco in search of a wife for his son, gulled her parents into giving away their only daughter, promising her first class passage to America on a luxury liner, a mansion with a dozen maids waiting on them at all hours, two chauffeured cars, a sailboat, and a trip to Paris every summer. Had such gaudy enticements not been persuasion enough, he showed them his "son's" picture—a face, it was said, of such inestimable grace and beauty that any woman would be happy to sail across an ocean in quest of its owner.

After the deal was struck, he whisked her off to the port of Y——, and she soon found herself aboard not a luxury liner but a freighter, in steerage, and her father-in-law-to-be had lost his refined accent for the guttural tongue of the southernmost provinces. When they were well out to sea, he laughed and informed her of her new life as a whore. She demanded he return her to her home and he told her she could jump off and swim, but not before she gave each of the crew a quick one. When she tried to claw his eyes out he tied her up in the hold for the rest of the trip and told her if she didn't work for him he would kill her and then go back and kill her family.

As one might expect of a woman in her situation, Kikue knew the secrets of many but volunteered few of her own. She knew, for instance, that Nakagami the saloon keeper had never been an army officer, as he claimed; in fact, he was rejected by the draft board for his "obesity and general slovenliness." By the same token, Mr. Kunihara's father was neither a Baron nor a former high-ranking bakufu official, as Kunihara was wont to boast in tearful, beery fits of nostalgia, but rather a low-ranking land-tax collector for the new federal government.

Perhaps because of the shady nature of her invitation to America, Kikue grew keen to all kinds of airs and pretenses. The off-beat pause in an affected accent; the effort behind a gesture; the seams in a constructed tale: in time, none of these escaped her eyes and ears. It was not hard for her to catch a man with his defenses wilted like the creases in yesterday's suit; since most of her customers tended to forget that she was a sentient being, they were all the more careless.

As she unraveled the lies that seemed to enwrap each new visitor, layer by layer, like a tightly wound obi, she began to wonder if there was anyone to be trusted, accepted at face value.

Her single-room clapboard shack had a door on the side, an 18" square portal braced with wooden bars facing the alleyway. A passerby could look inside and see her lying on a narrow barracks bed. A rickety deal nightstand was the only other furnishing; on it stood a kerosene lamp and an incense burner made of tin. The ragged remnant of a brown, fading tapestry drawn over the window meant she was entertaining.

Kikue's employer, a pimp named Kato, added a feature to all the huts that made his women all the more popular: an escape door in the corner of the far wall behind and below the bed. The idea came to him after that regrettable incident with Mr. Matsuda's wife, who followed him one night to Kikue's, and burst into the shack at a most unpropitious moment, catching her husband quite literally with his pants down. Screaming to high heaven, she dragged him, half-naked and red-faced, out by his ear, clinging with the tenacity of a snapping turtle all the way to their home. As more and more of the Issei were deciding to settle in America for good, brides from Japan were beginning to arrive in force, threatening the monopoly Kato had enjoyed when the local Issei population consisted almost entirely of single men.

The secret door was a godsend for men like Deacon Oshita of the

Japanese Methodist Church, who could not very well be seen traipsing in and out of a whore's shack. And it was a source of great fun for Takashi Arai, a silly young man who insisted on crawling in on his belly and startling Kikue off her bed whenever he came to visit.

In truth, he only surprised her once; after silently crawling into the shack, he began rocking the bed from below in a frenetic, bucking rhythm, sending Kikue shrieking and leaping across the room. But after a year of this, she was used to his stealthy entrances, and usually could hear him when he was still outside. Almost invariably, he would bang his head or bark one of his shins on the doorframe, or try to push the door in when he knew—or should have known—that it only swung out. Still, she always jumped on cue and scolded him for scaring her so in a convincingly angry tone of voice. She knew he would be sorely disappointed if he could no longer take her by surprise.

Kikue also knew the reason for his clumsiness: he always showed up drunk. She wondered if he was really as hard a drinker as he claimed, or if he just needed a quick dose of heart to bring himself to see her.

There were many things about Takashi that left her wondering. She didn't know why such a vain, empty-headed, but undeniably beautiful young man would keep coming back to her, an older woman, fearfully thin, with her knobby shoulders, her clavicle, and the sinews of her long neck protruding through her pasty skin; one with wrinkles gathering around her eyes and mouth; one with noticeable strands of gray in her dry, thin hair; one whose long, wiry hands might have been elegant, but were now coarse and leathery.

If Takashi was aware of the pain his face had caused—and still caused—her, he didn't let on. He carried his looks lightly and thoughtlessly, not out of great humility, but rather out of laziness. Though he prized his face more than anything—well, anything above his waist— he tried his best not to dwell on the curious power over others it lent him: that would be burdensome. He was like a king who relished all the trappings of office but dreaded its responsibilities.

What Kikue could least fathom was how such a refined, noble face could adorn such a dissolute, frivolous lout. On the surface, Takashi looked like one of those haughty snobs who never cracked a smile for fear of appearing plebeian. Instead, he was incorrigible; he had been expelled from prep school for stripping and hog-tying the schoolmaster's weak, pampered son and leaving him on the school lawn the morning of a visit by a local dignitary. He was audacious; after his father, disgraced beyond measure by the aforementioned incident, among many others, disowned him, Takashi demanded a round-trip first-class fare to America as his due. He was shrewd; he settled for one-way steerage, winning that concession from his father only by promising never to darken his family's doorstep again. He was irresponsible; he had gone through a dozen jobs in four years, staying at none of them more than six months. He drank every night, excelled in pool, went broke in fantan. Other men might have been too embarrassed to admit such an ignoble past, but Takashi delighted in recounting his prodigal life; in fact, he rarely talked about anything else.

For that reason, Kikue distrusted him. Men of candor, she had concluded, were the least trustworthy; they volunteered only palatable truths and held back the rest. Those who spoke with conviction were more likely than not deluded to some degree, and thus even more suspect. Truth could never be freely given; it had to be taken by force, snatched up by stealth.

Whenever she met one of these fellows who claimed to speak frankly, Kikue always thought of a painter in San Francisco who had recently enjoyed fame both in California and Japan for his hazy, swirling landscapes, which the immigrant newspaper *Nichibei Shimbun* compared to the paintings of the Frenchman Renoir. The artist angrily insisted that he was not an Impressionist, but one who sought to reproduce the world exactly as he saw it. Most people assumed he was merely being pretentious until he was run down by a streetcar on the day of his first public exhibit. Doctors who examined him discovered that he was near-sighted almost to the point of blindness—a fact duly reported in the paper. Nothing more was heard of him again, though some people who claimed to know him later said he had given up his art, become a derelict and drunk, and died in obscurity not long thereafter.

By his own account, Takashi was the scion of a successful merchant family that had made its fortune in soya and sake, brought up in an immense country house, surrounded by all the trappings of wealth, and schooled at one of the best, most expensive schools in their prefecture. If that were so, Kikue wondered, then how did he come to be a mere blanket-carrying dekaseginin?

She remembered the first time she laid eyes on him, more than a year ago. He was out cold and buck-naked, stinking of liquor. Three drunken, unshaven men, field hands from the look of their clothes, carried him unsteadily into her shack and dumped his limp body face down on her bed. One of them placed a neatly folded bundle of clothes on the floor.

"What's this? I don't do corpses," she protested.

The oldest of the trio, a stocky, leather-faced man with a pepper-gray beard, reached into his pocket and produced a wad of bills, thirty dollars in all. "Here," he said, holding out the money with an unsteady hand. "Humor us, please. We have an important favor to ask."

"What do you want? Who is this? What happened to him?"

The second man, a tall, sallow, bald-headed fellow, spoke up: "He is a sometime companion of ours; his name is not important. We met him this evening at a, er, social establishment, whereupon he declared to all present that he could outdrink the three of us combined. As this was, ah, something of an affront to us, we of course accepted his challenge. Although he is quite a, um, prodigious drinker, as you can see he was simply overwhelmed by our collective capacity." Discreetly, he suppressed a belch.

The older man spoke again: "Our friend here is quite a likeable sort, actually, a witty, lively fellow, truly enjoyable company for the most part. But he can also be insufferably boastful, arrogant even. He seems to think he is blessed with greatness, and has rather inflated notions about his innate superiority to the rest of us, whom he thinks of as being merely run of the mill."

Kikue marveled at these scruffy-looking men and their refined (if somewhat slurred) way of speaking. She guessed that they were professionals or scholars back in Japan who were ruined financially and came to America in a wild attempt to reverse their fortunes. In this country, where a Japanese education meant nothing, it was not uncommon to find janitors fluent in classical Chinese, barbers with degrees in medicine.

"It is true," the bald one hiccupped. "He believes himself capable of anything. We like to think his brashness is a function of his youth. But there is more: as you can see, he is quite a handsome, virile-looking young man. Unfortunately, he has allowed this whim of nature to go to his head. He fancies himself not only irresistible to all womankind, but entitled by natural law to their hearts' affections. Worse, he recounts incessantly his alleged numerous liaisons, sparing not a single detail. If what he says is true, he has had more lovers at the age of twenty-four than most men could possibly hope to have in a lifetime."

The older man smiled and said: "Naturally, we are skeptical."

"He's full of shit, is what." The third man spoke up for the first time. He was much younger than the other two, roughly the same age as the man on the bed and nearly as drunk. He was short and pudgy and wanting a neck. In the dim light of the shack, his long, stringy hair and his pock-marked face gave off a greasy sheen. "He's all talk and no cock," he said, letting fly a fine cascade of spittle.

The older man raged at him: "Damare! Mind your tongue!"

"What, she's just a whore," No Neck sneered, whereupon the bald man slapped him on the side of the head, nearly knocking him off his feet. "Please forgive our friend Isao," the bald man said, discreetly rubbing his fingers clean. "What you see here are the unfortunate side-effects of Westernization on Japan's younger generations. Regrettably, the great liberal thinkers, with all their emphasis on the individual, did not take into account the inherent baseness of mankind in general. To value freedom over civility absolutely can only lead to mischief." The older man nodded solemnly in assent. Kikue noticed that he was beginning to sway a bit.

"So what do you want?" she asked sharply. She was growing impatient with these long-winded fellows.

The older man said: "We would like you to determine for us whether our friend is telling the truth about his experience in carnal matters."

"You mean . . . ?"

"So. We would like you to find out if he is still a virgin."

"But how could I tell?"

The bald one replied: "Because you are yourself a woman of, er, experience. We trust you will be able to spot a novice by his lack of, eh, dexterity and, um, endurance."

Isao snickered. The older man cuffed him in the ear, eliciting a yelp. Then he said: "As you can see, we have already taken the liberty of undressing him, so as to spare you the difficulty. Needless to say, we are indebted to you for your indulgence, and we hope we have not caused you too great an inconvenience."

Kikue said: "Wait. What am I supposed to do with him? He's dead to the world."

"We leave that to you," the bald one said as he turned to leave. He stopped at the door and added: "Mind you, we are not being malicious; we are not trying to humiliate him. We simply want to know the truth. That he feels compelled to lie to us for the sake of self-aggrandizement is quite intolerable. Trust is precious, and not to be exploited. Friends should be honest with one another, wouldn't you agree?" With that, the three men bowed woodenly and said farewell, then staggered out of the shack, leaving Kikue with her comatose john.

The man rolled over onto his back, startling her, and began snoring, wheezing, snuffling, grunting not unlike a boar. His sleek, flawless skin, marred here and there by flushed, sanguine patches, shined like ceramic. He was tall and lean; his wiry muscles and sinews rippled, it seemed, with a barely dormant energy. His long, supple body reminded her of a rushing, white-water river as seen from a hilltop, his sex a dark, treacherous snag in mid-stream that could smash the sturdiest craft to bits. His face was elegant, finely honed. Shorn of any sign of chubby boyishness, it retained the smooth softness of youth, and was highlighted by bold, slashing eyebrows, long, down-like lashes, a subtle peak of a nose, and a firm, graceful arc of a jaw. His cheeks were flushed from the liquor, giving him the look of wearing rouge.

Kikue stared at that sleeping, expressionless face, and gasped. A palpable jolt emanated through her body, from the center of her chest down her limbs and up her spine all the way up to the base of her skull. Disbelief, anger, fear, humiliation, and grief—all of these flooded into her mind at once. She bent over him, so low that her nose was inches from his; sour whiskey fumes poured into her nostrils.

Kikue straightened up and backed away from the bed, wrapping her arms around her body. At that moment, she trembled with the urge to suffocate him with a pillow, then chase down his three friends and rip their eyes out.

She didn't, of course, nor did she tell Takashi when he finally awoke how his three friends had brought him to her or, more importantly, the cause of her shock. In time, as he kept returning to her, she grew fond of the Little Fool, as she liked to call him, punning on his name.

But she didn't forget, preferring to bide her time, planning all the while. She would determine when and how he would find out the secret of that night, when she saw for the first time in the flesh, there, lying on her bed, the promised son, the beautiful betrayer—the man who was to have been her husband.

Just a case of mistaken identity, Takashi Arai thought to himself as he crept lightly through the dark, empty streets. He hunched his shoulders and glanced cautiously from side to side. The collar of his peacoat (a memento of his brief career as a seaman on a pineapple boat) was turned up, partly from the chill northern California night, but mostly to hide his face from the shuttered, lamplit windows that seemed to wink at him as he walked by.

The streets were empty, and he was glad. Last night, when he was walking through China Alley a whore he'd never seen before had burst out of her shack and threw herself at him, babbling incoherently. She was a round-faced young girl, no older than sixteen, with droopy, hooded eyelids and a boy's body. The red, tassled dress was a size too large and made her look like a grotesque, shrunken doll. "It's you, it's you, you're finally here. Where have you been? Where have you been?" she sobbed over and over.

Takashi could only stammer "What? What?"

"Oh that terrible man—Saigo, he called himself—he said that you were ill and couldn't come, that he would take me to you. Why weren't you there? Now look what's become of me." She let out a short sob.

Abruptly she smiled and looked up at him. "Oh, how lucky I was to be looking out the window just as you were walking by!" Then, just as quickly, her countenance darkened. "And what do you think you're doing here?" she demanded sharply.

"I don't understand. I think . . . there's been a mistake."

She shoved him in the chest. "Yes, it was my mistake. I never should have married you! What kind of husband are you, bringing me all the way to America, then leaving me stranded?"

"Husband?"

A man approached. "Oi, what the hell? I was here first. You're gonna hafta wait your turn, boy," he growled.

It was Fuseda, the foreman at the local slaughterhouse. Even though he was a foot shorter than Takashi, and twice his age, Takashi knew better than to mess with him. Fuseda's grizzled face and thick, ham-like arms were intimidating enough, but Takashi had also heard that the older man came to America on the lam, after killing a man in a barfight in Hiroshima. And as foreman, Fuseda was rumored to hang men by their waistbands on meathooks if they weren't working to his satisfaction.

Fuseda grabbed the woman by the arm. "C'mon, girl. Back to work."

"No, this is my husband and I'm not your girl! You can't use me anymore." She struggled to free her arm.

Fuseda bellowed in laughter. "This is your wife, boy? What's the matter, ain't you got a job of your own?"

"No. I mean, she's not . . . I don't know . . . Ah, there's been a mistake."

The woman glared at him, then slapped him across the face. "Coward! Are you afraid of this pig? I thought you were a war hero. You said in your letter that you killed Russians with your bare hands."

The short burly man cocked his head back and folded his arms. Takashi pictured a slab of beef on a hook, all bloody and raw. He stepped away from them and started walking. "I have to go."

Fuseda hoisted the woman on his shoulder. "C'mon, I've had enough of this. Time to earn your money."

Takashi walked away. He could hear behind him the woman's shrill, panicked voice, calling him by someone else's name, with Fuseda's harsh laughter booming in the background. "Daisuke-san! Daisuke-san! Matte! Wait! Come back! I'm your wife, you can't leave me like this!" Then he heard a door slam and all was quiet again. His night thoroughly ruined, Takashi fled home in a panic.

What a nuisance, he thought now as he dug his hands into his pockets: a face confused, a name misplaced, and suddenly another man's life—his accumulation of debts, obligations, affections, and grievances—foisted on him.

Takashi wanted to believe that the woman was simply myopic, drunk, or mad, but he knew better. She was not the first woman to mistake him. There were at least a dozen other women before her, housewives who spotted him on the street and stopped dead in their tracks to gape at him in a most undecorous fashion.

Other men attributed this phenomenon to Takashi's face. It was a running joke among the bachelors and a sore point for the husbands; they called him Kao-sama, Master Face, the man who entranced women just by looking at them.

But vain as he was, Takashi knew there was nothing magical about his face. The way each of the women had looked at him—the contorted shock of recognition, the pained grimace clouding over, and then the black, icy bitterness—told him everything. It had to be the picture.

Three years before when the old man Kori offered Takashi fifty bucks for a photo of him and even agreed to pay the photographer, Takashi never foresaw his present dilemma. Kori told him that he had been looking for a picture bride from Japan and saw the perfect woman. The old man spoke as if he were describing the visage of a goddess instead of a wallet-size photo of an anonymous woman tacked on the bulletin board in the dusty, ill-lit office of the labor boss who doubled as a marriage broker for his hard-up, lonesome hires and anyone else willing to fork up the requisite fees. He couldn't remember her name at that moment, but it sounded high-class.

Unfortunately, the boss told him no chance. While Kori could no doubt provide a handsome wedding gift and a more than adequate living for any woman, all the gold in America couldn't compensate for his age and (Kori chuckled sheepishly) his looks.

It made sense to Takashi; Kori's face reminded him somewhat of a grizzled old fox: a pointed nose, two tiny, deep-set eyes, and long, angular ears. The only un-vulpine feature was his stark, shining head, which was shaped more like a squash than anything else. Takashi pitied the old man trying to catch a young wife, forced to mask his face in order to do so.

Kori was not the only one. On the mainland, Issei men still outnumbered Issei women tenfold, and the only way to find a wife—short of making the exorbitant trip across the Pacific—was by sending a photo of one's self to prospective brides in Japan; the importance of appearances was utmost. Naturally, the uncomeliest men—the hoary, hirsute, bald, fat, big-nosed, flat-faced—were at a decided disadvantage. So it was not uncommon for them to use outdated portraits that were taken at a more attractive age, or to hire a substitute. The families of the brides were not above this sort of practice, either.

Here Takashi hesitated. How many times had he seen a happy old man trailed by a crestfallen young woman who shuffled morosely and as deliberately as the tides so as not to overtake her doddering spouse? And how many times had he listened to a drunkard sitting beside him at the bar, mumbling a lament about his once-beautiful wife who had metamorphosed into a swarthy, basso-voiced giantess during the course of her trans-Pacific voyage?

Whatever misgivings Takashi may have had about engaging in this masquerade were quickly dashed by the wad of bills Kori flashed in his face. The woman who marries a man who carries so much ready cash will be set for life, Takashi reasoned—I'd be doing her a favor. Security is a wonderful thing; you can't take your looks to the bank, after all, he thought.

The possibility that he might one day come face to face with the gulled Mrs. Kori never occurred to him. Nor did the off-chance that Kori might be something other than a lovelorn, hopelessly ugly suitor in search of a wife.

What Takashi did know was that at least twelve women (thirteen, now) landed at the new immigration station on Angel Island, expecting him to greet them on the San Francisco pier, and looked for his face among the eager, anxious men queueing on the dock, who were probably in turn searching for the right faces on the ferry's deck, glancing down at the photos in their hands from time to time. Some of these women were taken home by jarringly homely husbands who bore no resemblance to their promises, and who were hard pressed, no doubt, to explain the vagaries of photographic mimesis or the transience of physical beauty. But some women, he now realized, were whisked off to saloons and whorehouses, where they were told, plain and simple, to work or die.

Takashi imagined an armada of immigrant ships steaming toward California, their steerage holds crammed with hopeful women, each of them clutching his photograph, eager to meet him but not him, some Taro, Jun, or Haruo wearing his face. He saw riots on the docks as the women, realizing they'd been had, fell on their hapless husbands, and the survivors, having just been told by their brides-to-be in no uncertain terms how wanting they were compared to the peerless man in the picture, set out, town by town, in search of this pretty despoiler, this dandy homewrecker, to tear him to messes in a jealous rage. And if they didn't get him, the women would, mobs of howling, teeth-baring women chasing him into the desert. A Society of Defrauded Brides would be founded, its membership in the thousands and spanning the entire West Coast, its sole mission to track down this treacherous Takashi Arai and bring him to justice.

Or, even worse—to bring him to marriage. Takashi shook his head as if to dissipate the vision that swelled in his mind: a wedding ceremony with a thousand brides and one groom.

One would expect that Takashi—who valued his looks more than anything—would be gratified at the willingness of so many women to cross an ocean to marry him. Instead, he felt like bait, thrown into the teeth of a hunting pack.

Takashi would not have given these women a second thought, if only he didn't keep running into them. After all, he was taken in as much as they were. One need not have been a genius to figure out that the glibly self-effacing old man had been sharing—or more likely, selling—Takashi's picture. That Kori would give this fellow Saigo the whore mentioned—a lowly pimp, of all things—license to use his face was intolerable.

Drunken laughter escaped from one of the windows high above the street. Takashi thought of Fuseda, and embarrassment coursed through his body; his face flushed; his armpits felt clammy; and his back prickled as if someone had stuffed cockleburrs down his shirt.

He clenched his fists and blurted out to the black silent night: "Isn't it natural for a wife to feel let-down by her husband once they're married? What difference does it make whether it happens sooner or later? Sure, everyone looks great during the engagement; but once the wedding's over, forget it.

"But they get over it. They must. Otherwise, all the husbands and wives would be running out on one another. There wouldn't be a single married couple left in the world."

As if in response, a dog barked in the distance. Takashi, realizing he'd been talking to himself, picked up his pace.

After all, Takashi thought, these women came here just like everybody else—chasing after their own little fortune. So the siren's song turned into a shrill mocking laugh; so the chest of gold proved to be a pile of shit; in this these women were not alone.

Even after six years Takashi could still remember the words of that sign he saw in the window of the S. Ban Company, a labor-export enterprise:

Kitare, Nihonjin!
Come merchants! America is a veritable human paradise, the ichi-ban mine in the world! Gold, silver, and gems are scattered in her streets!

Now that was a pretty picture. But it didn't depict him cutting cane under a scorching Hawaii sun, slicing his hands and arms on the razor-sharp leaves, or working as a houseboy for a churlish, dwarf-like hakujin widow, whose rancid breath was more stubborn than a painful memory. This was the life Takashi found awaiting him in this veritable human paradise. So why should he feel bad for these women who were just as gullible as he was?

Takashi stopped and realized that he'd bypassed the walkway between the tobacconist shop and the shoe-repair store that led to China Alley. He found himself before the Japanese Methodist Church, which stood at the corner of Third and J Streets in relative solitude, the closest buildings—Murakami's saloon on Third and Koyama's bathhouse on J—each a good thirty yards distant. The church was a one-storey affair, with white shingles and a tar-paper roof. Light flooded out from the square, single-pane windows. A cardboard sign, inscripted with bold, black kanji, hung by a nail from the white sandwich board that stood on the bald patch of dirt in front. ENGLISH CLASS TONIGHT 7:00–9:30. ALL WELCOME, it read.

Just then, he saw two people emerge from the main entrance, a middle-aged couple. The man was dressed in Western clothes: brown derby and overcoat, tartan scarf, pleated, grey pinstripe trousers, black shoes. The woman wore a red and white kimono with a simple floral design, and tabi. Her face was powdered white, with touches of rouge, and her hair was neatly coiffed. Takashi leaned against a lamppost and watched this incongruous pair approach. When they stepped into the circle of lamplight, the man's round spectacles glinted, and the woman's painted face seemed to give off a hazy, ethereal glow. Takashi bowed his head languidly in salutation.

The older man, no doubt noticing Takashi's insolent posture, nodded curtly and grunted. But the woman stopped, smiled, and pronounced a "*Good ee-ben-ning,*" in slow, measured syllables.

As they walked away, Takashi felt a sharp pang of annoyance, but he didn't know why. Was it the man's stodgy airs, which seemed to match his clothes, or the woman showing off her pidgin English? Whatever the cause, it quickly passed, and Takashi was relieved that she didn't stare at him like the others.

In a still night almost devoid of human traffic, voices carry for miles, it seems. Though the couple didn't speak until they were a presumably tactful distance away, Takashi could hear every word they said.

"Kugakusei ka?"

"Iya, branke katsugi soo da yo."

Indigent student? Migrant worker? Me? Takashi thought, astonished. He held out his arms and inspected his clothes. His once-elegant and expensive white linen shirt now had a dull, wheat-colored hue. He could see a pale crescent of it peeking out through a tear in the armpit of his coat. His shoes, once shiny as lacquer, were badly scuffed and creased. His blue trousers were faded and threadbare, nearly gauze-like in places; he could feel the wind tickling his buttocks. He scratched his chin and realized he needed a shave.

Still, Takashi was seething. He was on the verge of shouting something suitably coarse and defiant, when it occurred to him: what could
I say? *Fuck you, I'm a respectable . . . houseboy?*

Instead, he spat in disgust and stalked away. He was tired of being
seen as someone he was not; tired of worrying about who he was or
who people thought he was. He wanted nothing but to see Kikue. She,
after all, knew him better than anyone.

Empty Heart

Lois-Ann Yamanaka

He lay me down on the straw in the shed behind his papa's house, listen for awhile to the cane trucks passing on the plantation dirt road behind their property line, and the lychee tree moving crackly leaves in the early night time; chickens clucking low, low. He touch my forehead with his long fingers and make them crawl across my face like little feet.

And he turn the Eveready on. On his fingers as they track across my face. On my chin where he draw light finger circles. Down my neck, light shining, following a finger slide down my neck, and fingers light around each tit-ty. Spotlight left. And he smile, weak-like. Spotlight right, and his breathing rapid. His finger in my belly button and

LOIS-ANN YAMANAKA: "I write in the pidgin of the contract workers to the sugar plantations here in Hawaii, a voice of eighteenth-century Hawaii passed down to now third- and fourth-generation descendants of various ethnic groups. Our language has been labeled the language of ignorant people, substandard, and inappropriate in any form of expression—written or oral. . . . I met poet/teacher Faye Kicknosway in 1987 . . . and I was encouraged to write in the voice of my place without shame or fear. . . . My pidgin pieces have been published in many publications, journals, and anthologies. . . ."

swirl it around and around, eyes rolling, slow, flashlight fall and go off by itself.

I know what else he want to touch.

Crawl slow,
> slow there too
>> then stop
>>> in his finger tracks.

He groping around in the dark. Pretending like was one accident he touch me here and here and his fingers into there and there. Stop.

Take a fat red crayola he find in the corner of the shed and draw pictures in the asphalt right outside the door, wind pouring into us now, erasing our breath in the window-less shed. He say it will melt in the slope of the sun and stay there forever, and then he says,

Write your name
> *and mine*
>> *long*
>>> *and curvy.*

But I draw a school girl shampooing her hair with Prell in a tub full of bath oil beads.

Then I draw my name next to his:

Empty heart

Empty heart lov WillyJo

on the sidewalk in red crayola.

He not in school anymore but he drive his yellow Datsun with the 8-track tape player from Muntz stereo to the parking lot by the baseball field, far from the schoolyard and sneak across Alto's yard behind the school fence and hide on the slope full of dandelions and puffballs. He wait by the fence until the bell for recess time and I run to him fast and sneaky as I can, hide behind the hibiscus hedge and sit in the tall ironweed. I put my fingers through the chainlinks to touch his face. He kiss my fingers.

WillyJoe pass me cut persimmons so I can think in school. But I can eat um if, only if, I let him feed me. Then he sit there and teach me about places he think he seen. Words he learn from Uncle Penny:

The redpurple vein croton.
The story of the mouflon sheep tie-up in Felix yard.
The making of a Pontiac.
Beef cuts at Cosmo's like sir-loin tip.
Bangkok, a beach with waves like blacksands.
Or maybe he dream it,
Madrid, the Plaza Dee-chooca.
Or last Saturday he been there, places where the lights all blue,
Downtown Honolulu with Uncle Penny.
Yellow cities curling, places where he drank sunrise with mini pink
umbrellas and purple orchids in a cabaret, and the girls there no wear
panty. They kick their legs high and open (higher than the high school
cheerleaders), and ride one glass swing high above the audience.
Yellow lights and fingers through the chainlink.
More. Tell me. More. Tell me. And he tell me about
bells ringing,
the bell ringing, and the teacher yelling,
Get away from her before I call the cops, you mo-lester. Help, help
somebody help me. Trespasser! Quick, get the principal. This child mo-
lester's been after this girl for a long time. Scram, you big good-for-
nothing before the cops get here. The teacher grabbing my arm and
pulling me away. Scratch my arm on the hibiscus branch. My arm
bleeding.

Willy's fingers hanging onto the chainlink fence, his face, his lips
withering. And animal screams from his mouth like the sound I heard
his bunnies make when the mama rabbit step on them in the middle
of the night. We was sleeping next to his papa's shed.

Willy know plenny words he learn from his Uncle Penny who
teach him on Saturdays on the porch of his house. Willy bring the
Planters cocktail peanuts and six-pack Primo. And Willy learn all his
words.

And the drunker they get, out come the tequila, Cuer-vo, and fresh
pick pretend lime (from the kumquat tree), and rock salt. Then Uncle
Penny is Perfeser Penny.

A clot is a co-agu-late of blood.
Willy is himself.
　　Tell me about coitus.
Willy tell me come learn and I
　　　　can be
　　　　　　　myself
　　　　　　　　　too.

He the cherub come from St. Joseph's pink church on the corner across from Cosmo Meat Market and the post office, and the one bank in town. The church surrounded by jacaranda trees and African tulip trees. Get orange and purple petals on the gravestones the priest sweep everyday.

One day, Willy say he going read me the names on the stones, before the petal juice and black fungus fill the grooves and the names all gone.

And one day, he say he going ring the church bell for me.

One day.

He take me to St. Joseph's today to save me from Cain. We sit by the hedge of the graveyard and make mini-chure grave circles with tiny rocks and sprinkle mock orange leaves into the center. Ant graves or maybe a bigger insect if we kill one. So we waiting. And looking.

Then his fingers start crawling to the place between my legs.
Stop,
　　　he tell himself. *Instead,*
　　　　　I going cure the blood clot
　　　　　in your emp-ty heart.

By the saltwater ponds. Near the black sand beach. In the yellow Datsun. Late afternoon. Salt mist all around, the ocean rough and choppy today. A big hill of sea grass in front of the car, and Willy singing,

> *Some-where ov-a tha rain-bow,*

a cappella, he singing,

> *Good-bye yellow brick road,*

about his fuu-chur it

> *lie be-yond the yellow brick road.*

And he play a tape of Elton John. Like sound-track in a movie. Like background music that perfectly match what the actors doing. Like today.

But Willy, he say he have no brain. He say he stupid, he a drop-out with so-sho and emo-sho handicap. Willy say before in his special class, they dig weeds for the ag teacher all day so he can be

the Scarecrow long and soft.

Me, he say, I the star of the song. (Humming low and holding my fingers in his fingers.)

I Judy Gar-land.

I Dor-ty.

And my breath he say, smell like paprika.

He WillyJoe, the Big Scarecrow, scared

scared of a lot of things.

Scared of me.

Scared of my body.

Maybe one day I no

let him touch me anymore. Anywhere. Over there.

No fingers crawling no more.

Scared of my nostrils flaring.

So scared of me.

ScarecrowJoe.

he fiddling with his zipper again,
scratching it right in front
of the schoolyard fence

One day
I going write
about you,
I tell him.

Sitting under the tree in the schoolyard while the light from the softball game make the whole school like day. WillyJoe the scoreboard man but he tell my Uncle Reggie that he get one date tonight. Uncle Reggie tell Willy got the night off.

Willy hanging from the jungle-gym and make me sit at the very top. Right over his face.

No moonlight. The still shiver of tree leaves. His fingers gripping the bars and his legs too long, bent at the knees. Him sniffling and smiling. And loud cheering from the baseball field. And fingers moving. Stop.

> *Write about the way you*
> *walking down the road,*
> *rolling the cane truck tire innertube*
> *to take to the beach.*
>
> *One day,*
> *because you teach*
> *me so much*
> *new words*
> *and how to sing.*

In the grass, rolling together and laughing in the schoolyard, and making stepped on rabbit sounds until it echo and echo in the school buildings, and throwing glass and tinkling sounds. And licking each other's eyelids.

Everything feeling so red and looking red, all the lights and inside me.

> *One day,*
> *I going write*
> *about you*
> *walking down the road,*

bouncing the innertube
on the hot asphalt

right over the place
where we wrote
in red,

Empty heart.
            WillyJo lov Dor-ty.

That Was All

Wakako Yamauchi

Last night I dreamed about a man I hadn't thought about in many years. He was my father's friend, a hold-over from his bachelor days. As far back as I can remember, starting somewhere in the late twenties, Suzuki-san visited us—though not frequently—and my earliest memory of him begins with these visits when at four or five, I used to run from him. I hated the feel of his hands; they were rough and calloused from farm work. My father's bachelor friends were constantly reaching for me—perhaps they were amazed that he, bachelor of bachelors, had settled down to domesticity with this beautiful

WAKAKO YAMAUCHI: "I was born in Westmorland, California, a desert township near the Mexican border. I spent my early years there, where my father grew tomatoes, summer squash, and cantaloupes. In 1942 we were all sent to Poston, Arizona, one of ten camps where Japanese and Japanese Americans were incarcerated during World War II. After the war I moved to Los Angeles to study painting. I married there and, off and on during marriage, motherhood, and divorce, I wrote short stories about the Japanese in America. . . . During the seventies, I submitted 'And the Soul Shall Dance' to *Aiiieeeee! An Anthology of Asian American Writers*. I was encouraged to adapt it into a play and since then I have been writing plays. I write because I want to set down a time, a place, and a people, so I can get it right in my own mind."

woman, himself not so handsome, not so cunning (still not losing his bachelor ways—the drinking, the gambling), and had this scrawny kid, or perhaps they were recalling other children spawned in other wombs and brought to life only by seeing and feeling me and remembering. At that early age I suspected something sinister about their caresses, because I did not find this touch-touch attitude in men with families. Japanese people rarely touch, and my father . . . I cannot recall the warmth of my father's hand, except the sharp snap of it against my thigh when I misbehaved. My father acted as though I should accept these attentions from his friends as accommodations to him. I thought they were more for my mother's sake.

Raised on that desert farm under the patronage of two adults wrapped in their own set of problems and isolated from peer values, my imagination was left to run rampant. Although I cannot now believe it was entirely a misconception, I had the suspicion that all men were secretly and madly in love with my mother, who was the most beautiful and charming of all women. Magically emerging from that desert floor, she endured the harsh daylight realities and blossomed in the cool of the evening. After the bath. And I was sure no man in his proper mind could resist her. My father, I thought, was not in his proper mind.

My mother was a perfect Japanese wife except with my father in the bright light of day when she did the bulk of her nagging. My father's strength was his silence which he applied in varying pressures from Arctic chill to rock mountain imperturbability to wide open, no horizon, uninhabitable desert silence. My mother's emotional variances were my barometer: today she sings—fair and mild; today she remembers Japan—scattered showers; today he has made her unhappy again.

Suzuki-san lived in Niland 30 or 40 miles from us in a treeless landscape of sand and tumbleweed. I don't know why this area, not so distant, seemed more desolate than where we lived, maybe because where we lived there was a mother and father and a child, and where Suzuki-san lived, there was only him and two bleak structures, a kitchen and a bedroom, and the land beyond this complex and ranch was untouched from year to year, century to century—only the desert animals pocking its surface and the rain streaking the sand in a flash flood now and then. That seemed awesome to me.

I remember a visit to his homestead. I was six or seven. It was winter and my mother bundled me in a heavy coat and packed the car with pillows and blankets and we drove for what seemed hours. I was disappointed when we got there because there was no one and nothing to play with and in this incredibly boring place, the sun was blinding, the wind biting, and my mother was again in the kitchen cooking and mending Suzuki-san's clothes, and my father was walking up and down the furrows with Suzuki-san. I tried staying with my mother but the kitchen depressed me; without a woman's touch, it looked like the inside of a garage—no embroidered dish towels, crocheted potholders, nor a window with a swatch of dotted swiss fluttering.

I walked along with my father and Suzuki-san but their frequent stopping to examine plants, scratch the earth, turn over equipment, bored me and I wandered off to the desert. My father was not alarmed; on that windswept land a few loud bellows carried for miles and would quickly draw me back to him. Besides, there was no shrub taller than myself I could hide behind, no ditch I could drown in, and snakes and vipers were not considered a threat.

I wandered around looking for—I don't know what—maybe some indication that someone had been here before me and left something for me, and finding nothing, I stood by the fine pure sand the winds had pushed against a shrub and mused that it was possible I was the first person who had ever been on this particular mound of sand and put my shoe to that dust that began with creation and then my hand and then my cheek and then my hair and finally rolled myself on it and fell asleep.

My mother said later, brushing the sand from my coat with hard quick hands, "I think she rolled in the dirt," and my father said contemptuously, "Like a dog," and Suzuki-san looked at my mother with those bemused eyes that pretended to know something he didn't and I grew very angry and denied it all.

It was his mocking eyes that I disliked.

Intuitively I knew that my father, close to 40, and my mother, perhaps not yet 30, had abiding ties with Suzuki-san that started earlier than my arrival, perhaps somewhere back in Japan in Shizuoka, and perhaps on something less mysterious than appeared on the surface. I thought later maybe Suzuki-san had loaned my father a vast sum of money.

Suzuki-san was unlike my father's other bachelor friends, who still followed the crops along the length of California, cutting lettuce in Dinuba, harvesting grapes in Fresno, plums, peaches, and finally straw-berries in Oceanside and those little known places—Vista, Escondido, Encinitas. They spent their money as soon as they got it—drinking, gambling, carousing—until at the southernmost end of the state, they looked for us and stayed two or three months eating my mother's cooking, and drinking my father's wine, oblivious to my mother's sighs which grew deeper as the visits wore on. Although Suzuki-san drank with my father too, he never permitted himself the coarse laughing and out-of-control drunkenness characteristic of the other roustabouts. Also Suzuki-san leased a parcel of land and farmed it like a family man—although he had no family that anyone spoke of either here in America or in Japan—nor did he show any apparent need for family, nor did my father or mother show interest in seeing him married. The need only surfaced now and then when he would catch me unaware and hold me squirming in his sandpaper grasp. Or sometimes it showed in the way he looked at my mother with his amused eyes. Perhaps when these needs were strongest, Suzuki-san came to us and ate with us, often bringing something special for my mother to cook, examining each morsel on his *hashi* before bringing it to his lips and chewing slowly—movements as sensual and private as making love. Once when he caught me watching him, he laughed and slipped some food into my mouth in a gesture so intimate I flushed warm and my father coughed suddenly. Those days he would stay overnight, sleeping on a cot in the kitchen and leaving in the morning after my mother's good breakfast.

Then about the time I turned fifteen, something very strange hap-pened to me.

Suzuki-san was visiting us on this summer evening. We had finished supper; the day's warmth was still with us as we sat on the porch fanning away gnats and insects that flew past us toward the light of the small kerosene lantern. The air was still and the cicadas hummed without beginning or end. Suzuki-san returned from his bath stripped to his waist and sat next to me.

In the half dark I saw his brown body and smelled his warm scent and in the summer night with the cicadas' pervasive drone in my ear and the scent and sight of Suzuki-san's body assailing my better judgment, I fell in love.

I sat in the protective shadows of the night and watched the face I'd never before regarded as handsome and scrutinized the eyes that always seemed to mock me. I wondered about the wasted years this man had kept his perfect body to himself, never giving or receiving the love that was most certainly available to him. I wondered why he continued to work in his self-imposed exile and what future he hoped for himself . . . and whom he would share it with. An indescribable loneliness and sorrow came over me. I wished he would touch me again. He'd long ago stopped that.

Then he looked at me. My stomach turned and roiled with things terrible and sublime and sensual and sexual and rotten that I was unable to contain. They passed through me and fouled the still night. My father grunted and walked away. My mother glared at me and fanned the air away from herself and Suzuki-san.

I was mortified. I was betrayed by my mother, who should have found a way out for me. Instead she separated herself, denied me, and remained aloof, the lady of evening dew, and I . . . I was humiliated. Suzuki-san's eyes did not change. I went into the house.

That was all, that was all.

A few years later my father, unable to stave off the economic disaster that was our inexorable fate, moved us on to Oceanside. And a few years after that, war with Japan broke out and changed the course of our lives and we along with thousands of Japanese and Japanese Americans, were incarcerated in Arizona. Maybe Suzuki-san was also in the same camp. I don't remember seeing him.

And I fell in love at least three times thereafter—each time with the same brown body, the same mocking eyes—and the last time, I was drawn into a tumultuous love affair that spanned twenty-five years and ended on a rainy January morning. And perhaps I should add, I have not loved since.

And last night I had this dream:

I was living in a lean-to which I instinctively knew was part of Suzuki-san's house. The house itself was in terrible disrepair. It looked like a wrecking ball had been put to it. The floors buckled and the walls caved inward.

I felt I should offer to do something for the man who kindly shared his house with me, battered though it was. I was thinking of my mother who had so long ago done his cooking and mending. I went about gathering clothes I might wash for him. While going from room to room I passed a cracked and dusty mirror and in the fragmented reflection, I saw myself—older than my mother had ever been, older than I remembered myself to be.

I found two items to wash: an ancient pair of twills, moldy and stiff but unworn, and a sock, which I recognized as my own, half filled with sand.

Then I saw him in one of the rooms.

As it is with dreams, I was not surprised when I saw he was the same man I remember on the summer night when I so suddenly fell in love. He was naked to the waist, his body was tight and brown, he wore the same pants. In my head I thought, "He hasn't changed at all—still 35 . . . what would he want with this fifty year old woman I've grown to be?" But my mouth said, "I hope you're not paying a lot of rent for this place."

He said, "The rent is cheap."

It was my fault. I should not have started a conversation sounding so shrewish. I looked in his face to see if I could find some recognition of me . . . the me that he once wanted to hold . . . the me that was part of my mother's evening dew . . . the me that was gone forever.

I watched him until he could avoid me no longer and in my dream his eyes mocked me again . . . as they have always done.

Photographs
for an Album (Third Version)

John Yau

I.

O ne brother liked to watch a woman undress, while the other brother liked to wear women's dresses. There are some things you think you will never mention, but one day you begin talking about them, he thought. One day you begin talking about them knowing that it is not what you want to be doing, but you go on talking, go on as if there is nothing else to talk about, as if you were talking about someone else, someone you made up.

Made up, he thought. Someone you make up, someone in make-up. He made himself up as he put on his make-up. It was not make-believe, it was someone someone made up, someone you see looking back, looking back from that place in which you are encased, frozen face covered in something other than ice.

He was sitting on the floor in his apartment, looking at the photographs, knowing without wanting to know that the talking had already

JOHN YAU was born in Lynn, Massachusetts, in 1950, and now lives and works in New York City. An independent art critic since 1978, he has written for well-known American and European publications, including *Art in America, Art Forum, Interview,* and *Vogue,* and contributed more than a hundred essays and introductions to monographs and exhibition catalogues of contemporary art and artists. He is a recipient of numerous grants and awards and has been anthologized widely. His books of poetry include *Corpse and Mirror,* which was chosen by John Ashbery to appear in the National Poetry Series, *Radiant Silhouette: New & Selected Work 1974–1988,* and *Edificio Sayonara.* He is currently working on a book about Jasper Johns and a "notebook" about Andy Warhol, as well as collaborating on a book of poems and photographs with artist Bill Barrette.

started, that the voices had already entered his thoughts, had already become part of what he would or would not say. Now they were inside him too, photographs of his brother hanging in chains, wearing a shiny black dress, kissing the red shoes of a woman whose face was left out of view, long black whip dangling from her gloved hand.

II.

The brother who liked to watch a woman undress had removed the photographs from an envelope, expecting to see something else. An image of himself standing on the steps of his high school, twenty-five years after he graduated without honors of any sort, not the image of his brother hanging naked from the ceiling.

He had opened the envelope shortly after leaving the store. He was walking down the crowded street, and had carefully lifted the photographs out, like a deck of cards, and had started fanning them open. He did know who he was looking at, did not know this woman smiling at him like an old friend. He stopped, and then began walking faster, the envelope and photographs shoved into his pocket, his hand holding them so they would not get away.

You cannot speak of the deprivation of someone else as if it is something that happened to you, something you own. You cannot speak of the events that marked you or your brother, the things that made you up, the make-believe rooms you entered in order to get away from the ones you were in. You cannot tell either his story or your own. So you sit there looking at the photographs of your brother hanging in chains and wonder what you can say to him or anybody else about what you are looking at. You wonder who would listen to this if you began. You wonder why. You wonder what you would say, why you would say it. You cannot speak for others, he thought. You cannot take their place.

III.

The one hanging in chains and the one looking down at him are brothers. One in the air, the other on the floor. The one sprawled on the floor left their parents' house while in high school, the other moved back there after college. The one who left spoke to his parents about the one living with them and they laughed. Though he never admitted it, the one who stayed at home was angry with the one who left because one parent loved him and one parent hated him, and he was stranded between their choices. Or was it that the stronger parent hated and the weaker one loved the brother who stayed at home. Or was it that the one who stayed at home was loved and hated in other ways? he thought. Ways that he knew were in his imagination rather than his memory, because he had left as soon as he could, leaving them—father, mother, and his brother—behind. Had gone with the stronger parent's blessings. Or was this all part of his own make-up, what he wore when he walked down the street, and entered rooms full of faces unlike his own?

IV.

Once he wrote a story about a brother waiting for his older brother to return, an older brother he imagines having, one who left before he was born, and whose abrupt departure caused his parents to become what they had become, two listless shadows staring into themselves, two mouths speaking about what life was like before he was born. In his story, the younger brother is sitting alone on the porch, watching cars pass. It is late evening, near fall. The light has started to change.

After finishing the story he put it away and didn't read it again for many months. He told himself he had written a story, and he had wanted to write something else, something that would hold something else inside of it, something he had not been able to inject into what he had written. Was this when he first learned (but did not listen) that he could not escape into words, could not become a thing frozen in a white page of snow? Was it that he wanted to tell a story that held something inside of it? something that he was holding inside himself, something that he had not been able to speak about, had learned to believe it was wrong to speak about? Was it that he believed something else should be written? that the time for telling stories was over? that all the stories had been told? Or was it that he believed what he had been told about telling and because of that could not begin to tell? Or was it that for many years he had tried to escape into words and failed? had been unable to become an object held up to the light? Or now, seeing the form of his brother's escape, he wondered what it was he could say to his brother in the air or himself on the floor.

One morning he fished the story out of his desk and began reading it. What was about someone else, someone he made up, was about him and his brother, the one hanging in chains, the one in the photographs he had been holding, the one who never answered any questions. And now they were all inside him. In the story he had written, the older brother does not return. In the story he had not written, the older brother does not lower his brother to the floor. The brother hanging from the ceiling has been writing the same story over and over, he thought. He has not found a way out of his story, has not found a way to release himself from its words, has not found a way to make the ending change. He has stayed inside the story in which he makes himself up in a room of make-believe. He is listening to himself tell a story, and he is playing all the parts. It is a story no one else, not even his brother, the one looking at him, has heard. It is a story told to him over and over again until finally he believes there is no other story, and begins telling it to himself.

One brother inside the words of others, and one brother trying to escape into words he thinks are his own. This is their story, he thought. This is one that he has never told.

V.

The brother who liked to watch a woman undress had been beaten many times by his father. How many times is too many? he thought. When is enough more than enough? How far is too far? Once, while writing a letter to his father detailing each of the times he remembered clearly, he thought he should stop because he never spent a night in the hospital. Was he, as his father insisted, stubborn? Was he, as his father had repeated, bad? The brother who wore dresses never said if he had read the letter his older brother mailed to their father, the letter the father had read to the older brother's wife, a painter who believed it was possible for a blonde to become Chinese, like her husband. The brother who wore dresses never mentioned that his older brother's wife had come and stayed with him and their father during Christmas, and they had all spoken of the older brother's repeated desertions. The brother did not talk at all about the other brother's wife, blonde and blue eyed, the one who wore make-up and believed she looked Chinese. The brother who stayed at home never told the brother who had left that their father had given their dead mother's jewelry to the blonde wife, because, as the father said to the older brother later, he didn't deserve to have these things. Later, on the phone, his wife would tell him that she had been surprised by the calm, matter-of-fact tone of his letter, that the father had said to her after she had read the letter that his son was very spoiled when he was young, and that he was still spoiled or he wouldn't have left her? She would ask him why he couldn't see what had happened to him from his father's point of view. She would ask him when they could see each other again? She would ask him why he had run away from her. And he would listen, and wonder if he would ask her why she had not mentioned the things his father gave to her, the things his mother once wore, the things she had managed to carry with her when she left China, when she left her parents and a city turning to smoke and ash.

VI.

Do you or anyone else have to be there to know what actually happened? he thought. Is this what must happen for you to know what actually occurred in this room or that? The stories that never get told, the ones that each of us has kept—are these what must secretly be repeated in order for us to pass safely through each day?

He was looking at the photographs, but he was not in the room in which they were taken, basement of a suburban ranch home, formica paneling, and a bleached blonde in a red leather skirt, white satin blouse, and purple sunglasses, holding a whip and smiling. He was looking at the photographs of someone who could be a relative of his wife, a sister or cousin. He was thinking of the sunglasses she wore at the beach, of the wooden walls of her parents' house, of the stories they told. He was looking at the photographs and thinking that, though the blonde in purple sunglasses, the blonde smiling into the camera, looked like a relative of his wife, that she was not, and that neither her story nor his wife's was his to tell. He could see her smile, but not her eyes. He could see her clothes, and that she was thin. He could hold the photograph, but he could not hear what his brother and the blonde said to each other when the camera was pointed the other way or sitting on a shelf.

VII.

One brother knew he had been hit many times, the other brother never mentioned whether he was or not. One watched, the other wore. One moved from room to room, and house to house, while the other sat still or stood and waited. Neither of them spoke of that when they spoke.

Selected Readings

This is definitely *not* a complete listing of books by Asian and Asian American authors who write in English. I am happy to report that as of 1993 there are many more novelists, poets, critics, playwrights, and scholars than were around in 1973; bibliographies and "lists" such as mine, however carefully or casually drawn, need to be updated as often as possible. Obviously, some of these writers I have included have written many other books than I have noted here. *My selections are based on personal tastes*—these are books I have read over the years, books that have helped me comprehend and enjoy the depth and diversity of our vision and experience. Fortunately, some of these books have been reissued, and many are available in most bookstores and libraries. I also recommend checking out literary and scholarly publications such as *Amerasia Journal* (published by UCLA's Asian American Studies Center), *The Seattle Review,* and *Bamboo Ridge: The Hawaii Writers' Quarterly,* as well as books published by Hawaii's innovative Bamboo Ridge Press. I have included books by several Philippine authors who write in English; they are published and distributed in the Philippines and Asia by notable presses such as Anvil, Bookmark, New Day, and the University of the Philippines, to name a few. One thing all these books have in common besides the English language: they are worth the trouble of finding and are a damn good read. Here then, alphabetized by author:

Cruelty, by Ai; poems (Boston: Houghton Mifflin, 1973).

The Killing Floor, by Ai; poems (Boston: Houghton Mifflin, 1978).

Nampally Road, by Meena Alexander; novel (San Francisco: Mercury House, 1991).

Without Names: Poems by Bay Area Pilipino American Writers, edited by Shirley Ancheta, Jaime Jacinto, and Jeff Tagami (Kearny Street Workshop Press, 1985).

Making Waves: An Anthology of Writings by and About Asian American Women, edited by Asian Women United of California; various literary genres (Boston: Beacon Press, 1989).

Cebu, by Peter Bacho; novel (Seattle: University of Washington Press, 1991).

Random Possession, by Mei Mei Bersenbrugge; poetry (I. Reed Books, 1979).

Between Worlds: Contemporary Asian American Plays, edited by Misha Berson (New York: Theatre Communications Group, 1990).

Imagining America: Stories from the Promised Land, edited by Wesley Brown and Amy Ling; fiction (New York: Persea Books, 1991).

Visions of America: Personal Narratives from the Promised Land, edited by Wesley Brown and Amy Ling; nonfiction (New York: Persea Books, 1992).

Home to Stay: Asian American Women's Fiction, edited by Carol Bruchac and Sylvia Watanabe (Greenfield Center, NY: The Greenfield Review Press, 1990).

Breaking Silence: An Anthology of Contemporary Asian American Poets, edited by Joseph Bruchac (Greenfield Center, NY: The Greenfield Review Press, 1983).

America Is in the Heart: A Personal History, by Carlos Bulosan; nonfiction (Seattle: University of Washington Press, 1973).

DICTEE, by Theresa Hak Kyung Cha; experimental narrative (Tanam Press, 1982).

Aiiieeeee! An Anthology of Asian American Writers, edited by Jeffery Paul

Chan, Frank Chin, Lawson Fusao Inada, and Shawn Wong; various literary genres (Washington, D.C.: Howard University Press, 1974).

The Big AIIIEEEEE! An Anthology of Chinese American and Japanese American Literature, edited by Jeffery Paul Chan, Frank Chin, Lawson Fusao Inada, and Shawn Wong; various literary genres (New York: Meridian, 1991).

The Frontiers of Love, by Diana Chang; fiction (New York: Random House, 1974).

In the City of Contradictions, by Fay Chiang; poetry (New York: Sunbury Press, 1979).

Donald Duk, by Frank Chin; novel (Minneapolis: Coffee House Press, 1991).

Dwarf Bamboo, by Marilyn Chin; poetry (Greenfield Center, NY: The Greenfield Review Press, 1987).

Talk Story: An Anthology of Hawaii's Local Writers, edited by Eric Chock, Darrell Lum, Gail Miyasaki, Dave Robb, Frank Stewart, and Kathy Uchida; various literary genres (Honolulu: Petronium Press, 1978).

Filipinos: Forgotten Asian Americans, by Fred Cordova; nonfiction (Seattle: Demonstration Project for Asian Americans Press, 1983).

Forbidden Fruit: Women Write the Erotic, edited by Tina Cuyugan; anthology of various literary genres in both Pilipino and English (Manila: Anvil Publishing, 1992).

Killing Time in a Warm Place, by Jose Y. Dalisay, Jr.; novella (Manila: Anvil Publishing, 1992).

17 Syllables and Other Stories, by Hisaye Yamamoto Desoto (Kitchen Table: Women of Color Press, 1989).

The Third Woman: Minority Women Writers of the United States, edited by Dexter Fisher; various literary genres (Boston: Houghton Mifflin, 1980).

Brown River, White Ocean: An Anthology of 20th-Century Literature in English, edited by Luis Francia (New Brunswick, NJ: Rutgers University Press, 1993).

The Empire of Memory, by Eric Gamalinda; novel (Manila: Anvil Publishing, 1992).

The Bamboo Dancers, by N. V. M. Gonzalez; fiction (Manila: Benipayo Press, 1960).

Mindoro and Beyond: 21 Stories, by N. V. M. Gonzalez (University of the Philippines Press, 1979).

The Bread of Salt and Other Stories, by N. V. M. Gonzalez (Seattle: University of Washington Press, 1993).

Monkfish Moon, by Romesh Gunesekera; stories (New York: The New Press, 1992).

Air Pocket, by Kimiko Hahn; poetry (New York: Hanging Loose Press, 1989).

Earshot, by Kimiko Hahn; poetry (New York: Hanging Loose Press, 1992).

Yellow Light, by Garrett Kaoru Hongo; poetry (Middletown, CT: Wesleyan University Press, 1982).

The Open Boat: Poems from Asian America, edited by Garrett Kaoru Hongo (Garden City, NY: Anchor, 1993).

The Buddha Bandits Down Highway 99: Poetry, by Garrett Kaoru Hongo, Alan Chong Lau, and Lawson Fusao Inada (Buddhahead Press, 1978).

Before the War: Poems As They Happened, by Lawson Fusao Inada (New York: William Morrow, 1971).

Typical American, by Gish Jen; novel (Boston: Houghton Mifflin, 1991).

Mass, by F. Sionil Jose; novel (Manila: Solidaridad Press, 1983).

Three Filipino Women, by F. Sionil Jose; novella collection (New York: Random House, 1992).

The Floating World, by Cynthia Kadohata; novel (New York: Viking, 1989).

In the Heart of the Valley of Love, by Cynthia Kadohata; novel (New York: Viking, 1992).

Asian American Literature: An Introduction to the Writings and Their Social Contexts, by Elaine Kim; nonfiction (Philadelphia: Temple University Press, 1982).

The Woman Warrior, by Maxine Hong Kingston; memoir (New York: Vintage, 1977).

China Men, by Maxine Hong Kingston; nonfiction (New York: Knopf, 1980).

Tripmaster Monkey: His Fake Book, by Maxine Hong Kingston; novel (New York: Knopf, 1989).

Sister Stew: An Anthology, edited by Juliet Kono and Cathy Song; fiction and poetry by women (Honolulu: Bamboo Ridge Press, 1991).

The Buddha of Suburbia, by Hanif Kureishi; novel (New York: Viking, 1990).

the city in which i love you: poems, by Li-Young Lee (Brockport, NY: BOA Editions, 1990).

The Forbidden Stitch: An Asian American Women's Anthology, edited by Shirley Geok-lin Lim, Mayumi Tsutakawa, and Margarita Donnelly; various literary genres (Calyx Books, 1989).

Liwanag: Anthology of Filipino Writers and Artists in America, edited by The Liwanag Collective (Liwanag Publishers, 1975).

Pangs of Love, by David Wong Louie; short stories (New York: Knopf, 1991).

Expounding the Doubtful Points, by Wing Tek Lum; poetry.(Honolulu: Bamboo Ridge Press, 1987).

Woman, Native, Other, by Trinh T. Minh-ha; cultural studies (Bloomington: Indiana University Press, 1989).

Awake in the River, by Janice Mirikitani; poems and stories (Isthmus Press, 1978).

Sour Sweet, by Timothy Mo; novel (New York: Vintage, 1985).

This Bridge Called My Back: Writings by Radical Women of Color, edited by Cherrie Moraga and Gloria Anzaldua; various literary genres (Kitchen Table: Women of Color Press, 1981, 1983).

Woman from Hiroshima, by Toshio Mori; novel (Isthmus Press, 1978).

The Chauvinist and Other Stories, by Toshio Mori (Los Angeles: UCLA Asian American Studies Center, 1979).

Darkness, by Bharati Mukherjee; stories (New York: Ballantine Books, 1985).

The Middleman and Other Stories, by Bharati Mukherjee (New York: Ballantine Books, 1989).

A Male Grief: Notes on Pornography and Addiction, by David Mura; essay (Minneapolis: Milkweed Editions, 1987).

Turning Japanese: Memoirs of a Sansei, by David Mura (New York: Atlantic Monthly Press, 1991).

All I Asking For Is My Body, by Milton Murayama; fiction (Supa Press, 1975).

Bone, by Fae Myenne Ng; novel (New York: Hyperion, 1993).

No-No Boy, by John Okada; fiction (Rutland, VT: Charles E. Tuttle, 1957).

The Watcher of Waipuna and Other Stories, by Gary Pak (Honolulu: Bamboo Ridge Press, 1992).

19 Necromancers from Now: An Anthology, edited by Ishmael Reed; fiction (Garden City, NY: Doubleday, 1970).

State of War, by Ninotchka Rosca; novel (New York: Norton, 1988).

Twice Blessed, by Ninotchka Rosca; novel (New York: Norton, 1992).

Midnight's Children, by Salman Rushdie; novel (New York: Knopf, 1980).

The Satanic Verses, by Salman Rushdie; novel (New York: Viking, 1989).

The Day the Dancers Came, by Bienvenido Santos; fiction (Bookmark, 1967).

Scent of Apples: A Collection of Stories, by Bienvenido N. Santos (Seattle: University of Washington Press, 1979).

The Man Who (Thought He) Looked Like Robert Taylor, by Bienvenido Santos; novel (New Day, 1983).

You Lovely People, by Bienvenido Santos; stories (reprinted by Bookmark Inc., Philippines, 1991).

seasons of sacred lust, by Kazuko Shiraishi; poetry (New York: New Directions, 1975, 1978).

Dazzled, by Arthur Sze; poems (Floating Island, 1982).

River River, by Arthur Sze; poems (Lost Roads Publishers, 1987).

Strangers from a Different Shore: A History of Asian Americans, by Ronald Takaki; nonfiction (New York: Penguin Books, 1990).

Third World Women: An Anthology of Poetry, edited by Third World Communications (Third World Communications, 1972).

Time to Greez! Incantations from the Third World, edited by Third World Communications; poetry (Glide Publications, 1975).

The Words of a Woman Who Breathes Fire, by Kitty Tsui; poetry (Spinsters Ink, 1983).

Wings of Stone, by Linda Ty-Casper; fiction (London: Readers International, 1986).

Poems: Vol. 2, by Jose Garcia Villa (New York: New Directions, 1949).

Selected Stories from Footnote to Youth, by Jose Garcia Villa (Alberto Florentino Books, Philippines, 1973).

Ginseng and Other Tales from Manila, by Marianne Villanueva; stories (Calyx Books, 1991).

Talking to the Dead, by Sylvia Watanabe; stories (Garden City, NY: Doubleday, 1992).

Dreams in Harrison Railroad Park, by Nellie Wong; poetry (Berkeley, CA: Kelsey Street Press, 1977).

Homebase, by Shawn Wong; novel (I. Reed Books, 1979; New York: Plume, 1990).

Camp Notes and Other Poems, by Mitsuye Yamada (Shameless Hussy Press, 1976).

Through the Arc of the Rain Forest, by Karen Tei Yamashita; novel (Minneapolis: Coffee House Press, 1990).

Brazil-Maru, by Karen Tei Yamashita; novel (Minneapolis: Coffee House Press, 1992).

Great Philippine Jungle Energy Cafe, by Alfred A. Yuson; novel (Manila: Book Development Association, 1988).

The Music Child and Other Stories, by Alfred A. Yuson; short stories (Manila: Anvil Publishing, 1991).

FOR THE BEST IN PAPERBACKS, LOOK FOR THE

In every corner of the world, on every subject under the sun, Penguin represents quality and variety—the very best in publishing today.

For complete information about books available from Penguin—including Pelicans, Puffins, Peregrines, and Penguin Classics—and how to order them, write to us at the appropriate address below. Please note that for copyright reasons the selection of books varies from country to country.

In the United Kingdom: For a complete list of books available from Penguin in the U.K., please write to *Dept E.P., Penguin Books Ltd, Harmondsworth, Middlesex, UB7 0DA.*

In the United States: For a complete list of books available from Penguin in the U.S., please write to *Consumer Sales, Penguin USA, P.O. Box 999— Dept. 17109, Bergenfield, New Jersey 07621-0120.* Visa and MasterCard holders call 1-800-253-6476 to order all Penguin titles.

In Canada: For a complete list of books available from Penguin in Canada, please write to *Penguin Books Canada Ltd, 10 Alcorn Avenue, Suite 300, Toronto, Ontario, Canada M4V 3B2.*

In Australia: For a complete list of books available from Penguin in Australia, please write to the *Marketing Department, Penguin Books Ltd, P.O. Box 257, Ringwood, Victoria 3134.*

In New Zealand: For a complete list of books available from Penguin in New Zealand, please write to the *Marketing Department, Penguin Books (NZ) Ltd, Private Bag, Takapuna, Auckland 9.*

In India: For a complete list of books available from Penguin, please write to *Penguin Overseas Ltd, 706 Eros Apartments, 56 Nehru Place, New Delhi, 110019.*

In Holland: For a complete list of books available from Penguin in Holland, please write to *Penguin Books Nederland B.V., Postbus 195, NL-1380AD Weesp, Netherlands.*

In Germany: For a complete list of books available from Penguin, please write to *Penguin Books Ltd, Friedrichstrasse 10-12, D-6000 Frankfurt Main 1, Federal Republic of Germany.*

In Spain: For a complete list of books available from Penguin in Spain, please write to *Longman, Penguin España, Calle San Nicolas 15, E-28013 Madrid, Spain.*

In Japan: For a complete list of books available from Penguin in Japan, please write to *Longman Penguin Japan Co Ltd, Yamaguchi Building, 2-12-9 Kanda Jimbocho, Chiyoda-Ku, Tokyo 101, Japan.*